# THE PEACE MAKER

# THE PEACE MAKER

MARK J. LIVINGSTONE

BETHANY HOUSE PUBLISHERS
MINNEAPOLIS, MINNESOTA 55438

Cover illustration by Dan Thornberg,
Bethany House Publishers staff artist.



Published by Bethany House Publishers
A Ministry of Bethany Fellowship, Inc.
6820 Auto Club Road, Minneapolis, Minnesota 55438

Printed in the United States of America

**Library of Congress Cataloging-in-Publication Data**

Livingstone, Mark J.
The peacemaker / Mark J. Livingstone.
p. cm.

I. Title.
PS3562.I98P4 1990
813'.54—dc20 90-1083
ISBN 1-55661-156-0 CIP

To Carol Johnson.

Thanks for everything.

# CONTENTS

# PART I

# THE PRESIDENT

*The day of the Lord will come like a thief in the night. While people are saying, "Peace and safety," destruction will come on them suddenly.*

1 THESSALONIANS 5:2–3

# ONE

Darkness clung skin-tight to the shabby buildings.

Faint night sounds in the distance drew no response from the figure hurrying through a deserted alley. Reaching the opening onto the street, he slowed, inching forward alongside an abandoned warehouse.

He paused.

His breath pierced the frosty night in regular silent intervals, yellowed from the light of a pale street lamp.

Regaining his wind, he peered out, glanced to his right and left, and took off at a brisk walk, broken occasionally by a lumbering attempt at a jog. His hefty frame was unused to the effort, however, and could only sustain the pace for a block or two.

He darted into a shadowy recessed entryway. A profitable neighborhood market had once thrived behind these broken windows and boarded doors. The fugitive could easily have granted himself the momentary luxury of a few philosophical reflections on the decay of this side of town—his town—and on the deeper spiritual decay his new associates would say it symbolized. Was this secret that he alone knew really of such great importance? He'd watched all the old Cold War movies where the fate of the world hung in the balance time and time again. Was he truly in the midst of just such a real-life drama? Or would everything go on as usual no matter what he did? He didn't know. All he could do was play out the role that had seemingly been set before him and hope for the best. Meanwhile, his thoughts found themselves governed by more pressing concerns.

Trying to even his wheezing breath, he listened intently.

Yes . . . the footsteps still followed.

He'd taken the usual route. But after six such evenings, apparently they'd detected the pattern. He'd have to improvise, hoping his wind would hold out.

*I should get in better shape,* he chastised himself. Eluding his ever-present official shadows was no simple task, but at this moment he almost wished he had one or two of them along. If he had to make a run for it, no telling what might happen.

His Holiness Karil Lakota hadn't found it necessary to resort to such measures when he furtively haunted the streets of Rome. He simply changed clothes and slipped out. Unfortunately, this assignment had proven more rigorous. Besides which, the Vatican's security probably didn't match that of the White House. Especially a fictional Vatican. Of course, the Pope had *wanted* to see people. He hadn't been trying to camouflage a secret meeting. But what about those rumors about Jimmy Carter sneaking out late at night? How had he managed it?

Well, he'd just have to outmaneuver his pursuer somehow.

Gathering his strength for a supreme burst and praying it wouldn't bring on a coronary, he bolted noiselessly from the opening. Down the block he ran, diagonally across the street, and into another alley. It could hardly be called a sprint; nevertheless, his labored gait quickly widened the distance between him and his pursuer.

The stalking footsteps quickened, then shifted into a jog.

On he galloped, chest heaving, calves tightening, through the alley, onto the opposite sidewalk, then to his left. A block farther, across the intersection, another left for a short space, and into the alley on his right. Twenty yards into its darkness he stopped, creeping behind a garbage bin, hoping the blackness would conceal him. Bending his knees to the pavement, he crouched as low as his bulk would permit.

His lungs ached as he gasped for huge gulps of air. The stench of month-old refuse staggered his equilibrium, but he had to choke down the nausea . . . and wait.

The tennis shoes on his feet had proved the final advantage. His rubbery tread through the deserted streets produced only a whisper of sound, while the heavy-soled oxfords of his hunter echoed with every step.

Those steps had arrived at the intersection now.

They stopped, their owner obviously straining to catch the slightest disturbance of the deadened air. Uncertain, he turned, took a tentative step to the left, swung around and retraced his path back half a block, stopped again to listen, then resumed his jog in the opposite direction.

In the secluded alley, the sweating figure rose slowly, still panting. He stepped gingerly to the mouth of the alley and then to the intersection. Standing back in the shadow of a building, he could see the receding figure two blocks away. When the footsteps were no longer audible, he moved carefully across the street and continued on—walking now.

He breathed a mental sigh of relief. That had been close. Too close!

The riskiest night yet. In the future he'd have to take additional precautions.

*What am I doing here?* he thought to himself. *A sane man like me, sneaking around in the middle of the night to listen to—I can't even say it!—I must be crazy! How could I have come to this? If people saw me now . . .*

He did not allow himself to complete the unpleasant image of what such a revelation might mean. No one *could* see him! However this turned out, whether these people were right—especially if they were right!—the cloak of secrecy had to be preserved at all costs.

Thirty minutes later he stood before a run-down hotel whose chief function may at one time have been the provision of a clean room and a sound night's sleep. But it had clearly degenerated since then. Signs of seediness evidenced themselves from top to bottom. From the half-functioning neon sign to the threadbare maroon carpet to the ancient plaster chipping from the ceiling. As far as he could tell the lobby was vacant, so he walked in and hastened up the sagging stairs to the third floor.

He rapped lightly on the third door on the right. Immediately the knob turned and the door opened. He stepped inside.

"I'm sorry I'm late, Peter. Had a difficult time getting away, and then was followed. I had to take a rather circuitous route, to say the least."

"No problem," answered his host. "We all understood when we began that there would be contingencies."

"Nevertheless, your time is valuable too."

"Believe me, the time has been put to good use. Wherever two or three are gathered, you know."

"Yes, I believe you covered that last time."

"There, you see, Mr. President! Not a minute wasted. Now, come in and join the others."

# TWO

The peaceful sun of early May streaming through the windows in the West Wing of the White House contrasted conspicuously with the passionate discussion in progress between the two closest advisors of the president of the United States. The subject consuming them was the upcoming presidential election.

"I tell you, Dick, it won't be that simple."

"I've talked to Wilson's assistant," argued the other. "I'm sure he'll come along if we grant certain . . . reasonable concessions."

"What you view as reasonable, I'd call extreme!"

"Look, Jake, a year ago I would have been the last one to urge Jarvis to give Harley Wilson an inch. He's so stuffed with the power of UTAL he thinks he runs the country. I don't like the crook any more than you do."

"But you want to promise him a cabinet seat? Think what you're saying, man!"

Dick Howard and Jake Randolf were not only President Jarvis MacFarlane's advisors, they were also two of his oldest friends. After graduating from Columbia Law School and passing the bar exam, the three had pooled their funds and begun what in a relatively short time had grown into a successful and prestigious Manhattan law firm.

Since then, Howard and Randolf had risen alongside their friend into the halls of power. Now MacFarlane, in his first term as president, had entrusted them to plot out his reelection and political future. Though they were not in the national limelight, and few voters knew much about them, these two were among the country's most influential politicians.

Attorney General Dick Howard had masterminded MacFarlane's gubernatorial election victory in New York, a victory so unlikely at its inception that it was often likened to Jimmy Carter's run at the presidency in 1976. This earned MacFarlane an immediate national reputation.

At five foot nine, Howard was trimmer and fitter than most fifty-eight-year-old members of the Washington establishment. He worked out with weights twice a week, ran three miles a day, and neither smoked nor drank. Some thought him compulsive about his body, indeed about everything he did, but he didn't care a straw for what anyone thought. It was that very trait that had propelled him along in his successful career. From the top of his sandy crew-cut to the bottom of his spit-shined shoes, the man was an organizer, well aware that he himself did not possess the charisma to run for public office. Such was not his aspiration—leave that to the MacFarlanes. Just as long as they never forgot they needed people like him to reach the seats of power. He often likened himself to a ladder: "You can't get far in the only direction that matters without one," he would say.

The other man in the room was his closest friend, Presidential Chief of Staff Jacob Randolf. Although only three years older than Howard, he looked at least ten. Jake always blamed Dick for the discrepancy, bemoaning the fact that the latter looked so young. But the cigar clenched perpetually between Randolf's teeth (he still smoked Roi-tans, though he could well afford a more expensive Caribbean vintage) and the scotch-and-soda clutched habitually in his hand contributed more to the contrast than Howard's weight machine and well-worn Nikes.

Randolf possessed neither the drive of the attorney general nor the charisma of the president, but he lent a stabilizing force to the trio. He was solid and dependable and did his job well—when sober. And in faithfulness both to the president and the country, he kept off the sauce pretty well. But since his wife and two daughters had been killed in an automobile accident five years earlier, he seemed to walk an ever-tenuous line between sobriety and intoxication, the latter usually taking over once he closed the door of his home at night.

Now Jake shifted his overweight frame and shook his head. "I don't know, Dick," he said around his cigar.

"It's an extraordinary gamble, I'll admit. But these are unusual times. Everything's upside-down since the old days. You used to know where people stood. You could count on the unions and the white Southern vote and the rich California liberals. You had your Kennedys and Daleys, your Thurmonds and Johnsons and their various blocks of power. It made elections so much easier."

"Nixon and Carter, they're the ones who changed everything," assented Randolf. "Disrupted all the old balances. Nixon with his cover-ups, and Carter with his unnerving appeal to whole new constituencies. I agree, it's a whole new ball game now."

"Exactly! You used to be able to scope it out on paper. If you lost, you could see what had caused the crossover and analyze it for next time. But now thanks to Nixon, Carter—and who can forget Reagan!—who knows anymore? Labor's split to beat the band! Because of guys like Jackson, blacks are all over the spectrum. Republicans don't stick together, and Democrats are at each other's throats. You can't even tell a liberal from a conservative if your life depended on it. Bush proved that. And now you've got women and blacks running for president. No, Jake, something crazy's going on in this country. All the old lines are erased. If we're going to pull this one off, it's going to take some masterful inside stroke. Otherwise we're out of a job."

In response, Randolf drew two long puffs on his cigar. "But you're talking about putting the president of this country's most powerful labor union—a union with a century of reputed underworld connections!—on the president's cabinet. Entrusting a man like Wilson with upholding the Constitution . . . with making and carrying out law for heaven's sake! How can you be serious?"

"Because there's no other way we can win!"

Jake rocked back in his chair and exhaled, silenced temporarily. Then he sighed and resumed in a stymied voice, "Yeah . . . you may be right."

Neither man spoke for two or three minutes.

"Curse it all!" Jake burst out at last. "There's got to be some other way. The idea's just inconceivable! Remember Kennedy and Hoffa? You're proposing a marriage that simply couldn't work."

"No one's ever tried. Why couldn't we make it fly? If it didn't . . . well, there are ways for the president of the United States to keep someone like that under his thumb."

"You're talking about Jarvis MacFarlane, not Richard Nixon. The man still has a conscience after twenty years of public life. Besides, Wilson's no fool. He wouldn't put himself in a position where we could hang him out to dry after the election. He'd insist on substantial guarantees against our being able to do that. That's assuming Jarvis would even go along with the idea. Which I doubt. He's always hated Wilson."

"If he wants to win badly enough," Howard replied flatly, "one look at the polls will tell him some drastic measures are called for. No matter who the Republicans nominate, Jarvis is at least ten points behind. If Foster's the nominee, make that twenty."

Randolf glanced at his watch. "It's time for the meeting," he said. "We'd better be off."

"You go ahead," replied Howard. "I'll be along in a minute. I have to get a couple briefs together."

The chief of staff grabbed his briefcase and lumbered from the room. Before the door clicked shut behind him, the attorney general's thoughts were already leaping back over their conversation. One thing he had withheld from his friend was that he had already set up a meeting with Wilson. Just himself and the labor leader—no one else need know right now. He was anxious to feel the man out. He was certain he could come up with a deal they could all live with. *Wilson might be a weasel,* he thought. *But he has his ambitions like anyone else.* It would take slick negotiations, but that was what Howard did best. He had come too far to blow it now—they all had. Dick, the ivy-leaguer; Jake, the crusty cynic; and Jarvis, the down-home boy everyone liked.

Even back in law school days they were considered an odd mix. Mismatched, perhaps. But they had made it work. It was obvious from the first that Jarvis was a born politician. When the Democratic party approached him about the New York state senate, Howard made sure his friend accepted. When the gubernatorial race came along, Howard considered his friend's victory a foregone conclusion despite the fact that MacFarlane was a dark horse. And his instincts had proven accurate.

Now Howard faced a far stiffer challenge.

Though governor of a large state, MacFarlane, unlike his famous predecessor Mario Cuomo, had not built a national constituency and enjoyed little recognition outside the northeast. He had been a surprise choice for vice-president, obviously selected for his regional support and for the youthful balance he brought to the ticket headed by sixty-four-year-old Franklin Ryan. But after their narrow election, the vice president had served competently, had grown in the job, and had matured in national stature. When President Ryan had suffered a fatal stroke at the end of the first year of his second term, Jarvis MacFarlane—then fifty-five and a widower with a nineteen-year-old daughter in her first year at Georgetown—had inherited the reins of power.

Ryan had been enormously popular, and it was not without difficulty that Jarvis MacFarlane stepped out of the vice-presidential background and the shade cast by Ryan's overwhelming presence. Jarvis quickly discovered that magnetism in the courtroom and the state senate, or even eloquence as one of the nominating speakers at the national Democratic convention, did not automatically translate into popularity on a national scale.

He was quickly forced into presidential action in his own right by an unceasing barrage of crises, as if events had been gathering offshore like an impending storm awaiting Ryan's death.

MacFarlane was vaguely familiar with the phrase "wars and rumors of wars," though he could not have told you whether it came from Shakespeare, Plato, or an old Hebrew tax collector named Matthew. Neither was he familiar with the associated tribulations, famines, earthquakes, international disputes, military scenarios, and economic collapse predicted to accompany said rumors. Besides which, nobody was talking about war. This was the era of peace! If you had read him that New Testament passage the day after his swearing in, Jarvis MacFarlane would have dismissed the notion as archaic.

But now, suddenly, everything was changed, though he scarcely realized even yet to what extent. Jarvis MacFarlane knew neither the day nor the hour, nor did he apprehend the destiny that had been marked out for him to follow.

He had managed to weather the early storms capably. He'd coped with the first double-digit inflation since the late 1970s. He'd enlisted the banks' cooperation to keep the prime from climbing beyond twenty percent, although they were reluctant to give without pressure judiciously applied from the Federal Reserve. He'd even beaten back protests from the angry unemployed nine percent of the work force.

For a majority of Americans life was still great. If prices were rising and interest rates were high, what did it matter? Money was flowing, business was good, the world was at peace. But at the lower end of the economic spectrum people were hurting. And there were disquieting signs that this hurt was symptomatic of far deeper root problems than the United States had ever faced.

The failure of the Reagan and Bush administrations to effectively deal with the budget deficit had created an economic monster that was sucking the very lifeblood out of the nation's strength. Also, after years of warning, Social Security had at last come calling. The first of the baby-boomers were starting to think of retirement and would soon be collecting their pensions, further bankrupting the system.

And to further complicate things, not only was American industry facing the formidable might of Japan, which continued to erode the auto and electronics industries, but the united German nation had now reached full stride and was leading the economic community of Europe to dizzying heights of productivity. Even the Soviet Union had begun to export goods to the U.S.

For the great majority, who did not have to think about imports and exports or the budget deficit, peace in the world had created a mood of apathy, a malaise caused not by having too little but by having too much. "Why worry?" had become a popular slogan among affluent twenty- and thirty-year-olds. Things were fine! This was a new age!

Jarvis MacFarlane saw both sides and tried to be both realistic and optimistic. He'd worked hard to push energy legislation further than either Carter or Bush had dreamed of. For Carter it had been but a hope for future conservation; for Bush it seemed part of good stewardship. But for MacFarlane the energy package—addressing everything from surcharges at the gas pumps to acid rain to offshore oil drilling to the dreadfully depleted ozone layer—had become a matter of global survival. Somehow he had been able to twist the arthritic arm of Congress to get almost half his energy proposals passed, despite hundreds of interest-group pressures in every direction.

In the midst of all this he had even managed to avert a serious political conflict within the state of Israel between traditional Judaism and the rapidly growing Hebrew Christian groups. Those who analyzed and editorialized about such things found great interest in this Israeli revival, accompanied by a period of tremendous religious tolerance and awakening in Russia, at the very time when Christian values and ethics were on the wane in the U.S. They spoke of "cycles" and "swings of the pendulum." And who could deny that these days, to admit to being a fundamentalist Christian would have insured you of more than just a few skeptically raised eyebrows. If you were a politician, that was a statement you'd be better off keeping to yourself. At the same time, however, the cycle overseas seemed to be operating in the exact reverse. An explosive growth of Protestant evangelicalism, which now claimed to represent an astonishing forty percent of Israel, had taken the world by surprise and was attracting the hostile notice of the Arab states as well as Moscow. Such civil strife served as an open invitation for invasion. MacFarlane and Secretary of State Oscar Friedman had flown to Jerusalem last summer and had been able to effect some harmony between the two groups who claimed to worship the same God. How long it would last, no one could tell, but for now the Middle East remained calm.

Yet even if he handled everything that came his way with great skill, there was no guarantee the voting masses would absolve MacFarlane of responsibility for their own personal ills when it came time to walk into the voting booth. As an effective but not particularly popular chief executive, his was the fate of Hoover and Carter; he was blamed for events beyond his reach—and even, as some claimed in the case of the deficit, for events *caused* by Ronald Reagan, one of the most popular presidents. And the portion of the electorate that had no ills to worry about didn't care much for him either. They were looking for a more dynamic leader to unveil a vision of peace and prosperity for the future. Someone they could follow almost as a spiritual guru, who would intone the warm phrases of the new dawn and humanity's new reign on the earth.

"Dump MacFarlane!" cried the editorialists from the industrial cities. "Bring back the good old days!"

"A new age demands new leadership," wrote others. "We need a man with vision."

*Ha!* Howard thought. *The good old days! What a joke! Nothing but a hollow dream of a time that never was.* And what about the calls for new visionary purpose and direction? *Air-headed baloney!*

But you couldn't keep people from gobbling up such slogans and raising the banners proclaiming the need for a change in residency on Pennsylvania Avenue. It happened every four years.

Fickle though the people were, they comprised the electorate. They had to be coddled, spoon-fed pieces of the truth, and, one way or another, won over.

Jarvis MacFarlane was an honorable man. He took his public trust seriously. So Dick Howard knew a skillful handling of the temperamental voters must ultimately fall to him; that's what a crackerjack strategist was for. He'd done it in New York, and he would do it in Washington—no matter whose help he had to enlist.

He gathered his papers, tapped them sharply on the edge of the desk to straighten them, then laid them in his briefcase and snapped it shut. Exiting the room, he turned down the corridor toward the Oval Office.

# THREE

Hearing the hum of voices inside, Dick Howard entered the Oval Office without knocking.

Along with Jake, who was reclining in a leather chair with cigar in hand, six others were present. Sitting next to him was Avery

Lengyel, the president's campaign manager. On the other side of the room were Eugene O'Shea, presidential counsel; Duke Mathias, the president's chief economic advisor; along with Secretary of State Oscar Friedman and Secretary of Defense Martin Tucker.

"Come in, come in, Dick," said Jarvis MacFarlane, the final and most important member of the group.

Once Howard had closed the door and seated himself, the president rose from his desk and walked slowly, deliberately, to his favorite wood-backed chair, joining the circle of his closest confidants.

"Gentlemen, this isn't the first time we've been here like this," he began. "We've weathered some rough times together, and I'm sure before the election's over the political battles could get fierce."

He paused, sighed, glanced down at the single sheet he held in his left hand, then looked up to continue.

"You know how much I want to concentrate our efforts on the economy and the election. Not only will the opposition kill us if we don't get some things straightened out, but the country may never recover. The inflation, the debt, homelessness, interest rates, problems with the farmers, the environment, the poor—it's a mess! But I hardly need tell you that!" he added with an attempted laugh. "You're the guys coming in here every day telling *me* all your prophecies of doom! Like I said, it's these things I wish we could focus our attention on. Unfortunately, something has . . . come up. And frankly, it's going to require more energy and expertise than I alone can give it."

He allowed his small audience to shift in their chairs as they waited in silence for a few seconds. When he spoke again, each word seemed an effort.

"Two hours ago this communique came to the Pentagon." He held up the paper, half crumpled by now, obviously reread many times.

"It's a classified message, and Martin brought it over the moment it came in," he said. "You'll recall that two years ago a couple of our people raised questions about the Soviet military situation along the Caspian during the mutual verification tests. The Soviets talked their way nicely around the so-called 'problem,' and of course the rest of our delegation went along with their explanation. The anti-military groups in Congress casually dismissed the allegations that the Russians were cheating, claiming the report was a 'misunderstanding brought on by the zealousness of those yearning to return to the tensions of the Cold War era.' "

He paused, took a breath, and plunged on.

"But now it appears the Soviets may wind up answering that question for us and spare any further debates between the doves and hawks. Indications point to the necessity of a stronger response on our part than mere reprisals through the State Department. Incredible as it seems after these last ten or twelve years of superpower bliss, it looks as though we may have to square off against our old nemesis once again. And if the situation continues to build, the Soviets may force our hand into a more determined action than anyone in this town has considered since Kennedy's day. I don't like to think what that might mean—" His voice trailed away momentarily and he seemed to be focusing on something distant and removed.

An uncomfortable minute passed before Jake Randolf finally spoke, snapping MacFarlane's attention back to his colleagues.

"Mr. President, are you saying you want to change our position on their installations and troops in that area after all this time?"

"No, Jake. It's not just a matter of their having troops there. That's been part of the list of givens. They've got men around the world; we've got men around the world. They know where ours are; we know where theirs are. We check their installations; they check ours. All very friendly, this new World Alliance—just one big happy family. We're all allies now. The troops are just for decoration. We're even supposed to know exactly how many. And we okayed their request four years ago to shift twenty thousand men from the Baltic to the Iranian border. For humanitarian reasons—I think that's how they put it—cold winters up north. So no, it's not that I want to change our policy. They're the ones who appear to be dictating the change."

"Mr. President, what are you getting at?" asked Secretary of State Friedman.

The president glanced at Martin Tucker, the only other person in the room who knew the contents of the memo.

"I'm getting to it, Oscar. Give me time," he said. "Now you all know me pretty well. I try to be an optimist. I did my best to believe in Gorbachev and all he wanted to accomplish. In retrospect, I suppose I do believe he was for real, and maybe, had he lasted, we would have seen a peaceful new world order in the twenty-first century. It's hard to tell what might have been. But along with optimism, I also try to be a realist. If you want to hold this job for long, you'd better be. So I make it a practice to surround myself with those who represent the whole political spectrum. I want to get advice and hear opinions from a broad range of viewpoints.

Look at the six of you! I can't imagine you agreeing on anything!"

His advisors laughed, more out of a need to relieve tension than at the humor of the remark.

"So I've always tried to listen to both those who wanted to dismantle the Pentagon altogether the minute the Berlin Wall came down in '89, and those who have continued to speak words of caution about moving too quickly to undo our military, just in case Lenin and Stalin came back into favor in a post-Gorbachev Russia. To tell you the truth, I've never known exactly what to believe."

"Who has?" interjected Daniel O'Shea. "The changes in Russia and Eastern Europe took us all by surprise. It's been incredible—a whole new military framework since 1990!"

"Right, Dan," said the president. "Nobody knows what's coming. So, as I said, I've tried to be prudent and listen to all sides. Therefore . . . and this is the point I've been trying to get to . . . after that report two years ago I secretly authorized a small surveillance operation to monitor activities in the region."

Glances and a few raised eyebrows spread around the room.

"I know . . . I know!" he said, reading their minds. "I could be hung out to dry if this were found out, not only by the Russians, but by three-quarters of our own people. And I apologize for the necessity of keeping it even from you, my friends. I hope you'll be able to understand my reasons."

"And? What have you found out?" asked Duke Mathias.

"Well, after ten years of beefing up their economy, the Soviets appear to be thinking militarily again. We've been monitoring their movements very closely," replied the president, his voice and eyes sharp now. "Not only did they bring the twenty thousand troops down from the Baltic, it seems they've been gradually slipping in men from other installations also—from Siberia, from the Chinese border, from some of their remaining posts in Eastern Europe. Small numbers at a time, so as to go undetected. As you know, our last verification visit to the region was only two months ago, when everything was reported squeaky clean. With another visit from our officials not scheduled till the end of the year, this gives them a huge window of opportunity, *if* they are indeed up to something. So we've kept our eyes on them closely, apparently without their realizing it. Suddenly in the past two weeks they've upped the ante. Divisions have literally been pouring in, most notably along the Iranian border—all at night, of course. We're not one hundred percent certain, but—"

"If you'll allow me, Mr. President," broke in Secretary of Defense Tucker, "I would say we're as certain as you can ever be in such a situation."

Martin Tucker was a powerfully built stump of a man who looked more like a medieval battering ram than a summa cum laude graduate of Stanford.

"The report comes from this unauthorized intelligence source the president spoke of, headquartered in Turkey," Tucker continued, "and if we were still playing by the rules of the '60s and '70s, all indications would point to the likelihood that the Russians are positioning for an invasion of Iran. What it means in this new global context—well, that's what we have to find out."

# FOUR

Several low whistles, a gasp, and an audible sigh expressed the reaction to the defense secretary's astonishing revelation.

"It can't possibly be reliable, Mr. President," said Friedman. "The Russians haven't pulled anything since 1980. They've been—"

"It's reliable, Oscar," interrupted Tucker, "as much as it could be under the circumstances. Our network in Turkey includes some of our best people in the Middle East. They've been in close contact with our highest agent in the Soviet Union, and he assures them this is the real thing—the gamble the Russians have been waiting fifty years to take."

"I wondered the same thing, Oscar," said the president. "The whole thing hinges on the reliability of this communique. Clearly Martin would never have brought it to me if we didn't have solid substantiation."

"Could our agent's position have been compromised?" asked Howard. "Despite all this good will that's been flowing recently, I have no doubt the Soviets would love to trick us into a foolish move."

"Dick's right," added Randolf. "Now that the alignments have changed, in a sense we're both competing for the same allies and the same economic markets and the same raw materials. World opinion is the game now. They still want to be in control, to dominate. But for now they're just settling back to try it non-militarily, waiting for their economy to catch up and then pass ours. They get our aid and all our good will, and wham! Forty years later they're back in a position of world dominance. They're just following the lesson of post-war Japan, letting a former enemy finance their rebuilding. It's all a PR game."

"One foolish move on our part, and they could shout 'Aggression!' " added Howard. "They'd say we weren't keeping to the treaty, grab a bit more favorable press at our expense, and instantly they'd make further inroads. But I'm not so sure they've dismissed the military option altogether. What a perfect ploy in this era of good will to trick us into some confrontive action. Then they launch their forces in a limited way, knowing no one will do anything, and claiming all the while we started it."

"There's always the possibility that our agent's security has been breached, to answer your original question," replied Tucker. "But we have air reconnaissance photos. They've tried to hide their movements, but these stealth pictures confirm them. All your speculations are beside the point. We're dealing with facts."

"You've sent stealth missions over Russia!" exclaimed Friedman. "That clearly violates the 1994 Berlin Accords!"

"I had no choice, Oscar," replied the president calmly. "Only two brief missions, the most recent just last week. I *had* to be sure before I spilled this news to you all."

"But the treaty, Mr. President. The Russians could say—"

"I'm fully aware of the risk," interrupted MacFarlane. "The Russians! Just think what our own Congress would say! But I had to verify the truth of these intelligence reports. This is hardball we're playing here!"

Tucker opened his briefcase, removed a folder, and said, "I had these blowups made before I came over." He passed around several 11 x 14 glossies. "Compare the photo taken two months ago with the one dated last week. If you look closely you can make out some large, partially camouflaged buildings—probably portable—and what we have confirmed as a number of troop and equipment transport carriers."

As the photographs made their way around the group, nods and an occasional whistle of disbelief punctuated the silence.

"As of today, we're ninety percent certain our man's cover is intact in Moscow, and that this information is credible . . . *and* substantiated by these photographs," asserted Tucker. "I have experts going over them with a fine-tooth comb right now. Until we know differently, we have no choice but to treat this as a dangerous and imminent threat."

"Dick's comment is a good one, though," mused Randolf. "The Kremlin would love to catch us leaning the wrong way."

"What do you propose, Mr. President?" asked Mathias.

At thirty-nine, he was the youngest in the group, and his role was definitely that of the intellectual and aesthete, right down to the slender fingers that had won him a scholarship to Julliard as a concert pianist. He had chosen Harvard instead, where he had graduated at nineteen with a degree in economics. It was there that the unlikely macho nickname "Duke" had jokingly been applied by his friends. The label stuck when he became involved in the Reagan campaign in 1984, and since that time he had gone back and forth between the Democrats and Republicans several times, assessing where his conservative yet humanitarian views could be most useful. His religious preferences were well known, irritating many a pragmatic Washington politician, and he was one of the few in the higher offices of power who ever mentioned anything about his beliefs these days, occasionally drawing fire from those editorialists who compared him to Charles Colson and Jimmy Carter—all of whom, they said, should have no place in politics. But Duke was too astute an economist to be ignored, and MacFarlane trusted him implicitly. He knew Duke would play it straight with him no matter what the consequences.

"What do you think you're here for, Duke?" laughed the president. "You're supposed to tell me! That's what advisors are for."

The others joined in the moment of levity to ease the sober impact of the chief executive's words.

"The few in the Pentagon who are in on it at this stage think it's for real," the president continued. "Some have been claiming all along that the Gorbachev initiatives were nothing but a smoke screen to mask longer-range world goals. With an economy in collapse, and seeing that they weren't going to be able to maintain their grip on Eastern Europe, the Soviets pulled back and rethought their strategy. But they never really altered their basic objectives, and this is the practical result. With our military spending down and our whole priority structure as a nation looking in other directions, with NATO dismantled, their releasing Eastern Europe from their grip and dissolving the Warsaw Pact can be seen as part of the scheme. I'm not saying I've gone along with this reasoning, but that's how some see these developments. They're now predicting this will be like so many Soviet moves in the past, such as Afghanistan. Carefully planned, timed, and orchestrated, insuring our inability to come back with an immediate response. Knowing in today's climate they'll catch us off guard—again. By the time we get our wits about us, we'll be reduced to paper attacks through State. But—"

"I must say," interrupted Friedman in a measured voice, "that I resent the implication that our actions are so ineffective as to be termed—"

"Hold your horses, Oscar," said the president. "No one's ignoring the service you perform. But this is a serious matter, and we have to explore all the options. We'll talk about possible diplomatic procedures too, if you'll give us the chance. But first I want to run down the scenario from the military standpoint."

Seemingly satisfied, the secretary of state sat back in his chair with a "we'll-see" expression.

"As I was saying," the president continued, "the Soviets are gambling, like they have ever since 1945, that we won't be willing to back up our memos of outrage with guns."

"They'll have let go of a half-dozen satellites with the combined wealth and productivity of central Nevada, in exchange for one of enormous wealth and strategic importance," shot in Tucker, growing heated, his round, swarthy face reddening.

"What a satellite!" said Howard. "The oil fields, the gulf!"

"Iran's the ball game!" added Tucker. "Look at a map. Iraq's invasion of Kuwait was infinitesimal in comparison. There's no country on the globe—takeable country, I mean—that gives Russia as much as Iran. Access to the West . . . the East . . . oil. I have no doubt their taking of Afghanistan in '80 was seen as a steppingstone toward Iran, perhaps Pakistan. Things didn't work out so well for them. But I'm convinced their withdrawal in '88 was nothing but an inconvenience. They had to change their game plan temporarily, but I tell you, it's Iran they've been after all along. And these last ten years don't change that! What might have been had Gorbachev lasted, I can't say. But he didn't, and now I'm convinced they're playing by the old rules again, and we're not ready!"

"Which is why this leak of their troop movements is so vital," added the president.

"And why we must act without delay to plan a strong, affirmative countermove," said the defense secretary.

"They'll be prepared for worldwide flack, of course," said the president. "And they'll claim their move was prompted by Iran's recent instability. They had to move in to protect the world's oil interests."

"What do they care about flack," said Tucker. "A few sanctions, a few boycotts, what impact have they had? None. They still got precisely what they were after. When they left Afghanistan and East Germany and allowed the changes in Poland and Hungary, then eventually allowed the disintegration of the entire Eastern bloc, they did it because it suited *their* interests to do so. They weren't 'giving up.' They were just changing their strategy. Gorbachev was the first truly modern Russian leader. He understood the dynamics of the twentieth century and attempted to utilize that knowledge to the benefit of his country. But even then, *he* dictated everything. Reagan, Bush, Ryan, they were all bit players alongside Gorbachev. We've been powerless since 1945 to stop them from doing whatever they wanted—militarily, economically, diplomatically."

Attempting to wrest the discussion from the excitable Tucker, the president calmly tried to sum up the situation.

"England may have called Argentina's bluff in the Falklands. But that was hardly World War Three, either from the standpoint of the nations or the geography involved. When Bush squared off against Hussein, the stakes were obviously much higher, but then it still wasn't the same because we had everyone on our side, even the Soviets. But now *this* really could be explosive in a more major way—*if* we challenged the Russians, if they called our bluff, and then we refused to step down. Cuba was a long time ago, and Kennedy held more cards than Khrushchev. They've flexed a lot of muscle since then, and today most of the third world would line up behind the Soviets. We could find ourselves in a real bad situation. What makes it worse is the apparent diplomatic black-out the Soviets have instituted. It's subtle, nothing blatant, but I can't get through to the premier. Which makes their actions all the more suspect and ominous."

In the pause that followed the president's words, Avery Lengyel lurched to his feet and strode over to the wet bar.

"I can use a drink," he said. "Anyone care to join me?"

The only other takers were O'Shea and Friedman. But even as they were filling their glasses, the president spoke again.

"Listen, men. It's a few minutes after noon. I don't know about the rest of you, but I need a little break. Why don't you fellas get some lunch while I go upstairs for a bit. We'll kick around some options this afternoon, say one-thirty."

# FIVE

An hour and a half later the discussion quickly settled into the same channels where they had left it, zeroing in on the key question—what should they do?

"Mr. President, you're surely not suggesting the possibility of our defending Iran," said O'Shea.

"That's the rub. Iran's certainly no friend of ours," replied the president.

It was Duke Mathias who spoke next.

"There *is* another consideration, Mr. President," he said, "besides the strategic importance of Iran relative to oil and the gulfs. The only direct route from the Soviet Union to Israel lies straight across the Plateau of Iran."

"Israel the real goal? Come on, Duke! Where'd you get a cockeyed idea like that?" exclaimed Tucker. "Even they'd never dare such a thing!"

"Iran would bitterly resent our intrusion," said Friedman, still thinking of the previous comment. "The fanatics would sooner be exterminated to the last man than accept our intervention." His drooping eyes, long, creased face, and thick crop of white hair gave him the appearance of a grandfather getting ready to read a child a bedtime story. A distinguished Yale graduate, he had risen slowly in the diplomatic service, a fact not openly attributed to his Jewish heritage, but certainly related. Only after skillfully handling several hot situations in South and Central America had he come to the attention of the public.

"We can't give the Russians Iran, no matter how we feel about their ayatollahs and desert madmen, any more than we could allow Iraq to threaten the whole region," said Howard, whose distrust of the Soviets was extreme and usually outspoken. "I tell you, they're still determined to dominate the world. They couldn't do it with tanks, so now they're trying it in other ways. They can go over to a full-fledged democracy and I'll still believe that. They'll defeat us by democratic ballot if they can. Nixon was right about the unseen, seditious war. We've been losing it for fifty years. I tell you, men, it positively makes me shudder to project fifty more years into the future and think what the world might be like with the Soviet Union turned into an economic powerhouse as a result of the aid and technology *we* gave them!"

"Come on, Dick!" said an exasperated Friedman. "That argument's as passe as a Dukakis-for-President button! Haven't you been paying attention for the last ten years? The Berlin Wall is down. The Iron Curtain is no more. Germany is one. Free trade, free travel, scientific cooperation, and democracy are everywhere. What does it take to get through to some of you guys? The Soviets are our friends now! Diplomatic differences now and then, but *friendly* superpowers, not enemies! They're *not* trying to take over the world these days. The Gulag is history. Communism is dead."

"Don't you believe it!" snapped Howard. "They've just changed their tactics, that's all!"

"They've always been a crafty lot," put in O'Shea thoughtfully, "I'll say that for them. Gobbling up nations with natural resources, whose governments aren't powerful on their own and aren't friendly with us either. Even when they allow freedoms in, as they did with their satellites under Gorbachev, in most cases those countries keep their alliance with Moscow. I hate to think of that tactic spreading south from the Caucasus and west from the Zagros, through Iraq and to the Mediterranean. We think we've seen Middle East problems up till now. With the Soviets in the area, the place would be explosive!"

"That's where they're heading," assented Mathias. "The Bible guarantees it."

"The Bible! Bosh, Duke! It's Saudi and Iranian and Iraqi oil they want, not to mention control of Hormuz," said Howard.

"What about conceding Iran but drawing the line at Turkey, or with Saudi Arabia?" suggested Avery Lengyel, the blunt-featured black man whose voice of moderation and conciliation struck such a contrast with his activist predecessors in black American politics, and whose proposals always angered the military Tucker and the emotional and anti-Soviet Howard.

"You can't be serious!" exclaimed the latter.

"Look at the map!" said Tucker. "If we let them have Iran, Iraq is free for the taking. Especially with Hussein out of the picture. No mountains, no waterways to contend with. Talk about giving them an open highway into Israel! That would hand it over on a silver platter!"

"Taking Iraq wouldn't be that simple. Iran couldn't do it in seven years of war," countered Lengyel.

"You're comparing Iran's military strength with the Soviet Union's!"

"Okay," attempted Lengyel again. "We'll include Iraq in the line-drawing scenario. We'll go straight down from Yerevan to Hormuz, right through Kuwait, and if they so much as think of crossing that line, we shoot off an immediate ultimatum."

"An ultimatum!" scoffed the attorney general. "That'll scare them to death—after we've just let them walk off with Iran! I can't believe what I'm hearing! Are we sitting around in Number 10 Downing Street in 1936!"

"Some such response may be a recourse we have to look at seriously, Avery," said the president, ignoring Howard's outburst.

"It's hardly a solution, Mr. President—if you'll permit me to say so," said Tucker, with a tinge of sarcasm. "Drawing lines after the fact—it's the classic argument of appeasement. And against dictators it never works. Besides, all this ignores the fact that if we concede Iran, the Soviets would never need to go farther. They would have the oil fields, half the Persian Gulf coastline, and a clear shot at the Saudis and our Turkish airfields. We would have handed them vast oil reserves, plus the warm-water coast they have been after for their navy since before the Crimean War. Look at the map! Do you realize how vital that small stretch of coastline on the Gulf of Oman is? To their power in Europe they could add potential control of half the world's shipping lanes. They could exercise a stranglehold on world commerce, with the possible exception of the Americas and the North Pacific. I tell you, gentlemen, it's frightening. Iran is the plum they've been after for years, the most prized piece of real estate on their horizon. Iran's the ball game! Drawing a line *after* Iran is no solution at all. Suicide would be more like it!"

"But if we attempted to intervene," argued Lengyel, "Iran would be as likely to turn on us as the Russians. They hate us! Khomeini's death changed nothing in that regard. We'd be in the middle of a war against two adversaries."

"We could never hope to win unless we had Iran's support against the Russian incursion," said Randolf. "I agree with Avery on that."

"But the American people would never allow us to fight as Iran's ally," countered Mathias. "Our electorate would come down about split on whether it favored stopping the Russians or helping the Iranians. Either way, the president's chances for reelection could be damaged."

"Ah yes," sighed MacFarlane in the midst of the increasingly heated discussion among his advisors, "the election. There's always politics to consider in the midst of everything else."

"All this talk—as if a fight is even necessary. Don't you men realize those days are past? I would still argue most strenuously in favor of some diplomatic means of holding the line," said Friedman.

"Diplomatic means, my eyeball, Oscar!" countered Tucker. "Diplomacy is for treaties, embargoes, trade agreements, and even weapon reduction talks. But to stave off a war—face-to-face with a hundred thousand Russian soldiers and tanks and missiles—no way! That's what the Pentagon's for! Do you seriously think FDR should have said, 'Okay, keep calm everyone. We're still negotiating. If they attack San Francisco, then *that's* where we draw the line'? Wake up, Oscar!"

"But this is an imaginary crisis! The Russians aren't about to go to war! All this talk is absurd!"

"And the photographs?"

"I'm sure there's an explanation. If you would just allow me to explore the diplomatic channels, Mr. President, I'm sure—"

"Your whole argument's predicated on the assumption that the Soviet threat is over, that they are now and forever our allies. I don't buy that! As Dan and Dick both articulated, I think we still have a very serious Soviet threat to consider—different from the past, perhaps, but nonetheless serious. It's still there, a slumbering giant waiting for the right moment—when our guard is down—to wake once more! I tell you, the fifth column has been there all along—thousands and thousands of Communists who never bought into the Gorbachev fancy for peace and democracy. They've waited all this time for the chance to reassert themselves. Now Gorbachev's gone and they see their opportunity. I know some of you think these are strong assertions to make. They're our friends now, everyone says. Good old Gorby! Everyone loves Gorby! Gorby won the Nobel Prize for peace! Three cheers for Gorby! Well, Gorby's not there anymore, and I think we've still got plenty to worry about!"

"So that's your answer? Go to war? With no thought of the lives it would cost?" said Friedman sarcastically.

"Of course not, Oscar!" replied Tucker. "I'm not advocating war. I'm simply advocating backbone. I'm saying make a stand for freedom that has some teeth in it, like we did with Hussein. We keep our eyes open and don't let ourselves be lulled to sleep with this amnesia that has swept the country about what kind of foundation the Soviet Union is built upon. Compare 1776 and 1917! The foundation and roots of a nation tell a great deal about its priorities and direction and future. We just mustn't forget what kind of national heritage and structure we're dealing with—one founded on murder, deceit, ruthlessness, totalitarianism, communism, and conquest. A few years of peace can't alter that foundation. Russia is still Russia."

"Gentlemen, please!" said the president with a slight grin. "Points on all sides of the argument well made and duly noted."

He paused, turning serious once more. "The question seems to me a simple one really: How do we achieve peace? What are the parameters of the power we hold in our hands? Complex dilemmas. Reagan tried the tough approach in Grenada, Lebanon, and Libya, and lives were lost over situations that many considered hardly worth it. Well, is this 1938 or is this nothing but an illusionary crisis, as Oscar contends? I don't know. I *do* know that my name will be mud—as if I'm not already low enough in the public estimation!—if we even suggest military notions. The mood in this country is certainly different than it was a few years ago. Today people wouldn't even support something as small as Bush's incursion into Panama in '89, much less our deployment in Saudi Arabia a year later! Everybody's excited about peace. The Cold War is history. Freedom has broken out everywhere. No one wants to hear military news. The puppet dictators are temporarily gone from the world scene, and so everyone thinks we've got lasting peace. And who can blame them—I hope they're right! But we have to look at all the sides.

"Ten years really isn't very long in the scheme of world history. Ten years of peace and harmony do not change the intrinsic alliances of peoples. The Arabs and Jews? A piece of paper doesn't undo four thousand years of strife. The Camp David Accords between Egypt and Israel? They were set only twenty years ago, but it might as well be a hundred. The Russians? Look at their history. For a thousand years they've been a conquering people. Their whole ethnic and national outlook on life is so different from ours. When you look at their history you realize that Gorbachev was an aberration. Stalin was the quintessential Russian leader. So they debunk Lenin and Stalin for a time and hold a few free elections. But they can just as easily reinstate their former heroes. Nothing is permanent with these kinds of regimes. Has the militaristic fifth column silently crept back into power within the Kremlin without our knowing it?

"Where *does* lasting peace come from, gentleman? That's the question. *Lasting* peace. So on the practical side, where do we—you and I, *today*!—where do we draw the line? Where do we take our stand? How do we work for peace? Diplomatically, hoping that our information is false, or hoping there is some innocent meaning we don't see in it?

"Or—if this information *is* correct, and if the Soviets *are* determined to go ahead—then, to resurrect the old Cold War domino theory, do we yield this domino, hoping against hope that it's an isolated case, that the Cold War and the domino theory are still dead and buried, hoping that down the road—somehow—someday—they will listen to reason and pull back, and that even if they do invade, they will eventually withdraw like they did from Afghanistan? Or do we stand up and say, 'No, you can't do this, even if it is only one domino, and even though you have been good boys for fifteen years'?

"That's the situation, gentlemen—the ball game, as Marty has reminded us. The reality is that we may have to decide whether or not to militarily confront our old antagonist over a country most Americans despise."

# SIX

It was two in the morning and Jarvis MacFarlane could not sleep.

As he crawled out of bed he had to smile wryly at the irony of it. The first time in days he had a chance to get some desperately needed sleep, and it had suddenly become more elusive than the "auld broonie" in the land of his ancestors. The Scots might be a superstitious people, but none of that had transferred to him. He was a rational man. There was no such thing as magic, the supernatural, Scottish second sight, or anything of that sort.

At least he had been certain of that fact three months ago.

But since then everything had changed. Now . . . well, who could tell? His world had been turned upside-down, that's all he knew.

If only there *was* some miracle-working magic word he could shout to make everything come right! How could he face another crisis, especially a military crisis in the middle of this . . . this . . . he didn't even know what to call his secret dilemma! It was too bizarre even to have a name!

But he was the president. He *had* to face this crisis, and many others. He *had* to find an answer. There was no place to pass the buck beyond him. Why had *he* been selected to carry this terrible burden, this responsibility? He'd never been a religious man. He was the wrong person for the assignment. Why not someone like Billy Graham? It was like some gigantic cosmic mistake! How could *he* possibly know what to do? No matter what solution he ultimately chose, whether it had to do with the Russians, the farmers, the inflation rate, the banks, the military, the poor, the environment, or the state of the nation's cities, he would ultimately alienate a great many people. And that would cost him votes.

Jarvis MacFarlane knew better than anyone else that he could not afford that. He had to win the election! It was no longer a matter of personal desire or pride; that had all changed three months ago. It was not even a matter of what was good for the country—for either its economy or its reputation. He still had to win for those reasons. But it was bigger now. Even if some celestial foul-up *had* landed him in this unenviable position, the situation facing him was a matter of life and death—his life, his country's life, and perhaps the whole world's. This Russian activity on the Iranian border only accentuated the urgency of his finding some way through this quagmire.

He walked over to the large window overlooking President's Park, permeated now with nighttime shadows. The trees and shrubbery representing the tenure of past leaders were now dim and formless, serving to remind him that he wasn't the only man forced into the fray of impossible circumstances not of his own making. He wondered how many of his predecessors had stood at this very window, knee-deep in self-pity, wondering where the answers were going to come from.

He took a deep breath and let out a long sigh.

Well, he certainly hadn't made it this far by feeling sorry for himself. It didn't matter that he'd slipped into the White House by the back door. He stood on a pinnacle that only a handful of men in history had attained. When he thought about it, it always amazed him that such could be the fate of the son of an Oklahoma dirt farmer.

His father had migrated west during World War II seeking work in the lucrative wartime defense factories. Jarvis was but a small child at the time, but if he reached far enough back into the faint beginnings of memory, he could still picture that dusty, barren earth, where a man could scratch a lifetime and never amount to more than what he had been in the beginning—a poor dirt farmer.

After more than forty years in the West, primarily Washington state, his father still talked with an Okie twang. Even now the old man was apt to refer to a visit to the White House with down-home simplicity: "I'm goin' to visit my son down to his place fer a whal."

MacFarlane treasured as fond memories the unsophisticated nature of his life as a boy and young man. Waking up in the two-story frame house near Wenatchee, Washington, the fragrance of apple blossoms fresh in his senses remained as clear a vision as the sight of his face in the mirror that morning. Yet how that sandy-haired kid, with no greater ambition beyond making the little league team, had changed.

Although he reached maturity between Korea and Vietnam, he had enlisted in the service upon high school graduation. After discharge from the army he attended college, though he had no specific goals in mind. Then during his senior year he got a job as a clerk in a Seattle law firm, where he began to glimpse a world he knew existed but had never really experienced, even in his peaceful army stint. He saw suffering and human depravity and people with the capacity to help who clung to cold indifference. He could still vividly recall a nineteen-year-old black youth who had been assigned to the firm by the court. He was accused of attempting to hold up a liquor store and the case appeared fairly open-and-shut, despite the young man's protests of innocence. Then just before the case was to go to court, a new lead turned up. Substantiating it, however, would entail some legwork in the lad's infamous slum neighborhood.

"He's as guilty as Al Capone," said the senior partner who was handling the case. "And there's no way I'm going to risk getting my car heisted—or worse—in that neighborhood! Besides, I've got an important golf date."

"Would it be all right if I followed it up?" asked young MacFarlane.

"You!" The fellow laughed in his face. "What do I care? Go ahead. But you can't hold the firm liable for anything that happens there."

Swallowing his natural trepidation at entering the seamy slum, MacFarlane tried to check out the new information, but came up empty. The youth ended up with an eighteen-month jail term. MacFarlane was convinced that had someone with more experience done the investigating the boy would have gotten off. Eight months later he was proven right when evidence surfaced from another source and the youth was exonerated.

That incident deeply impressed the idealistic young law clerk, who wondered how many other innocents were condemned permanently because of such incompetence and indifference. And finally he knew the direction he wanted to take. Such injustices had to be countered; someone had to be willing to care and take a few risks for those in trouble. He saw no reason why *he* should not be that person, or at least give the thing his best effort. The G.I. bill made it possible for him to pursue his law degree at the prestigious Columbia Law School, where an army buddy by the name of Jake Randolf planned to attend. From the moment he entered his first year, his life had gathered momentum like a breakneck auto race, eventually landing him in this very spot on the third floor of the White House. But all along the way he had never forgotten his dream of doing something to change the world.

How much had he really done to fulfill his idealistic visions? Was the world a better place because of him? If not, perhaps he was being given one last opportunity to accomplish something lasting. Could he make a difference?

These were questions he'd asked himself over and over since that night when all his past perspectives had so suddenly been shattered. As incredible as that night had been, at times he still wasn't sure the episode had even been real. How *could* he believe it, after all? He, a rational, sane man. There was simply no way it could have happened!

He shook his head for the thousandth time in disbelief.

Yet no amount of doubt or even denial could change the imperative before him—an imperative caused by his own imagination . . . or by . . .

Words he'd read several days earlier suddenly interrupted his discomposed thoughts. What was that he'd read in the Bible . . . something Christ said: "O Jerusalem, Jerusalem, you who kill the prophets and stone those sent to you. . . ."

There was more, but that was all he could remember at the moment. Were those prophets crazy to keep on with their preaching, with trying to make the world a better place? Maybe they would have been better off to forget the whole thing. All their preaching and righteous living didn't seem to do the world any good. No one listened to them. It was the same with Washington. This city destroyed more . . .

*What am I doing?* he thought. If people had any idea what kinds of things he thought about in the middle of the night, the places he went, the counsel he sought, they'd hang him out to dry for having gone and got religion!

He chuckled to himself. Maybe his remembering the Scripture was nothing more serious than his subconscious trying to make sure he was ready for the visit of the leaders of the National Council of Churches next week. Maybe it had nothing to do with—that—that other thing . . . with his secret life.

He crawled back into bed, pulled the covers over him, and tried to get back to sleep. Returning to thoughts of war with Russia, collapsed economies, and lost elections was almost a comfort.

# SEVEN

Martin Tucker's footfalls echoed sharply against the cold, stark walls of the Pentagon hallway, each tattoo mirroring the aloneness he felt at this moment and heightening the knot forming in his stomach.

He had a tough, no-nonsense reputation, but in reality it all depended on his audience. To the sometimes-weaklings of the State Department, he appeared quick to speak of war; to the true hawks of the joint chiefs, he was perceived as a weakling. But with the president's advisors he had taken a hard line. Such was the role he needed to occupy in the Oval Office, bringing balance to the president's circle of advisors. Some things needed to be voiced, and he was firm in the convictions he'd expressed. He did believe there was a time to confront aggression militarily, and MacFarlane needed to be brought around to that view. That's what the military was for—to defend freedom. With his Pentagon peers, however, he had to don a different hat and speak for moderation; otherwise they'd have the country in a war next week. To the president he spoke for the Pentagon; to the Pentagon he spoke for the White House.

It was a tightrope he walked. Hard-as-nails general talking tough one minute and the next being seen as a hesitant military leader by the entrenched Pentagonites. And the price he paid for that was an ulcer big enough to stick a fist through!

Tucker had achieved his present position largely by squelching any hint of ambivalence within himself. He'd risen through the ranks by skillfully wearing both hats—not deceptively, but because he truly did possess convictions that went in both directions. Unfortunately, his stomach got caught in the middle.

At this moment, as was usually the case when in the privacy of his own thoughts the two sides went to battle against each other, his ulcer churned. World events were snowballing. Perhaps his response in the meeting yesterday had been out of proportion. But it seemed as though it was all going to fall right into his lap.

When he left the Oval Office yesterday evening, he should have felt a sense of exhilaration. The most important man in the world, the president of the United States, was looking to him for leadership and decision.

What man wouldn't give his eyeteeth to be in such a position? Hadn't he worked and prepared his whole life for this moment? He stood where few persons in history have the chance to stand—in the very center of the world's decision-making process.

*Yeah, it's great,* he tried to tell himself. *I wouldn't trade it for anything—except maybe a swig of Maalox.*

Today's was a far stiffer assignment than he had faced in his seven-year tenure as secretary of defense. He now had to gather his military people about him and arrive at a course of action to recommend to MacFarlane. He had to walk a fine line between the president's desire for action and strength, and at the same time moderate the military mood that had been forced to squelch itself for nearly a decade. With this news of the Soviet mobilization, the latter was bound to advocate taking on the Russians with aggressive strategic firepower.

General Emmit Howson, chairman of the joint chiefs, would no doubt argue in favor of just that. His outspoken view had been voiced with regularity back in the '80s, striking a positive chord among many high up in the Pentagon as well as with the public. When *glasnost* had changed the face of Eastern Europe ten years ago, shifting the military priorities of the global village with cataclysmic proportions equal to a 9.5 on the Richter scale, Howson suddenly found himself without a cause to champion. Iraq had been his last hurrah militarily, and since then he considered himself put out to pasture. Yet Tucker knew the fire still burned deep within the man, a fire even ten years of peace couldn't douse. He longed to be "back in the game"—Tucker was certain of it! This news from Iran was just what he'd been waiting for, and it was sure to exacerbate his own conflict with the man.

Tucker knew that Howson despised him. Tucker may have been the head of the defense department, but Howson felt nothing but contempt for a man promoted to the top primarily for his administrative abilities. Sure, he'd made all the necessary rotation points for combat time, but even in Vietnam and Lebanon his assignments had been easy. Nothing like Howson, who'd spent practically twenty years in the hot spots and battlefields of the world.

Howson clearly represented the classic military double standard: beneath the public calm that extolled the virtues of the world's new peace burned a hunger for war. Tucker had seen the man's eyes glisten when scanning the war-games map for alternatives. What besides war could bring fulfillment to a lifetime of preparation for conflict? Was not war the *summum bonum* of life for the staunch military mind? None would admit such a thing, of course, but Tucker had witnessed that gleam in the eye, that quiver of excitement at the thought of at last being free to execute what had remained on the drawing board for so long.

The secretary of defense did not share this zeal, however. Military preparedness was one thing—defense, deterrents, readiness. His was a defensive mind. If war became necessary as the last means to protect his country's freedom, then Martin Tucker would enter into it with the dedication and diligence he brought to every task. But he would never take it for granted.

He had always seen his job as an effort to use the military to avoid conflict, rather than as the tool of war. He hated the thought of having to kill to protect truth and freedom. True, there were times when you had to be tough. And it was his hope in this present crisis that an ultimatum, and perhaps the *willingness* to go to war for freedom's sake, would in the end back the Russians down.

But now was not the time to raise philosophical questions. Today the president of the United States was looking to him to orchestrate a politically viable military response to the Soviet threat. He must stand tall as the leader of his country's military and defensive arsenal. Never an easy task, especially with Emmit Howson, whose office he was now approaching.

---

Tucker swung open the heavy door and walked inside. As he had expected, Howson's secretary had not yet arrived. The general's early morning schedule was legendary. It was said he existed on three hours sleep a night, with an occasional catnap of five or ten minutes in between.

Howson's deep baritone barked out the command to enter in response to Tucker's knock on the inner door.

"Good morning, General," the defense secretary said briskly and confidently.

"Tucker," replied the chairman of the joint chiefs, rising and offering his hand across his well-organized desk. "Have a seat."

Tucker sat down in the chair Howson had indicated, reflecting a moment on the imposing six-foot-two figure and how dwarfed he felt alongside it. If Tucker was a battering ram, Howson was a bulldozer who could turn a mere battering ram into kindling. That is if he was given the space to do so. Tucker never intended to give the five-star general that much leeway. They butted heads constantly, not so much because they disagreed fundamentally on military issues. Actually their policies were remarkably harmonious. Their strife came from personality differences, from dramatically opposing political allegiances, and because they were both determined to better the other.

Howson was sixty-nine-years old, but with his steel blue eyes, salt-and-pepper crew-cut, and perfectly squared broad shoulders, he appeared nearer fifty-five. Add to this the rows of ribbons on his chest from two wars, including a Purple Heart, a Silver Star, and the Distinguished Service Cross, and you had an individual who would cause most men to shake at the knees and begin croaking like Vienna choirboys.

Actually, Tucker admired the general, if for no other reason than that the man was tough as iron and didn't carry an ulcer around with him. But neither that admiration nor Howson's physical *presence* could make him shrink from his own responsibility to the president.

"Well, Mr. Secretary, what's the verdict from the White House?"

Tucker took the time to place his briefcase on his lap, open it, and remove several papers before replying—possibly because the general's demanding tone irritated him.

"Well . . . what did the president say? What's our move?" Howson repeated.

"The president isn't going to make it easy for us," replied Tucker. "He wants a resolution. But he's still a long way from embracing any of the ideas we've kicked around. Don't get me wrong. He's in no mood to put up with any Russian aggression. He's in a position where I think we can work with him. He wants them stopped dead in their tracks. But how—that's the rub. He knows we have to stand firm at some point—"

"Stand firm!" echoed Howson. "I've been preaching that policy for forty years. Don't tell me MacFarlane is ready to listen?"

"Maybe a little more than in the past. He wants them stopped. At least that's the way I read him. But he doesn't want to have the end of this peace on his head. So I think the question of what to do is really wrenching his gut."

"Am I to assume from your words that our timid commander in chief is finally ready to heed the joint chiefs' recommendation for a military solution to the Soviet threat?" Howson asked.

"Now hold on, General," said Tucker, ignoring the derisive reference to the president, "the president's not about to throw away the past ten years and go back to Cold War posturing."

"Ten years of peace! Nothing but a diversionary plot to weaken us!" exclaimed Howson. "When will someone in this country start listening to me? Now we have a full-fledged Soviet mobilization, and they still think all that *glasnost* bull is for real!"

"General, we're not confirming a military solution here," Tucker said, determined to make his point.

"You used the term *stand firm*," said Howson. "The president wants them 'stopped dead in their tracks'—wasn't that the way you put it?"

"But in the president's opinion that does not necessitate a purely military response. I also said he's not about to throw away the peace we've achieved."

"Peace! You actually think there are other options available for stopping the Soviets once they roll their tanks toward a border?"

"I'm here to report what the president thinks," replied Tucker in a clipped, defensive tone, for which he despised himself. He was the head of Defense. These Pentagon guys worked for *him*! So how come they always managed to make him feel small? He should have the whole lot of them fired! It wasn't easy to maintain loyalties to the White House which compelled him to defend the president, even when his personal views were closer to Howson's than MacFarlane's. Why couldn't they understand the political side of the issues he had to consider?

"And what *does* the president think?" asked Howson, his steel blue eyes filled with challenge.

"The president wants a range of options explored. There's still a lot of fluff coming out of State. He listens to that stuff."

"Then he hasn't authorized mobilization?"

"He doesn't want war."

Howson stood and threw his hands in the air in a mock display of helplessness. "What good is a military at all if we're never going to use it?"

"As a deterrent, General. I don't have to tell *you* that."

"Bull cookies!" exploded Howson. "We deterred nothing with our pacifism of the '50s and '70s. They mobilized, they invaded wherever they liked, and we did nothing. Bush showed how the military *should* be used in '90—as an *active* deterrent, with substance! But when the Soviets backed off a little with all Gorby's peace stuff, we played right into their hands by cutting back on our own defense spending."

"Cutbacks that are going to get far worse and cripple our defenses more than we can even imagine if Rose's bill goes through."

"Those fool namby-pamby idiots on the Hill! How can they listen to a moron like that?"

"The whole country's listening, General. I tell you, the contented, gullible mood out there is dangerous. This might well be our last chance to prove the worth of the military, and I don't see how we can do it without getting behind the president. You may think he's soft, but he's the only game in town. We've got to work *with* him, not against him, or Rose and his people will sink us all—you, me, the Pentagon, the president—everything. MacFarlane's our only hope."

"So, what do you suggest?"

"The president wants us to explore a tough response," replied Tucker.

"But with only soft military alternatives?" said Howson. "Come on—we've had this conversation dozens of times, and as long as our commander in chief is going to be intimidated by—"

"General, I said that standing firm did not necessitate a *purely* military response," interrupted Tucker. "I did not say that military action was altogether ruled out, or that our troops can't be part of the final scenario. While I must make clear that the president is fully exploring every diplomatic channel open to him to ward off this renewed Soviet incursion against the cause of—"

"Can the crap, Marty!" said Howson. "There aren't any six o'clock news cameras rolling. Get to your point!"

"The point I'm trying to make is that our responsibility here in the Pentagon is to explore the military side of it. When I was with him, I gave MacFarlane both barrels. He heard the full military argument. But he has to make the final decision. He is the country's leader, and he is our boss. However, until he does make that decision, I'll continue to press for military action of some kind. I think in time, if we are subtle in our approach and not too anxious to overtly bury State's arguments, I think he may come around."

"But you said—"

"I said no mobilization on our part. You know what that would lead to. We were able to mobilize against Iraq because the country and the world were behind us. This is different. The Soviets would deny our claims, and Russia is still the apple of everyone's eye, especially the Europeans. Besides, our people don't want casualties. You saw how quickly support for Bush began to fade in '90 when the talk turned to body bags. No one is willing to pay the price. So we have to walk a fine line. Prepared we must be, even though we have to go about it quietly. The press knows nothing about these latest Soviet moves, and we have to keep it that way so the public response doesn't tie our hands."

"You say prepared, Marty," said Howson in a calm voice, sounding for the first time like he was carefully listening to what the secretary of defense had to offer. "Prepared . . . how and for what?"

Tucker paused a moment before answering.

"This may come as a shock to you, especially after what I've just said. But I believe—though he didn't say it in so many words—I believe the president is actually prepared to go to war if it comes to that. I don't think he's willing to concede the Persian Gulf to the Soviets. There's just too much at stake."

For the first time Howson had no response, other than a low whistle of disbelief.

"So I suggest," Tucker went on, "that we temporarily lay aside our differences and our political biases and get to work on some proposals and options we can realistically recommend to him."

# EIGHT

Jarvis MacFarlane closed the double oak doors, then turned and strode briskly across the carpet of his private third-floor sitting room to join his guest, who had just deposited an armful of papers and a briefcase on the low coffee table and was easing himself down into his customary chair.

"I think this is one of the first times I've actually looked forward to the lesson," said the president with a broad smile.

"Come now," replied the other, "you mean to tell me these studies aren't the highlight of your week?"

The president laughed. "I know it's something I must do—a task I set for myself—but it's been years since I've had to study a foreign language. The nouns, the adjectives, the ridiculous-looking alphabet! I'm just afraid I can't possibly learn enough in time, and with the election staring me in the face, I'm staring down the barrel of a shotgun! The exercise itself is a challenge—even fun. I only wish the stakes weren't so high and I didn't have so much else on my mind."

"So what makes tonight different?"

"A new crisis. Talk about things on my mind! This one's a real doozy!"

"Care to elaborate?"

"I can't. Top secret stuff, though I don't doubt it'll be all over the press in a matter of days. Let's just say—off the record and between good friends—that your old comrades are up to their old shenanigans."

"What crisis could the Kremlin possibly cause these days?"

"Don't ask! Just stick to your teaching and be happy you're one of us now. Leave the crisis to me, and make sure you get me competent in your mother tongue," said the president. "But this was supposed to be a diversion, and here we are talking about my presidential woes!"

"Is this—this new development—something you would want to talk over with my friends, Jarvis? It sounds like just the sort of thing they've been warning you about."

MacFarlane let out a long sigh. "I don't know," he said at length, his voice weary. "Your friends mean well, and I know they're sincere. But you've got to understand, it's still—it's doggone hard for me to know what to make of it all! What they—what you all have been telling me—it's tough to swallow! I mean, it goes against every bit of my upbringing, my political views, my whole consciousness of life. I mean it's just too bizarre!"

"I know. I applaud your openness—and your willingness just to listen."

"How could I not? If they convinced you, how could I *not* pay the most serious attention? You're one of my closest friends, one of the few people in this world I can really trust. When *you* tell me it's for real, then I've got to take heed. You, a Communist by birth—"

"Never a Communist."

"Well, a Russian anyway! And if you believe it, then—well—but you see, even then, I still don't know what to make of it all!"

"It's all tied together. None of this is happening by accident. Neither is the timing coincidental. Whatever has impelled you to feel the urgency about learning Russian—"

"I'd tell you if I could, you know that," interrupted the president.

"Of course. I don't need to know. But the point I was making is that whatever that reason is, along with what we've been telling you in the group, and now this latest crisis—it's all part of it. It's just what Daniel was saying the other night—things are not merely what they appear on the surface."

Again the president sighed. "That's sure the truth—if you and Daniel are right! Can you imagine what would happen if a transcript of one of those sessions was printed in the *Post*! They'd send every one of you to the funny farm! And me along with you! No one listens to that stuff nowadays."

"Don't worry. It's a very select group Daniel assembled. Every one of them is utterly trustworthy."

"And your friend from the embassy?"

"Dmitri is sworn to secrecy just like the rest. In his case, like yours, his political survival may depend on it."

"If only I can maintain *my* secrecy getting to and from the gatherings!"

"You are being watched over, my friend," said the visitor with a smile. "More than you know! I guarantee, no harm will come to you until you fulfill your purpose."

"You keep telling me that and I'm liable to start believing you," laughed the president. "Boy, I got myself into a lot more than Russian lessons when I called you and asked for your help!"

"As I said, nothing's by chance. I only met Daniel myself last year. And everything's turned upside-down for me too. I would never have predicted any of this either!"

"Well, I'm just glad we have these lessons out in the open so we can get together regularly. Not only do I have to learn Russian, and in a hurry, but I've got to have someone to talk to about the Legation between times—to help me sort it out."

"Has there been any problem with my coming? Do you regret the decision to carry on these studies here at the White House?"

"No, I think it was the right move. I know I wanted to try to do it in secret at first, but in retrospect, I think it's a good thing we saved my clandestine arrangements for my more scandalous activity!"

Both men laughed.

"How was I to know what you were going to drag me to after a month of language study!" continued the president. "But no, I don't think there's going to be a problem. You and I have been friends for years. If they ask, I tell people you're helping me brush up on Russian culture and history—all in the spirit of the new accords between our nations and all that. And I think it's causing less of a stir than if we tried to hide it."

"What if word does get out that you're learning the Russian language?"

"I'll handle it the same way. I'll say I'm just trying to get to know our new friends better, that's all—no big deal."

"There are bound to be questions raised."

"I don't think they'll be serious."

"Unless Foster gets wind of what we're doing."

"Yeah, you're right about that," said the president with a shrug. "But then I suppose that's a chance we're going to have to take. In the meantime, we have a lot of ground to cover, so we'd best get to it."

The two men loosened their ties and turned their attention to the papers on the table in front of them.

# NINE

Jarvis MacFarlane started awake.

*Good grief*, he thought, *how can a president who can't stay awake during an important policy meeting run this country?*

Fortunately Oscar Friedman was still droning on and no one had noticed his lapse.

". . . so, gentlemen, it is my considered opinion that the diplomatic channels can and should be viewed not merely as a formality which must be observed prior to more stringent measures but as a viable alternative which can be made to work."

The secretary of state shuffled the few papers in front of him into a neat stack, then sat down. The other four men in the room—Dick Howard, Jake Randolf, Eugene O'Shea, and Duke Mathias—shifted their positions and looked toward the president for a response.

Unable to fully resettle his thoughts on the discussion, and not quite sure how much of Oscar's dissertation he had missed, MacFarlane glanced around and then gestured with outstretched arm, as if to say, "Well . . . what do the rest of you think?"

Howard quickly took the cue.

"If you'll pardon my bluntness," he said, "under the circumstances I think it's a preposterous idea, nothing but more of the usual ambassadorial runaround that the consulates of the world dish out every day. No offense, Oscar. I know it's your job, and you're good at it. But this thing we're facing demands a response with teeth in it. The Russians will ignore our mere words, no matter how strong we make them."

"You missed the whole point I was trying to make, Dick," said Friedman. "We all realize it may come to the military in the end. Therefore, we have nothing to lose by trying a less combative approach first. I think we can rely on the joint pressure of the UN, the Western Alliance, and the European community to show the Soviets the error of their ways."

"Not a chance," laughed the attorney general. "The Europeans, and even the new Alliance, are rapidly going the way the UN went in the '50s and '60s—down the road of ineffective cowing to the Russians!"

"Don't be too hard on Oscar's plan, Dick," said MacFarlane, fully himself once more. "As far as diplomatic alternatives go, I think his recommendations sound rather brilliant—calling in our markers privately, sanctions initiated not by us at all but by India. It's a capital stroke—our staying completely out of the fray. With worldwide denunciation, I think the Russians just might be coerced into backing down."

"Economically it's possible," put in Mathias, his eyes reflecting enthusiasm. "Sanctions rarely worked in the past because they've never been done on a large enough scale. But with enough economic muscle brought to bear—as in the case of Hussein—anyone can be brought to their knees."

"No way," replied Howard. "Maybe you can make it work on paper, or with a two-bit dictator, but you'd never get worldwide cooperation against the Soviet Union. And you miss the key point here—Russia is no longer in the doldrums economically. They're nearly as strong as we are. They could hold out indefinitely. If Gorbachev's *perestroika* wasn't a brilliant success in and of itself, at least it opened the way for what he wanted—a revitalized Soviet economy—in large measure because of all the aid we gave him in the euphoric days of the early '90s. I still can hardly believe Gephart's inane plan—"

"For heaven's sake, Dick, it was the humanitarian thing to do! Russians were starving. Once they laid down their arms, what could we do but help them?"

"Laid down their arms! I won't even comment on *that* statement. But the point is, we rebuilt their economy and now there's no way we can stop them if we wanted to. History repeats itself—Japan, Germany, now Russia. We sacrifice our own future to give our former enemies enough strength to bury us. We keep doing it over and over again!"

Howard paused for a moment, then continued as he got up and walked over to fix himself a glass of tonic water with ice and lemon.

"And even if you did pull off the sanctions you're talking about, they'd have the oil reserves to buy anything they wanted once they had control of the Gulf. They could blackmail the rest of us. Plus, you've got to remember that even with Gorby gone, he's still the most-loved man of the past decade—the 'Man of Peace,' as *Time* called him. He turned Russia into the darling of the world. Everybody loves the peace-loving Soviets these days! I'm sure they already have the PR figured so *they* can invade Iran and leave *us* with mud on our faces!"

"But isn't the chance worth the risk to avoid military confrontation?" argued Mathias.

"Not if it's doomed to fail from the outset—besides making us look like fools."

"Haven't you been reading the think-tank historians these last ten years, Dick?" said Randolf. "It's economics that forms the power and undergirds the alliances of the world now, not the military. Everything's changed since 1990."

"I don't agree," insisted Howard. "Military strength is all they've understood for centuries, and these last ten years don't alter an entire culture. I've read a little Russian history, and I tell you—it's their past that scares me. They are a nation and a people destined to be ruthless, military, and autocratic. For centuries there has been talk of 'change' in Russia. Peter the Great tried to reform it, then Catherine the Great. But nothing changed. Russia remained Russia. And both of them were just as cruel in their despotism as all the czars before them. It's not a Western culture, with Western ideas, Western economics, Western freedom—they're just never going to fully take root there. Even when the Communists came to power in 1917, supposedly to throw out the past, what did they really accomplish? Only changing from one form of dictatorship to another. The Communist leaders have been just as cruel as any czar in history. That's why I firmly believe what Mac alluded to a few days ago—that Gorbachev was just a brief anomaly in this long historical pattern, and that as a culture and a nation they are sure to eventually revert to their militaristic and autocratic roots. What we're seeing now is something that we should have realized was inevitable. And besides—we haven't yet touched on the most glaring deficiency in this whole scenario."

"Which is?" asked Friedman, a bit sarcastically, tiring of the critical scrutiny of his plan.

Many considered Oscar Friedman a genius in international politics, and MacFarlane had immense respect for the man, his experience, and his often creative diplomatic ideas. But there was no denying that he was gradually losing his vitality, and he had never possessed much charismatic appeal. From his monotone voice to his impassive facial expression, he rarely displayed any range of emotion or enthusiasm. *He'd be a great poker player*, MacFarlane often said to himself—just the edge he needed in diplomatic circles.

"The problem is time," Howard said in response to Friedman's inquiry. "Even if your ideas were terrific and workable, they would take half a year to consummate. We'd be months just getting to the UN, and can you imagine what it would be like trying to get the UN, the European community, and the Alliance to agree jointly on anything! And even if you *could,* putting the mechanisms in place would take another year."

The attorney general had been pacing as he preached, glass in hand. Now he stopped for a moment to allow his words to sink in. Then seeing he still had the floor, he wound up his argument.

"The scope of the idea is appealing, Oscar—I grant you that—bringing that kind of pressure to bear on the Kremlin. I've maintained for years that if we could have stopped the open pipeline of technology that allowed the Russians to keep pace with the West in weapons and space, the Cold War era would have been much different. It's too late for that now, of course. For fifty years we let them maintain a dictatorial grip on half the world, while becoming our number one enemy, all on the basis of *our* technology! And now we're just aggravating that problem all the more with our new aid and cooperation packages. But a ten-year hiatus should not blind us to the fact that internally the Soviet colossus is growing stronger every day and is still a major threat, perhaps even more than before because now they have economic muscle to go along with their military machine. Under the proper circumstances, with time, we *should* be exploring ways to counter their growing influence in the world, before they are unstoppable militarily *and* economically. But now—today—this won't help us. The Russians are mobilized *now*, and we need something operational within weeks, not months."

Howard sank back into his chair, and silence filled the Oval Office.

The president stood and slowly walked toward the window overlooking the Rose Garden. He had absorbed the pros and cons of their discussion. Now he had to weigh their arguments, knowing the fate of the country could be at stake.

Finally he turned toward them again. "Gentlemen," he began slowly, "I'm afraid Dick's nailed the problem to the wall. Time *is* crucial. I like what you've offered, Oscar. Keep refining it. Turn it into a workable design. Meanwhile, we have to come up with an immediate course of action. Martin is over at the Pentagon right now trying to hammer out a military strategy with his people. If I know Howson and the others, that strategy will be confrontive and dangerous. They're military men with military minds. That's their job—to think militarily. Just like yours, Oscar, is to think diplomatically—and yours, Duke, is economical. But unless we come up with something better, an alternative to military action that will really *work*, then I'll have no choice—I'll either have to do nothing and concede Iran to the Soviets, or heed the Pentagon's advice."

"Do you truly think there is such a thing?" asked Howard, his voice noticeably softening from its previous hard line. "An alternative that will work?"

"I hope to God there is, Dick." The president rubbed his hands wearily across his face. "I hope there is . . ."

His words trailed off, and again there was silence.

"So what we need, Mr. President," said Mathias at length, trying to distill the information into a clear-cut set of axioms and priorities, "is an immediate proposal to meet the Soviet threat *right now* on the Iranian border. Then we need a long-range plan—perhaps economic—to back up whatever we do now—something more permanent that will stem the tide of this apparent sudden renewal of the Soviets' expansionary ambitions."

"Concisely put, Duke—your usual keen analysis," said the president. "That's precisely what we need. So, gentlemen, we have our work cut out for us. Bat this around on your own—keeping in mind the press blackout on the matter. Do your homework, and we'll meet again tomorrow afternoon. Come up with something for me. The boys from the Pentagon are sure to have their military prospectus on my desk soon, and I don't want to meet them empty-handed."

One by one the men filtered out until only the attorney general remained, intently watching the exit of his colleagues.

MacFarlane closed the door and walked toward the wet bar. "Want a drink, Dick?" he asked as he poured a small shot of Glenfidich.

"You know I don't touch that stuff, Mac," said Howard, holding up his empty tonic glass.

MacFarlane laughed feebly. "Guess my mind's not all here."

In aimless fashion he walked toward his desk and sat against its polished edge. Absently he took a sip of the drink and then, staring into his glass, he said, "I thought I needed this, but—" His voice trailed away as if he had spotted something unusual in the bottom of his Scotch glass.

"For God's sake, Mac!" Howard exclaimed, sitting upright in his chair. "What the hell's the matter with you?"

"Careful, Dick. You're mixing your metaphors. What's wrong with me may turn out to be for God's sake, but I won't intentionally do anything for the sake of the other place you mention."

"Your laid-back humor won't work this time, Mr. President. You look awful. You look like—well, I won't say it, out of respect for the office. But frankly, you're a mess—staring out into space half the time, when you haven't dozed off completely."

"You noticed?"

"Don't worry. No one else did."

"There's been a lot of pressure."

"That's fine for Avery to feed to the press. But I know better. You thrive on pressure. I *know* there's something else."

"What do *you* think it is?" As he spoke, MacFarlane leaned forward with an intensity that indicated it was no mere rhetorical question.

"I'm not about to play twenty questions," Howard replied. "If something's up that I ought to know about, then tell me. If not, tell me to shut up."

The president did not answer for some time, looking at his

friend and advisor thoughtfully as he emptied his glass and set it on the desk.

"You're my best friend, Dick," he finally said, "and you're right of course—there *is* something on my mind, and I wish I could tell you. But I have to work through it alone."

"You know I'm here for you."

"I know."

"Will it—" Howard hesitated a moment, leery of appearing too calculating. "Will it affect the campaign?"

MacFarlane smiled, and the smile turned into a hearty chuckle. Howard stared at him, puzzled, wondering if perhaps there was far more wrong with his friend than he had imagined.

"Affect the campaign?" MacFarlane ruminated when his laughter died away. Compared to the forces weighing down upon him, the campaign had grown distant and insignificant. "In other words—am I seeing a psychiatrist, or am I having an affair? Well, rest easy on both counts, Dick!" He smiled at Howard's relieved sigh. "But I cannot guarantee it won't hurt me in November either. It could. Or it may help. The election's six months away."

"Listen, Mac, don't snap on me now. We've got a long haul ahead of us."

"Don't worry, my friend. I want that victory as much as anyone."

# TEN

*At least I don't have to run for my life tonight,* thought the president as he strode briskly along 17th Street. Changing their meeting location regularly was not easy to pull off, but it kept the Secret Service off balance and usually enabled him to elude them.

He pulled the thick woolen stocking cap down tightly over his ears and broke into a clumsy jog as the light turned yellow at Connecticut Avenue.

Getting out of the White House was always the tricky part. If he could make it to the streets okay, he was safe—or had been till recently. This had required taking a few underlings into his confidence, which entailed risks enough. Yet in some ways they were more trustworthy than higher-ups; they didn't know enough to question what they were told. Too awestruck in finding themselves taken into the president's personal trust, "on a matter of national security," as he told them, which was the truth, they responded with blind obedience.

With the help of some mascara he'd pilfered from his daughter's cosmetic castoffs, a fake moustache and goatee left over from some past masquerade party, his variety of hats, some worn-out sneakers, and a pair of patched-up blue-jeans he kept for occasional tramps through the woods at Camp David, he'd managed to keep his appointments without drawing a second look out in the streets of D.C.

In a way the intrigue was kind of a lark—a game of wits and challenge. Or it would have been if the stakes weren't so high and he didn't have so much else on his mind.

Veering down Connecticut and then left on L, MacFarlane reflected on the irony of the string of events that had landed him in the middle of this political quagmire.

---

The peaceful years of his predecessor, Franklin Ryan, had set him up for a fall. From the moment of his swearing in, MacFarlane had begun to run into an unending string of situations—none of emergency proportions in themselves, but of lethal cumulative effect—which had steadily eroded his standing in the public eye.

It began with a month-long bull market on Wall Street that sent the Dow to a dizzying all-time high of 4369, with enough apparent inherent solidity that a week-long, profit-taking spree only knocked off 200 points. The rising inflation and prime interest rates appeared as only minor annoyances and seemed to do nothing to quell the jubilant optimism of the business and financial communities over the state of the nation's economic future. The alarming deficit problem, the Social Security shortfall, the import-export ratio, the deeply troubled auto industry, even the last stages of the gigantic Savings and Loan bailout—these were all things that would be rectified in time, given Wall Street's strength and the continued impact of the peace dividend. Or so said many economists and business experts. The buoyant and rising GNP was strong and dependable.

But MacFarlane wasn't so sure. He had tried to keep an ear tuned to what lower-income America was feeling and saying, and he saw danger signals of an American society increasingly polarized between the contented haves and the disgruntled have-nots. But in trying to be sensitive to both sides, he had made friends of neither.

His cautionary words about the underlying bankruptcy of an economy based on deficit spending—where drugs, welfare, Social Security taxes, and high interest were sapping the nation's working classes of the chance to succeed economically—were seen as doomsday prognostications by those on top. Yet working men and women complained that the president's lackluster policies were doing nothing to combat Japanese imports, unemployment, high interest, rising taxes, and inflation.

By the poor and lower middle-income groups, MacFarlane was seen as a friend of the wealthy; while to the wealthy he was a visionless prophet of doom, when their mood called for smiles and optimism.

Somehow Ryan had succeeded in riding the wave of idealism and hope following the first years of the U.S.-Soviet peace alliance, and it had not been until his death that this malignant polarization surfaced to boomerang against his successor. MacFarlane's cause was not helped by his predecessor's singular popularity, nor by his own difficulty in finding someone willing to be his vice-presidential appointee. And the eventual selection of Jacob Coombs was known by everyone to be a mere stopgap measure. Coombs was seventy-six years old, and while a respected former ambassador to several European nations and a six-term Congressman, he was clearly at the end of his career; he had only agreed to stay on until the next election. If the president decided to run again, Coombs said, he would have to find himself another running mate. The consensus was, however, that no matter whom MacFarlane picked, his chances of being elected to the office he had inherited were slim. "Caretaker administration" was a term heard often inside the beltway as the election drew closer.

The icing on the cake had been Congressman Rose's military spending bill. Everyone knew Rose to be a whacko, a time-warp holdover from the flower children of San Francisco and now representing one of California's rich trendy districts where common sense was not necessary to public acceptance. Dozens of such ridiculous bits of far-fetched legislation were bandied about every term. Yet this one, as sometimes inexplicably happens, suddenly took on a life of its own.

Rose called for a fifty percent cut across the board on all military spending, which was already at unheard-of lows. "We've been waiting too long for the appearance of the so-called peace dividend," Rose proclaimed. It was time to dismantle warheads, bases, tanks, carriers, and even half the Pentagon. The money saved should go immediately toward deficit reduction and to provide jobs for the unemployed. Where jobs could not be found, unemployment benefits should be doubled. "Put the peace dividend into the hands of the people!" became Rose's battle cry.

It was a typical liberal proposal, and was not even the first time such an idea had been floated. But suddenly it caught the fancy of both working people and wealthy idealists alike.

"The age of militarism as a necessity of survival is past," intoned Rose. It may have served its function—he was not unwilling to admit. With the U.S. and U.S.S.R. working in harmony, all major third-world adventurism had been stopped once and for all. Now the world was one community and there was no further need for huge military arsenals. Thus it was time for a wholesale dismantling of the war machines of the past. And the growing mood of the country seemed to be more and more supportive of Rose's idealistic views.

His bill first hit the nightly newscasts a month after MacFarlane had ordered the secret surveillance missions over Russia. He could not, of course, voice these hidden concerns. Instead, he responded to Rose's bill by pointing to the renewed outbreak of hostilities between Iran and Iraq and the concerns this raised about the world's oil reserves. The Soviet Union's request to add modestly to their troop supply in the region was also mentioned.

If the president had been seen as a cautionary doomsdayer before, now his talk of "moving slowly" and the need to "maintain a strong defense even in times of peace" were viewed as hopelessly archaic by the idealists of the country. While at the other end of the spectrum, those out of work were angered that he was hesitant to use military savings to help them. And the more Rose's movement to mothball the Pentagon gained momentum, and the more the president tried to stop it, the lower he slipped in the polls. Fortunately the bill still had not passed, although it appeared certain to do so before the elections, unless these new developments convinced Congress to reconsider.

*And I seriously think I have a chance at reelection!* thought MacFarlane. *I must be a fool!*

From the beginning he'd tried to do everything in his power to right what he considered a sinking ship. He'd called in economists from every position along the confusing spectrum—from Keynesian theory to the deceased Democratic government-side practices of FDR and LBJ to the ailing supply-side Reaganomics still being touted by one or two of the faithful. To all of them he put the simple question: "How can we be facing high interest and inflation, an apparent easy money supply, healthy housing starts, steady orders for new equipment and expansion, a solid index of leading economic indicators, and bullish Wall Street while at the same time layoffs are on the increase, along with unemployment, an unhappy work force, and a shrinking U.S. asset base from more and more foreign investment in real American wealth? How can these opposing factors exist simultaneously?"

The sole consensus was the same mystifying note voiced to a frustrated Jimmy Carter in the '70s—"It shouldn't be happening!"

MacFarlane tried to do what he thought was best for all sides of his diverse constituency, yet managed to satisfy no one. He knew that permanent healing of the problems underlying the budget deficit and permanent new directions brought on by military scalebacks all required time to work. Despite his unpopularity, he truly believed his recently instituted policies were the best for the country. A changing of the guard now would upset the nation's delicate balance, poised between the widely split segments of a complex economy. Thus, all personal concerns or ambitions aside, he knew the election in November was crucial.

Then in the middle of it all came that fateful night during one of last winter's blustery storms! How could he ignore *that?* The Voice had been too urgent, too compelling. It was not the sort of Voice you ignored.

How could he possibly pull it all together: stage an election campaign, keep the press off his back, and act as commander in chief of the United States military force in the midst of an impending threat from the Soviets and an impending threat from Congress to cut the heart right out of that force? How could he do all that and pull off this clandestine assignment at the same time? Why hadn't he chosen someone else to bear these importunate tidings to Kudinsky?

Talk about complex dilemmas! Ever since he'd become involved with the Legation, he'd realized how dangerous it could be to his reputation, to his presidency. If word got out, it would cause more of a stir than Nancy Reagan's astrologer! And Nancy hadn't had to stand for reelection! These just weren't the kind of people a president mixed with.

But he liked Daniel and the others. A lot of what they said made sense. And Dmitri Mujznek, the Soviet ambassador's top assistant, was in much the same position as he—with a great deal to lose if his secret allegiances were known.

Well, he'd have to ponder the fate of the world and his own personal celestial appointment later. He had arrived at his destination.

He knocked on the door and went inside. Twelve voices warmly greeted him as one.

# ELEVEN

Jarvis MacFarlane didn't even bother to look out the window as Air Force One touched down on the runway at Detroit Metro Airport.

Despite the efforts of the city fathers, the economically troubled Detroit boasted few distinctions besides the once-powerful auto industry. "Motown" would always be remembered for its factories and its racial and union tensions.

That was one thing to be thankful for anyway, thought MacFarlane. At least there had been no race riots to contend with. Nuclear annihilation was no respecter of persons or race or anything else.

But what was he talking about! Those kinds of thoughts were supposed to be a thing of the past! This was the rosy new dawn of mankind! And he was fighting for his political life. He would have to come up with a more hopeful message than reminders of mushroom clouds, no matter what the Russians were up to—especially in this industrial city that had been hardest hit by the economic boom in the Far East.

Even MacFarlane's political enemies had considered his announcement to campaign in Michigan an act of courage. It took guts to face this city's fourteen percent unemployed. As the president saw it, however, he had little choice but to make the attempt to fill these citizens with a ray of hope.

Michigan's primary was next week, and he was not unchallenged. If that fact made him bitter, he tried to swallow it and concentrate on other things. But it was not easy. Senator George DuBois of South Carolina was ripping the party to pieces with his unabashed challenge for the nomination. His audacity in the face of tradition had paved the way for two or three others to announce candidacies of their own. It was more brutal than Kennedy's challenge of incumbent Carter in 1980, and MacFarlane only hoped the results would not be the same—the election of the opposition in November.

He didn't mind a good scuffle. He had thrived on it during his law days and in the New York gubernatorial contest. But now higher priorities demanded his attention.

As MacFarlane unfastened his seat belt and stretched his arms and legs, Phil Schmidt, chief of the Secret Service detail, walked up to his seat.

"Sir," said the ex-Marine, whose voice, even after years in the Service, still betrayed awe in the presence of the nation's number-one citizen.

"What is it, Phil?"

"Sir, we just got a message from the airport officials. There have been several threatening phone calls."

"Oh, what next!" groaned MacFarlane, more from frustration than fear.

"I suggest we get you right to the limo and leave by the rear exit. The airport men will have cleared the way."

"These threats are pretty routine," said the president.

"That's true. But it never hurts to take what precautions we can."

The president glanced out the window and saw a crowd of at least five hundred gathered behind a chain-link fence. Some were waving flags, and all seemed to be eagerly anticipating the arrival of their chief of state.

Though never a demagogue type who thrived on the homage of the crowd, MacFarlane understood well the tactical importance of the populous in any election. He could ill-afford to lose even the five hundred votes of disappointed airport greeters.

"This is a campaign, Phil," he said, "and you can't get much campaigning done sneaking in and out of back doors."

"Yes, sir. But—"

"I know this makes your job all the more difficult," continued the president, "but I'm afraid you're going to have to cover it. I'll wait a few minutes before disembarking so you can coordinate something with the locals."

"Yes, sir," Schmidt replied crisply. But before he negotiated his about-face, he hesitated.

"Something else on your mind, Phil?"

"Well, sir, not exactly," Schmidt said, obviously flustered that his

hesitation had been detected. "That is . . . may I be frank, sir?"
"I wouldn't want you to be anything else."
"I guess I just hate election years, that's all."
MacFarlane smiled. "So do I, Phil. So do I."

# TWELVE

The suite at the Carlisle-Sheridan was adequate. It was the best in the house, and the Detroit Sheridan was the best house in town. Not to mention that the chairman of the board of the Sheridan conglomerate was giving the MacFarlane campaign substantial backing.

The president and his entourage had come to the hotel directly from the airport. Now that all the arrival flurry had died down, MacFarlane turned his attention to the sheets of paper his campaign manager had laid out on the coffee table. They contained the speech he would be delivering to the autoworkers in two hours.

"Mr. President, I think you ought to lighten up here in this section on unemployment and the plight of the workingman," Lengyel said as he straightened his wire-rims on his flat nose.

"You mean pretend it doesn't exist?"

"For crying out loud, sir, they *know* it exists. By making an issue of it, even in the context of trying to show your concern, it's only apt to rouse simmering emotions."

"I want to stir their emotions. I want them to know I have emotions capable of being stirred too. I want them to know I'm as sick of joblessness as they are."

"But you don't need to apologize for it. They'll interpret that as an admission that it's your fault."

"Isn't it?"

"Sir, that's crazy. You know very well it's not your fault."

"Then why am I powerless to rectify it?" MacFarlane sighed.

"You are doing what you can, and that's what you should emphasize. That jobs bill, for example. You initiated it—tell them!"

"That bill is about to die in committee, thanks to our old friend

Congressman Rose. The end of my bill will enhance the chances for his."

"They don't know that. Even if they did, that's not your doing either. You've got to let them see your heart's in the right place. Let them see what you *have* done, not reminders about unemployment."

Lengyel had been pacing as he delivered these last few lines. Now he sank into the cushions on the opposite end of the sofa from the president.

"You asked me what I thought of the speech," he said. "Well I'll tell you. This is not Jarvis MacFarlane, president of the greatest nation on earth, speaking. This is the speech of a loser."

Before MacFarlane could respond, commotion in the outer room of the suite caught his attention, followed by female laughter. But before he could identify the pleasant-sounding intruder, she was standing in the doorway smiling down at him.

"Karen!" MacFarlane exclaimed, jumping up. He reached her in two great strides and threw his arms around her.

"Hi, Daddy."

He stepped back and took her hands in his. "You're the best sight I've seen in days!"

He was beaming so, it was hardly necessary to say how glad he was to see her, but he did—several times—as he led her the rest of the way into the room.

"Well, hello, Karen," said Lengyel, rising and taking her hand. "This is a surprise."

"I love surprises," replied the president's daughter, "both giving and receiving them. School was such a bore. I decided it was time for some field work."

"Well, you couldn't have picked a better time. I need a friendly, familiar face in the midst of all this," said MacFarlane.

"You two probably want to be alone," Lengyel said as he gathered up the papers. "But about the speech—"

"You don't have much time," said MacFarlane.

"May I have your permission to give it a try?"

"No empty platitudes or egomania."

"You won't even notice the changes. But I guarantee they'll go down smoother with the crowd you'll be facing."

"Have at it, Avery. But get it back by seven. I want time to look it over."

"Consider it done."

The moment the door closed behind the campaign manager, MacFarlane turned back to face his daughter.

"Is there anything wrong?" he asked, as if he had to get the question out of the way before anything else could be said.

Karen smiled, and MacFarlane realized how proud he was of her. Her tanned features always possessed such a healthy glow, as if she had only moments before finished a tennis match—a sport at which she still excelled in the midst of her scholastic pursuits. Her short blonde hair swept back from her face emphasized her high cheekbones, fine nose, and graceful neck. Whenever she entered a room it seemed like a fragrant breeze followed her through the door. On top of such a lively physical attractiveness, she was extremely bright and knew how to make that intelligence work for her.

She would graduate from Georgetown University in June with honors and with a full scholarship to Cornell Law School already in hand. She joked with her father that by the time he got well into his second term, she would be ready to be made attorney general. Her real goal, however, was the State Department.

"Does something have to be wrong for me to come see my favorite dad?" she replied with an impish pout and a mischievous twinkle in her hazel eyes.

He smiled. "For you to come a quarter of the way across the United States, maybe. Hardly an afternoon's stroll off campus."

"To tell you the truth," she replied. "I was in a rut. And I love campaigning."

"I'm afraid this campaign's not going to be a lark, honey. Wilson's giving me fits in the press, and I have to face a crowd of union workers in a little while."

"The blue collars haven't written you off yet—at least not from what I've read."

"Some of them, perhaps. And this crowd's not supposed to be hostile. But in the end, Wilson calls the shots. Until we know which side of the fence he's going to come down on, this state's up for grabs."

"He's got that much power?"

"Remember Daley in Chicago? Need I say anything further?"

"Then you need me all the more. Who can resist a smiling daughter who believes in her father?"

"And an eligible one."

"I didn't say that!"

He put his arm around her. "Come on," he said. "Let's have something sent up to eat. Then we can sit down and talk about more pleasant things."

"I already told the S.S. men to send up supplies."

MacFarlane laughed at the sarcastic reference to her Secret Service protectors. He was glad she had come! Political disputes, this Michigan primary, the military crisis, and the agonizing secret he must keep from those closest to him—even his daughter. Just the chance to forget it all for five minutes would be worth triple what it cost her to fly here!

"Forget *pleasant* things," she said as they sat down on the comfortable couch. "I want to hear about the campaign. You look worn out. I should be asking *you* what's wrong."

"The last couple of months have been tiring," sighed MacFarlane. "But you already know that."

"I'd like to wring DuBois's neck for what he's putting you through! He has no right!"

As she stopped for a breath, her father laughed.

"How can you laugh? It's hardly funny," she went on indignantly. "The man's an outright Benedict Arnold!"

"No, it's not at all funny," he replied, still chuckling. "But I haven't been able to laugh like this for days."

"Maybe I should move back to the big white house on Pennsylvania. You need someone to liven things up for you."

"No," he said quickly, the smile instantly gone from his face. Then he grinned, trying to soften the edge of his answer. "You're better off where you are—out of the spotlight. I have a feeling the time is coming when things may get even tougher than they've been. I don't want you caught up in this any more than necessary."

"What more can go wrong?"

"Till now it's mostly been the economy. Wait till events brewing politically and on the international scene hit the fan. I'm afraid your old man may wind up a scapegoat for more than just this country's inflation and prime lending rates."

"It's making a wreck of you, Dad!"

"Thanks. You don't look so bad yourself."

"You know what I mean."

"And I love you for your concern. But aging comes with the job, my dear."

"Then why don't you bow out? Let DuBois and the others have the heart attacks and high blood pressure. You and I could move back to Washington state, and I'll find a law school out there."

"Oh, Karen," he sighed with a wistful look in his eye. "If only there was such an easy answer."

"Why couldn't you?" she prodded.

"Because there are . . . so many things—so many reasons. Too much depends on what happens. The country could collapse if . . . if—"

"If what, Dad?"

"If I'm not able to complete some of the things going on now."

"Oh, come on. Other presidents have felt the same way about their programs, but administrations come and go, and the country survives."

"It's different this time. I don't know how to make you believe me, because I know what it sounds like. But we really are right on the edge. If someone else comes into the White House not knowing—"

"On the edge of what? You're not talking about war?"

"I really can't say any more, honey. Let's just say times are serious—both here and abroad."

They were both silent a moment.

"Well, I'd still like to see you out of the pressure, that's all. But if you're determined to stick it out, I'm with you all the way. Why, I think you're the greatest president since—"

"Since Hoover! Don't say it, please," he joked.

A knock came at the door. It opened and a hotel attendant, accompanied by a presidential aide, came in wheeling a cart. The waiter uncovered platters of sandwiches and fresh vegetables, alongside a silver coffee service and a frosty pitcher of iced tea. A silver tray of rich pastries and petits fours completed the offering. It was enough food for a small, well-pampered army, but the waiter looked apologetic.

"Are you certain you don't want to see our dinner menu?" he asked.

MacFarlane shook his head in answer, thanked the man, and soon he and Karen were alone again.

As they ate, they chatted about inconsequentials—the food, her flight, the weather, plans for her graduation. But Karen could not be content with chitchat for long. She had traveled too far to be put off. And she cared about her father.

From her earliest years they had always had a very special father-daughter relationship. Even his frequent absenteeism and the demands of his work had never harmed that. And it was a good thing they'd been close, because after Elaine MacFarlane's death it was just the two of them—the only child and the widower father. It was his shoulder she'd cried on the first time her teenaged heart had been broken.

MacFarlane had talked to many men in politics who'd become alienated from their families because their jobs demanded such total devotion. Perhaps one of the reasons it hadn't happened in their case was that, in her own way, Karen was as devoted to his job as he was. Back when he had first run for state office and she was still a toddler, she had been thrilled with the excitement. And even though now—out of concern for him—she might occasionally try to persuade him to get out of the political arena, the strategy still fascinated her, and she wanted to know everything. Knowing her drive, he had little doubt that she would achieve her own goal to be involved in diplomacy at the international level.

He often recalled with nostalgia a conversation they'd had when she could have been no older than eight. He'd been trying to explain the workings of the electoral college, and at one point he'd used as an example the fact that it would be possible for a candidate to receive fewer votes than his opponent and yet still win the presidency.

"But that's not fair!" protested an outraged Karen.

"Nobody ever said politics was supposed to be fair," he'd replied.

How true those words were! Now his own presidency was in jeopardy for that very reason. So many things not of his doing were being laid to his charge. Yet that was politics—a fierce game, with more losers than winners. He had been a winner most of his life. Maybe this particular election year was fate's way of balancing the scales.

Whatever happened, he still had his daughter. MacFarlane knew he was a lucky man. Not only did he have her devotion, but also her ability to help him put things in proper perspective, to keep straight what the priorities in life really were. He needed that now more than ever, when perspectives seemed to be as out of whack as they could get. He wished he could tell her everything, but he dared not risk it.

"So what are you going to do about DuBois?" Karen asked as she munched on a carrot stick. She had kicked off her shoes and tucked her feet up under her on the couch.

"He has a right to challenge me. All I can do is give the campaign my best shot."

"He's a spoiler! And after you got the party to make him majority leader."

"I did that to get his support for my banking bill. Don't make me sound too selfless here; expediency is the name of the game, you know. DuBois and I may both be Democrats, but politically we're at opposite ends of the spectrum."

Karen shrugged. "I still don't like it," she said.

"I'll tell you something, Karen—something I'm certain of. He's not going to get the nomination. He's making things tough, making it so I can't sit back and relax. But he's not going to win. DuBois isn't the one I have to worry about."

"Are you thinking of Foster?"

"Patrick Harcourt Foster . . . ," MacFarlane uttered the name thoughtfully, as if he had been meditating upon each word long and hard. "Sometimes I wonder why I bother to run at all."

"Daddy!" Karen sat upright and sent her father a scowl of admonition. "Anyway, he hasn't won the Republican nomination yet."

"He's been as good as unchallenged in every primary since he took New Hampshire by a landslide. Opposed by no one but a few favorite sons here and there. Do you know what *my* margin was over DuBois in New Hampshire?"

"It doesn't matter," she answered firmly. "You won. And you've won most of the primaries since, except Florida and Georgia—"

"And most of the rest on Super Tuesday!"

"You've won everywhere else!"

"Won them by squeakers. Meanwhile, DuBois is piling up votes to add to his southern sweep. All it would take for him to pass me would be one huge haul in early June."

"Foster has no foothold in the South either," she tried to console him. "We knew you'd do poorly there."

"I shouldn't be doing poorly anywhere, honey." His frustration was clearly evident in his voice. "I'm the president. I shouldn't have to fight tooth and nail for my own party's nomination! We're dividing, while Foster stands by to take the spoils. Worse—public opinion toward this office falls lower and lower throughout the world. There are things I've got to do— things that—well, I need to be in a position of strength or . . ."

He stopped. It tried to come out whenever his thoughts turned serious. He would *have* to guard his words more closely.

Karen slid over to her father and put her arms around him. "You're a good president," she said. "As much as I'd like to see you out from under the burden, another part of me wants to stand up and say, 'Don't give up!' Especially when you're finally in a position to do so much good for this country."

He ran his hand over her silky hair as he'd done when she was a child, then gently kissed her forehead. "With someone like you on my side, how could I think of cashing in? So I'll warm up on

DuBois. And once we've made mincemeat of him, I'll send Foster flying back to Chicago on his . . . backside!"

"Spoken like the fighter you are!"

They laughed together, and MacFarlane realized again how glad he was she'd come. He purposely attempted to steer the remainder of the conversation away from politics, a singularly difficult task given Karen's passion for the subject. Though encouraged by her presence, more than half his renewed show of confidence was a front. It was one of the few deceptions between them, and he no doubt would have chuckled had he known she saw right through it.

Forty minutes later, Avery Lengyel knocked on the door, then popped his head inside.

"Mr. President, we've only got about an hour," he said. "We should look at the speech again."

MacFarlane glanced toward his daughter and shrugged, as if to say, "Sorry, but duty calls."

# THIRTEEN

Karen MacFarlane slipped into the auditorium followed closely by her personal Secret Service agent Brett Renfro.

She took little notice of his alert gaze probing the crowd of some fifteen hundred men and women. He'd said nothing to her about the threatening calls. But even if he had, she still would have walked with the same cool confidence, her finely chiseled chin tilted slightly upward with almost an air of defiance, which blended nicely with her athletic gait.

Renfro was concerned about the anti-administration feeling in the unions. The autoworkers had been hit especially hard by the import imbalance. He hoped none of the threats had originated from this quarter, and for this reason he had attempted to dissuade Karen from attending her father's speech.

But this was exactly what she'd come to Detroit for, and nothing could make her miss it. She brightened to see "MacFarlane's Our Man" buttons scattered throughout the crowd, although how many of them were Avery Lengyel's plants she had no way of knowing. Her father's campaign manager had not been adverse to such tactics before, and it irked her that he found them necessary. She was not blind to her father's unpopularity. But she believed in him. If people would only give him half a chance, he would prove himself—she knew that. She wished Lengyel felt the same and would let her father prove his merit without resorting to techniques of deception.

Her father had tried to talk her into entering the auditorium with him through the back entrance where security was tightest, but she didn't want to sit on the stage with the dignitaries. She wanted to see him, hear him, and feel the pulse of his listeners from the other side of the fence.

Now that her father was president, Karen realized she could never again be a mere face in the crowd. But at least her face was less known than his. And knowing the disappointment he felt at not being able to mingle with the people as he would like, she tried to fill that void whenever there was an opportunity. She was a good judge of character and had always been sensitive to what people around her felt. She knew crowds could be hostile. But it was the individuals who mattered. Were the men and women in the street really angry with her father?

She located a seat a couple rows from the back, between a middle-aged woman in a powder-blue pantsuit and a younger man in an open-necked, short-sleeved shirt and corduroy pants. They paid little attention, not recognizing her. The man did make a quick perusal of her figure, but before he could closely examine her face, a voice boomed over the microphone at the front of the hall.

"Welcome, ladies and gentlemen!"

Karen squinted but could make out none of the faces on the platform. She fumbled in her purse for her glasses.

"I wish we'd had this many at the last union meeting. But then what's a salary raise compared to the President of the United States!"

Half-hearted laughter rippled through the crowd. The man was obviously no stand-up comic.

"If I'd known you liked long-winded speeches, I'd have booked Harley Wilson for our last meeting." He laughed and turned toward a figure seated behind him.

With her glasses in place, Karen could distinguish the individual faces of the group. There indeed sat Harley Wilson himself. *How unusual for the UTAL president to come out for a Detroit campaign speech,* she thought. Especially given his acid remarks about her father in the press recently. He could hardly be here to demonstrate a show of support—not unless his stance had dramatically changed. Was he just trying to flaunt his power before the president?

Before she could ponder the enigma of Wilson's sharing the platform with a president he apparently despised, applause broke out around her—louder than before, but not deafening by any means—and she realized she had missed the introduction of her father.

Jarvis MacFarlane moved to the podium with a relaxed, easy step, giving the impression of a man who was comfortable before a crowd. Sheer numbers did not intimidate him; he could speak to hundreds or thousands as intimately as if he were with them in his own living room. That knack had won him New York—against all odds. He conveyed the impression that he was real, both with vulnerability and humble honesty, and people usually sensed intuitively that he could be trusted. Such had always been his strength. Since entering the White House, however, the public had grown more cynical in its assessment of him. His style was the same, but the response unpredictable.

The applause was mediocre at best, and scattered throughout the hall could be heard greetings of another kind. But the occasional boos and catcalls did not dim the enthusiasm he attempted to project. Fortunately the hecklers proved outnumbered by those who seemed determined to give the president a fair hearing.

He spoke for half an hour, then spent another forty-five minutes fielding questions from the floor. It was a dangerous practice, and Lengyel had argued strenuously against it. But MacFarlane believed it worth the risk, both to demonstrate his good faith and to show he was not afraid to tackle gutsy issues head on.

In his speech he was plain-spoken about how the nation stood economically, how times had never been better for a great many people, and how these same people overlooked the plight of the working man and woman with their rosy-scenario predictions for the future. But he understood, he said, and was clear about the only course of action that could balance the scales. And a solution would not come, he assured them, by weakening the nation's defense with a scheme like Congressman Rose's. He had initiated several policies which, he was sure, would turn things around for working men and women while sacrificing none of the success the business and financial segments were experiencing.

"Resist the urge to change horses in midstream in hope of a simple answer," he told them. There weren't any easy answers, he insisted, and he was the man to keep the nation progressing toward the goals they all shared: full employment, reduced interest rates and inflation, as well as continued industrial growth. With all elements of the country pulling together, they would be stronger in the end.

"I know this isn't the sort of thing you want to hear," he said, "and I know other candidates are telling you they can accomplish more than I can. But there are no easy solutions, and I'm in the best position to do what has to be done."

To Karen, as she listened, her father was both dynamic and down-to-earth, so genuinely sensitive and real. How could anyone doubt his sincerity or integrity to carry out the world's most difficult job? *They'd have to be both blind and deaf not to vote for him,* she thought proudly. How could anyone even think of stereotypical politicians like DuBois or Foster alongside her father?

But the questions, when they came, were pointed and critical of his policies, many blaming him for their woes. Her father fielded them deftly, reminding them of all he had tried to do on their behalf. But for out-of-work autoworkers with hungry children and scant unemployment benefits, his answers held little practical punch.

"We *can't* wait!" yelled one woman. "My kids need to eat *today*!"

"Yeah," chimed in a man from the opposite side of the auditorium, "what do we tell our wives and kids?"

"Why won't you endorse the military spending bill? Isn't it time to get rid of our nuclear arms and put some of that money into jobs for us?"

"I understand your heartache," her father replied. "I have no simple resolutions. But neither do my opponents. And I don't say that a vote for me will get some of you your jobs back or will increase our share of the auto market. Our country is in the midst of a time of change. We are discovering for the first time how to function in a world of peace, where the threats facing us are primarily economic rather than military. Yet we must retain a measure of military strength too. Finding the balance—that's the difficult thing. And the worst thing possible as we seek to discover that balance would be to change administrations.

"*No* vote cast today will create a job tomorrow—no matter *who* you vote for. We've got to look to the future not the immediate. Our country is strong. The optimism on Wall Street tells us that. But it takes time for that strength to filter down.

"To answer your question—I don't know what you tell your

children. I wish I did. I'm sorry I can't put a happy face on it. But that kind of gleeful cheeriness is far too prevalent today. You know that. You see it around you. So many parts of our society are so satisfied that apathy has set in. Yet here you are wondering how you're going to feed your kids tomorrow. It's a paradox. I don't understand it—no one does. So I won't lie to you and make promises no one can back up. It may sound good, but you don't need that either. You need results. You need jobs, not only for yourselves, but for your kids ten and twenty years from now. And I'm here to tell you that we can insure that—not tomorrow, but we *can* make it happen. *If* we stick together and go for the long haul."

Yes, Karen was proud of her father. When it was over, she immediately began making her way forward through the crowd. No more incognito. She wanted to stand proudly next to him. How could anyone even think of voting for anyone else! As far as she was concerned it had been a good evening. He had made his points convincingly and with the confidence befitting a president.

As far as Jarvis MacFarlane was concerned, his only moment of hesitancy came following the question-and-answer session when he and Harley Wilson stepped toward one another and shook hands. Wilson's expression vaguely hinted of gloating, as if the crowd was playing into his hands.

The two powerful men faced off for a mere instant, both seeming to say with their eyes, "If you're determined to make this a dogfight, you're tangling with the wrong man." Yet Wilson's smug half-smile indicated that he thought he held all the cards.

The moment MacFarlane saw his daughter, all political animosities were instantly forgotten, on his part at least. He took her hand and drew her toward him and introduced her proudly to those around him. In the compelling sense of exuberance the evening had imposed upon her, Karen took even Harley Wilson's hand without giving his opposition to her father another thought.

# FOURTEEN

One man who was giving Harley Wilson considerable thought was Attorney General Dick Howard.

Avery Lengyel may have been the official campaign manager, but Howard had taken it upon himself to fill in where the cautious Lengyel didn't go far enough. If he now had to covertly press things beyond limits Lengyel would deem acceptable, well, that was the price they would have to pay for ultimate success. All good things may once have come to those who waited, but these days the good things came to those who went out and got them. *He*, for one, was not going to let Jarvis MacFarlane down.

The day was a bright one and promised to be warm, but Howard scarcely thought about the weather. He was on a mission that might prove his most important of the campaign. It was a week after the president's speech in Detroit, and just two days after the Michigan primary.

Howard had said nothing to the president beforehand, but he'd had a bad feeling about Michigan all along. A bad feeling that proved prophetic, for MacFarlane had taken a shellacking in the primary.

Losing such a key state was a blow to the campaign, besides which all predictions had indicated MacFarlane strong in the Midwest. Nobody knew why the polls said he would run strong in the states hardest hit by the recession, except possibly because DuBois had always been weak in the Northeast and Great Lakes region. But Howard had doubted the whole business, and when the primary proved the polls cockeyed, he wished he'd said something earlier.

Now he could sense the rising momentum in the DuBois camp, and it worried him. If something weren't done, he was afraid the nomination could slip away in the two or three weeks of heavy primary activity in late May and early June.

Even more worrisome in the Michigan primary, however, was that the contest had not necessarily been between the incumbent and the southern usurper. The real contestants had been MacFarlane and Harley Wilson. The withholding of his endorsement had shown most graphically what Wilson's power could do behind the scenes. You'd think the man would be trying to *curry* the president's favor, but, then, that wasn't Wilson's style. Michigan would only be the beginning if some action weren't taken quickly.

Howard turned his rented Mercedes down the broad, tree-lined avenue leading to Wilson's estate. He let out a low whistle. Acquainted as he was with the labor leader's opulent life-style, he was still unprepared for the wealthy neighborhood that greeted his eyes; this had to be one of the most luxuriant neighborhoods between the Ohio River and Chicago. He wondered how the Bronx street fighter had maneuvered admittance to such society—bought and paid for no doubt with the retirement funds he'd been accused of pilfering five years ago. Though all the charges had been dropped when one of Wilson's flunkies had been caught living high in Mexico, Howard hadn't believed Wilson innocent for a second. Even as the nation's leading law enforcement official, however, his hands had been tied. Wilson commanded not only wealth, but that essential commodity which always accompanied it—power.

At the time Howard would have given almost anything for a charge he could slap on Wilson and make stick. Today's mission was precisely because of the man's power. He hoped to make an ally of his former enemy—each working toward a common goal, despite very different motivations.

At least the scandal from "the Mexican connection," as the press had dubbed it, had died away by now and Wilson was living in a respectable community as a politician, businessman, and union leader. Hopefully the public had forgotten all about it and no longer considered the man a crook.

If only Mac could forget! This Michigan fiasco—Wilson's refusal to endorse him, followed by a drubbing at the primary—was only likely to heighten MacFarlane's dislike for the UTAL president.

The UTAL speech, despite only a moderately enthusiastic response from the audience, had come off in the national press as a resounding success. The networks had lauded the president's guts and moxie for walking into the union stronghold with his head high and shooting straight from the hip with disarming honesty and humility. His handling of the question-and-answer session had actually raised him in the polls in several states, and for once the film clips chosen to receive air time had been complimentary to the president. Most newspapers, too, gave the president high marks for the evening.

Handled adroitly, the foray into Detroit could have turned the tide of union disfavor. But without actually endorsing DuBois, Wilson made very sure that didn't happen. He had successfully kept his role as a critically important power broker alive. One might almost say he held within his own hand the capacity to select the nominee, possibly even the next president. For, after Michigan, DuBois and the president were locked in a tight race, with the industrial vote seen as one of the most telling factors in the final decision.

Howard pulled into a long driveway and faced a ten-foot brick wall spanning to the left and right of a black iron gate. A guardhouse in front of the gate reminded Howard of the old Checkpoint Charlie in Berlin. A uniformed guard stepped out, and Howard braked to a stop.

"I'm Dick Howard," he said through his open window. "I've an appointment with Mr. Wilson." The respectful "mister" grated against his true feelings for the man.

"ID please," said the guard, who obviously took his job seriously.

Howard reached into his pocket, and the guard tensed imperceptibly, his training telling him to suspect everyone. His hand moved two inches closer to his prominently displayed sidearm. *Security's tighter here than at the White House,* thought Howard dryly.

He removed his wallet and held it out to the guard, who scrutinized it carefully.

"Thanks, Mr. Howard. Sorry for the inconvenience."

"No problem. Trouble in the neighborhood?"

"No, sir. Just routine procedure," answered the guard, stepping back into the guardhouse and speaking a few words through an intercom. A moment later the gates creaked open and he waved Howard on.

Two minutes later the attorney general pulled up before the union boss's sprawling mansion. He had barely stepped from the car when a uniformed attendant hurried toward him.

"I'll park your car," said the man crisply.

This was no slipshod outfit, that was for sure. Harley Wilson knew how to live!

"Thanks," said Howard, tossing the attendant his keys.

Once through the huge main door, a maid ushered him toward the rear of the house. The interior looked as though Wilson's only instructions to his decorator had been, "Do whatever you want, as long as it's expensive." And the decorator must have been having an identity crisis at the time, for the furnishings wavered garishly between provincial and ultra-modern, oak antiques sitting next to metallic modular units with dissonant incongruity.

Interior decorating may not have been Wilson's forte, but as Howard stepped out through huge sliding glass doors onto a spacious patio bordered with expensive Italian tile and extending all the way around an Olympic-sized pool, he decided the man could not be completely without taste. The complement of guests in the spring sunshine made up for any failings indoors. It looked like the swimsuit competition for the Miss America Pageant! Ten or twelve shapely young women lounged around the patio, sipping pastel-colored drinks and talking quietly.

As Howard was escorted to a wrought-iron chair at a glass-topped table, a young woman clad in the skimpiest of blue bikinis dove from the diving board. He watched the graceful maneuver in awe, waiting for her dripping figure to break back through the surface of the water. But before she did, another of Wilson's beauties approached.

"Are you thirsty?" she asked in a throaty, sensuous voice.

Howard pulled his attention from the pool with only momentary regret. The girl standing beside his chair was positively stunning. Auburn hair draped around bare shoulders and a short Hawaiian print sarong wrapped around her body revealed enough to make Howard's throat go suddenly dry. She was holding two frothy glasses filled with some Polynesian brew and smiling through luscious pink lips.

"That looks—delicious—" he began, before his voice caught. Feeling a little foolish for his reaction to her presence, he had to remind himself he was a married man. "—but I don't drink," he finally managed to add, more out of habit than conviction. At that exact moment, he thought, a drink might not be such a bad idea.

"Really?" she asked, drawing out the word.

"Alcohol, that is."

"Are you a reformed alcoholic or simply disciplined?"

"I just believe in taking care of my body."

"Oh." She seemed daunted for a moment, as if the idea were new to her. Then she smiled and added, "Well, Harley said to take good care of you. I'll go and see if I can't come up with something more your style."

"A Perrier would be fine," Howard said, returning the smile. He allowed himself to enjoy the sight of the girl swaying away to fetch him a drink, then leaned back wondering how long he might have to wait and what other "diversions" might wander his way.

He had barely sipped a third of his mineral water, however, when Wilson's bodyguard came for him. Howard cast one final, wistful glance at the enticing scene around the pool before stepping indoors. There were more reasons than one in favor of having Harley Wilson on the cabinet.

# FIFTEEN

Harley Wilson puffed on the stub of his cigar and drummed the fingers of his left hand noisily on the top of his dark oak desk. His slate gray eyes shot silent imprecations at the man standing before him who was speaking in high-pitched, disjointed sentences.

"I did the best I could, Mr. Wilson," said the man, obviously agitated. "I mean, you can't blame me if—"

"Can't blame you!" bellowed the union boss, adding a string of oaths only slightly less lethal than the ones his eyes left unspoken. "You messed up bad in Trenton, Gallagher. I've had to send five of my boys down there to clean up the mess you made. I don't like that!"

"It wasn't my fault, I tell you," insisted Gallagher, but the hesitancy in his voice betrayed his knowledge that he was a beaten man. "The FBI was breathing down my neck. I couldn't put any pressure on Stark's men with them watching every move."

"Yeah, the FBI," returned Wilson in a patronizing tone. He leaned back in his chair and rolled the four-inch cigar stub deliberately around in his lips. "Why don't you tell me all about the FBI, Gallagher."

"Hey, man, what're you saying?" For the first time Gallagher's apparent fear was offset with a brief flicker of indignation.

"I'm saying you and I both know you've been pretty cozy with them Washington boys."

"I don't know what you heard, but it ain't true!"

"True . . . true!" returned Wilson caustically. "Who cares what's true? I sent you to do a job, and it didn't get done! That's all that counts."

"I don't like you accusing me of—"

"And I don't much give a bleeding hoot what you like or don't like!" Wilson took a puff from his cigar, found it cold, took a gold-plated lighter from his desk, relit it, blowing the smoke toward Gallagher. "I heard all about your little meetings with those agents."

"Sure they talked to me! Like I said, they been on my back."

"And what did they talk about?"

"The Trenton operation, of course. They wanted to know about Jimmy Carranco's involvement. You know, they see a big mobster turn up in the same town we're trying to reorganize, right when we're having our election and trying to squeeze out them nonunion factories, and the Feds get suspicious. They've been watching Carranco 'cause of the Atlanta trouble he was in, so they was on his trail anyway and just stumbled in on what we was doing. But there's no way they can make any connection. Everything's clean as a whistle."

"No way they can trace the loot?"

"Not a chance," replied Gallagher, relaxing slightly, thinking he was at last making his case stick.

"And our boys you planted inside Granco and Allied Transcon Trucking?"

"No one suspects a thing. They'll both be unionized in a year." Gallagher's confidence was returning. "The boys know what to do. They'll have both them companies in an uproar within months."

"That so?" drawled Wilson. He didn't believe a word Gallagher was saying. He'd seen too many men try to buffalo him in the past to be easily taken in. He had his own spies too—layer upon layer inside his own network. He knew more about Gallagher's troubles in Trenton than Gallagher realized. The two companies may have been infiltrated, but the man had bungled too many other things, and the Feds had gotten too close this time.

Wilson took a long, slow puff from his dwindling cigar. He almost seemed to be enjoying himself. Gallagher was a big, broad Irishman, whereas Wilson was small in build—a mixture of English and Italian ancestry. At one time his five-foot-nine frame had been muscular. Now he was sagging in all the places where it counted. But he possessed a power more deadly than any that could be had from an expensive weight machine. Thus he took a small man's delight in watching a huge adversary squirm before him.

"'Course it's so," replied Gallagher defensively.

"I'm not sure I can believe you," said Wilson with just a hint of a grin. "You make it all sound so good."

"Hey, I been working for you ten years, Mr. Wilson. I don't deserve this."

"You're out, Gallagher," said Wilson flatly, the grin gone from his face.

"What?"

"You heard me! Out! You said it yourself—the FBI's on your back. You're a marked man. You've become dangerous to my reputation, not to mention that Carranco ain't gonna be thrilled about having the heat on him all over again. He went up to Trenton to cool off, the way I hear it. You botched it, Gallagher. Don't you see, I got no choice."

Gallagher stood slumped before his superior in silence, as if the blow of Wilson's words had knocked the capacity for speech right out of him. At length he turned and walked toward the door. Wilson had hardly even noticed his limp when he had entered fifteen minutes earlier; now it seemed pronounced, as if to exaggerate his exit from this scene of final defeat. But as he reached the door, he turned back toward his former boss.

"You'll be sorry," he said, although his words came out more as a confused afterthought than a threat. Even as the phrase left his lips, he seemed to realize the futility of trying to get even with a man like Harley Wilson.

As the door clicked shut behind Gallagher, another man stepped forward. He'd been leaning against the wall to the right of the door like a silent sentinel.

"You gonna let him go just like that, boss?" the bodyguard asked. His tone indicated respect for his employer, along with a certain right of familiarity earned after years of faithful service. He looked every bit the part he occupied at Wilson's side, from the taut, muscular bulk to the deep white scar on his ruddy left cheek.

"This is no time for us to get involved in anything messy," Wilson replied thoughtfully, crushing his well-chewed cigar in the full ashtray on his desk. "Not while we're trying to negotiate with MacFarlane. His man is waiting to see me right now, and I don't want anything to botch this up, Frank."

"Gallagher's mad—not to mention a little stupid. He could sell the Feds a mouthful."

"Ah, he's too scared right now to go shooting off his mouth. Plus he's got Carranco to worry about. And I think even Gallagher's got wits enough not to mess with him."

"Whatever you say, boss. You want I should send in MacFarlane's flunky?"

"Better watch your mouth, Frank," said Wilson with a laugh. "Howard's the chief cop of the country! Yeah, send him in. Then make sure Gallagher's off the grounds. And just to be on the safe side, put a twenty-four-hour surveillance on him. I want to know what he's up to."

---

The attorney general's conversation with the UTAL president was both predictable and brief. Wilson displayed quite a different side of his nature than was his custom when among his own cronies, and nothing particularly unexpected came out of their talk. Howard knew the man was trying to snow him. But where backs needed mutual scratching, things must be overlooked.

Howard drove away from the labor leader's mansion confident he could make the unlikely liaison work. Sure, the disparities between Mac and Wilson were so gigantic as to make any attempted harmony hopeless from the outset. But they could probably serve each other's interests better than any two men alive.

To call Wilson roughhewn was a gross understatement of the obvious. He was a street fighter who had probably never read a book in his life, and whose idea of a stimulating evening was watching Roller Derby or mud-wrestling at the local bar and grill. The man was no intellectual, that was certain. But he did possess brains. He had climbed out of a Bronx juvenile detention center to become one of the most powerful men in the nation. And he had managed to maintain his precarious position atop UTAL through ten stormy years of labor disputes, diminishing union influence, and personal scandal.

Howard couldn't say he liked the man, but he respected Wilson's powerful influence.

Tomorrow, Howard decided, he would arrange a meeting with Mac. Once he laid out the situation, especially given the shift in momentum the Michigan loss was bound to create, there was no way Mac could refuse.

Mac would never admit it of course. But everything was riding on Harley Wilson.

# SIXTEEN

Peter Venzke would never forgot that day long ago. Although it had been twenty years, the memories of his first trip to New York City and the KGB gunmen stalking him through the freezing winter streets were as vivid as if it had been yesterday.

The trip itself had been a star-studded miracle for the thin, pale, unathletic young Moscow professor who was uncomfortable without a book or pen in his hand. For years he had been totally absorbed by his research and study of ancient Russian tongues and linguistic development, and now he had wanted nothing more than to teach in freedom.

As the years went by, his research so absorbed him that he had never taken the time for marriage. His reading took him deeper and deeper into the roots of languages, and he began to find himself intrigued with certain historical developments which did not find favor with his superiors at the university. Attempting to publish his discoveries, he found his every effort thwarted. To make public a traceable linguistic link between ancient Muscovite tribes and the wandering Hebrews of Israel was not a finding deemed "appropriate" at the higher levels of the Soviet bureaucracy. Neither did it help his cause that his study had led him to further conclude that the ancient links between Israel and the Soviet Union would be renewed at some future time, if his supposition was correct that Russia was none other than the Magog of Ezekiel 38 in the Old Testament scriptures. That he was allowed a copy of those scriptures was not to be wondered at; he was, after all, a historical scholar. But to actually read them and—far worse!—try to interpret them! Such things were more than frowned upon!

Frustrated intellectually and irritated politically, he conceived the idea of defecting.

The very notion had terrified the timid soul of Professor Peter Venzke. On the other hand, perhaps that very perception would prove his greatest asset. Who would suspect him?

He had begun making plans immediately.

He had been denied inclusion on the first roster for the International Conference on the Origin of Languages, to be held in New York City, as an expression of disfavor for his subverted article. But at the last minute his name had been added to the list; it would hardly look good for the top Soviet linguistic expert to be absent from the international conference. He had, after all, authored several internationally acclaimed books on various innocuous topics, along with a scholarly thesis published in a number of countries exploring the relationship between Slavic dialects and those of the American Indians, which would be the focus of a workshop at the conference.

A month prior to his departure, a UN attache by the name of Valeri Kasantesev successfully defected to America. Suddenly security grew unbearably tight. Another top-level defection would bend Soviet pride to the limit, and he knew they would be watching all conferees unrelentingly. By this time, however, he was determined to run the risk. The mere *idea* of freedom became a motivation stronger than anything he had known in his life, eclipsing his fears.

Venzke chose the final night of the conference at Rockefeller Center as the moment. When the coordinator completed his closing statements at the podium, hundreds swarmed toward the platform to meet the speakers and panel members. It was the moment Venzke had hoped for, and in that instant of good-natured mayhem, he slipped away.

How he managed to slide by the Soviet agents who ringed the auditorium, he had never been quite sure. But suddenly he found himself alone in a long corridor which led him to a service elevator. Earlier that day he had managed to steal a few minutes to check out his potential escape route, but the elevator was as far as his plan went. Where it would take him was anyone's guess.

It was after eleven, so there were few people about. The only sign of life he encountered inside the building was a young maintenance man who bought his story about being lost and gave him directions. Within ten minutes Venzke found himself in open air on the ground level.

His heart pounded and his shirt was already drenched in perspiration, but he felt as though he were already free. He debated a moment whether to head for a dark back street or stick to main thoroughfares. He decided on the latter, thinking that if he could just get a cab, he'd make better time and be out of danger more quickly. Cautiously he made his way onto Fifth Avenue. Even in the middle of the night it was alive with neon, cars, buses, and pedestrians. But every cab was full. He walked half a block, crossed the street, and turned right to make his way down East 51st, still in search of a cab. Then he turned for one last look at Rockefeller Center.

With uncanny timing, just at that moment the two KGB agents who had been assigned as his bodyguards came running out the door, scanning the meandering crowd. If he had remained calm and continued to walk away from them, they probably would not have noticed him. Instead, he panicked and bolted. They spotted him immediately, and within seconds he heard footsteps in pursuit.

Even as he accelerated his pace and sprinted down the sidewalk, he thought: *It's over now! I'm a dead man!* Still he ran.

Within minutes his unathletic legs and lungs passed their limit. His only chance was to use cunning.

He turned into a darkened alley, leaving the staring but unconcerned pedestrians behind, ran through to the other side, across

52nd Street between the traffic, to the opposite sidewalk, and into another alley.

His pursuers were not fooled. Their leather-soled echo was not far behind. His only advantage was his three-quarter block lead.

Suddenly the sharp report of a gun split the night air.

He had forgotten about guns! They wouldn't even have to catch him! Just get close enough to have him in their sights for a split second. His government would be far more willing to explain a dead Russian than another defecting one. Unless some miracle intervened, he would soon be on a plane bound for the Moscow morgue.

Two more shots!

He was in another alley now, hardly even aware in which direction he had come. Frantically he tried every back door he came to, but all were locked tight. Out of the alley, he raced across a wide street. By now he had not the slightest idea where he was, how far he had gone, or if he had been running in circles. Why the two agents hadn't caught or killed him by now, he couldn't imagine. He tried several more doors, then suddenly one swung open. He staggered inside and shut it behind him as quietly as he could.

Pitch black surrounded him. In the distance he heard laughter and music. He inched forward, stumbled over something, and continued another two feet before he came to a wall. Feeling his way along it to the right for a space of five or six feet, at last his hands touched another door.

Peter Venzke had inadvertently found his miracle—Kelley's Bar. No one noticed him enter through the rear corridor, and he wondered philosophically about a city so accustomed to anomalies that nothing out of the ordinary could disturb it. The thought came in no disparaging manner, however, for at the moment New York City represented Paradise. If only he was allowed to live long enough to enjoy it.

He found an empty table, took a moment for a much-needed drink, and tried to collect his thoughts. Fortunately he had succeeded in exchanging some rubles into about fifty American dollars beyond what he'd been allowed for souvenirs. The KGB accompanying the seven Soviet representatives had watched their expenditures down to the last kopek, and he'd had to be very shrewd to pull it off.

As he sipped his vodka, he watched the back door. He knew the two agents might break through any moment. Certain they'd followed him all the way across the last street, he would not feel safe until he was inside the Federal Building surrounded by FBI agents. But he would allow himself a few minutes rest here, for he had taxed his sedentary constitution well beyond collapsing point.

Somehow he had made it through the rest of the night. The bar remained open till 2:00 A.M., and after that he spent most of the hours before dawn riding around in cabs, squandering nearly all his remaining cash.

At 7:00 A.M. his cab pulled up in front of the Federal Building. Even at that early hour activity enlivened the place. But before he noticed anything else, he spotted the two KGB men standing like statues on either side of his portal to freedom.

Of course! He should have known this would be the first place they'd look for him. He was nothing but a witless amateur! Why had he even thought he'd have a chance against these trained professionals?

He signaled the cab driver to move forward again, then ducked down in the back seat until they were out of sight of the building.

He had to think! Who could help him? He should never have attempted this on his own! One needed contacts—important contacts—to pull off something of this magnitude. Preferably governmental contacts. But he knew no one!

Suddenly a scene shot into his memory—a speaker at last night's banquet—someone from government. He was—what did the Americans call them?—ah yes, a congressman! A state official of some kind. He had spoken with the man for a few minutes before they were seated.

The congressman had mentioned where he was staying—if only he could remember! Let's see . . . what was the . . .

"Driver!" he burst out excitedly. "Take me to the Excelsior Hotel!"

Traffic clogged the streets by now, so reaching their destination took a long while, which was a good thing, because it took him the entire twenty-five minutes to remember the man's name. When at last the cab screeched to a stop, they were back within five blocks of Rockefeller Center where his odyssey had begun.

Venzke paid the cabby, which left him with only two American dollars and some small change, then turned toward the towering building. If this man should refuse to help him, the game would be over.

He walked toward the reception desk wondering what the man would think of a total stranger coming to him with such a risky request. The clerk was tall, lean, and appeared nervous. He seemed the type who enjoyed his days most when they progressed smoothly and uneventfully, not a person ready to warmly receive a disheveled foreigner asking to see one of Albany's new bright lights who was staying in *his* hotel for the first time. There was nothing Venzke could do about his rumpled clothing or the redness in his eyes or the shadow of beard on his face. He was a linguist, though, so at least he might be able to cover his accent.

He cleared his throat, and in the most diplomatic English he could muster said, "Good morning. I am here to see Congressman MacFarlane."

"Is he expecting you?" asked the clerk. Years of city life had taught him to trust no one.

"In a manner of speaking. We are friends, and he asked me to come by before I left town," Venzke said, stretching the truth.

"I can't send every Tom, Dick, and Harry up to our guests' rooms."

"I understand, but—"

"And I certainly cannot give you his room number."

"If you would please ring him and tell him his friend Peter Venzke from the banquet last night is here to see him, I'm sure he'll want to see me."

Venzke was sure of nothing. What if MacFarlane didn't even recall their brief introduction? How could he be expected to? The man probably met new people every day.

But Jarvis MacFarlane *did* remember. Venzke had not given his own international fame much credit outside the circle of his profession. But beyond that, something about the Russian had caught MacFarlane's attention from the very first, as if he could read the professor's intentions in his eyes. Moreover, when the clerk called his room with Peter Venzke's message about their being friends, MacFarlane found himself doubly intrigued. He told the clerk to send "my friend Mr. Venzke" right up.

The two men hit it off immediately. MacFarlane was not a man who remained a stranger to anyone for long, and he was both sympathetic to Venzke's resolve and willing to stick his neck out on the man's behalf.

First he found a safe place for his new friend to stay. Then began the tedious and frustrating process of plowing through the red tape to gain him asylum. This was no easy task, even for an attorney and congressman with MacFarlane's connections. Not everyone on the U.S. side of the fence shared his enthusiasm. The FBI would have been willing to go to the wall to aid a defecting scientist, a KGB agent, or a diplomat. An athlete or artist whose defection would make headlines around the world was nearly as good.

"But a linguist?" said one official. "That's a different story. There's no PR in it for us."

In the following two weeks MacFarlane made two trips up to Albany, followed by one to Washington. He called in several favors owed him, met for the first time several high-ranking officials in the State Department, which would come in handy later, and in the end helped secure political asylum for his friend.

Twenty years later, Peter Venzke still hadn't forgotten that he owed everything to Jarvis MacFarlane. He had enjoyed a successful career at the university here and had written and published several more books, including one detailing his Jewish linguistic theories. He and MacFarlane had remained close friends, but whenever Venzke mentioned his indebtedness, MacFarlane would dismiss it with a wave of his hand. What he'd done was nothing so astounding, he insisted; it wasn't as if he had risked his life or anything. Any American citizen would have done the same.

Perhaps. But Venzke would not forget. Thus, when MacFarlane brought up the subject three months ago, Venzke was both eager as well as curious. Especially when MacFarlane said the time had come when he had to call in his debt.

"You always said you wanted to repay me somehow," the president said one afternoon as they lunched together at Venzke's apartment.

"And you would hear nothing of it."

"I don't like mentioning it now. But something has come up."

"I will do anything you like," replied Venzke.

"What I ask of you will be unusual," MacFarlane said, "unorthodox. You will have to comply out of a sort of blind obedience. I'm not able to tell you completely what it's about. Only the basics."

"You mean, no questions asked?"

"Let's just say *few.* And I can promise no answers."

"You are my friend."

"What I require may stretch our friendship. I don't know yet where it may lead."

"I trust you."

"Can you trust me in the face of opposition?"

"When else does it matter?"

"When they find out what we're doing, people may say things that will cause you to doubt me."

"If there were no doubts, there would be no place for trust."

"There may be dangers. I doubt it, but one can never tell."

"You trusted me when I first came to you, and there were dangers then. You put your career on the line for me. What if I had been a KGB agent? I could have ruined you. But you trusted me . . . and I trust you."

"This trust I ask of you—my not telling you everything—it's for your protection as much as mine. The stakes are high, Peter, I will tell you that much. Total secrecy would be best, but I fear that trying to be too secretive would only complicate matters. Therefore, I'm going to begin inviting you openly and regularly to the White House and we'll *hope* few questions are raised. I'd prefer that no one except the two of us know what we're doing."

"Ask what you desire of me. I will do whatever is in my power to do."

"I need to learn to speak Russian," MacFarlane replied.

"That is all?"

The president smiled. "Sounds simple to you, I suppose," he said. "But it must be the best-guarded secret in town—and inside the beltway of this city there are very few secrets, you know that. I repeat—if at all possible, only you and I must know."

"How well must you learn the language? It is not the world's most difficult, but it is not without its complexities."

"I only need to become proficient enough to converse on a diplomatic level with high-ranking Soviet officials who have no knowledge of English. In other words, I need competent conversational Russian."

"And our time frame?"

"Our time frame is now, my friend."

"I thought you spoke with an urgency in your voice."

"We haven't a day to lose. In fact, I do not exaggerate when I say that our very lives may depend on our success."

"When do we start?" said Venzke.

MacFarlane clapped him on the back. "Thank you, my good friend. You are making this easier for me than I deserve."

# SEVENTEEN

How the president arranged over the ensuing weeks to clear his evening schedule twice a week and get Peter into the White House with only a minimum of stir was something his old friend didn't fret about. The few reporters who had noticed seemed comfortable with the president's reply that, with his daughter in school, he simply felt the need to rekindle an old friendship. He was prepared with statements about how Venzke was helping him gain a feel for Soviet culture and history, but thus far a more detailed explanation had not been necessary.

Venzke knew his friend was taking a risk and that his reasons must therefore be extremely vital. He would not add to his friend's troubles by allowing himself to speculate on the nature of those reasons. In the Soviet Union he had clashed on too many occasions with his superiors over political and ideological issues. That intellectual bondage had served, when he came to America, to make him a very tolerant man. This tolerance, combined with his implicit trust in Jarvis MacFarlane, prevented his curiosity from leading him down unnecessary paths. His belief in the man was great enough to see him over the hurdles of things he didn't understand and didn't need to understand.

No doubt it was that belief in the man—knowing him to be an individual of intellectual and moral integrity—which told Peter not long after the lessons had begun that he had to introduce the president to Daniel. After hearing what Daniel had to say, Jarvis might sever both the lessons and their friendship forever, but that was a chance he had to take.

He and Jarvis hadn't really seen each other much in the last five years, and during that time everything had changed for Peter. Everything! Thus, his friend's contacting him when he did could not be accidental. The Russian lessons were of minor importance. They had merely been the doorway into something far more significant.

Peter chuckled to himself. Jarvis didn't know that yet, of course. He still thought his future hinged on his ability to master the Soviet tongue. Peter knew, however, that their association was of far wider and deeper import.

How grateful he had been when Jarvis had not written off his friends of the Legation after their first meeting.

"What is it—a secret club or something?" Jarvis had asked. "Come on, Peter. You can't expect the president of the United States to get involved in something he knows nothing about."

"No, it's no club," laughed Peter. "Just some friends of mine I think you ought to meet, that's all. I'm not asking for involvement—just a hearing."

"Then bring a couple of them with you next time you come to the White House. I'll clear them."

Venzke laughed again, but this time his tone was somber. "No, that won't do," he said. "I would never do that, for your sake! Some of the men I speak of are known. If word were to leak out that you had spoken to anyone even connected with Daniel, for instance, even if just in passing, it could ruin you politically."

"It sounds dangerous," said the president lightly, following his words with a laugh.

"More dangerous than either of us know," replied Peter. "These are serious times. But please—I want you to hear what *they* have to say. I'm still a relative newcomer myself. I'm just asking you to keep an open mind for the moment. Then if you want to write me off and get a new Russian instructor, I'll understand completely."

"What do you suggest, my friend," asked the president after a moment's silence, "if an 'official' meeting is out?"

"Could you and I have lunch somewhere?"

"You mean out in the city?"

Venzke nodded.

"A novel idea," grinned MacFarlane. "But I'm the President. I ought to be able to do what I please!"

"And the Secret Service?"

"Oh, they're always around. But they don't have to sit with us."

"Okay, you remember that Italian place we used to go to, out toward the zoo?"

"The Big Four? Of course—big old converted house."

"That's the place. They have private rooms. I know the owner pretty well, though he's not connected to the group. I'll arrange to have Daniel there well ahead of time, hidden in one of the rooms. When you and I arrive for lunch, the owner will show us to that room, and we'll have lunch with no one there but the three of us."

"I'll say you and I are going out to one of our old haunts. We'll make it seem spontaneous. That way my people don't have time to case the joint for an hour ahead of time. It ought to work."

Thus had President Jarvis MacFarlane first met Daniel of the Legation. Daniel had been outspoken yet deferential and cautious, and the president had listened attentively for over half an hour, now and then asking a penetrating question. To Venzke it even seemed that he wasn't particularly surprised at the things he heard, almost like he was already familiar with some of Daniel's message.

When they stood to leave, MacFarlane shook Daniel's hand warmly.

"I hope we can meet again," the president said. "It may surprise you to know that I am very intrigued by what you say. It's all new to me, and I can't say I agree. But I am interested to learn more."

"I'm certain Peter will be able to arrange something," replied Daniel.

Two weeks later Peter had arranged to take the president to meet more of the group. It had been difficult to arrange, but he had managed to get everyone to the appointed spot at 1:30 in the morning. He gave the president directions during one of their lessons at the White House. How he had arranged to escape from one of the tightest security networks in the world, appearing at the meeting place utterly alone, Venzke could not imagine.

Nor did he ask. Peter knew the midnight excursions added tremendously to the risks his friend was already taking. Yet Jarvis seemed hungry to come again and again. He listened in rapt attention the first couple times, then began participating more and more in the discussions—always with a healthy skepticism and probing honesty.

Though he was a newcomer, the president set the tone for the meetings, for Daniel had gathered the select group specifically to meet with the president and to be at his service for as long as he wished. MacFarlane and Peter had set the times and places for later meetings, and each time all of the twelve were present.

And thus throughout the spring of the year Jarvis MacFarlane had lived two lives—carrying out the duties of his job and the politics of a reelection campaign in the midst of a secretive inner emotional and spiritual pilgrimage. Venzke could see the stress etched deeper into the lines of his friend's face every time he met with him. As if learning the Russian language wasn't difficult enough, the president was in the midst of having his whole world turned upside down—his values, his attitudes, his perspectives on leadership and the country. And through it all, Peter was certain some *other* cloud was looming over his friend, something bigger than all this—whatever it was he had alluded to during their first conversation that he'd said must remain a secret. It seemed to haunt him deeper than all the others combined.

---

Venzke glanced at his watch.

The president was late. He must have had difficulty getting away. The president had requested that the two of them meet alone for an hour before the others arrived tonight to squeeze in some additional grammar. Time was getting short, he said.

Peter opened his thermos and poured steaming coffee into a styrofoam cup. Then he settled back in the threadbare chair, stretched out his feet, and waited.

He looked around the shabby room and wondered how Jarvis came up with these meeting places. Each time they met in a different spot. Mostly they were sleazy, back-street hotels in D.C. But a couple times they had met across the river, though how the president managed to get to those without a cabby recognizing him remained another of the many mysteries associated with the whole affair.

The hotel in which he now sat was no better and no worse than the others. Everything was old and worn out. Though he had smelled alcohol in the hallway, at least there was no pervading odor of urine in the room as there sometimes was. Nonetheless, it was a fleabag, and no one would ever expect the president of the United States to show up within miles of the place.

A knock came on the door. Two taps, a pause, then another tap, a shorter pause, and three quick taps—it was the president's signal. Venzke rose and unlocked the door.

"Good evening, Peter," said the president in rather awkward Russian. "Late as usual. I'm sorry."

He stepped inside, locked the door, and began to remove his overcoat. Despite the advance of spring, a cold chill had swept over the East for the past three days.

"No apology necessary," Venzke replied in his native tongue. Jarvis had proved a capable learner, and the lessons had progressed to the point where they could converse almost entirely in an elementary form of Russian. "Now let's begin."

He poured the president a cup of coffee from the thermos, refilled his own, then shuffled through some papers on the card table.

"We were working on verbs last time, and as I recall you still were having difficulty differentiating between the various cases. Have you been using the tapes?"

"Nearly every moment I'm alone. Which isn't often, believe me!"

"I know it's difficult."

MacFarlane laughed. "The other day I had an appointment with a certain feisty senator. He walked in just as I was shoving the recorder into a drawer. He didn't say anything, but I know he thought I was getting ready to record our conversation on the sly. It took some fast talking, once I saw that look in his eye, to convince him otherwise—I'm still not sure he bought it. I hope I don't read about it in the press one of these days. I've got enough PR problems as it is. Though that would be nothing alongside the discovery of our middle-of-the-night encounters!"

"As difficult as it is, those tapes and your private study will make the difference in how quickly you pick up the language. Our sessions together mainly give you practical dialogue practice. But alone they will accomplish little. Whatever sacrifices you make on your own will be worth it in the long run."

"I know," answered MacFarlane with a sigh, then taking a sip of coffee. "How long before I can hold my own?" he asked, switching to English.

"Russian is a difficult language. Many subtleties—

"How long?"

"That depends on many things."

"I must be fluent enough to get me by before November, hopefully much sooner."

"You never mentioned that before."

"I said soon. I believe immediately was the word," laughed the president.

"Yes. Yes, you did. I had forgotten the immediacy."

"Can we make it?"

"The course we are following is the crash course used primarily by diplomats and missionaries. It takes two to three months, and during that time they study the language, and nothing else, night and day. You can see how much longer it might take at the rate we are forced to adopt. But if it's any consolation, if you were speaking with someone who made an effort to help you, I think you could 'hold your own' right now—make yourself modestly understood. The grammar and syntax would be questionable, but your meaning would come through. You can be encouraged about your progress."

MacFarlane leaned back in his chair, staring into his coffee for several moments. Finally he exhaled slowly and set down the cup.

"Well," he said, "I can't speed it up any more. I only hope when the time comes it will be enough."

He stood and walked to the only window in the room and stared out onto the deserted street. He knew that September or October was pushing it. What if an invasion—even war—broke out before then? What if Rose's bill passed and he was left with no troops to command? Congress was trying to dry-dock the Pentagon, while the joint chiefs were calling for mobilization! The country was flying apart in every direction at once, just like Daniel said. So many what-ifs . . . so little time! If hostilities broke out before he was able to complete his mission, all would be for nought.

On top of that, there remained the ever-present chance his clandestine activities would be discovered. Everything would turn against him then! Discovery of the Russian lessons he could explain. But with Peter involved in the other meetings too, any inquiry in that direction could unravel and eventually lead to the others. And his concern was not only for his own sake. He had to protect Dmitri as well.

Time was the most critical element of the entire plan!

But he had set his course three months ago. There was no changing it now.

The approaching hooves may not have caused an earthly echo in the region from which they had been sent with their divinely appointed messages. But their coming nonetheless impelled Jarvis MacFarlane to follow the path laid out before him. As yet, however, he remained unaware that they were drawing nigh, interpreting the compulsion upon him as one to be fulfilled through temporal not eternal means. The hour for his deeper realization of the difference and for his full apprehension of his true imperative would come later.

For the moment, he perceived no alternative but to push as fast as possible with the language study, try to balance the recommendations from State and Defense, and somehow arrange the secret meeting in the fall.

He turned back toward the professor and forced a smile.

"Well, the others will start arriving before long, and if we don't get down to it we will have wasted this extra hour. I believe you were talking about verbs. . . ."

# EIGHTEEN

Jake Randolf mopped his brow with his handkerchief. The cold front had swept offshore as quickly as it had come, and today it was hot, especially for late May. It would be okay if it weren't for Dick's fetish about open windows and fresh air and the 90° heat. Jake looked over at Howard and grimaced at the sight of his cool exterior. At least Mac seemed to be sweating a little between yawns, but Jake wondered why he looked and acted so tired.

"The press isn't helping our situation much," MacFarlane sighed, giving the morning paper a halfhearted stab with his index finger as he sat down at the luncheon table laid out for the three men. He was too sleepy to give full vent to his frustration, and followed his comment with a large gulp from his mug of strong black coffee, a regular habit these days.

"The *Post* hasn't been our friend since you took office," said Howard.

"I know, but this is ridiculous. Listen: 'Once again the president seems bent on twisting events for his own political gain. This time he has manufactured a so-called crisis in order to awaken fear of the Soviets. If the president would accept the new spirit of peace between the superpowers, he would be able to see that the unity of the races is no longer just a dream but a reality. We have conquered our worst enemy—ourselves—and now stand ready to achieve the harmony we have sought throughout history. President MacFarlane is as hopelessly wedded to the past as were the fundamentalist preachers of a decade ago. Well, we say good riddance to the archaic notions of both preacher and politician who cannot embrace the new age in which we live—' I can't read any more! The audacity of them—accusing me of making up the crisis. They know nothing about the complexities of this thing."

"All they see is that news leaked out about the Russian mobilization right during discussions on the military spending bill and at the height of the primary season when you badly need a boost," said Howard. "Given their slant, it's exactly the posture I would expect from the *Post.*"

"They were always pretty liberal down there," put in Jake, "but never like this. Why, the rag's turned into little more than a New Age tract."

"Ah, yes, the good old days of Woodward and Bernstein," said

Howard. "If only Katherine Graham were still running the outfit! Liberal through and through. They may have stabbed you through the heart, but you always knew which direction the knife was coming from.

"But seriously, Mac," he continued in a more measured tone, "this kind of palaver we don't need to worry about—"

"The country believes this stuff, Dick!" interrupted MacFarlane. "Nobody's worried anymore. Except for the unemployed, people think everything is rosy. In the last poll, eighty-one percent said they thought we were making too much of the Russian troop maneuvers, and sixty-three percent said they thought the whole thing was contrived. I tell you, we *do* need to worry about this syrupy foolishness."

"We don't need to worry about it as much as we need to decide what to do, Mac. It's been a week and a half since the news was leaked, and nothing's been done. The Pentagon people are just as annoyed with you as the *Post.* They think *you're* the one playing it soft."

"How can I possibly please both sides in this asylum!"

"I'm just relaying the perspective of the joint chiefs."

"I keep telling them our choices are severely limited," MacFarlane said. "The Soviets have made no hostile moves. What do they expect me to do!"

"We have to do something, Mac," replied Howard. "You're flat on your face in the polls."

"I'm sick of the polls! I'm supposed to be the commander in chief! Yet I have to rule my every move by those idiotic measurements in order to keep hold of the lousy job. I have no power at all except that conferred on me by Gallup or Harris!"

"Maybe you'd rather have a system like our adversaries used to have. Then you wouldn't have to worry about elections at all."

"I don't need your sarcasm right now, Dick!" the president snapped. "I need you with me, not fighting me like everyone else!" He dropped his fork with a clank onto his plate. He wasn't hungry.

A long silence followed, during which he regretted his words. He had always appreciated Dick's healthy discord on political issues. Why did it annoy him now? Was there an inescapable ring of truth to his friend's words? Maybe he *was* a powerless coward, afraid to move in any direction because of the repercussions. Most fearful of all was a military confrontation. To avoid that he would gladly sacrifice his presidency, his reputation, his very life.

Of course he was afraid. Most of the country could think what it wanted. In his heart, he knew the nuclear age was not yet over. Even if no one was talking about it anymore, he knew the threat was still there.

After these last three months—after what he had seen—after what he had been shown—after his frightening look into the future—how could *any* man remain brave? Having stared nuclear annihilation square in the face, he was afraid. He would admit it. Afraid for humanity.

No one wanted to believe in peace more than he! No one wanted to keep a cozy relationship with the Soviets more than he did. But a president had to be a realist. The final decision on how to achieve those goals would always fall into the lap of whoever occupied this office. All the pomp and circumstance, the ceremonies, and "Hail to the Chief" nicely camouflaged that single gut-wrenching truth. It was the ultimate bottom line: the man who sat in the Oval Office literally had the future of the world at the tip of his finger. The man in this office *had* to be capable of dealing with that level of responsibility and pressure.

Could he, Jarvis MacFarlane, take that responsibility if faced with it? What if his private mission, which seemed completely harebrained whenever he stopped to really think about it—what if it failed?

What then? What if it was no divine appointment at all? What if the whole thing *had* been a dream, as he had so often tried to convince himself? What if the world actually was on a collision course with World War III?

Doomsdayers used to shout that sort of thing, but their numbers had greatly diminished in the last fifteen years. In the mood of optimism and peace that flourished today, *he* was called a doomsdayer—he, of all people! He the pragmatist of pragmatists! And considering the people he had gotten mixed up with, maybe it was true after all and he didn't even know it!

What if this really was zero hour? The Soviet threat could not be ignored, notwithstanding the *Post*'s ridiculous statements. What if in the end—discussions and Russian lessons and visions aside—it all came down to his decision whether or not to push the button?

Could he ever do it? Suddenly his presidency seemed to be running squarely counter to the role of peacemaker he had been given. Did he have what it might require to achieve some viable alternative?

He looked up at Howard, who stood staring out the window. "I'm sorry for my sharp words, Dick," he said. "I suppose I'm edgy because I know you're right. I have been dragging my feet, both to avoid a confrontation and to buy time."

"You have something up your sleeve you're not telling us?" asked Randolf.

"In all honesty . . . yes, I do."

"Want to let us in on it?"

"I don't know. Nothing may come of it. And the timing—it'd sound so crazy to you that—"

"Come on, Mac," interrupted Howard. "Out with it. We can't help you if you're keeping secrets."

"Maybe you're right. But I warn you, if the boys in the Pentagon heard me say this, they'd swear I was a lunatic."

"Out with it, man! We know you. You know we won't think that."

MacFarlane hesitated but a moment longer, then burst out, "I want to meet with Kudinsky."

Randolf emitted a low whistle. "Howson and his entourage don't feel too kindly disposed toward him, that's for sure."

"Chamberlain walking into Hitler's lair, that's what they'd say," added Howard.

"But think of the other side," said Randolf thoughtfully. "Given the current mood in the country, the thing might play pretty well. You could be seen as falling in with the peace advocates for a change. It might take some of the wind out of their sails of criticism. It might even slow down Rose's spending bandwagon."

"Might is the operative word, Jake," replied the president. "These are volatile times. It's impossible to predict how the public would react, but it's something I know I've got to do."

"If DuBois or Foster ever got hold of it," said Howard, "oh boy! It'd be your head on a platter! I don't know exactly what spin they'd put on it, but you can be sure they'd make you look like a sap."

"I told you it was crazy. And there's no good time—with their troops mobilized, the campaign, the convention coming up."

"What if this crisis isn't as bad as everyone thinks?" suggested Randolf. "What if they're not preparing to attack?"

"Look at the situation realistically," replied Howard. "They're not going to massively build up troops for no reason."

"But they're doing nothing with them."

"That's part of the strategy—the waiting game! And I'll tell you what they're waiting for. They're waiting for just the right moment . . . till something happens here to weaken us—for a day, a week . . . just enough for us to be thrown off balance. Then in that moment, they'll strike."

"Maybe all the maneuvering is only to throw us off," suggested the president. "What if they're trying to lure our boys at the Pentagon into making a foolish move?"

"I don't buy it," said Howard. "No, they want Iran. I'm sure of it. And they're waiting for just the right moment to jump. It's just like Czechoslovakia. Why didn't they invade Prague in 1967 or 1969? Why 1968? Because it was our election year, and right when Vietnam was at its height. Johnson had just withdrawn from the race. The presidency was lame duck. Two assassinations. Student protests and riots. Our country was in the midst of its greatest turmoil since the Civil War, and they knew we would be powerless to do anything. And *that's* why they were able to take such an aggressive action in '68. They're waiting for the same thing now—a weakening of our position."

"Such as our defeat in November?"

"Such as your defeat at the convention! Can you imagine what an opportunity that would give them? Our own president defeated by his own party! It would be their engraved invitation to move without worry of a united stand against them from within the U.S. government. I tell you, Mac, this is why I wish you would let me explore—"

"I think there may be another explanation for their indecisiveness," interrupted Randolf. "Internal strife."

"Come on, Jake!" said Howard.

"We've all heard the rumors," said the president. "but if it's serious, they've been pretty good at masking it."

"I've told you about my impressions from my trip there last winter," said Randolf. "But something keeps nagging me from that visit. Kudinsky was an agreeable enough sort. As Soviet premiers go, we've seen worse, and frankly, I have to think we might do better with him than Gorbachev. He's continued with all Gorbachev's policies till now, making no waves until their next election. He's a caretaker in kind of the same way you are, now that they have elections in the Soviet Union, though the power struggles internally are fierce before the nomination process. I know it's too early to tell—it's been less than a year since Gorbachev died—"

"Yes," sighed the president, "but now a year's gone by and we've not yet sat down to talk. I only hope it's not too late."

"I think Kudinsky will win their election. As acting president, he's got to have the inside track, and I'm not so sure his coming to power might not be in our best interest—that is, if the rumors of strife in the Kremlin are false."

"Go on, Jake. What are you driving at?"

"Just a hunch, of course. Any interpretation of what these last ten years really mean historically hinges on the outcome of this present crisis. I mean if the Gorbachev era will prove nothing more than a Sadat-Begin interlude, after which U.S.-Soviet relations will go back to the pre-1986 jockeying for military supremacy, then that's one thing. If the changes are destined to be permanent, that's another. Although if the threat of invasion is for real, it's a moot point."

"Come on, come on, Jake, get to your point!"

"What I'm sensing is this: *if* we can avert war—weather this Iranian crisis—we may come out ahead in the long run, better than we would have with a 'peaceful' relationship with a Gorbachev-led Soviet Union."

"What do you mean, Jake?" said the president.

"Well, given his personal charisma, in another ten years Gorbachev would have amassed such an incredible bloc of power that, coupled with the industrial and economical strength he was fast bringing to Russia—well, I think they could have overpowered us on nearly every front. Western Europe couldn't run to him fast enough after the crumbling of the Wall and the democratization of the Eastern bloc in '89 and '90. You remember what it was like when he met the Pope in '89. Why, *he* was the one being worshiped by the adoring throngs! Picture it—we were headed toward a London-Moscow alliance, running straight through the Berlin of a united Germany! We were going to be left out in the cold. The Soviets would ultimately have achieved their goal of world dominion, but in a far different way than Lenin or Stalin would have foreseen. Gorbachev would have made them proud, once they wised up to where his strategy was leading! Though even his own people didn't see it at first. I heard hints when I was there that the assassination plot of '93 originated from within the Kremlin!"

"Wouldn't surprise me!" said Howard. "Moscow had its hard-liners, just as we did in Washington, who wanted no part of his reforms."

"The point I'm trying to make," said Randolf, "is that Kudinsky is a nice enough fellow, but not so public, not so appealing, doesn't have a pretty wife—isn't even married. My personal opinion is that we're fortunate Gorbachev died when he did."

"So what are you saying?" prodded Howard.

"I'm saying that there's a rising star on the horizon that we'd better start taking seriously."

"Leonid Bolotnikov?" said the president.

"Right! The second-in-command of the whole military machine," said Randolf. "I met him while I was over there, and he's pompous and bigoted and old-school Russian, as hawkish as they come. I'm convinced he wants to reestablish the Soviet Union as a superpower after this decade hiatus. And Bolotnikov's not alone. The peace-proponents and anti-Pentagon people don't realize how many of those guys remain in Moscow—there are still plenty of Stalinist, Brezhnev-types left. I can't imagine how Gorbachev managed to push through the first INF treaty with Reagan, and then succeeded in presiding over the dismantling of the Iron Curtain and the Communist stranglehold on the Warsaw Pact countries in spite of guys like Bolotnikov. He must have really been a power-brokering politician, I'll say that for him! Or maybe they just played it low profile, waiting for the pendulum to swing back in their direction. Maybe they *did* know that his demise was inevitable and that they'd be able to seize the rudder again before long. I don't know—I'm guessing here."

"So what does all this have to do with your original point?" asked the president.

"Despite attempts to keep a lid on reports of infighting, they can't hide the fact that Kudinsky and Bolotnikov are never seen together. If they appear together, they plant themselves at opposite ends of the room."

"It does make you wonder," admitted Howard.

"If things are so hot, then why doesn't Kudinsky just get rid of Bolotnikov?—is that what you're getting at, Jake?" asked MacFarlane.

"Exactly! If he had the power base he could. Gorbachev managed to get rid of people and pushed through all those changes we never would have believed possible. But what I'm thinking is that if we have two very divergent factions in Washington, why not in the Kremlin? Gorbachev may have been able to keep the hard-liners down for a while, but with him gone, they can mount a challenge to Kudinsky for the reins of power. And maybe that's exactly what's happened. Maybe they did get the upper hand temporarily, ordered up the mobilization, Kudinsky fought back . . . who knows!"

"Which is why they're vacillating about Iran right now," said Howard thoughtfully, rubbing his chin as he considered this new perspective. "It would almost be too good to be true—internal squabbling at the highest level, rendering their army temporarily impotent."

"I would hardly say impotent!" said MacFarlane. "Yet if it were true, it might give me the time I needed."

"Time? Time for what, Mac?" asked Randolf.

"Oh . . . I mean, it might give us a negotiating edge. You know, buy us some time. Possibly make a meeting with Kudinsky more feasible."

"Jake, what you say is all well and good," said Howard. "But from the standpoint of our press and our public, it still looks like the president's not doing anything. Mac, *we* know what you're going through, but try to convince Ted Scott at the *Post,* or the voters in the next primary."

"Well, come what may, I'm not going to do anything rash," said the president. "I won't start saying the words people want to hear just because it's expedient, any more than I'll try to act tough just to get reelected. And I don't really care how a visit with Kudinsky would 'play' as you say, Jake. I have to do what I think is right for the country—and right for me."

"We're not suggesting anything rash, Mac—or that you compromise. I'm only encouraging you to do something to hedge your bets."

MacFarlane eyed his friend skeptically. He could almost guess what was coming, but he asked the question anyway. "How do you propose I do that?"

"I was starting to explain that a few minutes ago," replied Howard. "You want to be able to act independently of the influence of votes, right? Do what you think is best for the country without having to worry about the political implications every five minutes?"

"Yes, of course," MacFarlane said cautiously. "To a certain extent. But not totally independent. We are still a nation of the people, by the people, and for the people."

"Granted. But you'd like the election assured so you'd be free to do what you consider in the best interests of the people?"

MacFarlane nodded reluctantly, waiting for the bombshell he could feel was coming.

"So," the attorney general said, "Harley Wilson can do that for you."

Randolf and MacFarlane both burst out laughing. Howard sounded like a salesman introducing a new laundry detergent.

Howard drained his coffee cup and slammed it down in its saucer. "You two make me feel like a headmaster in a prep school!"

"Sorry, Dick," laughed MacFarlane, dabbing his eyes with his napkin. "Forgive me on the grounds that I get so little amusement these days."

"By all means!" returned Howard with mock sarcasm. "Anything I can do to provide a good laugh." Then he smiled. "At any rate, it's good to see you laugh, Mac. It almost makes it worth being the butt of the joke. But I am serious about Wilson. Don't underestimate his power to help us."

"Oh, I don't underestimate his power, Dick. But as for working him into our plans—"

"He told me he was willing—" Suddenly Howard stopped. He hadn't meant to mention his meeting with the labor leader just yet.

"He told you what?"

"I met with him, Mac. I didn't want to bring this to you without knowing what his response would be."

"Okay, you saw him," said MacFarlane tightly. "No harm done. I only hope you didn't make any commitments."

"I wouldn't do that," said Howard. "It was just a little preliminary exploration. He could make a big difference. He could turn the tide. Michigan was a prime example of the clout he wields."

"I realize that, and I can't say it appeals to me."

"I'm not saying you have to like the guy—or even like his methods. But we need him, Mac. And the sooner we accept that, the sooner we can swing the tide of this campaign back in our favor."

"If that's what it takes to win, I'm not sure it's worth the price. Maybe my daughter's right. Maybe I *should* go back to Washington state and open a little law practice and grow apples."

"The country needs you, Mac! And you know it," said Howard.

The president hardly heard his friend's words. Already he had turned and was gazing absently toward the other side of the room.

Dick was right. He hadn't been serious. As soon as he spoke the words, he found himself wondering if what he *wanted* had anything to do with it any longer. Phrases like "the end justifying the means" tumbled into his mind.

Had he finally come to that? Had all his years trying to attain some kind of moral responsibility in his career been for nothing? Had his attempt to make a dedicated difference in the world gone up in smoke with the Russian mobilization? Now, face to face with the biggest dilemma of his life, would he have to throw aside integrity and morality and ethics in favor of expediency—in favor of boosting his own reputation?

He turned back and stared momentarily at his two friends. Could they possibly understand, even if he told them? How many times he had struggled, aching to share the burden of what had happened three months ago. Was his reluctance just further evidence of his own cowardice? Was he afraid to trust them, afraid to bear the sting of their ridicule? Even if they didn't accuse him of losing his mind, they would never sanction what he planned to do.

"Mac, what's on your mind?" Jake asked, sounding genuinely concerned. "You seem distracted."

"Yes . . . yes, I'm fine," he replied. "I just need a rest from all this. Maybe we ought to postpone the rest of our meeting until tomorrow."

"I don't know what's been eating you lately!" exclaimed Howard. "We're trying to understand, but you're making it hard."

"I'm sorry, Dick."

"Mac, I think what Dick is trying to say is that we want to help," said Jake. "Times are tough. But don't give up. We can get through this."

"I haven't given up," he said, though his voice sounded faraway.

"Well, then, you're doing a good imitation of it," snapped Howard.

"Dick!" admonished Randolf.

"You have an election ahead of you, Mac!" Dick said, ignoring the reprimand. "You better pull yourself together! DuBois will be a cakewalk compared to Foster."

"Foster . . ." mused MacFarlane. "As if things weren't bad enough."

"Listen, Mac, if you *have* given up, maybe we should quit busting our chops for you. Just give the word and we'll drop the whole blasted thing!"

In a quick and decisive move, MacFarlane pushed himself away from the table and jerked to his feet. He seemed suddenly to shake the fog from his brain as he glared down at Howard.

"Get this, and get it straight—*I haven't given up!*"

Taken aback but not cowed, Howard restrained a relieved smile. He stood and shook his friend's hand. "Fine, Mac! I'm glad to hear it. We're both with you all the way."

Mac's final statement was all Howard wanted to hear. Something definitely was bothering his friend and boss, but at least it hadn't knocked the fight out of him. And they had to keep him primed for the battle ahead.

Patrick Harcourt Foster was no lightweight opponent.

Meanwhile, as the door closed behind them, the president

slumped into his favorite stuffed chair, pondering his *own* private thoughts.

"I've got to tell somebody!" he said to himself at length. "But who can I tell? They would all think I've flipped!"

# NINETEEN

A silent cloud of smoke suspended lazily below the ceiling, shot through at intervals with fading beams of sunlight. It stood as a subtle reminder that the lovely summer day was quickly slipping away.

The four men in the penthouse high above Chicago's Loop had been cloistered together most of the afternoon.

"For crying out loud, Harv," Andrew Nyborg was saying in a decidedly heated tone, "playing games like that will land us all in the slammer!"

"Come off it, Andy. This is no church picnic. This league plays hardball. Do you think MacFarlane got where he is without some crafty plotting? You can bet he's made his share of deals and rubbed shoulders with a few shady ones himself. Believe me, he's not about to let us turn over his apple cart without striking back just as viciously."

Harv Bateman, stocky, balding on top, and approaching fifty rather ungraciously, often deadlocked with Andrew Nyborg over matters of ethical protocol. Nyborg, the tall, patrician Bostonian lawyer, usually urged wisdom and constraint in his cool, phlegmatic manner. Bateman, on the other hand, stood ready to roll up his sleeves and do almost anything to achieve his ends.

"I'm afraid I've got to go along with Andy on this one," said Hudson Hayford. The highly regarded Harvard economist had recently taken a leave of absence to join the inner circle of Patrick Foster's campaign staff. "Politics may not be my game, and I know I'm here to give advice on economic issues, but I feel I must say, with all respect, Harv, that we mustn't lose sight of the memory of Watergate."

"I'm sick of everyone squawking 'Watergate' the minute someone wants to show a little backbone. No one's suggesting another mess like that," rejoined Bateman, clearly irritated at the insinuation.

"We're all willing to stick our necks out for the cause," responded Hayford, "but none of us wants to attempt anything . . . compromising."

"Everything I've suggested lies fully within the law."

"Listen to yourself, Harv—to what you're proposing. There are similarities."

"Those Nixon bunglers broke the rules, obstructed justice, and they paid for it. My plan has none of those pitfalls."

"What you fail to take into consideration," broke in the final member of the group, a portly, balding man in his late sixties, Sam Lavender, ex-mayor of St. Louis, "are the subtle ramifications. Legal or not, what will the people think if they catch wind of all this? We may well be within the law and still damage the campaign if it became known."

"It won't. We'll take steps to insure—"

"That's what Nixon's men thought," put in Nyborg, "all the way to jail. It's called cover-up."

"Now just a minute, Andy!" said an affronted Bateman.

"Hold on, boys," interjected Lavender, who clearly considered his age and years of experience his license to act as a sort of fatherly overseer to the younger men. "We'll get nowhere this way. Andrew, you need to curb some of that righteousness. After all, this *is* a campaign, and we are allowed some latitude. There may be some problems with Harv's proposal, but we shouldn't throw it out altogether. And comparing it to Nixon's blunders is, I think, going too far."

Bateman's expression immediately grew smug, but Lavender gave him no chance to enjoy his victory, for he continued almost without a pause, "And you, Harv. You get so wound up in your schemes that you forget your good sense. Every campaign needn't be a blitzkrieg."

"Well, then, since you brought up the comparison, let me remind you all of one important thing," Bateman replied, taking the offensive again. "Except for the fact that they got caught, Nixon's campaign strategy worked perfectly in '72. The smear of Kennedy and Muskie, the bogus mailings, the use of the press. Nixon buried McGovern. And what about Bush's use of Willie Horton? Why not follow their lead. If we can stay within the law, keep a lid on, why not—"

"But who needs it?" insisted Nyborg, moderating his heated tone. "We're far ahead of MacFarlane in the polls. Pat is a shoo-in at the convention. Our best posture is to lay back and just wait for November 7. The only thing that can kill us is to blunder badly. If we run a nice conservative campaign, Pat's popularity will carry the day."

"I can't agree with you there, Andrew," said Lavender. "We're dealing with an incumbent. That will naturally swing things MacFarlane's way. For instance, if there's the slightest improvement in things for the work force, he'll get credit for the upturn. And it's not too late for him to ingratiate himself with the great contented masses. He may not have Pat's charisma, and he may not know the right phrases to plug into the country's mood like Pat does, but he's not without some savvy. And it's a well-known political curse that front-runner poll points evaporate through the fall when the race inevitably tightens. No, Andrew, we are going to need an aggressive campaign."

"Here, here!" cheered Bateman, lifting his half-filled tumbler of bourbon in a mock toast to his new ally in the debate. "Aggressive campaigning—I like it!"

"Aggressive, yes. An old political war-horse like me loves a good scrap. But we've got to walk warily," cautioned Lavender. "Like your proposed secret meeting with Bolotnikov. Something like that could blow up in our faces, Harv. Things are volatile with the Russians. I doubt the public would stand for that kind of back-room maneuvering, especially if—and you can be sure he would—MacFarlane played the outraged commander in chief, claiming that Foster was merely posturing to get elected and leading us toward war with his diplomatic games. Remember Jesse Jackson's loss of prestige from all his shenanigans with the Cubans and the Libyans."

"Not only that, but when you consider our strong peace stance, Patrick could look like he was capitulating," offered Hayford. "All these years he's promoted the peace movement, telling the country we must take Gorbachev at his word, using that stance to make MacFarlane seem like a gloomy Cold War holdout. So if we're not careful, MacFarlane's whole cause could be vindicated. People could begin to think he's been right all along. Up till now Pat's played the public mood perfectly. Now things could get tricky, depending on how people respond to these moves by the Russians."

"What *would* the response be if it got out that Pat had met with Bolotnikov to talk peace?" mused Lavender. "And behind the president's back. It might be a shrewd idea."

"Too risky," said Hayford.

"But imagine what a trump card it would be if Foster and Bolotnikov could meet and announce that significant steps to insuring peace had been achieved." Bateman's voice was both dreamy and insistent. "What a coup! Nothing could stand in our way then! The restlessness that has existed on the world front since Gorbachev's death, the wondering what's going to happen now, would all be resolved. Pat's been telling people to breathe easy, that the peace will last. Now he'd be giving tangible evidence to that belief for all the world to see. MacFarlane could complain all he wanted, but the fact would remain that within a few months we'd have a new president and we'd have made the transition into the post-Gorbachev era—still at peace. Pat would be the new 'man of peace' to replace Gorby—and might even win a Nobel Prize!"

"How would you rationalize Patrick's previous statements that peace is inevitable and that we don't need to worry about the few Soviet hard-liners who are still behind the times?"

"Who cares? They'll vote for the man who insures them peace. That's been the one criticism of Pat—that his high-sounding notions are impractical. This would take care of that too—show him to be practical in the midst of his global vision network ideas and his totality of beingness ideals. Practical enough to hammer out an agreement with a guy like Bolotnikov."

"I can hear him now," said Nyborg with a smile, "talking about the conscious evolution of humanity as we enter a new millennium."

"Forget it, Andy!" rejoined Hayford. "That stuff doesn't fit so well coming out of your mouth. Leave it to Pat. He's better at it, and the people buy it."

"And you don't?" queried Nyborg.

"Let's just say I believe in Pat's cause and leave it at that."

"Let's get back to business, gentlemen," urged Bateman. "As for Pat's flip-flopping, like I said, I don't think it'll matter. They'll vote for the man. Within six years Reagan did a one-eighty, from the famous 'evil empire' speech to the INF treaty, hands across the sea, and all that. And the people loved him just as much in both cases. And Bush—he had a reputation as a moderate hard-liner. Yet when the Gorbachev reforms came, he was there smiling and shaking hands and all for it. Times change. People expect their politicians to change too. That's Pat's strength. He's adapted to the public mood. Don't forget, he was hawkish on the Soviets too until he read Shirley MacLaine's book. That put the whole Gorbachev thing into—what does he call it?"

"Cosmic perspective."

"Yeah, right—cosmic perspective. That's my point. He's in touch with the public mood and has ridden the wave right to the forefront."

"It's a lovely fantasy, Harv," patronized Lavender, "but what makes you think we could trust Bolotnikov further than we could throw him? He's the Russian's prime hawk, KGB background, ruthless reputation. I have no doubt he's the prime mover behind this latest thing in Iran. He may have us at war *before* the election if MacFarlane doesn't do something. I've read up on this guy. He just sat quietly in the background throughout the Gorbachev interlude, but he's Stalinist through and through. It's all numbers to him, and he knows the balance is on their side."

"Precisely my point!" said Bateman, slamming his fist down on the table. "Don't you see the beauty of it? The world's leading hardliner and the world's most prophetic voice for peace in the new age, both in line to take over the reins of their respective governments—at least that's my perception of Bolotnikov's design—coming together to hammer out a peace agreement which makes everything before this moment obsolete! Gorbachev, Reagan, Bush, Ryan, INF, SALT, SALT II, the Helsinki Accords—they're all past, over! Now Foster and Bolotnikov prepare to take the world into the twenty-first century with even greater cooperation. Why, the thing staggers the imagination. If we could—"

Before he could complete his sentence, the large double oak doors swung open and in walked the imposing figure of Patrick Harcourt Foster, senator and presidential hopeful, the central character in the discussion at hand. All talk ceased immediately, and each man shifted to face him, as if coming to attention.

"Gentlemen," said Foster, closing the doors behind him and striding purposefully into the room. "I'm sorry to have held you up. The speech went well over its scheduled time, but a very successful afternoon otherwise." He moved a vacant chair to a central position and sat down. "Well, let's get right to it—I've a benefit dinner tonight. How're we doing?"

At fifty-two, Foster was tall, strikingly handsome, dynamic, innovative, and an unflinching adversary. Eight years earlier he had retired from the armed forces, a decorated military veteran. Since then he had become the Senate's most visible presence, possibly due to his embracing and propounding of certain mystical beliefs which had seemed to ring just the right note throughout the changing climate of the '90s. His charismatic, potent speechmaking often rallied important leaders to causes that were unquestionably his own. His campaign cry, and indeed the cry of his "mission" as he envisioned it, was simply that "a new world order has come."

"All history has been a prelude to this moment," he was fond of declaring. "The many paths to truth, as the sordid history of man has shown, have been uselessly fought over, but now has come the moment when they are converging into a grand global unity. The forces of perennial unity are drawing man into harmony even at the political and international level, and the responsibility of the world's leaders—indeed, their great opportunity—is to allow that energy of oneness to channel through them and flow out into their planetary brothers and sisters through their leadership and their international agreements."

Early in his career Foster had preached military supremacy. But then he had seen the light of his monistic beliefs through certain life readings which had been given him. From that moment on, his star had begun to rise on the national scene.

Foster had shrewdly incorporated bold new political themes into his message, taking it in many directions, always seemingly in uncanny tune with what the public relished hearing. He could advocate economic strength against the Japanese, originate a plan for the rebuilding of agricultural and labor and business coalitions within the U.S., taking the stand of American strength and might, while losing none of his visionary philosophical appeal.

Foster's bright promises of a "new sunrise for humanity"—another of his favorite phrases—went down easier than President Jarvis MacFarlane's worrisome talks on deficit dangers. Thus, this new hero on the horizon had all but overshadowed the president in the eyes of the fickle public.

---

In response to Foster's query, Hudson Hayford opened with a statistical summary of economic developments, which led into a less-than-lively discussion on appropriate campaign economic strategy. Once unemployment, inflation, and the national debt had been exhausted, Foster steered the group in a new direction.

"Harv, have you informed the others about the substance of your note to me?"

"No, sir, I hadn't," replied Bateman.

"Well then . . . yesterday I received a memo from Harv which I think bears looking into," Foster continued. "The president's apparently been making suspicious moves, and Harv thinks he's up to something. Why don't you fill them in?"

Lavender and Nyborg sat forward in their chairs with interest and anticipation. Hayford, still the outsider and uncertain how to respond to the political skirmishes so common at this level, merely shifted his position and looked to the others for a lead.

"Anything we can use?" asked Lavender.

"Possibly," answered Bateman. "There's something going on, but as to its substance, we're still in the dark. I have a connection in the White House. Half of what he brings me is useless. But he's moving up, and in fact is in line for a spot on the reelection committee, which would—well, you can imagine what that would do for our situation. So I've been applying no pressure and waiting, knowing when the time was right he'd stumble across something big we could use to tip the scales our way."

"And this is it?" queried Hayford.

"Could be—no way to tell yet," replied Bateman.

"Gentlemen, please," interrupted Foster. "Let Harv tell his story and then you can question him."

"Well . . . my friend called me a couple weeks ago," Bateman began again. "Said the president's been making some funny moves. All very hush-hush. No one on the staff has any idea what's going on. But strange movements have been noticed. Someone told him he suspected the president may be leaving the White House at night—late. Rumor has it he's even managed to give the Secret Service the slip. But the most amazing thing is this: he said he had gotten into the tail end of a conversation which implied the president had gone out without a bodyguard—I mean completely alone, on foot."

Bateman cast a knowing glance around at the others, all of whom were listening intently. "My contact says it's happened more than once. So if these reports are true, you can be sure something important is up. I mean, it's unprecedented. Presidents don't do that sort of thing!"

He stopped and tilted back in his chair.

"Is there more?" asked Foster.

"I wish I had more," replied Bateman. "Unfortunately that's it. My friend hasn't the slightest notion what it's all about. Apparently neither does anyone on the staff—even high up. He's done everything he could to crack it, and it's simply that no one knows."

"Someone *has* to know," insisted Lavender.

"Then whoever that someone is, they're not talking."

"What are you proposing we do with this information, Harv?" asked Foster, growing impatient.

"Well, I think the first order of business is obviously to find out what he's up to."

"Could it be an affair?" suggested Hayford.

"I've wondered that," replied Bateman. "But even Kennedy had a driver in on it when he snuck out incognito those few times. And considering MacFarlane's record, a midnight liaison seems unlikely."

"How I would like to get onto something like that!" said Foster with a grin. "The stuff a politician's dreams are made of! But MacFarlane is so clean he squeaks. I sincerely doubt that's it."

"Anyway, in this day and age a widower can have all the affairs he wants," commented Lavender. "Of course if it were something perverted . . ." he let a meaningfully raised eyebrow finish his sentence.

"True," mused Foster.

"It might be something even better for us," Bateman went on. "If it's so secretive and isn't an affair, then obviously it's either big or kinky. Could he be involved in secret negotiations? If so, by finding out we could undercut whatever he's trying to pull off. Arrange a speech where you'd advocate exactly what he's in the process of doing—take the wind right out of his sails. Whatever advantage to be gained would go to you."

"Brilliant," chuckled Foster. "You're cunning, Harv."

"Thank you, sir," responded Bateman with a sly smile.

"You really think that's it?" asked Nyborg. "It might be nothing more than party stuff—maybe a secret deal with DuBois. There's talk of his making overtures to labor."

"But what if it *is* more?" urged Bateman.

"Surely nothing to do with the Russians?"

"I don't know. Maybe it is an affair. Maybe he's just getting his jollies. Political, domestic—who knows? But this crisis is a tough one. He might be desperate. Things are hot in Russia too. I've heard that in some circles Kudinsky's no more popular than MacFarlane. The press there won't admit anything, of course, but there are hints."

"I've heard that too," added Nyborg. "But it's more likely either personal or internal. He's probably working on some deal with Wilson to sway the labor vote his way."

"That would hardly impact our position," said Hayford, at last feeling on secure ground to enter the discussion. "Even with Harley

Wilson's support, he's not going to dramatically alter the economic situation. The economy is still our issue, not his. The unemployed don't like him either, and the rest of the country's eating well, and they're ours. And from what I know of Wilson, he would be the last to help Jarvis MacFarlane with anything."

"I wouldn't bet on it," said Lavender. "If I know Wilson—and I do—if the price were right, or the payment, he'd throw in with the devil himself."

"Whatever is happening, we *need* to find out," emphasized Bateman.

"What do you propose, Harv?" asked Foster.

"I've already taken measures—"

"What kind of measures?" interrupted Foster. "Look, Harv, I want to beat MacFarlane. We must win for the country's sake. But no foolishness. We'll do what we have to, but some of your tactics in the past worry even me. And I'm pretty thick-skinned. I don't want to end up with my neck through a noose."

"Not to worry," Bateman reassured. "I'll be careful."

"What *have* you done?" asked Nyborg, with more than a trace of suspicion in his tone.

"I've enlisted the aid of a few . . . 'acquaintances,' shall we say. I positioned five men around the White House—a typical stake-out situation. They were experienced enough to blend into the surroundings. They waited all night. The first and second nights—nothing. But on the third, one of my operatives managed to tail him. He saw a man he assumed by build and gait to be the president leaving the grounds by a service gate, dressed in a shabby overcoat and worn hat—clearly a disguise."

"You're sure it was him?" asked Foster.

"It was dark, and there was some distance between them, but my man swears it was Jarvis MacFarlane."

The others whistled and shook their heads in disbelief.

"He followed, keeping a good distance back. The man clearly tried to be inconspicuous, taking side streets, jogging occasionally. Quite the cloak-and-dagger routine." Bateman's eyes shone. This was obviously his element.

"And?" prompted Lavender in anticipation.

"The president walked for more than thirty minutes, eventually heading straight for the Schorrline district. You know, the place that contractor Schorr is trying to renovate—pulling down the old and putting up condos and office buildings. It's pretty deserted right now, though some tenements are still occupied, along with a few hotels. It's the sleaze-bag part of town. A very curious place for the president of the United States to be in the dead of night, by himself, in tennis shoes and a disguise."

"So where did he go?"

"My man lost him. MacFarlane spotted him, made a run for it, and got away."

"Good work, Harv," said Foster. "This is definitely fraught with possibilities. If MacFarlane's trying to scoop us with something, we can only gain by possessing as much foreknowledge as possible. If for any reason it is something more sinister, I need hardly tell you what having such ammo would do for our cause."

"Sir," began Nyborg hesitantly, "I agree with you in most respects. But why should we waste our energies on all this chasing around when we are already so far ahead of MacFarlane? Winning the election will be like—"

"I know, Andrew," interjected Foster, "like taking candy from a baby. But you know as well as anyone, I leave nothing to chance. I've seen elections won or lost by something as inconsequential as a slip of the tongue, the birth of a baby, or a rumor that sneaks out and is later disproved. By the way, who's the expert on MacFarlane's daughter?" A sly glint flickered in the senator's eye.

"Twenty-two and attending Georgetown," answered Bateman. "What else do you want to know?"

"Attached?"

"Nope."

"Any likely candidates?"

"None I'm aware of."

"All the better," grinned Foster. "I want a tail on her. You never know what might turn up—a drug incident, a relationship we might make look like an affair."

"She's quite a looker," added Bateman. "Say the word and I'd feel duty bound to create a little back-alley affair for her." He cast a snide glance toward Nyborg.

Foster smiled, but a practiced listener could have detected an earnestness underlying his bantering tone.

"Don't get your hormones riled, Harv. I want you on MacFarlane."

"Aw, Senator, you take all the fun out of elections."

"Don't worry. Before November you'll have your share of fun!"

# PART II

# THE PRESENCE

*A word was secretly brought to me,*
*my ears caught a whisper of it.*
*Amid disquieting dreams in the night,*
*when deep sleep falls on men, fear and*
*trembling seized me and made all my*
*bones shake.*
*A spirit glided past my face, and the hair*
*on my body stood on end. It stopped,*
*but I could not tell what it was.*
*A form stood before my eyes, and I*
*heard a hushed voice:*
*"Can a mortal be more righteous than*
*God? Can a man be more pure than his*
*Maker? If God places no trust in his*
*servants, if he charges his angels with*
*error, how much more those who live*
*in houses of clay."*

JOB 4:12–19

# TWENTY

Karen MacFarlane inhaled the warm fragrant breeze and longed once again for the carefree days of summer—as she'd been doing frequently this week. So many exciting things awaited her out there that it had become extremely difficult to stay focused on her confining campus life.

Much of her discontent stemmed from the fact that she was so close to leaving this life behind. Already she sensed the emotional ties severing as she looked with anticipation toward the future. In addition, since Detroit she had been hounded by the feeling that her father was in trouble. His strong front was badly frayed. His laughter had grown strained. And his keen eyes were too often introspective and faraway.

It could be just the pressures of his office and the reelection campaign, the burden of public criticism, the anxiety over decisions he had to make. But it wasn't like him to cave in, even under that kind of strain. He thrived on pressure. Or so she had always thought. He was the strongest man she knew.

Perhaps that's what disturbed her the most. She had always looked to him for help, and he had always been there. Now it seemed the tables were turned and he was the one in need of support.

But here she was, stuck at Georgetown. Many times since that weekend in Detroit she had been on the verge of chucking everything and going to him, just so she could be there if he needed to talk. But she knew her father well enough to know that such a move would only intensify his misery. Her graduation with honors, only two weeks away, meant a great deal to him. He was proud of her, and she didn't want to take that from him. To be honest, it meant a lot to her too. Perhaps a sense of guilt at her own selfishness only added to her frustration.

Besides, wasn't it a bit egotistical and unrealistic to think that her father, surrounded as he was by the most intelligent and important people in the entire country, needed her? Yet he had looked so genuinely delighted—even relieved—to see her that night in Detroit. Had that been his way of crying out to her?

Karen sighed as she walked through the cafeteria doors and headed toward the serving counter, glancing along it at the array of food. What was she doing here anyway? This stuff was atrocious.

pumped up with sugar, salt, color, and preservatives. She wasn't even hungry. But it was three o'clock and she hadn't eaten anything since breakfast. She reached for a tray and slowly pushed it along the deserted line, mentally sorting through the selection.

A minute or two later when she sat down at an empty table, her tray held only a green salad, a handful of crackers, and a glass of iced herb tea. She sipped her tea and picked up a newspaper someone had discarded. It was a copy of the day's *New York Times.* Amid the various front-page headlines having to do with the primaries and her father she hardly noticed the feature article, "Earthquake Jolts Central Jerusalem."

Out of the corner of her eye she saw Renfro, her Secret Service man, take a seat against the wall. She knew he had chosen the spot for its strategically advantageous position, where he could survey the entire room and spring to action should it become necessary. How ludicrous that he should sit across the room by himself. Not that she had much in common with him; they weren't friends. She knew his job specs mandated that he not become too close to the subjects he guarded. Crazy though they sometimes seemed, she supposed there was some good reason behind the strict rules, and she was grateful that the agency men did their best to remain inconspicuous, since she wanted to live as normal a life as possible.

She also realized that she sometimes made life difficult for them with her occasional impulsive behavior. Often this was simply because she truly tried to forget they were there. Not particularly because they were there, but because of what they represented—the ever-present threat of danger. It was not something a vivacious twenty-two-year-old liked to live with every waking moment of the day.

"Hi—may I join you?" a deep voice said, startling her.

She glanced up at the tall form of a man she had never seen before. Without looking in his direction, she knew Brett Renfro was probably already on his feet. She judged the stranger to be in his late twenties, maybe thirty. His dark brown hair was conservatively cut and neatly combed, with the exception of one unruly strand which fell across the middle of his forehead. Dressed in gray slacks and a maroon sweater vest over a white shirt with navy pinstripes, he was the epitome of the young assistant professor.

Karen glanced around at the nearly empty room. "Well . . . ," she began reluctantly. On this particular day she was not sure her usual outgoing nature relished the chore of cranking up for a conversation with someone she didn't know. Quiet introspection really fit her present mood.

The newcomer hardly waited for a reply, however, but brashly slid into the chair opposite hers, smiling as he laid his books on the table. Actually it was a boyish grin—not at all unattractive, though a little disconcerting at the same time. He seemed aware of his presumption, but willing to brave it. In a certain frame of mind, Karen would have been put off by his boldness. Somehow today it struck her as intriguing.

"You're not just looking for a place to sit while you eat?" she said with a cautious smile.

"You've found me out!"

"Not that difficult in an empty room."

"To tell you the truth, I've been looking for an opportunity to meet you for some time."

"Should I be flattered?"

"I guess you'll have to answer that yourself," he replied with a laugh, then introduced himself. "I'm Jeremy Manning."

"Assistant professor?"

"Part-time only—and doing graduate work."

"Molecular biology?"

"Hardly! I'm in journalism."

"So now everything's explained! You're a reporter looking for a story. Sorry—end of interview."

"No, no, you've got me all wrong. Please, Miss MacFarlane, I'm not looking for a scoop."

"You're a journalist. What else would you expect me to think?"

"Only a journalism student," he corrected.

"Was there something you wanted then?" she asked after a moment.

"Only to meet you."

"You've done that."

"And perhaps share a cup of coffee."

"I don't drink coffee," she replied, still on her guard.

"You're making this extremely difficult," he said. "Do you realize how much nerve it takes to walk up to the daughter of the president, especially with that over-sized goon taking in my every move?"

"Somehow I get the impression you're not in short supply—of nerve, that is," she said with the hint of a smile on her lips.

He laughed. "I've been accused of that." He jumped up, leaving his books on the table, poured himself a cup of coffee, and planted himself opposite her once more.

"I have to confess something," he continued, as he dumped three heaping teaspoons of sugar into his cup, "I'm a Republican."

"That's okay," she answered. "The way you treat your body, filling it with that stuff, I doubt you'll last long."

"Maybe so, but at least I'll enjoy my life, however short it may be. I'm not sure I want to live to ninety if I have to drink herb tea and eat tofu."

Now it was her turn to laugh in earnest.

"It's not so bad," she said, lifting her glass toward him in a salute and then taking a swallow. "You get used to it, and it even begins to taste pretty good. As for the tofu, that's one transition I haven't made yet."

As Karen began to pick at her salad, her new acquaintance said, "Are you hounded by the media frequently?"

"Thank goodness, no! Except for my constant companion," and here she nodded at Renfro, "I doubt anyone notices what I do, and that's the way I like it."

"You didn't give that impression when your father was running for the vice-presidency four years ago."

"That was different. Campaigning is another story. It's two separate lives." She stopped. Why was she suddenly chatting away so freely with this complete stranger? "I'm through," she said, pushing her salad bowl across the tray.

Manning rose when she did and walked beside her toward the door.

"You have any classes this afternoon?" Karen asked.

"No, nothing till finals. I've only got seven units, mostly independent study stuff."

"Where do you work when you're not here?"

"Some free-lancing here and there—enough to keep bread on the table. But I promise I'm off duty."

"But can I trust your word?"

"I'll try to prove myself worth it."

Once outside, the day somehow looked fresher and more promising. Jeremy Manning's animated conversation and ready smile made her lay aside her earlier concerns. She felt as if she hadn't laughed for a long time, and the release of spontaneous energy felt good. It was only after reflecting on the day's events later in the evening that she realized how fully she had taken her father's anxieties onto herself.

"I need to head home," she said at length. "Want to walk me there?"

"I have my car over in the lot."

"It's only three or four blocks."

"Then let's go. The exercise will probably do me good—work off some of that dreadful sugar I put in my coffee!" he joked.

They walked along in silence for a time. Karen had no idea what was going through Jeremy Manning's mind, but she knew what Brett Renfro would be thinking as he dogged their steps half a block back. He would be furious with her! No doubt the report would get back to her father that she had behaved "imprudently" with a complete stranger. Well, she wasn't about to spoil the spontaneity of the afternoon because of the regulations and paranoia of the Secret Service.

"I never thought I could have such a nice time with a Republican," she said when they reached her apartment.

He laughed. "We're not such a bad lot when you get to know us. And who knows . . . I might even win you over."

"Never."

"In that case, maybe I could at least convince you to have dinner with me this evening."

"I don't know . . ." she hesitated.

"I promise I'll behave."

She cocked her head toward Renfro. "You'd have no choice. I don't go anywhere without my contingent of protectors."

"What kind of food do you like?"

"Mexican—French. Either one."

"I know a great little Mexican place—La Casa Del Rio."

"Oh, I go there all the time!"

"I know," he replied, a twinkle in his eye.

Karen never quite realized at what point she crossed over from caution to abandon, but almost before she had time to reflect upon it, she found herself saying yes. Jeremy Manning was intelligent, interesting, and good-looking. And though they obviously didn't agree on everything, he managed to make the differences stimulating rather than contentious.

She had only been inside her apartment long enough to glance through her mail when a sharp knock came at the door. It was Renfro.

"Who's the guy, Miss MacFarlane?" he asked in a professional tone.

"Just another student at the university."

"Name?"

"Jeremy Manning."

"Known him long?"

"As a matter of fact, I only met him about an hour ago. You saw the whole thing."

"You know the rules, Miss MacFarlane. You can't bring a complete stranger to your apartment."

"I didn't invite him in," she replied, growing frustrated with the whole procedure.

"He knows where you live."

"He could have found that out easily enough on his own."

"But you've made it all the easier for him. And what do you really know about him—no credentials, no background. How do we even know that's his name?"

"For heaven's sake, Brett! Do you have to be so mistrusting?"

"It's my job."

"Well I like Mr. Manning, and I can't help it if you don't like that. I've got my own life to live!"

"I'll have to report the incident, you understand."

"What's to report? There was no incident! You saw what happened. *Nothing* happened!"

"Nevertheless, I have to be thorough."

"Be as thorough as you want. Run him through your computer and do all the security checks you want. But be back by seven or else Evans will have all the fun tonight."

"What do you mean?"

"Why, Brett, didn't you know? I thought you Secret Service guys knew everything before it happened. We're going out for Mexican tonight!"

# TWENTY-ONE

La Casa Del Rio was the perfect place for an unexpected first date with an unlikely new friend. The out-of-the-way little Mexican cafe could have been in Tijuana instead of D.C., complete with the smell of grease, the dim lighting, and the rapid-fire Spanish dialogue coming from the kitchen. But anyone in the city who knew their Mexican fare knew that Señor Herman Juarez, along with his wife, brother, and various teenage offspring, possessed the gift all connoisseurs look for—that of being able to consistently put out the best food of its kind. Herman never spent a dime fixing up his place, but that merely enhanced the atmosphere—if it could be called that.

After Karen and Jeremy had ordered, she said, "You know, I got in trouble because of you earlier today."

"Because of me?"

"My SS shadow thinks I should be more careful—you being a total stranger and all."

"But I'm not a stranger now," said Jeremy. "Doesn't dinner together qualify us as friends?"

She laughed. "I suppose it must. But they're very possessive of me."

"What is it really like being the president's daughter?" he asked in a more serious tone. "I mean, do people hound you all the time—autograph seekers, photographers, reporters?"

"Not that much, really. Not as much as you might expect. I'm in the limelight, of course. And it's hard not to think I'm getting some kind of special treatment in my classes, though nothing's ever said. But I'm used to it. I love my dad and believe in him. I wouldn't want him not to be president just so I could live a normal life. So I adjust."

"You really believe in him that much, or is it just because he's your father?"

Karen paused a moment before she responded. "I don't want to be naive," she said at length. "He *is* my father, and I can't deny that probably does have its influence. But, yes—I believe in him as a president too."

"Despite the fact that he's out of touch with what the majority of people feel?"

"That's your opinion, not mine. Besides, you're a journalist. You must have followed world events over the last two or three years. You should know as well as anyone that what's happened isn't my father's doing."

"Maybe not totally, but—"

"As for being out of touch, I suppose you buy all that baloney Foster's always coming out with about the new era of mankind?"

"I didn't say that. Though his views do strike a chord with people. At least if you're going to mix politics with spiritual philosophy, Foster's brand goes down a lot smoother with more people than the hypocritical jargon the fundamentalists dish out," he said. "But that isn't what I was getting at. What I was going to say was that the nation's polarized economy would have begun to right itself by now if your father's government had done more."

"The deficit is hardly his doing, and that's the root of the problem."

"But if he'd been more willing to give private industry a freer hand—"

"You mean the way government used to give union leaders like Harley Wilson their way?" asked Karen, growing irritated at his arguments. She was fast beginning to resent people who were so quick to point a finger at her father for the world's ills. Before Jeremy could reply, a waiter approached with their order, and she was relieved by the diversion.

For several minutes they concentrated on their food. It was Jeremy who broke the silence, returning to politics and the economy.

"To answer your question—no, that was a mistake," he said. "I think everyone agrees they had too much for too long. Laissez-faire can only go so far. What I am saying is that you've got to be willing to play ball with these guys—unions, big business management, finance."

"But my father has tried. Everyone's so locked into their own private little sphere, not one of those groups will bend. And to achieve anything on a national scale means everyone has to pitch in."

"And the president should lead the way."

"He has. He is," insisted Karen. "He's made efforts in business and in finance. But without public support, it's like trying to drag a grizzly bear with a dog leash. You may have a very clear idea of where you want to go, but the bear can basically do anything he wants."

Manning thought for a moment. "I'd never really considered that before," he finally said. "I guess my notions of cause and effect might be rather one-dimensional."

"Well, that's a refreshing change," she said. "All most reporters will do is argue and try to defend and justify their position."

"I'm not a reporter, remember," he laughed. "Maybe I can afford to be more open."

"A *journalist* then—whatever that means. Same difference."

"Not really. Reporters are a different breed. I like to think of myself as a cut above the guy running around with a notebook and pencil in search of a story."

Now it was Karen's turn to laugh. "A journalist with an ego to match, huh?"

"Yep," he said. "Didn't you know—you can't be a writer without an enlarged ego? What else could make a person think he has something to say?"

"So, you're a writer. Now I've got two clues—a journalist and a writer. What more can you tell me?"

"I'll tell you anything you want to know—when the time's right. But right now I don't want to blur the issue. I don't want you to think of me as anything more than a friend—if I can presume to be that much."

"You can presume that much, Jeremy."

"Thank you," he said, and Karen sensed a ring of sincerity behind his words. "So then, tell me about your father, from the personal side rather than the political. It must be very hard for him, trying to achieve things and not getting the support of the country."

"If you only knew! He agonizes over this nation. He is so frustrated by our deterioration in international affairs too, on top of all the domestic troubles. He's afraid we're ultimately going to wind up in the midst of a full-scale depression once the deficit succeeds in swallowing us, and a war with Russia at the same time. Yet all the while the country goes for Foster's pie-in-the-sky ideals and calls Dad a forecaster of gloom and destruction."

"Why doesn't he take a harder stance against Russia?"

"Because he wants peace, not war, and he thinks peace can be arrived at peacefully. I don't know what he's up to, but I have a feeling he's got something in mind to diffuse the crisis in Iran. That ought to please even the Foster people."

"What is it?"

"Oh, I don't know. I just have a feeling. He's not talking. But he's been very preoccupied lately."

"That's interesting," Jeremy said. "Imagine what a juicy tidbit that'd be if I *was* a reporter: *MacFarlane's Daughter Says President Involved in Secret Negotiations . . . Mentally Preoccupied Chief Not Talking!*"

"You wouldn't dare," said Karen in alarm.

"No, of course not," he laughed reassuringly.

"Don't you breathe a word of what you just heard! I shouldn't have said anything. I don't have any idea if anything is going on. All I've noticed is that he's been quieter. I'm speculating, that's all."

"Well, I hope you're right—I mean, that he does have some peaceful solution in the works. Peace is the answer, not confrontation. The last ten years will mean nothing if we fall back into the old way of dealing with our brother nations."

"Come on, you sound like Foster!" exclaimed Karen. "Brother nations! We're more vulnerable now than we've ever been, even with nuclear arsenals fifty percent lower than in '85, and Rose calling for still more drastic cuts! The world can still be annihilated in five minutes with one push of the button. And now our defenses are down psychologically too, from so many people listening to all that inner-consciousness prattle of Foster's! We're not paying attention to the new generation of *new* threats to U.S. security."

"Is that your father's feeling too?"

"He wants peace as much as you or I, or Foster for that matter. But he believes in the long haul, in caution, in keeping our powder dry for a few more years till we see which way the wind's going to blow permanently in Russia."

"And so in the name of caution we should confront the Soviets and go to war? How can your father claim to want peace if that's his position? Hardly seems to make sense."

"Yeah, maybe it doesn't. But even if the answer's not a military one, I do think the time's going to come again when we might have to stand up to the Soviets, and the longer we wait, the more difficult it's going to get. They are the rising power in the world, we are on the decline—not just militarily, but in every way. I don't think it's too late, but the clock is ticking."

"Sounds like you've inherited your father's penchant for malaise-thinking. You could use a dose of Foster's optimism!"

"Spoken like a true Republican," said Karen.

"You won't hold it against me, will you?" asked Jeremy with mock concern.

"Oh, no. We Democrats are a tolerant lot. We can still be friends."

"At last! Detente between the warring factions."

"And it happened here, folks—over tacos and enchiladas!"

They both laughed.

"But honestly," said Jeremy, "I don't want to spend the whole time talking politics. Tell me about yourself."

"That's a line if I ever heard one."

"Come on! What am I supposed to say?"

"Okay, what do you want to know?"

"Well—for starters, what are your plans after graduation?"

*This guy's really something,* Karen said to herself. *He's not afraid to jump in with both feet. But somehow it doesn't sound corny coming from him.*

---

An hour later Karen had told Jeremy Manning a great deal about herself, and found out a great deal about him in the process. She learned that he was the fourth of six children and that his father was a Philadelphia policeman who, when Jeremy was sixteen, had been wounded in the line of duty and forced into early retirement. A proud Irishman, Carl Manning refused to let his wife go to work, so the family struggled to survive on his pension and any odd work his disability would permit. College seemed out of the question for his children. Jeremy's oldest brother was a cop, and the other two were factory workers. Both his sisters had married young.

But Jeremy wanted something more, he said. Ever since he could remember he had been fascinated with politics. There was no accounting for it from his background or schooling or family. But the older he grew the more obsessed he became with the notion of a political career. He knew what he wanted, and he knew a college education was the only way to get there.

So he had come up the hard way, working his way through college, joining groups and forming associations that would lead to political involvement. He took time off as necessary to bolster his finances and gradually worked his way toward the journalistic end of the political arena.

When he had finally graduated at age twenty-nine, his unemotional father wept with pride. Then two years ago, at the ripe age of thirty-one, Jeremy had received his master's in political science at Georgetown, and since then had been teaching a class or two each term in journalism or political science while he continued working toward his doctorate.

By the end of the evening when Jeremy left Karen at her door, without any overtures, not even a handshake, she found herself feeling very good. It had been a long time since she'd been close enough and comfortable enough with anyone to really talk like they had. True, their conversation hadn't been all that deep, but it had flowed both ways. Even superficial exchange, when it occurred in a relaxed setting of mutual give and take, could prove stimulating.

Jeremy *was* rather vague about what he did, and he *was* a Republican! But that was only two strikes against him, not three. And to balance the scales, he did seem honest, forthright, and even humorous when things threatened to become politically argumentative. He seemed to sense when to back off and let comic relief break into a discussion—placing a greater importance on relationship than on winning.

She respected that. Such balance was all too rare in the political world.

Karen locked the door behind her. If Brett wanted to talk, he'd have to wait till morning. Right now she just wanted to remember the evening, not justify it to her prying guardian.

She kicked off her shoes and fell back onto the couch. *He must have had an enjoyable time too,* she thought. *Why else would he have asked me out again so soon?* But she reminded herself that she had only met him a few hours ago. She wouldn't let anything happen too fast. She was still the president's daughter and must therefore take special care to remain sensible.

She would wait until tomorrow to fall in love.

# TWENTY-TWO

The clinking of china and silverware aggravated the silence that seemed to reign around the dinner table. It reminded Karen again that something was wrong. When she'd walked into the White House tonight, the air had been thick enough to cut. And it was like pulling teeth to get her father to keep up a conversation.

"When will you leave for California?" she asked, trying to find a diversion from the awkwardness in a discussion of politics.

"Day after tomorrow," he answered, hardly glancing up. His voice sounded faraway, as if he needed no assistance from Air Force One to transport him thousands of miles from his daughter.

"I wish I could be there."

"What about your finals?" asked her father.

"I didn't say I *was* going—only that I would like to. Besides, I had my last final yesterday."

"I doubt you'll miss anything!" he said. He sounded tired.

"Miss anything!" echoed Karen, trying to pump him up with a little enthusiasm. "The California primary is going to be DuBois's Waterloo—and that is one victory celebration I'd like to be in on! Where will it be?"

"The San Francisco Hilton. But you're making a pretty big assumption."

"Oh, Dad, what do the polls mean? Two or three percentage points?"

"In his favor! If they hold, he'll win the state, *and* the nomination by fifty or sixty votes. It's just like California wanted it when they changed back from an early spring primary."

"What do you mean?"

"They used to hold their primary in June. But then it seemed the race was always decided before it got to them. So they moved it forward. But then the races tightened up, and I think they missed the attention of being the big deciding factor. So they went back to June, just in time for this year's election. And now they get to decide between me and DuBois."

"Don't worry, you'll make it up. I know it!"

"I hope you're right," he said. "But we're not going to stop our lives for the sake of one primary. I'll be back in plenty of time for your graduation."

*Something is wrong,* thought Karen. Her father's fighting spirit was gone. The most important primary of the whole campaign seemed to him little more than a distraction. DuBois had pulled almost even in delegate count. Everything was riding on California, and he didn't seem to care.

Until recently she had never seen this side of her father's nature. She hardly knew how to respond to it. So she steered her thoughts momentarily into more pleasant channels.

It had been five days since she'd met Jeremy Manning. It hadn't taken long to realize that what began as a sensible relationship was turning into anything but. The more she saw of him, the more she looked forward to seeing him again. Falling in love was the last thing she would have anticipated, and the last thing she needed right now. But he was constantly in her thoughts, and someone resembling him had flitted briefly through a dream last night. It was becoming the sort of schoolgirl crush she would have laughed at in anyone else.

If only she knew more about him! But as open as he appeared about his feelings and reactions, he remained steadfastly silent about his life apart from the university.

Suddenly her father pushed his plate back and stood. "I've some pressing work to do before I leave," he said, "and a full slate tomorrow. So I must get at it."

"You have to go right now?" asked Karen, disappointed.

"I'm sorry. I shouldn't have invited you over, only to duck out on you so soon. I didn't realize."

"It's okay. But, Dad . . . is there—"

"What?"

"Is there anything you want to tell me about—something going on . . . I don't know—personally. You don't seem like yourself lately."

MacFarlane sighed and looked away briefly, then said, "No, honey, I'm okay. Just the pressures of it all. The usual stress of political life. You know how it goes."

Karen nodded. Her father kissed her lightly on the cheek, then walked toward the door. *I don't care what he says, he's definitely not himself,* she thought.

"I guess I'll be going too," she said. "Good night, Dad."

---

Renfro was waiting for her at her car. He wasn't such a bad guy, really. Sometimes she just wasn't in the mood, like tonight. But it was pointless to try to avoid him; this place was guarded from within and without like a stockade.

As she approached, he looked grim. Whatever he had to say, she didn't want to hear it. She walked briskly to her red Fiero and slid behind the wheel. Even as she did, however, her conscience reminded her that he was only doing his job.

"You're working overtime, aren't you?" she said.

"I'll see you home. Then Evans will take over."

"I'm so lucky."

"I have something I need to discuss with you, Miss MacFarlane."

"What have I done now?"

"Nothing, I hope," he answered, almost smiling. "It's regarding the security check we ran on your Mr. Manning."

"You're such a romantic," she commented dryly.

"I'm sorry. I'm just trying to—"

"I know, I know," she interrupted with a mock sigh of frustration. "Just doing your job. What is it? Is he a Russian spy or something?"

He handed a sheet of paper through the open car window. "You might want to read it yourself."

The color drained from her face as she read down the page. She looked up at Renfro, then reread it.

"Is this a joke, Brett?" she finally asked, forcing a nervous laugh.

"I'm afraid not. I wouldn't do that to you."

"Does my father know?" Her voice was tight, with none of its previous flippancy.

Renfro shook his head. "I wanted to tell you first."

"I appreciate that."

"It's the least I can do. I know it's a blow."

"Would you let me handle it?" There was a quiver in her voice as she spoke.

"I don't think that would be wise."

"Blast your military wisdom!" she half-shouted.

Renfro's cool posture never wavered.

"Listen," she went on, moderating her tone. "I'm in no danger, especially now that I know. I just want to deal with this, that's all. My father is leaving for California in thirty-six hours. He doesn't need any other burdens. Give me two days. I'll watch what I say."

"I can agree with that, but—"

"Then you'll let me take care of it?"

He deliberated a long moment, then said, "Okay, but I'll be out on a limb for you. I could lose my job. I'll be watching every minute."

"You do that anyway." She tried to infuse her usual light sarcasm, but it didn't work. Her final word deteriorated, and before she had a chance to say, "Thank you, Brett," she had to turn away to hide a muffled sob.

She hurriedly rolled up the window and started the engine, hoping the guard at the gate wouldn't notice her emotion. She wouldn't have Renfro or the gate attendant see her crying, especially over some silly infatuation.

"Stop it, Karen!" she muttered to herself. "He's not worth it!"

Yet despite her self-admonitions, her eyes continued to fill with the fluid that trickled silently down her cheeks. She stubbornly refused to call them tears.

# TWENTY-THREE

Karen and Jeremy had already arranged to meet at La Casa Del Rio the next day for lunch. Karen kept the appointment.

Jeremy was there ahead of her, sitting at the same place they had occupied only a few days before on their first date. The table was situated next to a trellis of artificial ivy that fell just short of being romantic. He waved and smiled as she entered, and she re turned the smile, inwardly gritting her teeth and thinking what a despicable snake the man was.

She had debated all morning about what to do. And now that she was here, she still had no more idea what course of action she would take than when she had awoke at five in the morning thinking about it. Would she dump a bowl of guacamole in his lap, or turn him over to Renfro to explain himself? That reminded her to glance around. Sure enough, there was her faithful watchdog at a strategic table across the room.

As she approached the table, Jeremy jumped up and gallantly pulled out the chair for her. She smiled sweetly and thanked him.

"I went ahead and ordered," he said. "Hope you don't mind."

"Fine," she replied. She hated this kind of subterfuge. She would rather have screamed at him, but of course that wouldn't be fitting for the president's daughter. And perhaps there was still a small optimistic part of her that hoped—in spite of the evidence—that he had been planning to tell her all along and that things weren't as bad as they looked.

"What's wrong?" he asked.

"Just hungry," she said, but she knew her poor acting wasn't fooling him.

"I've been wondering how a health nut like you can indulge in Mexican food," he commented in an obvious attempt to make conversation, something which had not been necessary between them before.

"We all have our weaknesses." Her words referred to more than food, and he knew it.

"Karen, I can tell you're angry about something." He reached across the table for her hand, but she pulled away. "You know, don't you?" he said, looking deeply and sincerely into her eyes.

"Know what?"

"Coyness doesn't become you."

"And *you* are the expert on masking one's true feelings and motives, right?"

"I wanted to tell you," he said.

"Right," she drawled the word. "But not before you had done a thorough job of spying for Patrick Foster!" Her voice had risen, causing several people nearby to look their way.

"Let's get out of here," he said. "Give me a chance to explain, okay?"

"I'm getting out of here!" she shot back. "But by myself."

She jumped to her feet and fled from the restaurant as gracefully as her fury and hurt would allow.

Jeremy threw a few bills onto the table and was after her in a moment, but he was stopped short outside the door when the huge presence of Brett Renfro loomed before him.

"Leave Miss MacFarlane alone," said the agent in a low, ominous voice.

"Let me by!" Jeremy flared back in his frustration. "I have to talk to her!" He tried to push his way past, but Renfro was immovable. For a moment they stood eye to eye. Renfro was clearly the more powerful of the two, but Jeremy was desperate enough to try something reckless.

"I don't want to hurt her," he implored. "Frisk me if you want. I've got no gun or tape recorder for heaven's sake. Just let me talk to her!"

Renfro held his ground a moment longer, then yielded. "Okay," he said. "But if you try anything, I'll be on you like flies on dead meat."

Jeremy didn't bother to respond. He rushed past the man and scanned the parking lot. Karen was just getting into her car. He raced toward it, managing to catch the door just as she was about to slam it shut.

"Get out of my way!" she yelled, trying to pull the door toward her.

"You've got to let me explain."

"No, I don't! There's nothing you could say." She started the engine.

"Karen, please don't do this! We have something special. I know—"

"Ha! Something special? You were using me!"

"No . . . please. Don't I at least deserve a chance to explain?" He realized too late that his words were ill-chosen.

"Deserve! How dare you—" She couldn't find the right words, and was only able to end her tirade with a sharp breath.

She jammed the car into gear and it lurched forward. The movement wrenched the door from Jeremy's hands, causing him to stumble backward. Instinctively Karen slammed on the brakes, but when a quick glance in her rearview mirror told her he was all right, she closed the door, threw her foot on the accelerator again and screeched off, this time not stopping until he was well out of sight behind her.

---

When Karen at last reached her apartment, Jeremy was waiting for her on the front steps. Several hours had passed since she had roared away from La Casa Del Rio, and it was evening. Sitting in the light of the street lamp, he reminded her of a lost puppy, dejected and homeless. But as she stepped out of her car, all her anger at his betrayal came rushing back—no amount of the man's dejected looks would soften her.

"I'm a fool," he said when she reached the bottom step, his voice as soft as the light from the lamp. "I really never intended for this to happen. I didn't want you to be hurt in any way."

Her fury subsided, though anger still lurked in her heart.

"Jeremy, I realize you're not a bad guy," she said, trying to handle *this* confrontation reasonably. "I wouldn't have liked you if you were. I know you have a job to do and all that—but you *won't* do it on me."

"I never intended to," he said. "If only I could make you believe me." He reached out for her hand, but she pulled back.

Only two days ago they had sat together in the moonlight on these very steps, talking and laughing. That had been the night Karen first realized that Jeremy was indeed someone special. That also was the first night he had kissed her. But now she did not even want him to touch her.

"I do work for Foster," he went on. "I'm on his press staff. Not a bad spot for someone fresh out of grad school and still struggling to get my feet planted in politics. Part time, of course. I do work for the university too. Everything I told you is true, I just didn't tell you *everything*."

He leaned forward earnestly, his elbows on his knees and his hands cupping his chin.

"In reality, Karen, I'm little more than a glorified errand-boy for Foster. But it looks good on the resume. I know you don't care about all that. But I want you to understand that my job is mostly pushing paper, doing a little research, fixing coffee. I'm not involved in the game, you know."

"And you think it matters whether you do it for a living or not? You did it. You *were* trying to use me for Foster's benefit, weren't you?"

"My motives were innocent. I didn't know you then."

She opened her mouth, but he spoke again quickly. "I *had* seen you on campus. And I *did* want to meet you. I hadn't yet tried to introduce myself because I was a little intimidated, not to mention that I don't have the kind of money I thought it would take to entertain the president's daughter. But then I was offered a bonus if I'd . . . well, keep an eye on you, and—"

"And what!" she snapped. "Entrap me?"

"No! Just . . . I don't know . . . find out what kind of person you were—that's all they wanted."

"I can hardly believe that!"

"I wouldn't have compromised you."

"Then you would have betrayed your own boss instead?"

"I didn't think of all that," he insisted. "All I thought of was the chance to meet you, and that the bill would be on Foster. Kind of ironic if you think about it."

"Forgive me if I don't laugh."

They were both silent, caught in the conflict between their feelings of attraction and their political allegiances, which were miles apart.

At length Jeremy exhaled a long sigh. "I can tell that nothing I say is going to make a difference," he said. He pulled himself up from the step. "I didn't think any of this through very well," he added. "I regret that very much. One thing I don't regret, and that's meeting you, and coming to . . . care for you—which I have, Karen. If you don't believe anything else, you can believe that." He turned and walked slowly down the stairs.

"I'm sorry it had to turn out this way, Jeremy," she called after him. He stopped and turned back for one last look. "But you must see, I just couldn't trust you anymore."

He nodded, then continued on down the steps. There was nothing more to say.

When Karen got inside her apartment, she sank onto the couch, laid her head back on a pillow, and cried.

## TWENTY-FOUR

The clacking of keyboards and electronic beeping of word processors buzzed in Jeremy Manning's ears. He had a huge list of phone calls still to make, with a headache to match.

He'd just come from a grueling fifteen minute session with Harv

Bateman in which the proverbial book had been thrown at him. The furious campaign manager had upbraided him for his handling of the situation with MacFarlane's daughter and he'd come close to losing his job. The funny thing was, he hardly cared. Being fired might actually be a relief.

"You were supposed to *tail* her for crying out loud!" Bateman fumed. "Do you know what that means? Watch her, get a line on her movements, her associations. Instead you go up and meet the girl, date her, for the love of Mike! And you don't even have the brains to use a phony name!"

"I thought you wanted me to get to know her, gain her confidence."

"How'd you come up with a notion like that?"

"When we talked the first time, you said—"

"You were supposed to know what I meant! There are rules to this game. When I gave you the assignment, I thought you had enough street smarts to show some finesse."

"I'd never done that kind of thing before. I thought I was doing the right thing."

Why hadn't he just told Bateman the job stunk and that he quit? The chastisement from his superior was all the more frustrating because it had accomplished nothing but anger on both sides. Now here he was—alienated all the way around.

After leaving Karen the previous evening, he had gone home to spend a miserable night in his own company, finally falling asleep about three in the morning. He lay there berating himself, Bateman, Foster—the whole dirty business. But mostly his anger fell on his own head. He knew what he had agreed to was questionable, whatever his own motives; this was not why he had always wanted to be in politics.

Over and over he tried to tell himself he was being stupid. What did he expect? They played a tough business in Washington.

Nothing eased his conscience, however. He still felt lousy about what he had done. And part of him had to admit being irritated at himself for blowing his good standing with Bateman too. He had been trying to play both ends against the middle—a slick technique used by all ambitious young movers and shakers. Save the wear and tear on your conscience. Don't look at the faces too closely. Get the job done. Impress those in power. Play by the rules. Do what you're told. It's all for the good of the cause.

But what was the cause, he wondered, other than your own promotion up the ladder of success and recognition and influence!

Was that all anyone was after—the illusive reins of power?

He remembered when such had not been his motive. Where had he gone wrong? When had he crossed over the line?

There had been a time when he'd had a bona fide set of ideals he carried around with him. He'd wanted his life to count for something. Trite as it sounded, he *had* wanted to make a difference in the world. He had studied the idealists of the '60s. They had preached peace and protested war, only to lose themselves ultimately in their own hypocritical brand of simplistic selfishness. Now here he was, a generation later, trying to make his mark on the world in new and different ways. He had determined he would not stumble into the same pitfalls.

His political consciousness had first awakened when he was a teenager. When other kids were writing book reports on *Huckleberry Finn,* he was reading *The Real War* by Richard Nixon.

His family background and upbringing did not tend to produce the Woodward or Bernstein sort of liberalism so common throughout the press corps since the '60s and '70s. Instead, he was a descendent of the new wave of young Republicans who emerged out of the conservative shift of the '80s. But like many of his contemporaries, he had wandered back from the right and now possessed a decided affinity for the newly emerging freethinking left of the political spectrum, where politics and life philosophy were doing so much business together these days.

He had begun to question many of his earlier views, assisted to a large degree by his best friend who was a staunch Reaganite. His friend argued that the underlying forces in the Soviet Union were still bent on global impact and assertive strength. At the time Jeremy had a hard time countering the argument, but his study of world events was leading him to different conclusions. He could see that the rules of the power game were changing, more drastically than most Americans understood. Military might was no longer the trump card, but one of a host of factors. Yet he was still unable to put these perceptions into a unified world view.

In attempting to voice his doubts and mixed feelings about the new world that was emerging, he got lambasted by his friend for being anesthetized along with the rest of the liberals into thinking that things weren't going to be so bad with the Russians after all.

"We're going to have to face the future as a second-rate world power," his friend said. "We'll have gone the way of so many great nations of the past if we don't wake up to the silent shift in the global balance of power. Militarism in Eastern Europe may have changed, but the dynamics of power hasn't. Russia is climbing to a position of economic might to match their military supremacy. We've got to wake up to the future. The hour to regain America's vigor and dynamism as the dominant economic, political, and social force in the world has come."

It didn't help that his friend was a born-again Christian, which made it all the more convenient for Jeremy to discount his right-wing political views along with his religious convictions. But Jeremy found that he had no viable substitute for the conservative mind-set he was leaving behind. His questioning continued. By the end of the '80s or early '90s, when Gorbachev's reforms and the dismantling of the Communist bloc were in full swing, Jeremy found himself in the midst of an all-out internal effort to locate some unifying set of axioms which would make sense out of all that was happening. He still loved politics, but he desperately wanted to make sure he was on the right side.

Patrick Harcourt Foster had first caught Jeremy's attention when he burst into national prominence in his first senatorial race. He had seen the limitations of his former views, said the former four-star general. He now believed that the changes taking place on the face of the globe were indications that a new dawn was about to emerge in the world's history, an era in which humanity would no longer be at strife, but would—as a united force—rise as one to occupy the destiny to which they had been evolving. These were the most exciting times in the history of the universe, declared Foster, and in his message young Jeremy detected much of his own inner quest.

Perhaps Foster did, as many throughout the country were saying, hold the key to an understanding of the "new" future that was descending so rapidly upon humanity. When Foster won the Ohio seat, Jeremy's own political bent caught fire once more. He was hooked and desired to be part of the political scene.

For years, however, finances seemed to stand in the way. One could not get into politics nor get an education at the sort of institution that looked good on a resume without significant bucks. His climb had been hard work every step of the way.

Perhaps it was that very struggle that had taken the edge off his idealism. The years of work had made him less attuned to the motives that had stirred him in the first place. He recalled how, after having spent a grueling year working at a steel mill in Bethlehem, Pennsylvania, he had managed to save enough money to enter the master's program. Then his youngest brother turned up in desperate need of money for an operation for his daughter. What could he do but help?

Such struggles might build character, but they also tended to make a young man think more of finally getting on his feet and making something of himself than of the lofty notion of helping mankind emerge into a new dawn of totality of brotherhood.

None of this dulled his enthusiasm for politics; it only made him look at things through less utopian eyes. He began working in the campaigns of several state politicians, and he significantly impressed Harold Means with his staff work after the congressman won his bid for the Pennsylvania state legislature. In fact, it was while he was visiting a friend in the state capitol at Harrisburg that Jeremy had met Patrick Foster for the first time.

Foster encouraged him, and from that moment Jeremy knew that one way or another he had to get to Washington. He tried several times for a place on Foster's staff, but was turned down. So he continued to work for Means in Harrisburg, kept plugging away on his master's, but always with an eye on Washington.

Finally, with letters of reference from Means, he transferred to Georgetown and began making his way in the nerve center of the country. Once he had his graduate degree, the job at the university kept him solvent while he worked on his doctorate and explored other avenues.

His chance came when one of his inquiries at last reached receptive eyes and he was offered a part-time position—at little more than minimum wage—as a journalistic assistant at the Foster for President campaign headquarters.

It was the break he'd been waiting for!

He threw himself into the work with vigor and quickly began to advance within the ranks of the lower echelon, even attracting the notice of some higher-ups—particularly Harv Bateman.

But it was not long before he began to detect a disparity between his belief that a new day had dawned and Foster's campaign of brotherhood and harmony. It was clear that ten years of peace were as good as a thousand to Foster. Something in Foster's manner was almost a little scary. According to his record he had always, even in his military days, seemed to take nuclear holocaust too lightly. And even in this so-called new age he took peace so entirely for granted that Jeremy couldn't help wondering whether he'd be a pushover as president—someone every little tin dictator in the world could take advantage of. Men were still men, after all, and still prone to the greed and lust for power that had driven the world's political conflicts for thousands of years. Foster seemed to think that somehow the unifying consciousness of humanity was going to rid individual world leaders of selfish motives altogether—or at least that was his line.

It sounded good, but Jeremy questioned whether such an ideal could ever become reality. His old friend, the born-again Christian, used to talk about "original sin"—the inborn bent of man toward evil. Well, Jeremy wasn't sure about *that* either, but he did think Foster might not be looking at the whole picture.

Then there were the discrepancies in the way things were done around campaign headquarters. For all the talk of brotherhood and higher-self consciousness that floated through Foster's speeches and public appearances, Jeremy couldn't see that there was anything different about the way his organization was run. In fact, he sometimes detected a greater ruthlessness here than he'd seen in the other political campaigns he'd been a part of. Where did ideals meet reality? *If the Russians are our brothers,* Jeremy asked himself, *then why do Foster's people treat mere political opponents as enemies?*

More and more often he had to remind himself that this was what he'd always wanted to do, that he had to expend his energies getting Foster elected rather than doubting the man's practices. He had to reassure himself that he just couldn't see the whole picture. A year from now he might well be working for the president of the United States! It had always been his dream. Suddenly he was so close! What could a few compromises in his ideals hurt?

Until a few days ago . . .

Until Karen MacFarlane . . .

Yes, he could squash, step on, and obliterate his own values if he chose—if that was the price to be paid to get where he wanted to go. But when he willingly compromised another person and put them at risk—either physically or emotionally—then something was wrong. He had crossed a line in what he had done with Karen. He had knowingly deceived her. He could not respect himself for it. And the bigger question was—could he be part of such tactics again?

He let his thoughts trail away. His head throbbed too much at the moment to face the inevitable confrontation toward which his mental quandary was leading him. He pressed his palms hard against his temples.

"You okay, Manning?" asked the pretty brunette at the next desk.

"Nothing a frontal lobotomy wouldn't cure."

She laughed. "Here," she said, tossing him a bottle of Excedrin. "You better take a handful. We have a meeting in ten minutes with CAPS."

He swallowed two pills, chasing them down with his fifth cup of coffee that morning. Now he was going to be *really* wired.

He was in great shape for the meeting, he thought mordantly. And it would be his first time in the presence of this elite group, overseen by Bateman himself.

The title—Campaign Auxiliary Planning and Strategy Board—probably had little to do with the actual function of the group. Bateman had a fetish for initials, and to get good ones he'd give an organization or committee almost any name. An appointment to CAPS, or even a temporary assignment there, was considered a definite step up the ladder around here. Were they possibly looking him over despite his bungling with Karen?

"Looks like it's time," called the brunette. "Bateman's just gone into the inner sanctum."

Manning dragged himself to his feet, taking his coffee cup with him, and followed her into Bateman's spacious office.

"All right," began Bateman without preamble, "the California primary is in a few days. DuBois is running out of steam. It's hard to tell—anything could happen. But MacFarlane could win it—could win it big. That would prove very uncomfortable for us—momentum and all that. If DuBois wins, we're in good shape. But we have to be ready for either outcome next Tuesday. If MacFarlane takes California by a landslide, he could be back on his feet and moving by convention time—and we can't have that. We want to make sure he goes to San Diego crawling on his knees—with the whole nation watching the pathetic state of his presidency. That's what we're after."

General murmurs of assent and understanding sounded through the ranks of the king's trusted servants. There were twelve of them, not counting Manning and the brunette.

"Now we've had most of our plans in place for some time," Bateman continued, "but despite our undercover activities, MacFarlane seems to be gaining ground. Something more is needed. Some last-minute counter-stroke, if you will. Time is short, but I want to bat this around and see what we can come up with that we can pull off immediately."

On cue, ten voices clamored for attention.

"Financial scandal?"

"The trade deficit's still a mess—could we bounce that off him again?"

"Anything more we can do with the Russian situation?"

Bateman sifted through the offerings one by one. "The president's finances are always interesting," he said thoughtfully. "But I've had someone on that for months, and they can't come up with a chink big enough to exploit. The economy . . . the Russians—there's nothing new there."

"What about his family? Any wedge we could use with his daughter?"

"Unfortunately," said Bateman, shooting a quick glance in Jeremy's direction, "that angle dried up too. I'm not giving up on it, but we haven't anything concrete to use as yet."

"How about something really messy—a sexual rumor?"

"Yeah," put in the man next to Manning with enthusiasm. "What about those rumors we've been hearing about the president's late-night goings-on."

Bateman nodded. "I've got someone on that. If it really pans out, though, I might like to save it for the general election. It may prove too explosive to waste on a primary. But I like the idea of dirtying MacFarlane."

"How about a gay? Get one of those Market Street weirdos to come forward claiming to have had an affair with MacFarlane during a campaign swing."

Bateman nodded, then his mouth cracked a grim smile. "You know, you might have something there. All it would take would be the hint. It could be proved to be totally erroneous and yet still do its damage."

"What about the gay vote? California's got enough gays to swing the election."

"Ah yes, you're right. The thing could backfire if we handled it wrong."

"Not if it were a black gay . . . or a Jew. That would split the gays wide open."

"A black, gay Zionist—I love it!" Bateman laughed. "We'd never be lucky enough to find such a perfect patsy."

"And in two or three days."

"Yeah," agreed Bateman. "I doubt there's time. But it's a promising possibility for November if MacFarlane's still around."

"We could incite the war in Iran."

"In three days?" sneered Bateman. "Let's get serious, folks. Besides, then Pat would look the fool."

When the conclave broke up an hour later, most members of the group left with an assignment. One man was told to follow up on the homosexual angle with his California contacts. Several others were given assignments having to do with members of the president's personal staff—a scandal there could suffice too, Bateman said. Bateman's best man was told to follow a lead on some linguistic prof at Georgetown, someone Jeremy had never heard of. And, to his consternation, a new man was put on Karen.

Along with two others, Jeremy was given the job of sifting through all incoming information and acting as a relay between the field and the brass. At least he wouldn't have to go out and get information by whatever unscrupulous means Bateman might lay out, thought Jeremy as he walked back to his desk.

But after what he'd heard today, he couldn't help wondering if he wanted to be around here at all. Homosexuals—scandals—lies! Something was wrong! Was this helping make the world a safer and better place?

Mud-slinging was one thing. Dirty it might be, but it was part of the campaign process. But this kind of slander and deception! Was this the new dawn of mankind? Or was Foster still a man of honor who simply didn't know what his underlings were up to?

Several times in the next few minutes Jeremy found himself on the verge of calling Karen. But then what would he say? There was no way she would ever trust him again, unless perhaps he told her he was quitting Foster. Even then, she'd probably think it was just another ploy to win back her confidence.

Several hours later, head still splitting, he was in the middle of his routine calls when one of the other low-level CAPS people strode exuberantly by his desk.

"Have I got something!" he announced.

"What?" Manning's lack of enthusiasm might have been disconcerting to anyone but the overconfident recent Harvard grad before him.

"One of my leads just paid off. Come on, wanna hear about it? Is Bateman still in?"

"Just got back," replied Manning, trying to ignore the huge knot starting to form in the pit of his stomach. He followed the staffer into Bateman's office.

"I've got something, Mr. Bateman," said the Harvard grad. "I didn't mention it at the meeting because I was still waiting to hear from a confirming source."

"What is it?" asked Bateman.

"It's on MacFarlane's chief of staff, Jacob Randolf. This happened when he was in private practice, and it never made the papers—I checked." He added this last defensively. "So it's never been a matter for the public record, and somehow they managed to keep it quiet. Anyway, about five years ago his wife and daughters were killed in a car accident. Randolf was a wreck afterward, started drinking heavily. Six months later he took an extended vacation. Went to the Catskills for several weeks. That was all my contact knew. But I began to put two and two together. I remembered an article I had read in *Time* about a place called Unicept located up in that vicinity. It's an old converted ranch where they run a chemical substance dependency program."

Bateman raised his eyebrows and shifted forward in his chair.

"I made a few phone calls. Sure enough, Randolf was admitted to the program about four and a half years ago. One source said he'd been suicidal at the time—really out of it. I know it's pretty circumstantial, but a trip to Unicept could easily substantiate it."

"This is good," said Bateman, almost to himself. "Real good." He paused, tapping his finger thoughtfully against his pursed lips. "Curious . . . nothing about this came out when MacFarlane took him on his staff two years ago. But this could be something hot."

He stopped again and seemed to be debating with himself. Then he spoke again, as if suddenly springing awake. "This may be just what we've been waiting for. I'll make a couple of calls, lay the groundwork for you. Then you book yourself on the next flight. Get out to Unicept and find out what you can. But make sure you're back here no later than tomorrow afternoon."

He turned to Jeremy. "Manning, I want you to follow up on the car accident. I want to know if drugs or drink could have had any part in it. Even the tiniest detail might be significant. Was Randolf's wife on the stuff too? Did they have an argument? Who was driving? Any speeding? Where was Randolf at the time? I want to know *everything!* I doubt we'd be so lucky, but if we should happen to have stumbled on another Chappaquiddick, I want to know."

Jeremy stood still, hesitating.

"What is it, Manning? Your assignment seems clear enough."

"Sir," began Jeremy, "I—I guess I'm having trouble seeing what this has to do with MacFarlane. Why drag the poor guy back through his grief?"

"I'm beginning to wonder about you, Manning," said Bateman, with obvious disdain. "This is *exactly* the sort of stuff that ruins politicians—which is precisely what we're after!"

"I can see it could discredit MacFarlane's judgment—though he could claim to have been blind about it and then fire Randolf on the spot. But to open up this kind of wound—it's cruel. And it may be completely unnecessary."

Jeremy was surprised at his own boldness. Harv Bateman was not the kind of man you talked back to.

"Listen, Manning," the campaign director shot back, "if you want to stay in politics, you better develop a stronger stomach!"

"There is the possibility it could make us look worse than MacFarlane," Jeremy persisted.

"So you think we'd allow our hand to be seen? Come on, Manning! I thought you knew the game. We know how to handle this sort of thing. The question is, do you?"

*I don't know if I want to,* thought Jeremy. But aloud he said, "I still think we could be making a mistake."

"You have a job to do, Manning. Either do it or pick up your walking papers." Bateman gave him no room for further response. He turned and picked up his phone and was immediately giving orders to someone on the other end.

Jeremy hesitated a moment more, then spun around and left the office.

In that instant he knew exactly what cowardice meant. But he had invested too much in this life to chuck it all in an impulsive moment of conscience. Besides, what about loyalty? He owed Randolf nothing, and he still believed in Foster's politics. Didn't the end justify the means?

Karen's face flashed before him. Would she have the guts to take Bateman on face-to-face if she were in his shoes? Probably. Even after only a few days in her company, he knew she was no coward. She said what she felt. She minced no words. He had a feeling that with Karen MacFarlane there were no gray areas where right and wrong blurred.

With him, on the other hand, everything lately seemed like one big mural of gray. Give a little there to get a little here—that's how the game was played. But he had to ask himself the same question Bateman had just thrown at him—did he have the stomach for it?

Still . . . he had come so far. He was so close to the real power. At least close enough to look at it. How could he back off now?

Another gray area.

He had a paper due in a couple days. Maybe he ought to drive over to the university and spend some time in the library. Perhaps the academic scene would help. Bateman would be steamed if he found his young underling leaving for any purpose other than to dig in the political mud. But before he was forced to stoop to that, maybe something miraculous would intervene.

# TWENTY-FIVE

"Mr. President . . . Mr. President!" called out an unidentified voice from the crowd. "Have you heard from Senator DuBois . . . has there been—"

"There's been no communication. It's still early—"

"Gentlemen . . . ladies!" shouted Avery Lengyel, raising his hands and trying to silence the crowd of press personnel. "When we know something, the president will make a statement!"

MacFarlane had just arrived at the San Francisco Hilton, where Lengyel was attempting to spirit him through the gathered throng and up to his room. It was 8:15 and nothing but a few scattered local tallies had trickled in.

"Just one question!" shouted out a young woman, thrusting her microphone toward the two men as they inched along between the bodies of their Secret Service coterie. "The latest polls show DuBois leading in all of Southern California. What do you think—"

"We think nothing, miss!" retorted Lengyel. "Except that we pay no attention to the polls."

"Did you hear DuBois's statement earlier in the day, claiming victory . . . and the nomination?" asked another.

"If the senator chooses to make statements he can't back up," answered the president with a smile, "that is his prerogative. But we are confident!"

"Confident, Mr. President? Or putting the best face on what looks to be an embarrassing showing?"

"No more questions!" shot Lengyel.

With the memory of Bobby Kennedy's assassination on this same night still fresh despite more than three decades, the well-screened crowd was kept at bay by the Service men. At last they reached the elevator, and in another moment the presidential entourage was safely inside.

"They're animals . . . bloodhounds!" exclaimed Lengyel.

"They don't let up for a second, do they?" laughed MacFarlane.

"I'm glad you can laugh," said his campaign manager grimly.

"Keep the faith, Avery!"

"I don't see what you're so cheerful about. You saw that poll yesterday as clearly as I did—DuBois ahead by eight points in LA and Orange counties!"

"Maybe the relief of having it over would almost be worth the loss," sighed MacFarlane.

"Sir!" chastised Lengyel. "If we should lose, the nomination's still up for grabs. In a brokered convention, you would hold the edge. Nothing ends tonight, even if he beats us."

The elevator stopped on ten. The entire floor had been blocked off for them, and the president and Lengyel made their way to the suite that had been prepared so they could monitor the returns as the evening progressed. Four television sets were already tuned in to CBS, NBC, ABC, and CNN.

"There's Novak," said MacFarlane as they walked in. "Turn up the sound on CNN."

"You don't want to listen to him, sir," insisted Lengyel. "He does nothing but criticize your policies."

"But he does it so intelligently," replied the president. "No, Avery, I think he's fair. I like hearing his side of an argument. He keeps me on my toes."

They settled into two easy chairs, while several other staff members scurried about preparing soft drinks and sandwiches. It looked to be a long evening.

---

By 9:45 results were coming in strongly from throughout the state. The president appeared to be carrying most precincts in Sacramento and Oakland. Fresno and the south valley had reported early, and the race there showed about even. Santa Barbara and the mid-coastal regions were running a percent or two in favor of DuBois. A computer malfunction had kept any returns from showing yet from LA County.

The surprise thus far had come from highly conservative Orange County, where the Democratic minority was thought to favor DuBois. With thirty-five percent of the vote tallied, the southern usurper showed a scant two percent lead. This represented an almost complete evaporation of the lead the polls had indicated only a day earlier.

The big question mark was still Los Angeles.

---

At 10:35 Bernard Shaw interrupted an interview with state patriarch Willie Brown to report:

"We have an update for you. It appears that President MacFarlane's surprisingly strong showing in Orange County will hold up, and we have just received word that most of San Bernardino County's votes are now in, showing MacFarlane running about three percent ahead. In the north, from Del Norte and Humboldt counties down through the San Francisco Bay area, Sacramento, and San Jose, the president is holding about a seven percent lead. These are unexpectedly strong totals, but must be balanced by DuBois's lead in areas of the south. However, at this point—wait a minute . . . yes, I'm getting a report . . . the problems with the Los Angeles vote seem to have been taken care of . . . yes, that vote is coming in now . . . it should be going up on our board momentarily . . . this will be for Los Angeles County alone . . . there it is, and as you can see President MacFarlane leads Senator DuBois in all LA precincts forty-eight percent to forty-two percent—a dramatic shift!"

A roar of shouts and applause erupted in the suite.

"Congratulations, sir!" said an ebullient Avery Lengyel, extending his hand to the president. One by one the others in the room began to file by and offer their congratulations as well.

"People . . . people!" insisted MacFarlane. "It's not over yet."

"Mr. President, you're carrying LA and San Bernardino counties, all of the north, the central valley's now inching up to about a one percent or two percent lead for you . . . San Diego. DuBois's only stronghold is Orange County, and that's just by a little. The rest of the state's yours! We've done it!"

Another round of applause rippled through the room.

MacFarlane hesitated but a moment longer, then smiled. "I hope you're right. Thank you all very much!"

---

At 11:07 the telephone rang. Lengyel picked it up, listened, then handed the receiver to the president, cupping the mouthpiece with his palm. "It's Senator DuBois," he said softly.

MacFarlane took the phone, listened, nodded with a serious expression, then finally said, "Thank you very much . . . yes . . . a tough campaign . . . well, thank you again . . . that's very gracious of you, George."

He handed the phone back to his campaign manager, glanced around the room at the expectant faces, then said, "I suppose it's time we headed downstairs. The bloodhounds will be waiting! And I'm sure they'll have heard of the senator's call by the time we get there."

He rose and walked toward the door. "By the way, Avery, I hope you've prepared me a good speech! Frankly, I hardly glanced at it . . . I didn't think I'd be needing it!"

# TWENTY-SIX

If California provided the miraculous for Jarvis MacFarlane, it had just the opposite effect on Harv Bateman. At Foster headquarters almost everyone avoided the surly campaign manager for days after the primary.

Then six days following the election upset, Bateman walked into the office wearing a smug grin. The hastily assembled group in Patrick Foster's plush office located on the top floor of campaign headquarters represented the elite of the elite—Bateman, Lavender, Hayford, and Nyborg, with Foster presiding behind his massive mahogany desk. The news they were about to hear could not have been timed better, for each of them still smarted from MacFarlane's stunning victory in California.

"The Randolf thing was a long shot," Bateman began. "And though it came too late for the primary, it might still be something we can use in the fall—that is if we haven't been able to derail MacFarlane before the convention."

"I don't think it would have helped in California anyway," interjected Nyborg. "They're pretty tolerant out there. And as to the rest, I think it would be a mistake using it at all. We'd only end up looking like the bad guys if we leaked it to the press."

"I disagree," said Bateman flatly.

"Maybe we should save it as insurance," said Lavender. "In case we fall behind in the polls."

"Which is unlikely enough," added Hayford.

"No," argued Bateman. "It ought to be part of our offense. It's good stuff. But I've got something better. That's why I asked for this meeting. I thought you all should know about this immediately."

"What have you got?" asked Lavender.

"A month ago I got a little memo reporting that MacFarlane had lunched with a linguistics professor from Georgetown, and I decided to follow up on it. Turns out this professor is one Peter Venzke, and he'd been to the White House to visit MacFarlane several times just before that lunch, and has been coming and going very freely ever since. Venzke's a Russian defector. Came here twenty years ago. When MacFarlane was still a freshman New York congressman it seems he helped Venzke defect, and they've been loose sort of buddies ever since."

"No news there," said Nyborg dryly.

Bateman shot him a venomous look, then went on. "I put a man on Venzke, but told him to keep his distance. We didn't want to spook him. Sure enough, the visits to the White House continued. But then after a few more tries we finally hit pay dirt. This guy Venzke went out sometime after midnight one night, and my man followed him to some sleazy hotel. Venzke went inside, and my man waited for a while outside in the shadows. Just when he was about to head inside and see what he could find out, another man comes walking down the street, and in he goes too. My man thought there was something odd about the second guy. His clothes almost seemed out of place—like a disguise or something. And there was something familiar about his walk. Then all of a sudden he realized who it was who'd come to meet Venzke, and then the disguise made sense."

Bateman stopped, waiting for the suspense to build.

"Well?" said Nyborg. "Are you going to tell us or keep us hanging all day?"

"The second man was none other than Jarvis MacFarlane himself." Bateman let the words drop like a bomb, then leaned smugly back in his chair to await the response.

His revelation elicited the expected bursts of exclamations, some vocal, some visual, around the group.

"And you think this explains MacFarlane's late-night excursions we've heard about?" asked Foster, leaning forward in his chair, genuinely intrigued.

"What else could it be?" replied Bateman.

"What do you make of it?" asked Lavender, looking toward Foster as he spoke.

"I'll tell you what it looks like," said Nyborg with a wink.

"The president involved in a gay liaison!" exclaimed Hayford. "It's too perfect!"

Bateman hardly took notice of the tantalizing suggestion but continued relating the events of the night in question, as if Lavender's question had been addressed to him rather than their boss.

"After MacFarlane went in, my man paid the desk clerk a big chunk of money to find out what room they were in. Then he rented the room next door. The walls were like paper. MacFarlane's not too smart to pick a flea-trap like that, or else he was dead sure he wasn't being followed."

"So what did your man hear?" asked Foster impatiently.

"Russian," replied Bateman, playing the word for all he could.

"What!" came several voices at once.

"That's right," he affirmed. "They were talking to each other in Russian."

"Is your man sure there were only the two of them in the room? I've never heard that MacFarlane could speak Russian."

"The clerk confirmed that no one else was there. And my man says it sounded like Venzke was teaching MacFarlane."

"Giving him lessons?" asked Foster.

"Yes, sir. That's what it sounded like. Like Venzke was making him repeat certain phrases over and over."

"This is unbelievable!" exclaimed Lavender, not a man easily ruffled. "The president meeting secretly with a Russian defector—and speaking Russian. Keeping it secret even from his own staff. I can hardly believe it!"

"Believe it," said Bateman. "I talked to the clerk himself."

"He recognized MacFarlane?"

"No. He was a dimwit. Probably doesn't know what the president looks like. But from everything he told me, I'm sure enough in my own mind to take it to the bank."

"Now *this* is something!" said Nyborg with unusual enthusiasm. "Really something! Unless the president has a good explanation."

"It better be a darn good one," said Lavender.

"Let's not get ahead of ourselves, gentlemen," cautioned Foster. "I hope none of you are thinking of making this public."

"Why not?" asked Bateman, already picturing the damaging headlines.

"Because, Harv, he just might have that good explanation," said Foster. "What if he's putting together some kind of goodwill ploy? What if it's not Russian at all but some other language? Some of the men you hire aren't too—how can I say it diplomatically," he said, glancing around the room with a wry smile at the others, "—aren't too bright, Harv."

A few suppressed laughs made their way around the group.

"He just might have an explanation which would make him come off smelling pretty good and make us look like fools," concluded Foster. "In this day and age, speaking Russian is hardly a capital offense."

"I don't believe it's that simple," said Bateman.

"Who knows? But you can bet he's already got some kind of response in mind, even if it has no basis in fact. Maybe he's learning Russian so he can demonstrate his commitment to cultural exchange. Maybe he's coming around to my way of thinking for a change! Maybe he finally realizes the Soviets aren't our enemies any longer and is planning to make a goodwill speech in Russian. Remember *Ich bin ein Berliner?* Kennedy scored a lot of points worldwide with that. We may differ with MacFarlane's politics, but I wouldn't put it past him to try some shrewd maneuver before November. He knows we're way ahead in the polls."

"If you'll pardon my bluntness, Pat, I think that's moonshine." Bateman knew he had something good, and he wasn't going to let it go so easily. "Nothing but some shady purpose would explain the late hour—and the location. It's just like you said—there's no reason for him to be so secretive about it if his purpose is merely international goodwill."

"You may be right," said Foster. "But we can't leak anything until we know more than we do now. And this is a late fall bombshell anyway, something we should reserve just in case he does start to build some momentum. Timing is crucial in a revelation of this magnitude."

"Unless our delay gives the opposition time to play out their hand."

Foster made no response.

"Maybe we should lean on Venzke—" began Lavender.

"For crying out loud, Sam!" cried Nyborg. " 'Lean on?' This isn't the Mafia. Listen to Pat. Knowing when to wait is as vital as knowing when to jump in."

"That's right," added Foster evenly. "I don't think it would be to our advantage to let on what we know in any way. Right now let's just watch and wait and keep our people on this. I want to know every detail before we move."

"You don't think—" began Hayford, then his voice trailed off.

"What?"

"No. That's *too* unbelievable," he replied. Then added, almost under his breath, "Although stranger things have happened."

"What are you thinking, Hudson?"

"It's too farfetched. But—well, with this Venzke being a defector and all—you don't thing there's a chance he could be a mole?"

"That *is* a long shot!"

"Can you imagine what that would mean! The president of the United States a traitor!"

"Or worse—a defector!"

"Gentlemen! Gentlemen!" said Foster, interrupting the speculations. "That kind of thing won't get us anywhere. That spy stuff is all passe anyway. No one cares now. With unrestricted travel, sharing of technologies, the day of the spy is over."

"Don't you believe it, Pat. There are still Russians watching our every move."

"Well, whether they are or not, I just don't believe there's any connection between that and MacFarlane." He paused and broke into a slow smile, almost evil in its intent. "Of course, the notion does have some appeal. Can you imagine our campaign ads if we could put just the right spin on it?"

He looked around the group. "Yes," he said at length, "that would be positively delicious! But I just don't believe it. MacFarlane may be a lot of things, but he's not a traitor. People would be more likely to accuse *me* of selling out America's strength than him. No, I just don't see that we'd be able to convince anyone that he's a willing lackey for the Soviets, even if we did leak this report. Nevertheless, keep your people working. I want to know everything!"

"This is another long shot," suggested Hayford, "but might it have something to do with all the hubbub this week in Israel?"

"You mean the earthquake?"

"I mean its political ramifications. The place is a hot spot—Syria, Egypt, the PLO, Lebanon . . . the whole Arab/Muslim world is ready to take Israel on at the drop of a hat anyway. It could be 1990 all over again. Now with the mosque in Jerusalem virtually in ruins—"

"How big was the quake?"

"Not that big really—6.2, I think. But it hit dead center under the Dome of the Rock. Which, by the way, is really peculiar, since there is no major fault line there. It was such a direct jolt that the place practically crumbled, though most of the rest of Jerusalem suffered only moderately."

"So what's your point?" asked Foster impatiently.

"Well, suddenly the whole country's in an uproar. The Zionists and the growing Christian contingent are sitting on their bulldozers waiting to level the place so they can start rebuilding the ancient Jewish temple, while the Arab world swears if they lay a hand on the Muslim sacred stones, they'll invade in force."

"I read something about that," interjected Lavender, "by some professor named Hagiz, I think it was. According to him, Hudson could be right. He was pretty outspoken in the interview about the Jewish right to the place."

"Just a local religious squabble! Those backward Christians, Jews, and Muslims—they're all alike. When are they going to wake up to the God within all men of all creeds. In this at least the U.S. is paving the way to a new order of spiritual consciousness. I see nothing involving us here—just unenlightened local bickering."

"I don't know, Pat," said Hayford. "I think it has the potential to heat up. The Jews have been waiting for years for something to happen so they can rebuild their temple there. So I'm wondering if MacFarlane's activities might have something to do with undercover negotiations—trying to keep a lid on all that."

"But why Russian?"

"Who knows? The Soviets might be involved."

"Seems doubtful to me. Why not use normal diplomatic channels?"

"A secret summit then?" suggested Nyborg. "Maybe MacFarlane wants to carry out some negotiations with the Soviets on his own."

"Why not use a translator like everyone else?" questioned Bateman, who was still hoping this would all lead to something juicier than a summit meeting or a religious history lesson.

"Yes . . . why indeed?" mused Foster thoughtfully. He rose slowly and walked over to the window. In the distance he could see the majestic dome of the Capitol. It was a scene that could inspire even the hardest of men. When Foster turned back to face his companions, he looked as if he had reached a long-debated decision.

"Gentlemen," he said, "MacFarlane has something up his sleeve. We can be sure, whatever it is, his success won't do us any good. Thus, we have to act cautiously until we have more facts—but aggressively at the same time," he added, with a nod toward Bateman. "Whatever he's up to, we have to knock the wind out of it. I don't want his shenanigans upsetting my karma. This is the incarnation in which it is my life purpose to be president!"

"What do you propose, Pat?" asked Nyborg.

"I think the time has come to proceed with plans for a meeting with Bolotnikov."

The others expressed only mild surprise. They had debated this strategy many times in the past, and with every discussion all had sensed Foster coming closer to a decision in the matter. It would be a bold stroke, not without great perils—but thus particularly well-suited to Foster.

"You'll take the risk of hanging yourself," warned Nyborg, scratching on his notepad.

"We'll move slowly," replied Foster. "But I want to get the doors open, lay the groundwork. Whatever MacFarlane does, I want us ready to jump. But with no commitments. If it looks like it's about to backfire, we want an escape route."

"Sounds as though you have it all thought out, Pat," encouraged Bateman.

"Andrew," Foster continued, gathering momentum as he spoke, "you get communications opened with the Russians. I'll give you some names that will be helpful. You'll probably need to take a trip there. I don't see any other way since we have to circumvent normal diplomatic channels. We'll make an announcement that you're going to Europe for a couple weeks with your wife—that'll get you out of the public eye here. Then hopefully you'll be able to slip over somewhere and make some contacts. As I said, these names I'll give you should be able to help. I don't need to remind you to keep a very low profile on this one.

"Now, Harv, you stick to the president. Get more men if you have to. Cover Venzke, too. See if you can't get someone who knows Russian. I want to know what's going on between those two!—I'll want daily reports. I want to know if he even uses a different toothpaste. Sam . . . Hudson, I want the two of you working with me to hammer out the substance of our proposed summit. It can't be just more talk. We've got to pull off a major upset, cutting MacFarlane off at the knees. That's going to take some planning," he concluded. "Well, that's it, gentlemen. Let's all get to work."

Bateman was unusually silent as he left the room. Foster's comment about the intelligence of his operatives had hit a little too close to home and kept him from revealing the final chapter of the story of the Venzke-MacFarlane meeting.

What he hadn't said was that his man had fallen asleep in the midst of his eavesdropping and didn't awaken till a few minutes before three. The meeting was just breaking up, yet he heard the confusing sounds of many voices in the room, not just two. And they were no longer talking in Russian, but in some other strange language. By the time he was fully awake and alert, the room next door was empty and all the footsteps had vanished down the stairs and faded into the night. He hurried outside in an attempt to follow, but all was quiet, and he began to fear he had dreamed the whole thing.

Bateman judged it best to say nothing until he had investigated further.

# TWENTY-SEVEN

Jeremy Manning had not had a pleasant week.

Since his last meeting with Bateman, he had spent his time on the assignment given him. At first he had tackled it halfheartedly, and it almost immediately became apparent to him that the auto accident involving Randolf's family was nothing more than that—an accident. But since his research into the event afforded some diversion, along with a good excuse to stay away from the office, he began doggedly pursuing every clue.

Today he had taken the opportunity to visit the scene of the accident, an area of the Shenandoah just north of Fredericksburg.

The drive proved fruitless as far as gathering information on the accident was concerned. But the beautiful wooded roads, crisp and new with the advent of summer, fragrant in the rising heat from the earth, acted as a tonic on his frazzled emotions. It had been a long while since he had allowed time for something like this. On his return he took the back roads instead of the interstate, and the soothing atmosphere helped him realize, like nothing in Washington could have, how one-dimensional his life had become. There were other things in the world besides his career—and certainly things other than Patrick Foster's cause. In fact, he wasn't even sure anymore just what that cause was. He had been attracted at first by ideology; now it seemed all that mattered was winning the election.

About two in the afternoon he stopped at a little cafe alongside the road. The area was isolated, densely wooded, and besides the cafe there was a filling station, a small market, and a campground. After a turkey sandwich and a slice of homemade blackberry pie, Jeremy struck out into the woods behind the building. He discovered a trail leading away from the campground on a circuit along the stream. It led him up the hillside and then looped back down. When he found himself back at the camp an hour later, he took another loop in the opposite direction and did not arrive back at his car until a few minutes before four.

Many things passed through his mind during those two hours. He reflected on where he had come from and the goals he had once nurtured. He thought about the men he was now involved with and about Patrick Foster himself. As he ruminated, an uneasiness crept in he couldn't account for—almost a sense of personal responsibility for the defeat in California.

Foster had, of course, walked away with the Republican primary hands down. But the MacFarlane victory on the Democratic side was considered a major defeat of their strategy in the Foster camp.

He had done nothing to help or hurt either Foster or MacFarlane, so what could he possibly feel guilty about? He knew it was an irrational response.

Did his guilt stem from his own wavering allegiances? Within himself he could sense his loyalty to Foster slipping. The kinds of questions that had plagued him had set doubts working. Were the ideals no longer worth fighting for? No, they were still important, though knowing Karen had certainly cast MacFarlane in a more favorable light. Or had his beliefs become muddled with his ambitions?

He had always been the kind of person who gave his best effort to a task, or no effort at all. He had grown up with his father's rugged injunction drummed into his ears, "If you can't do your best, it ain't worth doin'." Well, he had certainly not done his best for Foster in the last couple weeks, even if only in the privacy of his own mind.

The dilemma was: how far could one go for what he believed? How far could he push the limits of integrity, of ethics, of truth in order to achieve goals that were in themselves worthy and good? Perhaps equally basic: to what extent could the personalities involved be divorced from the issues they represented? Did it all boil down, in the end, to the probable choice the voters would be making in November—a choice between two men? A choice between Patrick Harcourt Foster and Jarvis MacFarlane?

Who was really the more respectable, the more trustworthy *man*, all politics, all elections, all idealogies, all party loyalties, all conservative versus liberal considerations aside? Did a man's personal character matter? Or only the platform he ran on?

The drive back to the city solved nothing, and when Jeremy sat at his desk the following morning, his dilemma was still unresolved. He almost wished the term at the university hadn't ended. Now they'd be expecting more of him here at headquarters. But there was only so far he could push his conscience. The time was bound to come when he'd *have* to take a stand—either that or snuff out his conscience completely.

His thoughts ceased abruptly as the brunette at the next desk hailed him.

"Have a nice day off?" she asked sardonically.

"Couldn't shake the headache," he replied. That at least was the truth. "I might be coming down with something." *A case of cold feet,* he thought dryly.

"Well, you sure missed some fireworks around here."

"Oh, yeah?"

"Big things going on upstairs."

"Fill me in . . . what happened?"

"Me! I'm nobody. It wasn't the CAPS committee this time—only the brass, you know. But when they came out of Foster's office, they were on fire and things started popping."

"What kind of things?"

"Assignments, orders, travel plans, press announcements—you name it! Bateman rode everyone around here yesterday—you'd have thought it was the last week of October."

"Any idea what's up?"

"The word is it's something big. No one really knows, but from the kinds of things involved, a friend of mine upstairs says he thinks it's international. He's heard some rumors about Foster meeting with the Russians. Nothing to do with primaries or the convention." She paused a moment. "And Bateman was none too pleased to find you gone yesterday. He came by here looking for you."

"Yeah," sighed Jeremy, "I suppose I'd better report in."

The brunette strolled daintily away from his desk, and he absently watched as she walked away. When he looked up, he saw Foster himself, along with Bateman and Lavender, emerging from the elevator. Suddenly he was out of his seat and moving toward them. He had just told himself the time would come when he'd have to take a stand. He might as well force the issue and make that time now—confront the man who was the object of both his commitment and his quandary. All they could do was fire him.

"Senator Foster," he said as he reached the three men who were engaged in conversation.

"Yes, young man," said Foster, "you're. . . ?"

"Jeremy Manning, sir. I'm on the press staff."

"Yes—Manning, of course. A good man too, I've heard."

Jeremy didn't respond to the compliment. Instead he asked, "Could I have a word with you, sir?"

"Of course, what is it?"

"In private, perhaps?"

"Listen, Manning," put in Bateman brusquely, "Senator Foster's a busy man, and—"

"That's all right, Harv," said Foster. "You and Sam go on ahead. I'll catch up." Then turning to Jeremy, he said. "Let's use Harv's office."

Jeremy followed the senator into the office, where they both remained standing. Foster was obviously anxious to make the conversation as short as possible, and by now Jeremy was feeling very foolish.

"I had a couple of questions, sir," he began, with more confidence than he felt. "About my work here."

"Yes?"

"Well, I hope you don't think me disloyal for asking, but I've been uncomfortable with some of the assignments I've been given lately. I'm having trouble putting it into the perspective of what we're trying to accomplish."

"Give me an example," encouraged Foster.

"Well, for instance, digging into a car accident that happened five years ago in order to discredit one of the president's staff."

"I see."

"I can't help wondering why we're using techniques like that. I've always thought our strength—your strength, sir, I should say—had to do with the issues, with a strong vision of the future, with a higher awareness of spiritual necessities, with man's duty to find the common ground with his fellows, both in this and in other nations. But lately, at least in the areas I've been involved in, it has seemed instead that such negative—if you'll pardon my saying so—such smear tactics have taken precedence over that message. You have a strong campaign, sir. We're way ahead in the polls. Your platform's sound. It seems we should want people to elect you president because of what you stand for, not because we've been able to ruin someone else's reputation in the public mind."

"You've raised some valid questions . . . Jeremy, isn't it?"

He nodded.

"Yes, Jeremy, some good points. I, as much as anyone, am committed to running a campaign based on issues. It is a grand cause we're fighting for. Certainly you agree?"

Again Jeremy nodded.

"Our foremost responsibility is to see that cause through to a successful fulfillment. That's our obligation to the American people, and to all the races of humanity. They are counting on us—on you too, Jeremy, for you are an important soldier in our fight to see that the truths of this new age prevail. We can't be weak or fainthearted. The truth and the future are on our side, and in that conviction we have to do whatever we must to further the cause—it is nothing short of a sacred duty. The future of this great nation, as a pioneer to lead the rest of the world, stands in the balance. We must not falter in the vision placed before us. Do you grasp the enormity of our calling?"

"I do, sir. I truly think I do. I have long believed that peace between nations had to begin with the superpowers. That's why I joined your campaign. But don't we have a moral responsibility too?"

"Our cause is a moral one. It would be nothing but immoral to waver in our dedication to proclaim these truths and lead people forward into our evolutionary destiny."

"Are you saying, then, that the end justifies the means?"

"Ah," said Foster, smiling. "The eternal question raised by all young idealists. I was sure that was coming." Here Foster chuckled in a patronizing manner that might have been meant to sound fatherly.

"Believe me, I understand your concern. And I share it. It is a dilemma all serious politicians wrestle with. But as one matures, one's idealism must always be energized with pragmatism. That's how you make things happen! That's the secret to accomplishment, to seeing your ideals reached—being practical along with your idealism."

"So you *do* believe the end justifies the means?" persisted Jeremy.

"I am saying that while we are admonished to be gentle as doves, we are also commanded to be wise as serpents. Of course I place no more value on the mythical character who was purported to have uttered those words than I would on any wise being. But wherever one can find wisdom to lead him into higher channels in his being, he does well to listen and heed. The point I am trying to make is that every general knows he must make sacrifices in order to win a battle. Is he immoral in doing so? Is he denying his higher consciousness? No. He is driven only by necessity, by the call of what he knows to be the greater good. Believe me, such decisions never come lightly. Above all things, I believe in the public trust. Was that all, Jeremy?"

"Well . . . I was wondering about one other thing," Jeremy replied.

He had to proceed slowly. He could sense that, despite Foster's outer calm, his questions had already pushed about as far as the senator would tolerate from such an insignificant underling. Besides, this was pure bluff—a gamble with his own political future in the pot. But he needed to see Foster's response firsthand.

"I heard about a new international phase of our strategy," he continued. "Something to do with the Soviets and—"

"That's top secret!" snapped Foster sharply, the friendly smile instantly gone from his face. Almost as quickly, however, he realized his error and attempted to recover himself. He smiled and, in a measured tone, asked, "How did you hear about that, Manning?"

"I've been working rather closely with Mr. Bateman and CAPS," Jeremy exaggerated.

"Ah, yes," replied Foster, seemingly relieved. "You folks have some important work ahead of you. Work of national importance—even national security. I'll be counting on all of you. Now, I hope that settles some of your anxieties, Jeremy. We'll talk again sometime. I must be going."

"But sir . . . about the Russians?"

Foster looked Jeremy full in the face, and his light blue eyes held an unmistakably menacing glint. "What I said before is true. This is absolutely top secret. You forget all about it until you hear otherwise from me!"

"Thank you for your time, sir," said Jeremy, knowing he could push it no further. "I appreciate your time and your candor." Actually, candor had been the last thing he'd gotten from Foster, but it seemed the right thing to say.

Foster's face suddenly relit with cordiality, as quickly as it had vanished a moment before. "Glad to be of help!" he said. "Keep up the good work. We can use more young men like you!"

The presidential candidate swept out of the room, leaving Jeremy standing alone, his head throbbing. His Excedrin headache had escalated into a full-blown migraine.

# TWENTY-EIGHT

Jeremy went home that night feeling exhausted and betrayed. He had believed in Patrick Foster. Believed him a man of principle and integrity, whose motives for seeking the land's highest office truly stemmed from his concern for the nation, the world, mankind—for the glorious and united brotherhood he talked about.

Foster's words rang in his head. Over and over the sound of that mesmerizing voice echoed in disordered snatches of rhetoric. Everything the man said made sense. Yet nothing made sense. He talked about truth, about the greater good, about ideals, about vision. Yet where was the truth in his trying to gloss over the issues Jeremy had raised? What had their little discussion been but a whitewash of the truth? Despite all his words, he hadn't really said a thing!

*The truth is on our side.* Baloney!

Then Jeremy's loyal side spoke up in Foster's defense. The man was right, wasn't he? Some things *did* have to take precedence over others. There *was* a greater good to be considered. Wasn't there? Wasn't that how all great accomplishments came about? Of course he was right when he said that idealism had to be balanced with pragmatism.

Jeremy closed his apartment door behind him, slid off his brown sport coat, and dropped it in a heap on the floor. He loosened his tie and kicked off his loafers with such force that one flew across the room. The exertion made his head throb painfully.

He walked to the kitchen and gulped down three aspirin. Then he opened the refrigerator and rummaged through the near-empty shelves for something to eat. It had been days since he'd shopped.

He grabbed a can of Pepsi and a hunk of jack cheese and ambled back to the living room. He picked up the TV remote control and began flipping through the maze of channels.

Right now he envied his brothers their factory jobs. He hadn't done a stitch of real work all day, yet he felt like he'd been jammed to the ground by a jackhammer. At least when they were worn out after a hard day's work they had something to show for their efforts.

Suddenly he let out a groan. There was the object of his mental conundrum, Patrick Harcourt Foster, leering back at him in all his senatorial grandeur. A speech he had delivered that morning was being replayed on C-SPAN.

He flopped down on the couch, hardly noticing when a splash of the soft drink flew onto his slacks. He found himself drawn into the speech, telling himself all the while that he'd had enough of Foster for one day and ought to change the channel.

". . . a past we can be proud of," Foster was intoning in his most sublime oratorical voice. "Certainly I recognize that the foundation of this great nation rests on moral values, expressed by our forebears in Christian terminology. But to understand not only our spiritual roots, but also the challenges of this new day, we must see that past in a historical, not a contemporary, framework. In other words, we cannot go back. We must always press forward.

"In all aspects of world and human history—biological, terrestrial, social, relational, *and,* I would contend, my friends, spiritual—in all these areas we can see the evolutionary process at work. There is a force propelling life in all its aspects—conscious and unconscious—forward and upward. Nothing is static. We are all familiar with what science teaches concerning the biological evolution of the species. But that represents only a picture of a much greater and more far-reaching evolutionary process in which the entire universe, with man at the center, is being drawn upward and inward into the center of light, of truth, where ultimately we will dwell in the fulfillment of that upward destiny.

"Man leads this forward march because man stands at the apex of the biological evolutionary ladder. Thus, man's destiny is to lead the way forward into higher destinies of spiritual consciousness. And as the species cannot go *backward* biologically, neither can man go back spiritually. All spiritual truths build upon former revelations in order to take man *forward* in his understanding. The reincarnative process, as an intrinsic part of man's evolutionary destiny, always tends forward and upward, the final result being the perfection of the species of humankind.

"This same process is at work in the gradual evolution of spiritual revelation through the ages. Thus man's religious history has progressed through sacrifice, through various myths, through an attempt to differentiate between good and evil. Many early peoples attempted to personalize what they called 'God' because it was the only means they had of making sense of the hugeness of the universe. Men came into this history of the human quest, men who were incarnatively in advance of their ages, who spoke light and truth to their contemporaries. But their contemporaries, being backward and unenlightened, misunderstood their messages and erected religious systems based on their teachings. Our great chal lenge now is to lay aside the untruths which have been done in the name of religion and to move forward in the truth that Jesus Christ and Buddha and Krishna and Mohammed taught—that the god-consciousness is within us all, not within a backward religious system.

"This great nation of ours has fallen victim more seriously to certain Christian myths than any nation on earth. And now we are at last waking to the fact that our destiny as men and women, even our destiny as Americans, demands that we lay aside its outdated relics of the past and move toward that truer, higher consciousness of the universal Power within each of us that Christ himself pointed toward.

"That brand of Christianity so prevalent in this country only a few short years ago was rife with backward notions that held humanity down, an antiquated throwback to ancient nomadic Judaism. It is a religion thousands of years behind the development of humanity's collective destiny. So it is with a great sigh of relief that I, along with millions in this new day, watch the signs all about us of its demise at last. I am truly thankful to the Bakkers and Swaggarts and others of their evangelistic brood who finally revealed the emptiness of their house of cards.

"New times are coming—new times *have* come! A new dawn is approaching. All history—biological and spiritual—has brought us to the threshold of this moment. Our destiny rises gloriously before us! It is no accident that peace has arisen throughout the world in this last decade. A new age, a new dawn for humanity is at hand. Societal changes will be vast as humanity enters an age of harmony with itself, with nature, and with the cosmos. This transformation is now taking place. It is a renaissance of Man's Consciousness throughout the globe. This peace which we have witnessed in recent years is but the beginning. Truly the evolutionary process is approaching its zenith, and we living to witness this new dawn are blessed to be able to help lead the way.

"A new generation of leadership is being raised up on the earth, individuals who perceive this purpose and this harmony, and who recognize man's destiny. This is the great cause to which I have committed myself, to help enlighten this nation, so that we might—as we have in the past—provide a beacon light to all the people's of the earth, helping to lead them out of the bondage of the past into the new era of peace and brotherhood and unity which is at hand."

It was mesmerizing. The man could sway anyone with his powerful tongue. Only the damp penetration of sticky Pepsi roused

Jeremy from his trancelike stare at the TV screen.

"Drat!" he muttered. However, it was not the spilled drink that bothered him as much as what he'd just heard. And what bothered him even more was the way he'd been listening, not even noticing how tightly his hand was holding the can of Pepsi—not even noticing when he spilled it. Foster's words could stir a man to a level of emotion that was almost frightening.

Three weeks earlier he would have stood and cheered.

But something was different for Jeremy Manning now. And he suddenly knew what it was.

*That man really wants to be president!*

Suddenly it was clear why Foster's soothing rhetoric hadn't soothed him earlier today. Foster was no different from anyone else—no different from him, no different from half the people he ran into every day. Foster talked about his "great cause," about vision, about truth, about the destiny of America and mankind. But what it all boiled down to was one thing.

Patrick Harcourt Foster's greatest cause was *himself*!

If the so-called new dawn of man's destiny, as he was so fond of rattling on about, had to do with harmony and unity and trust between adversaries, then what role did Foster's "top secret" ploy have? Where did the ruthless tactics of his underlings fit? Were all the smooth words chosen merely to lure the public to follow him because it was a message he knew they would swallow? Was it all a smoke screen to divert attention from his real motives?

It was all becoming so clear now: Foster would do anything to win the election!

Perhaps Jeremy would have been able to accept some of Bateman's shady deals and schemes in order to see a man like Foster—the Foster he had believed in—find success for the world's good. Perhaps he might even have convinced himself that Bateman was acting without Foster's knowledge. Perhaps he might even have crossed a few lines himself for Foster . . . if he could have maintained his belief in the man.

But what was left to believe in now? If Foster was going to use behind-the-back dealings, even outright deceit, to gain the presidency, then he was just like everyone else—a self-serving hypocrite.

Of course Jeremy had no proof that any of this was true. And was he any better himself? Any more honorable? Maybe he had believed in the cause, but he had also kept a keen eye on his own personal success.

Wasn't Foster right? After all, what politician in the world didn't have to deal and negotiate to get anything done? How could he expect Foster to be any different?

*Were* there any sincere, honest, straightforward people left in the world?

Jeremy rested his aching head in his hands, his temples throbbing against his fingers.

For years he had desired acceptance by the Fosters and Batemans of Washington. That had been his dream. Whether it was on their terms or his didn't matter. The only important thing had been to be part of the great Washington establishment so he could begin inching his way up through the ranks into positions of influence and power.

And he had crossed so many lines, walked through so many unexpected doors that he had begun to lose himself in the process. Just who was Jeremy Manning these days? Was he nothing more than an ambitious lackey to an ambitious power seeker?

His thoughts turned to Karen MacFarlane. She had seemed so sincere, so forthright—so honest. It was hard to believe she was a politician's daughter—especially the president's!

And that's the kind of person he wanted to be! The kind of man someone like Karen MacFarlane could respect; the kind of man he himself could respect. If it meant changing the course of his life, so be it. Whatever the perks, he didn't want to end up like Harv Bateman.

He slumped back on the couch and drained the remainder of the Pepsi from the can.

It was one thing, however, to talk about values, and respect, and integrity, and keeping yourself untainted, but quite another to know what to do about it in the midst of the battle. Was he prepared to give up his pursuit of a career in politics over these annoying twangs of conscience?

He could march down to Foster headquarters tomorrow morning and ram his resignation in their faces. But that seemed too much like running away. Besides, what good would it do anyway? What would it accomplish other than freeing him from the guilt? He had gotten into politics in the first place hoping to do some good. So what good would it do to run out on the whole thing?

He set the empty can on the table. It wobbled unsteadily for a moment, then tipped over. Slowly it rolled to the edge of the table, teetering precariously before finally tumbling to the floor. Jeremy watched the insignificant motion of the can with a sort of intellectual detachment. In the slow-motion, dreamy state of his consciousness it became peculiarly poetic. Suddenly there he was himself, his presence bound up in the little can, slowly but with utter certainty falling to calamity.

*If I was smart,* he thought recklessly, *I'd go and tell the president about Foster's possible involvement with the Russians!* Then he laughed at the foolhardiness of the idea. Him? Get to see the president? And he had no proof. At least nothing except Foster's unexpectedly violent reaction to his question. That was troublesome, but it constituted no real evidence.

He laughed again. *Well, if I'm going to get kicked out of Washington I may as well do it in style, via the White House! I must be going crazy to be coming up with loony ideas like this!*

Suddenly, without further thought, he jumped up, retrieved his shoes, jammed his feet into them, and stalked toward the door. He didn't bother to straighten his tie or put on a coat. He needed a shave and his pants were still stained with the soft drink, but he didn't care. He had to get out. Another minute ruminating over his failed dreams and confused ambitions and quandaries of duty would have sent him over the edge!

He ground his Mustang Fastback into gear and screeched out of the garage. At least he had a nice car, he thought, apropos of nothing. It was a silver-gray vintage 1967 model, very rare these days. His brother Larry had unearthed it at an estate sale in great need of an overhaul and body work. Larry's talent and Jeremy's money had turned it into something to be envied by any car buff.

He drove around the city for an hour. Finally the car came to rest, seemingly of its own accord, across the street from Karen MacFarlane's apartment building. He wasn't surprised. He supposed this had been his destination all along, without even realizing it.

He started to get out of the car, then stopped. Was that Secret Service thug around? Or worse, Bateman's man? Who cared anyway!

Defiantly he swung open the door and stepped out boldly. As he approached the steps he spotted a man in the shadows just to the left of the door. When Jeremy drew nearer, the man stepped up to meet him. It was not Renfro—probably his replacement.

"May I ask your business?" the man said.

"I'm just here to pay a brief visit to Miss MacFarlane," replied Jeremy. "Renfro knows me."

"Your name?"

"Jeremy Manning."

"Oh, yes, Mr. Manning. Brett did mention you. Go on up."

"Thanks," said Jeremy, and went up the stairs.

He hadn't thought about actually facing Karen herself until he found himself standing on her doorstep with hand poised to knock. He stood for a moment as if frozen in time. Then realizing he had little to lose, he let his fist rap on the door.

Even dressed in a bathrobe, hair mussed, and wearing glasses, Karen was lovely in Jeremy's estimation. For a moment they just looked at each other, only silence flowing between them.

At last Jeremy smiled sheepishly and said, "I know it's late but . . . I had to see you."

"You look awful."

"I feel worse."

She looked him over a moment more, then stood aside and motioned him inside. As she shut the door behind him, she asked, "Would you like something to drink?"

"Anything—what do you have?"

"I've got some instant coffee—and it looks like you could use some."

"Yes—please."

Leaving him standing in the entryway, she disappeared into the kitchen. He went on into the living room and sank down at one end of the sofa. A few minutes later she returned, holding a cup of coffee and a cup of tea.

"I always like to keep something handy for my derelict friends," Karen said with a slight smile. "And you certainly qualify tonight!"

She handed him the coffee. As he took it, their fingers brushed. He turned quickly away, trying to ignore the energy her touch generated within him. He took a long swallow. The warmth felt good.

"I'm surprised you didn't slam the door in my face," he said. "Our last meeting ended none too cordially."

"I've always had a soft spot for strays and vagrants."

"You won't let up on me, will you?"

"Just getting even for your chicanery the first time we met."

Jeremy started to let out a groan, but then caught something in her eye that told him her comment was meant in fun.

"Karen—" he began, "there's so much I want to say. I know I don't deserve a hearing, but right now you're one of the few people I can trust. When I'm done, you can throw me out if you want."

"Go ahead, Jeremy," she said simply. She sat down an arm's length away, feet curled up under her, facing him. "Talk."

He sat facing forward, then leaned over and set his cup on a coaster on the coffee table in front of him. He purposely did not look toward her, but could feel her self-assurance, mingled as it was with gentleness and honesty. He wanted to touch her. Instead he propped his elbows on his knees and stared woodenly ahead. Then slowly the jumble of thoughts plaguing him began to pour out.

"I've always wanted to be in politics," he said, "for as long as I can remember. At first I suppose it was the glamour of it. As I grew older the typical idealism came into play. You know—change the world, help mankind, make the earth a better place. I landed jobs here and there, worked for a state congressman in Harrisburg for a while. Then this opportunity with Foster came up and I really thought I had it made. The great cause . . . peace for the world—harmony for humanity and all that. But suddenly my train derailed . . . first you came along . . . then I got in trouble at work. Pretty soon all my plans began to unravel. Now I don't know what I'm about."

Karen said nothing, waiting for him to collect himself and continue.

Here he was, thought Jeremy—the bright intellectual graduate student and part-time professor—fumbling for words. He could hold his own in any political debate, but laying his soul bare in honesty and contriteness was an entirely different thing. You didn't learn this in school, or from a tough-cop father. Usually you didn't learn it at all. So when the time came, as it did for all honest persons sooner or later, you just had to reach down and yank it out. It wasn't a pleasant ordeal, to pull those frank confessions out of your heart. Nevertheless, he did. He told Karen everything, leaving out only the specifics about Bateman's and Foster's tactics. Those could wait. For right now this was his personal story, his confession. He would not whitewash his own behavior and self-centered attitudes by trying to focus attention on the misdeeds of others.

When Jeremy had completed his painful extraction, he sank back against the sofa, exhausted.

A long silence ensued, and he braced himself for the rebuttal he was sure he deserved. Instead, Karen reached over and took his hand.

"I don't know what to say, Jeremy," she responded tenderly. "I'm sorry I was so hard on you. Then again, these things you've been forced to think about will surely make you stronger in the end."

"You needn't be sorry. I acted like a fool, and you responded in the only way you could."

"Maybe you didn't think through all the implications of what you were involved in. But you don't have to keep punishing yourself for it. There might not be anything so wrong going on in the Foster campaign. In the meantime, you have to pick up and get on with life, learn from this, and go forward a better man."

"Does this mean you believe me?" he asked. "That I didn't set out intentionally to hurt or deceive you? And that you can trust me?"

"I believe you," she answered. "I should have believed you a week ago, but I was too hurt to see things sensibly. I had begun to think a great deal of you, only to have my feelings shattered suddenly. Trust is another thing. It might take time—but I feel as if I *could* trust you. I mean, I can see that you are trustworthy, that I *should* trust you. But trust also involves the emotions, and I'm not sure I can vouch for them just yet. I'm sometimes impulsive, and occasionally I can't foresee how I'm going to react."

Jeremy nodded in understanding.

"Trust—the real and lasting kind—has to be built up brick by brick."

"I thought about you often this past week, Karen," he said. "You became my touchstone to reality. I suppose you symbolized the opposite side of the fence for me. You reacted with such hostility to the deception, it somehow seemed you stood for the truth."

Karen laughed. "My, what a burden you place on little old me! Complete with pedestal!"

"Given the circumstances, it's crazy to expect you to trust me just on my say-so. But, Karen, I'm going to earn your trust."

"What about our different viewpoints? Have you forgotten that we come from opposite political poles?"

"That doesn't matter to me anymore. I'd rather cast my lot with a trustworthy man of integrity with whom I disagree philosophically than with a man who believes exactly as I do on every single issue but whom I can't put my faith in. It's all so clear now."

He brought her hand to his lips and gazed at her with deep intensity. "Suddenly earning your trust means more to me than anything."

She drew close to him and raised her hands to his face, pulling him nearer and nearer until their faces came together and their lips met.

After a moment they separated, then leaned back together against the arm of the sofa. Karen wrapped her arms about him and leaned her head on his chest.

"I didn't come here for this," he said, tenderly stroking her hair. "I don't want you to think—"

"I don't," she said, looking up at him with something very close to admiration in her eyes. "Don't worry. I'm a sensible girl. It just happened. Neither of us planned it."

"I just don't want you to think I came back for the wrong reasons . . . for—well, you know."

"You're funny!" she laughed. "Once you make up your mind to be forthright and full of integrity you feel guilty about one kiss!"

"I don't feel guilty. It's just that—well, I have to warn you, I think I'm falling in love with you."

She leaned up and kissed his cheek. "Well, let me warn you right back—I think the feeling is mutual."

"You sure it's not just pity for one of your derelict friends?"

"I know the difference."

He sat up, and she moved away from him a bit. "It's getting late," he said.

"You don't have to go so soon do you?"

"I should. I've got a lot to think about, and I don't want to rush anything."

Karen nodded, her disappointed expression conveying that she understood.

They walked slowly toward the door, and there he pulled her close again in one last hug. "Karen, there's more I have to tell you—about Foster. I didn't want to muddle things up with it tonight. And I have to be sure before I say anything. But do you think I could see you tomorrow?"

She nodded. "Are you going back?" she asked.

"I'm not sure," he answered with a frustrated sigh. "I hate to run away."

Reluctantly he stepped outside. "I'll call you tomorrow," he said. "We have to be careful—I'm not Foster's only spy."

"What do you mean?"

"He has someone else watching you."

"Oh, great!"

"Don't worry. He was furious with me for getting too close. This guy's going to maintain his distance."

# TWENTY-NINE

Not more than three hours after his daughter finally fell asleep, President Jarvis MacFarlane awoke from a troubled night.

It was a few minutes before five, but already the summer dawn had invaded the chinks of the bedroom's window shades. The moment his eyes opened MacFarlane knew he must be up. The still of the morning beckoned him.

He dressed in casual garb—slacks, knit shirt, and his well-used sneakers—and slipped quietly from the room and down the hall. Even at this hour there was activity about the place, but not much. He met a few of the staff on his way downstairs and was relieved to see everyone going about business of their own. He didn't want to talk just now. He needed to be alone.

In five minutes he was outside, exiting through the West Wing into the Rose Garden. Fortunately at this early hour there were few tourists about and he could walk through the expansive President's Park without fear of repercussions from the Secret Service. He just wanted to be outside, to hear the birds, to smell the grass, to feel the chill of the morning give way to the warmth of the sun . . . and especially he needed to think.

He had to talk to someone about his dilemma. He had never been a religious man. He simply didn't know how to interpret all this . . . what it might mean . . . and what he was supposed to do. It was maddening to be so alone! So alone with nothing but his own thoughts and his feeble prayers of helplessness.

Prayers . . . he didn't even know if that's what you called them! He'd never prayed before in his life. Really prayed.

Now his soul cried out from within him for help. But cried out to whom? A deity? The being called *God?*

No longer could he utter the name of the unknown Maker of heaven and earth casually, as merely one more expression of great feeling. Never again could he say *My God!* when what he really meant was *Oh, wow!* That word, that name, that sense of awful Presence could never be meaningless again.

But who was God . . . What was God? And why had *he,* Jarvis MacFarlane, an unbeliever at best, an outright pagan at worst, why had *he* been singled out? He knew nothing of how things were supposed to operate in the spiritual realm. Surely he was the wrong man for this dreadful burden!

On he walked around the circular path toward the south and west, passing between the willow oak that had been planted by Lyndon Johnson and the littleleaf lindens of Franklin Roosevelt. A little farther on he passed Nixon's giant sequoia, still in its infancy, Hoover's white oaks, and Dwight Eisenhower's pin oak.

What a heritage was here, he thought. Decades, even centuries, of presidents lived on in the very grounds they had inhabited. On the other side of the circle stood the magnificent American elm planted by John Quincy Adams, and up next to the South Portico grew Andrew Jackson's magnolia grandiflora.

Yes, a magnificent heritage! Now here he was at Jimmy Carter's favorite, a cedar of Lebanon he had planted toward the far edge of the walk. Jimmy Carter . . . now he'd been an outspoken Christian. Had he ever faced dilemmas like this—wondering how to balance politics and matters of faith?

*There's got to be somebody I can talk to who would know how to advise me,* he thought. *A minister, a priest, a rabbi . . . someone! But who! An author, a church official . . . maybe Duke—he's interested in religious things.*

On he walked, pausing at the fountain before slowly making his way back along the other side of the circle toward the White House. A few tourists were about by now, but he remained oblivious to the cameras clicking away outside the fence.

This was good, he thought, just the tonic he needed. He sucked in a deep lungful of the warm morning air. Somehow things never seemed as bad at this hour.

Nearing the great mansion again, the president detoured off the walkway to the right, entering the well-trimmed garden Lyndon Johnson had had planted in honor of Jacqueline Kennedy. He seated himself on one of the benches placed about its perimeter and continued his thoughts.

Yes, he had to sit down with someone knowledgeable in such matters and discuss this rationally and intelligently. It wasn't that he didn't think the world of Peter, or even that he hadn't come to respect and believe in Daniel and the others. But they were—he had to admit it!—radical in their approach. He had to get some balance to the input he was receiving. A second opinion. From more traditional circles. Someone who could talk to him about how God worked in human lives in more "normal" terms. The members of the Legation would have him carrying a doomsday placard and preaching in the streets! He wasn't ready for that!

But whom could he talk to? A string of names began filtering through his brain. The congressman from Virginia who had once had designs on this very house behind him; he'd run on the fundamentalist platform. Then there was Falwell, the old moral majority guy . . .

No, they wouldn't do. Given the current anti-evangelical mood in the country, just a visit from one of them to the White House would give Foster the election. How about Rabbi Epstein from up in New York? If anybody should know about God, a Jewish rabbi should. Or that fellow—what was his name?—chaplain of the Senate . . . Montgomery, that was it. He'd heard him pray several times in public. Sounded sincere . . . seemed to know his stuff. There was that religious author Lindsey whose book Dmitri mentioned frequently. No, that wouldn't work—that was futuristic and fundamentalist and he couldn't be openly connected to conservative Christian circles. That part of his life he had to keep secret.

None of them felt quite right. He doubted he'd be able to open up to any of those men. That fellow from the National Council of Churches who was just here . . . Sadler—he was definitely out. Sounded more like a politician than a religious leader.

MacFarlane looked at his watch.

No wonder there seemed to be so much activity about all of a sudden. He'd been out here nearly an hour and a half! It was quarter till seven. He had to get inside, dressed, and shaved. He had an eight o'clock briefing.

The president rose and made his way past the South Portico and to the West Wing doors from which he had come.

As he entered the White House, suddenly another face came into his mind—the face of a visitor who had been here recently.

*Of course!* MacFarlane exclaimed to himself. *That's it! I've always respected that man. And that look his eyes gave me a couple weeks ago when he shook my hand said that he cared more deeply than mere words would tell. He's perfect. And he's been untainted by all the scandal that put Protestant fundamentalism on the scrap heap politically and opened the way for all that spiritualistic nonsense of Foster's!*

He took the stairs two at a time to the second floor, then to the third.

When he descended from his living quarters an hour later, he went straight to the office of his personal secretary.

"Virginia," he said, "get me Billy Graham on the phone."

"The evangelist, sir?"

"That's right. His offices are in Minneapolis, but whether he's there or down—where is it he lives? South Carolina, I think. Anyway, I don't know where you'll find him."

"And when I reach him?"
"I want to talk to him."
"The briefing?"
"Break in. I'll take the call whatever I'm doing."
"Yes, sir. Do I tell him what it's about?"
"No, I'll do that. Just tell him it's personal."
The president turned and walked into the Oval Office and closed the door behind him. He sat down at his desk, glancing at the clock. It was five before eight. His advisors would be arriving downstairs already and would be here in just a minute or two.
Suddenly a case of cold feet overwhelmed him. *He's liable to think I'm loony just like anyone else would,* he thought. *Why should he believe me? He was so close to Nixon, and after that swore he'd never get so involved in politics again.*
A moment more and his resolve had crumbled. He reached across his desk for the intercom.
"Virginia," he said, "on second thought, cancel that call."

# THIRTY

Smoothly the elevator doors slid shut.
The two men inside remained quiet.
The steel cage lifted off the third floor, passed the fourth, then the fifth. Before it had a chance to reach the sixth, one of the two reached out and pressed the *Stop* button.
The elevator slowed to a stop.
"Melodramatics are not my style, Harv," said the larger of the two men, "but I had to be sure we were completely alone. This is about as safe as we can be. These walls must be nine inches thick."
"Safe? Safe from what, Pat?"
"Prying ears," answered Foster.
"You think our offices are bugged!"
"No, nothing as cloak-and-dagger as all that. But there are things leaking out. And I don't like it."
"We have nothing to hide."
"That's not exactly true, Harv. This Russian deal *must* be kept

under wraps. And somehow that young Manning kid's gotten wind of it."

"That's not possible!"

"Anything's possible in this town, Harv. You know that. When he wanted to talk to me yesterday—you remember, just outside your office?"

Bateman nodded.

"He asked some very pointed questions. And he mentioned the Soviets. He's none too secure—at least that was my perception. A troubled young man—mixed loyalties. He bears watching, and I have to tell you, I'm concerned."

"Why that dirty little—"

"Calm down, Harv, it's nothing we can't handle. What I want to know is how he found out?"

"I don't know. I can't imagine."

"We've got to find the leak. There were only the five of us in the room, and I trust every one."

"Maybe he was guessing, grasping at straws."

"I suppose it's possible. But even that's troublesome. Why is he doing it?"

"Well, what do you want me to do!"

"Do a little investigating—discreetly of course. See if there is any possibility this information has leaked. We've got to plug it! If even a whisper gets to the press, we've got big problems. It could be the whole ball game, Harv. So ask around. See who knows what and how they found out. Find out how far it's gone already."

"And Manning?"

"What exactly is his function around here?"

"Low-level press staff. I thought he had potential. Looked promising. Bright kid. Loyal, I thought. I gave him a couple of assignments. Thought he was a potential CAPS member and brought him in on a recent meeting or two. Although his fiasco over the MacFarlane broad rankled me, and I was beginning to have my doubts."

"Yeah, I remember you mentioning that. I wonder if she has anything to do with his pangs of conscience and all his talk of truth and integrity."

"Anything you want me to do about him?"

"We've got to keep an eye on him. Don't let him near CAPS or anything else substantive. Shunt him off on insignificant assignments if you can do it without him getting wise."

"Anything else?"

"Put a tail on him. Round the clock. I want to know everything he does. If he goes to the press, we've had it."

"And if he does?"

"Don't let it get that far. If it looks like he's going to unravel and go public on us, pull his plug, Harv."

"You mean—?"

"Do I have to spell it out for you? We've come too far! You've been in this game long enough to know how it works."

"Any preferences?"

"Use that guy from St. Louis. He's good with cars, brakes, that sort of thing. Then send our Mr. Manning on some assignment that's likely to tax his automobile to the limit."

# THIRTY-ONE

About an hour after Foster and Bateman emerged from the elevator on the sixth floor, Jeremy Manning walked into the ground floor of the headquarters building and took the same elevator up to his desk on the third floor. To call it reporting for duty was hardly accurate. He was there—still uncertain about what to do and hoping he didn't get pushed too hard.

He sat down at his desk. The brunette—she might be the key to this. He glanced around. She wasn't there.

What was her name! She'd been the first to mention the Russians.

There she came . . . let's see—Welling . . . Wellington . . . Weller. That was it—Weller . . . Linda Weller. He looked up and smiled as she approached.

"Good morning, Jeremy."

"Hi, Linda. What's up?"

"Not much. You?"

"I'm just finishing up my report on the Randolf accident."

"Find anything?"

"Nah." Jeremy hesitated a moment, then plunged ahead, trying to sound matter-of-fact. He had to keep a low profile, but he had to find out. "Heard anything more about the Russian deal?"

"What Russian deal?"

"You remember. You mentioned it yesterday. You said the brass had met and come out with something to do with the Russians."

"I never said that," replied Linda. "That kind of statement could get you into hot water around here!"

"I thought you did. Sorry."

"All I said was that I'd heard there was something international going on and that someone upstairs had heard a rumor about the Soviets. But it was two separate things—and just hearsay."

"Yeah, that's right. I guess I assumed," said Jeremy.

"Pretty bold assumption."

"Yeah," laughed Jeremy with a shrug. "Where'd you say you heard it?"

"What is this, Manning?" asked Linda, half playfully but with a hint of sincerity in her tone.

"I don't know. Just curious I guess. Come on, if you heard it here it can't be any big deal."

"Probably not. I just don't like the third degree. Besides, something I say might get back to Bateman, give him the wrong idea, and bang—I'm out of a job."

"Don't worry! I'm in Bateman's doghouse myself. I won't be going near him!"

She hesitated, then shrugged. "Oh, I suppose there's no harm in it. It's no big deal anyway. There's this guy up on four. We've dated a few times. Nothing heavy. Just a nice guy, you know."

"Yeah, sure. What's his name?"

"Mike . . . Mike Carson."

"What's he do?"

"He's on Nyborg's staff. Errands, clerical stuff. Nothing even as interesting as we sometimes get down here."

"So how did he get wind of it?"

"I don't know that he got wind of *anything*. We were out, talking, you know. I guess he was thinking out loud. It just wasn't that big a thing," she said as she moved back to her desk.

Jeremy nodded, then laughed. "Yeah, I guess you're right."

He made a pretense of work for a few minutes, then rose and headed toward the rest room. Once out of Linda's sight—he didn't want to arouse either her suspicions or curiosity any further—he made for the stairway. In another minute he was on the fourth floor, checking for the threatening presence of heavy brass. He remembered seeing a guy with Linda a time or two and assumed it was Carson. Now he quickly glanced about, looking for a familiar face. When he finally spotted the guy, Jeremy approached and introduced himself.

"Mike Carson?" he said.

"That's right."

"I'm Jeremy Manning. I work downstairs—for Bateman."

Carson extended is hand. "Pleased to meet you. Have a seat."

"I've only got a minute," Jeremy said, remaining on his feet. "But I wondered if I could buy you lunch?"

"Well . . . sure. But I'm not that busy right now, if you want to ask me something. Cheaper than lunch."

"That's okay," Jeremy laughed. "I would like to talk to you, but not here."

"What about?"

"I'd rather wait. If I told you, you might turn me down."

Now it was Carson's turn to laugh. "Okay. I'll bite. About noon?"

"That's fine," Jeremy replied. "I'll meet you down by the first floor elevator."

On the way back to his desk, Jeremy paused beside Linda Weller.

"Linda," he said, casually, "I'd appreciate it if you didn't mention our little talk to anyone."

"You sure are secretive all of a sudden, Manning," she grinned. "But that's all right with me. What's got you so wired about this thing?"

"I'll tell you about it someday," he said. "And thanks."

---

An hour and a half later Jeremy sat opposite Mike Carson in the corner booth of a downtown sandwich and chili shop.

"I'm sorry for the secrecy," Jeremy began. "I have my reasons. I hope you don't mind."

"What's it about anyway?"

"I work next to Linda Weller, and she mentioned that you think there might be some new international twist to the campaign coming up."

For a moment Carson looked at him doubtfully, then said, "I don't *know* anything. I was just saying to her that it wouldn't surprise me."

"Why did you say that? What did you base it on?"

"On a little hobby of mine."

"A hobby?"

"Yeah. A little game I play with myself."

"Care to explain?"

"I guess there's no harm in it," said Carson. "I've never made any big secret of it. I work for Nyborg—you know that, right?"

Manning nodded.

"Well, he has this habit—probably a carryover from his law days in Boston—of carrying around a yellow legal pad wherever he goes. He's always doodling, taking notes, writing reminders to himself. He's constantly scribbling away on that yellow pad," said Carson. "The odd thing is, he never saves the sheets. Anything that's a genuine memo he gives to his secretary. Anything that's even the least bit important gets typed and filed. But he never uses those yellow pages for anything except doodling, even though he occasionally does write some meaningful stuff on them. Of course it's all interspersed with nonsense. I suppose it's his way of killing time."

"So, what's this have to do with your hobby?"

"It's what he does with the sheets."

"Which is?"

"He tosses them . . . you know, the round file, deep six."

"He just throws them away?"

"Every last one, usually in the trash can by his secretary's desk. Sometimes I see him scan his pad, say a few things to his secretary to write down in a memo, then toss the sheet."

"And then?"

"Well, when I started noticing the pattern, my curiosity got the better of me. I wandered over one day when no one else was around and snatched one out of the can."

"Anything interesting on it?"

"Interesting, yes. Substantive, no. Just like I told you—doodling. A word or phrase here and there."

"So what happened next?"

"I couldn't help myself. I was hooked. I started collecting the sheets. He never crushed them into a ball—always whole sheets, like he was inviting someone to come along and snoop."

"And you obliged him?"

"You bet! Whenever I could, I grabbed them up and tried to make sense out of them. I made it a little game, trying to second-guess the brass and see if I couldn't figure out what moves they were going to make next, even before they announced them."

"And did you ever?"

"Oh, sometimes. Little stuff. Like I said, it's just a game with me."

"So tell me about your comments to Linda."

"Well, the other day when Foster and his lieutenants came down and started snapping everybody into action—"

"Day before yesterday?"

"Yeah . . . right. Well, midway through the afternoon I saw a couple of Nyborg's sheets slide into the can. I waited for my chance, got it about 5:30, and from a couple of the things written just figured there was something new going on."

"Things like what?"

"Oh, *international implications* was one phrase. Then there was a reference to Europe. It was curious, actually. Down at the bottom of the sheet was a 'Things-to-Do' list—almost like a joke. I mean lists like that are usually for mundane little chores. But Nyborg's list only had two entries: *Take wife to Europe*, and underneath it, *Secret Flight to ______________ (See Dierdorf)*. See what I mean—curious."

"Who's Dierdorf?"

"Only Dierdorf I know is the under secretary of state, Bill Dierdorf. But I don't know if that's who he meant."

"Do you still have the sheet?"

"Oh, yeah, I save them."

"Could get you in trouble."

"I doubt it. There's nothing on them. Well, not until this one."

"Could I see it?"

"I suppose," said Carson. Then he looked intently at Jeremy. "Say, what is this, Manning?"

"Let's just say I'm pursuing my own little hobby. Can you be satisfied with that, as long as I keep you up on anything I discover?"

"I guess that's fair enough."

"I appreciate it, Mike. You've been more than straight with me. I hope I can repay you."

"Listen, I'll put the sheet in an envelope and drop it by your desk this afternoon, sometime before five. Okay?"

"Great! It's more than I could have asked for. You're not afraid of betraying confidences?"

"Nah. I'm not a company man. I mean I'll vote for Foster all right. I'm a loyal worker. But basically this is just a job for me. Besides, I still don't see that there's anything that hush-hush about it." Here he paused a second, then said, "You know, come to think of it, there is one other thing on that particular sheet that puzzled me."

"Yeah?"

"Sort of a crude, political cartoon drawing. Interesting . . . well, you'll see it. Maybe you can figure it out."

# THIRTY-TWO

Jeremy tossed the single yellow sheet onto his coffee table for the dozenth time.

He had been going through this little ritual for an hour, alternately studying Nyborg's cryptic sheet of doodling, then throwing it down in frustration. But always he kept coming back to it, convinced that something on the page Carson had given him contained the clue to whatever it was he was looking for.

Two sketchily done drawings dominated the piece of paper. On the right side was what appeared to be a man riding a horse. The figures were rendered in stick format—Nyborg was certainly no artist. The rider appeared to be carrying an old-fashioned lance and wearing a suit of armor.

To the left of the horse and rider was a gallows, with steps leading up to the platform, a sturdily erected post from which the rope descended, with the victim clearly hanging from the noose. The curious thing, however, was that no hangman was present. The victim's hand was stretched out to the releasing lever on the post, as if he were in the process of hanging himself.

Between the two drawings were the large initials PHF, which must refer to Foster, with a large question mark above them. Had Nyborg been debating which of the two caricatures most suited his boss?

Above the whole thing, in large scrawled letters, was the simple injunction *Meet B!*, with the insides of the e's and the capital B filled in by the doodler's pencil.

At the bottom of the page, as Carson had described, was the curious things-to-do list.

Jeremy sat back in his chair, took a deep breath, rubbed his hands over his tired eyes, and exhaled slowly.

It had to mean something—if only he could figure out what!

*Dierdorf . . . Secret Flight to* ______________ somewhere. That had to be the key. Should he operate on the assumption that it was a reference to the under secretary of state? What could he lose? Only his job. And he'd already risked that anyway.

First thing tomorrow morning he'd try to bluff out some information.

*Meet B!* Who could that be, he wondered. Baker, the representative from Orange County? No, the California primary was already over. Certainly Bateman was a possibility. Then why the big to-do? Nyborg saw Bateman every day.

Suddenly a wild thought struck him.

He'd just been reading an article in *Time* about the Soviet hierarchy . . . but no—that was too fantastic! Not even Foster would have the guts to try something like that!

He leaned forward in his chair and picked up the yellow sheet. *Europe . . . Secret Flight . . . Dierdorf . . .*

Yeah, it might be possible! There was Foster riding off on Nyborg's version of a white horse to save the world, trying to pull off something so politically dangerous that he just might be hanging himself.

All the pieces fit! Of course, he still might be reading all his own fantasies into what was nothing more than what it appeared—the doodling of a bored man during a dull meeting.

---

The next morning at 8:05 Jeremy picked up his phone and dialed the number of the State Department.

"This is Jeremy Manning," he said. "I'm on Senator Foster's staff. Would you please put me through to Secretary Dierdorf?"

He waited for the connection to be made. After a minute's wait a woman answered. Again he identified himself as Jeremy Manning. She asked him to wait.

Then Jeremy heard a voice say, "Dierdorf."

"Secretary Dierdorf, my name's Jeremy Manning," he said. "I work for Harv Bateman at Foster headquarters, and I'm calling to confirm something for him on the European trip you're planning for Andy Nyborg."

He paused a moment, waiting to catch Dierdorf's initial response. There was a brief, awkward silence, then Dierdorf said, "That trip's top secret. I'm not allowed—"

"Yes, I know. As I said, I work for Bateman, and he's got me handling some of the details here," said Jeremy. Half-truths always led to lies, he thought, but he'd take his conscience out to the woodshed later.

Dierdorf hesitated, but finally said, "Yes? Okay, what exactly was it you wanted to know?"

Inwardly Jeremy exhaled a long sigh, but answered promptly. "There's some question about the flight . . ." he said, letting his voice trail off, hoping the other man would pick up on the thread of the sentence.

"Which one?" asked Dierdorf, but went on without giving Jeremy a chance to answer. "We're only handling the second one. He's arranging everything for his flight over through normal channels."

"Yes, yes, of course," replied Jeremy. "It's the second flight I'm referring to, taking off from Munich—" he said, taking a stab in the dark.

"No, no," interrupted Dierdorf. "They're not even going to Munich. Don't you people have your information straight? He'll leave his wife in Hamburg, be taken by car up to Kiel where he'll be ferried over to Stralsund. He'll be flown privately from there."

"Right! To where?"

Only silence met his question.

"Didn't Bateman brief you?" Dierdorf finally asked. "It doesn't sound to me as if you know much of anything about this meeting."

"Not on the details," said Jeremy. "Nyborg was supposed to brief me further, but ran out of time and asked me to call you." He was getting in deeper and deeper, but was by now so caught up in his desire to find out what he could that he hardly noticed. "Now, if you could just tell me his final destination, I'll be able to get to work on my end of it."

Dierdorf hesitated. At length he said, "It's a little place not far from Gdansk—just over the border. Kaliningrad. It's got a small airstrip."

"And that's where the meeting's going to take place?"

"Just the preliminaries—to set it up. They'll just be sending some unofficial staffer too, same level as Nyborg no doubt."

"And when's the meeting itself scheduled?"

This time there was tension in Dierdorf's voice when he replied. "Look, Manfrey, or whatever your name is, if you want to know any more about this, you come see me. And bring some authorization from either Nyborg or Foster if you do! Until then, you'll get nothing more from me!"

The phone clicked down and a dial tone pierced Jeremy's ear.

He hung up, sat back, and took a deep breath. This was turning into a whole lot more than he'd bargained for!

# THIRTY-THREE

When Jeremy called, Karen readily agreed to meet him. He had not seen her since he left her apartment two nights before.

"Meet me at the Jefferson Memorial," he said. "Go inside. I'll be there."

She laughed. "Why the elaborate subterfuge? Everyone knows by now. What does it matter if we're seen together?"

"I'm not sure," he replied. "Something just tells me we ought to be cautious."

"What is it, Jeremy?"

"Just be there. I'll tell you all about it."

Jeremy hung up and walked out of the phone booth that sat just outside the office building that housed Foster's headquarters. He hadn't dared chance the call from inside.

He'd told her to meet him in an hour. That would allow plenty of time to drive around, determine whether he had a tail—which he'd begun to suspect—and try to ditch him. He'd just as soon meet Karen with only her Secret Service agents in tow. They were a nuisance, but at least he knew why they were there. He couldn't say the same for Foster's men.

Fifty minutes later he walked inside the Jefferson Memorial and sat down to wait. Within just a few minutes Karen entered.

Karen took one look at Jeremy's face and knew this was no romantic rendezvous. His countenance was deadly serious.

"Let's walk down by the water," he said. "They'll be able to see us, but there won't be any way they can hear."

She followed him without a word.

They had walked for about three minutes in silence when all at once Jeremy burst out, as if releasing months of pent-up thought, "Karen, I know this may sound crazy . . . but I must see your father."

"So soon, Jeremy?" she teased. "We've only barely met!"

"Please . . . be serious," he replied, hardly noticing the implication. "This isn't about you and me. Something's going on I have to tell him about. He'd have every right to boot me out the door, or laugh in my face. But I have to try it."

"My father isn't like that," said Karen, sobering now in defense of her father.

"I'm still a Foster employee *and* an admitted spy. Why should he believe a word I say?"

"Because *I* believe you," Karen said.

"How can you? You haven't heard what I have to say?"

"Then tell me. I'll prove I believe you."

"I can't."

"Okay, then I'll say it's because I believe *in* you."

"You told me the other day it would take a long time to earn back your trust."

Karen hesitated before responding. "You're right. Trust is too deep a thing to be tossed about casually. Let's say, then, that I believe in your sincerity, in your motives. I'm *learning* to trust you. That strikes me as a good starting point for a relationship."

"So do you think your father would see me on that basis?"

"Of course. I'd make sure of it."

"He puts that much faith in you?"

"I don't know if I'd put it quite like that," she answered modestly. "But he and I are similar in many ways. He wants to know the truth, even if it comes from a Foster man."

"It's hard to believe any politician could be open like you are."

"Don't let your experiences with Foster sour you, Jeremy. There are many good and honest politicians."

"But once you enter the political arena, something happens to you. It happened to me, and I'm far removed from the real action. You can't help getting sucked into the big sell-out at one time or another, if only to save your political skin."

"I'll let that pass," she said, throwing him a sidelong glance, "on the grounds that you don't know my father. I'm sure he's made his share of deals. But he's cut from a different cloth. He's a man of integrity, Jeremy, all the way. I know that sounds corny, but I believe in him."

"I thought I believed in Foster," countered Manning.

"You didn't know Foster like I know my father," she said. "I'm not some star-struck, idol-worshiping kid either. I've seen him make mistakes. One of the reasons I love and respect him like I do is because he's human. I don't agree with everything he does just because he's my father. But I've seen him agonize over his command decisions, go without sleep night after night, skip meals—all because he cares intensely about everything he does. At this very moment something big is gnawing at him. I don't know what it is, but I know it's because he cares. You may oppose him politically at every turn, Jeremy, but once you know him you'll never be able to deny he cares for this country and for the integrity of his office. It makes me so angry when they say he's ineffectual and then demand a machine like Foster to replace him."

They had stopped walking, and she had turned toward him, her face animated with passion, her luminous hazel eyes flashing. Jeremy wanted to throw his arms around her, but it was the wrong time. That would have to wait for the proper moment.

They walked on for some distance in silence. At length he said, "Okay, I'm convinced. Which brings me back to what I asked to begin with. How does one go about getting an appointment with the president of the United States?"

"You're in luck," Karen replied. "It just so happens that I have an inside connection."

# THIRTY-FOUR

Jeremy straightened his tie for what must have been the sixth time. He couldn't help himself. Sitting on the edge of a plush yellow sofa in a room with walls and carpeting to match, he was sweating and knew it.

He had never expected to meet the father of a girl he might be falling in love with in a place like this. Formally called the Yellow Oval Room, this was more than some ordinary parlor. He was about to meet the president! As a young political devotee, he had entertained occasional lofty fantasies about the White House. But actually being here was another matter.

As he had walked past the elaborate security devices, he told himself over and over that he was going to stay cool. He had locked his jaw firmly shut and laboriously curbed his eyes from roaming to the ornate chandeliered ceilings and the paintings on the walls. He would not gawk at the people and offices he passed. He was no wide-eyed tourist. In fact, if these people knew who signed his paycheck every week, they would have clamored for his hide!

That thought alone was enough to produce his dry mouth and the clammy tremor in his fingers. The thought of facing the president of the United States only added to it.

He looked over at Karen sitting next to him—relaxed, confident, and lovely. It struck him again how remarkable she was. She looked elegant but totally at ease. She might have been dressed in jeans and a T-shirt sitting in her simply furnished student apartment.

He heard the doors open behind him, and he tensed noticeably. Karen reached over and lightly touched his hand, smiling directly into his eyes. As if energized, he stood and pivoted to face his host.

Jeremy immediately noticed the faintly dark area encircling Jarvis MacFarlane's eyes. He recalled Karen's statement about her father's sleepless nights, and now he could well believe it. The president's shoulders hunched forward slightly, adding to the general appearance of weariness. But as he strode confidently toward them, his easygoing manner made Jeremy almost forget that this was a man with tremendous burdens weighing upon him.

"Well, Mr. Manning," said the president, extending his hand and grinning warmly, "my daughter has spoken highly of you. I'm glad we finally have the chance to meet."

Jeremy took the proffered hand in his perspiring one. "I'm honored to meet you, Mr. President," he said, wondering how he even got the words out through his dry throat.

"Let's all sit down and relax," said the president. "I've ordered some refreshments. But while we're waiting, why don't you tell me a little about yourself, Jeremy? It is all right if I call you Jeremy, isn't it?"

"Of course, sir," Jeremy said.

He sat back down on the yellow sofa next to Karen, even more stiffly than before. The president took a seat in an adjacent Louis XVI chair, moving it a bit so he could face them more squarely.

That simple act helped loosen Jeremy's taut nerves. All at once he could visualize the president as a man in his own living room entertaining his daughter and a friend. He could move the furniture about however he wanted, maybe even put his feet up on a table if he chose. Somehow the notion made the place less intimidating.

Jeremy began a brief biographical sketch of himself. At one point the president interrupted with the comment, "Young Republicans, eh?"

Jeremy wondered just how much Karen had told her father about him. Not much from the sound of it. But before he could respond to the comment, a butler entered with refreshments.

"I ordered lemonade," the president said. "This early heat wave is taking its toll around here. We do have something stronger if you'd like."

"This is fine, sir," answered Jeremy. He took a long swallow. The icy lemonade soothed his dry throat, so he could at least talk without croaking like a frog.

"So, Jeremy," the president continued after sipping his drink, "you were born and raised in Philadelphia—a tough enough town at times. How did you happen to come to Washington?"

Jeremy hesitated. Now was the moment he'd find out just how much Karen had told him.

"I was active in student political groups during college and studying toward some kind of career in politics," he answered. "Not long after graduation I worked on Harold Means's campaign for the Pennsylvania state legislature. When he won the election, he took me with him to Harrisburg."

"Do you plan on running for public office yourself one day?"

"No, sir. I don't see myself in that capacity. I go in more for the technical aspects—strategy and the like—not the glory or the power—"

He stopped short when he realized the implication of his words. "Not that I consider anything wrong with public office," he hastily added.

"I know what you mean," chuckled the president, coming to the rescue. Then he quoted in a faraway voice, "Glory drags all men captive at the wheels of her glittering train. . . ."

He grinned and cleared his throat. "It's difficult to refrain from becoming philosophical in this job from time to time," he said, as if making an apology. "One of the hazards. No doubt you've made a wise career choice."

"I hope so, sir. But I'd be lying if I didn't say that the whole thing has disillusioned me lately."

The president leaned forward in his chair with apparent interest. "Care to explain?" he asked.

Jeremy said nothing for a moment, then turned to Karen. "Karen, would you be offended if I spoke to your father alone?" he said.

"No," she replied. She stood up and put a reassuring hand on Jeremy's shoulder. "I knew you had something private to discuss. This will be as good a time as any for me to make my graceful exit." She flashed a smile at her father, then left the room.

The two men remained silent for a few moments. Then Jeremy began speaking, with almost a confessional tone.

"In Harrisburg I chanced to meet Patrick Foster," he said. "He was a very dynamic man and I was immediately taken with him."

"Understandable," said the president. "He certainly does have magnetism."

"I desperately wanted to come to Washington to work for him. I believed in him. And, Mr. President, I have to tell you honestly that I still do believe in the philosophies he stands for, at least in part. I feel we've come to a point where we have little choice but to move toward the future with a whole new outlook."

He stopped, surprised at his boldness.

"I'm sorry," he said after a moment. "Perhaps I'm out of line here."

"I'd be a pretty poor leader if I couldn't accept honest criticism, Jeremy," the president replied. "Besides—you may be right—Foster may be right. It may all work out as rosily as his utopian, metaphysical ideals suggest. Yet sitting in *this* office I don't have the luxury he does of being able to bask in quixotic dreams; I still have a duty to be prudently cautious, even skeptical. Funny, it used to be the Republicans accusing the Democrats of having their heads in the sand about the Soviets—now it's reversed. But, please, go on—I didn't mean to get off on a tangent."

"I'm afraid it's me who's been stalling, Mr. President," replied Jeremy. "I'm still not quite sure how to tell you exactly why I'm here."

"Why not just tell me then?"

"I'm afraid it may sound crazy to you, alarmist over nothing."

"Try me."

"Well, I've been working at the Foster campaign headquarters," Jeremy began again, then paused for an icy gulp of lemonade. "I'm embarrassed to tell you all this . . . and—and I do want you to know that I *am* planning on quitting."

"Because of my daughter?"

"No, sir. It has nothing to do with that." He shifted uncomfortably in his seat. "It's a long story, sir. Are you sure you have the time?"

"I think I'd better make the time." For the first time the president sounded almost stern.

Jeremy continued, telling Jarvis MacFarlane everything he'd uncovered about Foster's dirty tactics, not leaving out his own part in them. He made no attempt to shadow his own behavior with Foster's duplicity. Finally he reached the point of his pangs of conscience, his conversation with Foster, his stumbling upon the Nyborg memo, and his phone call to Bill Dierdorf.

"I'm mortified that I've been a part of all this, Mr. President," he concluded. "However, I feel that it's now beyond me, beyond the election even. And this is where I'm hoping you won't call me loony and send for the men in white coats."

"No fear of that, Jeremy," said the president, his tone deadly serious as he edged forward in his chair. "Go on—what do you think it all means?"

"Well, sir, that's just it. I don't know what to make of it. Is it truly a matter of national security? Or even—I hate to use the word treason—but is it truly as grave as all that? Is he trying to usurp the power of the presidency . . . or is it nothing more than election posturing? I don't know, sir. But I have to be honest with you—I think Foster's planning a secret meeting with Bolotnikov."

He let out a long sigh and relaxed back into the cushions of the couch, exhausted. As he did, the president stood and walked slowly toward the window. He stood looking out for a few moments, then turned to face his visitor.

"Well, Jeremy," he sighed, "if you're right, we do have something of a problem. You know who Bolotnikov is, I take it?"

"High-ranking Soviet—"

"High-ranking indeed!" interrupted MacFarlane. "He's the most powerful man in Russia next to Kudinsky. And a devilish hawk. Yes, for Foster to meet him, secretly, without my approval, without Congress's knowledge, right now when tensions are so delicate . . . you're right, Jeremy, it goes far beyond the election. It certainly would impact our national security!"

"If I may, sir," offered Jeremy somewhat timidly. "I hope his motives would be peaceful."

"Oh, no doubt! No doubt!" replied the president, becoming animated. "And it would make him look good in the polls—to pull off a diplomatic coup for peace. But the fool doesn't realize how shrewd Bolotnikov is. That's Foster's one flaw, Jeremy. He thinks he's got the market cornered on savvy. He thinks I'm an idiot. But he has no idea of the forces I'm trying to hold together to keep this country out of war. Let him try it with his simplistic approach! Bolotnikov's no moron. He could have Foster for lunch around a negotiating table. The senator's liable to send us into a war in Iran if he's not careful!"

A heavy silence descended upon the room, and Jeremy was the first to speak.

"So you believe me, sir? You think that's what it might be?"

"I don't know, Jeremy," replied the president, calm again. "Looking at it logically, I don't suspect you of being sent here with false information, if that's what you mean. Beyond that, you certainly don't impress me as a liar. I can usually read people pretty well . . . as can my daughter," he added.

"I did succeed in deceiving her once," Jeremy countered with a modest laugh.

"Do you *want* me to throw you out?"

"I only want to make sure that from now on I'm completely out in the open."

"You're not alone there," the president replied. "But I'm afraid it goes on all the time on both sides of the fence. I don't condone the duplicity, the dirt, the self-promotion, but it's there. Sad to say, it's part of politics."

"I wish it didn't have to be. It seems there ought to be some more upright way of choosing our national leaders."

"How I wish there was, Jeremy," replied the president wistfully. As his voice trailed off he seemed to drift into distant thought. He then stood abruptly.

Reading this as his signal to leave, Jeremy rose also. "Well, I felt you should know about this, sir," he said, walking with the president toward the door. "I sincerely apologize if I'm pushing the alarm button for nothing."

"Even if there's nothing to it, I am still deeply appreciative of what you've done, Jeremy," said the president. "It took guts for you to come here, and I want you to know how grateful I am."

"I hope I'm wrong, sir," said Jeremy. "Notwithstanding my past loyalties, I would never wish harm to you or your position."

"Thank you. You've earned my trust, Jeremy, just by coming here and leveling with me. I hope you're wrong too—and not for the sake of my standing on election day. It's much bigger than that. There have been rumors—"

He stopped, then stared thoughtfully at Jeremy for a moment, as though trying to make up his mind about something. He appeared to reach a decision and plunged ahead.

"As I was saying, there have been rumors of a power struggle in the Soviet Union. We've not been successful in confirming it beyond the fact that Kudinsky and Bolotnikov have divergent ideologies. If Bolotnikov is trying to establish his own power base in preparation for a takeover, he might well consider some kind of agreement with the man everyone thinks will be the next president to his advantage. The Soviets may have elections now, but they certainly haven't adopted the checks and balances system of a full-fledged democracy. In many ways they still operate as they always did—and they have some fairly effective ways of making an unpopular leader ineffectual. If Bolotnikov developed some peace accord which circumvented Kudinsky altogether, it could reduce the premier to little more than a figurehead, with Bolotnikov holding the real reins of power."

He moved away from the window and crossed the rug to stand before the fireplace in front of Jeremy. As he began speaking again, he also began pacing, his hands in his pockets. He walked back and forth, staring straight ahead as he paced off the length of the fireplace, then turning to look at Jeremy and retrace his steps.

"But there's not a chance in a thousand Bolotnikov would honor any peace agreement, in my opinion. I think the moment he had enough power to get the Politburo to do his bidding he'd move on Iran, maybe even Turkey or Iraq, thus giving the Soviets both the Persian Gulf and the Mediterranean. He'd be convinced that a smiling new-dawn-for-mankind space cadet like Foster would never lift a finger until it was too late. But, you know, I think he might be wrong. If backed into a corner, I think Foster's old military background might flare right back up in an instant. I think both men would seriously underestimate each other, and that's why their supposed 'understanding' could eventually land the world in the middle of nuclear war. If this is what he's really up to, Foster *has* to be stopped. And I've got to figure out a way to win this election!"

"What would you like me to do, sir?" asked Jeremy.

The president gave Jeremy a long, assessing look, then said, "It would be nice to know a timetable on this Foster deal. You wouldn't have any information on that?"

"I'm afraid not, sir. But I'm sure following Nyborg's movements would give you an idea on the preliminary meeting."

"Maybe. But I'm sure Foster's moves will be closely guarded until the moment he leaves the country. Then we'd have very little time to make contingency plans."

"I might be able to find out more."

"I would never ask you to spy on your associates at Foster headquarters, Jeremy. We mustn't stoop to their tactics."

"Should I return to my job—and keep working *against* you?" asked Jeremy.

"I can't dictate your conscience to you, Jeremy. Do what you have to do. I'll respect you regardless. Even if you continue to work for Foster and he ultimately defeats me. You have shown yourself a man of conscience by coming here with this information. I'll ask nothing more of you. Follow your conscience. You can rest assured that I will be following mine as well."

---

Jarvis MacFarlane remained behind in the Yellow Room after Jeremy Manning had shaken his hand and departed. The young man did his daughter proud, even if he was a Republican! Honest and forthright. MacFarlane instinctively liked him. Manning had something else, too, he thought—he had heart, a refreshing quality these days. If he continued to be honest with himself, as he was struggling to be concerning Foster, Jeremy Manning would go a long way.

MacFarlane's thoughts about his daughter and her friend, however, were soon eclipsed by more pressing, more terrifying ones.

Everything was assaulting him at once. Along with this, the reality of his experience grew more graphic in his mind. Rather than fading, as a dream or even a hallucination might have done, it grew more urgent, more vivid, more compelling each day. Event piled on top of event, shouting that he must heed the Voice . . . he must take action . . . he must somehow, against the odds, succeed.

Yet, practically speaking, he still didn't know what it was he was supposed to *do*. He still hadn't even hinted at what he'd seen and heard to Peter or Daniel or any of the others in the secret nighttime company. He wasn't sure why—they were the logical ones to tell. But he was afraid of their reaction. He was afraid they would discount his experience, or think he was loony, or think he was trying to impress them somehow.

Why should they believe him, after all! *They* were the ones who claimed to have been given a "message"—prophetic words to deliver. That's what they said their cryptic name meant—they were part of a large host of messengers—*legates*, emissaries, envoys—sent to proclaim the coming of a new kingdom, but one vastly different than the new age of humanity proclaimed by Foster and his kind.

So why should they believe *him*! He wasn't even a believer! He knew how preposterous it would sound in their ears!

But he *had* to tell someone!

# THIRTY-FIVE

The following morning Jeremy reported for duty at Foster's campaign headquarters.

Bateman immediately took him to task for his recent absenteeism. Jeremy said he'd been ill, and his drawn pallor from poor eating and sleepless nights gave visual support to the excuse.

"All right, Manning," replied Bateman in his usual unsympathetic manner, "have Weller bring you up to date. You didn't give us much that's useful in that Randolf report. Maybe you'll do better next time. The senator seems to think you have merit, though I don't know why we bother." He turned brusquely and stalked away to his office.

Jeremy found his brunette neighbor loitering by the coffeepot.

"Want a cup?" she asked casually as he approached.

"Thanks," he answered. She filled a Styrofoam cup and handed it to him. "Bateman wants you to brief me about what's been going on."

"Sure," she replied. "That flu must have hit you hard. You look terrible."

"I guess so." He drank some of the black coffee. "So . . . what's up?"

"Not much really. Nyborg's off on a vacation all of a sudden. But the rest of the brass have been scurrying around for the last couple days, dishing out little assignments right and left. Nobody really knows what it's about. Last big push before the convention, I suppose."

"What have you been working on?"

"Oh, just a dull in-depth profile of some linguistics prof over at Georgetown. Maybe you know him?"

"Who is he?"

"Venzke."

"I may have heard the name. Never met him. What's the connection?"

"Who knows? They told me to dig up everything I could and write up a bio on him. Did you know he was a defector? Years ago."

"That's interesting . . . any political affiliations now?"

"Haven't found any. Other than the fact that he's a friend of MacFarlane's. Just a boring old bookworm."

"So why are we interested in him?"

"The guy's been going to the White House a lot lately, visiting the president. And then Mike just caught wind of a rumor that he's met secretly with MacFarlane too—and the two of them were speaking in Russian together."

Jeremy expelled a sharp breath. After a brief hesitation, trying not to reveal his reaction, he asked, "What's the big deal about that?"

"Nothing, if the president had enrolled in the Russian 101A course. No big deal. Speaking Russian's in these days. But why in secret? Meeting this fellow in shabby hotels in the dead of night! The whole thing's a little weird. If it sounds suspicious to me, you can imagine Bateman's reaction!"

Jeremy's mind reeled. His hands suddenly felt weak. He had to set down his coffee for fear of dropping it.

"But you heard none of this from me, Manning! I just happened to be around when Mike was puzzling to himself. If the president of the United States is speaking Russian on the sly, *I* don't know anything about it! All I was told to do was compile a report on Venzke, and that's what I'm doing."

Jeremy scarcely heard what she said. Absently he turned away and wandered toward the door. He hadn't intended to leave the office, but before he knew it he was standing in the fresh air.

He continued walking. No doubt the next time he entered that building it would be to have Bateman tell him he was fired.

What did it all matter now anyway?

With a sick pang he realized he had no place to go. He could never reenter the Foster camp. Even if Bateman never learned what he had done, inside—emotionally—he had risked his whole career based on Karen's faith in her father. He had laid all prior allegiances and motives on the line in that one moment of vulnerable openness with the president. He had thought the man was sincere. In spite of all his recent disillusionments, he had wanted to believe in MacFarlane.

Now . . . who *could* he believe in!

Had MacFarlane given him an even more subtle whitewash job than Foster? He'd been able to see through Foster's smooth words. But the president had been even more clever . . . more devious. He had *really* come across as believable!

MacFarlane had said it himself—there were dirty tricks on both sides of the fence. Had that statement been his way of cushioning Jeremy for the blow when the truth eventually came out?

He hardly seemed the type, but the president must be a terrific actor. He condemned Foster for his duplicity, coming across as so honest, all the time keeping from the nation, from his own daughter, something so blatantly controvertible.

Part of Jeremy was still an idealist. His mind didn't immediately turn into the low channels of a man like Bateman to think of affairs, homosexuality, or turning traitor. The crux of MacFarlane's deception had nothing to do with such nefarious possibilities, thought Jeremy. It had to do with his lack of openness in the very midst of a discussion about integrity and honesty. Was the man any more to be trusted than Foster?

Sure, the president owed *him* no special loyalty. Why would he be expected to tell an avowed Foster man the truth. But to deliberately deceive the daughter who trusted him, and to run on a platform of honesty and integrity, when all the time he was involved in secretive dealings even his staff apparently had no knowledge of. Perhaps worse scenarios than Jeremy had even dared imagine of Foster . . . the whole prospect was disillusioning to say the least.

Jeremy walked for more than an hour, paying no attention to the direction of his steps. When he finally became aware of his surroundings, the White House stood immediately before him. Subconsciously he had been heading in this direction all the while.

The brilliant white building gleamed in the morning sunlight, its lawns spreading out spaciously in all directions like green velvet. Was occupying this piece of real estate really worth so much? A news story a couple of months ago had reported on severe plumbing problems throughout the entire structure. And last winter the roof over one of the upstairs bedrooms had leaked. This prime piece of architecture had been subject to rot and fire and controversy throughout its years. An imperfect house with imperfect occupants.

Such could be said for every house in the country—why not this one? He remembered how he had determined not to be awed by the peculiar White House mystique as he had walked through its corridors yesterday. Obviously he had not succeeded. Like it or not, his expectations were higher than the reality.

When he left Foster headquarters earlier that morning, it had been with the feeling that he had no place to go. Yet, here he stood.

Could it be that although the road behind him was closed, the one ahead might still be open? Did MacFarlane deserve another chance? At least the benefit of an explanation? He had given Foster the opportunity to respond to his questions and explain himself. Did MacFarlane deserve less?

With more resolve and determination than he had felt in a long time, Jeremy marched up to the gate on East Executive Avenue.

"I would like to see the president," he announced boldly to the guard on duty. "My name is Jeremy Manning."

"What time is your appointment, Mr Manning?"

"I don't have an appointment."

"I'm sorry. No one is admitted without an appointment."

"It's urgent."

"You'll have to call the switchboard. They'll put you through proper channels."

Jeremy took a step forward. The guard tensed, his hands stiffening in readiness. Jeremy froze, realizing what his action might signify.

"Look," he said impatiently, "if you'll radio the information inside that I am here, I am sure the president will see me."

The guard ducked his head inside a small enclosure and mumbled something into his phone. After a few minutes, a burly man in a gray suit came striding toward him.

"Mr. Schmidt," said the guard, "do you know this man?"

"Good morning, Mr. Manning," said the Secret Service agent. "I understand you want to see the president."

"That's right. It's important."

"Everyone who comes to this gate thinks their business is urgent."

"All I'm asking is that you make one call to ask if he'll see me."

"Can you imagine what would happen if we did that for everyone who came up to this gate?"

At that moment Jeremy spotted Brett Renfro inside the grounds. He was about thirty yards away, walking toward his car. His encounters with Karen's bodyguard had not always been pleasant, but at least the guy had some idea of where he stood with Karen. And Renfro had helped him get beyond Foster's spies and into the White House yesterday, hopefully without their knowledge. It was worth a try.

"Renfro!" he shouted.

Renfro glanced up, closed his car door, and approached the gate.

"Is Miss MacFarlane here?" Jeremy called out. "I must see her."

Something akin to a smile flickered briefly across Renfro's stoic face as he answered, "It seems you always *have* to see her."

"Sorry to get you involved, Brett," said the one called Schmidt. "Mr. Manning was just leaving."

"Come on, Renfro," urged Jeremy, "tell these guys to let me in."

"The president's daughter does happen to be here, Manning. It's okay, Phil, I'll vouch for him. Let me just call inside and locate her." He ducked inside the guardhouse, reappeared a moment later, and the gates swung open. Suddenly Jeremy was inside.

Renfro led him into the East Wing of the house, upstairs, and to the waiting room of the family quarters. There he left him.

When Karen appeared, Jeremy's first reaction was, "I've got to see your father."

"Is something wrong?"

"I hope not."

Puzzled, but obviously concerned about his distraught appearance, Karen picked up a phone and called her father. After a brief conversation she hung up and turned to Jeremy.

"He says we're to come to his office immediately," she said.

# THIRTY-SIX

As they approached the Oval Office, the door opened and out walked the president's chief of staff and his press secretary. The looks on their faces revealed that they were none too pleased at being bumped from the president's timetable by his daughter. Karen nodded as they passed, but neither man spoke.

MacFarlane himself met them at the door. Before turning back inside he told his secretary to reschedule his ten o'clock appointment for later in the day. Glancing at his watch for the first time since leaving his office, Jeremy noted it was eight minutes to ten.

"I'm sorry to foul up your schedule, sir," Jeremy offered, wondering if his rash decision had been ill-advised.

"My schedule is *always* messed up, Jeremy," the president replied in his easy, unassuming manner. "Karen said she thought this was important. That's good enough for me."

All at once Jeremy's former vexation swept back over him. He'd had enough of all the cool, phony fronts. He was sick of politicians and their finely honed aplomb. Even Karen's father now seemed to be dishing it out to him. Without another moment's forethought, with Karen still standing by his side, he suddenly blurted out the first words that came to him.

"I'd like to know what in blazes you're doing sneaking around in the middle of the night with some Russian guy! You talk about honesty and forthrightness. Then why aren't you keeping *your* activities aboveboard?"

The words hung in the air for a long, tense moment. Karen looked back and forth between Jeremy and her father, seeing anger in one face, shock in the other, and not knowing what to think. Numbly she waited for her father to respond. At last he turned and walked slowly across the room until he stood facing his desk. Then, as if he could go no further, he rested his hands heavily on the polished surface, sagging almost as if for support.

"So they do know," he finally said, every word belabored, as if he could hardly breathe.

Karen finally forced herself into motion and hurried to his side. "Daddy, what is it?" she said in alarm.

He did not answer her.

Jeremy had never suspected such a reaction, and a sense of guilt now forced itself upon him. Still he waited, not saying anything, just watching Karen and her father.

At length the president spoke, although he did not turn, change his position, or even look toward either Karen or Jeremy.

"You have every right to feel as you do, Jeremy," he said. "This must seem like the final affront. You wanted to trust me . . . you *did* trust me by coming and leveling with me. Only to have me let you down, to find out that I was not leveling with you—or with anyone. Is that how you feel?"

"Yes, sir, I suppose it is," replied Jeremy sincerely.

MacFarlane turned and looked directly into Jeremy's eyes. "I would like you to know that I had good reason—at least so it seems sometimes. At other times . . . I'm not so sure. I have so little time, and so much pressing in. Karen," he said, looking down at his daughter next to him, "I pray that if no one else understands, at least you will believe I am doing only what I feel I must." There was entreaty in his tone.

"I don't understand, Daddy," said Karen in a soft, small voice. "What can be troubling you so?"

He reached out a hand and gently stroked her cheek. With the touch and the clear emotion in his face as he attempted a smile for her, Karen broke into tears. In that instant there was only a father and daughter, seemingly alone in the room where some of the world's most far-reaching decisions had been made. Everything else for the moment had disappeared—the stately Oval Office, the presidency, the personal struggles, the crises throughout the world, even Jeremy's presence. Only a girl and her father. There were no tears in MacFarlane's eyes, however, although he looked sad enough to weep.

Once more he turned away from the two, walked slowly toward the window, and stood staring silently out toward the south lawn for several minutes. When he faced them again, his expression was one of despair mingled with something akin to relief.

"I've told no one about this," he said in a soft, deliberate voice. "Perhaps I should have. I don't know. For the last four months I haven't known what to do. I was afraid of being misunderstood. Though more likely I would have been declared a raving lunatic. But now I see it's finally time I shared the burden with someone—and, Karen, you are the most likely candidate. You're the only person besides your mother who's always stood by me and understood me."

He paused, then focused his attention on Jeremy. "You wonder what I've been doing in the dead of night? Maybe you do deserve an answer. You risked a great deal for my sake yesterday. Well . . . now I'm going to take a risk for you. I'm going to trust you, Jeremy. Though I hardly know you, you strike me as the sort of young man who should be given my trust. So to answer your question—yes, I have been involved with a Russian friend of mine who's been teaching me Russian. My whole life is being turned upside-down, and by now it seems as though the lessons themselves are only a small part of it. But they are still an intrinsic part, because I've been preparing myself for a meeting with Soviet Premier Vladimir Kudinsky."

"But if that's the case, why the cloak-and-dagger routine, sir? I would think a meeting such as that to be perfectly acceptable. And why learn Russian when you have translators?"

"Because it's imperative I talk with Kudinsky one-on-one, face-to-face. Alone. No translators. No bodyguards. Nobody. Just the two of us in a secure place."

"But it's unheard of."

"True. And I have no way of knowing whether Kudinsky will even agree to do it. But it's something I have to try."

"You're just giving Foster more fuel to knock you out of this place," protested Jeremy.

"You may be right. But yesterday I told you to follow your conscience. And I must follow mine. I must do what I am compelled to do, even if there are a million sensible reasons against it."

"But, Daddy, why is it so important that you do this *right now*?" asked Karen. "There's the election, the Iranian crisis. For you to embark on this almost secret mission—what will people think?"

"But don't you see," said the president, a pleading quality in his voice, "it's precisely because of all those things that it must be *now*. What I'm proposing is the most important summit the world has ever known. Either Kudinsky and I come to a peace agreement, or the world may be lost."

The somber words fell from his lips in matter-of-fact fashion. He hardly gave them a chance to sink in before reinforcing them further.

"Do you understand? We are very close to war right now. There are forces in these two superpower countries that utterly misunderstand each other and are almost beyond our control already. If Foster is elected . . . if Bolotnikov comes to power in Russia, it's all over. World War Three is back on the option table. Don't you see—we have to take *immediate* steps to keep this peace or the world will explode!"

Jeremy was still puzzled. Politicians had been saying such things ever since the McCarthy era. But Bush and Gorbachev had made peace almost the status quo, and a year ago talk of war was passe. Was the president overreacting?

"What makes it so imperative to discuss these matters in private and in Russian?" Jeremy asked.

"What I have to tell Kudinsky is so fantastic . . . so positively—I don't even know what to say—I don't believe it myself—I can't even bring myself to tell a soul." He stopped. "It's not the sort of thing you go around telling people. At least not if you're president of the United States. You can't issue press reports from the White House about this kind of stuff. It would be political suicide! I have to tell him in private. I can't let the press get hold of it. That's why I've got to be able to speak to him in Russian, so I can tell him—just him!"

"But what does this have to do with a new peace initiative?" insisted Jeremy. "What's so fantastic and bizarre about that? You might lose the election, but no one's going to call you mad for arguing for peace."

"Oh, if it were only that simple! But it's bigger than that. Much bigger! It's not just peace on the Iranian border. It's the whole world, it's the future we leave our children . . . our grandchildren. That's why he *has* to believe me! There is no other way!"

"Daddy," said Karen, "he must want peace too. I don't understand. What is it you must tell him?"

MacFarlane sighed deeply two or three times, obviously distraught. He began to pace about the room, clearly debating about whether to proceed. No longer was he the unflappable image of the president of the United States, but just a weak mortal, desperately in need of unburdening his soul.

"It's a very long story," he finally answered in a strangely calm, almost other-worldly voice. "You had both better sit down."

Karen and Jeremy sank into the leather couch across the room from the huge presidential desk, looking at one another in some trepidation. In Karen's eyes Jeremy saw something he had never seen there before—fear. He couldn't tell if she feared for herself, for her father, or merely for the unknown.

MacFarlane himself did not sit. He continued to pace—from the tall, many-paned windows behind his desk to the bookcases on the other wall to the fireplace—as if gathering his thoughts before he spoke again.

Jeremy could sense that, though the president looked out the window, it was not the bright, cheerful sun reflected off the lawn that he saw. Nor was it the handsome jackets of the books, nor their titles, that caught his eye as he passed the built-in bookcases. His eyes saw something in the distance . . . at *great* distance. Jeremy didn't know if the man's eyes were focused on anything in this world at all. He seemed to have transcended time and space altogether and was now, even though he was still speaking to them, on some completely different plane of existence.

"It happened nearly four months ago," he began wearily, as if the mere remembering was draining what little strength he had left. "Winter was winding down. We'd just had a light snow, and there was a luminescence over the grounds outside. It was the end of a trying day. The new appropriations bill had only marginally passed the Senate and it seemed impossible for it to pass the House.

"As if that wasn't enough, word had just reached us of the terrorist bombings at Heathrow in London. Foster had delivered a stinging speech in New Hampshire to kick off his campaign, blasting me for being out of touch with the future.

"I so desperately wanted to sleep, but the moment I lay down, I knew sleep would be impossible. Something was in the air. I don't know how else to describe it.

"I felt something inside, some . . . some—*force*—some power, as if I should be hearing something and didn't know how to tune it in. I was keenly aware of *something*—out there—keeping me from sleep.

"Shortly after midnight I got up, threw on my bathrobe, and with a vague idea of fixing some warm milk with a dash of vanilla, headed toward the kitchen. But then I found myself, without even thinking about it, walking toward the Oval Office. At the time I thought I was just wandering, but now I realize something was drawing me. I knew I had to be alone, and I felt compelled to do as I did, as crazy as that must sound."

He chuckled dryly at the thought. "Of all nights to *want* to forget this . . . this responsibility . . .. this job," he went on. "It was not meant to be that night! I was to be made more painfully aware of my position than ever before. Yet it was something which had to come when I was alone. Just myself and . . . well, I'll let you pass judgment on that. Let's simply say that in the world we are normally accustomed to, I was alone."

He paused, then pointed to the window behind him and said, "I walked to this very window. The moon was full, and it brought out all the silent beauty of the thin layer of snow outside. It had been stormy and blustery for two days. Then suddenly a calm came in the midst of it, with the light snowfall. Gentle . . . peaceful . . . quiet. It reminded me of being a boy again . . . of Christmas. I suppose snow always does that. I found myself wondering how a scene could have the audacity to be so tranquil in the midst of a world full of heartache and tumult and confusion.

"I wondered when the last time was that I had known such peace. I looked up at the moon. Was that the only constant in our world these days, I wondered. The Eisenhower years . . . the Second World War . . . even Kennedy's missile crisis and Bush's Iraq crisis all seemed tame by comparison—linear . . . one-dimensional . . . right and wrong easy to discern. Now everything had a hundred contingencies. Sure, maybe we were at peace with Russia, but was the world at large really any further from war? Each side still possessed enough nuclear warheads to destroy the earth and there were two dozen countries with nuclear capability . . . besides terrorists all over the world. Maybe no time is more difficult than any other, but that's what I was thinking.

"Still I gazed at the moon. And as I did, I fell into what under any other circumstances I would call a trance. But on that night it was like being pulled into reality, not into a dream at all. The moon began to grow larger and was no longer luminous . . . the sky darkened, and everything faded away. The moon was all I could see, yet it wasn't glowing like a full moon, but reflecting colors and clouds and oceans and lands.

"Suddenly I realized I was no longer gazing at the moon, but at the earth, just like those photographs taken of the earth from the moon. I could see the continents—Europe, Africa, the Americas, Asia. Then it began to turn color. Not a change in light, but a discoloration. A reddish hue began to spread down from the North Pole like dripping paint. But it wasn't paint at all . . . it was blood!

"I stood frozen, at that very window, and watched as blood covered the entire planet. I wasn't dreaming, I tell you. I was fully conscious, aware that I was in the Oval Office, awake, with my senses working, standing there gazing out where the moon should have been. This was no film in a planetarium . . . no Hollywood stunt. I was actually watching blood pour out over the whole earth. I could *feel* the agony of the process—I could feel it, but was helpless to change it . . . to stop the flow.

"Was I looking into the future? Was I seeing the terrible result of some future war? These thoughts poured over me, but I had no chance to reflect on them. Was I looking *backward* in time, witnessing the earth covered in another's blood? But even as it came, I realized I didn't know what the question meant and had no way to answer it. It seemed an absurd question. Yet later—as I pondered these events—I could see its meaning.

"Then the terrifying thing happened. The moon—or earth now, changed again. The blood receded back toward the North Pole, but only temporarily, for the sphere slowly changed its form again. I no longer gazed on the moon *or* the earth. It began to take on human characteristics in place of the oceans and continents. Eyes began to glow out of the sphere, then a nose and mouth, not as a clearly distinctive face but fading in and out, always changing.

"Then, suddenly, I recognized my own features! It was *my* face . . . and the blood was slowly flowing down again, from the top of my head, down over my ears, onto my cheeks. My eyes held such awful sorrow and pain, and from them flowed gigantic tears, and I knew I wept because of what had come upon the earth and because I had done nothing to change it. Soon the tears were gone too . . . awash in a sea of red which now covered all the face.

"When I could make out the features once more, the face was no longer mine . . . others mingled back and forth—more rapidly now. I saw Senator Foster . . . I saw some of my own cabinet and staff . . . I saw other leaders—the British prime minister for one . . . a terrorist gunman . . . then Premier Kudinsky and many other world leaders—all of whom, like me, had done nothing to stop the blood . . . Bolotnikov was there, appearing cruel and heartless, and the blood flowed swiftly across the lines of his face.

"Again a change came. Without *seeing*, I was being carried back in time, and when I again beheld the features of a face emerging out of the swirling chaos of cloud and light, it was filled with an altogether wonderful expression of joy and delight. I felt for a fleeting moment as if I were looking upon God's face as the universe was being created eons ago.

"But it continued to change, and a sadness passed over the face and tears fell from the eyes . . . and then the blood came again, though not from the top this time, but from out of the face, as if the very cheeks and neck and head and ears had been mortally wounded and blood were being shed from within. And in the eyes was such a look of anguish and suffering . . . not from the pain of the wounds, but the sorrow of forsaken love. And I knew that this blood was blood that had already flowed. It was not, like before, a vision of blood that had not yet been spilled.

"And as I watched, my heart filled with a great sorrow—not for what I had *not* done, but in remorse for what I *had* done . . . for what I was. And rising up within me was an inexpressible longing for the blood to wash over me and cleanse me. For intuitively I knew that this was a healing blood, not the blood of retribution.

"Gradually the image of the face disappeared and again the sphere was filled with rapidly changing images . . . face after face . . . children . . . old men and women . . . black, white, brown . . . faces from ancient civilizations . . . faces of unborn infants . . . an endless sea of faces—with the blood from the joyful, sorrowful face flowing over them, cleansing them all. And I knew my face, though I did not see it again, was among them. And something inside me knew there had been a change.

"Slowly the faces and the blood faded and once again I was gazing at the moon, still transfixed, unable to turn to the right or the left, compelled to remain where I was.

"The moon was the moon again, yet still huge . . . out of proportion to reality and growing brighter and brighter. Its intensity was like the sun, yet I could keep my eyes on it and was not blinded.

"This blinding light was everywhere. Then suddenly I realized that the moon had become dark too, and this new brightness was not from the moon at all, but was reflected light coming off the moon but not coming from the moon. The sky was still black, and now the moon was dull . . . and a new light had arisen!

"I had not noticed it at first, because its source was behind me. But now I grew conscious that this new brightness, which I had mistakenly thought was from the moon, came from this new light behind me. Rays shot out through the window, across the night sky . . . rays of brightness illuminating the moon, the sky . . . everything . . . blinding light shooting from behind me . . . and all I could see of it was the reflected brilliance of the moon.

"I knew I should turn to face this new light, but I could not. I chided myself for being such a coward, but still I stood there staring out the window for what seemed an age . . . riveted to the floor, unable to move a muscle . . . terrified, yet awestruck . . . gazing out now upon nothing but blackness . . . for all the light—all the life—was behind me. Yet I could not turn to face it, for I was certain something terrible awaited me—as horrifying perhaps as death itself.

"Finally I knew I *had* to turn! I could not make myself turn, but I knew I had to.

"And now there are no words to describe what I saw. I can only attempt to make you understand . . .

"I would never describe what I saw as terrible . . . though at the moment it was terrifying enough. Terrifyingly glorious, perhaps! What I saw was light—pure light . . . *real* light, as if it were the source of all light. Not brighter than the sun, but more full of *life* than the sun. It filled my office and spread out in all directions, but its core stood in the very center of the room . . . right there." He pointed with his hand.

"I could not gaze at it steadily. The brightness was too great. But I could make out that it possessed definite shape—that is, the light emitted from a human form. But as far as I could tell, though the outline of a man was before me, there were no features other than the pure, radiant light. There *was* a form, but the form was only light. Not less real because of that, but more real! And for all the terror of the moment, a gentle warmth emanated from it, and I instinctively wanted to be near it—but I was far too afraid to move an inch closer.

"Then came the Voice, clear and crisp and commanding, from the center of the light.

"It was not a booming voice . . . not loud, rather gentle, almost soft, with even—if I can say it, because it seems so contradictory—a touch of the sorrowful in it. Yet with tones of joy and wonder and gladness. Contradictory because the Voice was full of such power and authority as I have never heard. Beside that Voice the president of the United States was nothing more than a speck . . . a fly on the wall. This was a Voice of energy . . . of authority . . . of creation . . . a Voice of one to be heeded . . . to be obeyed. But its power was not in its loudness . . . but in the quality of the Voice itself . . . a sound which must be heard, which no words can describe.

"Yet even as I recount the moment, I cannot say for certain whether I heard the Voice with my ears or whether I 'heard' it with my heart, my spirit, my mind. I don't know . . . yet whether it was audible or not hardly matters. I did hear, and that is enough.

"I remember thinking—*This is it . . . I'm surely going crazy now*! Yet of everything that had happened thus far—and I want to stress again that this was no dream; I was as wide awake and the vision of the moon and the earth and faces had been as utterly real as you are real standing here with me now—of all of it—the Voice was the most real . . . the most true . . . the most authentic part of the whole experience. I wanted to run toward it . . . to let the light engulf me . . . to let the Voice penetrate into my very being . . . as if the Voice itself, and the energy of the light coming from a Man I could not see, could somehow save me from the pain and sorrow of who I was, and might save the world from the horror of being engulfed in the blood of its own inhabitants.

"It said, 'The peace in the world is a false peace, founded not in love but in greed. Wars and rumors of wars must come at the hand of man, for the end of time is come. The blood you see shall be upon the heads of those who do not heed my voice, spoken through my chosen witnesses.'

"I was too numb to reply. What could I say? Mere human words seemed impertinent. How could a fly, a speck, a nothingness, as was I, address the Light, the Voice, the Source of power and love and authority—perhaps even the source of my very life itself?

"Yet against all reason, I found myself speaking. I asked, 'Is this thing set irrevocably in motion? Is there no hope for the world?'

" 'I will show you what must take place, my son,' the Voice replied. 'Before many days, the hand will be withdrawn which has held back the evil that would consume the nations. In that day, my earth will be ruled by violent men who do not look upon war with horror. But my time is not yet come. I love the world and spilled my blood for it. Behold, I am coming soon. There will yet be a few days of peace in which you must work. There is much to proclaim before that day which no man knows.'

"Again I asked, 'Is there then no hope?'

" 'There is always hope. The Peacemaker is coming. But the

peace I bring to you is not the world's peace, for I did not come to bring peace but a sword. Many will call out, "Peace here, peace there." But they are not my messengers. The peace they proclaim is no peace. Be not deceived by false peace.' All this the Voice replied. Then it uttered the words which have been so etched in my brain since—the last thing I expected to hear: 'There is always hope. Fear not, faint not. You shall be the instrument of hope, to proclaim my liberty to the captives, to proclaim that peace has come to the earth, yet not as the world gives, and to prepare my people for the sword that will fall upon the earth, dividing spirit from spirit, flesh from flesh, marrow from marrow, before the Peacemaker returns.'

"I felt like Moses in front of the burning bush. I wanted to argue and protest. 'But—but—but—' was all I could think to say. Excuses . . . questions . . . pleading for Him to pick someone else to do His bidding. *Who am I?* I thought. *I have no power to stop the destruction! God knows I have tried! The world is not listening to me. I am about to be ousted from power . . . even my own nation doesn't support me. I am unacquainted with things of faith . . . of hope. What could I proclaim? I know nothing about religion!*

"As if reading my thoughts, the Voice said, 'I will not leave you alone. I will send my servants to you to strengthen you. They too are my ambassadors of the truth. They will help you understand many things. All who speak with my anointing are my chosen servants, whose obedience is their strength. I will show you what I say. Listen to my voice. Obey what you hear. You are my chosen servant. You are my witness to the truth. The truth will be revealed to you, and thus you will be shown what to say and what to do.'

"I know I made no reply, but my fear, my uncertainty, my utter desolation must have been plainly apparent, for the Voice repeated: '*You shall not be alone in your task.* I have many servants who await my appearing. I will send them to you, to teach you, that you might proclaim my truths. And as the great nations of the world have always wrought ill over the lesser, so now shall the leaders of the power of the north and the power from over the sea be charged with the task of proclamation, healing, and preparation. Alienation has bred destruction. Now let the unity of my witnesses heal. Out of desolation will come hope. Out of desolation will come my presence. Be faithful, my son. The days of your testimony are numbered. Men will heed you. I am with you always.'

"That was all. Suddenly the light was gone. I was filled with a chill, as of warmth suddenly vanished. The Presence was no longer with me. Again I found myself looking out upon the tranquil south lawns bathed in the normal glow of the moon."

MacFarlane stopped and was silent for some time. A hush had descended upon the Oval Office. Neither Karen nor Jeremy dared break it, nor intrude upon the president's evident emotion as he relived the details of his experience.

"I might have left it at that," he went on at length, "chalking it up to nothing more than a bad dream, or at worse, momentary insanity—perhaps an hallucination . . . an over-vivid imagination.

"But this was nothing like that. I tell you, it was *real!* As real as the three of us together right now! In some ways perhaps even more so. I wanted nothing more than to forget the whole thing. I tried to force it from my mind . . . tried to tell myself I had imagined it all. People—and especially presidents!—just don't see things like that. If they do, they'd better keep it quiet! Can you imagine what the *Post* or the *Times* would do with a story like that? *Mad President Has Heavenly Vision!* Sounds more like *The National Enquirer*. That would *really* fix my standings in the polls!

"But how do you forget an experience like that? You don't!

"In the next week the vision came to me again two more times in dreams. Everything took place in the exact same sequence, though more shadowy, like looking at a scene through a slightly distorted mirror. But all the words were the same. That's how I can recall everything so vividly. It was imprinted upon me so that I *couldn't* forget.

"Still, I *tried!* I had primaries and Congress and Foster to face. The Lebanese, as always, were being troublesome. I had no time for a vision!

"The day of the last dream happened to be a Saturday night. The next morning I attended, as planned, the New York Avenue Presbyterian Church; it was some special occasion in the church's history in Washington, and I thought my presence would be appropriate. I suppose Dr. Johnson's sermon was routine. But it changed my life almost as profoundly as had the vision itself.

"He told about Joseph, who, in the book of Genesis, was the interpreter of the ancient Pharaoh's dreams. Those dreams, which foretold a terrible famine throughout Egypt and neighboring lands, had come to Pharaoh three times. Suddenly I broke into a cold sweat as the minister read the reason for this in Joseph's own words: '*And for that the dream was doubled unto Pharaoh twice; it is because the thing is established by God, and God will shortly bring it to pass.*'

"Those words cut through me like a jagged knife . . . '*because the thing is established by God, and God will shortly bring it to pass.*'

"In that moment, as I sat there, I knew there could be no ignoring the vision I'd had—vision . . . dream . . . call it what you will. Though I might fail, though I might become the laughingstock of Washington, though I might lose the election, I knew that I *had* to try to heed the Voice. I had to try to be an emissary of peace. I had to do my part to help prepare the world for what was ahead, whatever it might be, whatever the coming of His footstep meant. And I could see no other place to begin, according to His words, than with Kudinsky—than by attempting to find the unity He spoke of which would pave the way for the healing."

By now MacFarlane was emotionally spent. He collapsed in one of the overstuffed chairs adjacent to the couch where Karen and Jeremy had remained throughout the whole of his disclosure. He covered his face with his hands, inhaled a great breath, then let out a long sigh.

"God help me . . . that's what I've been working toward," he added in a voice, now so soft as to be barely audible.

The Oval Office was silent. He said no more.

Slowly Karen rose, approached her father, and knelt down beside him, laying a gentle hand on his shoulder. Her eyes, moist with emotion, glowed with something like pride.

Jeremy stared straight ahead.

When the three emerged from behind the closed doors thirty minutes later, none would ever be the same again.

# THIRTY-SEVEN

Jeremy Manning accelerated past the delivery truck, settled once more into his lane, then rolled his window down the rest of the way. The warm breeze felt good rushing all about him, through his hair, across his face.

The route he had chosen lay west into Virginia toward Charleston. There was no particular reason for that course. He could have taken any road out of Washington. He simply needed to get away—into the country, away from crowds and traffic. He wanted woods and fields and hills and trees and wind. Most of all he wanted to be alone.

The president's revelation had not disturbed him as much as it had sent him into a frenzy of thinking. It wasn't a matter of whether he believed MacFarlane or not. Despite the incredible story, there was no way Jeremy could doubt the man's complete sincerity. That something had happened to him was certain. That he was convinced beyond all doubt he had seen some kind of vision was equally beyond question.

But what had *actually* occurred . . . well, that was a question best left for a while. Besides, that was not really the focus of Jeremy's reflection at the moment. Such stories were not uncommon. He'd read his share of *Guideposts* accounts and was often moved by them. He wasn't the sort of person who automatically doubted at the first hint of the unusual. He could take what was told at face value, then wait to see what would come next.

The days, weeks, and months after a so-called revelation or "spiritual experience" were the proof of the pudding. Did life, did behavior, did habits, did attitudes change? Jeremy did not spend great energy trying to prove or disprove what he had been told. To do that, one needed facts. And in cases of this nature, facts were difficult to come by. Perceptions—they were the most important ingredients of all.

In the case of Jarvis MacFarlane, however, Jeremy could not sit idly by and take what he had heard as a matter of course. The startling revelation had consequences. Consequences for him!

He was now going to have to decide what to do!

Just when he had made the decision to break from the Foster camp, he was suddenly handed a story on a silver platter that would insure the president's defeat and Jeremy's likely advancement somewhere in the future Foster administration. He held in his hand information that could topple a government! Not that he had seriously entertained for even a moment the notion of disclosing to the senator what he had just heard. But the very thought of it showed how greatly he was caught in the middle of explosive developments at the very summit of power.

On the other hand, if he now cast his lot with the president, he would probably be jumping aboard a sinking ship, dooming his future political career in one wild leap.

And what of the matter of conscience? What about his duty as a journalist to the public?

Much to consider . . . not the least of which at the moment was the dark green sedan behind him.

Jeremy glanced again in his rearview mirror.

Yes, it was still there. The car had been dogging him for half an hour, almost out of sight—exactly like a good tail would be. A couple stops, a few turns, and it was still there. He'd seen the same car several times recently.

Jeremy rounded a bend, and the car behind fell temporarily out of sight. On impulse he slammed on his brakes and pulled off the road. A minute later the sedan whizzed by, slowing as Jeremy's Mustang came into view, but continuing on. Jeremy watched as the car passed. Two men, and one of them was Foster's all right! The other he didn't recognize.

He pulled back onto the road—cautiously, however; the brake pedal had gone nearly to the floor with that last stop. He got up to speed, then tested it again. Yes, the pedal went dangerously low under the pressure of his foot. He must need fluid; he'd check it at the next station.

Half a mile farther on, Jeremy flew by the green sedan pulled into a turnout, the occupants pretending to have engine trouble. When he glanced back about five minutes later, however, they were behind him again.

They'd come into a hilly region where the two-lane road wound back and forth. Jeremy had seen a sign advertising a service station and cafe about five miles ahead. He'd stop there. In the meantime, he'd round these curves carefully and keep it under forty. He'd have the fluid level checked while he picked up a bite to eat. That would also give him a chance to see what those two bozos in the green sedan were up to.

Suddenly the sedan speeded up and began bearing down on him.

What were those idiots up to! They were right on him now, but made no move to pass.

Wham! They rammed into his bumper, jolting Jeremy against his seat belt.

Jeremy accelerated, pulling slightly away. Again they came on, hitting him again . . . harder this time!

Those maniacs! Now they were on his bumper, pushing! He could feel the sedan accelerating, shoving him forward at greater speed. These curves were too tight to take at such a speed! Still the sedan pressed him faster and faster.

Frantically Jeremy pounded his brake pedal.

His foot sank flat to the floor! Pumping the pedal up and down brought no resistance.

Jeremy double-clutched down into second gear. The engine whined as he let out the clutch. Still the car behind continued to slam against his bumper. To take it down to first would rip his transmission apart.

A sharp bend in the road was coming up fast! He could never negotiate it at this speed!

Without time to think through his actions, Jeremy twisted the steering wheel to the right. Temporarily he was free from the sedan. He could feel the loose gravel of the shoulder underneath his tires.

Jamming his left foot onto the emergency brake lever, he cranked the wheel all the way to the left in one swift motion.

The silver Mustang spun around out of control, skidded back onto the blacktop, and screeched to a stop just a few yards short of the embankment that fell away on the other side of the road.

Sitting at a cross-angle to opposing traffic, which fortunately was light, he heard the squeal of the sedan's brakes as Foster's stooges slowed for the sharp curve, then sped off down the hill beyond.

Heart pounding, Jeremy started up his stalled engine.

"That was close!" he said aloud. "I must be in this deeper than I imagined. Apparently Foster's playing for keeps!"

# PART III

# THE PREMIER

*The godly have been swept from the land. . . .*
*All men lie in wait to shed blood . . . the*
*powerful dictate what they desire—they all*
*conspire together. . . . The day of your*
*watchmen has come, the day God visits you*
*. . . a man's enemies are the members of his*
*own household. But as for me, I watch in*
*hope for the* LORD, *I wait for God my Savior.*

MICAH 7:2–7

*Commit to the* LORD *whatever you do, and*
*your plans will succeed. The* LORD *works out*
*everything for his own ends. . . . When a*
*man's ways are pleasing to the* LORD,
*he makes even his enemies live at peace*
*with him.*

PROVERBS 16:3–4, 7

# THIRTY-EIGHT

A gray overcast sky hung over Red Square. General Secretary and Acting Soviet President Vladimir Kudinsky stared glumly out the window of his office. The great cobbled square before him was a stirring sight, able to move the emotions of even the most hardened Russian. The gloom lifted from his expression for a moment as he considered the irony of what the West had done in turning a simple reference to beauty into what they regarded as an evil symbol of Communism. For the Russian word for "red" was synonymous with *beauty*, and such it would always be for those who loved their expansive Motherland.

Yes, the colorfully domed towers of the Church of St. Basil were stunning, giving the Square a unique aspect. But with all its splendor, this was not the Russia Kudinsky loved most. Though he had been away from his home in the Ukraine for thirty years, except for brief visits, his tenderest emotions would always reside there. The farm near Kharkov where his parents had been workers, where he had played as a child in the fields of tall, golden wheat—how could streets of ancient cobbles compare with that?

*But you are a boy no longer,* he mused silently, still gazing out the window. *Your reflections prove it . . . for they could come from none but an old man.*

Kudinsky chuckled. If not gladly, at least with some humor. Far more than his reflections evidenced his age, of course, beginning with his thinning gray hair. True, it had been graying when he turned forty, but there had been much less of it clinging to his hairbrush back then. At least at sixty-nine he still managed to retain a somewhat trim physique. But he could hardly claim credit for that, since it was all due to a high metabolism that allowed him to eat anything without gaining a kilogram.

The thought of food made him glance at his watch.

Pavel and the others would soon be arriving. Best slip quickly into the proper party attitude, he thought dryly. Not that he didn't love the party and all it stood for; he had given it the complete loyalties of his long life and career. But there still came times when he would have preferred listening to his Barbra Streisand albums or relaxing for a few hours with an absolutely decadent Louis L'Amour novel. His most recent edition had arrived by his special courier only yesterday. If the others only suspected what those periodic parcels contained, marked *For the Eyes of the Secretary Only—Top Secret.* Ah, well, he had to keep some things to himself—one of the few privileges of his position!

In the midst of his thoughts, he heard a light tap on the door. The day had begun.

"Come in," he said, expelling a resigned sigh.

The door opened and in walked Pavel Soroka, secretary of agriculture, a stout, round-faced man in his early seventies. He waddled rather than walked into the room, giving the appearance of a pleasant nature, though he did not greet Kudinsky with a smile and spoke in a rather formal manner.

"Good morning, Mr. Secretary," said Soroka, standing stiffly before his leader.

"Ah, Pavel," Kudinsky replied, infusing more meaning into his tone than the words themselves implied. "It is a gloomy morning. It will rain before the day is out, and yet the month is June. Will the warmth of summer never come?"

"The rain will be good for our crops. God knows we need it after this dry spring."

"Pavel! What talk is this for a good atheist?" Kudinsky spoke more out of humor than rebuke, but Soroka coughed and sputtered before replying.

"Forgive me, Mr. Secretary. It is difficult to forget the ways of my parents. I meant nothing by it."

"Come now, Pavel, you have no need to apologize to me. We understand one another, do we not?" Kudinsky motioned his comrade to a chair, while sinking into his own. "We are of the same stock. We knew each other before we became surrounded by all the trappings of this grand Kremlin and its ways."

"Friendship aside, Vladimir," answered Soroka, relaxing a bit at last, "one can never be too careful."

Kudinsky smiled. "I am not yet in the pay of the KGB, my friend."

Soroka scowled reprovingly. "I was not worrying so much for myself as I was thinking of you, Vladimir. You speak too freely, even for the general secretary. You have always had that streak in you. But I fear with your present position you take your own immunity for granted. And as we know there is no immunity in the Soviet Union—for anyone. Do not become blinded by your position. You are only acting president thus far. Last year's incident should have taught you something."

"It taught me much, Pavel," replied Kudinsky, his features settling back into their former gloom. "When they elected Bolotnikov chairman of the Presidium instead of me when Szewinska died, it was a bitter blow. If I held any delusions of power, that surely crushed them. But I still will not grovel at any man's feet. I'll not bend against my principles, my desires for this country. I can't, Pavel. Especially now . . . I can't."

"Why not humor them a little?" argued Soroka. "That certainly is not groveling. It is simply good politics . . . good business as our capitalist friends in Washington would say. You have not lost your power base, but it is gradually slipping in Bolotnikov's direction. Some prudence on your part could halt the flow. For all his heated words, it is still you to whom many look for the voice of discretion and wisdom. Use that, Vladimir. You could have the opportunity in the meeting coming up soon. I came early so I might talk with you about that very thing."

"I know what you are going to say, Pavel. We've been over it before."

"The entire Politburo questions your reticence toward our Iranian commitment. When we planned the action and then moved forward months ago, you gave your assent—"

"My grudging assent," Kudinsky corrected.

"Granted," conceded Soroka. "But you did agree. And now you're pulling back. Bolotnikov will use this to crush you if he can."

"I must obey my conscience. And I still have *some* influence, Pavel. You yourself were saying so only a moment ago."

"And our comrade Leonid Bolotnikov has learned a few tricks during his years as chairman of the KGB. You must be wary."

They were interrupted by a sharp, imperative rap on the door. Kudinsky knew well enough who this would be—Bolotnikov and two or three of his staunchest supporters come to browbeat the general secretary. Kudinsky hesitated a moment, glanced at his friend, as if to ask, "Are you ready for this?" and then indicated with a nod that Soroka should open the door.

Leonid Bolotnikov strode into the room, followed by Andre Bragina, minister of defense, and Vasili Moiseyev, the secretary for ideology. These men represented a great deal of power within the party, and the three together were a daunting sight, even for the general secretary who was supposedly their superior. He had expected Bolotnikov and Bragina, two of the Soviet Union's staunchest militarists. But the appearance of Moiseyev was a blow. The heavyset Siberian, with his cherubic face and Asiatic eyes, had for years represented the moderate faction within the party. Kudinsky had expected him to be the last to fall under Bolotnikov's influence. He had, in fact, counted on Moiseyev's support to keep this Iranian thing from escalating beyond all reasonable bounds. But as Kudinsky greeted each one in turn and shook their hands, he noted that Moiseyev avoided his eyes.

What could have induced Moiseyev to enter Bolotnikov's camp? Could the former KGB chief have something on the ideology secretary—a position which must be kept free from stain? Was it possible Moiseyev hadn't given himself over completely but was being coerced into throwing his support against the general secretary? Kudinsky would not put anything past his rival, but it was a sad day for poor old Vasili when he was no longer his own man.

"You have heard of President MacFarlane's speech this morning?" asked Bolotnikov in a voice that obviously did not find it unusual to give orders.

"I have," answered Kudinsky in a civil but less-than-friendly tone. He had never liked Bolotnikov's strutting impertinence, and he refused to humor him as Pavel suggested.

"The Americans intend to humiliate us," continued Bolotnikov, undaunted. "I am here to insist that you do not act independent from the majority interests of the Politburo and to insure that you maintain the black-out. Has the American ambassador contacted you?"

"As to your first comment, Leonid," replied Kudinsky, unflinching and cool, "I accept your *suggestion* most gratefully. I have, in fact, called all the voting members of the Politburo other than the three of you, whom I was unable to reach." He paused and glanced at the two silent members of the trio. "As to your final question," he continued, "the American ambassador did attempt to telephone me, but I have continued to avoid contact."

Even as he spoke, Kudinsky wondered what his decision would be. He was still baffled by the American president's sudden and caustic response after nearly a month of silence from Washington following the release in the U.S. press about Iranian maneuvers.

In a hastily called press conference, MacFarlane had condemned the Soviet Union for its aggression in the Middle East, calling the mobilization of their troops a flagrant abuse of a nation's human rights, its autonomy, and its right to live with peace on its borders. Interesting worries indeed for an American president to voice in connection with Iran of all countries!

MacFarlane had then condemned the Soviet Union for failing to continue to uphold the peace initiated so boldly by their great former leader Mikhail Gorbachev, moralizing about all those everywhere who attempted to thwart the future of peace by seeking their own gain, adding curiously, "even those forces in our own government." He had challenged the Soviets—in more pointed and specific language than had been heard from the White House since the days of the Cold War and Kennedy and Reagan—to deny that they were acting as outright aggressors, revealing facts about the Soviet buildup they didn't realize U.S. intelligence even knew.

But then MacFarlane unexpectedly altered his tone, and Kudinsky had felt the shift when reading the bulletin, as distinctly as though he'd been listening to the American president's voice. Suddenly his words softened, sounding almost heartbroken over this turn of events, recalling to mind the goodwill that had existed for ten years. It was like two speeches by two different men, and Kudinsky could not help feeling that the second was directed at him.

Finally, in an odd mixture between the two, MacFarlane closed his remarks with what sounded like half invitation, half challenge to the Soviet premier himself, as a sign of good faith "in order to preserve the peace set in motion by our predecessors," to agree to an immediate summit on the matter of Iran and related issues. The American president had effectively sidestepped precisely what he meant by "related issues," responding to the questions of the press in only the vaguest of terms.

When questioned about why the United States had taken no affirmative action at this sudden new "hot spot" of tension, MacFarlane merely replied, "I am not anxious in the least to be the one responsible for a resumption of the Cold War. I am attempting to take action now by asking the Soviets to lift their diplomatic blackout and permit a meeting with Premier Kudinsky, in hopes of clearing all these matters up."

How did he plan to do so? He would say nothing further. His suggestions were for the Soviet premier alone.

What this sudden turn of events and the call for a meeting could signify, Kudinsky had no idea. It might well be some ploy with political overtones on the part of MacFarlane—it was, after all, an election year for the Americans and appeared to be turning into a very difficult one for the president. Still, he had never judged MacFarlane the deceptive or cunning sort.

Bolotnikov did not allow the momentary lapse in the discussion to last for long. "Do you mean to say you are considering his challenge?" then hurried on quickly, not awaiting a reply. "We cannot back down in Iran. It would bring humiliation to us all."

"Would it be so damaging to talk to them?"

"Talk about what! You know why we are there. I know why we are there. What is there to talk about? The Americans will only condemn us before the world. We have been bystanders on the world stage long enough, allowing democracy and capitalism to infect our nation and our own people with its cancerous greed. The Gorbachev interregnum is at last coming to an end! We must carry out our plans, begin to gain back what that fool gave away, and move on Iran and take it—*without* talk. The West will bluster and fume for a while, as they always used to. But the oil and the sea will be ours! Talk at this stage will only give them more time to prepare, and will bring humiliation."

"We might consider living with a little humiliation, if it will continue the peace."

"Peace, bah!" scoffed Bolotnikov. "You sound exactly like your mentor used to sound! It still fills me with anger and grief when I think how Mikhail swept the Politburo along in the train of his new ideals, as he called them. He set the Revolution back forty years!"

"Our economy is on sounder footing than it's been since 1917," suggested the premier. "Our people have food to eat."

"World events do not turn on food but on power!" stormed Bolotnikov. "We have food, but we are no longer feared. To the world we have become weak and ineffectual. The Revolution has come too far. I will not continue to stand by and watch the destruction of what our forbears established! We have kept our silence long enough. Power is the only way to peace! History proves it. When our own borders are secure with buffer nations surrounding us who pose no threat, when we are completely self-sufficient economically, when we have access to all the major waterways of the world, and when our own military is so vastly dominant over that of the United States that they would never dare any kind of force against us, *then* and only then, comrade, will there be true peace! And it will be a peace on *our* terms. Lenin and Stalin rejoice, as do I, that Gorbachev's weak-kneed interlude is over at last!"

"Leonid is right," said Bragina as if on cue. "To talk to the Americans now would be admitting we had something to discuss, the same as admitting we were guilty of wrong."

"Is that such a dreadful thing?" countered Kudinsky. "Do *we* of the high and mighty Kremlin, do we who sway world events from these halls and rooms hidden from view of the people—do *we* never make mistakes? Is it not possible that my esteemed mentor, as you call him, was not the fool you militarists thought him, but in reality a wise world diplomat with a vision for a much stronger, twenty-first century Soviet Union than your outdated policies could ever make possible?" He stopped, then turned to Moiseyev. "Do you agree with our esteemed colleague, Vasili?" he asked. "Do you too feel we must go back to tensions and hostilities and threats?"

Moiseyev looked wounded, though he refused to meet the eyes of his old friend. "The party was in favor of the action in Iran at its inception," he replied in a miserable tone that managed nonetheless to be noncommittal.

Kudinsky could not restrain a small wry smile. Moiseyev was assuredly in an unenviable place. He would push no further.

"Wise world diplomat, indeed!" scoffed Bolotnikov. "The future of the Soviet Union rests with me, not with the dreams of a fool!" He paused, looking Kudinsky directly in the eye. "So you intend doing this," he said quietly, his voice trembling with mingled warning and disdain for his counterpart.

Until the three men had entered his office, the premier had not known what he should do. The American president's announcement had taken him as much by surprise as it had the rest of the Kremlin, and apparently the U.S. press as well. Certainly calls for meetings were not abnormal. But he and the American president had not even met formally yet, let alone begun to discuss a summit. And something about MacFarlane's words had been different—commanding, urgent, inescapable. And after what had happened . . .

But he could not think of that now! That complicated everything so much further. Yet it did make seeing MacFarlane all the more imperative.

"So you intend doing this," Bolotnikov had challenged, and in that moment Kudinsky made his decision. Perhaps he was stubborn. Maybe it was impulsive. But it also made some sense. He would call the U.S. ambassador later today. It was time something was done; he had waffled too long.

"You will regret this decision," Bolotnikov continued ominously, witnessing the look of resolve in Kudinsky's eyes. "But if you must do this thing, let it be on *our* terms. You must choose the time and place of the meeting—"

"I have already chosen the place," put in Kudinsky almost smugly.

"As I suspected! You have taken leave of your senses even before my warnings."

"No, comrade. It is your insistence that has shown me that perhaps MacFarlane deserves a hearing. How does that suit your war-thirsty sensibilities, knowing that *you* are responsible for my decision?"

"Bah! You are a fool, Vladimir! You will surely regret this day!"

"Be that as it may, I *will* meet with the American president, and we will meet in Moscow. Here we will have the advantage, which should please even you. And if MacFarlane should be up to something, we want him at every disadvantage it is possible to achieve."

"If MacFarlane is up to something—as he certainly must be—then why place ourselves at his mercy in the first place?"

"The rules have changed," said Kudinsky, "whether you like it or not. The world has come to expect openness and fairness from us—not altogether a bad thing, perhaps. The Americans have an apt phrase for our position. They call it a catch–22 situation."

"You and your idiotic American phrases!" shouted Bolotnikov. "Not only do we have to play the part of a whipped puppy, withdrawing our people and our rule from those nations we vanquished, turning their governments over to democracy without so much as a whimper, now we must also put up with capitalism sprouting up in our own streets! McDonalds and Sears and Ford automobiles, all within a mile from where we stand! If Stalin or Brezhnev knew how fond you are of Westernisms and hamburgers, they would rise out of their tombs and throw you from power!"

"Our people are content."

"The people do not know what is best!"

"It is for our people that I will meet the American president and try to keep us from the war you seem eager for!"

"It is your fault we are in this position—call it by whatever idiotic term you will!—in the first place. Our advantage in Iran was swiftness and secrecy. Your procrastination has lost that for us, and more than likely Iran also. Now we must grovel at the Americans' feet. Fine! Meet whoever and wherever you like! But I wash my hands of you. Be assured, the outcome will be entirely on *your* head!"

Kudinsky visibly winced at these last words. He knew only too well how true they were.

Taking heart in the other's supposed weakness, Bolotnikov went on triumphantly, "If your meeting fails, you will not have a single supporter left in the Politburo."

"Is that all, *Comrade* Bolotnikov?" asked Kudinsky, indicating the session was at a close.

"That is all, *Mr. Secretary*," Bolotnikov answered with scorn. He swung around and made his haughty exit, followed by his still-silent retinue. Kudinsky stared after him, his cool reserve remaining intact until the door clicked shut. Then he slumped down into the chair at his desk and looked glumly at his friend Soroka, who had remained behind.

"He is right, you know," said Kudinsky.

"I know."

"The blood *is* on my head, Pavel. I cannot fail . . . I cannot."

"Is there any way you can succeed?"

"Do you remember the faith of our parents, Pavel?" asked the premier, and Soroka nodded solemnly. "It is in times such as these that I find myself wishing I had not abandoned it."

# THIRTY-NINE

Bolotnikov stormed from Kudinsky's office fuming. Despite his threats, he did not feel he had won much of anything.

When he reached the street, he left his companions, giving them a list of instructions to carry out before the important upcoming meeting. He would check with them again after lunch. He then climbed into his automobile and raced across town, all the while wondering if Kudinsky could indeed succeed. But even should he strike some damaging deal with the American president, thought Bolotnikov, two could play the game of peace as well as one. He still had a few things he could do himself, if he had to, that would cut Kudinsky off at the knees. For the good of the beloved Motherland, he *had* to get that man out of power!

What bothered him most about the premier was his self-assured imperturbability. It was especially irritating to a highly emotional man such as Bolotnikov who had stormed and bullied and shouted his way into the political arena, and held a natural suspicion toward one who seemed capable of achieving his ends with a quiet superiority.

That's what galled him more than anything—the general secretary's air of superiority. After all, Kudinsky was from a peasant background, and his Ukrainian birth made him something less than a *pure* Russian.

Bolotnikov, on the other hand, boasted a fine Leningrad pedigree, with parents who were both doctors. Unfortunately, Bolotnikov himself was not an educated man. And even though education was no prerequisite for leadership in this land, it had in the last twenty years become an increasingly desirable quality, if for no other reason than for the prestige one's credentials offered in Western eyes.

At eighteen he'd joined the military and moved up slowly in the ranks. When he distinguished himself during the 1956 Hungarian uprising, his career picked up velocity, and by the time of the 1968 Czechoslovakian invasion, he was a division commander with a well-established reputation as a decisive and brilliant strategist. Fifteen years later he became commander of the Warsaw Pact Forces, one of the youngest men ever to occupy that post, though considering the Kremlin's propensity for filling positions of power with octogenarians, the praise was somewhat void of significance. Shortly thereafter he was elevated to full membership in the Politburo, an advancement made possible by his friend and sometime mentor, the late Defense Minister Dmitri Ustinov. Ustinov had always seen great potential for leadership in Bolotnikov, and thus when the chairmanship of the KGB became available in 1984, he recommended his protege for the post.

Bolotnikov had no qualms about giving up his military career, for by now he had an eye on top leadership within the party. Anything that might propel him along that path was seen as advancement.

Now as Bolotnikov maneuvered his Mercedes onto Kalinin Prospekt through its busy morning traffic, he thought about his standoff with the premier. If all went well, he could take Kudinsky's place in the foreseeable future. All changes in top leadership did not come through death, although the deaths of Brezhnev, Andropov, Chernenko, and Gorbachev had made that the norm for thirty years.

Maybe that was one of the positive changes Gorbachev had made after all, thought Bolotnikov—the election process. He could get Kudinsky out using the West's own mechanism! Besides, Kudinsky's reign was never meant to be a long one. He had been chosen only to buy time and to shield the true state of the Soviet leadership from Western eyes as they prepared to gain back Gorbachev's losses.

Bolotnikov sensed himself standing tall as the new man for the hour. It was highly unlikely that the premier could recover from his wishy-washy stand throughout the Iranian fiasco. He had become weaker than ever, and if he now went against the clear consensus and made a deal with MacFarlane, the entire Politburo would likely turn against him.

Some of Bolotnikov's earlier feeling of triumph began to return as he parked his car. Before getting out, he donned a pair of dark glasses. It became more and more difficult keeping a mistress secret these days as he gained national recognition, and he certainly could not afford a scandal now. But then Tatyana was worth the risk.

He left his car and walked up the avenue two blocks to a modern high-rise apartment building. He entered unnoticed and headed directly for the elevator.

As the elevator soared to the nineteenth floor he mused that the most difficult part of this affair had been securing an apartment for Tatyana. But again, she was worth it. Grinning to himself, he stepped out of the elevator into the hallway.

His heart raced as he thought of the beautiful woman he would take in his arms seconds from now. He imagined her thick blonde hair draped against her soft bare shoulders and quickened his pace without realizing it. When he reached the door at the far end of the corridor, he fumbled for the key in his pocket and cursed when he had trouble fitting it into the lock.

"Tatyana!" he called when he had entered and closed the door behind him.

"I'm in here, darling," came a resonant throaty voice from the only other room in the small apartment.

He hurried to the bedroom, where limpid turquoise eyes and full lovely lips smiled a welcome he could not refuse. If he were a more reflective sort, he might have wondered what a beautiful young woman like this saw in a married sixty-four-year-old man. But as he walked past the mirror on the wall and glanced at his reflection it was not difficult to convince himself that he was still a handsome, even a desirable man. His thick thatch of dark hair was only slightly streaked with gray, and his muscular, six-foot-three build could still be considered fit by nearly any standards.

At that particular moment, however, his mind was able to focus on nothing but the bewitching woman standing before him in the pink cashmere sweater he had bought for her. She held out her hand, and in an instant he was at her side. She reached up and put her hands on his shoulders.

"Darling, you are so tense," she murmured.

"If you only knew the pressures this day has brought . . . and it will bring more before it is through."

"Tell me about it," she said as she began loosening his necktie.

"It would not interest you, my love," he answered.

"Anything that interests you interests me, Leonid."

"I am very close to replacing Kudinsky," he said.

"How wonderful!" Her fingers massaged his shoulders and she kissed his neck. "Poor old Kudinsky . . . he is not ill, is he?"

"Only in his heart. But soon it will not matter."

---

Forty minutes later, Leonid Bolotnikov found himself reflecting again on Tatyana's youth. At times such as these he felt his age most and wondered if he should give her up. But he couldn't.

"Will you stay for lunch?" Tatyana asked in a husky voice.

"Can't today. I have to see Bragina and Moiseyev soon."

"Leonid, you are in no danger are you?"

"What do you mean?" he asked carelessly.

"What you said before about Kudinsky. Could you get into trouble? Is there a coup brewing?"

He laughed. "The only one in trouble is Kudinsky. Hopelessly clinging to the memory of Mikhail's fading dream. The old fool! He has no idea how widespread was the silent opposition to Mikhail's reforms. Half the Politburo is against him. And if he carries through on this summit with the American president, he will seal the enmity of the others. He will be forced to retire in infamy."

"But, darling, what if things go wrong? They could, you know." Her brow wrinkled with anxiety. "What if it all goes suddenly his way and you are left with no backers."

"It pleases me that you worry so, my love," he said with as much tenderness as his manner would allow. He bent over to kiss her. "But no need to mar that lovely face with worry. There is no more chance of that than of a tropical heat wave in Siberia next Christmas. Kudinsky will not win. He cannot win! I will take care of him no matter what happens."

# FORTY

Tatyana Slerilnya watched from her apartment window as Bolotnikov reached the street far below and walked away toward his car. She stood there for several minutes, long after he had disappeared from view.

She had met Leonid about six months ago in a nightclub frequented by party loyalists and Kremlin underlings. He'd been there with several friends from his KGB days, while Tatyana was in the company of a girlfriend. They, too, frequented this particular club—for their own reasons.

Seeing the second most powerful man in the country seated with two single men apparently unattached, she and her friend had gravitated in their direction and proceeded to make themselves agreeable.

Tatyana found the other men dull, but Bolotnikov exuded power and passion. She could not resist the challenge of making him her mark, and thus the relationship had begun—far more designed a scheme than Bolotnikov himself ever knew. He was the kind of man who might be able to give her what she wanted, and more besides.

She assumed Leonid would have her thoroughly screened by his former associates at the KGB, but they would never guess the secret only her girlfriend knew. And Irina would never tell, for she harbored the same desire and had also been on the lookout for an unwitting Kremlin official.

Tatyana had never dreamed she would get someone so high up, for any of the lesser men in the nightclub would have served their purposes. In retrospect she sometimes thought it might actually have been better had Bolotnikov not become part of the scheme. But it was done now, and hopefully all would continue to go well.

A KGB investigation of Irina would have revealed that her parents were dissidents, and Leonid would never have trusted her. But Tatyana's background was as pure as the Siberian snow, and since no one could read her thoughts, the KGB passed her with a clean bill of health. That was her assumption, at least, since Bolotnikov contacted her several days after their first meeting and wanted to see her. Discreetly, of course.

Soon he was calling on her regularly, and after a month he had arranged this apartment. She felt badly that she could not share it with Irina, but by this time she had told Bolotnikov that Irina was only an acquaintance of whom she knew very little—a lie of course.

For years she and Irina had dreamed of going to the West to seek acting careers. They had been too young and indecisive in Gorbachev's early days when emigration restrictions had been lifted. And by the time the backlash set in against the freedoms given to Poland, Hungary, East Germany, and other former Soviet satellites, and visas for Soviet citizens were halted, it was too late for them. The further tightening of travel policies some time ago only increased their hunger to escape. They hoped a liaison with a government official might help them obtain even a temporary visa to travel to Paris or London, after which they would be on their own to try to change their identities and never return.

Tatyana soon learned, however, that even to hint at a trip to one of those decadent countries would have been considered betrayal by Leonid. She had been foolish not to acquaint herself with the man's ideology before setting him up.

She naively thought that most officials still welcomed the progressive ideas of the Gorbachev era. How wrong she was. Bolotnikov hated the West with such a passion that the mere mention of London could send him into a tirade.

"It will all be destroyed one day!" he said over and over. "Gorbachev was a fool, thinking he could adopt bits and pieces of capitalism without succumbing to its evil power!" The destruction of the West was Bolotnikov's religion, his god.

Yes, she probably would have been better off with some lesser-known Kremlinite, but she had found Leonid difficult to resist. Now she would have to make the best of it. If it worked, she would have pulled off a daring victory. If not—well, she would not worry about that now.

Irina had been the one to propose a solution to the dilemma several months ago. She knew someone, she said, who had an acquaintance who would pay well for inside government information. He might even agree to help them get out of Russia.

"You are crazy!" exclaimed Tatyana. "Giving out information is treason. We could be shot!"

"Who's to find out?" replied Irina.

"It's too dangerous! At least now no one knows we want to leave, and we have broken no law."

"If we're careful, no one will suspect a thing," Irina went on calmly. "You are a terrific actress, remember. That's what this is all about."

"It's easy to talk about being careful when I'm the one who will take all the risks. Sometimes I truly think Leonid would just as soon kill me as make love to me, if it suited his purposes. He's a cold man, Irina. I don't know why he attracts me."

"Power is a seducer," said Irina.

"Perhaps. But he frightens me sometimes."

"My friend says they will put a large sum of money in a Swiss bank account each time we give them information that proves useful. In a short time we'll have enough to live very nicely in the West."

"Leonid does not often talk politics when we are together."

"I'm sure you could change that," said Irina. "You are a clever girl!"

Tatyana smiled but did not reply.

In the end she had decided to do it. She desperately wanted out of the country. The years were marching on, and she was getting no younger. An acting career could not wait. She almost despised herself for deceiving Leonid so. Part of her did love him, she supposed, even if it was in a daughterly sort of way. And though she had experienced few qualms about trying to extract a favor from him with regard to a visa, this was out-and-out betrayal—a far more serious game and one for which she was not sure she had the stomach. She was not a dissident. She did not even hate her homeland or its ideology. She only wanted to be an actress—in France, or Italy, or maybe someday in Hollywood itself. She trembled at the mere thought of what Leonid would do if he ever found out.

She should only have to meet with Leonid another time or two before giving their contact word to begin preparations for getting them out of Russia. They had enough money, and she was afraid to push her luck much longer. Her last bit of intelligence regarding some of the maneuvers in Iran had proved a gold mine, and she figured one more tidbit would be enough to satisfy their employers.

This was surely it.

A coup against Kudinsky! They would gladly arrange her freedom for that. Then she would be finished with this deceitful life.

She dressed quickly and left the apartment building. Once on the street, she glanced as casually as possible to the right and left to make sure she was not being watched. Yet she knew she would not be followed. Not so much because Leonid trusted her, but because he could trust no one else with the secret of their affair.

# FORTY-ONE

His code name was Blue Doc.

He had received the odd epithet several years ago while on one of his first assignments in a seamy Yugoslavian port town on the Adriatic Sea. He had been seconds away from capture by the local KGB contingent when he boldly—insanely was more like it!—jumped into the icy sea. With bullets flying at him from every direction, he'd had no choice but to dive underwater and swim as far as his breath could take him. When he surfaced after three and a half minutes, he realized he had made good his escape but that they were still watching the dock area closely. He went under again and made his way farther down the coastline. He had kept swimming for over an hour until an Italian troller picked him up, half-dead, his skin as blue as the morning sky overhead.

Anyway, it made a good story, and the name, if not the color, had stuck.

The Moscow beat was a far cry from those days.

Well, maybe it wasn't Moscow. Maybe the changes were in him. At forty, diving into icy waters ahead of a barrage of bullets just did not seem as excitingly adventurous as it once had. The tedium of this assignment—not to mention the nice hotel, the restaurant meals, a fine bottle of wine now and then—was an easy R-and-R after ten years of deep-cover jobs all over the world.

Here his cover was his job as an innocuous American embassy attache, which consisted of sifting through miles of paper looking for . . . well, anything. A year ago, shortly after Kudinsky took power, he'd come across a bundle of Ivan Szewinska's trash, and there he discovered a memo regarding a doctor's appointment. Further probing determined that Szewinska was suffering from a terminal illness which would soon leave the chairmanship of the Presidium of the Supreme Soviet up for grabs. There wasn't much the CIA could do to influence the outcome, but the forewarning helped the U.S. government brace itself. Szewinska's passing revealed that Kudinsky's power was questionable and that he had a viable and perhaps dangerous new opponent in the person of Leonid Bolotnikov.

In recent months, however, the doldrums of sifting through discarded junk had given way to a fresh breeze—and a whole new direction for Blue Doc's Moscow assignment. A female acquaintance had approached him, saying that she knew someone who might be able to help them as a source. This tip eventually led him to the beautiful Tatyana Slerilnya.

She wanted to sell out her lover, Tatyana said. This kind of scenario was supposed to be reserved for the movies, and at first he was nervous about it. But how could he refuse once he learned the man was Bolotnikov himself? All she wanted in return was a back door out of the country and a little stake in a Swiss bank.

So far she had earned her money. She'd provided the CIA with its first clue that the Russians were preparing to invade Iran. That had enabled the agency to tighten its already crackerjack network in the area. It had been the best piece of intelligence work he'd seen in years; it wasn't his fault that neither the White House nor the Pentagon had seen fit to act on it. But cloak-and-dagger was Blue Doc's game, not politics.

Now that everything had stalled in Iran, even the Soviet's movements, he had been digging to find out why. Maybe Tatyana would have an answer—or at least part of one. He had sensed an urgency in her tone when she contacted him earlier today, but then her voice always sounded that way. And what a voice it was . . .

*Get your mind back to business!* he exhorted himself as he crossed Krymsky Most and saw the waters of the Moscow River glittering below. To his right he could see the lights on the giant Ferris wheel in Gorky Park.

Tatyana had said she wanted a public place, and this certainly fit the bill. It would be their third face-to-face meeting since her liaison with Bolotnikov had begun. Could their good fortune in remaining undetected last much longer? Tatyana always assured him she wasn't followed, but he could never say the same for himself. As a foreigner in the Soviet Union, especially one attached to the American embassy, he was always a candidate for some kind of surveillance, if only routine. Though he was careful, he could never be absolutely sure there wasn't someone back there. And if there was, being seen in the vicinity of the same woman three times in a row would raise questions. He had already decided this would have to be their last meeting; he hoped she wouldn't get greedy on him.

He turned into the park, where music from the Ferris wheel and the hum of voices filled the early evening air.

He walked aimlessly about for a few minutes, playing the part of a tourist taking in the sights. It would have been more convincing if he were with someone, but he'd had plenty of experience at looking like a sightseer. He spent a couple rubles in the concessions before spotting her.

She stood by the embankment gazing out onto the river. Another girl was beside her; no doubt she had assumed it would be less conspicuous if she appeared to be out for the evening with a girlfriend. He hoped the other girl could be trusted.

Blue Doc strolled to the rail, stopping a few feet from them. He took several moments to nonchalantly confirm that no suspicious figures were lurking in the shadows anywhere.

"I have something for you," she said in that throaty, exciting voice.

Staring forward without glancing in her direction, he replied, "What?"

"It's big. It's worth a lot."

"What do you want?"

"Before the end of the week my friend and I want to be out of the country."

"That's a tall order."

"You have our papers ready by Thursday and I'll make the exchange. It will be worth it."

"I'll do what I can."

"The Mayokovskaya Metro Station at noon."

"I don't like being seen together again."

"I'll risk it," she said.

"What about someplace less conspicuous?"

"No. I want daylight and people around. I have a feeling Leonid is watching me."

"Is he suspicious?"

"I don't know. It's nothing he's said. I just have a feeling it's time to get out."

Though she was staring straight ahead, he could feel the tension in her tone. She was scared. Maybe even desperate.

"It's my neck too," he replied lightly, hoping to ease the tension. "You're sure he's not onto you?"

"I'm sure of nothing. It's only a matter of time. He trusts no one."

"Okay. Listen closely." He wanted to look directly into her eyes but didn't. He wondered if she could pull off the plan formulating in his mind. "I'll be seated on a bench east of the main ticket counter at 11:30. There will be an overcoat draped over the back and a newspaper lying beside it. Do you know the place?"

"I'll find it."

"There's a phone booth beside it. You go to that phone booth. Pretend to make a call but leave the door open. I'll pick up my coat, leaving the newspaper behind, and saunter up. You talk into the phone and tell me what you've got. The moment I leave the bench, your friend must go and sit down. When you're through with the message, I'll play the impatient businessman who can't wait for the phone and I'll walk away toward the train platform. Pretend to talk for a couple more minutes. Then you will leave the phone booth and your friend will leave the bench, but in opposite directions. But she must remember to take the newspaper. Everything you need will be inside it."

"All right," she agreed.

"Is everything clear?"

"Yes."

She and her friend turned and walked idly away from the railing, leaving Blue Doc alone watching the lights on the river.

# FORTY-TWO

There's something about it I don't like."

"You want us to take some action, sir?"

Bolotnikov strode to the window, planted his feet almost a meter apart, clasped his hands behind him, and stared outside in silence. Could he order his old colleagues in the KGB to put a tail on his own mistress? He knew what they were like when they sniffed an informant. He should know—he'd toughened the agency considerably during his tenure.

Besides, the woman they were watching—Irina something or other—was just an acquaintance of Tatyana's. She'd been honest about that, hadn't she?

Leonid Bolotnikov was not one who would admit to the possibility that he had been duped. Seduced by a woman! Never! He'd been the one to charm *her*!

No, he refused to believe it. To prove he was right, he *would* subject Tatyana to the scrutiny of the most feared agency within the Soviet Union—his own KGB. They could tail this Irina all they wanted, and Tatyana too. She'd come out clean, and their quiet little affair could go on as usual. He'd just have to monitor the agency's activities closely and wait until they had backed off before making another appearance at her apartment. If it got to be too long, he'd step in, assess their progress, decide what to do with this Irina person, and then order the case closed.

"You say you've already been watching this young woman by the name of Irina?" he said finally, his back still turned toward the room.

"For some time, yes, sir."

"And the other one—what's her name?"

"Tatyana Slerilnya."

"Yes . . . and you think she's—"

"They've been seen together quite often. Most recently in the vicinity of a fellow we could not help wondering about. His movements were curiously nonchalant and disinterested for one in such close proximity to two beautiful young women."

"Do you know his identity?"

"Not yet, but soon—he is being shadowed."

"Good work," said Bolotnikov, masking his growing concern.

"Shall we continue to observe both women, sir?"

"Those were the instructions from your superiors, were they not?"

"Yes, sir. They merely wanted you informed."

"Then I suggest you continue. I'm sure their guilt or innocence will be established soon enough."

"And if there is trouble, sir? If we see either of them trying to contact the British or the Americans?"

"I doubt it is of such magnitude."

"It is wise to be prepared, sir. One of your lasting maxims at the agency."

"Yes, of course," replied Bolotnikov. "Full readiness at all times."

"And if contact is made?"

Bolotnikov was silent a moment before replying. He would not believe any of this nonsense in connection with Tatyana! It was too absurd. She loved him! Even the KGB would find nothing on her.

"Then follow standard procedures," he answered at length.

"You mean—"

"I mean standard procedures," interrupted Bolotnikov, growing perturbed with this lackey they had sent to his office. "Standard procedures . . . do I have to spell it out for you? Now, get out of here and on with your business! Don't you have more important things to do than stand here arguing semantics with me?"

Without another word, the young KGB lieutenant spun around

and walked from the room, leaving the Soviet Union's second most powerful man alone to consider the tenuousness of his hold on the power he so desperately hungered for.

# FORTY-THREE

Three days after the meeting at Gorky Park, Blue Doc entered the Mayokovskaya Metro Station at 11:10. The midday crowds were fairly heavy and would nicely camouflage the unobtrusive drama he had planned.

He walked slowly, looked at a schedule, bought the all-important issue of *Pravda,* and curled it under his arm. He glanced at his watch and walked back and forth a bit as if waiting for a train. Finally he sat down on the appointed bench.

He spotted Tatyana Slerilnya about twenty minutes later—right on time. He did not see her friend.

Tatyana went directly to the telephone booth, deposited two coins, dialed a number, waited an appropriate time, and then began to talk. She was good, he thought to himself—calm, following directions to the letter.

He looked down at his watch again, for the sake of anyone whose eyes might happen to be on him, appeared to think for a moment, then rose and walked to the phone. He took up a waiting position where he could hear Tatyana clearly, hoping no one else would suddenly decide to queue up for the phone.

"Kudinsky's hold is weakening," she said into the phone. "Bolotnikov says most of the Politburo is against the premier on the Iran situation . . . that Kudinsky's stalling is hurting the Soviet position. He says he's almost ready to make a move . . . to take Kudinsky's place. I asked if there was going to be a coup against the premier . . . he said it wouldn't be necessary, but that he was determined to have his way, and that it would be disastrous for Kudinsky to meet with the American president. Leonid is passionately angry about their failure to carry through with the invasion of Iran, and he said he was determined for his plans to succeed. He has always boasted that the Politburo would side with him against Kudinsky."

She paused.

"That is all. I presume it is worth two forged passports."

Glancing around as if impatient but disinterested, Blue Doc nodded his head twice, then glanced at his watch in frustration and walked away.

Tatyana's friend was already at the bench, but she had picked up the newspaper and was glancing through it. A minor glitch in the plan. No problem. But she should have done exactly as he said.

Blue Doc walked onto the platform, stopped to glance at some magazines on display. Out of the corner of his eye he saw Tatyana's dark-haired friend stand, tuck the *Pravda* under her arm, and then walk casually toward the boarding platform. A train soon came rumbling to a stop before her.

Just as he was about to move away from the magazine stand, he spotted two plainclothes KGB agents. They went straight for the girl.

One of the men grabbed her arm roughly. The other went for her bag. She struggled. The newspaper fell to the floor, and the second agent reached down for it. He shuffled through its pages, then turned to show his comrade the travel documents.

Blue Doc should have made his move to get clear of the nasty scene right then. But he hesitated, feeling responsible for the girl's plight. Yet he could do nothing from where he stood.

Suddenly the girl twisted her arm free and gave one of the men a vicious kick, breaking loose from their hold.

In a confused instant, with the crowd shouting and scattering, she sprinted down several steps and onto the adjoining platform.

Blue Doc saw one of the agents pull his gun, and all his years of discipline and training left him.

"No!" he shouted, forgetting even to use Russian. But it was too late. Before the echo from his voice had died out, the explosive crack of the pistol shattered the air, and Tatyana's friend lurched forward as she ran, an ugly blotch of dark red spreading across the middle of her back.

He didn't see her hit the floor, for the reality of his own peril was immediately upon him. He turned and fled, a sickening feeling already welling up inside him that this whole miserable thing was his fault.

He did not stay to see the two agents walk toward the blood-stained body. One of them turned her over with his booted foot, as if with this final insult to humiliate this traitor, even in death.

Nor did he see Tatyana's horrified face, watching from behind a pillar as her friend fell and her hopes of a new life in the West evaporated.

He quickly eluded the backup KGB agent—he was good at that sort of thing, after all. But not good enough to keep a young girl from being shot to death in the middle of one of Moscow's most public places. Not even good enough to keep from blowing his own cover and perhaps placing the rest of the Moscow network in jeopardy.

He swore under his breath when he reached the street and was safely in the clear. He had gotten lazy in Moscow! He had forgotten what a brutal, life-and-death game this could be. Ten years of Soviet nonaggression had lulled him to sleep. He had forgotten that even now the Soviets did not ask questions when it came to traitors. A young woman's death was proof of that—and of his carelessness.

With an awful pang he realized he had misread the whole scenario. Tatyana would have been safe. No one was following her. Bolotnikov would never have risked the exposure. But Blue Doc had never checked on her dark-haired friend! Foolish! Idiotic! The friend was the one under surveillance, and she'd led the KGB right to them!

About a mile from the metro station he began to think seriously about what to do next. He couldn't go back to the embassy. The KGB might have spotted him—he couldn't know for certain. He'd have to lay low for a while.

He found a telephone and dialed the only number he knew to be safe.

"This is Blue Doc," he said. "My fishing trip washed out. I'm coming home."

"Sorry, Blue Doc," said a voice on the other end. "It's raining here too. We're making other arrangements. Call back in an hour."

He hung up the phone and sagged limply against the booth. He had no safe place to go, and now his colleagues would have to risk their positions to get him out of the country—certainly out of Moscow.

For the next hour he tried to piece together exactly what had happened. Could Bolotnikov have learned about Tatyana? Was this little incident his way of cleaning up the mess. Despite popular opinion in the West, Blue Doc knew the Russians still maintained a few hidden Siberian gulags. A man in Bolotnikov's position would wind up in one of them if word ever got out that his mistress was a CIA informant. Tatyana's life must be in danger too, but there was no way he could warn her. She had been careful to conceal the whereabouts of her apartment. And to make too much of an effort to find her could only make matters worse, if her fate wasn't sealed already.

But even now Blue Doc had not pierced the self-possessed mind of Leonid Bolotnikov. For, once aroused, the evil man's suspicions could not keep from gathering themselves about the fair face of his mistress. With the suspicion came doubt. And with the doubt came yet more evil thoughts.

---

An hour later he had at least learned his own fate. The KGB hadn't ID'd him. His cover was still intact. But the embassy was under heavy surveillance. He would have to wait until nightfall to come in for debriefing.

The wait seemed interminable. He could not have been more relieved when 10:30 rolled around and he was able to slip into the embassy unnoticed.

He met his supervisor in the basement headquarters. The man, ten years his superior, looked drawn and haggard, but his manner was calm and restrained.

"You okay, Danny?" he asked, using his proper name in these safe confines.

"Yeah, Frank, I'm fine," Blue Doc replied, but his tone and defeated expression did nothing to corroborate his words. "But I blew it bad."

"None of us are perfect, Dan. And Berlin Wall or not, we're still behind the line. It's still their territory, and it's still a mean business. Allies or enemies, the Russians still play for keeps."

"That's just it—I forgot."

"All right, fill me in on what happened."

Blue Doc recited a play-by-play account of all that had transpired at the metro station. When he was through, he dismally shook his head—it sounded even worse in the retelling. So many things had by now come to mind that he could have done to change the outcome.

"You're certain they were tailing the friend?" said Frank after a thoughtful pause.

"You mean—?"

"Is there any chance they were onto you?"

"I don't think so," he said. "Yeah, I'm pretty certain they were tailing her." Blue Doc paused, then added. "Any word . . . there's no chance she—?"

"No. Dead on the spot," Frank replied. "They claimed she was armed and dangerous. But it won't make the newspapers."

"No, I'm sure not," said Blue Doc dryly. "What about my informant, Tatyana?"

"Found shot to death in her apartment."

Blue Doc groaned and shook his head.

"Somebody out there means business."

"Yeah . . . Bolotnikov."

"Did you learn anything from the girl before the fireworks started?"

"Yeah," answered Blue Doc, thoughtfully rubbing his chin. "And if my assessment of this fiasco is right, what I learned scares the pants off me."

Frank leaned forward in his chair.

"She thinks Bolotnikov is planning an inside coup against Kudinsky."

"You can't mean it!"

"That's what she said."

"You think she was on the level?"

"I have no reason to think otherwise—and especially not now. She really wanted out of the country."

"Blast! That's all we need right now with the president planning a trip here!"

"My feeling is that Bolotnikov's plans might hinge on the success of the summit. But I think he'll go for Kudinsky no matter what happens. Tatyana said he'll stop at nothing to get what he wants."

Both men sat for some time, talking through the implications of the day's events.

Bolotnikov was a dangerous man—that much they knew. While the doors inside the Kremlin were closed to the West, the moderate stance of Premier Vladimir Kudinsky appeared to be largely responsible for the restraint shown by the Soviet government since Gorbachev's death. Neither man wanted to imagine what might happen were he toppled from power. The thaw in the Cold War seemed about to ice over again . . . before exploding apart.

At length Blue Doc verbalized the immediate fears both men shared.

"Without Kudinsky, there's no way we'll avoid war in Iran," he said with a sigh.

How many more factors might have entered the equation had Blue Doc known Tatyana had been on her phone, her fingers frantically dialing his number, when her apartment had been broken into by the KGB hit squad. As one last bargaining chip for freedom, she had wanted to tell him something she had forgotten earlier—that Bolotnikov had mentioned a "summit of his own" in connection with the small city of Kaliningrad.

But now he would never hear it from her lips.

# FORTY-FOUR

Two men and a woman stood on the brink of a dark pit. Clustered about them were a dozen or so laborers, some holding picks and shovels, others clutching brushes, brooms, and trowels. All gazed down into the abyss, waiting—waiting for what each hoped would be the greatest archaeological discovery of all time.

Shimeon Hagiz, archaeology professor and temple expert, gave the extension ladder a final tug to assure it was firmly in place, then glanced at his two colleagues.

Rachel Leventhal appeared sad, probably thinking of her father Yakov, who had been Shimeon's mentor at Jerusalem University. He it was who had planted in both Rachel and Shimeon the near-obsessive hunger after the past and had willed to them the dream that had led them to this very spot. Rachel must be thinking that Yakov deserved to stand here with them on this momentous day. Death, however, had taken him only last year.

Beside Rachel stood the American rabbi, Jacob Cohen, who was still a puzzlement to Shimeon. Here was a rabbi, a Levite, and a fundamentalist Christian all wrapped up in one thick, muscular package. His eyes glowed like an eager child's from his tough facade. Beneath him lay the treasure of a lifetime of devotion to two faiths.

Only a month ago it seemed this moment would never come, for the fulfillment of their quest was blocked by an impenetrable thirteen-hundred-year-old shrine of an opposing religion. Yet suddenly, in one swift devastating stroke of nature, all that was changed.

In the aftermath of the powerful earthquake, the Israeli government acted hastily, if in somewhat clandestine fashion, anxious to stake their claim before the dust settled and the Arabs or the United Nations could protest. It was, after all, in the center of Israeli jurisdiction and had been since 1967. A crack team of Israeli investigators, temple historians, scholars, and laborers was quickly assembled—headed by Shimeon. By the time the ultimate fate of this controversial piece of real estate came before international courts, the Israeli team would be solidly entrenched.

Millions of Jews and Christians the world over longed to see this ancient place of worship restored, holding to the tradition that God's biblical command to rebuild the temple was irrevocable. And even for the more orthodox—who believed that the Messiah, not man, would rebuild the temple—did not the Jerusalem Talmud say that Jews could construct an intermediate edifice before the Messianic era?

For years no group had been more zealous in its advocacy of rebuilding than the Temple Institute, whose spiritual leader, Rabbi Israel Ariel, was one of the first Israeli paratroopers to reach the sacred mount when the Old City was captured in 1967. For a dozen years the institute's American-born director, Zev Golan, had said, "Our task is to advance the cause of the temple and to prepare for its establishment, not just talk about it." And for almost as many years, an expensive miniature temple replica had lured tourists to Jerusalem's Holyland Hotel, keeping fervor for the notion central in the public consciousness. No group had shown more enthusiasm than the evangelical Christian tourists, for the rebuilding of the temple played as vital a role in their faith as it did for the Jews.

Thus the rebuilding of the temple was a cooperative affair, and the Knesset backed their united efforts to see the historic edifice erected on its original site, the very place chosen by King David himself.

The Israeli parliament did have to maintain appearances, however, in order to keep from offending the Arab world into an armed invasion. Only last month an official at Al Aqsa had said, "The Prophet Muhammad's followers will defend the Islamic holy places to the last drop of their blood." So the shrewd members of the Knesset had fallen in supportively with UN negotiations and discussions of the matter, while behind the scenes they gave tacit approval to the low-profile excavation. Their only stipulation was that if the subterranean exploration was discovered by the city's hotheaded Muslims, the Israeli body of lawmakers would disavow all knowledge of the proceedings. But the Jerusalem police had taken up guard positions around the entire perimeter of the disaster site and had thus far kept out radicals and curiosity seekers alike.

*Soon the dreams of nearly two thousand years will be fulfilled,* thought Shimeon as he peered into the blackness before him—since that time when Roman troops obliterated Herod's gilded temple. The prayers of tens of thousands of pilgrims at the ancient Wailing Wall would at last be answered!

"We need more light!" he called to one of the laborers, a tremor of anticipation in his voice.

Although the idea of temple reconstruction had been important to Shimeon's people for centuries, it had reached fervid heights when the Zionists reclaimed their homeland in 1948. For many Jews the establishment of a new temple lay at the very core of their faith and was a necessity before their long-awaited Messiah could make His appearance. For the Christians of the world, among them a rapidly growing number of Jewish Christians, the rebuilding of the temple was seen as a necessary prelude to the second coming of the Messiah, who had already come two thousand years before in the person of Jesus Christ.

Even after the Six-Day War of 1967, however, when Israeli forces captured the Old City and the temple mount and Jews were allowed to visit their holy sites for the first time in nineteen years, any plans toward reconstruction were forestalled by the presence of the mosque. Jewish law strictly forbid disturbing in any way the shrine of another religion. Still, plans for rebuilding had continued in hopes that somehow, someday the time would come.

Meanwhile, excavations had been carried forward outside the perimeters of the mosque. Additional segments of the Wailing Wall had been unearthed, revealing large new sections of Herod's temple. Plans had even progressed to the point where stones were being stockpiled in readiness for the actual construction. And Yakov Leventhal, Rachel's father, was one of those who had been instrumental in locating the ancient cornerstone of Herod's temple.

Despite all these preliminary efforts, however, the two key ingredients which both Jew and Christian agreed would signify the time when construction could actually get underway remained unfulfilled. The mosque still sat directly upon the old temple site, and the precise location of the original Holy of Holies had never been pinpointed with certainty. Now suddenly an act of nature—the staunchest believers among the diggers would have said an act of God—had substantially eliminated the first obstacle, and Shimeon's team of archaeologists hoped to solve the mystery of the second.

They had entered the area of rubble from a westerly direction, for it was traditionally believed that the Holy of Holies lay closest to this side. The excavators spent more than two weeks clearing away the recent layers of earthquake damage, taking painstaking care to harm none of the beautifully carved stone of the mosque. Then Shimeon had called his years of temple research into play in order to fix the most probable direction for the second phase of excavation.

He ordered the first shaft started just southwest of where the Dome had but recently stood. If the Stone of Foundation, on which tradition placed the ancient Altar of Burnt Offering, did indeed sit beneath the Dome, then the Holy of Holies should be located behind it. Shimeon preferred not to approach it directly from above, but from the side. To his colleagues he said this would protect the find, which was true enough, but in his heart he was also concerned about human entry into the holy place. This matter had been much debated by Jews over the centuries, and though Shimeon was by no means orthodox, he could not completely discount the idea that the Shechinah, or Divine Presence, still dwelt in this holy place—even after two thousand years. It was one of the reasons he welcomed the addition of their resident Levite, Jacob Cohen, to the team.

The shaft burrowed down thirty feet then slanted west in a subterranean path. Just before today's afternoon break the laborers had come to the stopping point predetermined by Shimeon. After a hasty council with Rachel and Jacob, it was decided to move into the final stage of the excavation that night.

Now the Jerusalem sky was dusky gray as the workers assembled at the edge of the shaft. One of the young assistants, a student volunteer, jogged toward Shimeon with flashlights, which Shimeon, Rachel, and Jacob attached to their belts. Other lanterns and tools had been stowed in a gunny sack to be lowered by rope after the three descended.

Jacob entertained a slight smile, reflecting only half the ecstasy he felt inside.

"I am reminded of an account in the Babylonian Talmud," he said in his mellow bass voice. "Rabbi Akiba, with several other sages, had come to the ruins of Herod's temple not many years after its destruction. A jackal was skulking about in the place where the Holy of Holies had been, and Akiba's associates wept and rent their clothes. But the wise rabbi looked upon the charred temple with hope. 'The prophets foretold both the destruction of Jerusalem and its restoration to glory,' he said. 'Now I have seen the first prophecy come to pass, and I know the second will also be fulfilled.' "

"Amen!" several in the group breathed reverently.

"Amen and amen!" said Shimeon. "Jacob, if you will." He stretched out his arm to indicate that the Levite Christian should proceed first.

---

For two hours the group above ground offered patient vigil. Some paced idly about, others worked by lantern light on sketches and descriptions of minor items uncovered during the dig. A few dozed off, leaning against heaps of rubble.

The night deepened, and a quarter moon rose. Though light conversation characterized the early part of the watch, the small group gradually fell silent, as if in reverent anticipation of what was to come.

All at once Shimeon's dark shaggy head emerged out of the ground, a broad smile spread across his face.

"Praise God! We have found it!" he declared. "We are standing above the Holy of Holies."

By the time his brief announcement was spoken, everyone had gathered around the edge once more. All fell to their knees, Jews and Christians united together, giving their silent thanks to God as Shimeon murmured the words of the prophet Isaiah.

"And it shall come to pass in the latter days that the mountain of the Lord's house shall be established in the top of the mountains, and shall be exalted above the hills; and all nations shall flow unto it."

"Blessed be the name of the Lord!" replied the others in unison.

"The temple *shall* be built!" exclaimed Shimeon. "We standing here this day shall see with our eyes the fulfillment of Isaiah's prophecy!"

# FORTY-FIVE

Mohsen Ali Pevlahvi slammed his fist down on the rickety wooden table.

"This is the final injustice!" he shouted, spitting upon the newspaper he had just thrown on the floor, where headlines announced a three-way oil deal between Great Britain, the United States, and Saudi Arabia, the intent of which was to cut Western dependence on Iran's oil fields to an all-time low.

Pevlahvi's small dark eyes glinted wildly, and his voice shook with passion. "We must stand for our country now, before the imperialist thieves trample it under their stinking, greedy feet! It is time for us to bring to completion what visionaries like Kaddafi and Hussein were only able to dream of!"

He glowered at his two companions in the dimly lit Tehran apartment.

"The Communist warmongers must also be destroyed! Standing at our borders even now, waiting to plunder all that is ours! Both the powers of the East and West must be put to death. The hour has come for a new order, rising out of the dung heap of the Soviet and American lust for power and world domination. Now it is time for *our* power to arise, I tell you!"

Pevlahvi's compatriots shifted uncomfortably as if they were the object of their leader's fanatical outcry. All three were, in fact, leaders of a small cell of the large Islamic socialist guerrilla band called Mujahedin-e Khalq.

Five years ago the Mujahedin had begun an all-out offensive against the Tehran regime still wedded to the ideas of the former Ayatollah Khomeini. But the offensive had been poorly timed, and Saddam Bani-Sandideh had brutally crushed the Mujahedin, leaving them weak and leaderless. Forced deep underground, the group still lacked its former strength and for some time had been completely ineffectual in destroying the Bani-Sandideh government.

But this small cell of maniacal subversives had a design far greater than the mere forming of a new administrative order for their homeland. They believed that a corrupt and brutal Ayatollah—hardly better than the Shah he had replaced—was not the major ill festering in their land. They saw their beloved nation as a pawn in the hands of greedy world leaders who would suck away their oil and leave them desolate. They could not sit idly by and see their homeland ravaged.

Mohsen was the most fervent of the three, but he had good reason for his hair-trigger emotions. At thirty-one he bore the scars of a violent, bitter life. He had lived through Khomeini's overthrow of the Shah's regime and at the age of fourteen had joined the Basij suicide corps. By the time he was twenty he had shed more blood than most of his cohorts and had survived missions that would make most men retch.

Then his own parents were murdered by the Ayatollah for persisting in their Baha'i faith in defiance of the mainstream fundamentalist mullahs. At that point Mohsen's wild fanaticism turned upon the government he had once fought for and hate became his driving force.

"Our course is set!" he shouted to his comrades. "Nothing will stop us!"

Ahmed Pevlahvi stared up at his brother with unabashed awe. His smooth, finely featured face revealed not only youth, but an innocence that stood in glaring contrast to his elder brother's scarred and pock-marked visage. Ahmed had been only eight years old at the time of their parents' terrible death, but in the years since his brother had protected him from his own brutal lifestyle.

Three years ago Ahmed had insisted on joining the Mujahedin, and Mohsen could act the role of protector no more. Already the younger Pevlahvi had seen a dozen assassinations of the Ayatollah's officers.

"Mohsen, I do not recall that the details of our course, as you call it, are so firmly set," said the third man, who appeared unimpressed by the zealot's flaming words.

"We have known all along what we must do," replied Mohsen. "The news from our sources in Jerusalem, along with everything else, only confirms that we must delay no longer. Our underground friends say that now the infidels dare to defile our sacred mosque. It is the supreme sacrilege!"

"You have *known,* Mohsen. I have only considered many options."

"Pah! You and your semantic debates!" He shook his fist within a few inches of the other man's face. "I tell you, Seyed, your Harvard education will do you no good here! Those Jewish fools shall never lay one stone of their demon temple upon another so long as I have power to stop them!"

"Let the Jews and the Egyptians kill themselves over Jerusalem. It's not our fight, Mohsen."

"Anywhere the name of Allah is profaned is our fight! Muslims must stand together the world over!"

"I know you hunger for blood. But violence is not always the best way."

"It is the *only* way! How else will that fat bear in Moscow and the beleaguered donkey in Washington be made to listen? How else will the sham nation of Israel finally be decimated so that the servants of Allah can once more worship in the city they claim as their own? Only by destruction can we throw them all into the turmoil that will topple their hollow systems and pave the way for the new order!"

Seyed Gilani folded his arms across his chest and leaned back against the wall, looking both smug and amused. Though only a year younger than Mohsen, his life had progressed along a far different course. In 1979, Seyed's father—a staunch dissenter—had fled Khomeini's bloodthirsty guerrillas, taking up residence in Paris. A wealthy man and a supporter of the Shah, he knew their homeland was no longer safe for his family. In Paris they wanted for nothing, and Seyed grew up in luxury, far removed from the squalor and strife of war-torn Iran. Unlike Mohsen and Ahmed, who had been acquainted with poverty all their lives, Seyed had led almost a jet-set existence. Everything had come easily. While it was true that he was an exile from his homeland, in reality he hardly knew the place, and he had suffered none of the agonies of the bitter and useless war with Iraq. So the exile in Paris was hardly a punishment.

Following Khomeini's death, Seyed's father was asked to return to Iran to help lead the resurgence of the Mujahedin and was instrumental in reestablishing the terrorist group and providing it a base from which world events could be altered. Seyed's father fought for several years in the underground, praying daily to Allah that his son, now a student at Harvard in the United States, would catch a vision for the cause.

Upon graduating from Harvard, Seyed traveled to Iran to visit his revolutionary father. It was then that a curious thing happened inside the soul of the urbane young man, for the moment he stepped off the airplane in Tehran he suddenly felt as if he had touched his true home.

Perhaps blood *was* thicker than water. By no other means could Seyed explain the change that came over him. It certainly had nothing to do with the intrinsic attraction of the place. Tehran was crowded, dirty, violent, foul smelling, laced with crippling poverty, and steeped in such bizarre customs that he sometimes felt he had landed on another planet.

Despite all this, something began drawing him into its vortex of turmoil.

Before long, his love and respect for his father sealed his fate. In truth, he took up fighting for *his father's* cause more than the Mujahedin's. He believed in his father, and he loved Iran because it *was* his father's land. When his father died in Seyed's arms following a street riot, he found himself pledging everlasting fidelity to the cause of a new Iran. A cynic in many respects, Seyed would never grow cynical enough to turn his back on a sacred promise to his father—even when that promise might now mean committing himself to an insane and fanatical undertaking.

"What you are suggesting is too fantastic to be seriously considered. Besides which, it would alter nothing in Jerusalem," said Seyed, ignoring Mohsen's venom, which by now he was more than accustomed to.

"You are afraid, perhaps?" snarled Mohsen.

"You should know me better than to make such an accusation. I have proved myself. The blood I have spilled may not match your own evil count of bodies in which you take such pride, but I am no coward. And you know it."

"Pah!"

"My objection is that it will not work. We will—"

"You believe I cannot do what I say!" screamed Mohsen in a white heat of passionate rage.

"I have little doubt that you can do all you say, and more . . . that you can kill as many leaders as you choose. But for what purpose, that is what I ask?"

"To bring their nations to their knees!"

"Will it rebuild the Dome of the Rock?"

"It may keep the desecration of their own temple off the sacred ground."

"You will succeed only in bringing their combined wrath down upon us, and possibly bringing about our own destruction as well."

"I knew it—you are a coward!"

"You know better, Mohsen. But you cannot expect me to leap on the bandwagon of every scheme you hatch without some deliberation."

"Bandwagon!" Mohsen spat again, this time coming disgustingly close to Seyed's boot. "When will you forget those decadent Americanisms? I do not know why I continue to endure your compromising and cowardly face!"

Seyed smiled, inwardly gritting his teeth. He could put up with Mohsen's personal attacks most of the time. But one of these days the insolent fool was going to go too far.

"Because my father was a great man," he replied tersely. "And you know my loyalty to him and our country is irreproachable."

"And because you are brothers," put in Ahmed rather timidly.

"Yes, Mohsen, because we are brothers," repeated Seyed. During the years of fighting while he was in America, his father had grown close to the two young Pevlahvi's, to the point where, as he lay dying, he addressed all three as sons. And while Ahmed might not have been referring to the brotherhood of familial blood, Seyed knew that something deeper than nationality had drawn and kept the three together despite their divergent personalities and views of how to achieve the ends they all desired.

"So, what is it you find so objectionable in my plan?" asked Mohsen, striking an uncharacteristic moderation in his tone, seeming to make an effort toward conciliation. He too was aware of the bond between them, but would only begrudgingly admit it.

Seyed burst out laughing. "Absolutely nothing!" he said as he continued to chuckle, "other than the fact that you want us to assassinate the world's two greatest leaders at the very moment when they will be under the heaviest protection imaginable, in the heart of a country where an ant would have difficulty moving freely, much less crossing the border to make an escape. Do you seriously think they will let three Mujahedin terrorists out of Russia after an explosive event like that? No, no, my friend—come to think of it, your plan is not objectionable—it is insane!"

"So insane it might work."

"And if not?"

"No one promised us a long life in this business."

"A wild fantasy," said Seyed.

Mohsen sat down across from his comrade and, leaning forward, fixed an intense gaze on him.

"But consider the beauty of it," he said. "Killing the United States president and the Soviet premier while they meet together. What better way to show the world that we will not be haggled over like a piece of meat! And when our own people finally see the will and the power of the Mujahedin, the Ayatollah will no longer be able to stand. The Arab world will unite behind us. The Jews and Americans will be left in ruins, the Russians driven back, and once again the power of ancient Persia will rise to rule the world. In a single stroke we will have advanced toward our goal and will stand on the threshold of ultimate power!"

"Have you considered the reprisals those countries would initiate if the rest of the Arab world does *not* unite behind us? In a single breath, hardly even exerting themselves, they could wipe us off the face of the earth."

"You know the weakness of the Americans. They have allowed terrorism to reign throughout the world, they have let the Russians and the Libyans do whatever they pleased. We have nothing to fear from the weakling imperialist Americans. As for the Russians, what does it matter? They are at this moment perched at our back door, and nothing can stop them from overtaking us at their will. At least we will have made a statement the world will not soon forget. Our boldness could be the catalyst to unite all the Arab nations against the American *and* the Russian *and* the Israeli pigs!"

"I shouldn't have to remind you, Mohsen, that we sit directly between the Russian troops and the Israeli warmongers. It is the blood of *our* people that would be shed. You have perhaps heard of Armageddon?"

"Bah! A foolish infidel superstition! It will not come to war, I tell you. Even the Russians will not be willing to alienate the third world—because we possess a weapon stronger than all their nuclear warheads. They fear terrorism more than anything."

"You're crazy."

"To be a revolutionary one must be a little mad, my friend. Your father and I often spoke of this."

"I know," replied Seyed. He found it difficult to believe his father would have sanctioned such a wild tactic, but he knew it was true. Yet he resented Mohsen using that as a point in his argument.

"All right," Seyed said slowly. "I concede to the possible effectiveness of eliminating the president and the premier. But the timing and the proposed methods only invite disaster."

"It is the very daring of the plan that will make it effective."

"Spoken from the heart of a true fanatic," said Seyed sarcastically.

"Perhaps you consider your life more valuable than your father's?"

"Don't even think it!" snapped Seyed, losing his composure for a brief instant. He jumped from his seat on the wooden bench and paced frantically back and forth, as if he could somehow walk away his sudden agitation. Finally he took a deep breath and turned toward Mohsen. "Doesn't it frighten you . . . even a little?" he asked.

"There is no room for fear in a cause as great as ours," replied Mohsen flatly, refusing to yield even an atom to whatever emotions might lurk unseen inside him.

Seyed looked directly over to his brother. "And you, Ahmed? Are you willing to go to your death because you believe in your brother?"

"I have always known it would happen this way," replied the boy in the same unflinching tone.

Seyed sighed deeply. Despite his differences with these two, their cause was his cause too. He knew that. How could he look upon such courage, fanatical as it might be, and not resolve within himself to meet it with like courage? The moment young Ahmed spoke, he knew he had no choice but to follow the bleak path of his destiny in the footsteps of these two wild-eyed Iranian brothers.

# FORTY-SIX

Jarvis MacFarlane made his way carefully up the dark, narrow flight of stairs. Between the two of them, he and Peter had certainly picked some quirky spots for these meetings!

He knocked on the door as he always did, then entered. As usual all twelve men were already there. They greeted him warmly, and he reciprocated. In the eight times they had been together, he had barely managed to get every name straight. Yet the men in this small room were fast becoming the individuals he could trust most in the whole world—and that despite the fact that each of them were avowed born-again Christians while he was not.

"Welcome, Jarvis," said Daniel with a smile. Then as soon as the president had taken his seat with the others, he began the meeting.

"Tonight, gentlemen, it is imperative that we bow earnestly before the Lord before we begin," Daniel said. "We pray together each time we meet, of course. But earlier today I felt the Spirit urging me to share something that may be difficult for Jarvis to grasp, because of his position."

"More difficult than everything else you've been bombarding

me with?" laughed MacFarlane. "That will take some doing!"

The others joined him in laughter.

"I know we have taxed your brain and your heart with what must seem inconceivable and fanatical ideas," replied Daniel.

"To say the least!"

"Yet I hope your association with us has shown you that we are not unhinged lunatics full of hysterical, imaginary ideas."

"That I grant," said the president. "Though I still don't know what to make of your interpretation of life, world events, and the future, I would have to say you are among the most level-headed persons I have ever met."

"Well, tonight's time together may cause you to wonder afresh at that perception! So shall we go before our Lord and ask that His wisdom and mind be present among us and in us tonight? And we must bind the strongholds of the enemy, who would work confusion and discord at any opportunity, and ask the protective hand of our Father to be over all we do and say."

After several moments of silence, the men began to take turns praying. As always, MacFarlane listened without offering any prayer of his own. The first time he had participated in the spontaneous prayer time—which resembled a round table discussion with some invisible host who had invited them to his house—the president had indeed fancied himself fallen among a band of crackpots. His only thoughts that first night were variations on the single theme: "What did I let Peter get me into!" and he scarcely remembered a word that was said. By the second meeting, knowing a bit more what to expect, he was able to listen more attentively, though still comprehending little. By the third and fourth meetings, he had begun to absorb some of what was being said and realized why Peter felt so compelled that the group be formed for his benefit. By then, too, he was growing accustomed to the notion of twelve men praying aloud together and was able to listen to the words being uttered.

And as he listened, the realization gradually stole over him that none but sane, mature, selfless, intelligent, and truth-loving persons could pray the prayers that came out of their mouths. He heard no loud incantations, no shouting like the TV preachers, no asking God for favors, no long, pious pulpit orations. Their prayers were simple, humble, and focused on the single request that God would reveal His wisdom to them. The cry of their hearts seemingly had nothing to do with themselves or their personal desires. They were willing servants who had placed themselves under God's dominion and now asked Him to instruct them in all they did.

MacFarlane had never seen the like of it in his life, bearing no resemblance to what he had always thought of as "religion."

By the fifth meeting he had become an active participant, mostly voicing the many questions which came to him, sometimes arguing, pointing out opposite points of view, asking them to help him understand.

Always his questions were met with acceptance, with never a hint of condemnation. The twelve knew they had been brought together largely for this man's benefit, to love and support and pray for him, not convince him regarding any specific set of ideas. They treasured MacFarlane's open heart far more than his agreement or disagreement at any particular point. All things needful would be revealed. There was plenty of time for accuracy of perspective as the Lord opened His mind to each heart. For the present, they were more concerned with nurturing the relationship, while speaking gently of the things they were given to say.

As he listened and questioned, what gradually began to unfold before Jarvis MacFarlane was the most fantastic story he had ever heard. Had it not been for the vision he had seen, he would probably have dismissed their prognostications of the future—a future which, according to them, held anything but peace. Indeed, their incredible message predicted a great apostasy, as America deserted its spiritual heritage, and a resultant judgment because of it—a judgment not unlike that prophesied by Jonah against the great city of Nineveh in the Old Testament.

At one meeting MacFarlane's mouth gaped open in astonishment as Daniel spoke.

"God told Jonah to go to Nineveh and proclaim His message of judgment against it. These were God's words to Jonah, *Go to the great city of Nineveh and preach against it, because its wickedness has come up before me.* Jonah did so, and remarkably the people of the city listened and believed God and repented. Then the king issued a decree."

Here he paused and turned toward the president.

"And here, Jarvis, may perhaps be a word for you, for we all know that it is no accident that you are here among us seeking God's truth for this nation. Listen to the proclamation of the king: *Let everyone call urgently on God. Let them give up their evil ways and their violence. For who can tell, God may relent and with compassion turn from his anger so that we will not perish.*"

The small room was silent. Jarvis required no one to make the application to his present position. Would he ever have the guts to do such a thing?

After another minute, he quietly asked. "So how does the story end?"

Daniel smiled. "As always with the things of God—just as it should have! Let me read it. *When God saw what they did and how they turned from their evil ways, he had compassion and did not bring upon them the destruction he had threatened.*"

As the meetings continued, MacFarlane came to realize that the Legation was not offering a message of doom but of warning—like Jonah's—of the need for repentance, and of the promise of God's love and compassionate purpose. If what they said was true, the significance for the world was enormous. But the implications for a man who just happened to be president of the United States were positively staggering. Along with the vision, these nighttime meetings were unmaking every single thing Jarvis MacFarlane had ever believed, and were turning his world upside down.

On the present night, when they were through praying, Daniel spoke again.

"Tonight I feel the Lord would have us talk about peace. Our friend Jarvis will soon embark on a trip to the Soviet Union to seek peace among the two most powerful nations of the world. The peace which the Lord means to bring, however, is an altogether different peace, and we must ask the Spirit of Christ to help us discern between the two. And we must—the twelve of us—join together in lifting up Jarvis in prayer in the coming weeks, that he would come to apprehend the distinction clearly, for the Lord has placed him in the position of great responsibility, and has placed us in the unique position of being able to pray actively and personally for him."

He paused, took a deep breath, then looked tenderly into the president's face. "Jarvis," he said, "I don't think I even need to tell you how much we all love you and respect you. I hope you know that."

MacFarlane nodded.

"What we have to say right now may stretch your trust in us. But we feel the time is short and that these things must be said."

"I will do my best to keep an open mind."

"We have no doubt of that," said Daniel. "Much of what we have spoken of together up till now has primarily had to do with how we, as Christians, view our lives with God, how personal we take it, how every facet of our being we consider as coming under the

Lordship of Jesus Christ. And that, in and of itself, is a radical view these days. The notion of a personal God who has a claim upon our allegiance and a right to our complete obedience—such is not the prevalent view of our times, to say the least, nor the accepted American 'world view.' "

"To say the least!" laughed MacFarlane. "As I've said before, if word got out that I was receiving counsel from the likes of you, the political fallout would be irreparable. People would be more comfortable if I consulted the stars for advice!"

"Well, it's going to get even worse, Jarvis," said Daniel, "because now we need to begin considering in more depth the political and social import of some of these things. And tonight we want to share what we believe is the Lord's word for you as you think and pray and prepare for your trip to Moscow."

"Go ahead," said MacFarlane. "I am eager to hear anything you have to tell me."

"It is a simple message really," Daniel said, "but a prophetic one. And the message from God is this: *Peace is not what it seems. The world looks for peace and thinks it has found it, but it has found no peace. The world's peace is a false peace proclaimed by false messengers. They have no peace to offer. Do not be deceived by their smooth words. The peace they proclaim will bring with it a sword, a sword dividing spirit from flesh, a sword that is coming unexpectedly upon the world. The sword will bring with it judgment. Now is the hour for preparation, for obedience, for purification, to make ready the bride for that day which no man knows. These tranquil days are not what they seem. Do not be lulled to sleep, My people. Rise up! Awake, for the time is short. The hour is at hand for the fulfillment of all things! Proclaim the day of the Lord, My son, while there is yet time, while there are ears to hear. Be not afraid. Faint not, for I am with you. My words shall be in your mouth, and My fire will burn your tongue, anointed for My purpose. You are My witness to these things. Though no one seems to listen, your faithfulness will carry My message of peace to the four corners of the earth. Warn them that the kingdoms of man are as dust. My kingdom is coming. The day is at hand. My people will join together, that the world may know. Fear not. The day will come with great rejoicing.*"

The flow of words from Daniel's lips stopped abruptly, and he bowed his head. In the silence of the room Jarvis could hear the rapid pounding of his heart within his chest. He knew that the words Daniel had spoken had been meant for him.

For ten minutes the heavy silence was broken only by faint whispers and murmurs of prayer. At length the Russian Dmitri slowly rose, walked to where MacFarlane sat, and knelt down beside him

"Such are not always easy words for us to hear," he said quietly in his broken Russian accent, "the likes of you and me—political men. It is perhaps more difficult for us to shake ourselves loose from the kingdom of man to see the things of the kingdom of God. You have no idea of the struggles I have gone through in the consulate, maintaining my job on the surface, all the while deep inside realizing that this peace between our two nations is destined ultimately to go the way of all so-called peace of man's devising."

"Must it be so?" asked MacFarlane, a forlorn sound in his voice. "Why can't we bring peace among men, among the nations? Why can't this peace last?"

"Because man is man," replied Dmitri. "Without God, it is impossible for men and women to put others ahead of themselves. Greed and power and self-interests always take precedence over good to one's neighbor. Because of this, the kingdoms of man are doomed to fail."

As Dmitri rose and returned to his seat, the president shook his head in frustration, staring at the floor.

"Then—then is *peace* in the world—is it a bad thing? Is it wrong to seek it?" he finally asked.

Daniel spoke again, his voice filled with calm compassion.

"Wrong? No, Jarvis—peace is not wrong. Any harmony is far better a thing than fighting and strife and hatred. There is nothing *wrong* with this last decade of peace. It is a wonderful thing that these two mighty nations have laid aside their differences for a season. And as president, you do right to seek peace. As long as you occupy that position, such will be your job, your responsibility."

"But—I don't understand. I thought you said such peace was doomed to fail. What about the judgment and Nineveh and all that?"

"The peace that man devises *is* doomed to fail in the end, Jarvis. But that does not mean that it is not better to seek peace than to allow open warfare. We must simply remember where *true* peace is found. True peace, lasting peace, peace which truly binds the hearts of humanity in the unity of brotherhood—such peace only can come from God. We can never artificially create it by signing a piece of paper. In other words, in the kingdom of man, true peace can never be achieved. It can only come in the kingdom of God. What God means by peace is not what the world means by peace—the two are totally different."

"But I've spent my whole adult life in politics working for peace—or what I thought was peace! Now you tell me it's all been for nothing?"

"Not for nothing, Jarvis," answered Daniel softly, lovingly. "All those years have been preparing you for this moment—I truly believe that. Perhaps those years seeking peace in man's domain have uniquely prepared you now to take the message of God's peace to the world."

Again MacFarlane shook his head. "This is all—it's too overwhelming. I hardly know how to cope with it! Everything I thought I knew, everything I thought I believed is being tossed out the window."

Again the room fell silent, and it was MacFarlane's friend Peter Venzke who spoke this time.

"What you are feeling, my friend, is perhaps one of the effects of man's peace," he said. "There is almost a danger to it, not because—as Daniel said—it is in any way a bad or a wrong thing, but because we unknowingly allow a counterfeit sense of security and well-being to obscure deeper realities. Peace in the world can be an analgesic, numbing us to God's voice because everything all about us is so rosy. All around us in this country we can see signs of that very thing. People have been lulled to sleep. They do not realize that judgment is coming, that this peace cannot last. Their hearing has grown dull, their eyes dim, to the things of God. And in many ways, the peace of man only deepens their slumber. In that sense, though it is not a wrong thing to seek in itself, earthly peace is something the enemy can actually use, because peace in the world is a fleeting delusion that turns people's eyes from their need to seek God's kingdom."

"Let me add this to what Peter has told you," said Daniel. "In no way are we disparaging peace, or you in your job as president. But we feel we must be faithful to tell you, to warn you, that there can be no peace—no lasting peace—as long as Satan rules the world. This peace between the U.S. and the Soviet Union can be a mere smoke screen of the enemy. The Bible says that certain things *will* come to pass in the latter days, and one of those prophecies is that Russia is going to be a major player in a bloody and gruesome war. Therefore, this peace *cannot* last. It is not wrong nor even inappropriate for you to seek it, my friend. That, only God speaking to your heart can determine. But you must understand that this is just the calm before the storm. The time for preparation is now—preparation for times vastly different than what Foster calls 'humanity's new dawn'! The kingdom of God is coming, not some New Age utopia. The prophetic events foretold in the Bible must be fulfilled, and that means that Russia will still one day be Israel's enemy. Despite the present peace, therefore, you would do well to be wary. As a man who must walk among the rulers of the world, you must walk warily. And my word to you as one whom I sense God raising up to walk among the people of God is—walk faithful in the calling wherein God has called you to speak His truths."

MacFarlane said nothing more. There was little to say. He knew that all twelve members of the Legation were praying for him. It was a good thing, for he could not have prayed for himself right then even if he *had* known how! He felt as though the whole secure world he had known was crumbling beneath his feet.

# FORTY-SEVEN

Mr. President, why do you think Premier Kudinsky *really* wants the summit to take place in Moscow?"

MacFarlane smiled at the man from ABC. Dustin Michaels was a crack reporter, always looking for an angle, but this was one time he definitely wanted to curb the newsman's investigative urges.

"I have heard the Russians are extremely hospitable, Dustin," MacFarlane replied with a subtle twinkle in his eye. He would not give Michaels the opportunity to nail him for his nifty side-step.

This was some act he was putting on, MacFarlane thought to himself. After last night's Legation meeting, he had hardly slept. But today's press conference was already scheduled, so he had to carry on, despite his sleepless night, the bags under his eyes, and his distracted mind. He'd gotten out of bed at six, taken a cold shower, and was now doing his best to pretend this was a normal presidential day. In the back of his mind, however, lurked thoughts of prophets dressed in sackcloth and an ancient city called Nineveh.

This was the third time he had faced the press in the span of one week.

He had called the first meeting himself, issuing a prepared statement with no opportunity for response or questions. This gave him a platform for his hard-line censure of the Soviet threat to Iran. He then stunned both the press and the nation by ending with the unexpected announcement that he would be contacting the Soviet premier with the offer of a summit meeting in Washington. Neither his opponents nor his supporters imagined he had it in him to get so tough, especially after his long inaction over the issue.

It had been a curious speech, an unlikely mix of tough anti-aggression talk coupled with the summit idea, and had played well throughout America's heartland. His approval rating immediately shot up ten points.

The very next day both Howard and Randolf urged him to take to the stump again, giving the press the opportunity to question him. Howard argued that it was the perfect, not to mention free, chance to drive home some important election points. MacFarlane agreed, and the second press conference was equally successful.

But then three days later came Kudinsky's left-handed affirmative, which essentially said, "I'll agree to meet, but you must come to Moscow."

MacFarlane shot off a quick reply giving tentative approval to the premier's offer.

"You're not serious, Mac," said Jake when the three met to discuss it.

"If you go to Russia, you'll lose the ground you've gained," exclaimed Dick. "You're in a strong position right now—calling the summit, your tough speech. You haven't polled this good in three years!"

"The polls can do what they will. I don't want to risk the Soviets backing down. I have *got* to meet with Kudinsky."

"The world is watching, Mac," Howard argued. "Going to Moscow will be interpreted as a sign of weakness. Especially in face of impending war. It's just plain risky. Make them come to us."

"I think you're overemphasizing the possible negative reaction. If I can gain substantive concessions from the Soviets, no one will care where the meeting took place."

"Fat chance! You don't seriously think they're about to back down in Iran?"

"I don't know. What have I got to lose?"

"The election, Mac!"

MacFarlane did not answer. For the first time in a long while it suddenly dawned on him how different he and Dick Howard were, and for a long moment he stared at his old friend, both amazed and appalled. Dick might not know the whole picture, nor what was so urgent about his meeting with Kudinsky, but surely he should know that more was at stake than his own political security. Was more changing for him than he even realized, causing this almost overnight separation from a friendship that went back years? Though he hardly knew them, it was as if he suddenly had more in common with that small group of Christians than with some of these men he had known half his life.

He sighed deeply but still could think of no words with which to answer Dick's frustration. In that moment there were no words to bridge the gap between them.

Thus, this third news conference had been called.

Another hand shot into the air. This time it belonged to Maggie Warner of the *Los Angeles Times.* "You can't seriously believe there is no ulterior motive in the premier's invitation, after you specifically invited him to Washington. Wasn't that his condition for agreeing to the meeting at all?"

"It might well have been, Ms. Warner," replied MacFarlane. "But you must understand that the Soviets are clearly entering this summit on the defensive. When I announced my proposal, I was hardly mild in my denunciation of their action on the Iranian border. We have now brought world opinion to bear against them. It is not illogical that they at least want to be on their own turf. And I am willing to be flexible, even go to Moscow, in order to protect the peace that has been established in the last decade."

"Are there no political motives in your timing of this whole thing?" shouted a voice from the back.

MacFarlane laughed. "I was expecting that one!" he said. "And it's a fair question, to which I would like to respond. First of all, I certainly didn't engineer the Soviet military buildup on Iran's border six weeks ago. The fact that their action came at the height of the political fray was hardly our doing.

"But we have to respond in some manner. That's the president's job. And the fact that this is an election year does not change that essential fact. Since news of the Soviet mobilization, I have been blasted by you esteemed members of the press and by my Democratic and Republican colleagues for *not* taking any action, *and* by my worthy opponent for threatening the peace, for not believing in—what does he call it—the brotherhood of man. But now when I am attempting some action which I hope will result in a peaceful settlement of this crisis, I am taken to task for politicking.

"So I ask you"—and here he chuckled lightly to diffuse any sound of accusation in his tone—"what's a president to do? I see no alternative but for me to move ahead, do what I feel is in the best interest of the nation and the world, and let the election take care of itself. Those of you who would read political motive into every breath won't want to believe that, but I honestly mean it.

"Of course I want to win in November—if I can just get my own party's nomination first," he added, as an aside, which brought a ripple of laughter from the assembled press corps. "I feel I must win, for our country's health and security. But I tell you honestly that what I intend with Premier Kudinsky has no political basis whatsoever. I am committed to peace even above politics. At this point, my own political future is secondary to me."

"You seriously expect us to believe that, Mr. President?" said Michaels. "A politician involved in a fight for his survival, and you're saying you don't care about your political future!"

"Mr. Michaels, I'll be very forthright with you," replied MacFarlane. "I really don't care if you believe it or not. You can put me on the evening news and add your ever-piercing editorializing to my comments—call me a liar or whatever you want. But I'm simply telling you in all sincerity that right now my political future is secondary to me. I did not say I didn't care about the election. I hope I win in November. I want to win. I should win. In all honesty I think I am the best man to sit in the Oval Office at this stage of our nation's history. But that's all secondary."

"Hasn't your own staff advised against a Moscow meeting?" asked Sylvia Buchannan of the *Post.*

"My own staff, Ms. Buchannan, is one-hundred percent behind me!" As he spoke, MacFarlane let a half smile form on his lips. The press would know his statement was bunk. But then the smile assured them that he wasn't trying to put anything over on them. "Seriously, yes—there have been some heated debates among my people. And yes—there are those who think I am crazy to even think of it. But they are—and here we come back to Mr. Michaels' question—thinking of the political implications, and that is not primarily my focus. Those who doubt my wisdom are worrying about what the polls will show if I go to Moscow and get slapped around by the Russians and come off looking like an idiot. Well, that's certainly a possible scenario! And these advisors of mine worry about what political hay my esteemed colleague, Senator Foster, would make of such fumbling around, so I suppose their concerns are legitimate. But again, that's the political argument—and I happen to think it's worth the gamble. If peace is preserved but I lose the election, then maybe I have done what was best for the country in the long run."

"And if peace isn't preserved. If the summit is a flop and they're determined not to withdraw their troops?" asked Michaels.

"That *is* the biggest question of all, isn't it?" MacFarlane replied.

He paused for a moment, and the room was unusually quiet. No hands clamored to be seen.

"I said a moment ago that I was committed to peace," he continued. "I meant that. I truly am. But along with peace I am committed to freedom in the world. That's what America has stood for on this globe for two and a quarter centuries. When another power threatens freedom on an international scale, we have always seen it our duty to step in. In other words, freedom must be preserved as well as peace. As the president of this nation, I must stand for both. Therefore, two things are necessary for this crisis to be resolved. Their troops *must* be withdrawn. And there *must* be peace."

"But if that proves impossible, Mr. President, will you rule out military options?"

"I'm sure you can understand my reluctance to give specifics, for security reasons. I will close by merely saying that I plan to go to Moscow to make sure such is not necessary . . . ladies and gentlemen, our time is up."

# FORTY-EIGHT

Following the press conference, Dick Howard sidled up to the president in the corridor of the White House.

"We have to talk," he said softly but urgently.

"Can't it wait?" replied MacFarlane. "I'm exhausted. How about this afternoon—say three o'clock?"

Reluctantly Howard conceded.

---

He was at the door of the Oval Office at exactly three.

"Well, Dick, what's on your mind?"

"All right, Mac," said Howard, clearly agitated, as if he had been stewing over this speech for hours. "I'm willing to go along with this summit thing—"

"Willing to go along!" MacFarlane repeated the words with obvious sarcasm. "Three days ago you thought this was the best thing since the Declaration of Independence."

"That was before you started pulling your tricks and talking about giving in and—"

"I pull no tricks!" snapped MacFarlane. He could take the flack that was hurled at him from his enemies, but he'd had just about enough of it from his friends and colleagues.

"Okay, wrong choice of words," Howard conceded, though the effort at apology was clearly halfhearted. "I'm sorry. That wasn't the point I was trying to make anyway."

"It's what you feel, isn't it?"

"Forget it."

"I can't. What's happening with us, Dick? Don't tell me we're under pressure. I've heard that excuse—and used it myself!—too often lately. Some fundamental differences are cropping up between us. We've got to do something about it before it destroys not only our political ambitions, but our friendship as well."

"Mac, I'm supposed to be your advisor, as well as the attorney general," said Howard after a moment's pause. "That's what you said you wanted from the very start. But you never listen to me anymore." He took a sharp breath and tried hard to restrain his frustration. "We butt heads at every turn. What good am I doing here? I could ensure the election for you, but you won't let me do my job. Instead you seem bent on doing everything in your power to thwart me. I don't know what's going on inside your head anymore. You seem so distracted. Maybe we *are* at cross-purposes. I want to win, and you . . . I don't know what you want. Mac, this Moscow thing—your intransigence over my proposal about Wilson—your refusal to come out with a strong denunciation of Foster . . . I don't know—it almost seems you don't want to win, like you've got your head in the clouds."

"I *have* to win," said MacFarlane, almost to himself. "And I have to go to Moscow. It may be my only chance, Dick. Call me a fool! What can I do if my own goals are at cross-purposes with each other? You may be right—what if the Moscow trip costs me the election and Foster lands us in a war? I've lost on both counts! Yet what alternative do I have? You face choices, Dick, and you have to do what you think is best at the time. You can't hedge every bet. What else can I do—sit down and cry over my lousy lot in life?"

The ridiculous picture this conjured in Howard's mind forced a smile to his lips, diffusing some of the tension.

"You know, Mac," he said in a more relaxed tone, "you're just the kind of man this country wants for its president—you've got honesty, integrity . . ."

"Just what they want, huh? Yet my approval rating is still only 29%. Harris said last week that Foster would beat me 63% to 35%. Even after my speech those figures had only changed to 59% and 39%."

"Well, that's true. You're the kind of man they want, only trouble is—they don't know it! It's a rotten irony that you have to fight tooth and nail for the office."

"But I am willing to fight. I *will* fight."

"Then let me help."

"You can't think I don't want your help . . . that I don't *need* your help," MacFarlane answered emphatically. "You're the best, Dick. If you can't pull this off, no one can. But I'm the candidate. It has to be my campaign. You can't squeeze it into your mold. If I let you do that, then I'd not be much of a candidate at all, and certainly not one you'd respect."

"I respect you! But it's not getting us very far."

"Come on, Dick, let's sit down. We're standing here like two cocks in a fight. Come on." He nudged Howard into a chair and took the one adjacent to it. "You want to advise me—well, advise me on Moscow. What do you think the Soviet stance will be?"

"I think you're humoring me," replied Howard skeptically.

"You're one of the best Soviet analysts around."

"Okay, I'm humored!"

The two men laughed together, and when Howard spoke again, it seemed more like old times.

"I think Kudinsky's looking for a chance to back down in Iran," he said. "Don't get me wrong—I don't trust him any more than the rest of them. But whatever his reasons, I have the sense he'd prefer nonaggression. I think they got into this without realizing they bit off more than they could chew. Just a guess. But then Kudinsky could be the minority on this one."

"Would he break under pressure from the rest of the Kremlin?"

"He's agreed to the summit," Howard answered. "That's something. It shows he's still got some pull over the hawkish element."

"I wish we knew the true extent of his power."

"Our sources indicate rumblings in the Politburo—that Kudinsky's hold is shaky."

"Their intelligence could say the same of me," laughed MacFarlane. "And they'd be right."

"So tell me, Mac—what are you planning to propose to him?"

For a brief instant MacFarlane came very close to telling his friend. He felt as if he were trying to trick Howard by keeping his actual plan a secret—and he hated the feeling.

Jarvis MacFarlane was attempting to walk a tightrope even he himself did not always see clearly. His soul yearned for peace. He had been given—he could hardly even say the words—what amounted to nothing less than a heavenly imperative to find a way to keep peace in the world. Wasn't that what he had been told to do? What else could the message mean? What else could the *truth* the Voice spoke of refer to? Yet after the last Legation meeting he could not help but be confused. Daniel and Dmitri and Peter had spoken words that shed an altogether different light on the scope and possible purpose behind the vision.

How could he possibly doubt that God was speaking to him, as fantastic as the very words sounded! The uncanny resemblance between what the Voice had said and Daniel's words at the last meeting! There could be no other explanation, even though it defied all that was rational and logical. He was still a babe, but would quickly grow into the sonship for which he was even now being prepared. The soil of his heart was good soil, rich for hundredfold reproduction. And now that the seed had been planted, its fruit was sure.

Until the last meeting he had gradually come to interpret his priorities as twofold: talk to Kudinsky and make every effort to find a permanent and lasting peace between the two superpowers while at the same time standing firm against further Soviet expansion if his talks with the premier failed. Two seemingly contradictory resolves.

If the public interpreted what he was trying to do as weakness and condemned him for it, so be it. Since his revelation to Karen and Jeremy Manning, he had gained a renewed confidence in the direction he must follow. When doubts came—and after this last meeting he had a host of new ones!—they were offset by the support and loyalty of his two young confidants, and his knowledge that throughout the city, though they knew nothing of the vision, twelve men were praying for him.

If only he had more experience with this sort of thing. Going to church on occasion, or even reading a passage now and then in a Bible was *nothing* like this! To hear the voice of . . . of Jesus . . . or whoever it was!

What he'd seen and heard that night in the Oval Office was from another world—he was sure of that! And it was like nothing he'd ever heard from a church pulpit! Every time he replayed it in his mind, he wondered all over again if he was going loony!

Yet even that thought could not stop the imperative . . . the urgency . . . the accountability he somehow knew was resting upon him.

*Witness*—that's what the Voice had said . . . witness to the truth. Witness to the truth and prepare the way for peace!

Yes, he *knew* what he must do, even if he didn't grasp all the implications of that night. He *had* to tell Peter and Daniel. They could help, they could pray, they could give him advice. Yet he wished he could work more of it out himself first.

There were times—rare enough, but increasing in frequency—when he almost felt confident enough to take the story of his visionary experience to the world. But that *would* be crazy, especially at this juncture in time. His own people would leave him, Foster would make mincemeat of such an announcement, and the Soviets and other world leaders would laugh him to scorn. If he went public, there would be *no* chance of peace.

No, his best course was still to keep quiet.

He had to keep as many options open as possible, for he remained uncertain what his exact course should be following what he hoped would be his private talk with Kudinsky.

Because no matter how the premier reacted, MacFarlane still had a long and rocky road ahead of him.

All these thoughts and more raced through his mind as he briefly debated about telling Dick Howard the whole truth. But he knew in an instant that his revelation would be too much for his old friend. He knew Dick Howard pretty well, and he gave the term "no nonsense" new meaning. If he acceded at all to the validity of the vision—which was highly doubtful—he would never agree to MacFarlane actually acting on it. And his more probable reaction would be to think his friend had gone off the deep end.

So MacFarlane opted to reply to Howard's question only on the level of partial Plan A, followed by Plan B. It was this portion of the summit the world would be watching. If he couldn't somehow arrange what he had been scheming and preparing for these last four months—a private and honest exchange with Kudinsky about *genuine* peace—then there might be nothing more he could do in Moscow than what he now revealed to Howard.

"I'll beg him for the good of mankind to consider their course in Iran, and to withdraw their troops. Then I'll ask him to join me at the peace table and go much further to insure *permanent* peace than Bush and Gorbachev did in Berlin in '94."

"And when he says, 'No deal. Our troops are necessary in the

Persian Gulf region to protect the security interests of our nation'?"

"Then I will go to Plan B and demand that they back off from Iran and pull their troops into a stand-down mode at least as far back as the Aral Sea."

"They will never agree to that! They'll claim you're infringing on their national sovereignty."

"Then I'll have no choice but reluctantly to step into the role of commander in chief. I've already put 20,000 troops on alert, and before leaving for Moscow I would instruct the joint chiefs—in secret, of course—to get another 200,000 men ready to pour into the Middle East at a moment's notice."

"What if Kudinsky calls your bluff?" asked Howard.

MacFarlane sighed, rose from his chair, and walked toward the window. He stared out for a few moments without speaking. All he could think of was that fateful night in February. What would *He* have him do? How would *He* have him answer the agonizing question Dick had just put to him? When finally he turned back into the room, his face bore the strain from the uncertainty of his tentative steps of faith.

"I don't know, Dick," he said. "I honestly don't know. Just a month ago I was willing to listen seriously to the military option. And to a certain extent I must still consider that. I will not put troops on alert for the sole purpose of a bluff. Perhaps our being willing to fight a limited war now over the right of the countries of this world to exist freely without outside domination might well prevent a more catastrophic holocaust later on. Might that be the price of a lasting peace? I don't know. It's a course I have to consider. Vietnam made us lose sight of being willing to fight for freedom. It's that willingness which made America the country it is. But I don't want war. How sincerely I pray it doesn't come down to a military confrontation. I pray Kudinsky is wise enough to see that we must keep peace together. Anyway, if the talks get to that point, by then he'll probably think I'm crazy enough to take military action."

"What do you mean?"

"Oh, nothing," MacFarlane answered vaguely.

"One thing I can say, Mac—you've got guts. If you pull this off, you'll be more popular than Jimmy Carter after Camp David. Even if you have to order troops in, your ratings will surge. Any strong action can only help you. This could be the best thing for you politically. But if you fail, or if the Russians make you look weak, the election's Foster's for the taking."

MacFarlane rubbed his eyes. He was exhausted, and he still had a lesson with Peter tonight, to continue touching up his opening remarks to Kudinsky, which he was in the process of memorizing. It was becoming more difficult to concentrate on his studies. He wanted to sit down with Peter and talk about spiritual things instead.

"Maybe I'm not in my right mind, threatening war on the eve of a possible change in the leadership of our country," he said at length.

"Don't talk like that, Mac!"

"I don't know what to do sometimes, Dick. It seems I have few choices. Boy, I wish I had the likes of Henry Kissinger to help guide me through this one!"

"You still do have some choices where the election's concerned, though," persisted Howard.

"That's what I like about you, Dick—you've got a one-track mind. So what are my choices?"

"Harley Wilson is still waiting for your call."

MacFarlane turned away again, then paced about for some time in silence.

He had not wanted to think about what he would do if he failed in Moscow. The need to win the election would be even more imperative in that case, to give him another four years to work on the Soviets. Yet failure would almost certainly destroy his chances of victory. A classic rock-and-a-hard-place scenario.

Some outside force seemed to be pushing him toward a union with Harley Wilson. Perhaps such an alliance wouldn't be as bad as he thought. There were ways to keep men like that in tow.

Suddenly the Voice in his vision echoed in his mind—that Voice so pure and compelling, so urgent yet so full of peace. Instinctively MacFarlane knew that *He* would never sanction alliance with a man like Wilson. So how could he, with a clear conscience, use Wilson to achieve the very ends the vision was driving him toward?

At last, in a moment of frustration and weakness, perhaps the result of the pounding in his temples rather than any overt decision, MacFarlane offered a compromise.

"Dick, there is no way I can have that man on my cabinet," he said with resignation. "I don't like him, and I think he's crooked. But if you can get him to agree to some lesser terms, I'll at least talk to him when I get back from Moscow."

Howard grimaced. MacFarlane saw it and knew why his friend was not pleased with his answer. Everything was stacked in Wilson's favor, and the union boss was well aware of it. He didn't have to agree to anything lesser, and thus there was no way he would.

To Dick Howard, MacFarlane's token compromise mounted to nothing better than an outright rejection.

# FORTY-NINE

What do you want to do? Shall I cancel your trip?" asked Andrew Nyborg.

"No, dammit! We're going to go ahead with it!" Foster shouted at his colleague. "So the white-livered fool wants to try to steal my strength and boast himself as the bringer of peace! Well then, if he makes peace the issue of this campaign, we'll beat him at his own game! No—no—I'm going to meet with Bolotnikov as planned."

Patrick Foster was far too agitated to sit down. He raved about the room like an angry bull, venting his wrath against the opponent he scorned.

"If word of this gets out," cautioned Lavender, "you'll look like you're undercutting the peace process."

"Word won't leak out! Besides, when that fool MacFarlane comes back from Moscow with his tail between his legs, the time will be perfect for us to step in and announce that *we* have been successful in concluding an agreement with the chairman of the Soviet Presidium. Who knows, it may turn out even better for us this way. But damn! How could MacFarlane have found out about our plan!"

"Who's to say he has?" asked Nyborg. "His summit may be a completely independent action."

"Baloney!" put in Bateman pointedly. "You don't really believe that, do you, Andy? MacFarlane's not clever enough to have thought of it on his own. And neither is he clever enough to pull it off. I think Pat's right. He must have found out what we were up to. There must be a leak somewhere."

"No one knew our plans," insisted Nyborg.

"Obviously someone got wind of it. I can't help thinking of that Manning kid. Something about him bothered me. Anyone seen him around lately?" asked Foster.

"You heard about what happened?"

"Yeah. Did he make out our boys?" asked Lavender.

"They think so. He got a good look at them."

"Has he been back?"

"Only to pick up his things and leave word he was quitting."

"Enough! Enough!" interrupted Foster. "Harv, I thought I told you to make sure that Manning kid didn't cause us any problems!"

"Don't worry. I'll put some other guys on it, and next time they won't mess—"

"What's done's done! Don't try anything more with the kid now. Once, maybe he'll chalk it up to dirty politics. Twice, he'll probably go to the cops—or the press. No, leave him alone and let's get on with it. Andy, I'm depending on you to have this Bolotnikov thing set up. And, Harv, I want more on this deal with MacFarlane and his idiotic Russian lessons. He may have trumped us with the summit announcement, but if we can dig up the dirt, we may scuttle him yet. I want MacFarlane cut off wherever he turns—whatever it takes! Do I make myself clear?"

# FIFTY

At eleven o'clock at night the 88th Street subway station was nearly deserted. The last train would be along soon.

Kenny Gallagher glanced nervously at his watch.

He'd been jumpy all day—and with good reason. For the last few weeks he'd been conscious every minute of Wilson's ever-present tail. Either Wilson was waiting for him to mess up or just looking for the right time and place to waste him. Day after day he'd lived with the fear and uncertainty, and at last could take it no more. He'd had enough of not knowing when he woke up in the morning, if it might be his last morning. He was scared, and he knew that was right where Wilson wanted him.

Yesterday the moment had come when he'd made the fateful decision. Whoever the guy was behind him, he was sick of him! It was time for Wilson to be scared for a change! Gallagher had debated with himself for weeks, and finally he was ready to take action. They'd left him no choice!

When he'd walked out on Wilson—or more correctly, when Wilson had thrown him out—he had not gone empty-handed. He'd made photocopies of certain incriminating records—papers that could put Wilson away for a lot of years if the Feds got hold of them. Yesterday he'd finally decided to use them, but not for the FBI. First he was going to bleed Wilson with them—make him sweat. In the process he'd stash away a nice little bankroll to retire on. After all, he deserved it. For ten years he'd worked his butt off for the illustrious labor leader, done his dirty work, and even taken the rap on that embezzlement charge five years ago—for which he'd served eighteen months in Leavenworth.

Trying to do a number on Wilson was a big risk. Probably would wind up getting him killed. But he had a kid who wanted to go to college, and Wilson had cut him off with nothing. Besides, Wilson might still be intending trouble for him regardless, so at least he could try to go out with a few bucks for his kid.

Yesterday Gallagher had telephoned the New York office. His plan was simple: he told his former boss that he would take what he had to the FBI unless Wilson met him that night in the alley behind the old United Grocers building off Manhattan's East 137th Street with $50,000 in cash. But Gallagher wasn't stupid. He had some insurance. He'd put a few of the papers into an envelope, addressed it to "The FBI, New York," and stuffed it into a mailbox on his way to the meeting. A few others he'd given to a friend. He wanted to spread his security around.

Not stupid, maybe. Just dumb. Of all the idiotic places to arrange a meet with a streetwise man like Wilson. Yet back alleys and deserted warehouses were what Kenny Gallagher knew best. Neither did he have the savvy to realize Wilson's man had seen him at the mailbox, had called Wilson, and that before the meet even took place the unopened parcel was being retrieved by one of Wilson's inside men at the post office. The labor leader had so many people—from union leaders to street thugs to government officials—in his pocket that the penny-ante tactics of a lowlife like Gallagher merely amused him.

Now Gallagher heard the train approaching. His eyes darted around; he was completely alone. This was one time he would have liked a crowd around. Maybe he should have taken a cab.

In a moment the train ground to a stop before him and he climbed aboard. The car was empty. He found a seat on a graffiti-carved bench and, sitting on its very edge, drummed his fingers against his knee. At the next stop an old lady carrying a grocery bag boarded. Though she didn't even glance at him, he felt better having some companionship.

The train stopped again and the old woman stiffly rose from her seat and inched her way off the train. Then two men came aboard through the open door at the other end of the car.

Gallagher went cold. They were Wilson's men!

Instantly he jumped from his seat. Even as he did so, the men started toward him. He raced forward, following the old woman, shooting his hand out between the closing doors. The sensors reopened the doors briefly, long enough for him to squeeze through before they slammed shut and the car lurched forward again. The two thugs remained trapped inside.

But even as the big Irishman sprinted for the stairway, he heard the screech of locking train wheels on steel tracks, and he knew his pursuers had pulled the emergency cord. When he was halfway up the flight of stairs to the street, he could hear two sets of footsteps pounding after him.

He brushed past the grocery-bag lady, emerged onto the street, glanced quickly to his right and left, then shot across through the thin night traffic. Only a couple horns blared their annoyance. Turning to the right, he sped away, with no clear destination, only frantic to cover distance. He was not fast enough, however, his lame leg impeding his progress, and within moments he spotted the two men behind him.

In a cold panic, Gallagher did the one thing he should never have done. Rounding a corner, and hearing the footsteps gaining behind him, he darted quickly into an alley. His labored gait was now almost beyond his own control, his leaden legs barely able to interpret the signal from his brain screaming, "Danger!" Hardly noticing, he tripped over something in his path. He heard the faint tinkle of coins scattering across the opening of the alley, hardly distinguishing it from the clank of the tin cup which had held them. In such a terrified stupor, he neither heard nor responded to the startled groggy voice calling out into the night: "Hey! Watch what you's about! Can't you leave an old man what little he has?"

But the old beggar, sensing trouble, kept his peace when, a few seconds later, two more sets of footsteps entered the darkened alley. Whatever all the commotion was about, he'd best wait till it was over to look about for his scattered wealth.

He saw nothing and heard nothing more, other than the brief

sound of a struggle, a dull thud, a choking sound, and then two sets of steps—walking this time—leaving the alley the way they had come. As they rounded the building where he sat crouched in darkness, he heard a voice say, "Well, that's the end of this rotten assignment, Smitty."

"Yeah, I'll call Frank as soon as we get back to the place."

"He better pay us what he said."

"Don't worry. Frank may be a bruiser, but he's nobody's fool. He knows to keep his end of the bargain or he'll end up like Gallagher!"

When the voices had died away in the distance, the old man began to grope about the filth-strewn alley for his cup and the few nickels and dimes he had lost. He never knew that only ten yards away, lying in a pool of blood from a knife wound straight through the heart, lay a three-time losing Irishman who would never send his sixteen-year-old to college.

# FIFTY-ONE

The phone rang in Dick Howard's ear.

He rubbed his eyes and glanced at the clock on the bedside table. It was 5:00 A.M.

He grabbed the receiver on the third ring, his wife mumbled something incoherent, and he urged her back to sleep. Then he turned his attention to the caller.

"Howard here . . . who is it?"

His statement was followed by a series of grunts and nods, finally concluding with, "Okay, put him through. I'll decide if he's a crank."

He waited a few seconds until a muffled voice came through on the other end.

"Is this Mr. Howard . . . the attorney general?"

"Yes, it is. What do you want?"

"Can't talk over the phone. I've got to see you in person."

"What's this all about?"

"Harley Wilson."

Howard's lips twitched. That name was beginning to haunt him. "What about Wilson?" he said.

"Not over the phone." The voice was clipped and breathless, as if the caller was genuinely scared stiff. "I'm in New York, but I can be there in three hours."

"Who are you?"

"Nobody you would know. Name's Jack Hensley. Please, you've got to see me."

"Okay," resolved Howard. "Eight-thirty, my office in the Justice Building."

"No. I can't be seen going in there. Wilson may have a tail on me. Make it in front of the Washington Monument at nine."

---

Three and a half hours later, Dick Howard was standing before the great obelisk commemorating the father of the nation. Small knots of tourists had already begun to mill about. It was warm and muggy, even at that hour of the morning, and Howard glanced impatiently at his watch every now and then.

By 9:30 he was beginning to wonder if the whole thing was a hoax. Just as he was about to head back to his car, he spotted a nervous little man approaching. He had never laid eyes on the man before, but he knew beyond doubt that this was Hensley. The stranger emitted intense anxiety. He walked with jerky, uncertain steps, his eyes darting back and forth.

He seemed to recognize Howard immediately, probably from news photos, and edged up to him like a dog who had spied a strange object but wasn't quite sure if it was safe.

"I'm Hensley, Mr. Howard," he said in that same breathless, fretful voice.

"It's 9:30," answered Howard sharply. He had never had much patience with tardiness.

"I'm sorry . . . I got hung up getting out of New York."

"All right, what do you have? I'm on a tight schedule."

As they strolled slowly around the monument park, Hensley poured out a stunning tale—crooked books, blackmail, all sorts of rackets, extortion, skimming money from union pension funds, even murder. By the time he was through, Harley Wilson came off looking almost as bad as Al Capone.

"Why should I believe you?" asked Howard at length.

"Because I used to work for the scum," replied Hensley, by now relaxed a bit.

"And now?"

"No more."

"Why the change of heart?"

"Because Kenny Gallagher was a friend of mine."

"Gallagher? Who's that—someone I should know?"

"Like I said—a friend. He used to work for Wilson too."

"Used to?"

"They found him in an alley last night. Stabbed in the heart."

"Any witnesses?" asked the attorney general.

Hensley shook his head.

"Then there's no proof Wilson was behind it."

"It was Wilson all right! I know it had to be. Kenny was going to blackmail him with what he knew."

"You have proof of that?"

"Kenny gave me these." Hensley pulled some papers out of his pocket. "He said he was giving me these few, just for insurance."

Howard took them, glanced through them briefly, thought a moment, then said, "Even if we could prove some blackmail scheme, you can't prove murder on hearsay."

"Are you telling me there's nothing you can do?"

All the while Hensley had been spinning out his tale, Howard had been unable to shake one thought from his mind: What if the press got hold of this story? He hardly bothered to ask himself if there was any truth to what the nervous little man was telling him. All he could think of was that if Wilson was destroyed, with him would vanish the small hope Mac might have at a second term.

At length, in reply to Hensley's pleading question, the attorney general answered with a bold-faced lie: "You can believe me, Mr. Hensley, if these things you have told me are true, and especially if Wilson was behind the murder of your friend, there is nothing more the Justice Department would like than to nail him. You can be assured we will investigate thoroughly."

"But you said none of this would do any good?"

"If what you say is on the level, I'll do my best to put him away."

"I'll do anything to help," offered Hensley.

"You'd better let the Justice Department handle it from here on out," said Howard. "By the way, have you told anyone else what you just told me?"

"Not a soul, sir. Kenny once said that the only way to get Wilson was to go all the way to the top, because he has nearly every other official in his hip-pocket."

"Good," replied Howard. "That is, we'd better keep it that way for a while. If Wilson had any idea we were watching him, he'd clear his tracks real fast. This way, we can wait for him to slip up. So don't mention a word of our little conversation to anyone."

"Yes, sir. Thank you for seeing me."

The two men shook hands and walked off in different directions. While Hensley was visibly less agitated than when he came, Howard's palms were sweating. He had to think, to sort all this out.

Why did this have to come up right now?

---

Dick Howard went back to his office, made a few calls to see if he could verify Hensley's identity, then called the NYPD to verify Gallagher's death. Everything had gone down just as Hensley told him.

Then he sat down to take a closer look at the photocopied records Hensley had given him.

The papers showed unquestionable abuse of labor funds and certainly indicated more than sufficient probable cause to proceed with an investigation of Wilson. No jury would indict a man for murder on such evidence, but it was a place to start, a handle. There was enough for the foundation of a case. A murder weapon (no doubt lying at the bottom of the Hudson River by now) and an eyewitness would help. But enough digging might turn up something. At the very least, he could make life miserable for the union boss.

That is, *if* he pushed it.

Wait a minute! Here he was, the highest law enforcement officer in the land. How could he even entertain the notion of doing less?

Yet from the moment Hensley's story began to unfold, his mind had raced with schemes of how he might keep all this under wraps—at least until after November. By then Wilson would be expendable. But until the polls had closed, though he hated to admit it, they needed the man. He was simply too influential.

The only problem now might be this Hensley. If he got impatient or shot his mouth off, it could kill their plan. And he didn't seem like the sort who could be bought off.

Howard paced around his office, his thoughts drifting toward the election. Try as he might, he could not think of any plan for victory half so effective as gaining Wilson's powerful endorsement. It was the only chance they had! If he could only get Mac to see it his way.

Suddenly a whole new train of thought exploded in his mind.

It made him feel weak all over, and suddenly cold, as if all the blood had drained out of his heart.

There might just be a way to turn this incident into the *assurance* of victory in November. A fantastic, outlandish, horribly evil way! To entertain the merest notion of it, even for a fleeting moment, was unthinkable.

But . . . it just might work!

The first thing would be to discreetly put some meat onto the bones of his case. It wouldn't have to stand up in a court of law. He merely had to have enough to put a righteous scare into Wilson. Then with enough evidence in hand to keep him in line, he would make another call on the labor leader.

The whole possibility made Howard tingle with exhilaration. Just the thought of making Wilson squirm was a satisfying enough feeling. It kept him from thinking through the total ramifications of his plan. All he could think was that they had Wilson now.

When he was finished with the labor boss, Wilson would not only agree to support MacFarlane, no strings attached, he would go down on his knees for the privilege!

"Ha, ha!" he laughed out loud. "We just might be able to pull this win off after all!"

# FIFTY-TWO

Jeremy was the first to arrive at the White House, and Karen approached him with a warm smile.

"You're looking better than the last time I saw you," she said, slipping her arm through his.

"You mean my pale face and palpitating heart . . . I tell you, that was some frightening drive!"

"Any verdict on your beautiful Mustang?"

"It's okay. My friend checked the suspension and said it was undamaged, but it'll need a little bodywork where I grazed the embankment before I spun out across the road."

"And the brakes?"

"A tiny hole had been punctured in the fluid line, so it would leak out slowly. That's fixed now too."

"I'm just glad you weren't hurt."

"They tried!"

"The whole idea of you being run off the road gives me the creeps," she said with a shiver. "What kind of hoodlums—"

Just then the other dinner guest arrived, along with their host, and she was unable to continue.

"You remember my daughter, Peter?" said the president.

"Yes, though it's been a while—and you've grown into a beautiful young woman!" said Peter Venzke. "You remind me of your mother."

"Thank you," Karen replied. "It's nice to see you again, Dr. Venzke."

"Please—no *doctors* tonight!"

Karen laughed, and the president turned to introduce the professor to Jeremy.

After the two had shaken hands, Peter said, "My good friend tells me you have joined his staff."

"Yes," Jeremy replied. "I guess when he heard I was no longer with my former employer, he felt he should take me on as a charity case," he added with a grin. "I'll be working in the press room."

"So you are a journalist?"

"Not exactly, but journalism *is* more or less my stock in trade. And I have had some campaign experience," he added lamely. To tell the truth, Jeremy was not sure what his exact job around here would be, or why it had been offered him.

"And did you meet Karen as a result of wanting to come work for the president?"

"Actually, professor, I was involved with the president's campaign for quite some time before I met Karen," said Jeremy. "Although I'll have to admit that it's largely because of her that I'm where I am right now."

Karen burst out laughing at Jeremy's elastic way of trying to keep to the truth with his responses.

"Come, come!" said MacFarlane, laughing himself. "We can have no secrets between us. Until a couple days ago this young man was on Senator Foster's campaign staff! What do you think of that, Peter? His first major assignment was to spy on Karen. That's what got him into trouble and started all this!"

"Well, well! That *does* make for interesting conversation, I would think."

MacFarlane wondered if either of the young people had caught the irony in his statement. If only his secret could be dispensed with in a couple of swift sentences! It was with relief that he heard his private line begin ringing, and he excused himself to answer it.

"Sorry," he said, striding back a moment or two later. "A little snafu regarding the hotel accommodations in Moscow."

"Nothing serious, is it, Dad?"

"The Cosmos Hotel was having some difficulty clearing a wing at such late notice. We'll have to make a switch. But the Rossia can handle us."

"I still can't believe we're going!" exclaimed Karen. "I can't believe *I'm* actually going!"

"Moscow or bust—!" said Jeremy blithely, then stopped short, realizing the implications of his statement.

But the president was not easily daunted. "You hit it on the nose, Jeremy!" he said, laughing. "And if we can get a score of rooms on three week's notice at the height of the tourist season, who knows what other wonders we'll be able to perform."

The dinner was enjoyable, and the conversation easily settled into grooves that only the truest forms of friendship can carve out. Karen was happy to see what seemed a return of her father's old buoyancy. There were still brief moments when she detected him turning inward and thoughtful, but in general his mood was light and relaxed. She concluded that sharing his burden with them, and perhaps taking some action in the form of the Moscow trip, had at least made his heavy responsibilities more tolerable.

From the president's perspective, the dinner was a success. By inviting his old friend and his new associate to the White House for an informal social occasion, he hoped to diffuse the increasing speculation that something "out of the ordinary" was going on between him and the professor. Plus, he had already made public mention of his attempt to learn "a few Russian phrases" in advance of his trip, for which he had enlisted Professor Venzke's help.

Secondly, deep inside Jarvis MacFarlane knew he was standing on a threshold in his life. Looking back he saw the faces of his old friends, Jake and Dick, and his political associates and colleagues from over the years. But as he looked ahead, the eyes he saw looking back into his were all new. And unexpectedly he realized that these new eyes saw deeper into his soul and understood more of this path that had been laid out for him to follow than his former associates ever could. Though he was still reluctant to make any commitments, even to himself, or to actually walk forever *through* the door at whose threshold he stood poised, yet he sensed himself being drawn, pulled, stretched forward into a world which for him was unknown. And he wanted those who, for better or worse and for whatever reasons, were part of this process of growth with him to know one another. Destiny . . . fate—maybe God!—had made these three his closest compatriots in this insane sojourn of the soul, and he now found himself looking to them for the companionship, solace, understanding, and advice that he had previously sought from his political advisors.

For now, getting Peter on familiar terms with his daughter and all of them getting to know Manning better was at least a place to start.

Lastly he hoped—though it was a wild idea—he might find some suitable way to tell Peter about the vision. He needed to tell him—and before the Moscow trip. He needed Peter's full spiritual support, not just his language expertise. He was afraid he would be very much alone on the Russians' turf. That was one reason he was taking Karen *and* Jeremy along. He would need all the help and support he could get from people who really understood what he was about.

Toward the end of the evening as they sat chatting over coffee in the comfortable living room of the president's private quarters, MacFarlane looked around in satisfaction. Jeremy and Peter seemed to be hitting it off, for which he was deeply thankful. As the others carried on a discussion concerning a book all three had read recently, he found himself drifting into introspective reflections regarding the last few months.

He recalled the private meeting Peter had set up where he first met Daniel. He had been full of questions—and reservations! Everything had been so new and strange. Yet as the weeks passed, he had found many of the words of that first encounter coming back to him out of his subconscious. And each time a piece of that original conversation returned to his memory, it carried with it deeper and more far-reaching meaning.

"Who are you?" he had asked, once Peter had introduced him to Daniel and given him the briefest of sketches of their purpose in speaking to him.

"We in this city call ourselves *the Legation.* But that is merely a designation of convenience. It has no significance beyond that."

"What does the name mean?"

"A committee, a collection of emissaries, delegates—an embassy established in foreign territory to carry out the mission of its King."

"Is it a society?"

"No."

"But it *is* an organization?"

"Not as such. Only a knitting together of men and women of common purpose."

"There is no structure?"

"None."

"Are you a church?"

"We are part of *the* church, but we are not *a* church."

"Who is your pastor, your clergyman?"

"We have none."

"Where do you meet?"

"Nowhere."

"A church that doesn't meet!" exclaimed MacFarlane.

"I said we are not *a* church," answered Daniel. "We are individuals, some of whom meet, some of whom, I presume, never do."

"What are your rules, then—your guidelines for existence?"

"We have none."

"What makes you part of the church then?"

"That we do the work of our head, the King in whose name we have been sent."

"And who is this king?"

"Jesus Christ."

"What is your creed?"

"Jesus Christ."

"What do you believe concerning Him?"

"We believe *in* Him, not *about* Him. We believe that He is alive, that He is among us, and that He is presently raising up a vast host of men and women, like us, to proclaim His presence and prepare people for His visible return again to the earth."

A lengthy pause followed. And though they were meeting together over lunch, MacFarlane found it difficult to eat.

"But you must have some tenets," he insisted at length, "some doctrines or beliefs that hold you together and make you what you are?"

"Only obedience."

"Obedience to what?"

"To what He has instructed and commanded and shown us through His life, and to what He now tells us to do."

"Is the Legation nationwide?"

"As I said, our local group, if you want to call it that, is known by that name, but only to ourselves. As a name, a title, no—the Legation is not nationwide."

"But you say there is a vast host of you?"

"Indeed, vaster than you or I can comprehend."

"Nationwide?"

"Worldwide."

"Who are the *we* you speak of? If there is no organization, no connection, no earthly leadership, I do not understand how you can speak of being knit together in common purpose."

"We are but a small part of a worldwide network of envoys of the truth. In the physical world, we are not connected as such. But in the world of the spirit, where we function, every tiniest facet of our work is in harmony with every other, because God our Father and the Father of Jesus Christ guides every detail. We have no need to know all He is doing, only to faithfully obey in the sphere of His work to which He has called us individually. God is raising us up independently, but always the message given is similar—one of preparation, of putting houses in order, of proclaiming true peace. It is a message of preparation for the coming of our King, of readying ourselves to be His bride, of warning those that are asleep of the coming judgment."

"And you say you are not the only ones speaking these things?"

"You could go to any city in this land, to any country on the globe, and—if the Spirit of God were guiding your footsteps—find men and women being called out, speaking prophetic messages, feeling the same urgings, their hearts opened to the same truths, their spirits seeing the same visions, their hands and feet being led to the same totality of obedience to their common Master."

"Are you their leader?"

Daniel laughed. "God is raising up people in every city, in every country, on every continent to proclaim this message of unity and preparation. There are no human 'leaders.' Granted, there are some in high places—even within the governments of the world. But there are probably more among the poor and powerless. God is raising up this message to go forth within the clergy, in the laity, among Catholics, among Protestants, even among Jews—among those in big churches, in tiny ones, and even among those with no church affiliation at all—in cities, in the country, among the educated, among the ignorant. Everywhere throughout the world men, women, even children are being raised up—always with this message on their hearts. Those of us right here—some of whom I hope you will be able to meet—are but a small part of this huge movement of God's Spirit. No one is greater, no one is lesser. All listen to the same Voice, for there is but one message, though it has several components—unity, warning, preparation, judgment, obedience, purity, readiness!"

"Well, I would like to hear more," said the president at length. "From the little Peter has told me, and from what I have heard today, it strikes me that I would do well to learn more. I have my own reasons, which I'd rather not go into at the moment. But if we could arrange it, I would like to meet with you again."

"Peter has already spoken to me about gathering together several of our number to meet with you—that is, if you so desire."

"I do," replied MacFarlane.

"For your protection, and ours, it will be imperative that any future meetings be held in absolute secrecy."

"Is it such a clandestine affair as that?" asked the president.

"The times are not what they seem. There are many forces at work who would seek to discredit you, Mr. President. There are among us several men of reputation, one of whom has published a book concerning these matters. For you to be seen with any of us, to meet openly, to invite us to the White House—considering the things some of our number have said publicly—I fear would spell an immediate end to your chances of reelection."

"I appreciate your concern. But I can hardly believe—"

"We are known as a radical organization, Mr. President. I hope you will wait to make that determination for yourself. But I must make sure you understand the potential danger to yourself if you associate with us. Also, it is imperative that we are not perceived as having any political leanings—for the sake of the message we need to give to the widest possible audience. Thus, for our benefit too, I would hope to keep our association hidden for a season. And the life of one of our number—a Russian attached to the embassy—has been threatened as a result of his outspoken spiritual views. He already meets with us secretly. So you see, there are a number of consequences involved."

"What do you propose?" asked MacFarlane.

"I would like to assemble several of our most trustworthy men. We will come wherever you like, whenever you like. We will be at your service, Mr. President, and will share in greater depth these things we see, while we continue talking and praying and seeking wisdom from one another. You will be welcome among us."

"Agreed."

"I will leave it to you and Peter to make whatever initial arrangements are necessary. I understand you are seeing one another regularly already."

The president nodded.

As Daniel rose and shook MacFarlane's hand, he added, "I consider it a privilege to serve you in this way. I pray we have the opportunity to meet again, soon."

When he had exited by a side door, the President turned his gaze across the table to his friend and exhaled a long sigh.

"We didn't eat much, but this is certainly a lunch I'll never forget!" he said.

Drifting back to the present, MacFarlane saw that Peter was making signs of leaving. He had stood and was shaking Manning's hand. MacFarlane wondered how long he had been daydreaming and was grateful that his lapse did not seem to have distracted the others.

# FIFTY-THREE

Joint Chiefs Chairman Emmit Howson had just addressed a distant, right-wing offshoot of the VFW, formed only five years earlier to voice concern felt by the most conservative of veterans that the U.S. was getting soft militarily. It was one of the few places where the chairman found receptive ears for his stubbornly hawkish views, and the gathering was not widely attended nor publicized.

Ironically, Howson's most important engagement of the evening followed his speech and took place far from public eyes. Indeed, the subjects of the two appointments could not have been more divergent. But politics, as the pundits said, made strange bedfellows. And the chairman was about to discover just how strange—surprising even himself by his decision. Some gut feeling, however, told him it was the right thing to do.

---

"I owe you one, Emmit."

"Just so long as you understand I don't make a habit of divulging top-secret information," said the chairman of the joint chiefs somberly, raising his tumbler of bourbon toward his companion.

Patrick Foster raised his own martini in return and smiled. "Understood perfectly," he replied, and sipped his drink. "I am curious, though, what prompted you to do so on this particular occasion."

General Emmit Howson pondered the rim of his glass a moment before attempting to frame a reply. For the time being at least he dropped his military facade. He was speaking to an equal now—perhaps more than an equal. This could well be the man who would shortly be his boss.

"I'm sick of all the pussy-footing around by this administration," he finally said. "Up until just a couple weeks ago MacFarlane had turned down every last recommendation made by the joint chiefs regarding the Iranian situation. Suddenly he's talking tough, but if you ask me, it's only for political purposes. When push comes to shove, I don't think he has the guts to face them off. I know the man's my so-called commander in chief, but I tell you, I've had it with him! And you know what scares me the most? With all the talk of peace, he's going to lead us into a war. But because of his ineptitude, it'll be a war we can't possibly win. If we're going to have to get involved militarily, which looks likely to me, I wish he'd let me do my job and run the show!"

"Given my positions, this sounds like a speech you should be making to DuBois," commented Foster dryly.

"DuBois! He's finished. Even if he stole the nomination from MacFarlane, which I don't think he will, you'd beat him by twenty points. No, I'm afraid the future of this country doesn't rest with either of the two Democrats."

Foster smiled but waited for the general to go on.

"I consider myself a decent judge of character," Howson continued. "You and I may differ considerably on the philosophical aspects of the military, but I think you know what you're about a whole lot better than MacFarlane does. You've got a solid military background."

He paused to sip his drink, then added, almost as an aside, "I've got to tell you, Pat—I can't make heads or tails of all this new dawn malarkey you've been spewing out lately. But I know the people eat it up, so I guess you have no choice. But when push comes to shove with the Soviets, my instinct tells me your past background will come to the fore. And I'd sure rather have you in my corner than MacFarlane! So all this is just a roundabout way of saying that I've decided to put my money on you, Pat."

The general drained off his bourbon in a single gulp. "I've been in three wars and won every one of them," he said. "And I'm not about to lose the next one because of some lily-livered, pantywaist.

Whatever you say about the evolution of mankind's consciousness, or whatever the heck it is, I just don't think you'll let that happen."

Foster merely nodded, and refrained from commenting that Vietnam could hardly be considered a win. Instead he beckoned a waitress to refill their drinks.

"So," Foster said when he had a fresh martini in his hand and the waitress had departed, leaving them alone in their dim corner of the Dome, a secluded watering hole not far from the Capitol, "what is that, ah . . . tidbit . . . you wanted to pass on to me?"

"It may not be of much actual help beyond giving you some lead time to formulate a response," Howson replied, "but in a campaign like this, knowing what's coming before it gets there can put you in the driver's seat."

"True," replied Foster with a knowing smile.

"Well, here it is," said the general. "MacFarlane ordered the CIA to report directly to the joint chiefs as well as to him in matters concerning Iran. Understandable enough, the situation being what it is." Howson paused, either for effect or to gather momentum.

"Anyway, that's how this 'tidbit,' as you call it, found its way to me. And it's possible you could benefit from knowing it. It doesn't violate national security that I can see, and that's why I feel free to pass it on to you."

"I wouldn't want you to place your own position in jeopardy, Emmit," said Foster, with a smile that was less than sincere.

"Not to worry, In a nutshell this is it—our agent in Moscow has reported that Kudinsky's in trouble."

"You mean in the Kremlin—leadershipwise?" asked Foster, as if this were news to him, although he had already surmised as much from his own sources.

"That's right."

"Any details?"

"Only that there have been some very heated meetings of the Politburo recently, with Bolotnikov making serious waves. Five days ago he apparently spoke out quite boldly and caustically against Kudinsky, and the premier, not Bolotnikov, rose and left the hall. Apparently he no longer has the clout to deal with him."

Foster let out a long, low whistle—his scheming mind already far away, wondering how he could best put this information to use.

"And you think a coup is imminent?" he asked at length.

"No one's actually used the c-word yet. But it looks very close."

"The talks are only three days away."

"And any shake-up of the Soviet leadership would blow Mac-

Farlane's hopes right out of the water."

"You're right there, Emmit," said Foster, brightening. "Very right indeed! It would hardly be MacFarlane's fault, but it would still make him look bad. A no-show summit is never a good vote-getter. By the way, how did MacFarlane react to this communique?"

"I thought you understood, Pat," replied Howson cagily, "this is fresh off the presses—my eyes only. The moment I got it I intercepted it, saying I'd inform the president personally. The point is, to my knowledge he isn't aware of this yet."

Foster's lips twisted into a cunning grin. "I owe you one indeed, Emmit!"

The two men deliberated in silence while they nursed their drinks. Then Foster continued.

"The elimination of Kudinsky would serve our purposes in more ways than one. Is there any way the CIA could stop it? Might MacFarlane try something like that?"

"Well, naturally, if we were talking about some Central American Republic there'd be no problem. But the Soviet Union . . . that would be a tall order, even for the CIA. But you're right—MacFarlane needs Kudinsky. A man like Bolotnikov wouldn't give him the time of day on peace talks. So it's conceivable he might order the Moscow network to attempt to stop, or at least delay it."

"*If* he knew Kudinsky was in trouble . . ." Here Foster's sly smile reappeared.

"Yes," said Howson, catching Foster's train of thought. "And you'd be amazed at how many communications such as this are lost in transit, or even waylaid."

"Didn't just such a snafu occur at Pearl Harbor?" Foster queried. "It would be ironic, but after all this to-do, MacFarlane could well be going to Moscow to negotiate with a lame duck Soviet premier. Even better, one who's already on his way out."

Howson merely nodded, and the two men toasted each other once more, very pleased with themselves.

---

An hour later Patrick Foster was back in his office. Placing an overseas call to the Soviet Union wasn't easy no matter who you were, but in this case it was difficult to be patient. With the president leaving for Russia in three days, there wasn't a moment to lose.

"Andrew . . ." he finally said into the receiver, "Andrew . . . is that you?"

The voice at the other end seemed to answer in the affirmative

"And how are the accommodations in Kaliningrad?"

A moment's pause, after which Foster laughed. "I don't blame you! But she'll have a good time in Hamburg. Besides, aren't there any cute little Russian peasant girls up that way? . . . Yes, of course . . . I should know you better than that." Foster laughed again.

Another pause.

"Listen, Andy," Foster went on, immediately turning serious, "I've just got wind of something here. Word is things may be moving fast in Moscow . . . no, no, the summit's going on as scheduled. This is different . . . internal Kremlin disputes . . . a shake-up . . . possibly even a change in leadership."

Another pause, while Foster listened intently.

"Yes . . . yes . . . that's similar to what I heard. Look, the point is, we've got to move on this thing as quickly as we can. See if you can't get something set up for me immediately, even within the week if you can. I don't know what Bolotnikov's posture is. But if he and I can meet and come up with something, it could help both our respective positions . . . that's right . . . no, I'll have to come up with some kind of official statement . . . that's all right, you just do what you have to do."

Again he listened to the voice at the other end.

"At this point, I don't care," he replied. "Sure . . . yeah, the press'll be on me like a glove, but that won't matter. If we can pull it off, it'll all be out in a week or two anyway . . . no, under wraps till MacFarlane leaves."

Another pause.

"Yes . . . yes . . . that would be terrific! If you can do it, I'd love to be in Kaliningrad while MacFarlane's in Moscow . . . just perfect . . . you just get Bolotnikov's people to nail it down and I'll be there!"

Foster hung up the receiver and leaned back in his chair, a wide smile of satisfaction spreading over his face.

Perfect, he thought. A simultaneous summit between the next two leaders of the superpower nations. While the two lame ducks are strutting around Moscow in front of the press, the decisions which will *really* impact world events will be going on six hundred miles to the west in a little town on the Baltic nobody's ever heard of. The perfect, ironic way for one political career to end and another to be launched!

*History will remember Kaliningrad as the turning point,* he mused. *And Patrick Harcourt Foster as the U.S. president who made it happen, even prior to his election!*

# FIFTY-FOUR

Vladimir Kudinsky hung up his phone with the forced reserve of one who would rather have tossed it across the room.

Bolotnikov would be in the premier's office momentarily, he had said. Without a "by your leave" or an "at your convenience." No—just a curt and imperative, "I'll be there in five minutes!"

The man was irritating beyond all limits. Now he had some trivial complaint about the presidential visit. After the grilling Bolotnikov had given his policies last week, followed by that humiliating denunciation in front of the Politburo, specifically regarding his planned meeting with the American president, Kudinsky didn't know how much more of the man he could take.

He should never have walked out; he had realized that almost immediately. It was the ultimate sign of weakness. He should have stood and faced Bolotnikov down on the spot. Yet he was none too sure whom the other members would support.

He'd hoped that Bolotnikov would back off for a time following his minor victory, but apparently his belligerent foe was going to push until it came to blows. If he didn't succumb to the pressure and proceed with the Iranian invasion, Bolotnikov would no doubt be occupying this office in less than a month. And he himself would be . . ." He shuddered to think. Without some breakthrough, his would be the fate of Nikita Khrushchev, to die in ignominy.

If only . . . if only. . . ! But how could a man like President Jarvis MacFarlane, who only three weeks ago had condemned the Soviet system itself . . . how could he possibly make a man like that believe?

If he could only talk to the American president alone. *Might* it be possible to convince him? For the chance at such a breakthrough, he would willingly risk everything—even his own reputation, his own perilous future.

He wished he was able to converse more fluently in English, or had time to learn. How could he ever hope to get through on any profound level while surrounded by interpreters? Somehow, beyond all reason, beyond all historical stumbling blocks that would be in their way, he and MacFarlane *had* to break the impasse. If only he could make the American head of state believe that in his heart he, too, yearned for peace.

*If only* . . . life was full of *if only's*! If only this had happened to him before the Iranian maneuvers. Then he might have had time to ponder the implications, to plan a private meeting with the president. But now the whole Communist world sat poised, watching, waiting for him to exercise the strength of his leadership in the Persian Gulf. Now, when peace was most imperative, his colleagues in the Kremlin awaited his word to launch what could well become World War III.

If only he had time . . . if only he could convince the military to stand down their troops from full alert.

If only Leonid Bolotnikov was not so close to seizing power and launching the attack himself!

Kudinsky fingered the manila envelope lying on his desk.

How could he have been so fortunate as to have such a document fall into his hands? Could that Providence—in which he kept trying to convince himself he didn't even believe!—have ordered it so? Was this the means he was supposed to use to destroy the forces that would bring war to the world?

He was not a violent man, nor a malicious one. He disdained weapons of any kind, though as a pragmatic politician he could not deny their value. Yet this weapon he had before him was in many ways more terrible than any the military held in its arsenal. For the use of this weapon lay completely at the mercy of his own personal hatred or benevolence, whichever he chose. He knew that with a few phone calls and a few photocopies of its contents, he could destroy Leonid Bolotnikov.

It was not that he would condemn a man for keeping a mistress, as long as he was discreet—although he would never choose to do such a thing himself. But when a man was an important public official, there could be repercussions. And if that mistress should turn out to be a CIA informant . . .

Disastrous was too soft a word to describe what it could do to a good party man's future. He had little doubt that Bolotnikov had been set up because of his seething dislike for anything remotely American. Still, that fact would not save him if less forgiving members of the Politburo and *Tass* chose not to believe him. They would say he could never be trusted again. His loyalty and judgment would remain forever in question.

If the information in that envelope should get out, it would be the end for Bolotnikov. His own leadership problems, at least for the present, would be over.

Kudinsky smiled a grim smile. *I should be delighted,* he thought. He only wished the contents of the envelope had fallen into another's hands so that such a degrading method of destruction would not have had to rest on him. He doubted he could ever himself employ such means.

Yet, if things became desperate enough. . . ? What might a man be compelled to do?

At the very least, it provided him with a safety valve. He had to move with extreme caution. It would never do for a hint of this to escape prematurely.

In the midst of his thoughts, there was a sharp knock on his door and Bolotnikov stormed into the room, his face florid, his hands clenched into tight fists.

"You have gone too far now, my esteemed premier!" he shouted. "I have just been told that you ordered out the honor guard for tomorrow, as well as a band and—" here he gritted his teeth and raised his fist, "and given the airport permission to allow several hundred citizens into the reception area to greet the American president! Can this folly possibly be true? Tell me I have heard wrong!"

Kudinsky nodded his head in the self-assured manner he knew drove his adversary to distraction.

"You have not heard wrong, my friend," he said softly.

"What do you think this is, I would like to ask!" insisted Bolotnikov.

"We are receiving an important foreign dignitary," Kudinsky answered calmly.

"He is our enemy!"

"Wake up, Leonid! This is a new era. He is the president of the most powerful nation on earth besides ours!" countered the Premier, growing heated himself, "a nation that has for ten years been considered our friend. Gorbachev walked the streets of New York City. Their President Bush shook more Russian hands by ten times than the small welcoming contingent I propose to have at the airport. You are living in the past, Leonid! What would you have me do, send the KGB to greet him and deposit him in a gulag and feed him on bread and water?"

"He has denounced us publicly and is coming here to exact an unconditional retreat from us," the deputy premier continued to rant.

"That is how politics is played. We made an aggressive move; he denounced it."

"It is hardly necessary to wine and dine him!"

"Presidents and premiers have been eating and drinking as friends for years! We have learned to live together in spite of our differences, and I intend to continue doing so!"

"Bah! Spoken like the true weakling you are! You will do nothing but place us at his mercy."

"You would suggest a hostile reception I assume?"

"A chilly reception is no more than he deserves. The coziness your predecessor felt with Western leaders was nothing short of demeaning! A stiff greeting now would demonstrate to the world that we have not lost our backbone, that strong men are now back in control, and that our strength is a force to be reckoned with again."

"It would only reinforce what so many Americans used to think of us—that we are uncivilized animals. When will you and the other stone-age Stalinists realize there is a better way? Mikhail brought us into the twentieth century from Brezhnev's nineteenth-century ways!" Kudinsky spoke each word firmly, powerfully, as only a quiet man can when he is aroused. "No, my friend, I would show to the world a Russia that can be gracious as well as strong."

The calmness with which Bolotnikov spoke his next words was not the result of any sense of intimidation on his part, but of his decision to try a new approach.

"Very well, Mr. Secretary," he said. "As I said before, the summit is yours. Do with it what you wish—what you can. You have this last opportunity for the world to see what a fool you are. I will not stand in your way. But be assured, you are sealing your own doom. The future of Russia lies with me!"

"Thank you for your consideration, comrade," replied Kudinsky.

Bolotnikov swung around to make his exit, but Kudinsky's words stopped him before he reached the door.

"One more thing, Leonid," he said. "I would like you to represent me to the presidential party at the airport."

The deputy premier spun around and glared at his superior with fire in his eyes, looking for a brief instant as if he would bodily attack him.

"You think for a moment I would comply with such a demeaning request!" he said, spitting out each word with contempt.

"I am telling you that is what I want you to do," said Kudinsky firmly. "If you choose to do otherwise it will only confirm your disloyalty."

"Think what you will! I call it patriotism to refuse such a loathsome bowing to a hated enemy of our Motherland!"

"Then you refuse me? The council will not take it kindly."

"They will side with me! The time for such a reckoning approaches. To answer you again—I will not do it!" he cried. "You may kiss the hand of our foe, but I'll not be party to it!"

"I had hoped, in the spirit of conciliation, to give you this opportunity to be a part of history."

"Conciliation!" fumed Bolotnikov. "You scheme to relinquish the superiority of our nation's might by your refusal to march upon Iran, while entertaining an enemy bent on our destruction, and you talk of *conciliation*! You have indeed lost your senses! I will listen to no more!"

He stormed from the room in a flurry of white-hot anger.

*He is even more dangerous than I imagined,* thought Kudinsky. *I should be careful not to provoke him so.*

His hand fell on the manila envelope. *But I too can be dangerous.*

He picked up the packet. He knew clearly now that he could only use these contents at the peril of his own life. That fact alone would make him cautious.

He rose from his chair and walked with resigned steps toward a cabinet, where he unlocked a drawer and laid the envelope inside. For the present, his weapon would have to remain hidden. He was not yet desperate enough to use it.

First he would talk to Jarvis MacFarlane. Everything hinged upon his ability to make the president grasp the urgency. If he could conclude an agreement with him, perhaps—just perhaps—he might then be able to undercut those in his own government who seemed bent on a new era of militarism. If he couldn't do that, then Bolotnikov was right—he would be sealing his own doom and the future of Russia would go on without him.

Again his thoughts turned to his former comrade Nikita Khrushchev. There had been unsubstantiated rumors floating about that the aging leader's fall from power had something to do with a "religious experience."

Nonsense, no doubt! Or an invention of the Americans who loved such gossip about the Soviet leaders.

But he couldn't help wondering whether he was destined to follow the same pathway to oblivion.

# FIFTY-FIVE

How did you become involved with our mutual Christian friends?" asked Jarvis MacFarlane.

He and Peter Venzke were seated in the president's private compartment on Air Force One with the door closed. The drone of the plane's engines, despite the soundproofed interior, added to MacFarlane's sense of security that no one could possibly overhear their conversation. For he had determined to tell Peter everything!

Venzke thought for a moment, then replied, "You ask a question with many complexities. Are you sure you want to hear? The answer may take me a while."

"We have a long flight ahead of us, my friend," smiled the president.

"And you would rather spend it in this manner than on a final brushup in preparation for your time with the Soviet premier?"

"I'm afraid my Russian is as good as it's going to get. Besides, my mind is too distracted to worry about the language. I'm too occupied thinking about *what* I have to tell Kudinsky to worry about how I'm going to say it."

"Anything you want to share with me?"

"Yes. But I want to hear your story first."

"Okay," said Venzke with a smile. "I'll try to give you the abbreviated version."

He paused, thought for a moment, then launched into his story.

"I suppose the changes that have come upon me had their beginnings back when Gorbachev came to power. You can imagine what it was like for me then, a native Russian. Everything changed for me. I don't mean the way it changed for everyone—I mean everything changed *internally* for me. Suddenly all my reasons for defecting were erased. Freedom had come to the Soviet Union! It was too incredible even to comprehend. Everything I had wanted, hoped for, fought for within myself—suddenly it had come to pass!

"I should have been elated, wouldn't you think? Instead, I had a great sense of confusion and disorientation. It was like my *persona,* my sense of who I was, my *raison d'etre* had been jerked out from under me and I fell into a void. I watched the conservative political movement in this country struggle with the very thing—watched with interest, because it was going through the same thing I was. With the demise of Communism throughout the world, there was nothing more for the conservatives to fight. A vacuum was the result, a floundering for a message, a purpose. What were the conservative editorialists supposed to write about once their enemy had been defeated. The Cold War had been won! Yet the victors often did not seem to know what to do with their victory. And that was exactly how *I* felt. My life, my very being, my reasons for defecting had all been vindicated. I had won! Yet I found myself tossing and muddling about. The foil against which I had sharpened myself all those years was gone.

"It was easy for me to understand how the mood in this country shifted so dramatically after 1990. It was like contrasting the U.S. mentality in 1944 with the mentality in 1954. The whole world had shifted, and people had changed their whole outlook. The changes in mood and perspective triggered by the end of the Cold War created such an obvious 'spiritual' vacuum—that is, spiritual in the broader, philosophical sense. The 'new age for mankind' ideas were able to slide right in, and people ate them up. They were ready; they were hungry. With the failure of the Christian evangelical movement, coupled with the changing world situation, the stage was set for those like MacLaine and Foster to sweep people right off their feet with a message of light and peace and a new era."

Venzke paused and looked out the window into the distant blue, obviously reflecting deeply.

"I have to admit, I listened to that stuff for a while. I'm telling you, I went through a very difficult time for two or three years when I really wondered about . . . well, about everything. Life, what is its meaning, who was I, what was my purpose, what did the future hold for me? It was not easy for me to pay attention to my students and my research. Inside I was struggling, groping for answers, for reality, for a meaningful bedrock to which I could attach the roots of my life now that all my previous foundations had crumbled beneath me.

"So I listened to many of the so-called prophets of the new era. I read books. I listened to things my students were saying. Perhaps it sounds odd for a grown man to say, but I was *searching* for meaning. And it was a struggle. I did not know where to turn.

"Part of me wondered if I should go back to the Soviet Union. I could not deny that a piece of my heart had broken when I left, and that corner of my being had always yearned to set my eyes and feet on my homeland again. Now, suddenly, it was possible! You cannot imagine the perturbation that knowledge caused me, my friend! My search for—what shall I call it?—a new identity, a search for meaning—everything was exacerbated tenfold by the realization that I could now go back if I chose to a free and—I can scarcely say the words even now!—a democratic Russia!

"I tell you, my mind and emotions were being stretched and pulled and torn in a thousand directions at once. I was in more turmoil than before making the decision to defect. That had been a single-dimensional decision—either yes or no. But now what I faced had too many facets. There were no straightforward decisions. And it wasn't as simple as just, 'What do I *do*?' It was a quandary of 'Who *am* I?' "

"Why didn't you come to see me?" asked the president.

"I thought of you often. But we had not communicated for some time, and you were swiftly being drawn into national events. To tell you the truth, I was embarrassed. Saying you are searching for meaning in your life is not something most men go about voicing openly."

"You would have had nothing to fear from me."

"I know that now. But at the time, I tell you I was in miserable shape inside, and I just kept most of this to myself."

"So what happened? What did you do?" asked MacFarlane, by now on the edge of his seat. So much of his friend's quest paralleled his own.

"I thought long and hard about returning," answered Venzke. "Yet I could not help but be concerned too. I read about an East German border guard who had escaped to West Berlin just a few months before the wall came toppling down. He longed to go back, to see his family and friends and reestablish his life in a free East Germany. But he was afraid he would be arrested for defecting. How many thousands must have faced a similar quandary. Freedom came to Eastern Europe—yes. But were those who had escaped the old regime truly able to participate in that freedom? It is a question perhaps we will never know all the answers to. In my own case, I did not fear arrest so much, for during that time the Soviet government was showing remarkable openness toward those of the intellectual community. My real fear was that I might return home and find that things had not changed as much as I had expected.

"My emotions were all over the place during those days. I cried on that fateful October 3 when the Germany's were reunited. Yet I must admit that there remained within me an honest skepticism whether the same level of freedom could ever happen in Russia. I was delighted to see the changes within the Kremlin. I rejoiced with those first free elections of 1990, when the Communist Party was dethroned of its monopoly! But at the same time, I was too much a student of my own country's history to believe that democratization could be achieved overnight. We Russians have a history, a culture, a national identity as a collection of peoples that goes utterly against the grain of democracy. Frankly, I did not think it could work. And if it was to work, it would take fifty or a hundred years to break the chains of the past, not five or ten. Whatever was presented to the world, I knew the internal pressures had to be severe, and I knew that Gorbachev's power, like the power of all Russian leaders since time immemorial, hung by the slenderest of threads. And I knew that without him the *new revolution* of 1989 could collapse. This current crisis but confirms that. The fifth column has been there all along."

MacFarlane nodded, with a look of grim agreement. He knew only too well! That's what this trip was all about.

"But you know what I was even more afraid of? In another sense, with free elections in Russia came an even greater, more subtle danger. Do you remember when Gorbachev was elected 'President' in 1990 by the Congress of People's Deputies in what they called the Soviet Union's first free elections? No longer was he just going to be the Premier or the General Secretary of the Party. Now he was even going to have a democratic title! Yet such vast new powers were immediately bestowed on him as president that it was clear the way was open for an even more sweeping dictatorship at some future time under a less scrupulous man. In all fairness to Gorbachev, I honestly believe he was a great man and carried himself honorably. But the possibility was there for trouble, despite the outward moves toward freedom. And the internal trouble was always there—as evidenced by Gorbachev's ongoing problems with the Baltic states and others who wanted to follow Lithuania's example and break away. The place was a tinderbox for a while.

"Well, the point is, I wanted to go back, yet I was deeply reluctant. And this just intensified my internal questions and struggle."

"So we're back to my question of a minute ago," said MacFarlane. "What did you do?"

Venzke sighed. "I kept reading, kept listening, kept thinking, and finally I decided to try something bold."

"What was that?"

"I went to see Aliyandr Minkovitsyn."

"You actually got to him?"

"It took some doing. But after a number of inquiries and some correspondence, he agreed to let me come to the New Hampshire hideaway where he's been since his defection."

"I'm impressed!"

"It was certainly a day I won't ever forget!"

"Can you tell me about it?"

"To tell you everything that went on that day, Jarvis, would take hours and hours! It was positively remarkable. I heard things the likes of which I never dreamed of! The man was amazing! He had such a grasp of the historical and cultural factors that he showed me vast pieces to the political picture I had never even considered. He had the whole thing so nailed down—ancient Russia, the Revolution, the Second World War, Stalin, the '50s, the Cold War, the U.S./Soviet history, and now the changes that had occurred. It all fit perfectly for him into a harmonious flow, and he helped me understand many things."

"I would like to have heard *that* conversation!"

"But that wasn't really the most significant part of the day."

"What was?"

"The spiritual dimension he gave to the whole thing. Minkovitsyn's a Christian, you know, besides being one of the foremost Russian scholars in the West."

"I guess I'd heard something like that, but never thought of it much before now."

"He kept himself in the background, but he was right in the middle of some very important things going on in this quiet *movement* into which you are now being drawn yourself. In fact, Daniel was there that day too."

"Was Minkovitsyn telling you the same kinds of things I've been hearing—you know, warning of judgment and so on?"

"No, not at first. That only came into it a little that day. It has only been in the last year that I've been going to the meetings of the Legation and have been hearing more and more of that message."

"Then what was it you talked about—spiritually, I mean—on that first day?"

"I suppose what it boils down to is simply this: he told me about an altogether new way of life, something I'd never heard of—a more intimate and personal way of viewing being a Christian. It was just remarkable! You have no idea how good it sounded—'good news' was just what he and Daniel called it!—and it gradually began to make some sense out of all the questions and doubts I'd been going through. Do you want to hear about it?"

"More than you can know," answered MacFarlane eagerly. "Please go on."

For the next thirty minutes the president listened in rapt attention. No longer was he aware of jet engines, Moscow, or an upcoming election as his soul drank in every word that fell from his friend's mouth.

At length Venzke stopped and drew a deep breath.

"Don't stop now!" urged MacFarlane.

"Have no worry," said Venzke. "I'll finish the story. It's just that I can't even think about the events of that day without losing my composure. Out of respect for the esteemed company I'm in—" he paused and flashed a smile to show that his comment was tongue-in-cheek, "I'll try to refrain from tears!"

"Hold nothing back on my account," said the president. "I'm already struggling with my own! I hope that door is locked!"

Venzke laughed. "Well, the evening ended with me on my knees, Daniel and Aliyandr beside me. And I tell you, on *that* night there were tears, and plentifully! But my life has not been the same since. I finally knew who I was, where I was going, and who my Father was."

The president's private cabin fell silent. Neither man spoke for perhaps ten minutes.

At last MacFarlane said, "I am deeply moved, Peter. I don't know what else to say."

Venzke nodded.

"And now it would appear that it is my turn—if *you* want to hear *my* incredible tale!"

"As you said earlier—it is a long flight!"

"It happened in February," the president began. And there, locked away and soundproofed by the drone of the plane's engines, MacFarlane told Peter everything.

Slowly he recounted the events of his visionary experience, as he had earlier with Karen and Jeremy. By the time he was finished he was almost shaking with emotion.

"So you see," he said in conclusion, "it's bizarre. Am I actually claiming that *God* spoke to me! Am I saying that the God who made the world picked *me* to reveal himself to? Who would have the audacity to make such a claim? And why me? I'm not religious. You know that, Peter. If God has some urgent message for the world, why wouldn't He take it to the Pope or somebody like your friend Daniel or some theologian or church leader or priest? But me! The thing's absurd! 'Much to proclaim before that day . . .' What day? I don't even know what He was talking about! I have no idea what to proclaim."

"I think I may have some idea, Jarvis," said Peter softly. It was the first time he had spoken since the president began his story, and tears were not only standing in his eyes, but trickling unashamedly down his cheeks.

"God's hand is upon you, that is clear. Now much of what you said that first day when you came to me about teaching you Russian begins to make sense. Indeed, neither of us knew where that day would lead us. God be praised, His work in you is bigger than I could ever have imagined!"

"If it hadn't been so *real*," MacFarlane sighed, "I would have dismissed it as a dream. But I tell you, Peter—it *happened*! And in spite of the warning, the blood, the gloomy prophecy of what will come to the world if there isn't a change, the feeling that has stuck with me strongest since that night has been the great *peace* of the Voice . . . I felt—and I know that sounds crazy—but I felt He *loved* me, cared about me, and that in the midst of the prophetic message that love was *really* the message, the essential core of what the experience was all about. I couldn't help identifying a little with those guys in the Old Testament that God spoke to—Noah, Abraham, Jeremiah, the prophets. I know what that must sound like! But since that night I've been reading the Bible, hoping to find some clues or answers. And I've learned that most of those men faced the same doubts I have, wondering if they made the whole thing up, worrying about what people would think. It seems that whenever God speaks to people—though I've never heard of Him doing it in these modern times—they don't believe Him at first. So maybe . . . I don't know . . . I mean, *could* there be something to this? *Can* God actually talk to people? I just don't know what to do with it all!"

At that point a deep silence descended upon the two men. Finally Peter spoke gently to his friend and spiritual comrade.

"Have no doubt, Jarvis, what has come to you *is* real. There is a scripture in the Old Testament prophets in which I think you will find great comfort, for I truly believe the prophet was foretelling these very days in which we live: *'I will pour out my Spirit on all people. Your sons and daughters will prophesy, your old men will dream dreams, your young men will see visions.'* "

A pause followed.

"This is but the beginning, Jarvis," Peter added finally. "The hand of God is upon you. He will continue to show you what course you are to follow."

# FIFTY-SIX

Jeremy Manning looked across the aisle of Air Force One to the window opposite him. As the plane banked for its final approach to Moscow International, he could see a portion of the city's skyline. He felt an undeniable surge of excitement.

Here he was, a trusted confidant of the president of the United States!

Well, perhaps that was overstating it just a bit! But he *was* a part—if only a very minor part—of the most important diplomatic mission in several years, perhaps in all of history. The feeling was heady to say the least.

Yet he could not avoid a corresponding uncertainty, even trepidation. A nagging question mark still loomed in his brain—just who was this man to whom he had suddenly given his unreserved loyalty?

When he considered the vision the president had described, he could not do so without a measure of skepticism. If there was a God, certainly in this day and age He would be too sophisticated for such crazy displays. If, on the other hand, He was the God that Cecil B. deMille had contrived to speak to Charlton Heston out of the glowing bush, then what could such an old Hebrew deity have to do with modern presidents? Either way, the thing was preposterous!

Wild desert patriarchs had visions, not American presidents! So what did this say for Jarvis MacFarlane who was staking his reputation and even the future of his political life—and possibly a military confrontation—on the validity of his experience?

Jeremy pondered over something he had once heard which had never left his mind. Back in the 80s, as an eager young political aspirant, he had gone to hear ex-White House hatchet man Charles Colson speak. He'd had no idea the thing was going to turn into a ranting fundamentalist tent meeting! But one thing at least had stuck with him. Colson had been quoting from some book he said had exercised a tremendous impact on his life. Jeremy couldn't remember the name, but it was written by some Englishman who'd died the same day JFK was shot.

Colson had quoted the author's view of Jesus Christ, one of the most outlandish things Jeremy had ever heard—perhaps that's why it had stuck with him. The Englishman had said that when one considered the claims Jesus made about himself, there were only three possible conclusions to be reached: He was either telling the truth and was exactly who He claimed to be; or He was the greatest deceiver the world has ever known—a liar, a devil straight from hell; or else He was a lunatic. There just weren't any other options available.

Well, Jeremy couldn't help thinking the same might hold true for the president and his "experience." Wasn't this what it boiled down to? He couldn't believe MacFarlane was lying; the man was too sincere, too honest. Therefore, he was either insane or he was telling the truth. The only difference was that MacFarlane didn't have two thousand years of history to back up his claims.

So why had he thrown away all his past notions to give the man his support?

He looked over at Karen, sitting beside him, gazing out the window.

She had never once questioned her father's experience. Her faith in him remained undaunted.

He liked Jarvis MacFarlane. It was amazing how quickly ideological differences had settled into the background in the face of personal loyalty. He knew he would go the limit for MacFarlane—and not merely because he was Karen's father. Yet he could still not honestly bring himself to accept the validity of the vision. Over and over he had tried to rationalize it all, but he knew he still had only two options—insanity or truth.

But if it wasn't real, then this whole trip meant nothing. Jeremy hated to even think about that.

He sighed deeply, and Karen turned toward him.

"Is that a sigh of contentment I hear?" she asked.

"I wish it were."

"Having misgivings about coming?"

"No, not about coming. I was just thinking about—you know—everything that's happened. There's still a lot on my mind. It'll take time for it to settle. You have to realize this is quite an about-face for me. Every time I think I have my loyalties all worked out, something upsets my equilibrium."

Karen nodded in understanding.

Just then the plane touched down smoothly on Russian soil, and soon they were taxiing toward the terminal.

Jeremy could see a large crowd pressed against a chain-link fence adjacent to the official greeting area. At the end of the runway itself, next to the terminal building, were several rows of Red Army troops decked out in their finest regalia. With them stood a party of dignitaries, obviously government officials and perhaps Soviet press representatives, along with U.S. embassy personnel. All told, perhaps four or five hundred people awaited the arrival of Air Force One.

Jeremy had a feeling that privacy would be a commodity in short supply on this trip.

# FIFTY-SEVEN

The president of the United States stepped off Air Force One, waving to the cheering crowd. It wasn't large by U.S. standards, but then this was the Soviet Union.

With his translator, Professor Peter Venzke, behind him, MacFarlane descended the stairway, extended his hand, and smiled warmly at Soviet Premier Kudinsky.

"*Dobro pojalovat!* Welcome in kindness!" said Kudinsky, shaking the American's hand firmly.

"Thank you," said MacFarlane in Russian.

"I am honored," he continued, this time in English with Venzke translating, "that you came to meet me yourself. It is an unprecedented accolade, for which I cannot adequately express my gratitude."

"Protocol was not written for historic events," replied Kudinsky. "Your coming pleases me greatly. It was only right that I welcome you personally."

"Thank you again," said MacFarlane, then added, telling Venzke to speak softly to the premier as he translated, "but won't such a breach, especially toward an American president, cause concern among your colleagues?"

MacFarlane thought he might as well test the waters immediately to see how open the premier was going to be to a straightforward approach. The Russian leader's response was encouraging.

Kudinsky laughed. "Not to worry, Mr. President!" Then *he* said something softly, almost as an aside, which translated into, "My chief adversary is not even in Moscow. He was so outraged by your coming that he took off yesterday morning for someplace on the Baltic, making excuse about the need for a vacation. But it is good—this will give us all the more freedom to talk between ourselves!"

Kudinsky, too, was testing the waters.

MacFarlane drew Karen into the inner circle of dignitaries and introduced her. Then after more handshaking all around, the retinue made its way to the waiting limousines, and in a few minutes they were speeding toward the Rossia Hotel.

---

From his vantage point near a magazine rack in the lobby of the Rossia Hotel, Seyed Gilani watched the presidential arrival. He appeared every inch the well-educated, well-appointed French businessman. No one would ever suspect that in the last year alone he had played an active role in three airport bombings, two assassination attempts, as well as a handful of executive kidnappings, most of which had ended in gruesome executions. Indeed, no custom official ever gave him a second look, despite the fact that he was nothing less than a cold-blooded killer. Yet he would always be less comfortable with that role than his natural role as a suave, urbane Frenchman.

Two weeks previously he and Ahmed had flown from Tehran to Paris, where they had begun making their elaborate preparations for this excursion behind enemy lines. Using his Parisian contacts and his already established reputation as a world traveler, Seyed obtained passports and visas for himself and Ahmed, who was posing, quite believably, as a student.

None of Seyed's associates could do anything for Mohsen, however; his face and reputation were already too well-known by the authorities, and Interpol was looking for him throughout Europe. He was making his own way into Russia, for he, too, had his contacts. If not as reputable as Seyed's, they were equally effective.

The three terrorists had planned to arrive in Moscow at different times and would rendezvous at the Rossia, where one of Mohsen's contacts had confirmed that the American president would be staying.

Thus far, their plan had gone smoothly. This morning Seyed had arrived at Moscow International on Aeroflot flight 528 from France and had cleared customs without a hitch.

Now as he watched the president's party enter the hotel, the first thing Seyed's trained eye noted was the extremely tight security. The chief executive was flanked with more than the usual number of Secret Service agents, and he knew that behind their dark glasses they were being ever-vigilant. He breathed a hasty prayer of thanksgiving to Allah, in whom he had only a perfunctory belief, for his fair skin and rather innocently boyish features. One look at a dark and hardened countenance such as Mohsen's and the U.S. agents would probably have drawn their weapons.

Despite security, the president did manage to greet and shake hands with several of the hotel patrons milling about the lobby. A group of Americans entering the hotel rushed innocently toward him, creating a momentary confusion. The agents tensed and moved in tightly, but the president waved them off and extended his hand and friendly smiles to his countrymen.

For a brief instant a seething, blinding anger welled up within Seyed, threatening to overwhelm him. The little scene, played out so graphically before him, with the smiling, joking, hail-fellow-well-met president ignited something basic inside him.

This ridiculous imposter had no idea of the pain and suffering being caused by his hateful country! His bland American face was all smiles, but in the *real* world his aggression and policies of imperialism kept three-quarters of the earth's people hopelessly bound in poverty so that his three-hundred-million rich, fat countrymen might live lives of decadent consumption! Turmoil, hatred, poverty, and the pain and hunger of starving millions abounded all around them. The world could blow up at any moment because of their nuclear weapons which further fattened the coffers of their greed. Yet this arrogant American could strut about as if he owned the world, smiling and waving his greetings as if all nations should be at his feet!

"Monsieur!" intruded a voice at his elbow.

Seyed turned sharply, quickly bringing his raging emotions under control.

"The magazine?" said the hotel attendant in very poor French. "Did you intend on purchasing the magazine?"

Seyed's gaze dropped quickly to the copy of *L'Equipe* he had been holding. It was crushed in the vice-like grip of his fingers. Crushed, as he would crush the arrogant oppressors of his people!

"No," he replied in a tight, pale voice. "I mean—yes—yes, of course," he added, suddenly realizing that to do otherwise might cause a scene.

He thrust some coins toward the man and walked away, looking down once more at the crumpled magazine in his hand.

*You are acting more and more like Mohsen every day,* he thought. *Before long it will be you who is shouting the slogans of hatred and terrorism from the stumps and alleys where willing ears will listen.* He wondered if such a notion was a blessing or a curse.

# PART IV

# THE PROPOSAL

*"I will pour out my Spirit on all people. Your sons and daughters will prophesy, your old men will dream dreams, your young men will see visions. . . . I will show wonders in the heavens and on the earth, blood and fire and billows of smoke. The sun will be turned to darkness and the moon to blood before the coming of the great and dreadful day of the* LORD*. And everyone who calls on the name of the* LORD *will be saved; for on Mount Zion and in Jerusalem there will be deliverance, as the* LORD *has said. . . ."*

*"Proclaim this among the nations: Prepare for war! Rouse the warriors! . . . Let the nations be roused. . . . Multitudes, multitudes in the valley of decision! For the day of the* LORD *is near. . . . The sun and moon will be darkened, and the stars no longer shine. . . . But the* LORD *will be a refuge for his people. . . ."*

*"Then you will know that I, the* LORD *your God, dwell in Zion, my holy hill. Jerusalem will be holy; never again will foreigners invade her."*

# FIFTY-EIGHT

"*Vladimir . . . where are you? Vladimir . . .*"

He could still hear her voice calling from beyond the little wood. She couldn't see him where he sat on his favorite grassy knoll. But she no doubt knew where to find her seven-year-old son.

"Vladimir . . . the rain is approaching. You must come in."

He looked around with a sigh of satisfaction, then rose and began walking slowly down the hill toward his mother.

This particular memory came back many times. Not so much for the place itself, although that was a memory he cherished too: the foot-worn path leading away from their peasant cottage, through the edge of the pine and fir wood, up the bare, grassy hill, and to his favorite spot, the knoll with a rock on its top just the right size for a boy and his dreams. When he closed his eyes and breathed deeply, he could still almost smell the sweet fragrance of the ground, the trees, the decaying needles underfoot, the sun-warmed branches during the months of summer that were all too short near the Ukrainian village of Kharkov.

And though it was not a large wood, it had held mysteries and terrors enough for the young Russian boy, causing him to reflect upon many things. It was these dreams, meditations, and reflections that came back most often to his memory, even before the lovely smell of the wood.

He had never been like other boys. Whereas others wanted to play or hunt, young Vladimir preferred being alone—to think. He would stretch out on the grass and examine each tiny blade of green and wonder how such delicate things could survive the harsh, frost-bitten winter and then force themselves back through the stubborn sod again . . . and again . . . and again.

Many times, sitting on his rock, he found himself wondering where the rock came from. If it was on the top of the knoll and was clearly too heavy for any five men to lift, how did it come to be there?

The trees he mostly just enjoyed. Perhaps, though he loved the wood, he did not ponder its depths as frequently because he was usually on his way either to or from his thinking place when he passed through it. He did like to pick up the small cones that fell from the trees, to open them before the birds and forest creatures got all the seeds.

Ah, seeds! There was a mystery that sent him ruminating time and again. How *could* such magnificent things as trees, carrots, and apples come from such tiny beginnings? And where was the life in the seed, he had wondered, as with fingers and fingernails none too nimble he had probed to the limit of his youthful dexterity the very beginnings of life.

But try as he might, the seed could never divulge to him its unspeakable secret. So he had to content himself to sit on his rock and wonder—where the grass derived its strength, where the seed obtained its life, where the sky got its blue, how the clouds remained in the sky, and how the snow could look so peaceful and yet be so deadly. And always in the back of his mind was the question, from what seed had *he* come? Who had imagined him before making him? He remembered his mother talking about a God who lived somewhere in the sky who had made everyone and everything. But that had been a long time ago, and she hadn't spoken of Him recently. But he had always remembered, and wondered if this God, whoever He was, made seeds for little boys to come out of as well as trees.

---

Vladimir Kudinsky's family had been Ukrainian peasants from the village of Kharkov before 1917 and were still peasants in 1938 when the world was in the midst of something they called a depression. He had been a dreamy seven years old then, when the Revolution was hardly past its infancy, and he knew nothing of it.

What was that to Vladimir's family? Food was scarce, but they had enough to live. They worked hard and managed to stay alive. But they talked no more of God. That much about the Revolution his father did understand. Times had changed. God was no more. Moscow must be obeyed.

But young Vladimir could not stop his mind from wandering where his father said it must not go. By the time he was fourteen the questions, unspoken and inward, had become increasingly profound. He had moved beyond his knoll now and taken to lengthy walks up into the high hills on the other side of the village, and down into the valley and along the river into the pasture land beyond.

How many times since then had he wondered, in his pensive moments, what might have become of him had he been allowed to follow the rambling train of his musings. Might a different course in life have been his had he continued to ask if there wasn't a greater

Someone who made all the seeds . . . and even him? Even now, though it wasn't prudent to verbalize such thoughts, there remained some deep reservoir within his being that said: that seed cannot have created itself, nor can it have come from nothing.

It made of him an unlikely Communist.

But he had not followed such a path, outwardly at least. His father saw in the new regime an opportunity to better himself. He became an active party loyalist and took his bright son with him.

Vladimir became active in the Communist Youth League as a teenager, and later joined the party himself. By 1950 he was a promising young man whom his father would have been proud of, had he lived past 1944. Vladimir moved to Leningrad in that year to begin working as a propagandist and quickly became interested in politics.

His youthful energy channeled itself, and by the time he was thirty, he had all but forgotten the ramblings and musings of his childhood. There was a world to enlighten, after all. Who had time for childish fancies?

In 1955 he was transferred to the Moldavian Republic to work under former General Secretary Konstantin Chernenko, then head of the local party, rapidly becoming his trusted assistant. In 1956, when Chernenko was summoned to Moscow by Leonid Brezhnev to be given a succession of posts on the Central Committee and the Supreme Soviet, Kudinsky moved up to fill his post at the local level. There he remained until 1966.

In 1965 when Brezhnev took over the party leadership and Chernenko joined his personal staff, the latter remembered his loyal assistant. He brought Kudinsky to Moscow, where he rose steadily but quietly in the ranks of the Moscow bureaucracy, was named to the party's Central Committee in 1971, was handed increasingly important posts in the Central Committee's foreign affairs section, and in the late 1970s was chosen by aging President Brezhnev to deliver the keynote address on the anniversary of Lenin's birthday—a singular honor that marked Kudinsky as a public figure to be watched.

As a member of the "younger" generation of rising Soviet leaders, along with Mikhail Gorbachev, Grigori Romanov, Geidar Aliyev, and others, Kudinsky occupied the fringes of power during the era of the Brezhnev, Andropov, and Chernenko. But with Gorbachev's accession to Russia's highest office, Kudinsky was promoted to full Politburo membership.

Up to that point Kudinsky's status had derived almost entirely from his friendship and proximity to Chernenko. But after 1986 his performance was impressive on his own, particularly as the head of the party's ideology and culture committee. By the late 1990s, he was clearly the leading candidate to succeed Gorbachev, even though aging military czar Dmitri Ustinov had been grooming his own version of the new military leader in the person of his protege Leonid Bolotnikov.

Upon Gorbachev's death a bitter power struggle ensued. Kudinsky emerged on top, but the Politburo remained more seriously divided than at any time in memory, with Kudinsky and Bolotnikov representing two extremes of ideology.

The struggle for leadership had forced Kudinsky into periods of depression and self-evaluation, and without even realizing it he began to think again of things that hadn't been in his mind since he was a child. Coming out the victor only served to increase his introspection for a time, and he became, in the view of certain of his colleagues, a reclusive and isolated leader. In truth, he was struggling with the very thing that he had so long been a spokesman for—Soviet ideology.

All at once, that hidden place in his heart, which he had closed over in his youth, opened up, and from within it came again many questions about life. Now, however, they were not the unintelligible broodings of a youngster, but full-blown philosophical and religious quandaries which cut across the very grain of everything Communism, and he as Communism's leader, stood for.

Desperately he tried to force his troubled brain into silence. But it was no use. The questions *would* come in spite of themselves! Once, in the privacy of his room, he fell to his knees in despair and cried out, *"God, whoever you are, show yourself or let me die!"*

Then suddenly, realizing what a cardinal sin he had committed, he quickly rose and glanced about, as if wondering whether he'd been seen.

From that moment, however, something in his approach to Soviet policies began to change.

Kudinsky steadfastly maintained that his tastes were strictly orthodox and Russian. But in his heart he knew his leadership was in trouble. He had hoped to move his country forward toward peace and technological independence, and closer to the West in other areas as well. But the divisions in the Soviet halls of power between those eager to improve relations with the West and those desirous of using the military supremacy they had at last achieved was simply too great.

Would he be able to make a difference? Would he have the courage? Was he doomed to the exile of his own mind, or was there someone with whom he might share such questions, such aspirations, such dreams? Was he fated to a short-lived tenure that would end like those of Georgi Malenkov and Yuri Andropov?

---

Vladimir Kudinsky sighed and forced his mind back to the present. Whenever he began thinking about his boyhood, his mind raced across the intervening years in a few split seconds. But the mental journey always took something out of him. It had probably all been brought on by that poem he had read today by the American poet Robert Frost—about two roads diverging in the yellow wood. He always had wondered what might have been different if he had followed the heavenly meanderings of his fanciful brain rather than the pragmatic path of his father . . . two roads in a yellow wood . . . a vivid analogy.

He should go over and greet the American president. Even from a side view he could tell MacFarlane was wearying of this supposed gala event. He ought to play the part of a good host. And he had much he hoped to talk to MacFarlane about.

If only he could speak English a tenth as well as he was able to read it!

# FIFTY-NINE

*If I have to smile through one more vodka martini, I'm going to crack,* thought Jarvis MacFarlane.

For years he had tolerated these political social gatherings as part of the game, a necessary annoyance. Talk was superficial, smiles were forced, and the general interaction plastic. Rarely could you penetrate the facade and manage to engage a colleague in meaningful dialogue.

In addition, tonight he was on display for the gawking eyes of the Soviet brass, and the protocol was stifling. The Russians seemed to enjoy following the diplomatic rules to the utmost. Showing consideration for the rigors of travel, they had postponed a state dinner until the next evening, but this was trying enough!

First there had been the long, tedious reception line, then the photo session with him and Premier Kudinsky smiling and shaking hands. Smiling—always smiling! And now for the last two hours he and his American entourage had been mingling with the Russian dignitaries in the huge, ancient, ornate hall which seemed to have been designed for this very purpose. Several other major embassies were also well represented, and he estimated that by now he had been introduced to at least seventy-five individuals and had shaken over two hundred hands.

Throughout the evening he had hoped for an opportunity to find Kudinsky alone, even for a brief moment. If he could just mention the possibility of a one-on-one session before the schedule was set in stone. That was the whole purpose of his visit, after all, and he had to establish it quickly. They were only going to be here for four days. Time was of the essence!

That was the trouble with being a president—or a Russian premier for that matter. You were *never* alone! The thought of *two* such leaders simultaneously being granted such a luxury was almost unthinkable!

MacFarlane looked over the rim of his glass to note how his associates were faring. Secretary of Defense Martin Tucker was, naturally enough, involved in an animated debate with Defense Minister Andre Bragina, their two translators barely able to keep pace. He hoped things between the two would remain friendly until they got down to more substantive talks—if they indeed got that far. Secretary of State Oscar Friedman appeared to be engaged in a much calmer conversation with an elaborately robed representative from Kenya. Chief Economic Advisor Duke Mathias, looking especially elegant and urbane, was talking with two very attractive women, probably British, although MacFarlane hadn't met them and couldn't tell what their role here might be.

Jake Randolf, the remaining member of his advisory staff present in Moscow, had just lifted a martini from a tray borne by a passing waiter. He and Vasili Moiseyev, secretary for ideology, were engaged in a jocular conversation despite the language barrier and lack of assistance from any of the two dozen bilinguals floating about the hall. The secretary looked as if he had already imbibed too heavily to care much about comprehension, and MacFarlane hoped Jake was not doing the same.

Funny, thought MacFarlane. Here they were, decked out in

their finery, smiling, shaking hands, exchanging pleasantries, pretending that all was well in the world and between their two countries. Yet even at this moment the Soviet army was at full military readiness for an invasion of a strategic neutral country, and his own forces were only awaiting his command to step up their own readiness. The world was on the edge of a serious military confrontation and here they were playing party games.

At least Karen and young Manning seemed to be enjoying themselves, although their exchanged smiles in the secluded corner they had found seemed to have little to do with the adventure of being in Russia. But that was all right. MacFarlane was glad for his daughter; he liked Jeremy Manning.

Although they had run the gamut from one end of the hall to the other, his reflections had taken only a few seconds and were suddenly interrupted by Kudinsky's voice.

"You are enjoying yourself I trust, Mr. President," he said in halting English, referring to the smile MacFarlane had worn only a moment before.

"I am enjoying the happiness of others," MacFarlane replied. "But your English is very good, Mr. Premier. I had no idea."

"Not so good, really. I know but a few poor phrases."

"You speak very well, sir," insisted MacFarlane in hesitant but adequate Russian. "But you must give me the chance to try my Russian out on you."

"Ah, so you are trying to keep pace with me with such diplomatic amenities," laughed Kudinsky, now speaking in his native tongue through his translator, who had just come up beside him. To MacFarlane's delight, he realized he understood Kudinsky's words even before the translator repeated them.

He joined the premier in the good-natured laugh. "No, I was just saying that I hoped we might have the opportunity to speak more . . . personally, at a later time."

"Indeed, we shall," replied Kudinsky. "I too had hoped for such a time, to speak privately with you—"

MacFarlane gazed deeply into the Russian leader's eyes. His words seemed sincere indeed. This was more than he had hoped for!

"—even," Kudinsky was continuing, "if we dared attempt to speak without . . . without the benefit of our ever-present companions." Here he cast a nod toward his own interpreter and Venzke who had been standing silently at the president's side.

MacFarlane felt a surge in his pulse. How he had hoped for just this moment, and now it had come without his even saying a word. He was about to express his wholehearted approval of just such a tête-à-tête, when the premier spoke up again.

"That is, if we can refrain from trying to outmaneuver one another in language as our two nations seem to be doing with our tanks and planes."

From his tone, MacFarlane judged that the premier was speaking in jest. Yet the mere mention of the pall hanging over their talks seemed to sober both men unconsciously, and without realizing it, each pulled back a step and the cloak of diplomatic formality closed between them once more. Having begun to feel a tentative rapport springing up between them, neither man was now able to conjure up appropriate small talk, and they fell silent.

Just then the cherubic Secretary of Agriculture, Pavel Soroka, joined them.

"There you are, Mr. Secretary," he said breathlessly. "Please pardon the interruption, but you have an urgent phone call. It is from Kaliningrad. I think you should handle it personally."

Excusing himself, Kudinsky turned and left the room, followed by Soroka.

When the premier returned, his face was ashen. It was clear the phone call had disturbed him.

He did not speak to MacFarlane again that evening, except to wish him good night forty minutes later when the reception was over.

---

The following afternoon at one o'clock the leaders and ministers and secretaries and advisors of the two superpowers met formally for the first time. The president and the premier sat opposite one another at the center of the twenty-foot-long conference table, flanked by the secretaries of state and defense and their Soviet counterparts.

Kudinsky opened with a prepared speech of welcome, followed by MacFarlane's prepared text, which he read with little emotion, scolding the Soviet Union for seeming to bring back its policy of aggression. His carefully measured words were not especially confrontive, containing the kind of rhetoric that had flowed freely between the two nations throughout the Cold War and detente periods. Both men seemed to be speaking more for the benefit of their own constituencies than for one another. Their words were expected, ideological, and dispassionate.

The Soviet Minister of Defense took the floor next, delivering a more pragmatic account of the burden of necessity placed upon the Soviet Union to rigorously defend her borders. Their purpose, he emphasized, was purely defensive, as it had been throughout the entire nineteenth century.

At this point Martin Tucker interrupted with a blow-by-blow accounting of the offensive nature of the Hungarian invasion, the Afghanistan invasion, and the present threat to Iran which could not, he said, under any circumstances whatsoever, be interpreted as anything but an act of aggression and a threat to the free commerce of the Persian Gulf.

For the next seventy-five minutes the two sides exchanged increasingly heated words, each pointing steadfastly to the other's intransigence, without so much as a mention of the reforms of the past decade. It was as though ten years of bottled hostility suddenly surfaced on both sides of the table.

Nobody seemed to notice that neither Kudinsky nor MacFarlane said another word beyond their introductory remarks. If anything, they seemed bored by the meeting.

When the meeting finally broke up, in the midst of the bustling activity of gathering papers and scooting back chairs, MacFarlane noticed the premier trying to catch his eye. When he saw that he had the American's attention, the Russian stretched his hand across the table quickly. MacFarlane held out his hand, and in the course of the ostensibly innocent handshake intercepted a folded piece of paper. Their eyes remained fixed upon one another for but an instant more, then each turned away.

An hour later, when he was at last alone, MacFarlane took the paper out of his pocket and unfolded it. In awkwardly constructed English characters were the words:

*You said we should speak privately. I agree. We must do what others cannot. We must find a way! Please, after tomorrow's meeting, meet me to talk. Follow me and I will show you where. I will not be able to be alone until then.*

MacFarlane took a deep breath and smiled. An enormous weight had just been lifted from his shoulders.

# SIXTY

Vladimir Kudinsky rose from his bed and glanced at his watch. It was two-thirty—the dead of night.

Slowly he walked to his window.

Usually his insomnia resulted from fear of war. Tonight, however, he was unable to sleep for fear of man. One *particular* man!

Curse that Bolotnikov!

Step down indeed! Did the pompous zealot actually think he was going to resign in favor of the likes of him? The man's ego and presumption knew no bounds!

The phone call could not have come at a more inopportune time. Of course, Leonid knew that. He was fully aware of the diplomatic schedule and had purposely picked that very moment to interrupt him.

What could he possibly have meant—*"I can bring you down at will, comrade. You are falling from power anyway. But I warn you, a deal with the American president will seal your fate all the sooner and ensure your disgrace. And in the Soviet Union, my friend"*—here he had laughed that hateful, evil, scornful laugh—*"you know what that means!"*

Yes, he *did* know what that meant. A small apartment with an even smaller pension. In Moscow if he was lucky. If he wasn't—somewhere considerably farther to the east where the frigid winters were the cruelest exile of all.

Worse—it would mean his political nemesis, that war-hungry madman, would command the seat of power in the Kremlin with a willing Politburo behind him. Chances for a lasting era of peace in the world vanished! Bolotnikov's Napoleonic ego and lust for conquest would lead him to war as surely as it did all rulers with that twisted nature.

It was a fool's game they played with their scorecards of weaponry! Even if the Soviet Union out-tallied the U.S. in "kills," what would be accomplished?

Only death . . . death . . . and more death! Men killing men. What a travesty against . . . against—he couldn't say it even to himself. He wasn't supposed to believe in such things. But even if it wasn't a travesty against man's Creator, it lessened the evil of killing not a straw. When was killing *ever* a thing to be desired—for anyone!

He groaned to himself.

He was the wrong man for this position, for this time. He should have been born in another place. Probably in the West. He was not even thinking like a loyal Russian peasant, much less like the leader of the Soviet Socialist Republic. He sounded like one of those American peace demonstrators!

Oh, the irony of this position in which he found himself! His nation poised on the brink of nuclear confrontation, and him thinking of peace . . . everything was upside-down!

*Perhaps Bolotnikov is right!* he thought. *Perhaps I am the one who is going mad!*

Ah, but the pomposity of the man was unbearable!

*Persist in your folly and both you and MacFarlane will be finished forever,* he had said across the six hundred miles of phone line. *Do not be a fool, Vladimir. Take this opportunity, with the world watching, to resign, and I will see that you are treated kindly. Otherwise, I can guarantee nothing.*

Yet . . . no doubt he was right. The American president had been talking tough lately. Surveillance showed they were stepping up military readiness. For all he knew this peace initiative was merely a smoke-screen. Hadn't they been taught—and told their people—that it was the Americans who were pushing the world toward the brink of war? Furthermore, even if he could arrive at some understanding with MacFarlane—of which there was no certainty—such an accord might mean nothing. If Bolotnikov truly had the backing and chose to take matters into his own hands, the results could be beyond his control, no matter what happened in these few days.

Yet somehow . . . some illusive something in the American president's eyes told him there *was* hope. When their gaze had met, there was—a look—almost a *bond*, an unspoken understanding.

If he *was* going mad—as he had told himself he must be at least five dozen times this year!—this sense of camaraderie with the enemy only served to complete the delusion.

*Vladimir, Vladimir . . . how did you come to this place? You are truly caught between the Siberian winter and the animosity of an evil rival. To whom will you turn for help?*

Sometimes he longed for a chance to walk again through the woods, to be alone, to smell the fragrance of the earth after a warm rain. But now, though he occupied one of the most powerful positions in the world, he was a prisoner. He could not so much as leave this room without falling under close scrutiny. Even if he could manage to speak with the president alone, what could they hope to accomplish? Today's meeting demonstrated all too clearly that the leaders on both sides were intractable in their positions. Tomorrow's session would likely be more of the same.

Bolotnikov was probably right. If he tried to effect some peaceful settlement, it would be viewed by the rest of the Politburo as a backing down. Then Bolotnikov would step in and wrest control out of his hands. He could no doubt pull it off.

Similarly, he knew MacFarlane was in trouble in his own country, even in danger of being ousted from office. So what if the two were able to come to some understanding? It would mean nothing but a private meeting of minds. The result would probably be no more successful than Sadat and Begin had been in the months following Camp David. And Sadat wound up assassinated for his trouble!

What was the use?

Still—he had to try! Even if he and MacFarlane could just . . . communicate . . . as two individuals, wouldn't that be a victory of sorts? Letting their guards down long enough to become friends!

Ah—what incredible possibilities . . . two world leaders who in a moment of time laid down the trappings and cloaks and preconceptions of their offices, and drew together as fellow pilgrims on the earth. What a historic, personal triumph!

Yes, he *would* see MacFarlane alone. Somehow! It didn't even matter if the president called him a lunatic. He must unburden his heart, on a personal level. To do so was unheard of in the Soviet hierarchy. To show emotion was regarded as the supreme weakness of the dominant male.

But for too long he had disguised his true thoughts and feelings. If MacFarlane thought him crazy, then perhaps he would do well to follow Leonid's advice and step aside voluntarily.

If only he could make the American president believe him!

# SIXTY-ONE

The day promised to be lovely and warm. Perhaps Moscow would enjoy a fine summer after all.

Jarvis MacFarlane and Vladimir Kudinsky looked like two old friends out for a quiet stroll, enjoying the warm sunshine of a summer afternoon in Moscow's Vorontsovo Park. In the distance, swimmers splashed about in a deep, glassy pond while others sunbathed along the water's edge. They paid no attention to the two men, nor did they seem to notice the other two brutish looking young men in dark suits and sunglasses, following some yards behind.

Had the scene been played out on American soil, a mob of media personnel would have been scrabbling to press as close as possible. But Kudinsky had given orders for the press and everyone else to stay away for the day, so the scene was almost a quiet one. Only a few ambitious American photographers were trying to capture the private moments with huge telephoto lenses, but even they were a great distance away.

The private meeting had been hastily arranged after today's morning session when, during a five-minute photo interlude, Kudinsky had inconspicuously suggested that MacFarlane meet him after luncheon at the entrance to Vorontsovo Park. Bring only a bodyguard and his interpreter, the premier said, if he would not feel too vulnerable, and he would do the same. MacFarlane had readily agreed. In the United States such a private encounter might have been fraught with danger, but with the park well-patrolled by troops there was little risk for either man.

Every now and then as he and the premier walked along the path winding through the towering oaks and ash, MacFarlane thought he caught glimpses of the suits of his own security agents among the foliage, along with the black jackets he had come to associate with the KGB. The entire park, in fact, was heavily staked out. But the premier had given strict orders that everyone keep their distance. He did not want to be overheard. What the American president might say he had no idea, but if his words were heard by the wrong ears, it would mean an instant end to everything he hoped for.

"So, here we are," said Kudinsky, as if enjoying himself. His interpreter was by his side and he spoke in Russian. "Who would have thought it possible? An American president and a Soviet premier strolling together in the park!"

MacFarlane laughed, then replied, also in Russian. "The barriers of custom, office, and diplomacy must come down between us, and between all men. Otherwise the day will surely come when we will destroy ourselves."

"Truly spoken," replied Kudinsky. "But so much separates the people of the world. And we leaders especially are hopelessly bound up by the vestments and pressures of our positions. We become imprisoned and cannot do the very things we want to do."

"Not to mention language and cultural differences."

"Ah, but you handle my language very well. I must say, I am surprised at your proficiency."

"I am not as proficient as I would like to be," replied MacFarlane.

"You must have acquired this skill recently. There has been no news of it."

Again MacFarlane laughed. "*Very* recently! And with much hard work, believe me."

"But why?"

"Because, as I said two evenings ago at the reception, I came to Moscow with the hope of speaking with you alone—completely alone. To do so, I knew I must learn as much Russian as I could."

"But you cannot have learned so much in the three weeks since we have been planning this summit?"

"No. I have been studying four months."

"Four months?"

"Yes. Something happened four months ago which made this talk with you imperative, so I began immediately to study your language." He paused and Kudinsky cocked an eyebrow inquisitively. "But that I will have to explain when we are *completely* alone," the president nodded toward the men who were still with them.

Uncertain as to what the premier was thinking about his previous statement, MacFarlane finally added, "You understand about the necessity for privacy in our talk?"

Kudinsky nodded.

"I am glad you have chosen the open air. It is exactly the kind of setting I would have hoped for."

"To avoid indoor bugging devices, I assume?" said Kudinsky.

"I meant no disrespect, but it is the kind of world we live in, and you and I are both pragmatic men. In positions like ours one soon learns to live with a certain amount of paranoia."

"Ah, yes," sighed the premier with a knowing nod. "A sad but true fact of leadership. But though the open air cannot be bugged, a premier might be. A man's clothes, you know? Are you not concerned about that?"

"You would have had good reason. I might even have considered it myself in your position. But it is a risk I must take. What I have to say to you is too important to worry about such things. If you choose to use my words against me afterwards, I will take no steps to stop you."

"Spoken like a gentleman who is sure of himself," replied Kudinsky. "I applaud your stout heart. In truth, my associates tried to force a bugging apparatus on me, but I declined . . . for my own reasons. So I suppose we are relegated to the somewhat uncharted territory of trust."

"Trust is a weighty burden."

"You are a philosopher."

"I was only thinking that *now* the burden rests on my shoulders, but before this afternoon ends it will sit squarely on yours."

"In what respect, Mr. President?"

"After what I have to tell you, the fate of . . . many people may be determined by whether you laugh in my face or call me a madman."

Kudinsky was silent a moment. "Very mysterious," he said at length, then paused again. "You have obviously gone to a great deal of trouble to obtain a private meeting with me. The lessons, the summit, speaking so forthrightly to a man you scarcely know—even an enemy, some would say." The premier stopped and faced MacFarlane. "I will accept the challenge that lies ahead. I assume you have no choice but to accept the one set before you right now."

MacFarlane smiled. "I have a feeling it won't be such a challenge for me after all. You are an open and honest man. Forgive me for casting doubt on you."

"These are difficult times," answered Kudinsky. "Caution is a virtue not to be despised."

"I see you are also a philosopher."

The two men laughed, and in that moment took the first important step, which was to cease being adversaries. They were not yet friends, but they were no longer strangers.

As they continued walking, MacFarlane removed his handkerchief from his pocket and mopped his sweaty brow. The weather was warmer here than he had anticipated.

"There is a bench up ahead where we can sit," suggested the premier. Then he turned and spoke to his interpreter and to the two bodyguards who had been following about five paces back.

Meanwhile MacFarlane spoke to Peter Venzke and his own Secret Service man with him.

"The premier and I are going to talk privately for a while," he said, giving Peter a knowing glance. "So I'd appreciate it if you'd stay back there with the others till we're through."

He rejoined Kudinsky and the two men walked the forty or fifty yards to the bench and sat down. For the first time they were completely alone. No one could hear a word they said.

"I think we'll manage fine without the interpreters," said Kudinsky. "Your Russian is really quite splendid."

"Thank you," said MacFarlane, easing his frame onto the bench. "Ah, it feels good to sit. I keep telling myself I should exercise more."

He paused, knowing the time had come to set aside small talk. He had been preparing for this moment for months. Yet more often than he cared to admit, he had feared that when the time came he would not be able to summon the courage to go through with it. It would be so easy to write the vision off as fantasy. He could quickly draw up a whole list of good reasons for doing so—all logical and sensible. But none could dispel the glaring fact that to deny the vision would be an act of pure cowardice.

He sucked in a deep breath of warm air, as if it might be his last, and then launched out into that uncharted territory Kudinsky had spoken of earlier.

"Mr. Premier," he said, "I think you will agree with me that as each year passes, our world becomes a more dangerous place in which to live. Our capacity for utter destruction has been refined to near perfection. In the name of peace we have made ourselves stronger and stronger. With the exception of your immediate predecessor, Mr. Gorbachev, whom I greatly admired, the leaders of both our nations have not *really* sought peace. My own predecessors have built up vast nuclear arsenals while trying to conduct SALT and SALT II and INF treaties. And, if you will pardon my being so blunt, the leaders of your nation have lied about the true nature of their intent—speaking of freedom and peace, while taking freedom away from sovereign nations by most unpeaceful means. Even the great advances made by our Mr. Bush and your Mr. Gorbachev represented the merest beginnings, only tentative steps toward a permanent peace. And now with them gone, I fear it may rest with us to determine what course we take on this uncharted path of recent peace, whether we continue on or whether it becomes a mere asterisk of history—a brief but temporary respite in the hostilities of man against man."

He paused and glanced over at the premier, concerned about both his language skill and the effect of his words. He was taxing his Russian to its limit, but it appeared he was making sense and not giving offense.

"Thus far we have been lucky," he continued. "Men of restraint, if not always complete honesty, have kept our respective nations in tow for over fifty years. Daily I pray that some madman doesn't get hold of this capacity for destruction we have invented. You and I both know there are men out there who would have few qualms about using it if they dared. Men in countries of the third world, angry men, violent men—even men in our own nations—who have no fear of the horrors of war. You have heard all these things before and have no doubt pondered them yourself."

As MacFarlane spoke, he fumbled for the right phrases, occasionally substituting an English word or sentence. When he did, Kudinsky seemed to sense his hesitation and nodded for him to continue. Thus, in an unorthodox mixture of Russian and English, the two leaders were able to make themselves understood.

"I would have resigned myself to this dilemma—as leaders before me have done. Resigned myself, that is, to the impossibility of *doing* anything tangible and practical about it. Peace is such an elusive dream. It sounds so easy. Who wouldn't want peace? But let's be honest with ourselves . . . there has never been a lasting peace throughout the whole history of man. Politics does not make for peace; it makes for conflict. And here *we* sit—two politicians—talking about peace. What *can* we do? I don't know. But it seems that someday—somehow—*somebody* has to turn that tide if mankind is to survive. Why should it not begin with us?"

MacFarlane was so intent upon finding the words to communicate what was on his heart that he had hardly noticed Kudinsky's increasing agitation as he spoke.

"It *can* begin here . . . now," the premier finally burst out. "I agree most heartily! I cannot tell you the joy it brings to my tired old Russian heart to hear you say these things. Indeed, you give voice to the very longings of my soul—longings I am afraid even to tell to my own people. For so long I have hungered for just this of which you speak, but I feel the constant frustration of knowing all do not yearn for peace as I do. At this very moment there are men who would unseat me from power, as there are those who would wish for you to be defeated in your election—men who are bent on domination and destruction."

"Given these realities, what can we do?" posed MacFarlane.

"We must go beyond negotiations and limiting arms," replied Kudinsky. "Like you, I feel the futility of all this. For months I have been fighting a losing cause in the Kremlin against this problem in Iran. How can there be peace when we are threatening war? But they listen only to false and lying voices, and I have become impotent. Do you feel such frustration with your own Congress and Pentagon?"

"Of course."

"And what you said in your recent speech was absolutely true. Our action on the Iranian borders is inexcusable. It is an aggressive move, contrary to the cause of peace, contrary to all my beloved Mikhail accomplished."

"I said what I said out of diplomatic necessity."

"I understand."

"But then I don't . . . perhaps *I* don't understand. You sound as though you are against what your country has been doing?"

"Much has changed for me in recent months. I have had . . . what shall I call it? . . . an experience, perhaps, which has profoundly altered my outlook about many things. Since then I have been a lone voice in the Politburo, pleading for a continuation of our course of peace among the disgruntled hard-liners who have been silent longer than they like. But to little avail. I fully understand the concerns you must have. As long as our Soviet troops are massed in an aggressive posture, how can we talk of peace. But beyond that, something must change in the fundamental way we view our two nations. Oh, if only I might tell you . . . everything! Then you would see!"

"Would a total peace between us ever be possible?" asked MacFarlane. "Can you imagine not just an arms reduction, but elimination? A peace treaty of genuine alliance and mutual support? I can hardly imagine such a thing! But I too have much to tell you. I have a story to tell you that will seem . . . incredible—unbelievable. You might *not* believe me! But that is the risk I take."

"But if you could only first hear what I was about to tell you," said Kudinsky.

"Please . . . if I don't go on with it now, I may never get up the courage to tell you my story again," said MacFarlane. "As you will see, it is not an easy tale to tell."

"You are my guest," conceded Kudinsky. "I will yield to you. But only if you promise to hear me out in full later. To tell you *my* tale is why I insisted upon a private interview."

"Granted," said MacFarlane with a laugh. "But after I am through, you may not want to tell me anything. As difficult as it will be for me to tell, it will be even more difficult for you to believe."

He paused. The moment of truth had come. He began to perspire once more, this time not from the heat.

"Samuel Butler, an English satirist, once said, 'There's but the twinkling of a star between a man of peace and war.' I find that to be truer every day," he began. "Sometimes I even question where

I stand myself. I only know that I ache for my world. And perhaps that is why . . . why I experienced what I am about to tell you. You may well think me insane. There is nothing I would like to do more right now than to forget the whole thing—to go back to our utterly futile little so-called 'peace' talks and somehow muddle along, and if we are lucky leave our problems to the next generation to solve. But I didn't come ten thousand miles to . . . ah . . . to chicken out."

"Chicken out?" inquired Kudinsky, again with raised eyebrow.

"Yes. It means to—well, to get cold feet—to back down from something. Like cowardice."

"Ah, I see—hmm—*chicken out.*" Kudinsky mused, tapping his lips thoughtfully. "An interesting way of putting it. But go on, I did not mean to interrupt you."

"It's very difficult to express what I want to say, but it's vitally important that you understand. So interrupt if I am not making myself clear. But I took special care to make sure of this one word, because everything hinges on your grasping what really happened." He paused, as if to summon one last measure of courage before going on.

"I suppose you could say it all began with the twinkling of a star. Not a star, actually, but the moon. I was up late several months ago and, unable to sleep, I wandered into the Oval Office. I found myself at the window staring out at the moon and the blackness of the night, pondering the day's events and the future of the world, when . . . and here I don't know how to tell you this except to say the word I told you I wanted to make certain of. Mr. Premier, I experienced what in both our lands we refer to as a . . . a *vision.*"

MacFarlane released a long sigh, as if the worst were behind him. He had *said* it, and to his complete astonishment, Kudinsky had not laughed. In fact he had not responded in any way at all except to knit his brows in intense interest. There was a glow in his eye which MacFarlane could not account for, but he said nothing.

The president then went on to recount his entire experience on that fateful night, leaving nothing out.

As he listened, Kudinsky sat still as a stone, and toward the end MacFarlane could hardly tell if he was comprehending him at all. He moved scarcely a muscle throughout the recital. When the president finished with the final account of the minister's sermon, he suddenly felt a sick pang. Had Kudinsky understood a word of it?

The only sounds were those filtered to them from the rest of the park and the muffled traffic from beyond the lawns and woods. Yet they might have been a thousand miles away. The two men were alone in the universe, side by side, still as statues.

MacFarlane had expected many things in response, but not this. The utter silence was almost more than he could bear. He wanted to say something to break the heavy pall, but there was nothing left to say.

The summer heat became oppressive, and MacFarlane removed his jacket and hung it over the back of the bench. Suddenly he was desperately thirsty, yet at the same time rebuked himself for thinking of something so trivial as water when the survival of the world was at stake.

Finally, after nearly five minutes, Kudinsky spoke, weighing his words carefully.

"I have a question for you, Mr. President," he said.

"Yes."

"You were very precise in your account. But you left out one rather key point—the time of your . . . uh, vision."

MacFarlane opened his mouth to respond, but Kudinsky held up a restraining hand. "Let me see if I can guess."

This was hardly the time for games, thought MacFarlane. Was the premier making sport of him? Yet there was something in the Russian's tone that matched his expression. It was extremely disquieting, but carried no ridicule.

"By all means," said MacFarlane rather doubtfully.

Kudinsky noted the skepticism and a brief smile flickered across his features.

"Thank you," he said. "My guess would be that it occurred around February twenty-seventh—no, February twenty-sixth—in the very early morning, perhaps twelve or one o'clock. Computing time differences is such a nuisance. I have never been very proficient at it—my watch is invariably off when I travel. What is there, nine or ten hours difference between our two countries?"

But MacFarlane scarcely heard the premier's question. His mind was reeling with the man's astounding estimate of the date and time of his vision. It was correct, down to the exact hour!

Quickly he reviewed whether he had let the date slip. He was certain he had not. In fact, he couldn't even remember telling it to Karen or Jeremy—somehow the precise date had never seemed that important. He might have mentioned the time, but not the date. And he had certainly never said anything about it to Kudinsky.

Seeing the president's dumbfounded expression, Kudinsky chuckled lightly, and a full grin spread over his face.

"You are baffled, no doubt?" he said.

The president nodded, still speechless.

"It is now time for *my* story," said the premier, settling back comfortably against the bench.

"It was the twenty-fifth of February, and the day had been an impossibly long one. For the first time, it had fully dawned on me what a threat my comrade Leonid Bolotnikov truly was. And it was on that day that I became filled with a fear that was new to me—the practical, realistic fear of impending war. I did not get to sleep until after two in the morning and slept poorly all night. Finally around dawn I settled into a more restful slumber and managed to sleep for several more hours. When I awoke it was as though something had startled me out of a deep sleep. It must have been 9:00 or 9:30 . . . which, as you have by now surmised, was almost exactly the time of your . . . shall we say, your experience."

MacFarlane stared blankly at Kudinsky, unable to believe what he was hearing. The Russian premier now wore an extremely serious countenance, as though the reliving of his own personal memory was pulling emotions from somewhere deep inside him.

"A great light filled the room—but it did not come from the morning sunlight streaming through the windows. Then, as I slowly rose from the bed, I realized I was not alone. Someone was in the room with me, but I could not see His face—for the light was coming from Him, blinding me. I was terrified, and yet I could not take my eyes off the wondrous sight. I do not know if the Voice spoke to me then or not. I only know that He was leading me to the window, where He pointed out toward the sun. Beside the light coming from the man in my room, the sun seemed almost pale. Somehow I could look at the sun without being blinded. That was one of the things that kept telling me the whole thing was a dream. Suddenly the sun turned dark for a few moments—pitch black. Then gradually billows of smoke began to seep from around its edges. Then the smoke gave way to flames, and I knew it was the fire and smoke of war."

He stopped for a moment, took a deep breath, and labored on.

"I looked at the sun—and then the Voice spoke to me as I stared out into the morning sky. Gradually the sun changed again, and as the Voice spoke, I found myself arguing with it, saying that I could not possibly be the one to do as he said . . . but there is no need to tell you all the Voice said, because you have already told me—for He spoke the same words to us both!"

Kudinsky stopped, overcome by emotion, and MacFarlane looked into his face. He could not believe what he saw. Tears were gathering in the old Russian's eyes, threatening to spill onto his cheeks.

"Do you grasp what I am telling you?" he said at length, his voice barely under control. "Do you understand *who* this man was . . . who the Voice was? I do not even believe such a power exists! The Communism to which I have given my life steadfastly denies the existence of any supreme being.

"Yet—yet—what can I say? All my attempts to convince myself that I was dreaming have now been utterly dashed. It *did* happen, my friend! He spoke to us! To you and to me. He came to us both . . . spoke to us. How will we ever be the same again?"

Kudinsky buried his face in his hands, weeping freely now.

MacFarlane reached over and gently laid his right hand on Kudinsky's shoulder in a simple gesture of comfort and brotherhood. With his left hand he wiped away the moisture beginning to gather in his own eyes.

# SIXTY-TWO

That evening the three U.S. networks as well as the major cable channels opened their newscasts with reports from either their Moscow or White House correspondents who were covering the talks. The headlines astounded the world.

Standing in front of the backlit Kremlin, floodlights upon them as they held their microphones, a bevy of reporters and anchormen spoke to the American people:

> The diplomatic world in Moscow was stunned today with an unprecedented move by President Jarvis MacFarlane and Soviet Premier Vladimir Kudinsky. . . . Taking both sides by surprise, the two leaders issued a joint statement calling for a cancellation of all further talks between their staffs and departments of State. . . . Early this afternoon the two leaders left officialdom behind and went walking together in Moscow's Vorontsovo Park for approximately two hours, leaving interpreters, bodyguards and Secret Service agents to watch from a distance. . . . A round of discussions was slated for four o'clock this afternoon, but at the last moment both the premier and the president instructed their staffs and department heads that the meeting would be postponed.

> Nothing more was said, but it is thought that the two men conducted further private meetings. . . . At seven o'clock this evening the two men appeared in front of the Kremlin and issued word for word statements in both Russian and English, saying that there would be no further talks. . . . Apparently the only two men in Moscow who know what is going on are the president and the premier, and they are keeping their thoughts and their whereabouts a closely guarded secret.

A report, taped earlier in the evening and filed by veteran Moscow correspondent Mark Phelps, was run by CBS:

> Theories of what President MacFarlane and Premier Kudinsky are up to are as numerous in Moscow tonight as there are people. It was first thought that the cancellation of this afternoon's session indicated a stalemate between the two leaders. Sources close to the president, however, indicate that his spirits seem upbeat, that he is smiling and optimistic, and this has led to speculation that perhaps the two men are attempting to circumvent the traditional diplomatic process by arriving at some mutual agreement between themselves. Indeed, though press cameras and microphones have been kept far away from the two men during their private talks this afternoon, long-distance glimpses of the two leaders seem to confirm the very opposite of discord. One photographer's comment was: "They seemed like two old friends out for a walk and enjoying themselves." So we continue to wait for more light to be shed on this highly unusual situation. Meanwhile, a press conference has been scheduled for tomorrow afternoon at three o'clock.

---

Some three hours later as the morning sun broke over Moscow, the air in the presidential suite of the Rossia was almost jubilant.

"I haven't slept like that in months!" exclaimed MacFarlane to his smiling daughter across the breakfast table. "It's like a burden's been lifted off my shoulders!"

"What about the burden you've placed on everyone else?" laughed Karen. "You and Kudinsky turned this city upside down! Do you know how hard it's been for me to play dumb to what's going on?"

"I'm sorry," he said with sincerity. "But it'll all be out in the open soon."

"And then what?"

"The way I have it figured, one of two things. Either I'll be a hero, or the minute we get home they'll tar and feather me and run me out of Washington."

"Are you and Kudinsky going to go public about your visions?"

MacFarlane didn't answer immediately, and when he did, his words were measured and serious. Yet at the same time they conveyed a new level of confidence. Deep inside things were beginning to align themselves. The new spiritual perspective with which he was viewing the world and his mission was gradually coming into focus. What Peter had told him on the plane was having its impact in his soul, and though there remained a great deal of uncertainty, his tone reflected calmness and poise.

"I don't know, Karen. That's something we still have to decide. These are unknown regions—for both of us. First, trusting each other enough to actually tell what happened. Then trusting—I don't know, a higher Power, I suppose—for what to do next. The only thing we're both agreed on is that we want to do what's right . . . right for both nations and right for the world. How to achieve that, we don't know. We're merely two men—two men who have seen something, who have seen an urgent truth. How to go about leading our nations and our people into living that truth, when there are powerful forces in both our governments trying to do just the opposite, that's the new challenge. And we just don't know. There's a great deal we have to work out. But at least on a personal level we are allies—friends—brothers. We know that now, which makes it much easier."

Karen smiled understandingly at her father. She was truly proud of him. She believed in him now more than ever.

"I don't know if you do this kind of thing or not, dear," MacFarlane went on. "Heaven knows it's new to me, and I feel like a little child when I try it by my bed at night. But if you do—if you can—will you pray for us, that we will make the right decisions?"

"I already have been, Dad," was Karen's simple reply.

---

By 10:30 that morning, MacFarlane had summoned Jake Randolf, Peter Venzke, and several of his most trusted Secret Service agents to his room.

"I'm going to need to ask you men to trust me," he began, once they were seated. "I know all this looks pretty kooky, and I imagine the press is making it even worse. I'm going to tell you as much as I can. Premier Kudinsky and I have decided to take matters into our own hands, so to speak. We're going to cut through all the diplomatic baloney and try to come up with a lasting, long-term settlement on our own."

He held up his hand to forestall a comment from Randolf. "I know, I know, you're going to say we *have* a peace with the Soviet

Union that they are now on the verge of breaking in Iran. And that's the problem! All the summits, treaties, and talks and everything else over the last fifty years has resulted in nothing *lasting*. 'Permanent' peace is what we need. Even Gorbachev could only make beginning stabs at it, and now here we are at it again—the militaries of both nations on full alert. Well, we think it's time for a new era of peace—*real* peace. Lasting peace. The sort of peace Gorbachev and Bush only saw dimly. And we're determined to make it happen, by executive fiat if necessary. Now I have about four more hours to meet with the premier to work things out, and I need your help before it all hits the fan this afternoon at three. So . . . are you with me or not?"

"We're with you, of course, Jarvis," replied Randolf. "But look at it from our standpoint, how do we know—"

"Trust, Jake," interrupted the president. "How do you know Kudinsky's not using me? How do you know this whole thing isn't some kind of set-up? How do you know I'm not being made a patsy? Right?"

Heads nodded everywhere around the room, with the exception of Peter Venzke.

"I can't give you a good answer, gentlemen. But we've got to start trusting each other sometime. So I'll put it as simply as I can. I trust Kudinsky. He's playing straight with me. And I'm being up front with him too. We're no longer an American and a Russian—we're two human beings—two brothers on a common planet. Trust. That's the answer to your question. And as for me, I'm ready to start living by it. So I'm asking you—can *you* trust *me* for another four hours and help me bypass the press, state, defense, even our own people? I have to get out of here and over to an apartment near the Kremlin where Kudinsky's waiting for me. And I need to do it secretly if possible. So I ask you again—are you with me?"

---

When MacFarlane walked into the sparsely furnished fifth-floor apartment he half expected to see Kudinsky surrounded by three or four KGB agents. Years of conditioning still operated despite his efforts to shake them off. But the premier was alone in the room, and MacFarlane dismissed the next immediate thought that flashed through his mind—was the room bugged. Their relationship was certainly beyond that now.

Kudinsky rose to meet him with a smile. They shook hands, then embraced warmly.

"It is good to see you again, my friend," said the premier.

"We have much to decide upon, and the time is short," said MacFarlane. They each continued to use a mixture of Russian and English, trying only to make themselves understood and not worrying about propriety, protocol, or grammar. "But I must tell you," he continued, "I slept marvelously—the best night's sleep I've had in months . . . since February!"

"I was a baby again!" agreed Kudinsky. "To have that weight lifted—to have actually *told* someone!"

"And to be able finally to say—*I'm not crazy*!"

"Or at least to know that if you are, then you have company, for surely we must both be thus afflicted," replied the premier.

MacFarlane laughed. "Believe me, I have wondered about my sanity more often than I care to remember during these past months. I kept these incredible things to myself for so long that I was convinced I'd be shipped to the funny farm if anyone knew, all the while half wondering if that wasn't where I belonged anyway."

"Funny farm?" repeated Kudinsky.

"An asylum for the insane."

"Ah, yes," the premier replied. "I have wondered the same things myself. In my country most such places, especially those reserved for public figures and dissidents, have Siberian addresses."

"I hadn't thought of that. It must have been agony for you."

"Most of my life I have been an atheist. At least I have forced myself to believe I was an atheist. I have spent my life convincing my unwilling brain that such places as heaven and hell, and the supposed beings who are said to inhabit them, do not exist. But in recent months I have begun to wonder whether any man truly can be an atheist, down in the very foundation of his being. I wonder whether those who call themselves atheists are in reality simply expending intellectual energy trying to convince themselves that there is no Maker of the soul they deny having, yet whose existence they feel inside themselves—fighting against the feelings that make them what they are, different from a tree or a bug or a dog."

"Yesterday you called me a philosopher," said MacFarlane. "It would appear, however, that you are the philosopher-theologian among us!"

Kudinsky laughed brightly. "I have been forced to think about these things, whether I want to or not."

"As have I."

"Yet now that I have thought seriously of these things," continued Kudinsky, reverting to his native Russian, "I have to realize that all along some inner voice cautioned me against the teachings our young Soviet children have forced upon them. Even as I grew into manhood, though I did not recognize it, I now see that something was telling me to heed my boyish—I was about to call them 'fancies.' Something was telling me to heed the truths that perhaps only a child is able to perceive."

"This recent experience must certainly have shaken you then."

"Until about a week ago, most of my effort has been spent trying to refute the entire affair."

"How do you interpret it now?"

"At first yesterday as you began to recount your experience, I listened in dumbfounded silence, trying to find some way to discount the thing. But . . . I could not. Two men, separated by thousands of miles, strangers from two utterly opposite ideological and cultural and religious backgrounds—for us to have the precise same experience, at precisely the same time. It is too incredible to explain away. I had not told a soul what happened to me. Thus, you could not possibly have known. The only rational conclusion that can possibly be drawn is that some—some supernatural power must have machinated such a phenomenon."

"You are convinced then?"

"Convinced that—?"

"That this is a message from God, which we must heed?"

"Though I have never consciously *believed* in God, yet . . . yes—I suppose that is what I consider the vision to be. Though how to—as you say—*heed* it . . . how to obey that Voice, that man of light—knowing what He would have us *do,* that is another matter."

"What else can we do? I thought we were agreed yesterday that the only option before us is peace? That we had been selected in order to bring peace to our world?"

"Peace—yes, of course. But what of the other things the Voice said—the coming of His footsteps—preparing—much to proclaim—what can it all mean?"

"I have pondered those same questions, but I have no firm answers yet. However He said we would be shown and that He would send people to us. And that *has* happened in my case. Suddenly I have met some very interesting people and they have been telling me remarkable things that coincide exactly with the vision."

"You must tell me of them."

"I will. We must find time for that too. And we'll get my friend Peter Venzke in here who can *really* talk to you!"

"And how do we proclaim the message of peace? You might

think that to bring disarmament would make of me a national hero. But I am in a most precarious position in my country. I fear a sudden move toward conciliation would only signal my demise and perhaps drive us even closer to war. Especially if word got out that I'd had a so-called religious experience—that I claimed God had spoken to me. Ha! I would be finished! On the next train to Srednekolymsk! And one is waiting in the wings who would scorn all talk of visions and sneer at even the suggestion of dealing with an American president with trust."

"Do you mean Bolotnikov?"

"I do," said Kudinsky.

"Do you think he possesses the power to overthrow you?"

"I have no doubt of it. He has eyes everywhere—and a great deal of support in the Politburo. He is probably already planning his rejoinder to our talks. Not all men favor peace, my friend."

MacFarlane sighed wearily. "Yes," he said. "The same might be said of some in my country. Though they talk of peace, they spend their lives and energies preparing for war, and the fate of self-fulfilling prophecy draws them ever toward it."

"There will be those in each of our nations who will insist we are being duped, that we as leaders are selling out, that we are being lured into helplessness by a cunning and unscrupulous enemy, especially after this latest breech of the previous attempts at peace."

"I know you are right," said MacFarlane. "We have spent generations erecting massive walls of distrust."

"And we must look prudently and honestly at any agreement, even any attempt to form a treaty of mutual benefit—even the most stringent safeguards could not guarantee compliance in the face of continued mistrust. There must be fundamental commitment to any plan, originating on *both* sides, with trust and brotherhood remaining the guiding principle. Men like you and I must be at the forefront to lead the way in each of our nations."

"Yet if we move too quickly, we may lose all that we have gained by our personal alliance. Remember the Camp David Accords. So much gained on the level of friendship and brotherhood, but all lost so quickly because of the continued self-interests of the respective countries and their governments. Within two years, all three men were out of power."

"I watched the demise of Mr. Carter's valiant efforts with sadness," reflected Kudinsky. "Of course I could say nothing publicly—but I greatly respected that man."

"You are right though," MacFarlane said, responding to the

premier's earlier comment. "If we don't move quickly, within six months I might be out of a job. And the man who would succeed me is, I am afraid, no more to be trusted than your would-be successor."

Both men paused to consider their dilemma.

"We must reeducate our people," offered Kudinsky. "We must make public our friendship, show that there is no fear between us, teach them to trust by offering an example."

"We have no time for all that."

"Yet could that not perhaps provide the key," suggested the premier. "We are the leaders of our people. They look to us. We still control much public response. And you are in a position to control policy."

"Not as much as you might think. We are both in many ways at the mercy of our own political systems."

"There must be a way," said Kudinsky. "Why else would we have been given the vision?"

"Let's forget for the moment the long-range implications," said MacFarlane. "Right now our big problem is Iran. If we can solve that dilemma, then we can announce the more personal elements of trust and work our way toward a genuine and permanent peace."

"You are right. Iran is the immediate issue," replied Kudinsky. "We, of course, have no right to have troops threatening there, though many in the Politburo would strongly disagree with me."

"If you agree to pull your troops back, however, you will lose face and incur the wrath of your military men—who may then defy you and march across the border anyway. Yet if I cannot show my own people that I am strong enough to force you to retreat, I will lose the election."

"At this point," said Kudinsky gravely, "I think I must risk incurring some wrath. There is no way to settle the issue otherwise, even if we had at our disposal the greatest geopolitical minds."

"If only there were some other way . . . but whatever hope we have must come from you and me or my daughter and a young man named Manning, or my friend Peter Venzke. No one else knows of the vision."

"I am not concerned," said Kudinsky in a more positive tone. "There is always the hope of a divine messenger."

*"There is always hope,"* MacFarlane quoted. *"You shall be the instrument of that hope."*

He paused and let the words surround them, permeating their minds and hearts with an assurance that help, at the time it was needed, would indeed come to them.

"I have never been a man of faith," MacFarlane said, "even though I come from what used to be called a 'Christian nation'—though I think few would make the mistake of calling it that now! But when I reflect on that Voice, a great peace comes over me. I *know* we'll find a way. Or perhaps—I know a way will be revealed to us."

The sound of approaching voices intruded upon the silence of the room, and Kudinsky walked to the window and looked down.

"It appears your aggressive free press has found us at last," he said.

"I didn't think we could remain secluded the entire day. But I have good men outside. No one will get in."

"I too have a strong contingent surrounding the building."

"The press will see us soon enough. Though I imagine my own people are just as anxious to know what madness has overtaken us. They didn't appreciate their meaningless meetings being cancelled. They all thrive on what my State Department calls *dialogue*."

Kudinsky laughed. "Yes, I fear we did steal their show."

MacFarlane looked at his watch. "It's almost noon. We have three hours."

"I'll order a light lunch," said Kudinsky. "Then we must sit down and plan more decisively what we will do . . . and what we will say when we place ourselves at the mercy of their questions."

"I think too, my friend, that we should pray."

## SIXTY-THREE

The main hall was filled. Every seat was taken, and people filtered into every conceivable corner and standing place.

The front three rows had been reserved for MacFarlane's and Kudinsky's staffs and departments and ministries of state whose "dialogues" had been so summarily preempted by their bosses. Silently, almost stiffly, they filled up the rows on either side of the center aisle—the Americans on the left, the Russians on the right—while the press corps and other officials jammed in and jostled for position in the rows behind them.

At twenty minutes after three, the president and the premier strode onto the platform together and took their positions, side by side, behind two podiums. Immediately the room fell silent.

"We will each deliver a prepared statement," said Kudinsky in Russian. "We will speak in our native tongues. Then we will open the floor for questions."

MacFarlane repeated this same statement in English, then motioned for Peter Venzke to join him, while Kudinsky's interpreter also came forward.

"When I came to the Soviet Union," began MacFarlane, "I came with a sense of desperation, but also with a sense of optimism and hope. There had been several personal concerns on my heart which convinced me the time for a major new breakthrough in American-Soviet relations had come. Two weeks ago I spoke tough politically because I was not certain whether what I had to say to Premier Kudinsky would be received. If it was not, though I dreaded the very thought, I could see no alternative but an increasingly tougher U.S. military stance. In my heart, however, I knew a lasting peace could only be achieved on a profoundly personal level. I knew that we had to move beyond political and economic necessities toward a lasting relationship of peace that can take our two nations, and indeed the nations of the world, into the twenty-first century and beyond. I came to Moscow seeking just such a permanent solution, though I let no one know of my plans."

The flashing and clicking of cameras was the only sound in the room. Very few of the press took notes, relying instead on pocket recorders to accurately chronicle the historic session.

"I came hoping to meet with Premier Kudinsky alone—completely alone. For that reason I have been intensively studying the Russian language for the past four months—"

At this announcement a slight buzz spread through the room, while several of the American contingent shifted uneasily in their seats; the State Department did not appreciate being in the dark about affairs they judged vital to the national interest.

"And while I cannot by any means claim proficiency in this very difficult language, I can say that the premier and I have managed to communicate most admirably. He knows just enough English to make sense of my fumbling Russian, and vice-versa.

"The language, however, was not the primary ingredient for the success of our talks. Americans have spoken Russian, and Russians have spoken English for decades, yet our two nations have remained hopelessly separated. What we have not sought to become familiar with—and the blame lies on both sides—is something which Premier Kudinsky and I have taken the first tentative steps toward this week. I am speaking of learning the universal language of trust and brotherhood.

"I came to Moscow with a deep desire to speak this language. And unbeknownst to me, Premier Kudinsky desired precisely the same thing. And so we mutually sought a time when we might be alone to share personally and honestly our deep concerns. As we did, we discovered that within the Russian and the American beat the hearts of two fellow human beings who shared a hope that mankind might truly know not only peace at the international level, but compassion and unity on the personal level as well. In short, we became . . . friends."

Here MacFarlane glanced toward Kudinsky with a smile. The premier stepped forward, took the president's hand, and shook it vigorously and meaningfully, looking deep into MacFarlane's eyes for a brief instant, as if to say, "This is it!" He then stepped back to his own podium, and began.

"Since the time of World War II when our two nations fought as allies, we have followed the self-seeking path of watching out for our own interests only. Both nations are guilty. We in the Soviet Union, in our paranoia over what we term American imperialism, have sought to surround ourselves with puppet governments we control, all the while failing to ask ourselves what value should be placed on freedom—"

He paused only long enough to allow the ripple of disbelief and consternation in the Soviet ranks of listeners to settle itself.

"—while you of the West, in emphasizing that freedom, have not adequately taken into consideration the historical and cultural differences which make your form of democracy a workable impossibility not only in our land but in many other countries throughout the world.

"Remaining entrenched in our own systems, our own fears, our own selfishness, our own greed, we have—as the two wealthiest nations on the face of the earth—brought mankind to the perilous brink of destruction."

He paused, apparently gathering strength for what must now come.

"We should be ashamed of ourselves," he said. "If there is such a thing as an ultimate reckoning to be given, then we who have occupied positions of leadership in the United States and the Soviet Union in this last half of the twentieth century—*all* of us—are indicted for our self-seeking ways. We will be held accountable for what we have done. And we have not done well! We hold the wealth and technology to eliminate world hunger, to cure disease, to end poverty, to make great strides in medicine and energy research and space exploration. Yet you Americans spend a fifth of the unfathomable wealth and prosperity granted you forwarding a military system to make guns and planes and ships and other instruments of war and to build up nuclear arsenals that would destroy half a dozen planets the size of the earth.

"Why have you done so? Because *we* have forced it upon you with our military budget which is vastly more out of proportion than yours. The lunacy of our false priorities is no more clearly demonstrated than when we celebrate our national holidays by parading our huge missiles and tanks and troops through Red Square, even as our own people cannot buy the very staples of life.

"False priorities! Priorities of destruction and selfishness!"

Kudinsky stopped and wiped his perspiring brow. He knew he could be committing political suicide. Yet his course was set. There was no turning back. With a deep breath of courage, he continued.

"It is time we stop that evil trend. It must begin somewhere, at some time. And we propose—my friend here and I—that it begin today, in this room. We propose that we jointly dedicate ourselves to an altogether new set of priorities—not only as nations, but as individuals. We propose that we begin to assess national policy not by what is best for *ourselves* based on misconceptions and a mentality that views the other as an adversary on the world stage, but rather by that which seeks the good of both nations. We propose a free flow of information and leadership between our two nations. We propose an alliance of peace and harmony. We propose, in short, a revolutionary and altogether untried relationship between two traditional conflicting powers."

He stopped for a moment, seemingly spent, then concluded, "But before I yield the microphone once more to the president, I must say one thing more. As he stressed earlier, this is the factor upon which everything is based—and thus I reiterate what he said about trust. It is necessary . . . vital. But this trust is not some abstract philosophical entity—it is personal and real. I want to say that I do trust President MacFarlane. He is my friend . . . my brother. Therefore, I ask—how can our two nations continue to be enemies when we hold within our hands the capacity for something so much greater?"

He stepped back, and MacFarlane spoke again, turning first to his colleague.

"Thank you, Mr. Premier. Your trust means a great deal to me."

Then he once more addressed the audience before him.

"But we would not have you misunderstand us. When we speak harshly about the past leaders of our two nations, seeming to lump them all together, we do not discount the advances of this recent decade of good will. Certainly Mikhail Gorbachev and Joseph Stalin cannot even be considered in the same breath, any more than the United States of John Kennedy can be viewed as the same United States as that of George Bush.

"Yet even during these past ten years, even at Malta in '89, and the European summit of '90, and their cooperation at Helsinki over the Hussein affair, and in Berlin in '94 . . . even in the midst of those historic times one ingredient out of the past—yes, out of the Kennedy-Khrushchev Cold War past—still remained. Mistrust remained, ladies and gentlemen—simple mistrust. Therefore, despite all the troop reductions and the dismantling of NATO and the Warsaw Pact, despite the travel freedoms, despite free elections in the Eastern European nations and the Soviet Union, despite the collapse of the Berlin Wall and the reunification of Germany—underlying all that, on both sides, remained a silent question mark, a silent reluctance to fully trust the other. We said to ourselves, we'll keep our weapons systems ready . . . 'just in case.' Maintaining a 'scaled back but highly efficient' military was the subject of many a Washington discussion in the early '90s.

"We were skeptical! And, ironically, we freedom-loving Americans were reluctant to let go of the past. We didn't *want* the Cold War to end! We only fell in with Gorbachev after mind-boggling world events forced our hand. But we kept our suspicions fully in place. Around Washington—and I heard such things throughout the '90s—you could hear discussions to the effect: 'Well, of course, I'm all for Gorby and freedom and peace . . . but what would have happened if Israel had dismantled her army after Camp David, in the aftermath of the Begin-Sadat euphoria? Where would Israel be today? No, Israel kept her powder dry, kept her military strong, and so should we! They're still Russians, after all.' We're skeptical even of peace!"

"And not altogether without reason," put in Kudinsky. "In all honesty, and this will come as no surprise to you given the recent events on the Iranian border, there are powerful elements in my government who never did embrace my predecessor's reforms and who waited patiently and silently for the end of his tenure. So the Egypt-Israel parallel is perhaps apt. The events of this year demonstrate that those mistrusting Americans were right not to trust us."

A rumble of shock ran through the room at the premier's bold admission.

"The point is, we're not trying to affix blame," MacFarlane went on. "There have been violations of trust on both sides. In my government, too, notwithstanding the vast cuts in troops stationed in Europe, and the great reductions in missile strengths on both sides, and the tremendous reductions in military spending, the fact still remains that we—this year!—will spend over two hundred billion dollars on our military. As delighted as I am about the developments of this past decade, and though that's less than half of the level of ten years ago, the fact remains that we are spending that staggering sum essentially targeted *against* the Soviet Union. Don't you see what that means? Despite all the recent changes, our perception of one another is still adversarial. Militarily, we are still enemies!"

He paused, took a sip of water, and allowed his words to penetrate. Then he took a deep breath and continued in a softer tone.

"Well, our hope today is to fundamentally *end* that adversarial relationship which, in spite of the treaties, necessitates military posturing against one another. We want to put to rest, once and for all, the skepticism and mistrust that are still present. What our predecessors began, we now desire to take to deeper and more permanent levels, because we know that unless peace does come on a fundamentally deeper plane, it can never last. History proves it. The Camp David Accords prove it. The enmity and strife over borders and between peoples and among world leaders for all time proves it. To last, there must not merely be a diplomatic peace, but an altogether *new* kind of peace—a peace founded in trust and brotherhood."

He paused again and looked over at the Soviet premier, giving him the opportunity to speak. But Kudinsky gestured for him to continue.

"Now to those of you who are asking what all this will mean, be assured that Premier Kudinsky and I intend to give substance to our words. Palaver about trust and friendship and putting the other's interest on a par with one's own will mean nothing if we return to our respective offices and go on with our affairs as if nothing had changed. We intend to make substantive and permanent alterations in practical policies—cultural, military, and trade—which will not only signal an end to these temporary hostilities between us, but will signal a new era of active and aggressive friendship. Some of these we will simultaneously consummate by virtue of our executive powers. Others we will have to execute through approval by other branches of our respective governments. But it must be understood that we are in dead earnest about each of these policy changes we intend to bring about.

"Now . . . with that as an introduction, we will proceed to outline the specific tenets of actual policy which we envision as paving the way for this new alliance between the United States and the Soviet Union.

Clearly these are only beginning steps. From them, it is our hope that even deeper aspects of healthy change will take root and grow."

President MacFarlane stopped, took a drink of water, followed by a deep breath. Then he embarked on an outline of the specifics of the plan he and Kudinsky had adopted. For the next forty-five minutes the two leaders shared the podium, speaking in turn on arms reductions, total elimination of nuclear weapons, a joint-protection agreement, freedom, Communism, the world's historical and cultural differences, verification, trade agreements, major military restructuring, the peace dividends, nuclear energy, world terrorism, and a plan for the leader of each nation to visit the other twice yearly—addressing its body of leaders and mixing with its people. They ended with a proposal to establish a worldwide body whose sole purpose would be to band together to solve various world problems—beginning with the United States and the Soviet Union, who would invite the participation of any and all interested nations.

## SIXTY-FOUR

When the leaders of the world's two most powerful nations had finished presenting their initial proposals, the room fell deadly silent. The men and women in the front rows appeared stunned. However, it did not take long for the members of the press to begin jumping to their feet, shooting questions at the two men.

"Mr. President, I'm sure we all sense your sincerity," said ABC's Moscow bureau chief. "But realistically, do you actually believe *any* of this will fly past Congress? Seventy-five percent cuts, Mr. President—with our missiles pointed at their targets and theirs at ours!—do you seriously think Congress will even consider it?"

"I don't know, Mr. Jacobson," replied the president. "Perhaps not. But I do believe both the American people and the Russian people desperately want the sort of relationship we have outlined. Maybe if Congress listened to its constituency, there would be approval."

"Come on, Mr. President," shouted another reporter, "you make it sound as though the Cold War was Congress's fault, when we all know it was the direct result of Soviet expansionism and militarism.

And now we have Soviet troops threatening again."

"You've stated the traditional American view, and I would not dispute it," responded the president. "However, I would add that we have done our fair share to contribute to the spread of nuclear weapons. But that is now past history. The Cold War *is* over. It died ten years ago, and this thing on the Iranian border is but an aberration, which we are going to snuff out here and now."

"Premier Kudinsky, I would like to ask you a question," said the American correspondent from CNN, then waited for his words to be translated into Russian. "When you and President MacFarlane were alone, in which language did you speak?"

"We spoke mostly in Russian," answered the premier in halting English and with a slight smile. A ripple of laughter followed, and he added, "Your president speaks very tolerable Russian, and combined with my limited English we managed quite well. But I am determined that when I come to Washington—and we have spoken of a meeting again next month—I will be able to do much better."

"Does the timing of these announcements have any political overtones, Mr. President?"

"None whatsoever," replied the president.

"Mr. Premier, surely this proposal will send major shock waves through the Kremlin. Do you honestly think your hard-line colleagues will back you up on any of this? Immediate withdrawal in Iran . . . *unrestricted* military verification? Monthly meetings with the president! It all signals the most major departure from Soviet policy for the past eighty years, at the very time when we've been hearing that a backlash has already set in—not to take reform further, but to retreat from Gorbachev's liberalizations."

"I answer with President MacFarlane," said the premier. "It is my conviction that the people will support us. *Glasnost* left a lasting mark on our society. We have begun to listen to our people. While it is true our first free elections were carried out only by the Congress of People's Deputies, today our people can also be heard. Such could not have been said twenty years ago, nor even ten. But today, with the people behind us, even in Russia, I believe the leadership can be swayed. Following your example, we are slowly becoming responsive. We either go forward, or we will see a second Russian revolution—this time *against* Communism."

"Is there any sense, Premier Kudinsky, in which your comments today and your plans for the future—the joint manufacturing, for example, and shared technologies, the trade agreements and economic suggestions—indicate a further softening in your attitude toward the democratic system? I know in recent years you have opened your doors to many Western ideas, Western companies. You have even begun to allow private ownership in industry. All steps which we applaud and which have strengthened your economy. And you have allowed a diversity of political viewpoint as well. Yet the Communist party still represents a 79% majority in your People's Congress, and there has never been a disavowal of the intrinsic values of Communism itself. So are you now recognizing to an even greater degree that democracy is a system which allows for greater freedoms—a system which is more humanitarian and which simply *works* better? And on the other side, I would ask you, Mr. President, if today's comments indicate on your part a more liberal attitude toward what we might call a new brand of Communism?"

"Ah, Mr. Forbes," answered the president with a laugh, "you reporters are determined to get us into hot water with our colleagues."

"These are the questions on all of our minds, Mr. President," said Forbes. "We want you to succeed in this. But the people will want to know."

"I understand. We'll try to answer as best we can. But you have to realize that we're in uncharted waters here ourselves. We don't have every detail worked out by any means, nor have we had time to analytically assess every minor point. There are, I'm sure, a hundred holes in the few proposals we have just set forth. We will not be able to give totally consistent and plausible responses on every issue. So long as you can take our answers on that basis, without trying to rip them apart, we'll do our best. Agreed?"

"Agreed, Mr. President."

"And to that I might add that as soon as we're through here, we intend to submit all this to experts in every field whose express purpose will be to blow every hole in these proposals they can, so that we *will* know what's wrong in these ideas. Then we'll be able to modify them accordingly. The point is unity of purpose and common vision, not perfection of the initial plan. Our idea for a commission, a world problem-solving body, for example. What a cockeyed idea that sounds like on the surface! Something like that could never work, right? It never has in the past. The League of Nations . . . the U.N.—no one has ever been able to make such a thing work. Well, we'll bring in experts from around the world to help us avoid some of the same pitfalls, to help us learn from history and from the progress we have made in understanding one another. And hopefully we will be able to truly create an apolitical body with teeth to make a difference. Can it be done? Who knows! So, I would say you're right to ask questions, and to pinpoint flaws. Just so long as you realize the flaws don't undermine the foundation of what we're trying to accomplish. Agreed again?"

"Agreed again," several reporters responded in unison, followed by a round of laughter.

"Then perhaps I'll give my friend a go at the very difficult questions Mr. Forbes posed about changing attitudes," said MacFarlane, turning toward Kudinsky with a grin. "He can hang himself, then I'll follow his lead."

Again laughter filtered through the audience.

A serious look spread over the premier's face as he pondered the implications of the reporter's question. Then he began to speak slowly.

"Certainly my attitude has changed—toward many things. At issue here, I would say, is not so much my attitude toward the democratic system but toward the people who are part of that system—your president in particular. What we have come to see is that relationships must in the end outweigh systems. Certainly democracy contains many inherent strengths, but so does Communism. There are greater freedoms in a democratic state, more of what you would call individual opportunities. Yet in our system we do not have the accompanying ills which freedom inevitably brings—crime, unrest, dissent. These last fifteen years have been a time of 'reevaluation' for us as we have come to realize the bankruptcy of much that we once held dear. But we have not thrown it all out. We have sought since then both to learn from your ways and to find a balance between our system and the old-style Communism of our fathers. And we are still seeking what will work best for us."

He paused, and the president took up the same theme.

"You see," he said, "we are in no way advocating any sort of future political oneness insofar as a system is concerned. For too long we of the West have insisted that democracy is the only viable political system, while the Soviets have steadfastly maintained the same thing about Communism. That dispute has led to this untenable position of conflict which has dominated the world for fifty years. We simply say it is time for such dogmatism to end. Each system has its strengths and its weaknesses.

"It is much like a marriage. A man and a woman are vastly different. Yet they come together and agree to unite in spite of those differences. It is in the joining of those very differences that the uniqueness and joy of marriage shows itself. Similarly, we will not try to impose our specific brand of democracy and our Constitution on the Soviet Union, nor will they try to spread their mix of socialism and capitalism to America. To answer your question, yes—I think this does signal a more understanding attitude on each of our parts toward the other's system. But in no way do we view a fundamental altering of either system as part of the package. We feel it is time for a harmony in the face of differences. That's what unity is—a coming together and merging of different things. We must lay aside the notion that we are bound to promulgate our own system and destroy the other. Both systems are here to stay, and it is time we accepted that."

"That's all well and good, Mr. President. And it sounds very open and peace-loving and magnanimous. However, it misses a key point: the Soviets have expressly avowed as one of their fundamental goals, from the very beginning in 1917, to force the spread of Communism throughout the world, with the ultimate goal being world-wide domination. Now granted, Mr. Gorbachev significantly altered that process. Yet there has never been any formal statement, even by him, that such has ceased to be their goal. As you very well know, many argued that the Soviets were merely taking the struggle to the economic battlefield once they saw that the goal could not be achieved militarily. There is much within your proposals which could be seen as playing right into their hands—the technological implications, especially—*if* such conquest were still their unspoken aim."

MacFarlane opened his mouth to answer, but Kudinsky cut him off.

"Please, Mr. President," he said, "perhaps it would be beneficial for me to try to answer. This is something which really must be clarified. Certainly much has been said through the years about the Soviet goal of so-called world domination. In the early years of the Communist movement this was thought to be the ultimate, practical goal. And there are those in my country who still hold to the goals you speak of, I will not deny it. Some still avow the military method as best. Others, backing the policies of *glasnost* and *perestroika*, view these changes as means—however different—to work our will in the world, to advance Communism more subtly than with tanks and guns. But you have never heard either from my lips. That philosophy of conquest probably reached its zenith during the Brezhnev years. But twenty years later, my predecessor took a more pragmatic view. Afghanistan was perhaps the turning point, when we realized the Soviet empire had overreached itself. Suddenly on every front we began to recognize that the Communism we had fought for was not working. Our economy was collapsing, our people were discontented, our cities were stagnating, while throughout the world we could clearly see capitalism flourishing. Gorbachev focused our attention again on ourselves and our own problems. He forced us to look at the weaknesses of our own system. Against unbelievable odds and opposition in the Kremlin—opposition which still is not dead—he displayed a vision for the future. He knew that freedom had to come to Eastern Europe, that self-determination had to replace Soviet domination. He could see the very survival of the Soviet Union in the balance. The Brezhnev brand of socialism was dying, and capitalism and democracy, where religious and social freedoms existed, were destined to outlive it. Thus, he brought sweeping changes to the Soviet Union. He brought a new revolution. And it was a healthy, vital, necessary change. He did not throw out Communism, but he changed Communism forever. Perhaps now is the moment to take that change a step further still. Thus, I tell you in the clearest terms possible, as premier of the Soviet Union, world domination is *not* my goal for the Soviet Communist system. The past is past! The time has come for us to live harmoniously while we maintain our distinctions.

"Having said that," continued the premier, "let me ask you to exercise the open-mindedness you Americans are so proud of; let me ask you to look at this issue from another vantage point. You have said in the past that we were bent on world domination, which I have not denied, pointing to Communist regimes that have sprung up in Europe and Central America, in Cuba and Africa and the Far East. However, we in the U.S.S.R. saw the rampant spread of democracy and capitalism throughout the '50s and '60s and feared it just as greatly as you feared Communism. We saw it not only in the United States and Britain, where modern democracy originated, but in dozens of nations whose history has not always been democratic—France, Italy, Japan, Germany, Korea, Israel, Spain, Mexico, Africa, Indonesia. Everywhere the democratic system was making incursions into countries where it was as foreign as Communism would be to your nation. We saw billions upon billions of dollars pouring out of the United States under the heading 'foreign aid,' yet to our eyes it looked as though you were trying to buy democracy throughout the world. The spread of democracy, equally bent on world domination, was something we feared. So you see, my friends, it is all a matter of perspective. While you saw our role as aggressive, we saw it as defensive. We of the Soviet Union have always viewed the U.S. as the aggressor.

"I offer none of these thoughts in hostility, but in friendship. As I said, the past is past—on both sides. I merely point out this difference in viewpoint in order to equalize perceptions about what we must now lay down in our mentalities. You Americans will no doubt think it is a greater reach for you to adopt a new view of a non-conquest oriented Soviet Union. I do not think that is true. I want to emphasize that we must *both* lay down the mentality that our own system is best for the rest of the world. At the same time we must lay down our paranoia that the other is seeking to destroy us. At one time such was perhaps true. But no longer. Times, leaders, and our national agendas have altered with the passage of years. We must accept once and for all that the changes of the last decade can become permanent, if we will let them. And here we once again come back to *trust.*"

"Well then, let's say for a moment we buy this," responded UPI's Monica Schaeffer. "We believe the two of you are sincere. The two governments agree to implement the majority of your proposals, and everything goes along wonderfully for a few years—the scale backs, the friendship alliance or whatever you'll call it, the wheat and oil deals, the humanitarian spending of the peace dividend, everything you talked about. Let's even say it all works, and your world problem-solving council solves the ozone problem and makes great inroads against poverty and pollution. But what then? Twenty, thirty years from now, when neither of you is in power and a new generation of leaders comes along and sees an opportunity to secretly get on top, suddenly one of us is in a very precarious position. Wouldn't it be better to maintain our military parity now so as to keep that possibility from happening? After all, it has kept the world out of a major war for fifty years."

"Out of war, but constantly on the verge, Ms. Schaeffer," replied the president. "Hardly a healthy state of affairs, to my way of thinking. Nevertheless, your point is well-taken. Admittedly what we're talking about here is a huge gamble—there are no guarantees. But is the fact that it might not work permanently a sound reason not to try, when it just might turn out to change the world for all time—for the better? The point is, change has to start someplace.

"In 1945, Japan and Germany were our enemies. Then for the next thirty or forty years they were strong political allies. Today we are struggling with each of them to achieve a harmonious equality in the face of extremely competitive economic differences. Some even argue that Japan has become our adversary again. The point is—times do change, and there are no guarantees. What might Marshall and Truman have proposed in 1946 had they foreseen that their rebuilding of Japan and Germany would one day create a serious economic threat to the United States? I don't know. They did what they felt the world needed right then—in the interest of good and right and truth. That's all any leader can do.

"Of course, we are well aware that dozens, maybe hundreds of leaders in our governments will object, for the reasons you have stated and more. Thus it will be incumbent upon us to build into this agreement safeguards at every point which will severely hinder and penalize either nation the moment it begins to think aggressively. Yes, we *will* maintain parity, but at a dramatically reduced level—a parity of allies rather than adversaries. Numerous checks and balances will have to be phased in, just as we have in our constitutional system to keep either a bad president or an over-zealous Congress from gaining an upper hand. Our system proves that checks and balances can work. There is no reason we cannot take them up to the international level as well. There will be constant watch-dogging on the part of each nation, joint committees and commissions, constant military verifications, and a great deal of personal interplay between the president and the premier so that the two leaders always have the opportunity to be friends. These factors alone should keep the relationship on a far sounder footing than it has been till now.

"But what if they don't?" said the president. "I don't know. No one knows. I would think a jointly drafted statement of purpose and intent, which we made mandatory upon future leaders to read and re-sign every two years, would be a place to start. How did the founders of our country know that the document they drafted—with many questions and uncertainties and negotiations—would last for over two centuries? They didn't, of course. What is before us is *not* impossible . . . if we share a common commitment to see it through to the end.

"But I admit—there are no guarantees. We are suggesting a starting point. And I would hope future leaders would catch the same vision of harmony and unity and would desire to carry it even further."

"If I may respond too," said the premier, "I would add this. Intending no disrespect to my homeland or our heritage or my colleagues in the Kremlin, both past and present—but we have been a stubbornly suspicious lot. We have accused the Americans of everything we could, knowing in our hearts that half of what we said was fabricated. We wanted to believe the American system was weak, so we imputed motives that were mostly fiction.

"It is time such mistrust and suspicion ended. I think it is built into the very fabric of the Soviet system. Thus, these proposals, by forcing openness and interplay between our governments and people, by forcing cooperation through joint agencies, by forcing us to each consider the other's best interest along with our own, by forcing regulation not merely from within but at a shared level, by forcing regular dialogue between leaders, by forcing our premier to visit the States at least several times a year and vice versa . . . all these factors will combat this cancerous suspicion which characterized our relationship throughout the Cold War period. We will force these things upon our future leaders by mandating them into law through the treaty and trade and diplomatic agreements we will conclude together.

"Thus future leaders, in both the Kremlin and the White House, in both the Congress and the Supreme Soviet, will be less likely to fall back into the pit of mistrust than we have been. A Soviet leader fifty years from now—having been raised in this atmosphere and taught the strengths as well as the weaknesses of the American system, knowing the English language, perhaps having friends he met in Chicago or Los Angeles during a soccer match; a leader who has stayed in American homes, walked the streets of America, talked to its people, saw its landscape, and even come to love it—such a leader will be far less likely to misjudge the American system and American motives than we who have grown up under the shadow of Stalin and Khrushchev and Brezhnev.

"As President MacFarlane has stressed, this is all a gamble—but a gamble in our favor. These actions will dramatically increase the likelihood that future leaders will be able to do much better than we have done in the past. These actions should decrease the chances that future leaders will revert to suspicion and antagonism, and will serve as a model for resolving conflict in the world for future generations.

"I beg of you Americans—trust your president. He is a courageous and patriotic man. He loves your country, as I love mine. He wants only the best for you. And if you can find it in your hearts to do so—trust me. I ask this of you and of my own people as well. I ask you . . . I beg you . . . you leaders from both our great nations who are listening to us at this fateful hour . . . lay aside your preconceptions of politics and history for a moment and ask yourselves if you cannot find it in your hearts to become a vital part of the most historic step for peace ever taken between men. Is not such a challenge, such a legacy, such a destiny worth the risk?"

As the premier spoke his final, forceful words, he and the president looked at one another, shook hands again with a smile and a nod, as if to say, "There is no turning back now," and then turned and left the room, side by side.

# SIXTY-FIVE

Well, your father really stunned them today," said Jeremy.

"I must admit, I wondered how he would ever pull off his grand plan," replied Karen. "I'm still not sure how he was able to orchestrate it—maybe I should say, how it was orchestrated for him—but it certainly happened."

After the press conference Jeremy and Karen had returned to the hotel to wait for her father. Side by side on the sofa in the sitting room of the presidential suite, they could talk of nothing but the astonishing announcements which had all Moscow and the whole world buzzing.

"Aren't you . . . I don't know . . . not skeptical exactly—but don't you wonder about it all?" asked Jeremy. "I mean, it's too incredible . . . the kind of thing that might happen in a novel, but not *really* happen. I mean—how *can* it have happened?"

Before Karen had a chance to answer, a voice boomed out from behind them.

"Don't you believe in miracles, my boy!" said the president, who had just entered the room and heard only Jeremy's final question. His face wore an ebullient smile.

"Oh, Dad!" exclaimed Karen, jumping up and running to hug him. "You and Kudinsky were marvelous!"

"Thank you, dear," said MacFarlane, then turned to shake Jeremy's hand. "Hello, Jeremy. And what do you think of all this?"

"Oh, I agree with Karen. Whether I believe in miracles or not, today's performance was truly moving. I've already heard talk about a joint Nobel Prize. What kind of response have you been getting?"

The president's face clouded momentarily. "Mixed," he said, "as you might imagine. Very mixed! The premier and I went out for a walk in Red Square after the press conference, to let people see us . . . to demonstrate that the bond we feel is real—touchable. People swarmed about us, at least as much as we could persuade the guards to permit. Old Russian women came up with tears in their eyes expressing gratitude, reaching out just to touch their leader. But then, as I expected, my own people—State . . . Defense . . . the guys who see their bureaucratic colossus in jeopardy and their power and budgets scaled back—they're full of mistrust and skepticism and warnings that it's a Soviet plot and that I'm being played for a sucker. Dick Howard telephoned me from home the minute he could get through and pretty well summed up that viewpoint. 'Mac,' he said, 'have you taken leave of your senses!' Actually, that's putting it mildly compared to what I've heard others are saying. Martin Tucker, I understand, is already on a plane heading back to Washington so he can get a jump putting the spin on this to turn public opinion against me."

"And on the other side?" asked Jeremy. "Any positive feedback from official circles, or only old Russian women?"

"That would make a great campaign slogan for Foster, don't you think?" MacFarlane laughed. "Yes, there has been some gratifying response. They're quieter about it than those who are hot to cut me off at the pass. But I've gotten little comments, even some anonymous notes and letters voicing support. The press is about evenly split, and on the whole seems willing to give the thing a chance to fly. It's uncharacteristic of them, actually, but no one wants to put the kibosh on this if, in fact, it turns out to be the historic turning point the premier and I hope it is. Most of the correspondents are reporting it factually, interviewing both the pro and con people, then adopting the proverbial 'wait and see' posture. I understand Tucker did a barn-burning interview with Jacobson of ABC and really lambasted me. But then Oscar Friedman made some comments which could be interpreted as positive in an NBC interview. It'll take time for all the dust to settle."

"What are you going to do in the meantime?" asked Karen.

"I'm going home. Kudinsky and I will simultaneously initiate everything we can by executive order. We'll talk by phone every day and plan our moves so the opposition can't weasel in and thwart anything because of miscommunication or goofed-up timing. What we have to get approval for, we'll submit to Congress and to the Supreme Soviet or Politburo, as the case may be, and see what happens. We're planning to move fast—strike while the iron's hot."

"And if there isn't support?" said Jeremy.

"We'll take our case to the people. I'll travel through Russia with the premier, and he'll come over and stump the States with me. I know the people want this. So we'll have to get them to make their pressure felt in Washington and Moscow. It *has* to happen! It is meant to happen! Otherwise why . . . you know—why the light—the Voice?"

"What about the election?" asked Jeremy.

"The election hardly matters. This is far more vital! This is what I became president to do. If there is a 'divine plan' behind all things, then this is my 'divine destiny,' so to speak. My future is in *His* hands—the election, the success of our peace initiatives. The people will decide who they want as their next president on the basis of who I am, what I stand for, not because of some campaign speech. I intend to be nothing more, nothing less, than the man I am—the man I am becoming. The people will see that and make their choice. Miracles—that's what it's all about. What happened in February is no more a miracle than what I feel going on in my own heart. That a man can be so changed so late in life, so unburdened . . . I tell you, I feel young again! I feel a peace in my heart—a love, not only for those close to me, for Kudinsky, but for all humanity. There's been a fundamental change in my heart, and somehow I'm convinced that this change is the example God wants in the world. Kudinsky and I, maybe you two, who knows how many others—we're supposed to be witnesses to the truth that peace can come—peace *has* come! If we will only take it into ourselves, make it real, make it happen. It's been here all along—

the light—the truth. We've just refused to see it for two thousand years."

# SIXTY-SIX

Two hours later Jeremy and Karen headed out of the Rossia for an evening alone. Alone, that is, to the extent that Brett Renfro and his partner would permit.

The president had invited Jeremy and Karen to a party the British embassy was throwing that evening, but sensing that the two would rather be alone together than stuck at a stuffy diplomatic reception, he had suggested they have, in his words, "a night on the town."

As they walked arm in arm, Karen thought how handsome Jeremy looked in his well-cut gray cashmere suit. It reminded her, with a slight twinge, that not long ago he had been a young man with great ambitions and a wardrobe to match. Yet he had given it all up on the wildest gamble a man could take.

Today, that gamble had paid off—for her father at least. For Jeremy, however, the burden of destiny seemed to be settling more heavily. She had noticed a quiet solemnity coming over him, as though something was troubling him, although he was making a brave attempt to mask it with lighthearted banter.

They dined at the Slavyansky Bazaar. It was crowded and noisy, in the fashion of Moscow restaurants, which more accurately resembled night clubs. Thanks to Renfro they were given one of the best tables, and their bodyguards also saw to it that Karen and Jeremy had a table to themselves, despite the Soviet custom of seating strangers together to make the best use of limited space.

The orchestra playing mostly popular Western tunes and the general bustle of the place presented a sharp contrast to the vaulted, cathedral-like ceiling that rose above them. The merrymakers filling the place were laughing, dancing, talking, relaxing, socializing.

*This is no gathering of little Communist puppets or tin soldiers,* thought Karen. She noticed a small group nearby engaged in an especially animated conversation. Not knowing the language, she was unable to guess at the subject under discussion, but it was clear these people had minds and thoughts and feelings of their own—opinions, curiosity, desire, ambitions. No system of government could take those from you—unless you let them do so, she thought. These people wanted the same things she wanted, the same things people everywhere wanted—peace, security, love, and freedom to be themselves.

Suddenly she noticed Jeremy staring at her.

"Profound thoughts?" he asked.

"I was just noticing all these people," she said, "and thinking what our world could achieve if we could all get together like Dad and Premier Kudinsky have done. I don't mean just the leaders, but the ordinary citizens. These people are just like a gathering of Americans. That's the part of what Dad said today I like best—interaction between the common people of our two nations."

Jeremy did not reply, but after a moment he rose and said, "Let's dance."

Karen took his hand and followed him out to the dance floor, where several other couples were gliding along to an old Bacharach number. She closed her eyes and laid her head on his shoulder. Neither spoke. When they returned to their table at the end of the song, a waitress had already begun to serve their meal.

"Looks . . . interesting," said Jeremy, with questioning enthusiasm. He attempted to strike up a conversation with the waitress, but his Berlitz vocabulary of ten or twelve words did not get him far.

Finally Karen asked, "Jeremy, what's wrong? Something's on your mind, I can tell."

He made a pretense of enjoying his soup, which was some bland concoction made from cucumbers, hardly worth all the attention he was giving it. Finally he laid down his spoon, rested his chin on his folded hands, and looked into Karen's eyes.

"I suppose it boils down to not knowing what to think of it all," he said.

"You mean the press conference, their proposals?"

"No—none of that. Everything they suggested was great. It's the most remarkable thing I've ever heard. All the Fosters, Kissingers, and Carters combined couldn't have come up with something so sweeping in a month's time—and they did it in a couple of hours! It's incredible. Who knows! It could turn out to be as significant as our own Constitution, paving the way for a whole new era in international relations. It's almost as if it were . . . *inspired*. And that's the rub. That's where I don't know what to think of it all."

Karen gave him a puzzled look, inviting him to continue.

"What happened yesterday—today," he went on, "it's just what your father said, isn't it? It was a kind of miracle."

Karen nodded.

"Okay, then, let's cut right through and say what no one has dared to verbalize up to now. If it really was a 'vision'—if the Voice really was who we all think it was—then what we're talking about is *God* coming to earth and actually talking to a man!"

He stopped, letting the force of his words catch up with him.

"Do you understand the improbability—the unthinkableness—of what I just said? And your father—I mean he's a fine man, and I respect him—but it's not as if he's some religious guru. Why would God come to him? And in the middle of the night when . . . you know . . . when dreaming and sleepwalking and strange sights are . . . well, more likely. Look at it from a down-to-earth perspective. Aren't you just the least bit skeptical?"

"But then what about Kudinsky? When Dad told us about it last night, he said—"

"I know! I know! That's the real rub! Without Kudinsky's part in this, your father could be written off as a kook. I'm not saying *I* would do that—that's just how most people would react. That's what the press would say if they ever got hold of it. But once you bring Kudinsky into it, then the whole scenario changes. Then you have . . . I don't know what you have, I guess! It's spooky!"

"Are you saying you don't believe it? That you think my father made the whole thing up?"

"No. How could I say that? But it goes against all my conditioning. How can it not be the truth—yet I can't bring myself to believe it. I can't help it. I'm skeptical."

"Then how *do* you explain it?"

"Don't all kinds of things come to your mind?"

"Like what?" asked Karen, a trifle annoyed.

"Like your father telling Kudinsky about the vision, him buying it, and then your father telling us Kudinsky had the same vision."

"That's as good as calling my father a liar!"

"Okay, then how about both men wanting peace so badly—and I don't fault them for that, it's a great objective—that they interpret their individual desires in a similar way and it becomes a 'vision' to them?"

"Jeremy, that's ridiculous! They'd never discussed it before, never met in private. Either my father's telling it exactly like it happened, or he was dreaming, or he made the whole thing up.

The same applies to what he said about Kudinsky. He either made it up or he's telling the truth. You can go and interview Kudinsky if you want to—if you can get near him. But I'm putting my money on my father. I believe him."

"Okay, let's take a giant leap and look at it from another angle. If what happened was supernatural—if it really was God or Jesus speaking to your father in a vision—then why, if He wants peace in the world, go through this elaborate gimmick with two men who probably won't be able to do anything about it anyway. Why not just use His supernatural power and clean the whole mess up?"

"I don't know. Who am I to say why God would do something a certain way? If God is God, then wouldn't whatever way He chose to accomplish something automatically be the best way? How could He do anything but the best?"

"There must be a thousand things He could do to bring peace to the world."

"Maybe He doesn't work that way. What if He wants us to figure it out for ourselves—to make it happen ourselves—rather than by imposing it through some worldwide, instantaneous, supernatural miracle? Maybe that's the only way it's worthwhile."

Jeremy shook his head, then thought a moment before answering.

"Look, I respect your father," he finally said. "But all along I have to admit I've had my doubts about the vision. All at once I find myself confronted with miracles, with a supernatural intervention here in today's modern world by a divine being I've never really believed in anyway. Then I come crashing headlong into something else. Say it is all true . . . say I do believe it . . . then what do I do with the fact that this all-powerful being has allowed mankind to struggle through centuries of war and pain and suffering when He had the power to stop it?"

Their waitress arrived with another course, and Karen thought that perhaps at that moment she was the only tourist thankful for Moscow's notoriously slow service, which was giving them time to talk all this through. Jeremy had a wonderful way of opening up his heart, especially for a man, but you had to drag it out of him at first. Once he got started, however, he was refreshingly earnest.

"Maybe the answer's in the vision," she suggested as the waitress departed. "Maybe He's making us bear the responsibility for our own actions. If it's our mess, why shouldn't we have to clean it up? It makes perfect sense to me, Jeremy. In today's world where nobody's responsible for anything anymore, I think that could be the most appropriate divine response of all. If we're going to think in terms of the supernatural, let's look back to the very beginning when God created the world. In Genesis it says that God gave *man* dominion over the earth. I looked it up in the Bible just this morning."

"You carry a Bible?"

"No, but I may start. However, this morning's revelation came courtesy of the Bible my father has with him."

"So, tell me what you read."

"It said that God not only created the earth, but that He also gave man power to rule it. Which is like what I said before—maybe He wants us to take responsibility for cleaning up the problems we have brought on ourselves."

"Sounds more like a cranky parent than a divine being."

"Isn't He kind of like a parent?" Karen replied. "But a wise rather than a cranky one."

She paused, reflected a moment, then went on. "Once, shortly after I got my driver's license, I got a speeding ticket. My father was vice-president at the time, so with my best seventeen-year-old tact I asked if just this once he might pull a few strings for me."

"What did he say?" asked Jeremy. "Although I think I can guess," he added with a grin.

"He put a fatherly arm around me, smiled, and calmly shook his head. 'Not in a million years,' he said. And I didn't have to ask why. It was my doing—my fault. I was responsible. I couldn't be above the consequences of my actions just because I had a father powerful enough to bail me out. So I wonder if that's sort of the way God works with us."

A smile played at the corners of Jeremy's mouth. "You've given this some serious thought."

"There's more to the story."

"Tell on," he said with a wave of his fork.

"Though my father wouldn't use his power as vice-president to bail me out, he did loan me the eighty dollars for the fine. I had to pay back every penny, with interest, but he did help me as much as he could and still remain within the bounds set by him."

"So are you saying the vision is God's eighty-buck loan?"

"You have such a way with words!" she laughed. "That isn't exactly how I'd put it, but in a sense, maybe it is. We have to take responsibility, but He will reach out and guide us and help us if we are able to hear His voice. At least that's how I've come to terms with it."

Once again they tried to take a superficial interest in the meal, but finally Karen laid aside her fork.

"Are you up to an evening stroll?" she asked.

"Maybe we can work up an appetite."

Jeremy paid the bill and told Renfro that they were going to walk back to the hotel.

Outside in the cool evening air they slowly made their way down 25th of October Street without giving the most important date in Russian history so much as a second thought. Despite the fine summer weather, they encountered few other pedestrians. It was 9:30 and the citizens of the working city of Moscow usually entertained themselves with their families at home and retired early. If the public bars and restaurants seemed crowded, it was because there were so few of them, and the night owls of the populace would stay until closing time at ten or eleven.

Karen could hear the steady rhythm of the bodyguards' footsteps behind them, but tonight she didn't mind. She had too many other important things to think about. She sensed something happening inside her, and inside Jeremy too. A deeper bond seemed to be forming between them, a kind of love that she couldn't begin to explain in the usual words.

"Karen," said Jeremy, picking up the threads of their conversation, "I don't want you to get the wrong idea. This is all going to take a lot of getting used to, that's all."

"I know."

"You wouldn't respect me if I wasn't honest about my doubts—and I want to believe. But wanting something to be true can't make it true. Truth is truth. There's no halfway with it."

When Karen didn't respond, Jeremy asked, "What is it?"

"I'm just trying to find the right words," she said.

"Come on, just spit it out."

She hesitated again, then said, "Remember how I told you I'd read a little in Dad's Bible this morning?"

Jeremy nodded.

"Well . . . I want to know if you'd do something—for me, if you want to look at it like that."

"You want me to read the Bible?" laughed Jeremy.

"Not exactly."

"What then?"

"Promise you won't laugh? I'm serious."

"I'll try."

"Well, I stumbled onto something when I was flipping through the pages that I haven't been able to get out of my mind. Two things actually."

She paused.

"Go on," he urged.

"The first was in a book called Proverbs—right in the middle of the Bible—a collection of little sayings on all kinds of things. What caught my eye was one that said, 'Those who search for me find me.' It really hit me between the eyes. I thought to myself, 'Okay, if I really want to find what the truth is, then what I need to do is search for it, and one way or another I will find it—find God, if He truly is behind all.' "

"Pretty heavy."

"I know."

"What's the second thing you read?"

"It's even heavier."

"How so?"

"Because it's the one I want to ask you to do something about."

"Okay, I'm game. Don't turn back now."

"Well, the other thing I read was clear in the back of the book. I don't know how all these passages struck me—one from the first few pages, one in the middle, one at the end. I was just unconsciously turning pages. But I haven't been able to shake the words. I found this last one on the first page of a book called James. It said, 'If any of you lacks wisdom, he should ask God, who gives generously.' "

"What's so revolutionary about that?"

"Don't you see? It's so practical—so down-to-earth. I always thought the Bible was stuffy and churchy and boring and having nothing to do with real life. But here we are in the midst of a quandary we can't make heads or tails of—"

"You mean the vision?"

"Yes. We don't know what to make of it. We are reasonably intelligent people, and then here comes this experience that contradicts everything we have ever thought."

"And?"

"Don't you get it? Those words in the Bible say we can ask and God will give us wisdom . . . they say that if we search, we will find the truth!"

"So what is this thing you want me to do?" asked Jeremy.

Again Karen hesitated.

"It can't be all that bad," he prompted lightly.

"I would like to ask you," she began slowly, "to do what that

Bible verse says. Do it with me. I want to know whether the vision is real. I want to know if God is real! I want to ask God for wisdom, just like it says."

"You mean *pray?*"

"I don't know what to call it. Maybe. I just mean to ask God for wisdom. That's all it says."

"But I don't even know if I believe in God."

"After the vision?"

"That's my whole dilemma."

"All the more reason we should ask—pray—call it whatever you like. If there is no God and it's all a hoax and my dad and Kudinsky are being duped somehow, or are trying to dupe the rest of us, then nothing will come of it and we've lost nothing except maybe a little pride. Nothing ventured, nothing gained—right? But if it is real, and God is behind it, and we do ask for wisdom—then maybe He'll somehow show us what the truth really is here. It says we have to 'search' to find the truth . . . to find Him!"

They were crossing Red Square now. The vast expanse of cobbles was nearly empty, and Karen couldn't help thinking what a strange place it was to be talking about God.

"I'll go along with you," said Jeremy at length. "What should we do?"

"I don't know," she replied. "I've never prayed, except for the little prayers I learned as a child, for bedtime and meals. You know, like 'Now I lay me down to sleep.' "

The Rossia showed itself in the distance, but before they reached it, they came to the medieval basilica of St. Ann.

"Well, this looks like as good a place as any," said Jeremy, pulling Karen down beside him on the wide stone steps. "So, here goes," he said, and after a brief pause plunged in. "God, we don't know much about you. I can't even say I know you exist. But if you do, and if you are behind this vision, then we ask that you'll show us."

He stopped abruptly, then exhaled a long breath of air as if to punctuate the fact that he was glad the frightful little experience was over.

"Oh, God, I too ask for wisdom," Karen began. "I want to know the truth—about you and about the world and whether the Bible is true. And about my father and Premier Kudinsky and if it really was you who spoke to them. So I'm asking you for wisdom, just like it says in the Bible."

Jeremy turned toward Karen, studying her face, as if wanting to say something which had caught somewhere between his heart and lips.

"Karen," he finally said, "everything has been so uncertain lately. I've been afraid to believe in so many things—in the vision especially—but then, too, whether I had the right to think of . . . whether we might possibly have a future . . ."

He paused, and Karen's heart began beating an ear-splitting tattoo.

"But tonight I don't feel so bogged down with my doubts," he said. "Maybe it helps just saying it. But I feel I don't have to be afraid anymore—of God, of the vision . . . or of you."

He exhaled deeply, then reached over and took her hand. She laid her head on his shoulder, and no more words were necessary.

# SIXTY-SEVEN

The British embassy had laid out all its finery for this occasion, with no thought for the sagging economy at home. The British were determined to play some part in this momentous Moscow summit.

Even Phil Schmidt was impressed, and he had seen his share of splendor in the two years that he'd been head of White House security. He forced his attention away from the fourteen-karat-gold table service and crystal candelabra. Tonight he was on duty, along with twenty other agents, and it wasn't going to be cushy duty like most state dinners. Despite the grandeur, something gnawed at his gut. He had a funny feeling about this night.

For one thing, the ambassador had changed the guest list at the last minute, adding ten names to the already ponderous list of one hundred. There hadn't been time to run more than a cursory security clearance on the new names, and he didn't like to do things that way.

Then this morning a water main had broken. Half the plumbing in Europe couldn't have stood up to even 1940s codes in the U.S., and Moscow was even worse! The place had been swarming with workmen, and he had been forced to detach half a dozen agents to clear them and secure the building. He would have needed twenty-five men to do everything adequately, but that was nearly the whole White House detail here in Moscow, and the majority had to be at the Kremlin to guard the president during his talks. If the British hadn't lent him some of their men, he'd never have made it through the day.

Late that afternoon he had tried subtly to convince the president to speak to the British about cancelling or at least postponing this affair. The talks had taken such an unexpected turn, the city was in such an uproar over it, and the embassy really needed a much more thorough going over, he argued. The timing of this reception simply couldn't be worse. The president had said that the ambassador would have a stroke if he cancelled out at this point, and he suggested that Schmidt enlist some of the embassy people to run a final sweep of the building and grounds. That was fine, but Schmidt would have felt much better if he had his own people to do the job. This was makeshift security at best.

Then there was MacFarlane's daughter. Why she had come along on this trip in the first place, he couldn't tell, but it only complicated things. Not only did he have to keep a detail on her, but tonight she had opted out of the dinner and was off somewhere with the president's new aide, taking two of his best agents along with her when he desperately needed them here.

He kept telling himself he had more than enough manpower—a wraith couldn't get close to the president tonight. Maybe it was just that these social functions always made him nervous. Everyone was having such a good time—drinking, laughing, chatting, joking—that they weren't the least cognizant of potential dangers. There were only he and nineteen others between the most important man in the world and disaster.

Oh, what was he worrying about anyway! This was a party. Nothing was going to happen.

---

Everything depended on the dancers. They were lucky to have such a trustworthy diversion.

Seyed had argued against the plan at first, but it was finally beginning to make sense to him. And he had argued with Mohsen so many times through the years that he hardly expected to be listened to anyway. Mohsen insisted that it happen while both leaders were together, in the same room, at the same moment. And since Mohsen was interested in impact, not sanity, the plan did possess a certain flair. No mention was ever made of the possibility that they could be killed in the process, but then Seyed had come to accept that as a daily fact of life.

Mohsen had entered the embassy earlier that day with a crew of workmen sent to repair broken water pipes. It had taken several hours for them to fix the damage Mohsen himself had done earlier to the water main—a nice piece of work. Mohsen had smuggled their weapons in with his tools and then concealed himself within the embassy.

Seyed smiled to himself. He didn't know how the wiry ape managed to do what he did, but there could hardly be a more resourceful man.

He himself had gained entry to the embassy with a forged French press pass, none too difficult to obtain given his passport, his looks, and his connections. His biggest problem was avoiding recognition. There were several in attendance here from the circles in which he had once moved, so he hoped his moustache, trim goatee, and wire-rimmed glasses would disguise his identity.

Ahmed would come in tonight with the small company from the Bolshoi that would be providing entertainment after dinner. The medley from Swan Lake and other of Tchaikovsky's most famous ballets would never see its final act, however. Before the curtain went down on this evening's performance, the embassy would be in chaos and the two most powerful leaders in the world would be dead.

Security people were everywhere, and before the second shot was fired, the whole embassy would be sealed off. Nevertheless, Mohsen had three escape routes planned and had drilled into his comrades every confidence that they would all reach the rendezvous point on schedule.

Flimsy as the whole thing looked on paper, somehow the Mujahedin terrorist always managed to take into account every detail. He was an evil genius.

But Seyed couldn't think of all that right now. He had to concentrate on playing the role of French reporter, while continuing to await his cue. He hadn't seen Mohsen yet, but he was certain that when the time came, everything would be ready. Mohsen was a genius in planning evil as well as an expert in carrying it out.

Suddenly Seyed heard commotion in the corridor. He shot a glance at his watch. It was about time for the dancers to arrive.

---

Phil Schmidt had stationed himself by the main doorway of the embassy dining room. He wanted to be on hand when the ballet company arrived, and then he wanted to give the ballroom where the performance was to be held another once-over. Dessert was being served, and everything appeared under control, but an additional hundred guests would be coming just for the ballet. They had all been cleared, but the new influx of people weakened the security chain.

Why couldn't they keep it simple? he wondered. A dinner would have provided more than ample opportunity for everyone to shake hands and talk. The situation was just too tense for all this pomp and circumstance. In the last two weeks terrorist activities in Iran and Europe had accelerated with frightening speed. The president had, in the last week alone, received thirteen anonymous death threats, most of them pointing with particular venom to his plan to visit Moscow.

Matters of state couldn't stop because of kooks, of course. Threats were part of politics. Still, this didn't seem like the time to party. Perhaps his nervousness was without basis, but deep inside something gnawed at him. Perhaps it was the little voice telling him there was no surer way to infuriate a terrorist than to ignore him.

Voices in the distance, outside the door, brought him to abrupt attention. He turned and stepped into the corridor.

Nothing appeared amiss in the immediate vicinity, so he proceeded down the hall and entered a large foyer, which opened toward the main entrance of the embassy. Three or four uninformed security guards clustered about a figure Schmidt could not readily identify. As the guards shifted their positions to make room for him, however, the object of the commotion became plainly visible. He saw an older man, sixty-five or seventy, of diminutive stature, with a thick clump of white hair atop a forehead and round cheeks red with more than annoyance at the embassy guards with whom he was arguing heatedly.

Schmidt recognized the man as Vasili Moiseyev, one of the Soviet ministers. He had obviously been drinking heavily.

"What's the difficulty?" Schmidt asked one of the British guards. "Trying to crash the party?"

"No," replied the guard, "he has an official invitation. But he arrived late, and . . . well, you can see his condition."

"He'd make a rousing entrance all right," chuckled Schmidt.

"It's a bit sticky, sir," the guard went on. "We don't want to disrupt things in there. We've sent for a Russian official to sort it out, but in the meantime we've been trying to restrain this chap. None too successfully as you can see."

"Maybe he'll pass out and save everyone the trouble. Can you use my help?"

"I suppose it's under control," the guard replied. "Only you might hurry someone on. We need a Soviet interpreter."

"I'll see what I can do," replied Schmidt. He swung around to leave and nearly ran headlong into a newcomer.

"You must be the interpreter," said Schmidt.

The man responded with a peculiar half-smile. He was tall, well-dressed and refined looking, and sported a neatly trimmed moustache and goatee. There was the definite air of a foreigner about him, though he spoke in flawless English.

"No, I am with the press," he said. "What is the problem?"

"I think you reporters ought to keep a low profile on this one," suggested Schmidt.

"A drunken diplomat?" said the man in an aloof tone. "Hardly front page material."

"I'm sure the gentleman will appreciate that," replied Schmidt. He turned and went in search of an interpreter.

---

Perhaps in a few years—if he lived that long—Seyed would laugh over what had just transpired. At the moment, however, his heart raced and his knees threatened to buckle. He had overreacted when he heard the argument in the hallway and had immediately jumped to the conclusion that Ahmed had run into trouble, which only pointed out just how overwrought he was. If he fell to pieces over a simple drunk, how would he react when it counted? He comforted himself with the fact that he was usually keyed up before an operation but had always come through in the past.

He glanced once more at his watch.

Ahmed should have arrived by now, and it was time for him to make his way to the ballroom for the Bolshoi performance. He ambled away from the little scene after the interpreter arrived and began trying to calm the Russian minister.

The dinner guests were now filtering through the wide corridor toward the ballroom, and Seyed blended in with the flow.

Until now he had only seen diagrams of the room. He glanced about, trying to pinpoint all the spots he and Mohsen and Ahmed had discussed in such detail. Where the two heads of state would be seated, the location of the stage, what positions would be most advantageous for a sniper—every possible aspect had been rehearsed many times.

The layout was precisely as Mohsen had reported. An enormous central area filled with rows of folding chairs faced the temporarily erected stage. Along two sides of the room ran rows of Grecian pillars. Above, a mezzanine circled the room with a wide staircase coming out from it and sweeping down onto the ground floor just behind the stage.

That mezzanine greatly complicated their task. It would make a perfect perch, but guards would be stationed around it because of its overview of the room. If there were only two or three guards, their plan might work. But the guards would have to be taken out right at the beginning—simultaneously.

Seyed glanced up as casually as possible. Two guards—positioned on either side of the staircase, in about the middle of the mezzanine. That had been Mohsen's guess. He was right again. The plan called for him to enter directly onto the mezzanine from a second floor corridor, and Ahmed would be in position opposite to take out the second guard.

Seyed began inching his way toward the front. The moment the fatal shots were fired, it would be his job to jump up and grab two hostages, a Russian and an American if possible, preferably women, shield himself behind them, and move toward the foot of the stairs. Mohsen and Ahmed would cover him from the mezzanine, and unless there was someone inside crazier than Mohsen, no one would dare come near them. The hostages would provide passage out of the building, and they'd make their escape through a side door into the waiting van. Three blocks away they would ditch the van in favor of a rundown 1984 BMW.

Timing was crucial. Mohsen and Ahmed had to eliminate the mezzanine guards at precisely the same moment so the element of surprise worked *for* them. And Seyed had to be properly positioned to grab the hostages. The curtain was scheduled to rise at 9:30, but they would wait until the second portion of the presentation, when both wine and drowsiness had begun to take their effect. Mohsen was to fire his first shot at exactly 10:40.

It was now 9:20, and the seats were already filling up. The premier and the president would be the last to arrive and would be seated in a roped-off section in the middle of the front row.

Seyed glanced up at the mezzanine, wondering if Mohsen and Ahmed were there already . . . somewhere. Would everything go smoothly, or would it all blow up in their faces?

Seyed breathed a prayer to Allah—though in his anxious state he could dredge up little more than a perfunctory utterance—and then made his way to the most advantageous seat he could find.

# SIXTY-EIGHT

Phil Schmidt shook his head as he recalled the earlier debate about who should enter the ballroom first, the president or the premier.

The aides on both sides had mustered their own logical arguments as to why their man should have the honor. The moment President MacFarlane caught wind of the dispute, he had sighed in disgust.

"Don't you guys get it?" he said. "Didn't you hear anything we said at the press conference? This kind of petty bickering has got to end! How about if we go alphabetically?"

"Using our alphabet or theirs?"

"For crying out loud!" the president nearly exploded. "I'll solve this here and now. The premier goes first. Otherwise, I don't go at all!"

So Kudinsky would lead the procession.

Schmidt turned down a corridor and mounted a flight of stairs, passing the premier and his retinue on their way toward the ballroom. Down another hallway and he arrived at the door behind which the president waited. He knocked. Jake Randolf answered, and within a few moments they were all making their way downstairs. It was 9:28. They would get there just at curtain time.

The president was in a particularly jocular mood this evening. At any other time Schmidt might have chalked it up to the fine dinner wine, but he had been this way ever since the press conference.

They had to wait another minute at the door to the ballroom as several latecomers were admitted. It was 9:35 when the president finally took his seat. Almost immediately the lights dimmed and the orchestra struck its opening chord.

Schmidt remained by the door, ever-vigilant, as the first act passed without a hitch. Then a brief intermission, some milling around, the resumption of seats, the dimming of lights, and the sounds of the orchestra once again.

Glancing up toward the mezzanine, Schmidt thought it was about time to check in with the guys up there. Everything was routine, but he'd better play it by the book.

As he scanned across the mezzanine his eyes suddenly caught a glimmer of light.

He jerked his head back, trying to locate the source. It had been so fleeting, so faint, that he began to think he had imagined it. Glancing mechanically down at his watch, he saw that it was 10:37.

He sidled up to Walker, the agent posted nearby.

"Did you see that?" he whispered, cocking his head toward the mezzanine.

Walker shook his head.

"I thought I saw a flicker of light."

"I haven't noticed anything," said Walker.

"Maybe—" Schmidt stopped short. His mind raced to organize the shadowed patterns in the darkness above him. By the time he realized that the glimmer he had seen had come from the scope of a miniature high-powered rifle, his revolver was in his hand.

He fired two shots as he shouted to Walker, "Get to the president!"

---

Seyed heard the first shot, but it hadn't come from the right direction—above and to the right, where Mohsen was supposed to be.

As he jumped to his feet, another shot followed. Then another, this time from the mezzanine. He looked up. There was Ahmed!

A volley burst from the gun of one of the American agents now racing up the stairs.

Mohsen's body toppled from the mezzanine. Ahmed shrieked mournfully and began wildly firing his Uzi submachine gun. Shattered glass from a chandelier rained upon the screaming, frantic crowd, now running in panic toward the exits.

Three more explosions burst from the floor of the ballroom. Seyed saw that Ahmed had been hit. His shirt was red with blood, but he continued to spray the crowd with gunfire.

A Russian agent creeping up on him from behind now lunged for the gun. Ahmed spun around, screaming like one possessed, and riddled the man with bullets. By now more than twenty agents had located the terrorist and had him in their sights. Fatal slugs shattered his chest and head, and he crumbled to the floor.

Seyed watched it all—transfixed, unable to make any move toward carrying out his own part in the plan, knowing he could do nothing to help his comrades.

The instant Mohsen fell from the mezzanine, Seyed knew their mission had failed. Even if Ahmed's crazed gunfire had somehow brought down their targets, they had still failed—for they had lost two of the best fighters in the cause.

Had Mohsen been standing in Seyed's shoes at that moment, he would have pulled his gun and rushed to sacrifice himself. But Seyed had never been one for suicide missions. Besides, it would be a senseless sacrifice.

He and Ahmed could both have retreated when Mohsen fell.

Ahmed had chosen his course. Now Seyed must choose his.

And what choice was there but vengeance?

Not now, however. Vengeance would be impossible if he too lay in a pool of his own blood. He would wait until his act could count for something greater. Unlike Mohsen, he wanted no part of blind terrorism. If he was going to die for the cause, he wanted his death to serve some purpose.

Scarcely a minute had passed since the action began. In all the chaos it was easy to stash his pistol in a planter and slip out a side door along with the dozens still fleeing madly in every direction. He looked back fleetingly toward the front of the ballroom where the president and the premier had been sitting.

Had Mohsen and Ahmed died in vain?

Perhaps not. The floor was strewn with bodies.

A crowd of yelling agents hovering together in the front made it impossible to tell what was going on. All the seats were now empty and several bodies lay prostrate in the immediate vicinity.

Seyed didn't stick around long enough to learn any more.

---

Jeremy and Karen were crossing the lobby of the Rossia toward the elevators when they heard the screech of tires on the street outside, followed by slamming doors and shouting voices. Almost immediately the hotel door burst open and four agents ran inside. One grabbed Brett Renfro, who had just followed Jeremy and Karen inside. The other three rushed across the lobby to where the two young people stood.

"Miss MacFarlane—Mr. Manning, will you please come with us?"

"Why, what's—?"

"Immediately! There's no time. We'll explain on the way!"

Karen glanced apprehensively at Jeremy as they followed the agents toward the door.

Karen stopped beside Renfro.

"Brett, what's this all about?" she asked. "Do you know what's going on?"

"I'm sorry, Karen," he replied distractedly, as though he hardly heard what she had said.

"Brett—what is it?"

"I'm so sorry, Karen—there's been an attack on the embassy . . . your father's been wounded."

"Oh, no—please, Lord, no!" she cried. Jeremy grasped her arm to steady her.

"Is he . . . what's his condition?" asked Jeremy.

"We don't know," replied one of the other agents. "He's alive. That's all we know. We'll go straight to the hospital. They should be there by now. The premier was hit badly too."

"Premier Kudinsky?"

"Yeah. They don't expect him to make it."

# PART V

# THE PLEBISCITE

*Then Samuel said to the people . . .*
*"You said to me, 'No, we want a*
*king to rule over us'—even though*
*the* LORD *your God was your king.*
*Now here is the king you have*
*chosen. . . . If you fear the* LORD
*and serve and obey him and do not*
*rebel against his commands, and if*
*both you and the king who reigns*
*over you follow the* LORD *your*
*God—good! But if you do not obey*
*the* LORD*, and if you rebel against*
*his commands, his hand will be*
*against you, as it was against your*
*fathers. Now then, stand still and*
*see this great thing the* LORD *is*
*about to do before your eyes!"*

1 SAMUEL 12:6, 12–16

# SIXTY-NINE

THE MIRACLE OF MOSCOW! The *New York Times* headlines sang the words boldly and brightly.

Patrick Foster flung down the newspaper with a venomous curse and strode across the office to his desk. He struck the intercom button as if it were an opponent and shouted all his ire into it.

"Where the blazes is Bateman?"

"He just walked in, sir," came a timorous female voice. "Mr. Lavender is with him."

"Send them in."

When the door opened, the cocky confidence was gone from Harv Bateman's tough countenance, and Sam Lavender's fleshy jowls were taut with the recent anxious hours.

All three men had read the papers, heard the news reports, and watched the repeated replays of *Air Force One* landing at Andrews Air Force Base, returning the wounded hero. The whole scene had been a nightmare for the Foster campaign. No one had shown much spark for a week, least of all their surly leader.

"This *has* to stop!" Foster seethed as he picked up the *Times* and waved it in his cohorts' faces.

"We talked about the importance of timing," replied Bateman evenly.

"The *Times* has always been partial to MacFarlane—he being their favorite son," put in Lavender. "Here are a few you'll be more pleased about." He held out three newspapers which had been tucked under his arm.

Foster took them without comment, opened each in turn, and scanned the headlines. The *Chicago Sun Times* read, "MacFarlane, Hero or Patsy?" The *Kansas City Register* asked, "Can the Soviets Be Trusted?" And the *San Francisco Chronicle* stated, "Moscow Summit Raises Hopes and Questions."

He dropped them on his desk.

"Are our people responsible for these or are they the real thing?" he asked flatly, showing none of the delight Lavender had hoped to elicit.

"This is the approach we discussed," said Bateman guardedly.

"I know," replied Foster. "But I've got to know if these are plants or truly representative of the public mood."

"The *Sun Times* and the *Register* are ours. For days now I've had our boys subtly getting the message across, making sure it's coming from no one directly connected to the campaign. Just like you said. Whether it actually represents the public mood isn't as important as if it shapes and molds the mood to make it receptive to your counterpunch when it comes."

Foster reflected a moment, seemed to take a certain begrudging reassurance from the words, then asked, "And the *Chronicle*?"

"You know California. They question everything. They didn't need our help! But I tell you, Pat," and here some of Bateman's old animation returned, "the skepticism is widespread, and not only because of our efforts. Everyone was dazzled for the first few days after the Moscow stuff hit the fan. And the assassination attempt didn't help—"

"Wounds will heal long before November," interrupted Foster. "I'm not worried about that. Besides, I have a feeling MacFarlane will underplay the shooting because it only emphasizes the futility of his peace plan. Russia is not our only enemy in the world."

"With Russia as an ally, not many would dare cross us," said Lavender.

"First they would have to accept Russia as our ally," rejoined Bateman.

"Exactly!" interjected Foster. "That is what we're going to see *doesn't* happen. It's my bet that most people in this country are downright nervous about such a prospect. Those are the hidden fears I'll exploit tonight."

"You think the time is right to go public with your objections?"

"I've played the consoling, supportive adversary long enough," replied Foster, sinking back into his comfortable, upholstered chair.

"You've got to be careful," warned Bateman. "You don't want to come off looking either unsympathetic to his wound or bitter about his peace plan. I know he stole the message you've been touting all these years, but in the public eye you can't be perceived as harboring a sour grapes attitude for political purposes. Somehow you might have to adjust your stance to get in line with this sudden swing in his direction. We're still in that touchy period when sentiment runs high. There could be backlash if you hit him too hard."

Foster picked up a manila folder and hefted it thoughtfully. "Not to worry, Harv." He handed the folder across the desk to Bateman. "I've had my writers working on this all day. I think even you will be pleased."

"Your speech for this evening?"

Foster nodded. "You and Sam have a look at it. Make sure it includes everything we need to cover."

Lavender, who had been quiet for several moments, now cleared his throat.

"What is it, Sam?" asked Foster. "You don't usually go reticent on me."

"I'm not sure you'll like what I have to say."

"Out with it."

"Listen, Pat, I know you're steamed about that starry-eyed *Times* headline, but—" Lavender paused to take a short breath. He wasn't used to the role of campaign watchdog. "—you'd better be careful not to rush it. If what MacFarlane's done *is* on the level, who can knock it? I don't trust the Russians for a second, and I know the whole thing's probably a set-up, but what about the one-in-a-million shot that it *does* work. I wouldn't want to be the man who stood against it. And all that aside, even if it is a setup, you still gotta be careful. You were way ahead in the polls two weeks ago. They'll come back your way by election time—*if* you don't say anything that angers—"

"Read the speech, Sam," Foster broke in impatiently. "Then you can deliver me your lecture."

Bateman handed the folder over to Lavender, who pulled up a chair and flipped open the folder. Five minutes later he looked up and smiled.

"Okay, I'm a believer!" he said. "Great stuff!"

Bateman reached out and snatched the speech from Lavender. After scanning it in his hasty but thorough manner, he too looked up with a grin.

"You are a genius, Pat," he said, a sly glint in his eyes.

"It's only a beginning," replied Foster. "We're still facing an uphill battle. MacFarlane pulled a fast one on us, but *we're* going to win this thing. We just have to pull a faster one."

"You have something specific in mind?"

"Several things, Harv. But first of all I want to put a stop to garbage like that." Foster cocked his head at the *Times*. "Then we have to gear this campaign back up. Watching those favorable polls all spring made us soft. We've got to get back in fighting trim. When Andy gets back from Europe, we'll decide on what action to take on that front. Up till now peace has been *my* platform, and now MacFarlane's trying to grab it! Well, we've got to make sure it backfires on him, while closely watching the mood of the country to see that we stay right in tune. It could be time to make an adjustment in the 'new dawn' theme. We'll have to see what the public's going to respond to. But in the meantime we have to make MacFarlane seem soft, a pushover, like he's being duped by the Russians. That should hardly be difficult. Everyone knows he's been wishy-washy since this Iranian deal came up. So for starters, I want you to begin working on a program to see that his judgment is scrutinized from every possible angle. Dig up everything. Get some of your contacts from Albany to find us some shaky decisions he may have made when he was a state congressman. I don't care if it happened when he was ten years old!"

"We can use the dope we have on Randolf," added Bateman eagerly.

"Yeah, but go easy on that one. See if you can compromise him publicly rather than dredging up something on his family."

"You mean get him drunk in public?"

"Yeah, perfect!" Then, spotting the expression on Lavender's face, he challenged, "You got a problem with that, Sam?"

"No, Pat," answered Lavender. "I'm just offering the voice of reason, that's all."

"To blazes with reason!" exploded Foster. "The gentleman's game is over. This is war! An all-out blitz against Jarvis MacFarlane. No holds barred. You got it?" He pounded his fist on the desk, and without missing a breath he jerked his eyes toward Bateman. In an instant ten years of enlightenment and higher consciousness and new eras for mankind and Patrick Foster's peaceful new-age demeanor all evaporated.

"Another thing," he went on, "I want MacFarlane's organization infiltrated. With something of this magnitude, there have got to be some dissidents on his staff, some unbelievers. Get to them! Find out who they are—their weak spots. We've got to get these people to talk, to undermine MacFarlane from the inside. And who knows, maybe there's more to what happened in Moscow than they're letting on to the public. We've got to dig, I tell you. So, Harv, get your electronics wizards rounded up. I've got several places I want bugged."

"Consider it done!" answered the loyal storm trooper.

Two hours later Foster's limousine cruised along the freeway toward the Hyatt-Regency and the annual convention of NASA's Washington-based cousin, the Space Defense Research and Deployment Agency. SDRDA would provide him the perfect platform from which to launch his subtle counterattack against that milksop of a president!

Foster smiled to himself as he thought of his speech. Even as he did so, however, his face remained taut, primed like a precision weapon. His was not a countenance that could, even smiling, appear altogether congenial. He emanated force and unwavering drive. A determination to conquer, to vanquish all foes whatever the cost.

# SEVENTY

In closing then, ladies and gentlemen, I stress to you again that my heart yearns for peace as much as any person's on this earth. Peace has, in fact, been my predominant message as I have traveled through this great nation of ours speaking out on the issues of our time. It has been my steadfast goal to point with vision toward the new times ahead. So that sentiment of peace, despite the reservations I have alluded to this evening, I certainly share with our president. I have a wife and children, and grandchildren too, whom I want to see grow up healthy and happy in a world secure from war."

Foster paused, seemed to reflect for a moment, chuckled briefly, then continued as if the homey illustration had only that instant occurred to him.

"You know," he said, "I could not help thinking just now of my little four-year-old granddaughter, Mandy. She got a new kitten recently. She brings that little ball of fluff to every meal, she sleeps with it, talks to it—why she even wrapped it up in a baby blanket and paraded around with it in her doll carriage!"

Here the crowd of men and women stirred with easy laughter. Foster beamed. He had them in the palm of his hand, just like Mandy had her kitten, which he had given her a couple days earlier in case anyone checked his story.

"Don't think I won't do all in my power to make sure little Mandy *and* that scruffy little kitten are able to grow up content and peaceful in a world free from the fear of holocaust. Peace means everything to me, as I have stressed all these years, as I know it does to you, too, for the sake of your loved ones. But I could never allow that desire to blind me to the harsh realities of this world in which we live—harsh political realities of . . ."

Jarvis MacFarlane leaned back in his chair and exhaled a long sigh.

Foster's speech was nothing less than a masterpiece. Opening with a nostalgic series of reflections on some of the country's most contented times during the past fifty years, he had progressed adroitly up to the present, painting with a deft hand his perceived need for visionary firmness and caution in the days ahead.

". . . As your next president I will not be swept away by currents and cross-currents blowing here and there about the political land scape. I will do as I have always done—look at things squarely and realistically. A president must be a realist, and President MacFarlane's plan—as much as I applaud his efforts—has caused me to give serious thought to some things. That is another quality a president must have—the capacity to modify his views when it becomes necessary, and the capacity to draw upon his experience in many areas. Which is why I now find my background in the military coming back to give balance and long-range perspective to my desire for peace, so that as we truly enter the new era of the twenty-first century, we do so with our freedoms intact and our belief in the brotherhood of man strengthened by . . ."

Yes—a masterpiece! thought MacFarlane. With just a slight twist to his own holistic views, Foster was attempting to keep his hold on his portion of the electorate while sowing seeds of doubt among those who were MacFarlane's strongest constituency. Who could have listened to his oratory without walking away wondering what there possibly was about the man to disagree with. Jarvis almost found himself asking that very question.

But he'd expected no less. He was only surprised that it had taken Foster so long to get to it. The senator had given him ten days to bask in whatever glory there was to be had from Moscow.

Glory—that's how Foster would see it. But Jarvis knew the peace plan wasn't about glory. The terrorist attack, if nothing else, proved that. Six people had been killed, including a Bolshoi ballerina. Another twelve had been hospitalized. Two of his own secret service men had died while protecting him. And the premier's condition was still precarious.

No, Moscow had been deadly serious business, and the attack had turned their initiatives into an urgent necessity.

But Foster was even now twisting it to suit his own purposes. As he had used the concept of a united global community to build his own political base, now he would subtly distort the peace effort to make MacFarlane appear the inept fool. This speech was only a subtle beginning—MacFarlane knew that. The attacks would heat up once Foster regained his stride and the positive public sentiment generated by the events of recent weeks ebbed. MacFarlane knew how men like Foster played the political game. Every move calculated, timed to precision.

As long as everything was going smoothly, Patrick Foster had been able to talk about peace and new eras and everybody loved it! But let a crisis arise or let someone speak of peace in practical, workable terms, and suddenly Foster—the man of peace himself—

did an about-face. And the papers that had raved about the senator's impractical palaver now had no use for a *real* peace plan! Peace was not nearly so saleable a commodity in reality as in the idea. And he supposed even he was coming down to earth a bit too—perhaps like everyone else. Maybe Foster was right to sound a note of caution. Even he himself had been swept along somewhat by the enthusiasm, the glow, the excitement contained in the sheer possibilities of the so-called "Miracle of Moscow."

That night of terror at the British embassy had forced reality upon him. Was the world not ready for peace? Was it possible that even his own freedom-loving fellow Americans were no more ready for true world peace than those two dead Mujahedin terrorists? If only they could have heard the truth in Kudinsky's voice and read the desire for brotherhood in his eyes. But such things did not translate well to television screens ten or twelve thousand miles away.

Oh, they had cheered him as the conquering hero when he returned from Moscow, treating his sling-bound arm and deep thigh wound as badges of honor. But this was an election year. And the good senator wasn't going to let even an assassination attempt blind the public eye to glaring holes in his adversary's proposals.

Maybe it was a good thing, thought MacFarlane. He wanted rational, thoughtful support, not emotional, gutless ratification by a populace and a Congress too caught up in the drama to consider the hard realities of the work it would take to achieve peace. Such support would only fizzle in the end.

On the television screen Foster's speech droned on, as if to punctuate MacFarlane's thoughts. After another moment, his attention was diverted as Karen entered the room. He smiled, reaching out his hand as she came to him.

How glad he was to have his daughter living in the White House with him again! Right now he didn't know if he could make it without her presence and support. How much her love meant to him!

"When are Peter and Jeremy due?" he asked.

"Ten or fifteen minutes," she said. "Dinner's almost ready. But are you sure you want company so soon, Dad? You can hardly walk yet. I could still call it off."

"No! I'm about to go stir-crazy. I need some people around to talk to. There's too much going on inside my head to keep it all bottled up."

"Got Foster on the brain, eh?" asked Karen, nodding toward the TV with a smile.

"A lot of what he says makes sense," her father replied with a sigh, "at least to people who don't know what *I* know. How can I communicate to them what is in Kudinsky's heart? How can I make people who have never met the man trust him? How can I make them trust *me*? They've never met me either! How can I get them to fathom the friendship that has grown between us? It's not an experience that is even on a level most people can grasp—I don't even fully understand it myself."

"You're certain about not revealing the vision?"

"For the moment—yes."

"It won't matter to me what you do, Dad. I'll love and believe in you no matter what."

"I know that, Karen, and I appreciate it." MacFarlane sighed. "Now that I know the vision was real, I'm not so worried inside about what people might think. If it were only the negative reaction, I probably would tell. I want people to know there is a God and that He cares about His world. Yet at the same time I know if I went public, Foster and the press would not only make mincemeat of me, they'd also ridicule the vision. The end result would be dragging God's name through the dirt on my coattails. The vision is too sacred, and God is too . . . I don't know . . . too holy, too pure, too compassionate for that. One day I might be required to tell about it, and I'll do so gladly, without fear for my reputation or what anyone thinks. But I don't believe the time is right. I don't have the conviction that what God wants me to do first is tell what happened, but rather to work for peace through the political and diplomatic process. I may be wrong, but that's what I feel right now."

"What about Kudinsky?"

"I know. I've thought a lot about what it would mean for him if I were to say anything. It would go far worse for him than for me—that is, if he survives his wounds. It would ruin him, and probably endanger his life all over again."

"It's so incredible that a Russian—a Communist—could have a vision from God," said Karen.

"No less incredible than that a faithless American would. I still wonder why He chose us."

"I've been thinking a lot too lately, reading—even praying, Dad. I just wish I understood more about God."

"I know what you mean. But you have to admit—suddenly people are coming out of the woodwork to help us along! It's remarkable. I just didn't realize there were so many closet Christians around. I told you about Duke?"

"You mentioned that you've had a couple talks with him."

"I guess I always knew he was a Christian, though he never said much. But that guy's as sold out to the cause as any of the others I've met. He could easily be part of the Legation. Then I find out he's part of some other group that meets in the Executive Office Building—right out in the open!"

"Are you thinking about joining them?"

"Well, I'd at least like to go see what it's about. I don't want to be limited just to what I hear from Daniel and Peter. You know—always get a second opinion!"

"In things medical *and* spiritual, huh?" laughed Karen.

"Can't hurt to have more than one perspective. Want to join me?"

"You bet. But are you going to do it publicly? You know what people are liable to say."

MacFarlane sighed. "Always the fickle public to contend with. If it was just me or the election, I'd say hang it all and let them say what they want. But for Kudinsky's sake, and the sake of our proposals, probably it *would* be better to keep it under wraps. I don't know. It's so confusing. But I do know that one of the most inescapable sensations I had that night was that before me stood a Person who would lead me to all the answers of life. So I'm convinced the answers *will* come."

"Why didn't we know any of this before? How could we have been so blind to the spiritual side of life all this time?"

"Because the kind of 'spirituality' that's floating around nowadays is that ridiculous stuff of Foster's. If anyone talks about a personal God or about Jesus being alive or anything like that, they're branded as kooks. And besides, speaking for myself, I know that I never paid much attention to spiritual things because I just wasn't interested. To my shame, I now realize. So if anyone had told me God was a personal God, a friend, I probably wouldn't have heard them anyway."

Karen rose from her father's side. "I think Peter and Jeremy are probably here by now," she said. "I'll go greet them and we'll meet you in the dining room."

---

An hour later the four were finishing their dinner in the midst of a lively discussion.

"But what *are* we going to do about the Legation meetings?" the president asked Peter. "This dead-of-night stuff can't go on forever."

"Daniel and I have discussed this," replied Venzke. "I don't know yet. Dmitri's situation is still quite tenuous."

"Couldn't he—perhaps—not come for a while, or meet with some of the others at a different time?"

"It's a lifeline for him, Jarvis. What would you say if I told you not to see any fellow Christians for two or three months?"

"I see your point! Right now I feel I've got to talk with someone every day!"

"Besides that, Dmitri's a strong link to some connections we have in the Soviet Union right now. But it's not without dangers. The spiritual climate may have opened up over there, but officialdom still frowns on the kinds of things we're doing. So we've got to be very careful not to compromise Dmitri's position. If his connection to us were discovered, he would be yanked out of the Soviet Embassy and on his way back to Moscow within hours."

MacFarlane thought for a moment. "Yes . . . I see the problem. It's bigger than just my role in it. And I had been hoping, too, to be able to get Jeremy and Karen involved with the group. But it seems that would only add to the complexity."

"What about the group Duke's in?" suggested Karen.

"That's a good possibility," mused Venzke thoughtfully. "Daniel knows several who attend it, as do I. Christianity may not be particularly popular around Washington these days, but there are certain expressions of it that are more acceptable than others. This group Duke's involved in falls into the more or less acceptable category—kind of an outgrowth of the old prayer-breakfast idea."

"He tells me they discuss some of the same kinds of things as the Legation," interjected the president.

"That's true. But it's a more traditional approach. In a way it's an excellent cover for some very significant things that are starting to develop throughout this town. Whereas the Legation and the prophetic message we're trying to promote would be perceived as pretty farfetched stuff, the prayer-breakfast kind of thing is not seen as a threat, or even as peculiar. This could be an excellent way for you to begin to become involved in spiritual things publicly, Jarvis."

"But what about the Legation?" asked MacFarlane. "I need to know more about what this country's headed toward if I'm going to . . . well, you know . . . be a voice to proclaim the truth, to promote healing, to help people get ready, to help lead toward true peace, to be a *witness* to these things to people everywhere. I feel so inept! I know so little, and yet the task seems so huge. Look how my first attempts in Moscow are already unraveling!"

Venzke laughed. "Have no worry, my friend. *His* purposes do not unravel! All is taken care of—all is in His plan—all will accomplish His purposes."

"But how!" exclaimed a frustrated MacFarlane. "How am I to know what to do?"

"You will be shown. Just as He told you." The professor paused, then continued. "Did you know I was a Christian four months ago?"

MacFarlane shook his head.

"How about Duke? Had you ever spoken with him about spiritual matters?"

"No."

"Did you know Daniel, Dmitri, or any of the others you have met?"

"No."

"Had you heard of the Legation?"

The president was silent.

"Karen . . . Jeremy," Venzke said, turning toward the two young people. "Had either of you even considered having a personal experience with God's Son? Or that your lives were about to be turned upside down?"

They both shook their heads.

"There—you see! The Lord's hand is mightily at work in your lives! None of you have engineered any of this. It's God's Spirit at work. Your hearts are receptive, and He is sweeping you into the flow of His great work. Nothing can stop it! The purposes He spoke of in the vision, Jarvis—they're *His* mighty purposes. You can no more stop or alter them than you could have brought about the unity between you and Kudinsky on your own. Don't you see? You are not alone. You are being led—guided by God's unseen hand in all you do."

"But what am I to *do*?" asked MacFarlane again.

"He will show you. Your only responsibility is to take the *next* step. That is all you need worry about. He will then show you the next—and when you have done that, the next. Everything is part of a bigger plan than you or me."

# SEVENTY-ONE

The following morning MacFarlane was seated in the Oval Office attempting to resume his schedule in spite of his wound when Duke Mathias was announced.

"Is this an official call by my chief economic advisor?" asked MacFarlane with a smile.

"Let's just say I received a phone call from Professor Venzke late last night," Duke replied.

"I see. And what did the good professor suggest?"

"He thought it might be fruitful for us to talk about some things."

"Such as the economy?"

"How about the spiritual economy?"

MacFarlane threw back his head and laughed. "So now *you've* been made part of this plot of concern for my spiritual growth too, eh!"

"I'm simply at your service, Mr. President."

MacFarlane quickly became serious. "I know, Duke. I didn't mean to make light of it. And I appreciate your concern."

"I wanted to put your mind at ease about some things," said Mathias. "First of all, I think the political fallout will be minimal if you begin attending the prayer time we have in the EOB. It's been going on for years and nobody pays us that much attention."

"If I go they will."

"True. But only temporarily. And after Moscow, I think people will be prepared to take any more 'surprises' in stride."

"No doubt!" laughed MacFarlane again.

"I know the country seems to have gone bananas over all the new age ideas, but—"

"New age? I thought that was just a general term for modern—I don't know—modern ways of looking at things."

"Hardly just a *general* term. No, 'new age' is a definite cult—almost a religious movement, if I can use that term. Extremely dangerous! We should spend some time discussing it because it's vital that you understand the deceptions being foisted on the American people."

"Is that what Foster's been preaching these last few years?"

"Foster's speeches are filled with new age deception. Whether he personally buys into the whole movement and its philosophy, I don't know. But what I was going to say is that despite the rampant new age ideas, there still are a good many groups like ours. Some have continued on from their charismatic and evangelical roots in the '70s and '80s, while others are springing up as part of a sort of underground revival."

"I would never have known."

"It's going on in schools and places of business all over the country—quietly, personally."

"Must be one of our best-kept secrets."

"I suppose," said Duke. "But once you're in the stream of what God is doing, suddenly you realize how widespread the grass roots really are."

"A hidden world that few see—like faith being personal," said the president thoughtfully. "But tell me, Duke, what do you do at your meetings?"

"What we do is try to understand more about what it means to live as a Christian. I mean *all* the time, in *every* decision, in a way that God would want us to, rather than just putting on a spiritual suit of clothes every once in a while to wear to church."

"But you're an old hand at it, aren't you? Haven't you been a Christian for years?"

"Yes, but that doesn't mean the hunger isn't in my heart to live more completely in obedience to God's ways," said Mathias earnestly. "That's what a brand-new Christian and a twenty-year Christian share in common—that hunger to know God more intimately. So when we come together, we pray, we study the Scriptures, we talk, we question one another, and we try to discern God's voice and what He would say to us."

MacFarlane let out a long sigh. "My, oh my, Duke! What is happening to me? These are hardly the sorts of things that traditionally concerned the men who have occupied this office!"

"If more presidents—not to mention senators and representatives and Supreme Court justices—*had* paid attention to the voice of God, we wouldn't have drifted so far away from the spiritual values upon which this nation was founded. Washington and Jefferson and all the rest would be shocked and appalled to see how their words and their values and priorities have been twisted and distorted today, all in the name of separation of church and state. With apologies to you and your position, Mr. President, it's unbelievable what a godless nation we have become at the leadership level! We've completely lost sight of the fact that, at *every* point, this nation was founded on spiritual values. Now in the name of freedom we are banishing every reminder of that spiritual heritage. We are no longer a nation 'under God' at all, but under someone else whose name I am loathe even to mention. It's even against the law to pray, for heaven's sake—when prayer was *the* single undergirding priority of life for the men who framed our nation's beginning!"

Mathias paused, then looked at the president sheepishly. "Sorry for the soapbox sermon."

"Next you'll be telling me that judgment is at hand."

"I think it is, Mr. President."

"Like Nineveh?"

"The parallel can hardly be ignored. And you may well be a modern-day Jonah whom God is preparing to deliver a similar message."

MacFarlane sighed. "I have to tell you, Duke—I'm none too comfortable with any of this."

"Neither was Jonah. He hated God's injunction so much that he tried to run away and hide, and you know what happened to him!"

"Yeah, I guess I don't want to make the same mistake he did. But I just don't know what I'm to do . . . what I'm to say!"

"Neither did Moses. None of God's chosen messengers *enjoyed* the call God placed on them. It's no fun being a prophet—the uncertainty, the ridicule, the soul-searching. Just read through the prophets in the Bible. Every one of them resisted what God told them to do, sometimes for years. But in the end they knew they had to obey. And none of them knew what to say either. But God gave them words. As He will for you."

The president did not reply. He was thinking that now he knew he had to tell Duke about the vision too—when the time was right. The Lord had said He would send people to help make the vision clear, and He had. And they all seemed to speak the same language!

"The other thing I wanted to do was to give you this book," said Duke as he opened his briefcase and pulled out a paperback. "It'll give you a good historical basis for coming to grips with what many of us think is coming very soon to the United States—a widespread prophetic message like that of Jonah to Nineveh, with the two identical options before us that they had."

"Which are?"

"Repentance or destruction."

MacFarlane let out a long sigh. "Pretty heavy stuff, Duke."

"The times are not what they seem, Mr. President."

"I've heard that before too."

"Whoever speaks that word speaks the truth," said Mathias, then looked at his watch. "But I have to go, and you have work to do. But please try to get to the EOB prayer meeting. I promise I won't put you on the spot."

"Thanks, Duke," smiled the president, "but I'm not going to be able to avoid the hot seat indefinitely."

# SEVENTY-TWO

The day could not have been a better one for Karen. She still bubbled with enthusiasm over the events of that morning as she and Jeremy ordered their dinner at La Casa del Rio. She could hardly believe the changes that were happening to her. Today she had actually heard her father pray aloud!

It was no easy thing for the president of the United States to admit to confusion and personal struggles, especially during the heat of an election. Even if he said nothing about the vision, one unguarded word from a member of the EOB group could send a newspaper headliner scurrying for the red ink.

When her father had announced his plans to attend the EOB prayer group, there had been the usual bureaucratic hubbub, along with complaints from people like Jake Howard because of its affect on his image and how it would "play" to the nonreligious majority. But her father had waved off their concern, saying he was determined to go. It was enough that he had to tolerate the usual Secret Service business, security checks of the facility, and clearances for the various people involved. All in all, fewer eyebrows seemed to be raised over the affair than anyone had thought.

The meeting itself had been simple and short, only thirty or forty minutes in length. Neither she nor her father nor Jeremy had said a word. However, when Mathias asked for prayer requests and personal concerns, her father had briefly requested prayer for wisdom and guidance in several decisions currently before him. He hadn't elaborated. Then several members of the group had prayed, including her father, and it was over.

"Jeremy, did you hear my father this morning?" said Karen after the waiter had delivered a plate of nachos. "I've never heard him pray out loud like that—from his heart, you know, not from something prepared by a speech writer for a state dinner."

Jeremy chuckled. "I believe Phil Schmidt and the other agents still think this was some kind of campaign caucus."

"I can't think of anything better to happen to the campaign."

"You're really enthusiastic about all this, aren't you?"

"I can't help myself, Jeremy. Since that night you and I prayed together in Moscow I've felt so much more complete than I ever have before. We asked to be shown the truth in all this, and I suppose I feel like that's what's really happening. As much as I didn't expect it, I think my prayer is being answered."

Jeremy appeared thoughtful, then spoke in a measured tone. "For me, I guess, the shooting kind of derailed my focus."

Karen sensed that Jeremy was trying to express his own doubts. She knew there was more on his mind than the terrorist attack.

"I was shattered by it too," she replied. "You saw me. But after the initial shock wore off—"

"You don't have to tell me," Jeremy said. "I saw it in you." He reached across the table and took her hand. "You *were* different. I could tell. A peacefulness came over you I'd never seen before . . ." His voice trailed away as if the answers he sought were too distant for the questions even to have formed fully in his mind.

"We haven't had time to talk much since then," attempted Karen.

"It's not your fault. I've been avoiding it."

"Avoiding me?"

"Not *you* . . . Him! . . . God, prayer—the whole confusing business!"

"But you came to the prayer time this morning?"

"I still want it, Karen—the peacefulness, the answers, the assurance that it's all true. I want to believe . . . I think maybe I even do believe, in a way. I'm not fighting it skeptically like I did at first. I'm just struggling to really be sure. Can you understand that?"

She nodded.

"Maybe I'm more hardheaded than you. I've done plenty of soul-searching these last few weeks, and there have been a lot of changes in my outlook. But part of me has to be sure intellectually—you know, analysis versus emotion. I just want to be sure."

"I can understand that, Jeremy. This is not something to be taken lightly—like a political campaign."

He smiled. "Exactly! And I have a feeling this is going to require a lot more from me than Foster ever did, so I want to make certain my head is in the right place."

"That's one of the things that appeals to me about Christianity," said Karen. "I mean this new, personal way of looking at Christianity . . . or should I say this new way of living Christianity? It satisfies both your emotions and your intellect. At least it does for me. It makes sense to my brain and feels good in my heart. Maybe that's one of the reasons I'm so enthusiastic and really do believe—because God seems to care about all of me . . . my whole person, from emotions to intellect . . . all of the person I am."

"Have you talked to your father about all this?" asked Jeremy. "Does he feel the same way?"

"Only a little. I'm still in the thinking stages myself. I talked to a couple of the women there this morning who've been Christians a long time. They gave me a couple books to read. In a way, too, I suppose, my dad's struggling with it on a level you and I don't have to face."

"How so?"

"Well, you're still wrestling with whether it's all true or not, right?"

"I suppose so," answered Jeremy.

"Well, I think my father came to terms with belief some time ago. He's different. There's a look in his eye. He still talks about his doubts, but he's a different man. It's something I can almost see visually—a growth, a sense of increasing stature, a look of purpose in his gaze. I've never witnessed anything like it before, but I can tell the vision is taking hold of him in more far-reaching ways than even he realizes. It's almost like I sense that he's going to become . . . I don't know . . . a modern-day prophet or something."

"So what's the struggle you mentioned?"

"I think he's struggling with what to do with it. Where does he go from here, what's he supposed to do—as president . . . the election . . . the peace proposal. There's so much resting on his shoulders. How does the vision work itself out in the daily grind? Along with everything Peter and that Legation group are telling him."

The waiter arrived with the main course, and Jeremy waited until their Tostadas Grande had been served before he spoke again.

"Seeing your father there this morning, listening to him pray, did something to me. I can see the change too. I know what you mean—that look on his face. Political battles and the horrors of a violent world may rage around him, but . . . yeah, I think you're right . . . he's won his inner battles, or close to it. It's clear from looking at him that he's found the truth. He didn't have to say anything—it was there, even in his mannerisms. He's living on a different plane now."

"So where does that leave you?" asked Karen.

"I think I really do believe," answered Jeremy. "But for me it has to be more than believing because you or your father do. I want it to be Jeremy Manning's personal discovery—for himself. So there are still some things I have to think through. Is that unreasonable?"

"No, of course not. I'm convinced that's what it's all about—making that discovery for yourself. My father would say it's discovering that Person for yourself . . . encountering your own personal vision of Him . . . of the light and truth which are His essence."

"That does sound like something your father would say."

"Not long ago he told me that he felt the vision he'd been given was nothing more than the physical manifestation of an experience all men and women were destined to have one day—if not in the flesh, then in the spirit."

"What experience?"

"A personal encounter with God himself."

# SEVENTY-THREE

Jeremy Manning was by nature a perfectionist, and an analytical and self-reliant one at that. He always pushed himself to his limits, depending on his own skills and insights and abilities and hard work to get him where he wanted to go. Trusting his personal and professional fortunes to another was no easy assignment for a man like Jeremy, even if that One was perfection embodied.

Now, however, the medium in which he had lived comfortably all his life was gradually losing its power to sustain him. A certain intermittent choking sensation somewhere deep in his soul called for a new kind of air. His moral lungs were undergoing an unseen metamorphosis, requiring a new form of life sustenance in order to breathe.

As he walked up to his apartment building that evening after taking Karen home, he found he was breathing easier. Even his step was lighter. The talk with Karen had helped. He sensed he was getting closer to what he was looking for.

When he bumped into the building superintendent as he approached the elevator, he offered the man a friendly smile and sincere greeting.

"How are you this evening, Mr. Eastman?"

"Oh, you know," replied Eastman, a former truck driver who had several years ago retired to the easier life of apartment management, "pretty much the usual. Yourself, Jeremy?"

"Actually, I feel pretty good."

"You look chipper. Better than a few weeks ago." The elevator reached the ground floor, opened, and both men entered. Eastman raised his hand to the controls and pressed the button for Jeremy's floor.

"Going my way I see," said Jeremy lightly.

"I left my clipboard up there this morning during all the fracas."

"What happened?"

"Phones on the whole floor went dead. A big mess. Phone company was here all morning."

"Did they get it straightened out?"

"Yep. Everything's back in order. Had to let them into your apartment though."

"Just mine?"

"No, all the ones on your floor."

The elevator slid to a stop and the doors opened.

"Now I've got to find my clipboard or there will be an even bigger mess," said Eastman. "Why'd I ever leave my eighteen-wheeler?"

Then without waiting for a reply, he scurried out and down the corridor to his left.

Jeremy turned down the hall to the right. When he unlocked his apartment door, he was relieved to see that everything was in order. At least the workmen had been neat. Absently he lifted the phone receiver, reassured to hear the dial tone. He paused for a moment, thinking he heard a faintly discordant hum, but decided it was his imagination and hung up.

It was late, almost eleven o'clock. No wonder Eastman had sounded frazzled. Well, tomorrow was Saturday. Maybe they would both be able to sleep in. At least he knew he would. His day had begun at six that morning and had gone full clip until dinner. He had not even had time to come home for a shower before his date with Karen. Instead he had used the facilities at the Executive Office Building, where he now shared a small office with two other presidential staff members. The busyness did serve to remind him that he was beginning to feel like a useful part of the president's staff, for which he was thankful.

He didn't have all the answers yet, but he knew they were out there waiting for him.

---

At nine o'clock the following morning Jeremy's phone rang. He had slept solidly, and the sound jarred him out of the pleasant semi-wakefulness of Saturday morning. He grabbed the phone by his bedside, doing his best not to sound groggy when he spoke.

"Hello."

"Good morning, Jeremy. I hope I haven't called too early. This is the president."

Jeremy shot up in bed as if a thousand volts of electricity had just coursed through him. In spite of a supreme effort to sound calm, his voice cracked.

"Mr. President—this is a surprise—and really, the time—the time is perfect."

"I just spoke to Karen a few moments ago," the president said, mercifully ignoring Jeremy's obvious discomfort. "It's been wonderful since she moved into the White House. We've had so much time to talk. This morning at breakfast she mentioned her conversation with you—no details, mind you. I hope I'm not out of line calling you like this—"

"Oh, no, sir," interrupted Jeremy, fully himself now. "That's fine."

"She happened to say you were struggling somewhat in your search for the truth. I wanted to encourage you, son, for whatever it's worth."

"Thank you, sir," he replied, genuinely touched by the president's gesture. "That means a great deal to me."

"I think we both got into all this at about the same time," MacFarlane went on. "We were both confronted with startling facts our pragmatic intellectualism could not explain. Speaking for myself, I had to make an about-face. That wasn't easy. I fought it for months. Perhaps it was even worse for you—I don't know. At least I had the personal encounter to fall back on during my worst doubts. Nevertheless, I think I understand what you are going through."

"You have no more doubts, sir?" asked Jeremy earnestly.

"Not about God, son," MacFarlane replied. "Not since Moscow. I should say, I have no doubt that God is real, that His Son spoke to me, and that He now has a claim on my life. No doubt that from this moment on I am nothing less than compelled to live for Him, to proclaim His truth. No doubt that He is involved with me personally, that I am seeking to allow His Spirit to live in my heart. In other words, at last I am gradually coming to peace with the Giver of visions, even though it's an ongoing and deepening process."

The president paused. Then Jeremy heard a light chuckle on the other end of the line. "But don't get me wrong," he said. "Doubts about what it all means? Oh, boy, I'm full of those! How to live this new life, what to do in a given situation, how to be a strong president while I'm groping around as a new Christian. I tell you, Jeremy, this is not an easy time for me." He stopped again and now laughed outright. "Can you grasp the enormity of the unpleasant dichotomy, Jeremy? If I wasn't caught in the middle, I'd think it was the most hilarious thing I'd ever heard. Here I am trying to run the most powerful nation in the world, and I'm a mere novice, so to speak!"

"If you'll pardon my saying so," interjected Jeremy, "you don't sound like a novice to me."

The president's sigh was audible. "Well, if that's true, I'm immensely thankful to God. He does seem to be filling me with His perspective and His wisdom. I have this sense there is something He wants me to do, something urgent—perhaps something which even extends beyond the peace plan with Kudinsky. In the meantime, however, I'm confused about many things. Doubts? You bet . . . every day. Struggles, questions. I often wonder if I am seeing things the way God intends. Just this morning I read in my Bible that God's ways are not our ways. That made me wonder if I was going about this effort for peace all the wrong way, if I'd somehow misinterpreted the vision altogether. I struggled in prayer over that for a good while—just a couple hours ago."

"At least you're doing something. At least you're confident about the road you're traveling," said Jeremy. "At this stage, for me, even that seems rather enviable."

"It'll come for you too. When an honest heart searches for the truth, I have no doubt He reveals it in time."

"Well, sir, let me just say that it's reassuring to see you responding to what God told you."

"I am trying. I can only follow a step at a time. But knowing what that next step is can be downright puzzling. And now with Kudinsky laid up in a hospital in Moscow, it's difficult to know what we're to do next."

MacFarlane paused.

"Listen, Jeremy, this isn't the kind of conversation to have by phone. Why don't you come over for dinner tomorrow night. I'd like to talk more. We're all so new at this—it helps to talk it out. Perhaps we might all be able to encourage one another."

"I'd like that, sir."

"Good. I'll let Karen arrange it with you."

Jeremy hung up the receiver, thinking how much the president had changed in such a short time. Whatever questions remained, it was clear the weight of doubt had been replaced by a solidity of purpose whose foundation had to be something . . . some *One* more powerful than he.

# SEVENTY-FOUR

Monday morning dawned with thick clouds and the promise of a hefty summer thunderstorm.

Jeremy felt good in spite of the gloomy weather. The warm rain was cleansing and lent a tangy, refreshing fragrance to the atmosphere.

The president had suggested that he begin reading the Bible each day, and he had decided to start that morning, using the black book he had been given when he was ten years old. Its leather was hardly worn, though he'd had it twenty years. How he happened to have it with him was a mystery. But perhaps it wasn't an accident after all. His mother had helped pack the boxes of books he moved from home, and he could just picture her slipping it in.

He had begun reading in Matthew, which Duke Mathias had suggested during their meeting the previous week. He had nearly finished the book before suddenly realizing he'd be late for work if he didn't put it down and get going. By the time he showered, shaved, and dressed there wasn't time for breakfast. On most days he enjoyed his morning coffee and toast and a brief scan of the newspaper.

He didn't miss it on today, however. To Jeremy, who had never read the Bible in his life, the Book of Matthew had been as compelling as a good mystery. But now he was late, so he plucked the *Washington Post* out of his mailbox as he hurried through the lobby of the building. As he walked to his car he began scanning the front page.

Halfway to the parking garage he stopped, as though stunned by the force of a physical blow. Black type stretched across three columns of white page.

PRESIDENT VOICES DOUBTS OVER PEACE BID, read the headline.

Forcing his eyes to read on, Jeremy's horrified features grew more ashen with each incredible sentence.

> Sources close to the White House revealed yesterday that President MacFarlane has had curious second thoughts about his bid for peace with the Soviets. It was just two weeks ago when he and Soviet Premier Vladimir Kudinsky stunned the world with their historic and unorthodox proposal.
>
> The president is quoted to have remarked to a close aide: "I wonder if I am going about this effort for peace all the wrong way." The president went on to say that he has been praying about how to interpret recent world events and how to cope with the rigors of the presidency.
>
> The radical steps toward peaceful coexistence outlined by MacFarlane and Kudinsky in the Moscow summit were initially lauded as hovering between the revolutionary and the miraculous. However recent polls indicate that confidence in the peace proposal has dipped nationwide.
>
> MacFarlane's recent comments may sound the death-knell for the ill-fated U.S.-Soviet treaty that had been regarded as suspect from the outset by many Washington political analysts.
>
> In a recent campaign appearance in Boston, presidential hopeful Patrick Foster stated that "though peace is every sane man's heart's goal, we as a nation must seek a peace whose basis is reality. With Soviet troops menacing the Iranian border, one must ask what is the true species underneath—the wolf or the sheep?" That question is becoming more dominant around the country.
>
> One that is likely to be asked with it is this: If the president has now taken to prayer meetings as his means of seeking guidance for his decisions, to what extent may his judgment in Moscow be relied upon? A Gallup poll . . .

Jeremy could read no further.

Searing white-hot anger blinded his eyes. The blatant bias of the article was bad enough—sure to cause scandal among those to whom any hint of religion was tantamount to losing one's mind. But even worse was the quote that had been lifted directly from the president's private telephone conversation with him two days earlier. As this fact sank in, Jeremy's anger gradually was replaced by numb horror.

The president would read this and think he had been betrayed. He probably already had seen it!

How could it have happened? Jeremy knew from experience that Foster had an effective spy corps at his command. Surely the president took precautions against common eavesdropping. Any way you looked at it, thought Jeremy glumly, the finger was going to point straight back to him.

What could he possibly say to the president? The words from the article repeated themselves unmercifully over and over in his mind: "death-knell for the ill-fated U.S.-Soviet treaty . . ."

Was this one breach going to ruin it all? Again he asked himself how it was possible someone could have overheard his conversation with the president.

Suddenly his mind cleared with a sickening jolt. He jerked around and ran the half-block back to his building, took the stairs to the lobby two at a time, and raced to the elevator. He pressed the "Up" bottom several times, sweat breaking out across his forehead. How he hoped he was wrong!

Finally he turned and raced to the stairwell. He attacked the four flights at a run. By the time he stood in front of his own door, his lungs were aching painfully. He could hardly get the key into the lock fast enough. He flung open the door and ran directly to the telephone, grabbing the receiver and unscrewing the mouthpiece.

He was right! The leak was right here, not in the White House!

Jeremy tipped the bug, no larger than a watch battery, into the palm of his hand, then dropped the tiny disc into his coat pocket. Then he went to the bedroom to check his second phone. Finding an identical plant there hardly came as a surprise.

With a heavy step he turned and left his apartment for the second time that morning, dreading what he knew he must do next.

---

Jarvis MacFarlane had already guessed how the quotes had been leaked.

"I don't know what words to use to apologize," said Jeremy remorsefully as he dropped the tiny electronic microphones on the president's desk. "I feel dreadful about this."

"It's not your fault, son. These things happen in politics. We'll just have to be more wary in the future. To tell you the truth, I'm almost relieved to see those bugging devices."

"What do you mean?" asked Jeremy.

"I knew there were only three possible ways the leak could have occurred. Either my phone had picked up a bug, or yours had, or you had talked. Those were the only three options. So you can see how relieved I am to learn that the White House hasn't been infiltrated and to know that it didn't come from you."

"Ah," smiled Jeremy, "I see your point. But I would never knowingly compromise you, sir."

"Oh, I know that, Jeremy. I never believed you had. I only wondered if something might have been said between you and Karen that had been overheard. You never know about these things. Anyway . . . no sense in dwelling on it. The point is, I'm relieved it's only a bug."

"Do you think this will hurt the campaign?" asked Jeremy. "The article said—"

"It said the president is a human being who struggles like everyone else and who sometimes has to look outside himself for help. It says that to people who will read it correctly," added MacFarlane. "To others it will say I'm weak, or that I'm a religious fool. I'm sure that was Foster's intent—for who else could be behind this? And the people who will read this into it are the ones who think I'm weak anyway. To some it will make me look frail, ill-equipped to be president. Others will perhaps be more sympathetic. But I'm not overly concerned about public reaction."

"I thought you'd be devastated."

"I'm sorry to disappoint you," said MacFarlane with a grin.

"I'm not disappointed, believe me!"

"Probably a year ago I'd have hit the roof, called in my press secretary, and fired off a carefully worded rebuttal intended to blur the issues all the more, couched somewhere between an outright lie and a skillful political rejoinder. But no more. I can't play the game that way any longer. Someone else is in control now, and I care more for His reputation than my own."

"I must say, it's a relief to see you so calm, sir. But I think if Foster heard you, he'd be disappointed. He must have thought he really hit pay dirt to use our conversation so overtly and risk arousing our suspicions so soon after the bug was planted. He had to know we'd find it sooner or later."

"It's a good sign, don't you think?" said the president. "For a change Foster is running scared."

"I hadn't considered that."

"It reminds me of Watergate. Nixon had the election in the bag, but he was so scared of losing that he risked his entire reputation on something they never needed to do. If Foster's desperate enough to try this, it means he's worried."

"A shrewd analysis."

"When you've been at this as long as I have, you begin to see all the angles."

"Well, Mr. President, here's an angle you might not have considered," said Jeremy, shifting in his seat, not feeling altogether at home in the role of presidential advisor. "Why don't I put the bugs back in place and give our eavesdroppers a real earful?"

"You mean feed them bogus information?"

"We could make Foster look like a real bozo."

"Jeremy, do you hear yourself?" said MacFarlane, his tone a fraction sharper than before. "Do you realize what you are saying?"

Jeremy shook his head with self-reproach. "It's so easy, isn't it? To get sucked into that game you talked about."

"Especially when you know your cause is just."

"I only thought . . . well, it is an election year, and we all know how vital it is that you win."

"Would we be winning if we used deceit to achieve our goal? Would that be His way?"

"But how can you hope to defeat a man who will stop at nothing to get what he wants?"

"I've asked myself that many times, Jeremy, and there's no easy answer. But take those listening devices and flush them down the toilet—I think that's a reasonable beginning. Winning isn't up to us anyway. Our part must be to live with integrity, live by the truth, live by what He would have us do. Don't you think a God who could do what He did with and for Kudinsky and me, not to mention a God who could effect the changes of heart you and I are experiencing, could enable the man of His choice to win a simple election? We need no tricks or angles—or these." He flicked his hand toward the bugs sitting on his desk. "Speaking for myself, I only need His strength."

These last words sounded more like a plea than a declaration.

---

When Jeremy left a few minutes later, MacFarlane remained seated behind his desk in the Oval Office, thinking back over their conversation. It had made him more aware of the fact that the importance of the election was slowly paling in his mind. Politics—even the election—were beginning to feel almost . . . he hated to even think it . . . irrelevant.

He had to win—of course. But what seemed altogether more vital now was that he grow in his newfound faith. And somehow the two goals—winning the election and deepening the spiritual part of his being—seemed more at cross purposes every day. He could not even talk on the phone to a friend without it hitting the front pages. Which made him realize that he'd have to be extremely careful in the morning devotional meetings he'd been attending in the EOB. Foster would probably have spies planted there too.

But it went beyond these issues.

Beyond the election . . . beyond Foster . . . beyond the Legation . . . beyond his faltering attempts to learn to pray . . . beyond all that into the nebulous region of his own inner being, into that core of self where no one could go with him except God. And when he delved deeply into that spiritual personhood in his heart, he could not yet grasp all that was going on.

Since Moscow, a kind of regeneration had begun to occur within him. Could it be as simple as passing from his old life into the new, as spoken of in the Bible? He didn't know. But he sensed it was more than that. He was being led toward something he could not see, pulled toward some higher purpose—more than the election, more than the presidency—some greater destiny. Even as the thought occurred to him, he realized its gross presumption. Yet—yet—if it were not so, then why the vision?

Words spoken first by Daniel, then Peter, and finally Duke began to tumble into his consciousness from out of his memory: *"Peace is not what it seems . . . be not deceived . . . a sword is coming unexpectedly . . . now is the hour for preparation, for obedience . . . your faithfulness will carry my peace to the four corners of the earth."*

*My peace* . . . what *was* His peace, thought MacFarlane. Hadn't he attempted to accomplish just that with the Moscow proposals—carry peace throughout the earth? But what about the words *"peace is not what it seems"*?

What did it all mean? *"My fire will burn your tongue unto its anointing for My purpose. You are My witness of these things."*

"What things, Lord?" MacFarlane found himself crying out. "What purpose—if not peace with the Soviets?"

More statements came ringing through his brain: *"Warn them that the kingdoms of man are as dust . . . you are my witness . . . in the kingdoms of man, true peace can never come . . . peace means something different . . . peace in the world is a fleeting delusion . . . you may be a modern day Jonah . . . none of God's messengers enjoy the call . . . God gave them the words . . . as He will for you."*

Slowly Jarvis MacFarlane slipped out of his chair, and, wincing in pain from his leg, went down on his knees behind the huge presidential desk and clasped his hands together, as he had done as a child, and quietly wept.

"Oh, God!" he cried out softly. "Help me to know what You want me to say . . . what You want me to do!"

As if in answer to his plea, the words the Voice had spoken to him that fateful night came back to him: *"You shall be the instrument of hope . . . to proclaim that peace has come . . . and to prepare My people for the sword that will fall . . . I will show you what to say. Listen to My voice . . . you are My chosen servant . . . you are My witness . . . you shall not be alone in your task."*

When at last he rose to his feet, a flame of new purpose and strength sparkled amidst the tears in his eyes. He walked slowly to the window and looked out, as he had that night. He drew in a deep breath and smiled.

He was a new man! He could tell. The process begun that winter night in February had just taken a significant step. Somehow he sensed a deep assurance inside that he would be shown how to proceed. His prayer would be answered! And perhaps that in itself was part of the answer.

He felt stretched, pulled beyond the changes of new birth, new relationships, new priorities. The fluttering wings of his spiritual being were at last shedding the dark confines of the chrysalis.

Yet toward what new life would this fluttering of wings lead him?

# SEVENTY-FIVE

I don't care what it takes," Foster yelled into the phone, "I want to know everything!"

The senator held the receiver to his ear in a vise-like grip, pacing behind his desk to the extent the phone cord would allow. He listened to the reply, but apparently did not like what he heard.

"Then plant a new one! I shouldn't have to tell you . . . okay, okay! Maybe you're right. Then try something less risky—don't you guys have wall taps now that can penetrate into a room? . . . Yes, that might do it . . . one side of the conversation would be better than nothing."

He listened again, seeming to relax a bit as he sank into the chair behind his desk.

"I see. That *is* good . . . well done. Let me know the second you have something from that angle. Now, what about the impact of going even more public with this disclosure, that is *if* we can substantiate this religious experience thing? We need to get some polling information immediately. What's likely to be the impact with the conservative white Christian vote. I want to know—"

The speaker on the other end of the line interrupted with a comment to which Foster nodded emphatically.

"Yes, I saw that piece against MacFarlane . . . yeah, what magazine was it—one of the evangelical rags—" A brief pause. "Right—that's exactly my point. We need to determine if there could be any potential damage here, in all directions. If MacFarlane starts getting religious, how much of the evangelical vote are we likely to lose? I know it's minuscule in comparison to '80 and '84, but right now we've still got most of them because they're more Republican than they are Christian, and I don't want to lose any of them. On the other hand, who knows! Maybe if MacFarlane gets religion he'll hang himself without us lifting a finger. And then there's the question of the potential negative backlash against us if we play up his religion and try to brand him a fanatic or a phony—or just loony tunes. There're so many ways we can play this thing. But we've got to have some figures before we move on it."

Once again Foster listened carefully.

"Right—right—first we've got to know for sure what MacFarlane's up to . . . I don't want him stealing any of my lines! Get some of your Christian contacts to interpret all that prayer and vision stuff . . . right, the plants may help. But before you do anything further or release any statements on the religion issue, make sure you get some figures about the impact. We can't afford to mess up at this point. That evangelical vote is tricky. It went against Carter, even though he played up the born-again strategy, taught Sunday school, and said he asked God for advice on decisions. And yet the evangelicals were behind Reagan like he was the Messiah, even though he and Nancy fooled around with horoscopes and his Christianity was as shallow as his platitudes. Figure that one out! They're more loyal to conservative politics than to their own people! They're an unpredictable lot and we've got to know what MacFarlane's about. If we're clever, we can play both sides of the religious fence—and we'll keep both the New Agers and the Christians. It's okay to mingle in a little Bible with that new age stuff—no one even notices and you keep everyone happy. But you've got to know what you're doing. We might have to import a Christian or two to help with the speech writing for a while."

Foster hung up the phone, propped his feet on his desk, and gazed thoughtfully into the distance.

*What is MacFarlane up to?* he wondered. *And what is all that kinky stuff about God's Son speaking to him?*

*This tape is dynamite,* thought Foster, a smile spreading across his face. They had MacFarlane in the bag!

# SEVENTY-SIX

The call came just as MacFarlane was preparing to leave for a briefing with several key senators over the peace proposal.

"Something has come up," said the voice on the phone. "The group is slated to meet, and you've got to be there. Are you up for one more midnight ramble?"

"I suppose. But what's it all about?"

"Something came into Daniel's hands yesterday from Romania. He says it confirms everything. It's imperative that you hear it."

"Right. Okay then, what do you suggest?"

"Remember our second meeting?"

"Yes."

"I think we could use the same place again."

"Sounds fine."

"Same time?"

"Yes."

"Tonight?"

"I'll be there," said the president.

---

Fourteen hours later, in the dead of a Washington night, sixteen men sat in a circle on the floor of a run-down hotel room. After the urgency of Peter's call, MacFarlane hadn't known what to expect. Something big was obviously afoot, for Duke Mathias was present, along with two other men he had never seen before.

"This tape came to me from some of my underground sources in Romania via our connections in the Soviet Union," said Dmitri as Daniel held up a small cassette player. "The speaker is a Romanian who was imprisoned in the old days several times for Bible smuggling and who was nearly executed three times. Miraculously, he was delivered. At one point, during his last imprisonment, a vision came to him in the form of a bright light. It surrounded him in his cell, and a voice spoke to him. He says it was the voice of the Lord himself. And what this man now speaks on the tape, through his interpreter because he does not know English, is what the Lord said to him."

Daniel set the small cassette recorder on the floor and turned it on. They heard a voice speaking in Romanian, a sentence at a time, followed by the voice of English translation.

Jarvis MacFarlane could scarcely believe his ears. Had he not known differently he would have sworn the Romanian had been told of *his* vision and what the Man of Light had told *him*.

". . . 'Do not be discouraged. Have patience. There are many people I want to wake. America will burn . . . do you see Las Vegas, New York, Los Angeles, Florida? This is Sodom and Gomorrah. One day it will burn. When the Americans think all is peace and safety, there will be an internal revolution, and while the government is busy with that, from across the sea will come forces from other nations, and America will burn.'

" 'But what about the church?' I said.

" 'The church has forsaken me,' He said. 'I am no longer with the church because the people give praises to themselves. The honor that is to be given to Christ, the people take upon themselves. In the churches there is divorce, there is adultery, there is homosexuality, there is abortion, there is every kind of sin. Churches have been turned into moneymaking businesses. Their evangelists preach only salvation and happiness and blessing, but they refuse to show the destruction and the hard times I will bring upon their land. Through your mouth, and the mouths of others of my servants, I want to wake up the multitudes. I love America, and I desire to save its church.'

" 'How will you save the church if America will burn?' I asked.

" 'Just the way I saved my three children in the furnace of fire. Just the way I saved Daniel from the lions in their den. I will save them the same way. Tell them to stop their sinning. Tell them to turn toward me. The Father never tires in His forgiving. They must look to the Lord their God with all their hearts, because it is only a short time before everything will happen which I have told you. Tell them not to be afraid. I will go before all those who speak the words I give them, and I will work powerfully. I will heal. I will open doors for them to speak my words.

" 'The trumpet will sound. The church in America will awaken because America has been greatly blessed. America took the Bible all over the world. Americans went as missionaries to the ends of the earth. But America fell from truth, and the church in America fell from the truth. I want to save them and heal them, if only they will turn from their sin. I desire to pour out My blessings upon this country. But the people refuse to recognize Me. They persist in their sin. Judgment will come if they do not turn and recognize their Messiah.

" 'Read Jeremiah 51 and Zechariah 14 and Revelation. Everything has been prophesied before. The American preachers and evangelists do not preach the true word of the Lord, because if they spoke these truths to the people, the people would leave their churches. The people do not want to hear this message. But they will all have to answer before the Lord."

The tape went on for about another ten minutes. When it was over, the room was utterly silent. Then some began to pray softly. At length Daniel spoke.

"With something of this sort, there is always difficulty discerning the true word of the Lord from the human chaff through which He must speak. We know ourselves how prone we all are to the weakness of human opinion. How difficult it is for God to break through our own views and opinions to truly speak His word to our hearts! In the same way, we must recognize that the man on this tape is just that—a man. He is not an infallible vessel, for none of us are. In addition there is the difficulty of language, of translation. What I am saying is that each of us must weigh these words carefully as we humbly and prayerfully seek the Lord's mind, not our own. However, I do sense the Spirit of God speaking to us through this man."

When Daniel had finished, a man whom the president knew only as Richard asked, "Might I add a word or two?"

"Of course," replied Daniel.

"Mr. President," he said, turning to MacFarlane, "I feel it is important to clarify something especially for your sake, because of your position and influence and also because you have openly expressed to us on several occasions how new this all is for you."

"Indeed!" said the president. "I'm eager for any enlightenment you can provide!"

"These days in which we live are among the most significant in the history of God's people—for a multitude of reasons. God is actively at work, speaking in a variety of ways. But no single man, no single woman, no single church or movement or group will ever be given *the* message of God, *the* full truth, *the* complete perspective of God's plan. God works through His *whole* body throughout the *entire* earth, throughout *all* time. Many, many parts of His body, hundreds and thousands of men and women, are all given pieces of God's truth to proclaim to the rest. Our responsibility as God's people is to discern God's voice, to receive what He has to say to us, and to live faithfully as His people. So many Christians take a piece of this truth or a piece of that truth as the *whole* truth and then run off at full speed with only that little part of God's revelation. They blow it all out of proportion, and what God intended to be a true portion of His total will and plan, to work in harmony with the rest but not to be mistaken for the whole, becomes an untruth because it is not seen for the *part* of the truth it is.

"I have been praying for you these last months since we met, Mr. President, and as I have, the conviction has grown upon me that God is raising you up as a mighty voice, though not necessarily a political voice. To tell you the truth, although I love you as my brother and have come to feel a deep fondness for the humility of spirit I sense in you, your success or failure in the upcoming election is not of great concern to me. I wish you well. And if God has led you to serve Him in the political arena, then my prayers will be with you daily, I assure you of that. But I sense that God has something greater than that on your horizon—some greater purpose.

"Therefore, I feel it is imperative that you see a wider, broader perspective, that you not be swept away by this teaching or by that idea. Do not allow yourself to become narrowly defined as a Christian by rigid confines of message as so many are, even some of us here.

"What I'm trying to say, Mr. President, is that you must earnestly seek the Lord himself to reveal His full truth—not those of us in this group. Take this tape, for example. I believe this is a message from God. I sense the Holy Spirit as I listen to this man. I sense that he has suffered for God and that through that suffering has come purification. However, at the same time I can hear the man himself. I can hear his own opinions coming through. Such does not invalidate the message from God. It only tells us to be prayerful and discerning and to receive our wisdom from God, not man. This tape, then, does not represent God's full message to us here. It is just one part of the whole.

"The same holds true for us, Mr. President. We who call ourselves the Legation speak a certain message of preparation to God's people. But we are only a small part as well. God is speaking in and through and among His people in such an incredible multitude of ways and means. We have been given a piece of the whole to communicate, and we must be faithful to do so. But you, Mr. President, must see a larger vision of the whole. You must listen to the Lord speaking through many parts of His family. And above all, seek God for truth, not men.

"Judgment coming to America—yes, perhaps this is a true message from God. But it is only one part of the message, for great revival is coming too, great hope. You, I believe, can be a voice to proclaim both. There are so many things God wants to say and is saying. You can—and I believe the Lord has shown me this—you can be an instrument through which God's people begin to see bigger and more complete parts of the whole."

When Richard finished speaking, Daniel added, "In Jesus' name, I concur, Mr. President. Do not let our human limitations limit your perspective of God's huge work. The time is coming when you will have to step out and take these truths beyond what even we are capable of seeing. God's anointing is upon you, and you must step into your calling."

# SEVENTY-SEVEN

Part of Jarvis MacFarlane wanted to just chuck the whole political business. Everything Richard and Daniel had said just confirmed the sense he had of being drawn toward some unknown destiny. Yet without any firm indication about what he was "supposed" to do, he saw no alternative but to continue forward on his present course. Perhaps against all odds he might win the election after all—perhaps this was to be part of his "calling." Perhaps it was not too late for the peace initiatives. Perhaps as a second-term president he would have the strength he needed to achieve some impact.

But if the importance of the election had begun to dim and become confused with a host of new factors in the priority structure of Jarvis MacFarlane's mind, it grew to almost obsessive proportions in the consciousness of the nation.

July drew to a close with the solemn rites of the two national political conventions. The Democratic gathering in San Diego proved a heated forum for widely divergent views right down to the end. In many ways it was reminiscent of 1988, featuring the race between Dukakis and black activist Jesse Jackson. On this occasion, however, one of the participants happened to be the incumbent president, harking back to Ted Kennedy's bid to oust President Jimmy Carter from the party's nomination in 1980. Like Jackson and Kennedy, DuBois vowed not to go down without a skirmish, though it was clear he did not have enough votes to mount a serious challenge. And, dogfighting to the end, the large vote he garnered justified his clamoring for second spot on the ticket.

Jarvis MacFarlane had other ideas, however. For over a year he had known he would have to replace ailing, seventy-six-year-old Jacob Coombs when the election rolled around. Coombs had emphysema which was steadily growing worse, and though he might survive another term, his health was such that he could no longer fulfill the obligations or withstand the rigors of the office.

With this eventuality in mind, MacFarlane had embarked on a personal investigation to find a running mate, not only qualified and experienced, but a person of integrity and honor who would be capable of discharging the duties of the nation's highest office if necessary. In the months since the vision, once he had fully faced the enormity of the challenges ahead of him, he had privately widened his search beyond the confines of his own party. He had scoured through resumes and briefs on all fifty governors, all one hundred U.S. senators, and about half its representatives, narrowing the list down to fifty names he felt worthy of further investigation. He had then requested more detailed files on each of these, and by June 15 he had it down to twenty names. Surprising even himself, he discovered DuBois still on the list.

At this point, after requesting additional information and detailed personality profiles on each man, MacFarlane sought no more counsel on the matter of the vice-presidential selection. Both Dick Howard and Jake Randolf did their utmost to probe his thought waves, but to no avail. By July 10, after much thought and a great deal of prayer, MacFarlane had narrowed the choice to four men.

Knowing that his every move was being scrutinized for clues to his potential selection, MacFarlane was unable to formally meet with each man. Instead, he discreetly arranged to have each of the four present at numerous functions throughout the month of July. Under the guise of informal and social exchange, he was able to become better acquainted with them all.

Finally, just five days before the opening of the Democratic Convention, employing several of those who had been instrumental in helping keep his nighttime meetings confidential, MacFarlane effected a private meeting with the man he had selected—Charlie Backman, three-term senator from Oregon.

At the end of this rather lengthy, face-to-face encounter, MacFarlane rose, stretched out his hand, and said, "I'm sure you've wondered what this little inquisition was about, Senator. And it boils down to this—I'd like you to share the ticket with me, as my vice-presidential candidate."

Stunned, Backman groped for a reply. "It's no secret I've not been a Foster man, Mr. President. But to run . . . with *you*! It's unprecedented!"

"Not as unprecedented as you may think," said MacFarlane with a smile. "You know about the Federalists and the Democratic-Republicans?"

"They hardly shared the ticket!"

"They shared the executive branch. Besides, it's time this government of ours was stretched. We need to see that governing is about people, about integrity, about leadership more than it's about partisan politics. And in my judgment, Senator, after me, you're the person best equipped to run this country. I know a great deal about you. I applaud your record, I admire you personally. And I believe the country will be stronger for my choice."

"I appreciate your confidence, Mr. President. Needless to say, I'm honored. I will have to talk to my wife about this. It's a big decision. And if you don't mind my saying so, I'll have to pray about it as well."

"Those were the very words I hoped you'd say," rejoined MacFarlane. "If you hadn't wanted to seek higher counsel, I'd have doubted whether I was properly interpreting the answer to *my* prayers."

---

It was on the second night of the convention in San Diego that MacFarlane invited his closest advisors to his room to inform them of his decision. As he had anticipated, most of them nearly went through the roof.

"A Republican! Mr. President! Tell us you're joking!"

"It's no joke, Avery," replied MacFarlane to his campaign manager. "I'm convinced Charlie Backman's the best man."

"I must say, Mac, I'm hardly surprised," laughed Jake Randolf. "At every turn this year you seem determined to defy the political pundits."

Most outspoken and vehemently opposed was Dick Howard.

"Aside from all the obvious problems with this, Backman gives us no regional leverage, Mac!" insisted the attorney general. "What good will he possibly do? You've already got the northwest sewed up. I've told you all along, pick DuBois to erode Foster's southern base, and the election's yours."

"DuBois isn't the presidential timber Backman is. Neither do his views—politics aside—line up with mine as well as Backman's."

"I tell you, Mac," said Howard in frustration as he tossed his hands up in the air, "I sometimes think you're trying to throw away the election!"

"Look, Dick, I know we've had our differences lately," said MacFarlane calmly. "But I'm seeing a lot of things much more clearly now than I did a couple years ago. I'm changing, and I think for the better. One thing I know, and that is that leadership, courage, and integrity have to mean more than party politics. If we're not big enough to look beyond ourselves—beyond our own views, beyond our own dogmas and biases, beyond people who are merely clones of our own value systems—then we're not fit to lead ourselves. True leadership is about people, not party loyalties."

Only Duke Mathias offered no opinion on the president's decision to select a member of the opposite party to run alongside him. He merely sat back with the hint of a peculiar smile on his face.

"And the bottom line," the president went on, "is that in a way even I don't exactly know why Backman turned out to be my choice. I prayed long and hard throughout the entire process, and as much as some of you may not understand how I can say such a thing, I feel strongly that Backman is the man God wanted me to choose. Ultimately, it was *His* choice, not mine."

---

The acceptance speech of the vice-presidential nominee, usually a dull ritual, became the highlight of the week. At the end of MacFarlane's nomination speech, when he had built up to the dramatic moment and dropped the name of Senator Charles Backman onto the roaring crowd, the huge hall was almost silent. The hall full of Democrats didn't know whether to boo or cheer as the Republican senator, whose arrival in San Diego had somehow been kept secret, strode onto the platform to join the president. But his speech, which stressed unity, his support of many of the party's planks, and his enthusiasm for the president's peace proposal and the treaty before Congress, seemed to win them over in the end.

By contrast, after MacFarlane stunned the nation with his announcement of the first joint Democratic-Republican ticket in history, the Republican Convention a week later in Minneapolis proved a rather tedious affair. It could hardly have hoped to measure up to the drama provided by what some called the MacFarlane-Backman show, which still had the nation buzzing when the networks opened their coverage in Minnesota. And in spite of Foster's attempt to infuse the proceedings with what theatrics he could in a rousing acceptance speech, his unchallenged nomination drew low ratings on all four of the major networks.

---

During the August lull prior to the traditional opening of the fall campaign on Labor Day, Patrick Foster focused all his back-room Senate experience on one objective: the defeat of the president's treaty.

After eight years in that enclave of power he had accumulated a good deal of old-fashioned clout, not to mention countless favors owed him. Knowing sentiment was still riding high in favor of the president, Foster's short-term objective became the destruction of the treaty's chances before Congress adjourned in October, hoping that its defeat would pave the way not only for a drop in MacFarlane's standing in the polls, but also for him to offer his own peace initiative. The polls would then swing his way in late October, just in time for a victory on November 7.

When Foster boarded his private jet to fly out to St. Louis for an old-fashioned Labor Day celebration, complete with several stump appearances and photographs, he could not have been more pleased. The treaty had been stalled, largely on account of the back-scratching, potential favors, and even blatant blackmail his people had used as they prowled the back halls on Capitol Hill. Debates from the floor, often televised nationally, were dominated by anti-treaty rhetoric, and those defending the president's proposals were slickly edged out with effective filibuster maneuvering. Foster saw to it that MacFarlane's defenders gained the floor only during slack times when the cameras weren't running.

Although the president's approval ratings were higher than they'd been in more than two years—surging to a twelve-point advantage immediately following the San Diego convention—the public was divided over his vice-presidential selection. And by Labor Day most pollsters rated the race a toss-up once more, with the momentum gradually swinging back to early leader Foster.

If only he'd had one more week back in June, thought Foster. One more week and it would have been *his* peace plan now dominating congressional discussions! He and Bolotnikov had come so close to hammering out a mutually advantageous arrangement.

Not that he trusted that beady-eyed Russian—not for a minute. But he would only have had to keep him in tow until after the election. At that point, as president-elect, he would have had the power to do anything he chose.

But MacFarlane's inane summit had thrown the proverbial wrench into his designs. Suddenly the weakling's show of guts had won back the esteem of the voters Foster had worked so hard to erode. Suddenly the election, which earlier seemed ripe for the plucking, was a close race again. He couldn't afford to ease up now. He had to continue sniping away at MacFarlane's credibility, undermining his treaty attempt, making him look like a religious nincompoop, keeping up his own stance as the standard-bearer of the new era of peace, all the while hoping circumstances would permit him to cut his own deal with the Soviet heir apparent.

*If only Kudinsky had been killed by those Iranian terrorists,* he thought, *I might be on my way to Moscow right now for meetings with the new premier!*

---

As Jarvis MacFarlane handed Karen his crutch and eased into his seat on Air Force One in preparation for their flight to Seattle for Labor Day, his thoughts too were on the Soviet premier. The two leaders had maintained regular communication since June. Yet he had heard nothing from Kudinsky in well over a week, and he was growing concerned.

Rumors had been circulating that the premier had suffered a relapse from his wounds and had been re-hospitalized. But even the American ambassador had been unsuccessful in ferreting out the truth.

# SEVENTY-EIGHT

The Soviet premier had in fact *not* been re-hospitalized. Though his recovery had progressed well, he still spent a great deal of time in bed and was under the daily supervision of his physicians. Reports, however, having their origins in political motive rather than medical reality, had been cunningly filtered out of Russia, exaggerating the premier's condition. The man at the center of all this hearsay, however, knew nothing of what was being said of him outside the borders of his own homeland.

The days of summer had been bleak ones for Vladimir Kudinsky. The only bright spot, besides his ongoing conversations with his friend MacFarlane, had been the opportunity to spend a great deal of time at home reading, away from the pressures of the Kremlin, while recovering from his wounds.

The doctors hounded him daily, it was true, but he was reasonably sure they were honest men and not Bolotnikov's lackeys, so he accepted their rituals, tests, and potions.

Time was passing, however, and there was much work to be done on behalf of the treaty. He had begun easing back into his schedule, working daily on a speech he planned to deliver to the meeting of the Party Congress in September, stressing the urgency, the necessity, of an enthusiastic ratification of the peace proposal with the Americans.

He had not spoken to MacFarlane in ten days now. He'd made numerous calls, but each time his operator had come back with the report that the lines into the United States were jammed and it was impossible to get through. He'd made the attempt from home as well, but found the call was routed through the Kremlin, with the same result. He hadn't heard of a change in Moscow's phone system and had certainly not authorized any alterations to his own line, so he determined to look into the matter the moment he was back in his office on a permanent basis. Once or twice he considered using the Moscow-Washington hot line, but thought better of it. Every call would be taped on both ends, and he could not run that risk to either of their reputations. No, he would just have to wait, continue trying to get through, and in the meantime complete both his speech and the insurance package he was preparing with respect to his chief adversary.

If Kudinsky had any doubts about what he had done, his time

of recuperation at home after leaving the hospital served to dispel them once and for all. The sixty-nine-year old widower lived alone, with only a housekeeper who came in daily to prepare his meals and to clean.

Though Anna had worked for him a number of years, he had never had the time to get to know her well. She was married and had several children, but he didn't even know their names. She prepared and served his breakfast each morning and they exchanged their daily two or three sentences. He was seldom home at midday, and when he returned in the evening it was the same routine.

But on one particular day, about a week after his release from the hospital, Anna had spoken to him in very uncharacteristic fashion. All morning he heard her about her work keeping the house in order. He dozed off before lunch, and when he awoke he saw her brown-gray head poke through a crack in the door.

"Oh . . . I am sorry! Did I wake you, sir?" she said, flustered.

"Don't give it a thought, Anna—I was already awake. Did you want to clean this room?"

"No—not while you are resting, sir," she answered, before pausing awkwardly. "But I have brought lunch, if you might manage it."

"Brought lunch?" asked Kudinsky, surprised by the unexpected gesture. "You certainly didn't have to go to the trouble."

"I am pleased to, sir. May I bring it in?"

His pensive face transformed into a broad grin and she scurried back into the hall. A moment later she returned carrying a heavy-laden tray, complete with a vase of fresh flowers. The tray contained enough delights to please any red-blooded Russian man, from borscht to rich homemade brown bread.

Kudinsky chuckled his pleasure, thankful that he could do Anna's effort proper justice. She placed a tray in his lap, lifted lids, poured his tea, and fussed like a mother over her child.

"I am very touched by your kindness, Anna," said the premier.

"Please, it is my pleasure . . . my honor, sir."

She lowered her eyes as if embarrassed, then stepped back. She started to leave the room, then stopped and spoke again in a halting voice.

"Sir . . . Premier Kudinsky . . . I want to tell you that you are a great man. Perhaps it is not proper for me to speak to one such as yourself in this forward way, but I must. I think maybe you do not hear enough times what people think."

Had it not been for the seriousness of her effort, Kudinsky might have laughed outright at this understatement.

"What you and the American president have done," she went on, "for our countries—for the world—is like a divine gift. My family and I are afraid sometimes when we hear about all the terrible weapons. My children wonder if they will have a future. But, sir, you have given us reason to hope. For that I thank you, but my little attempt to show my gratitude seems now so paltry beside what you have given the world."

---

Kudinsky thought of Anna's simple but sincere words now as he sat in his office, reflecting on the tenuous state of his position in the Kremlin, staring outside where the chill of autumn had begun to grip the Soviet capital. It did indeed at times seem as if he stood entirely alone in his quest for peace with the nations of the world. Anna's words reminded him that no matter how the government might try to repress them, there were Russian citizens—millions of them—who yearned for the same thing. While Anna's words had been the most personal comments he had received, rumors of positive public sentiment had been slowly trickling to his ears since he first woke up in his hospital bed two days after his surgery.

Unfortunately, in the Soviet Union it was the government rather than the public that counted in such matters. Public sentiment could not move Kremlin policy. It was one of the fundamental lessons Russian leaders had to learn. A crack in that structure, however slight, and the whole system could topple.

In the case of the proposed treaty with the United States, Kudinsky felt sadly alone. He knew there were those on the Politburo who supported him, but they were reticent to voice their thoughts and had become even more so in the last few weeks. Moiseyev's capitulation had been only the beginning. The premier was certain that Bolotnikov was making shrewd and effective use of his years with the KGB to collect damaging information on members of what he considered his opposition, using it to bully, intimidate, and even blackmail them into silence. Those who were above his petty scandals would get the message: destructive stories could just as easily be invented against them if they did not toe the line. And they all knew the danger of alienating themselves from the heir apparent to the reins of power. This was way the game was played; he knew it well.

A soft knock at the door interrupted Kudinsky's thoughts. He looked up, hoping it would be a pleasant diversion.

"Come in," he called, grinning when he saw his friend Pavel Soroka. "I am so glad to see you!" he said, struggling to his feet to embrace the secretary of agriculture warmly.

"Ah, Vladimir, it is good to see you also."

"It has been too long."

"I am sorry."

"Never mind. I am on the mend now."

"I should have come to see you, but—"

"Think nothing of it, Pavel. You were busy and I needed my rest."

"I am happy your recovery has been so rapid. At first we were told many things about your condition, none of them good."

"That is all behind us. Come, sit down." The premier quickly pulled two chairs together so they could sit informally. He took no more than passing notice of the grim look clouding his friend's usually pleasant countenance.

Pavel sat heavily in the chair offered him. "What do the doctors say?" he asked.

"You know the physicians—always gloomy. But other than a scar in my abdomen—" here he patted himself on the stomach to indicate where he had been wounded most seriously, "and a few more months with this ankle cast for the bone to heal properly, they say I'll be back to normal."

"I am happy to hear it." Pavel paused momentarily. "We are told, however, that your condition continues to be grave."

"Grave! Nonsense!" exclaimed Kudinsky. "I feel wonderful! As long as I move about slowly."

"That is not what I heard."

"I see," said Kudinsky, nodding knowingly.

"The rumors circulate, Vladimir."

"And has *Comrade* Bolotnikov already reserved my resting place in the morgue?"

"It is no joking matter. You must think about changing your position."

"Pavel, what you ask is impossible," Kudinsky replied.

"Why impossible? You must save your skin while there remains a chance!" Pavel pleaded, a note of desperation in his oddly intense manner.

"What is it, Pavel?" Kudinsky asked compassionately.

"I—I am merely concerned for your welfare," answered Pavel lamely. Silence filled the room for several uncomfortable moments.

At length Kudinsky reached for the crutches which would be his companions for another three months, pulled himself out of his chair, and walked to the window. With his back to his friend, at last he spoke.

"Pavel, I will tell you something. Perhaps because you are my friend, you will be able to understand. It is something I have told no one else in our country, and it is this: I believe it is God who constrains me to follow my present course."

Pavel gaped at the shocking words. Slowly he shook his head, and when he spoke again it was with audible defeat in his voice. "As if you are not in trouble enough, will you now begin speaking about God? Oh, Vladimir . . . Bolotnikov will bury you!"

"Perhaps . . ."

"Then do something about it!"

Kudinsky turned and hobbled to the ornate antique cabinet sitting against the wall opposite his desk. He paused, raised his hand thoughtfully, and touched a locked drawer.

"Pavel, perhaps it is providential you have come today."

"Must you speak in such terms?"

"I think you may be right. Perhaps it is time I did something," the premier went on, ignoring Pavel's question. "I have refrained thus far because I despise such tactics. And, too, I do not think that the God who spoke to me would necessarily approve—"

"God speaks to you!" exclaimed Pavel.

Suddenly Kudinsky realized his error. But Pavel was his closest friend. Even if he couldn't fully understand, surely he would not betray his trust.

"It is a long story, Pavel, and quite incredible. Suffice it to say that I do believe God has told me to do the things I am doing, and above all to make peace with America."

"Oh, Vladimir!" groaned Pavel.

"You think I am insane?"

"I do not know what to think," replied his friend miserably. "What does it matter what I think? It is what your opposition thinks! They would destroy you with this!"

"Well, perhaps it is not important that you consider it at all," said Kudinsky, thinking perhaps he had spoken unwisely. "It is not at all the point of what I have to share with you now."

Pavel stared at his friend without answering.

"What I intended to say was this . . . I have a way to stop Bolotnikov. It is highly distasteful, but I think the situation is desperate enough to call for it."

"What is this thing?" asked Pavel.

"It is nothing to do with God, I assure you. Far from it." He took a key from his pocket and unlocked a drawer in the cabinet. "I have some compromising information on our comrade," he said as he removed a large manila envelope from the drawer. "I believe the time has finally come to put it to use."

"What could you possibly have?" Deep creases in Pavel's round face mirrored his inner anxiety.

"Read it for yourself," said Kudinsky, handing him the envelope.

Pavel took out the contents and began scanning the pages. His eyes became wider and finally he let out a sharp breath.

"A CIA informant?" he said. "I cannot believe it."

"The evidence does not lie."

"You surely cannot be serious about using this. Bolotnikov will tear you in pieces and toss you on a floating iceberg off Siberia."

"I think not, Pavel. Even his supporters would have to question his integrity, or even his loyalty, upon seeing this."

"You take too great a risk . . . your plan could easily backfire."

"The risk is warranted," replied Kudinsky flatly. "Nothing must hinder this effort for peace which the treaty affords us."

"Vladimir, I believe you are losing your . . . perspective." The slight pause before his last word was nearly imperceptible, but the premier caught it and winced. For friendship's sake, however, he let it pass.

"Vladimir, we have lived with the Cold War for fifty years. What will a few more hurt? It would be foolish to destroy yourself over it."

"I have no choice," answered the premier firmly.

Pavel clamped his mouth shut and said no more.

"I need your help, Pavel," continued Kudinsky. "What I ask may involve some danger, but I have no one else to turn to. Will you help?"

"Go on."

"I need you to take this envelope and keep it secure. I plan to speak to Leonid this afternoon at four o'clock. I will arrange to meet again with you here in my office at six. If I am not here—if our worst fears are confirmed and he truly has gained the degree of power you say—if something does happen to me, then you must immediately make this material available. Deliver copies not only to my supporters, but to Bolotnikov's as well."

"But Leonid will surely suspect that you have confided in me."

"Speed will be your ally, Pavel. You must not give him the opportunity to act on his suspicions. Have several messengers ready to instantly take their copies in various directions to the other key members of the Politburo. He will not possibly be able to run down every copy in time."

"I do not like to sound selfish, my friend, but what about me?"

"You will need to lay low for a few hours until the documents have their effect. Then you will be safe, I think. Bolotnikov will be too worried about his own skin to be concerned with you."

"You have overlooked one thing, Vladimir," said Pavel. "If your plan progresses far enough to require my active participation in it, that will mean you yourself have been . . . removed from the picture."

"That is the one fact I have *not* overlooked," replied Kudinsky soberly.

# SEVENTY-NINE

Kudinsky entered Bolotnikov's office at precisely four o'clock. His rival welcomed him expansively. This worried the premier, but his course was set, not to be easily deterred.

"This is a rare privilege," said Bolotnikov, his cold eyes negating any genuineness in his voice.

"I appreciate your seeing me on such short notice."

"You are the premier. My schedule is at your disposal. Please, sit down."

Beneath the facade of politeness, the atmosphere between the two men was icy as a Russian winter.

Bolotnikov walked slowly around to his desk and sat, while Kudinsky took the chair in front of it.

"I will get right to my business," said Kudinsky.

"I expected nothing less."

"I am concerned with the lack of support the peace treaty is receiving," began the premier.

"I am hardly the one to see about that." Bolotnikov chuckled patronizingly. "Our comrades are simply pragmatic men."

"My staunchest supporters have turned."

"Can it be helped if they have come to their senses?"

"If I were certain they had experienced a true change of heart for reasons of deep loyalty to the Soviet Union, then I would remain silent. But I believe they have not been left entirely with their own consciences in the matter."

"What do you infer, Kudinsky?" Bolotnikov's tone suddenly altered and filled with menace.

"You know as well as I do that they have been intimidated into opposing me."

"Surely you entertain delusions, comrade."

"I will not waste time and point fingers, Leonid."

"Point all you want, Mr. General Secretary. It will get you nowhere!"

"I will not stoop to a shouting match. Suffice it to say that I want such tactics stopped." Kudinsky ended the sentence with his own quiet menace clear in his tone.

Bolotnikov leaned back and smiled. Slowly the smile gave way to a light chuckle, a sound totally devoid of humor.

"I do believe that you are not in full possession of your faculties. A persecution complex perhaps—"

"Enjoy your amusement while you can, comrade," replied Kudinsky coldly. "You will accede to my demands or you will be finished here."

"You have it wrong, comrade. It is you who are already finished!"

Kudinsky had hoped, however futilely, that he might be spared his next move, but it was clear his rival was not about to bend. Bolotnikov was intent on forcing him to take the contest between them to its potential deadly conclusion.

Slowly Kudinsky took an envelope from his breast pocket and handed it across the desk to his adversary.

"I truly did not want to resort to this, Leonid," he said with regret in his voice, "but you leave me no choice."

With great deliberation Bolotnikov picked up a long, slim letter opener and inserted its sharp edge under a corner of the envelope, then sliced meticulously through the paper. He removed the contents and shuffled through each paper. Then he turned his icy gaze on Kudinsky.

The premier found himself nearly unnerved by Bolotnikov's expression. Not by the look itself, but by the fact that the man registered not a trace of emotion, no reaction whatsoever, at the contents of the envelope. Even a man so viciously unscrupulous as the ex-KGB chairman must realize the deadly implications of Kudinsky's information.

"I am appalled at the use of such despicable methods," said Bolotnikov, his pretense of shock mocking Kudinsky.

"I am only following your own example," the premier replied.

"But you do it so artlessly," rejoined Bolotnikov, his mouth cracking once more into the hint of a grin. Then just as methodically as he had slit open the envelope, he began to tear its contents into tiny bits.

"There are copies." But even as he spoke, Kudinsky knew, with a sinking sensation in the pit of his stomach, that everything was going terribly wrong.

Bolotnikov laughed. "Left for safekeeping in the hands of a friend, I presume—to be distributed should harm befall you?"

Kudinsky said nothing.

Seconds later Bolotnikov's features snapped once again into their grim alignment.

"What friend do you have left in Moscow?" he sneered. "What friend loyal enough to take such a risk? Ah, yes—Soroka, your dear and loyal friend—" He laughed again. "You choose your friends in Moscow with as little care as you do your so-called friends in Washington!"

His hand moved toward the intercom on the desk. He pushed a button and said, "You may come in now."

Still the premier did not speak, but turned toward the door, half-expecting what he would see when it opened.

Pavel looked miserable—at least Kudinsky had to give him that much. He walked in, head hung down, eyes purposefully avoiding those of his old friend.

"So, Pavel, you have fallen also."

"I did it for your own good, Vladimir," Pavel replied, his eyes still downcast, "and for the good of our country. You are not yourself, my—my friend. You need a rest."

"Oh, Pavel!"

Kudinsky wanted to weep, but he would not bare his emotions before his enemy.

"You should never have attempted to play at the master's game," jeered Bolotnikov. He dropped the scraps of torn paper into his wastebasket. From a desk drawer he took a larger envelope—the very envelope Kudinsky had earlier given Pavel—and threw it in also. Finally he struck a match and tossed it in with the now impotent evidence. In a moment a bright, hungry flame shot up from the metal can.

"What now?" said Kudinsky in an inexplicably calm and composed tone.

"I have affidavits," said Bolotnikov, producing a folder, "a dozen or so, all verifying your incompetency to direct the government."

"Dear Lord!"

"Yes, that particular imbalance figures into it quite heavily. A lengthy confinement is called for—psychotherapy, perhaps, electroshock—anything that will restore our beloved leader to his former self."

"You promised you would not harm him!" broke in Pavel. "Demotion or retirement, nothing more!"

"You are a fool, Soroka!" rejoined the aspiring Soviet leader. "You have both become an embarrassment to our country."

"Oh, Vladimir, what have I done!" moaned Pavel pathetically.

"I am sorry to have brought this on you, my old friend," said Kudinsky, laying a sympathetic hand on his shoulder.

But Bolotnikov had no time for such sentimentalities. He was using his intercom once more. "It is time," he said into the speaker.

At his command, three burly, black-jacketed men stalked into the office. The KGB officers did not hesitate to take their premier into custody. Two grabbed Kudinsky's arms, pulling him to his feet, while the third firmly clutched the forearm of a broken and unresisting Soroka.

Vladimir Kudinsky, Chairman and Premier of the U.S.S.R. and man of God's choosing, did not resist the inevitable. He pulled himself loose from the restraint of the guards, picked up his crutches, and began making his way toward the door—his head held high, chin taut with determination—defeated but not broken.

All seemed lost. The country he loved would soon be under the thumb of an evil and unscrupulous man. At the same time, everything he and Jarvis MacFarlane had risked so much for appeared all but destroyed. Yet since that singular night in February, Vladimir Kudinsky had learned that one could not always judge matters on their external appearance. Sometimes the ethereal and dreamlike—to earthbound eyes—was in truth the most real and concrete. And thus, perhaps what seemed horrifying and hopeless was only a dream that would in the end usher him into an existence more real than he could presently imagine.

# EIGHTY

The mighty yellow and green tractors, bulldozers, and giant earthmovers that had rumbled so unceremoniously into the area a few days earlier now stood in silent abeyance on the temple mound.

All was quiet as Shimeon Hagiz approached the microphone to deliver his few prepared words to the crowd that had gathered at the ground-breaking for the construction of the temple. Shimeon was no public speaker, and he felt especially out of place with the Israeli prime minister, defense minister, and many other notable dignitaries, both political and religious, standing behind him. Yet the prime minister had deferred to him, insisting that Shimeon was the one to do the main honors this day. He was, after all, largely responsible for their being here at all.

Shimeon gripped the silver-plated shovel firmly in his hands, cleared his throat nervously, and began.

"I need not say what a great moment in our history this day signifies," he said. "We have waited nineteen hundred and thirty years for it!" He paused, gazing over the crowd.

A number of Gentiles mingled with the Jewish onlookers. This day held some significance for Christians too, he supposed, but their longing for the rebuilding of the temple was on a completely different plane.

There were also a few head-wagging Hasidics milling about, no doubt lodging their disfavor with the proceedings. The most orthodox of the Jewish population still believed Shimeon and his crew were trampling with profane feet on what should remain holy ground. For was it not the Messiah himself, *after* His coming, who would rebuild the sacred edifice and drive the desecrating foreigners from the land? No mere man could take the place of God's holy Anointed One, especially a mere archaeologist.

Despite the heated protests of such Jewish conservatives, and with the unlikely support of the Gentiles, Shimeon had persevered in his vision. Since that day months ago when they had discovered the Holy of Holies, he had known what he must do. How the problem of the Arabs and their fallen mosque would be solved he would leave to the political leaders. How to satisfy Jewish fundamentalists and liberals as well as the vocal Christian element, he would leave to the religious negotiators. Shimeon only knew that *his* duty, *his* calling, was to dedicate himself to the task which suddenly God had miraculously made possible.

To Shimeon, the rebuilding of the temple had but one meaning—one that transcended everything else. The temple—that central place of worship the Jews had lacked since it had been razed by the Roman emperor Titus in A.D. 70—was the ultimate symbol of unity for his beleaguered race, and would, as nothing else could, solidify their claim on the tiny chunk of earth which God had given to Abraham four thousand years ago, and which had proved so difficult for his descendants to hold ever since.

Shimeon continued with his speech, raising his voice so every significant word would be clear to these spectators.

"We are standing upon holy ground, consecrated since the days of our brother and father David. Here shall the temple of our God stand once again. I pray as Solomon did on the day when he dedicated the temple which his hands had built: 'That thine eyes, O Jehovah my God, may be open toward this house night and day, even toward the place of which thou hast said, My name shall be there, that thou mayest hearken unto the prayer which thy servant shall make toward this place. And hearken thou to the supplication of thy servant, and of thy people Israel—' "

All at once angry shouts rose on the perimeter of the gathering, and Shimeon stopped short as his eyes jerked up.

A mob of Arabs was pouring down the narrow street in front of them, heading toward the ceremony. Publicity for the event had been guarded, the precise date kept quiet until the final moment to prevent just this sort of upheaval. But Shimeon was not surprised—it was bound to happen. The Muslim world had been up in arms ever since the Knesset had announced that the Dome of the Rock would not be rebuilt. There had been protests and skirmishes since the day the Israeli government went public with its plans for the temple six weeks ago.

Shimeon raised his voice above the din. "—and of thy people Israel when they shall pray toward this holy place." He paused to gather momentum to finish, but before he could open his mouth to speak again, a rock hurled toward him. Shimeon ducked, but not quickly enough. It grazed his head. Instinctively he reached toward his forehead and felt blood on his fingers.

Armed police units rushed toward the intruders, attempting to cordon off the approaching mob. But as the Israelis had learned from half a century's fighting over this land, angry Arabs and Palestinians and Muslims were often oblivious to threats and clubbings.

Several more rocks flew, while the crowd of spectators jostled its way toward safety.

Behind him the prime minister and other officials had crouched down, but Shimeon did not move. He stared defiantly at the usurpers.

"Hear, O Israel!" he cried. "The Lord our God, the Lord is One!" Oddly, only the handful of Hasidics stood firm, joining him in the ancient Sh'ma.

# EIGHTY-ONE

Scorching heat seared down upon the jagged mountains. The lone traveler made his way gingerly across the rocky incline. He had journeyed for weeks, mostly on foot, occasionally on a camel or donkey when he could steal one. A motor vehicle was out of the question because of the attention it might draw, and also its need for petrol. There were few fuel pumps along the barren and deserted paths he had been forced to traverse.

The traveler's heavy, dun-colored desert robes hung over his wasted frame in deeper folds than they had a month ago, and his dirty, once-white howli framed a gaunt, blistered face, nearly black now from the constant exposure to the sun's relentless rays.

Seyed Gilani had never been further removed from his past Western lifestyle than he was at this desolate moment. He looked like a wild desert mullah, and as each day passed the likeness went deeper than mere surface appearance.

"Allah preserve me," he muttered into the cloth wrapped tightly around his mouth.

Suddenly his foot slipped and he flailed desperately at the rock ahead of him as the ground at his feet crumbled away. His sandaled foot frantically grabbed for a foothold, the bare stones cutting at his toes. Slipping down a yard or two on the hard-gained path, he tumbled back several feet until he slammed against a flat upright slab of rock which checked further disaster. The rock had broken his fall and saved him, but the impact knocked away his breath, and he could not move for some minutes. His endurance was not what it had once been, a fact he was well aware of as he looked up despairingly at the small peak he was having such difficulty conquering.

*These mountains should end soon,* he thought—the great Kopet Mountains which formed the border between Iran and the Soviet Union east of the Caspian Sea—though he wondered if he would ever come out of them alive.

Once he got through this tortuous terrain, it would then be only fifteen or twenty miles to his destination—fifteen or twenty miles of the merciless Kara Kum Desert. If the mountains spared him, the desert wouldn't. He had so little strength left, and his goatskin water bag was not nearly so fat as when he had begun. Still he did his best to shake the depression born of heat and agony and fatigue.

He must not let the elements defeat him!

His was a holy quest, blessed by the Great Prophet. He knew that now, even if he had argued so often against Mohsen's fanatical outcries. Now he alone remained to avenge the injustices to his people, his country, and to the Holy Rock from which the Prophet had ascended into heaven.

"Oh, Mohsen . . . Ahmed . . ." he whispered, though there were none to hear him but a handful of desert ants, "your lives will not have been spent in vain."

The words grated at his parched throat. He coughed violently, only stopping after he put his water bag to his lips and sipped some of the precious liquid.

*Pull yourself together, Seyed,* he silently admonished.

His thoughts seemed all at once to come into brief focus. Suddenly his mind glimpsed the man lying there among the rocks and dry shrubs—a stranger. This man was but a copy of a Mujahedin terrorist named Mohsen Ali Pevlahvi, or perhaps it was Rhevlah Gilani, revered father and courageous warrior. *Or am I merely a pathetic caricature of those two great men?* he thought mordantly.

Seyed shook his head. In truth he had nearly ceased to know who he was. Perhaps this leathery, desert nomad was the true Seyed, and that other man from the now-distant past was the true stranger. The dreams and hopes he had once entertained were but faded memories of trivial aspirations—a Manhattan law practice, a Park Avenue penthouse, and a sleek Ferarri. What drove him now in his private holy jihad were matters closer to the source of life . . . and death.

He chuckled grimly to himself. "What a fool you are," he said aloud, and the sound of his own voice seemed to bring the impassioned desert traveler to himself.

Seyed moved his aching body, but his pack was too cumbersome and he had to slip it off before he could gain his feet once more. He swayed precariously as he stood upright, swirls of light momentarily blinding him. In a moment or two he was steady and bent over to retrieve his pack. As heavy as it was, it could not be left. Its contents were vital to his mission. The American-made weapons, the explosives and the submachine gun, had cost him forty-three hundred U.S. dollars on the Tehran black market. The back alleys he had been forced to prowl to make the right contacts had been perilous, and the brokers themselves, even by the standards of the terrorist world, had been murderous and loathsome.

As Seyed turned to face the rocky incline once more, his eyes glanced toward the left and he noticed a gentler slope winding around the peak he had been trying to climb. Why he had not seen it in the first place he could not imagine. Hitching himself into motion, he determined to have a closer look.

"Allah be praised!" he cried aloud. It was a perfect pass directly through to the other side. The rocks jutted out at just the right angle so that he could never have seen it from his previous approach. The easier way through was only noticeable from the spot where he had landed after the fall.

It took another half hour to reach the peak, and before beginning the final slow descent from the mountains, Seyed paused to take in the scene spread out below. The fierce desolation of the Kara Kum Desert stretched unendingly before him, the heat from its floor rippling the stagnating air above it into menacing waves of death. Tomorrow he would have to cross that furnace—and either conquer it or be consumed by it.

Miles away he could just make out the Soviet border city of Ashkhabad—"the city of love"—in the fading daylight.

"I will make it a city of hate," murmured Seyed. "It will become a despised byword among cities, for here is where it will all start . . . fire and destruction and death!"

He knew now beyond all doubt that his quest was a holy one, to be compared to the historic jihads of old. Allah had directed him here, led him, protected him. The desert would not defeat him. He was the Prophet's chosen one!

*Mohsen . . . Ahmed . . . I will not fail you! I will bring death to our enemies—death by their own hand.*

# Eighty-Two

"This is Terry Farmer reporting from Red Square, Moscow." The camera zoomed in for a close-up of the CBS correspondent as he delivered his report in the dank autumn drizzle.

"These ancient walls of the Kremlin standing directly to my left are still ringing after yesterday's stunning announcement of the abrupt change in power at the top of this nation's hierarchy. Early this morning Leonid Bolotnikov officially assumed the reins of leadership, following the sudden death of Premier Vladimir Kudinsky two days ago from complications resulting from the wounds he received during the June assassination attempt."

The newsman paused while the camera angle widened to take in the entire scope of the majestic backdrop.

"Bolotnikov began his career in the military," continued Farmer, "becoming the youngest man ever to command the Warsaw Pact forces. Later he migrated into party politics as head of the KGB, and for the last year has served as Chairman of the Presidium of the Supreme Soviet. Bolotnikov's outspoken criticism of Premier Kudinsky's moderate policies is well known in political circles here in Moscow, thus it is yet to be seen how this change in power will impact U.S.-Soviet relations."

The monitor switched back to the CBS newsroom in New York and anchorman Dan Rather.

"Terry, has there been any mention of the treaty currently being negotiated between the two nations?"

"No, Dan," answered Farmer. "In fact, in today's speech before the Politburo, Premier Bolotnikov made no mention whatsoever of the treaty. Embassy sources speculate that this silence may provide a statement in itself."

"Thank you, Terry."

Rather turned a page of copy and looked directly into the camera. "Back in Washington, the president has been unavailable for comment. But White House Press Secretary, Rich Bonner, issued this brief statement this morning."

The monitor quickly focused on Bonner in the White House press room.

"The president is deeply grieved over this great tragedy," said Bonner in his easy Southern drawl. "The death of Premier Kudinsky will not only be a terrible loss to the Soviet Union, but to the entire world as well. President MacFarlane characterized the premier as 'a large-hearted and peace-loving man, a man whom I considered a friend and who will be remembered as having moved the world several strides closer to a lasting peace among the brotherhood of nations.' The president strongly believes that the late premier would not want his passing to disrupt the ongoing peace process. 'The fitting legacy we can offer him,' says the president, 'is to bring his dream of peace between our two nations to a successful conclusion.' Thus President MacFarlane will continue to work tirelessly to see the Moscow treaty quickly implemented. To this end he will deliver a nationally televised address before both houses of Congress tomorrow."

---

Patrick Foster turned from the bank of television sets in his office where he had been viewing all four networks' renditions of this most recent upset in the world situation. He picked up the steaming mug of coffee his secretary had just poured for him and grinned.

Things could not have gone better if he had planned them himself. A few days ago all had seemed lost—or at least more dismal than he liked this close to the election. Now, suddenly, he was back on top. Of course, no official polls had yet been taken to verify his optimism. But Kudinsky's demise could only mean one thing: MacFarlane's glory train was about to derail.

Bolotnikov would never deal with MacFarlane, that much Foster knew. The president's short-lived sideshow was over. His peace plan was as good as dead and buried. And his bid for another term could be thrown into the grave along with it. Foster's only regret was that he had not been able to be there to see MacFarlane's face when he heard the news of Kudinsky's death.

Regardless of this apparent boon, Foster knew there was still no time to sit back and relax. He still had plenty of work to do before November 7. The failed peace plan would knock a few points off MacFarlane's standing, but that was not enough. Foster wanted a return to the sweet lead he had enjoyed last spring. He wanted no "ifs" left when November 6 drew to a close.

The senator gulped the remainder of his coffee, picked up his phone, and instructed his secretary to put a call through to Harv Bateman. Moments later the campaign manager was on the line.

"Harv, I want you to put the Randolf set-up into motion . . . yes, right away."

Foster paused to listen a moment.

"Yeah," he answered at length, "sounds good. No connection to you, is there? Good . . . take care of it then."

He hung up, had another call put through, and soon was speaking to Andrew Nyborg.

"I'm afraid I've got another urgent job for you, Andrew." He paused and smiled. "No, I don't think it will require you to take another trip to Russia. A few phone calls ought to do it. What I want is for you to finalize those Kaliningrad negotiations. It's time *I* met with our friend Bolotnikov myself. And time is of the essence, Andrew—you realize that, of course."

# EIGHTY-THREE

Eight days later Patrick Harcourt Foster stood before correspondents and reporters at the press conference he had called the previous afternoon.

"Ladies and gentlemen, these recent months have been uncertain, even perilous ones for our nation and our world. The issue of peace has been raised on every front and has been on everyone's mind. Yet we still feel little sense of security.

"The thinking person knows peace is no simple thing to be achieved overnight. Especially between two nations that have been at ideological, moral, and spiritual odds for over fifty years. You all know that I have sought to offer practical solutions, combining my long-standing call for peace with a down-to-earth prudence regarding changing world affairs. Thus, I have been at the vanguard of the growing movement that would give the president's peace proposals a hard scrutiny. If we are to see humanity's future on this planet rise to the levels I believe destiny has marked out for us, a strength must undergird our optimism. We cannot allow our generosity and desire for peace to be taken advantage of. Prudence and mutual respect must be fortified with realism and potency.

"Yesterday the validity of these convictions was brought home to me more clearly than ever—"

Here Foster paused for effect, making sure all eyes in the room were riveted upon him before he dropped his bomb.

"—when I received a telephone call from the new leader of the Soviet Union," he said, pausing to allow the hum of surprise to settle. "Leonid Bolotnikov is also a man who believes in strength. In that sense, we think alike." Foster chuckled softly in order to let the news people make what they would of the statement. "We are pragmatic men who will not sacrifice the security of our countries to some Pollyanna notions that years of strife can suddenly be healed with a smile and a handshake."

Though Foster was hardly thinking of Howson at the moment, the general's instincts had proven true in the end. "You and I may differ," Howson had told him, "and I can't make heads or tails of all this new dawn malarkey. But when push comes to shove with the Soviets, my gut tells me your military background will come to the fore." The general was indeed a good judge of character!

"The world could be on the brink of holocaust," Foster went on. "Something must be done. But it must be something sane, reasonable, and workable—not some cockeyed dreamy notion out of an old Frank Capra/Jimmy Stewart movie! To that sane and reasonable end, the new Soviet premier and I have entered into discussions of our own. He has made several unofficial suggestions to me—including a ban on further strategic defense research, along with joint space explorations. He also feels his government would support a five-year plan to reduce overall missile strength well below present levels. These, as I have said, were unofficial statements, but Premier Bolotnikov is anxious to talk again with me in a more official capacity."

Foster paused, turning his gaze on the group assembled before him. "Are there any questions?"

A dozen hands shot simultaneously into the air. Dustin Michaels of ABC was acknowledged first.

"Senator Foster, did the premier say why he did not contact the president regarding all this?"

Nods and verbal assent indicated that Michaels was not the only one with this question.

"The premier and I have met on other occasions," answered Foster smoothly, "most notably three years ago when several other senators and I visited Moscow. We established a certain rapport at that time, and have maintained a loose contact since. But—and I must be frank here—the premier told me he has sensed a definite hostility from the White House toward him, and, desiring peace as he does, Mr. Bolotnikov felt his best chances for a breakthrough lay with me. He hoped I might act as a kind of liaison between his government and, if not the president, at least the Congress. I told him I would do what I could, given the constrictions of our system and, of course, the parameters of the election process."

"Have you spoken with the president?" asked the UPI correspondent.

"I spoke with him this morning," said Foster.

"What was his reaction?"

"The president, as would be expected, was dismayed to learn of such negotiations secondhand. He . . . uh . . . denied Bolotnikov's allegations about White House antagonism. And I, myself, received a rather stern reprimand for my part in the dialogue, regardless of the fact that I had no part in initiating it."

Foster stopped, cleared his throat, then went on in a softer voice, as if he truly were an injured party but was trying honestly to make the best of it.

"For years I have been proclaiming my belief that we stand on the very threshold of a new era of peace. Such is my message, such is my commitment. I think it ought to be clear to everyone that, in a deteriorating world situation which threatens that future, it should not matter who helps the process along, just so long as peace is indeed the result. I personally have a difficult time understanding the petty political motivation which would criticize a sincere attempt to right the course of dangerous international tensions. Premier Bolotnikov impressed upon me firmly that the Kudinsky-MacFarlane treaty had been almost unanimously rejected by his government. I felt I had no choice but to seize the opportunity offered me—perhaps the only such opportunity our world might have for peace."

Cameras flashed, video tape whirled, as Foster made his point for all the nation to see. Here was a strong, practical, reasonable man, in touch with the world scene, on intimate terms with the new Soviet leader, on the verge of a major breakthrough at which the president had apparently failed.

Just the kind of man who should be in control of the reins of government.

# EIGHTY-FOUR

Dick Howard needed a drink—a good stiff one.

He didn't care if he wasn't a drinking man or if it might take the edge off his time when he went out for his daily run. He walked to the liquor cabinet, reserved for guests, and poured himself a double scotch. The clear amber liquid burned his throat and he coughed as he gulped it down, realizing the futility of the gesture. This was indeed strong stuff, strong enough to fuel a nation's passion, as it had the old highland Scots during their long fierce winters. But it would take considerably more than one swallow to numb the horrible sense of defeat he felt at this moment.

He set the glass down and walked over to the window of his office. As things stood now, he wouldn't be enjoying this particular view of downtown Washington much longer.

Foster had pulled the coup of coups.

Nothing could possibly top his announcement yesterday. With the election so close, there was just no time to recover and mount a serious counteroffensive. To beat him would take a whole new campaign strategy, and that wasn't something you began in October. Mac would probably never go for any of his suggestions anyway.

Foster had as good as won.

Only one thing could possibly pull the election out of the bag now. Even that was a long shot—but it was the only shot they had. Before Howard could resume the long-standing debate with himself regarding Wilson, a knock at the door interceded.

"Come in," he said testily.

Jake Randolf walked in, took in the scene at a glance, noting with particular interest the half-empty glass of scotch on the desk.

"You too, eh?" he said glumly. "Or are you just contemplating the possibility of jumping?"

Howard grunted unpleasantly. "Sounds great," he said, "but I'm afraid getting drunk is just not my thing."

Randolf closed the door behind him and sank into the nearest plush leather chair.

"No, Dick. You better leave that to the experts—like yours truly."

"You're joking, right?" Howard tensed, his tone earnest.

"On the last count—yes. On the first, no."

"What are you talking about?" Howard was too impatient and

surly to put up with his friend's cynical repartee.

"I fell off the wagon last night."

One look at Jake's red, puffy eyes and tremorous hands told the attorney general that his colleague was not joking.

"That's all we need!" groaned Howard.

"I'm going to turn in my letter of resignation today."

"Is that on the president's order?" asked Dick.

"No, but I thought I'd spare him the trouble."

"I suppose I am to assume you didn't do it in the privacy of your own home?"

Randolf rubbed his forehead miserably and shook his head. "There was this . . . lady," he said in a forlorn tone. "I don't know how I let her talk me into it. Before I knew it, I was sharing a drink with her . . . then two—"

"For all Washington to see, no doubt?"

"What else? There were even two or three reporters there. I know it was idiotic of me."

Howard strode from the window to his desk, picked up the glass, and in one quick motion flung the expensive crystal across the room where it shattered against the wall. Randolf stared with gaping mouth. It was a rare moment indeed when Dick Howard ever displayed such a lapse in his tightly controlled reserve.

"I guess I should be relieved you didn't aim that thing at me," Randolf said.

"You're a fool, Jake!"

"I hardly need you to tell me that."

"Get out of my office!"

Randolf heaved his tired frame from the chair and shuffled toward the door.

Watching his shattered friend, Howard was ashamed of his outburst. He added, as if continuing his previous sentence, "I gotta think."

Randolf paused and turned. "I am really sorry, Dick. I know that doesn't help, but . . ." He didn't bother to finish. Instead he turned and this time made good his exit.

Howard dropped wearily into his chair. This was about as close to despair as he had ever come in his life.

When Jake had attempted suicide three years ago, Howard had lost nearly all respect for his old friend. That was the coward's way out, and he was anything but that. Although right at this moment, jumping out a window did not seem an altogether remote possibility. He began to wonder what it would be like to be back out in the world of commerce, tackling the courtroom beat again, fighting with judges and writs and deadlines, jockeying around with some corporation's legal department.

He groaned. The thought made him sick.

He *belonged* where he was. He made a good attorney general. It would be a waste for him to occupy a less significant position—This realization had nothing to do with ego. He merely knew himself and was honest enough to be able to look his credits straight in the face. The pity was that he had to depend on others in order to stay here. If Mac fell, he fell.

Howard slammed his fist on his desk. "Not yet!" he said aloud. "We're not finished yet!"

He glanced over toward the locked drawer in his file cabinet as if it held all the answers to ward off his present frustration. He had been sitting on evidence that could convict Harley Wilson of everything from interstate commerce fraud to murder. He kept telling himself that he was waiting for more conclusive proof. After all, you don't convict a man for murder on hearsay, much less hearsay that had come from a wimpy little man who happened to accost him at the Washington monument. So he sat on Hensley's information, while the weeks turned into months . . . and now it was October and he had still done nothing.

As head of the nation's legal and justice system, he could not continue to ignore what lay in that file and maintain his integrity. Still . . . no one else knew the implications of the contents. Didn't men in positions of power have obligations which sometimes reached higher than the detailed scruples of the law? What about the greater public good? What about the benefit to mankind if he could insure Mac's reelection?

The minute that information became public, any chance of using Wilson would be lost.

No, there had to be some other way.

Perhaps he could convince Mac to do some "aggressive" campaigning. Mac wanted to win, and he wasn't blind to the desperation of the situation.

At least he should talk to Mac, try one last time to make him listen to reason. It was either an immediate denunciation of the Foster campaign in ruthless go-for-broke fashion, or get Wilson onto their team.

Those were their only options. It was do-or-die time.

---

Half an hour later, Howard walked into the Oval Office. From the beginning he knew it would be an uphill battle.

"Look, Mac," he began after settling himself into his customary chair with a cup of coffee in hand, "we've got to make some strong response to this move of Foster's. And soon!"

The president sat back calmly, a look of contentment on his face. His very expression of serenity galled Howard, but the attorney general kept his annoyance to himself.

"I don't suppose there's any chance you'd reconsider the Wilson option?"

"You know better than even to ask, Dick," replied the president with a peaceful smile. "Winning the presidency isn't worth sacrificing what I believe in."

"I thought as much," muttered Howard. He took a deep breath, then tried the alternate game plan he had hatched. "Okay, then how about a frontal attack on Foster?"

"I won't stoop to personal injury, Dick."

"You do agree that his meeting with Bolotnikov behind your back was damaging to the country."

"Seriously damaging," agreed the president.

"Treasonously so."

"I wouldn't use that word yet," replied MacFarlane. "But close. Certainly it hinders the peace process and undercuts my authority as president."

"Precisely! That's why we must—for the good of the country and for the future of the peace process—stop him . . . show the people he is not to be trusted with the highest office in the land."

"What do you have in mind?" asked the president warily.

Howard sucked in another breath before continuing. This was his last chance to persuade his friend. "I've been keeping this in reserve," he said slowly, "but I think the time has come to put it to use."

"What is it?"

"It's some information I've gathered on Foster's running mate—"

"I told you, Dick, I will not stoop to mudslinging or personal attacks," interrupted MacFarlane.

"The voters have a right to know about a man's questionable military record, especially if that man could one day succeed to the presidency."

"Questionable in what way?"

"Involvement in a drug investigation in Vietnam."

"That's already been raked through the papers months ago. He was cleared of the charges."

"A rich father and a four-star uncle got the charges dropped," retorted Howard. "But I've come into possession of new evidence, testimony from the other defendants and witnesses in the preliminary court-martial proceedings." Howard said nothing about how such so-called evidence had come into his hands.

"I don't care, Dick. I will not stoop to those measures. You ought to know better than to ask." MacFarlane let out an impatient sigh.

"By your own admission, we have a presidential candidate flirting with the edge of treason. Meanwhile, his running mate was probably involved in criminal activity while representing this country's military and obstructed justice in using family influence to escape the consequences—and you want to ignore it! You want to let these two men win the two highest offices in the land! I don't understand you, Mac! I'm not talking about mudslinging . . . I'm talking about the right of the people to know. What about your obligation to tell the people the truth?"

"I can't try to win that way, Dick, don't you understand," answered MacFarlane. "Everything's different for me now. I'm under compulsion not to take matters into my own feeble hands. There is a higher power controlling the destinies of men, and I for one am no longer going to interfere with His design for my life."

In exasperation Howard rose and paced about the room for a moment. When he spoke again, he did not sound like a longtime friend.

"Let me see if I can phrase this so it will penetrate that thick skull of yours—Mr. President!" He let out a sigh of frustration and vexation, knowing full well he was overstepping both the bounds of friendship and professional duty in speaking thus to the president of the United States. But what more did he have to lose? "You've lost the election—need I be more blunt? You may as well start packing now! Foster has pulled one over on you, and there is no way to recover. No way, that is, unless you decide to part with some of that lofty moralism of yours!"

"I can't do that." MacFarlane's words were quiet but firm.

"I don't believe you, Mac!"

"Let *me* try to get *you* to understand something, Dick." In contrast to Howard's passionate outcry, the president's voice was soft, calm, and self-assured. He paused, then rubbed his chin thoughtfully. "Dick, we haven't talked much about this before, but I'd like you to know that I've recently come to take very seriously my belief that God is active in the detailed affairs of men's lives . . . of my life."

"So I've gathered from some of your comments recently," replied Howard without interest.

"It may be none of my business, Dick, but I'd like to know if you believe in God."

"Come on, Mac!" grimaced Howard. He had no time for such tripe.

"You don't have to answer if you don't want to. I just thought knowing might help me get my message across."

"I'll tell you what I believe in, Mac," rejoined Dick defiantly. "I believe in winning. I believe in keeping my job. That's all there is. And you're as crazy as the rumors say if you think you can mix politics and all this religious mumbo jumbo!"

"Maybe you're right."

"I know I'm right!"

"I meant about not being able to mix politics with matters of faith. About spirituality being mumbo jumbo, you're dead wrong. My newfound walk with God is the most real thing I've ever experienced in my life."

"Maybe it's a good thing for you, Mac, but—"

"There's no good-for-me-but-not-necessary-for-you to it, Dick. Reality is reality. If it's true, it's true for all people, whether they recognize their need for God's presence in their life or not."

"Maybe so," mumbled Dick, shifting uncomfortably. "All I know is—"

"And, on second thought, I don't think you are right about not being able to mix politics with matters of faith. Our founding fathers built every aspect of this government on faith! Yet we have surgically removed all vestiges of spirituality not only from government and education, but from our very society. It's no wonder things are such a mess. Bringing God's sovereignty back into government, back into education, back into society at all levels is precisely what we must do if we are truly to preserve, protect, and defend the Constitution."

"That's yesterday's news, Mac. It doesn't work that way anymore. This is a modern age."

"A modern, godless age!" said MacFarlane. "You're right in your assessment about one thing, Dick. This country is headed toward defeat and impotency, but not because Foster's about to be elected. Rather it's because we as a people, as a government, as a society, as leaders, as common men and women have *all* lost the spiritual base upon which this nation was founded."

He paused, then continued in a profoundly serious tone. "I took an oath with this office, Dick. All of us in government do. I swore to preserve, protect, and defend the Constitution *so help me God.* During all my years of public office I have ignored that oath . . . ignored the fact that I promised to allow God to help me. I lied, Dick. I promised to do something I had no intention of doing. I said the words, having no idea what I was saying . . . having no idea that the Constitution was at root a *spiritual* document, written by men relying on God's guidance in their lives to order their ways. How can we so-called modern leaders preserve, protect, and defend it when we don't even understand or acknowledge the very basis for the Constitution's being—that it was God himself who breathed the miraculous life into it? Well, Dick, whether I have another month or another four years, I intend to allow God to help me do my job, as I promised."

"So if you feel that strongly about all this," said Dick, trying a new angle, "then isn't it of paramount importance that you win the election so you can get your message across?"

"Not as important as becoming the sort of man God wants to make of me."

"Come off it, Mac! Your back's against the wall, and all this talk about God and morals isn't going to save your neck. We've been tiptoeing around the issues of this election for months. But now push has come to shove and you've got to decide if you're in this thing or not! You can't win any other way."

"If I'm meant to win, I'll win."

Howard's almost unconscious roll of the eyes did not go unnoticed by the president, but the attorney general refused to relent.

"Maybe it's time you realized you're not the only one to consider here. Have you ever stopped to look at the selfishness of your righteous approach? When you go down, you're going to bring a lot of others with you. Jake is in his office at this very minute writing his resignation in order to save your backside. If you had some solid, aggressive game plan, we wouldn't have to worry about the minor scandal of Jake's binge. This job is Jake's life. Without it—"

"I won't allow Jake to resign, if that's what you're really worried about."

"Okay, I'm worried about my job too. We've sweat blood for you, Mac. We deserve some reciprocation."

The president pushed back his chair, stood, and then walked over to the windows looking out onto the rose garden. He remained quiet for several moments, and Howard, thinking that perhaps some of his words had finally sunk in, did nothing to interrupt the solitude. Finally MacFarlane turned to face him again.

"Try to understand me, will you, Dick?" he said, his eyes pleading with his friend. "Not too long ago I felt exactly as you do. Winning was everything . . . stay on top at all costs—for the good of the cause, of course . . . peace . . . the country's stability. I believed everything depended on my power, however puny or ethically questionable. But lately my vision has broadened. I see—or at least I'm beginning to see—a portion of the larger picture. I've come to realize that I am not in control at all. It is the Lord God, Dick, whether you choose to believe in Him and His dealings with man or not. His Son, Jesus Christ, has promised that the Father will be faithful. All that is required from me in return is to live by His laws, His truths. Yet even when I don't, He is still in control."

"Sounds rather fatalistic, if you ask me."

"Just the opposite. It's trust, not fatalism. It is the security of knowing I no longer have to depend on my flawed and finite power. Imagine what that means! Think of all the mistakes we have made in the past—mistakes which might have been avoided had we depended on Him."

"Even your fanatical Christians make mistakes, Mac."

"Of course they do. But He makes them come out right—"

MacFarlane stopped abruptly and hurried to his desk. "I just read about it today!" he said excitedly. He opened a drawer and pulled out a Bible, thumbing quickly through the pages. "Have you ever read the Bible, Dick? I mean really read it? This is amazing stuff—here it is! Listen to this, it's just what I want to tell you: 'We know that in all things God works for the good of those who love him, who have been called according to his purpose.' You see, He takes our mistakes and turns them to good. But there's more! Listen—you'll appreciate this: 'What, then, shall we say in response to this? If God is for us, who can be against us?' "

MacFarlane closed the book and leveled his eyes, shining with enthusiasm, at his friend. "Dick, I believe God is directing me . . . leading me. I'm not entirely certain yet what His purpose is. But I know God is bigger than Foster or Bolotnikov or muckraking newspaper articles—bigger than the peace treaty Kudinsky and I attempted to forge. Who knows, perhaps that attempt of ours was but a steppingstone in the purposes of God toward something that our earthbound eyes are not yet capable of seeing. The point is—I'm not worried about the election. I intend to continue running the kind of race I believe will please God. He will take care of the result."

"But, Mac, you can't . . ." Howard let his sentence trail away unfinished. He had detected something odd in the president's eyes, and a sudden realization hit him. *The rumors are true. Mac has gone off the deep end.* Words were useless now.

"That's it then?" he said tightly.

"You know where I stand now, Dick. Can you live with it?"

Howard hesitated only a brief instant before replying. "I guess I'll have to," he said, rising from his chair.

MacFarlane strode toward his friend and grasped his hand affectionately. "Dick, think about what I've said . . . okay?"

"Indeed I will," replied Howard.

---

Once outside the Oval Office, Dick Howard's thoughts ranged far afield from what the president might have hoped. Foremost in his mind was the certainty that he could no longer depend on MacFarlane for rational action. Something in the man had snapped. All this talk about God and—of all things—reading the Bible! Good grief! These were not the arguments of a sane man.

Still, it did not occur to him that if MacFarlane were insane, then he was not fit for the presidency. Howard merely concluded that the task of insuring victory must now rest exclusively with him. He only hoped Mac had enough sense not to go public with all this religious prattle. For if that happened, even *he* might not be able to save his skin.

As Howard returned to his own office fifteen minutes later, his thoughts were already solidifying into a definite course of action. And, as if on cue, he was drawn once more to the file cabinet. Inside lay the solution to all his problems. That is, if he chose to ignore what those files held and perjure his own stature as the nation's chief law enforcement official.

Could he do that? Was the situation really as desperate as he had intimated to the president? Were there any other choices?

He took a key from his pocket and slipped it into the lock. The drawer opened easily, perhaps too easily. He lifted out the folder. It was all there—Gallagher's ledger pages showing Wilson's illegal handling of union funds, a letter from Gallagher to Hensley indicating Gallagher's intent to blackmail Wilson, and also evidence known only to Howard linking Gallagher's murder to Wilson's lackeys. Howard had made discreet inquiries into the hit, learning enough to solidify his own conclusions and to assure that he'd be holding a pretty solid case should he choose to pursue it.

Glancing through the papers, he realized again the danger of one very prominent loose end if he did decide to drop all potential charges against Wilson. That Hensley fellow would certainly start squawking if, instead of going to jail for killing his friend, Wilson suddenly ended up on the president's cabinet.

Though Hensley didn't have to be an insurmountable obstacle. One judiciously placed word to Wilson about the mousey little man would take care of him. Of course, Howard in no way kidded himself about what that would mean. Wilson played for keeps. At least that way, if anything ever did leak out, the administration and the Justice Department could deny any foreknowledge. Wilson could hang, but the election would be over and he would have served his usefulness anyway.

All at once, without him consciously realizing it, an ethical line had been crossed within the heart of Dick Howard. He carried the folder across the room to the shredder, turned on the machine, and began feeding Wilson's incriminating folder into it.

After two pages had gone, suddenly he stopped. He had convinced himself he'd be able to handle Mac and override his objections. But come to think of it, maybe he ought to retain some of this material, just in case he ever needed leverage to blackmail Wilson and keep him in line. After the election it might become expedient for Wilson to resign.

He turned off the machine, and slowly a smile spread across his lips. *Yes, I'd better keep my grip on the man after all!* All he had to do was select the proper time and circumstances to inform Mac that the decision had already been made—sometime just before the election . . . leaving just time enough for Wilson to endorse the president, but leaving Mac no time to respond!

Five minutes later Howard was on the phone line he knew was secure and not tapped.

"Harley . . . Dick Howard here," he said when Wilson's secretary had put him through to the labor leader. "I've got some good news. The president has just approved you for the opening as secretary of transportation. . . ."

# EIGHTY-FIVE

Ashkhabad.

The ancient city rose from the desolate Kara Kum Desert like a mirage, the graceful spirals of its mosques looking like a scene from *Arabian Nights*. Fifty years ago the entire city had been rebuilt following a devastating earthquake, but it still retained the seamy and exotic flavor of a border town on the edge of nowhere.

Prostitutes, black marketeers, and drug dealers congregated in its maze of back streets and alleys. Here too roamed the soldiers of the Soviet invasion force, surly and disgruntled, drinking too much vodka, looking for some excitement now that the prospect of military action had been stalled. If only something would happen . . . to go to war . . . to be sent home . . . anything would be better than being stuck in this hole.

Seyed Gilani had been in the area for several days. Reconnoitering . . . waiting for the right moment.

It had come two days ago when he learned that General Leon Milyukov, commander of the invasion force, would be celebrating his birthday. There was to be a party at the Kanal Geldy, a nightclub the soldiers frequented. The event would provide the perfect backdrop for his demented plan.

Seyed had spent the time since gathering detailed information as well as buying or stealing the plastic explosives and other materials he needed.

Before entering the city, Seyed had slit the throat of a sentry and stripped him of his uniform, then had buried the body in the sand. Now dressed in the garb of a Russian corporal, he moved through the town with relative ease. If anyone wondered about his burned and blistered skin, they asked no questions. Perhaps they sensed that if a man had been caught out in the torturous Kara Kum, he had suffered enough.

As dusk descended on the day of the general's birthday, Seyed began putting the pieces of his three-pronged attack into place. It did not take much to position his hastily constructed device on the Iranian side of the border, jamming the two contacts into the plastic and setting the ten-dollar alarm clock for two hours later.

With a final lingering look out across the desert night at his homeland, he turned back toward the city, where he next had a date with a multi-storied barracks housing hundreds of Russian soldiers. A fire bomb ought to do nicely there.

Fifty-five minutes later everything was in place as Seyed wandered toward the nightclub.

He stashed his duffle bag of weapons behind a pile of garbage in an alley. Even in his soldier's garb he might look suspicious roaming about too heavily armed, especially carrying the American-made Springfield he'd purchased through a black-market dealer who had lifted it off a dead CIA agent. At about eight he ambled into the club, ordered a vodka, and sat in a dim corner where he wouldn't be noticed. The general wasn't expected to arrive for another thirty minutes, but Seyed wanted to be sure he was in place.

He leaned back in his chair and sipped his vodka, rehearsing the details of his plan one last time. It was simple enough really. Most of his work was already done. All he had to do was wait. He had carried out similar operations many times before. A straightforward assassination, requiring nowhere near the scope and complexity of their failed attempt in Moscow. Get in, wait till the right moment, kill the general, and, if possible, get out.

Whatever happened, the shooting *must* be linked to the CIA. Besides the purchase of the CIA-connected Springfield, Seyed had gone to great pains to establish himself with the U.S. agency. Shortly after returning to Tehran from Moscow, Seyed had hired himself out as an informant and had worked closely with two CIA operatives. But his long residence in America would be the clincher. Once the Russians identified him, which he would make sure they did, they'd have no doubt the assassination was CIA inspired. After that, nature would take its bloody and historic course. War between the two nations would be inevitable.

Seyed smiled and jerked back the rest of his drink.

The plan was flawless. Perhaps if they had tried it in the first place . . . but no, Mohsen's attempt had its own merits, even if it had failed. Actually, it had turned out rather successful after all—the Russian premier *was* dead. And now Bolotnikov, with all his hatred of the West, would be even more likely to fall into Seyed's trap.

Seyed glanced down into his empty glass, then raised it in silent toast to his departed friends. "Peace to the mighty dead!" he murmured.

General Milyukov and his entourage soon clamored into the nightclub. Seyed watched the party with quiet detachment, thinking only of the grand finale awaiting them. The vodka flowed, and music filled the room as the handful of women hired for the evening entertained the Russian officers.

General Milyukov was a broad-chested, roughly hewn sort with a deep gravelly voice that sounded like a growl even when raised in laughter as it now was.

"A toast!" cried one of the officers. "A toast to Milyukov!"

Several glasses were thrust into the air in response.

*"Nu Budem!"* shouted a chorus of voices.

*"Budem!"* laughed the general in reply, tossing off his tenth glass of vodka.

The dull state of drunkenness did not take long to set in. Seyed glanced at his watch—it was almost time. He rose and slipped out, unnoticed. The shouts of laughter and music from the carousers followed him as he crept around to the alley to retrieve his bag.

With hasty but nimble fingers he loaded the rifle, then slowly made his way to the opening of the alley, from which he could enjoy just the right vantage point.

He glanced at his watch again. Any second now and . . .

A sudden blast in the distance rent the quiet night! A glow from the explosion lit up the southern sky, followed almost immediately by faint shouts and cries, then machine-gun fire erupted at the border.

Instantly a soldier dashed out of the Kanal Geldy, looked toward the border, then ran back inside shouting. Before the merrymakers had a chance to respond, another explosion blasted through the night, followed by shouts and screams from the direction of the Russian barracks. The sky above was suddenly ablaze from the effects of the firebomb.

A roar of voices went up inside the nightclub as the soldiers, many wobbling on their feet, began to pour outside.

Seyed took a breath. He was unaccountably calm, not at all keyed up as he usually was before an operation—and he knew why.

"Allah," he silently prayed, "bring me quickly into the bosom of my brothers."

Crouched in the shadow of the alley, he shouldered his weapon, peering along its sight toward the well-lit door of the club. The general was emerging now, barely able to stand, a girl on each arm supporting him. He looked around as he exited, his glassy eyes struggling to make sense of the confused sights and sounds.

Seyed stepped out of the shadows, his rifle spitting deadly fire.

# EIGHTY-SIX

Acting President Leonid Bolotnikov shot up in bed out of a dead sleep, groping for the screaming telephone. He did not come fully to himself until jarred by the urgency of the voice at the other end.

"What!" he exclaimed. "General Milyukov? . . . I can hardly believe the old windbag would—"

He paused to listen.

"Confirmed . . . You are certain? . . . What? . . . CIA connections!" The new premier was fully awake now.

"You've captured the assassin?" Bolotnikov groped around the bedside table for his cigarettes. "I see . . . but you are certain of the CIA ties?"

He nodded his head several times while attempting to get his cigarette lighter to ignite. "All right—keep on this. Call me if there is *anything* further, do you understand? In the meantime, set up a meeting of the ministers in my office in . . . let me see—what time is it anyway?" In response to his own question, he glanced at the clock by the bed. It was five in the morning. "Have them there in two hours," he ordered, then slammed down the receiver.

His wife stirred and mumbled something incoherent in her sleep, and Bolotnikov thought fleetingly of Tatyana . . . but she was gone now and he had all he had ever desired. He was leader of the most powerful nation on earth, an aphrodisiac far more potent than the love of any woman.

---

In two hours the premier was standing in the center of the largest and most spacious of the well-appointed set of rooms in the Kremlin reserved for the head of state. The stunning news had by now had time to filter through his analytical mental system.

Last night an assassin—an Iranian national apparently, but with ties both to the U.S. and France—had crossed the border, entered Ashkhabad, placed two bombs, and then shot General Leon Milyukov. The assassin had himself been shot down by machine-gun fire at the border while trying to escape into the desert. He had died instantly.

The military intelligence station chief had been able to identify the killer within hours after the incident. The young fool had very ineffectively covered his tracks. He was one Seyed Gilani, a known terrorist with ties to several fanatical Muslim organizations. He had been found with an American-made rifle, and his pockets contained American money as well as two papers they were able to trace. Shortly before the call to Bolotnikov, a KGB operative from Tehran had been located who confirmed Gilani's recent involvement with the CIA.

Why the assassin had bombed the Iranian headquarters across the border and firebombed the Russian barracks was unclear. In any case, great damage had been done. The fire had spread to six buildings, and a hundred and fifty Soviet soldiers had died in the blast. Many more had been hurt.

Across the border, apparently thinking the Russians responsible for the initial explosion, the Iranian border contingent had immediately opened fire on the Soviet aggressors, and the fighting had spread quickly. It had now become a full-blown border skirmish, with heavy loss of life on both sides. Intelligence had it that Iranian troops were already pouring toward Ashkhabad from outlying encampments, and General Milyukov's second-in-command had placed his forces under full alert and was now awaiting further orders from the Kremlin.

The whole dirty incident reeked of the CIA, thought Bolotnikov. But what could the U.S. possibly have to gain by such a move? They had been trying to keep Soviet forces out of Iran. So why incite a border riot that would only inflame hostilities? Nothing about it made sense.

Maybe it didn't have to, he thought. He didn't need to understand the perverted U.S. motives anyway. The facts were all that mattered, and they were clear enough.

He had been urging the invasion of Iran for over a year. Only that weak-livered Kudinsky had stood in his path! Here was clear provocation. An act of sabotage and aggression on Russian soil, sanctioned by the United States! This was all Bolotnikov needed to justify what he had called for long ago.

Bolotnikov laughed to himself. "Do they actually think they can stand against the might of Soviet Russia? The idiots . . . fools! And that senator is the biggest fool of all!"

A talk with the front-running presidential candidate was one thing; sitting still for American imperialist subterfuge was quite another. Now was the time to seize the oil and ports they had coveted for years, all as part of the expressed need to defend Russia's borders from American hostile intent. Kudinsky had wavered them into an impossible stalemate. As a result the element of surprise had been lost.

"I will not make the same mistake!" declared Bolotnikov aloud, hardly caring that he was alone.

When the ministers assembled in an adjacent conference room a few minutes later, their new leader presented the kind of aggressive decisiveness they had found so lacking in recent years.

"The time has come at last, comrades," Bolotnikov said, after briefly apprising them of the situation in Ashkhabad. "The opening we have hoped for has been handed us. If we move without delay while the Americans are mired in the throes of their election, Iran will be ours without opposition. Alert your assistants and your staffs. I will summon our best military men to join us. We will meet back here in three hours to finalize plans for the mobilization and invasion. By nightfall I want Soviet troops in Gurgan and troop carriers standing off Resht and Pahlevi. Within thirty-six hours I want thirty divisions in Tehran and the capital under our control. Needless to say, our navy will by then be in control of Hormuz."

He paused, the fire visible in his eye. Indeed, thought more than one of the ministers, their new premier seemed a direct descendant of the line that had passed from Lenin down through Stalin, Khrushchev, and Brezhnev.

"We are the mightiest nation on the face of the earth," he said. "And before this day ends, the rest of the world will know it!"

The room was deathly still. Not a single voice was raised in protest.

# EIGHTY-SEVEN

Washington D.C.

It was 3:37 on the afternoon of October 31st. Tuesday. The sun shone out through clear blue skies. Temperature inside the beltway stood at a crisp, invigorating forty-six degrees.

In four days the Redskins would take on the division-leading Eagles in hopes of moving into a tie for first place. And in exactly seven days the nation would elect a president.

At that moment, however, no one was thinking of either the temperature or football.

Word had just exploded off the news wires that the Soviet Union had invaded Iran. Tehran and the entire northern coast of the Persian Gulf had fallen within twenty-four hours. The Strait of Hormuz had been closed by Soviet warships. At least two dozen tankers were trapped inside the gulf, including five American vessels, and Soviet submarines had blockaded the Gulf of Oman between Muscat and Karachi.

Words of menace from the Kremlin had accompanied the action, warning that Soviet missiles were aimed at Turkey, Iraq, and Saudi Arabia. Any hostile action toward the Soviet Union would be met by a ballistic counterattack.

The invasion, reported *Tass,* was a direct retaliation for American and Iranian attacks on Soviet troops stationed peacefully in Ashkhabad. The Soviet Union must protect its borders against Western aggression.

---

Jarvis MacFarlane sat at his desk and wept.

He could neither ignore nor deny the feelings of failure which now washed over him. A dozen times, two dozen, he lashed himself with the tormenting question—*Was there something more I could have done?*

*O God!* he cried in his silent despair. *What are you doing?* He and Kudinsky had been so close to world peace! *So close!* Now his friend was dead and the world was in turmoil once again.

Thoughts of Kudinsky made the president's tears flow more freely. The premier had been a good man, a caring man. Now he was gone, taking with him so much of MacFarlane's hope for lasting peace between their two countries.

Then with Bolotnikov's seizure of power and his alliance with Foster, even the president's deepening faith had undergone the crucible of testing fire. Still he did not lose hope that God was indeed the almighty Lord of the earth. His belief in God's personal supremacy in his life and his growing relationship with the Master was too real to be easily swayed by the roller-coaster tide of world politics.

But now, in one evil moment, everything he believed God had wanted him to achieve—peace in the world—had been dashed to dust under the conquering footsteps of invading Soviet troops.

Even if he won the election, there would be no peace with Bolotnikov ruling the Kremlin, hungering after the old Soviet objective of conquest.

What was he to do?

His own military leaders would be looking to him for some response. And what of his words of five months earlier, warning that any Soviet act of aggression would be met with U.S. force? Could he still utter those same threats? After all, he was not the same man he was then.

What was he to do!

---

Dick Howard heard the stunning news on his car radio and broke out in a cold sweat.

No matter that he had an appointment at the justice department in five minutes. He had to pull over somewhere . . . anywhere. He had to think!

He should have waited . . . listened to Mac. He was caught outside the loop. Events had suddenly conspired against him. Now they probably wouldn't need Wilson at all. Yet he had already made the commitment, jeopardizing himself ethically, morally, politically . . . and legally.

He wondered if it was too late to back out on the deal . . . pull the plug . . . tell Wilson there'd been a mistake.

Probably not. That would make it all the worse . . . infuriate Wilson . . . possibly even place his own life in danger.

Best just to let things sit. There was no turning back at this point.

But how would he tell Mac?

What a mess! If only he'd waited!

---

The triumphant smile had long since faded from Patrick Foster's face.

The climbing polls, the rosy future, and his reputation as a wise and clever negotiator had vanished like a puff of smoke . . . like a mirage on desert sands. His certain victory had been cruelly snatched from him!

*Bolotnikov!* He cursed the man. *Why couldn't the maniac have waited a week? One week!*

Bateman, Lavender, and Nyborg were all trying to comfort him. Their sappy commiseration only made it worse.

Foster was finished . . . and he knew it.

He could visualize tomorrow's headlines after the invasion

news, of course. Patrick Foster . . . the great senator . . . the five-star general . . . the man who would be king . . . duped! . . . tricked! . . . played for a sucker!

What a fool he'd been to trust Bolotnikov!

Even one of Bateman's gutter pranks wouldn't save his hide now.

---

Jeremy Manning and Karen MacFarlane walked hand in hand along the river. The Lincoln Memorial rose majestically across the parkway to their right. They could not help wondering what he might have done if faced with the Soviet threat.

Silently they walked.

Words seemed useless. Even at this moment Karen's father was wrestling with events and decisions that would crush the sanity of most men. What could either of them say that would not pale beside the fate of freedom which potentially lay in his hands? What could they do but offer their own silent entreaty to the Master above that His servant would discern His voice in the midst of chaotic world events.

The president's decision would deeply affect their future together. Yet neither Karen nor Jeremy could find the right words to sort through the emotions generated by consideration of that subject.

Content in their love, they could only wait and see what tomorrow would bring. Yet on both their minds was the overriding question. How many tomorrows would they have left to share together?

---

Martin Tucker was angry.

Had the secretary of defense analyzed his present disposition, he would have seen it to be childish.

This situation wasn't the president's fault. No one could possibly lay Bolotnikov's move to MacFarlane's charge. Now was the time to pull together. Unity of spirit.

But Tucker had been angry at the president since June, ever since he left Moscow following the announcement of that ridiculous peace plan. This latest Soviet action only confirmed what he had known all along—that the president was letting himself be played like a mere pawn in the great Soviet scheme of conquest.

He had told the president so . . . on numerous occasions since. But would MacFarlane listen?

No! He just jabbered on about trust . . . about peace . . . about God! The fool!

Well, maybe this would bring him to his senses!

Now he would have to pay attention to the military options he had been ignoring like an ostrich for months!

*What could have happened to the man?* thought Tucker for the hundredth time. He had seemed so reasonable last May—had even sounded off about military force himself. Why Tucker himself had defended the president's blend of caution with military preparedness.

Then suddenly the Moscow trip, and he was a different man.

What could have come over him?

---

The scene in General Emmit Howson's office looked more like a "situation room" than the plush quarters of the chairman of the joint chiefs.

Maps had been spread out over every available inch of desk space. The general had long since thrown his jacket over a chair, loosened his tie, and rolled up his shirt sleeves. The same could be said of most of the other occupants of the room.

A couple of the men worked cigars between brown-stained teeth, probably in subliminal simulation of the great English hero of World War II.

But no external emulation of Churchill could make of these men national heroes. For the strategies they had been hotly considering and contesting for the past hour might more likely be considered treasonous. More than once during that time the question had been raised: How will we respond if the president backs down?

Emmit Howson was not thinking of peace . . . or of war. Or of presidents, freedom, life, death, politics, diplomacy, or elections for that matter.

His eyes glowed with the thrill of the game! He had trained thirty years for this moment.

Men to command . . . troops to move . . . strategies to devise . . . battles to win!

Oh, this was great fun!

Where was that Tucker anyway!

Not the most brilliant of military minds, thought Howson. But a tolerably decent fellow, now that they were together in the same camp. Besides, they could hardly move without the secretary of defense.

---

Something was wrong. Somewhere he was missing a signal, thought Jarvis MacFarlane. God must be trying to tell him something that he wasn't perceiving.

He had been to several more Legation meetings. They had even decided to be more open about it. Daniel had come to the White House for lunch with Peter, and MacFarlane had gone to a larger meeting and met many more people—of course Dmitri hadn't been in attendance. He had even told the original group of twelve about the vision and was regularly attending the devotional prayer meetings in the EOB. He had grown more and more comfortable praying and talking in each group about his deepening faith. He had also sought out and attended several different church functions in accordance with the advice Richard had given him that night when they'd listened to the tape.

Howard was furious, with the election so close, but MacFarlane wasn't worried. There was some public reaction, of course. Foster had seen to that, making sure word continued to spread about the president's new religious fanaticism. But somehow the public didn't seem all that concerned when talk of war was suddenly in the air.

Yet even with the gradual steadying of his spiritual rudder, something still troubled him—something that all the prayer, all the discussion, hadn't succeeded in getting to the bottom of. A peculiar sense that God's work in his life, God's transformation of his heart, didn't have to do with the election at all, nor with the invasion—and possibly not even with the Moscow peace plan.

Something more . . . something greater . . . some deeper historical consequences . . . something far more encompassing than his mind had been able to fathom . . . perhaps more stupendous than any human mind could fathom!

The night he had told the twelve about the Lord's appearance to him, Daniel had fallen to his knees and cried out, "O Lord, our God! To what great purpose have You called this humble man, Your servant? Reveal Your mighty, mysterious way to him, O Lord!"

Then he and the other eleven had joined in a circle around the president and laid hands on him and prayed for God's purpose to be accomplished through him. It had been an emotional moment, and even as MacFarlane recalled it a surge of warmth rushed through him.

Yet what was that purpose? What was that calling?

Something was stirring deep in his heart. Something he couldn't pinpoint. But his heart fluttered in joyful, frightful, eager anticipation that whatever it was would soon be revealed.

In the meantime, how was he to be God's man *and* president of the United States? That was the critical question. What was he to *do*?

God's man . . . trying to discern God's will, not man's, while sitting in the Oval Office contemplating potential war.

"Dear God," he murmured through his tears, "You spoke to me once in a vision, in a blaze of light, before I even knew You. You have spoken to me since in quieter ways—in my heart, through Your word, through the men You have sent to encourage and help me. O God! Speak to me now! I must hear Your voice! What would you have me do?"

Only silence filled the room as the echo of his agonized words died away.

At first the quiet lay heavy upon his soul, as if in accusation against a God who refused to speak in answer to the entreaty of His child.

Then gradually a kind of expectation began to flood over him . . . God *was* trying to tell him something!

All the events of the last months began to tumble through his brain, playing themselves out again in words, images, ideas, visions, Scriptures, faces . . .

MacFarlane sighed deeply, trying to put the pieces together in his mind. One thing seemed clear—in the world, according to the values and perspectives of man, he and Kudinsky had failed.

They had brought the world closer to permanent peace than it had been in decades, yet public sentiment had been divided against them. Even as president he had not been able to ignite Congress into action—and it had gone worse for Kudinsky, who had never been able to rouse even token support from his government.

He'd even wondered about Kudinsky's death . . . didn't it seem almost too fortuitous? . . . too timely for Bolotnikov's purposes? He'd had a weird dream a few nights ago in which he had seen a man who resembled Kudinsky wasting away in an eerie medieval dungeon, bound with chains from hands to feet. What an image of impotence, for as leader of his nation, Kudinsky had indeed been powerless.

*As I feel powerless myself,* thought MacFarlane.

Yes, perhaps they had failed in earthly terms. Still . . . God *had* given him the vision. Was the bringing of peace the only message of the vision? What kind of peace? How was it to come? What about everything else he had heard through so many other prophetic mouths of God's people? How did it all fit together?

As he recalled that night in February that now seemed so long ago, the memory increased the feeling of anticipation building within him. There *was* some purpose . . . perhaps a different purpose than he had yet apprehended.

The Lord had said he would be an instrument of hope. And, He had said he would be shown truth and that he *would* be heard.

Now that he reflected upon it, the Lord hadn't said that *he* must make peace happen, but rather that he should proclaim peace . . . that he should make preparation, whatever that meant. Preparation for what? The whole message sounded like he should be getting ready for something, getting ready in the short time that was left.

"So . . . have I failed?" he asked himself again.

All at once he sensed an answer to his question, coming from within his brain, but originating on a higher plane.

"Yes . . . Jarvis, the president has failed."

"I don't understand, Lord."

"The president has failed to make peace. But I gave the vision not to a president, but to My son and My servant, Jarvis MacFarlane."

MacFarlane was about to protest further in this silent dialogue of prayer in his mind, but then he stopped. He had been waiting to hear the Lord's voice.

"I'm listening, Lord," he murmured humbly.

The impression of being spoken to continued, more strongly now. "I speak to *people,* Jarvis, not to titles or positions. There is never failure when a man or woman remains open, ever listening for My voice. Now you must make others listen. Not by exercising human authority. That can never accomplish My purposes. But rather in the mighty power of God's Spirit. You must tell them, Jarvis."

"Tell them what, Lord? How can I possibly—"

"It is the hour of preparation. I have given you the charge of telling them."

"But, Lord, what is the message if it is not the message of peace?"

"The message *is* peace, Jarvis. But not as the world knows it."

"What would You have me say?"

"You have had glimpses through My other servants. You will know more when the time is right. Others will heed you, for you will speak with My anointing upon your lips."

Again the room seemed silent. The thoughts and prayers and

voices within his heart had stilled. But now Jarvis MacFarlane knew he was not alone.

He sank to his knees beside his chair and poured out his heart to God.

---

When Jarvis MacFarlane rose to his feet thirty minutes later, his face was full of purpose. He had not seen everything, but the next step he was to take had been shown him. Now he just had to summon the courage to carry it out.

He picked up his telephone intercom and spoke to his secretary.

"Virginia," he said, "get me the Pentagon. I want a conference call with Tucker and Howson. Then call Duke Mathias and Peter Venzke. Tell them to meet me here as soon as they can. Tell them I said the three of us need to talk."

# EIGHTY-EIGHT

Tuesday. November 7th.

In Washington the president still slept. Surprisingly sound. Surprising because an hour and a half earlier, with the stroke of midnight, this day had become the first Tuesday after the first Monday of November. A day that made all presidents nervous.

In Moscow the sun was approaching its meridian. It was 11:23 A.M.

Blue Doc snatched up the telephone receiver on the first ring.

His quick reflexes had more to do with taut nerves than with efficiency. Everyone at the embassy had been on hair-trigger fuses these last ninety-six hours since President MacFarlane's ultimatum.

At any moment, should Bolotnikov so choose, he could launch a further aggressive move against the United States or one of her allies, effectively ridiculing the president's message. Should this happen, members of the diplomatic corps could suddenly find themselves at the mercy of the Soviet government. They were all waiting for orders to evacuate.

The veteran agent thought this call might be it.

"Yeah, this is embassy security," answered Blue Doc.

"I must to speak someone on matter very urgent," said an imperative male voice in broken English.

"Are you a U.S. citizen?"

"I have information! Please to tell who I must speak!"

Blue Doc instantly switched his cap from embassy staffer to CIA agent. "This line isn't sterile," he said. "Call back in ten minutes at this number—"

"Fifteen minutes please. I must to change telephone device."

Blue Doc gave the caller the number, then grabbed his coat and hurried out of the Security offices.

---

Election day dawned in Washington with a persistent rainstorm and blustery winds. News commentators speculated that the nationwide inclement conditions could seriously affect voter turnout. No one went so far as to indicate whom they thought this would favor—they had become leery of speculation these days.

As one voter made his way to the polls, he was followed by an entourage of news personnel. And when President MacFarlane stepped out of the voting booth, the reporters immediately barraged him with questions.

"Who'd you vote for, Mr. President?" asked one with a grin.

MacFarlane returned the smile. "Every four years you folks try to find a new story when the president steps out of the booth. I'm sorry to have to disappoint you, but you'll find nothing new here. I'm afraid I cast my ballot in a very traditional manner becoming incumbent presidents."

A roar of laughter went round the room and several cameras flashed. More than one headline would report that the president was in high spirits this election day.

"Have you any comment on the Iranian situation?"

"The world has heard my reply. I have been as lenient as anyone in my position could be. A permanent solution rests in the Soviets' hands."

"Too lenient according to some?" suggested another newsman.

The president laughed. "You've been talking to the Pentagon!" he chided.

"It's no secret Secretary Tucker's furious about your dismissal of their recommendations."

"No secret at all!" rejoined the president. "Nevertheless, the Pentagon will have to learn to live with my decision too—that is, depending on the outcome of today's election! In any case, I have asked for new recommendations and a revised strategy from the joint chiefs to be on my desk by week's end."

"Will you commit our troops?"

"If that becomes necessary. But the parameters of a U.S. military response were clearly spelled out in the text of Sunday's speech. I'm afraid I cannot give any more specific information than that, for reasons of national security."

A handful of others threw hopeful questions into the air, but by now the president was outside and ducked into the waiting limousine.

The questions emphasized once again for the president just how dangerous the situation was. Despite strong U.N. censure of the Soviet action and several failed attempts by MacFarlane to contact Bolotnikov, the new leader of the Soviet Union had remained staunchly "unavailable." A show of force was clearly called for. The tense stalemate regarding the status of ships and oil tankers in the Persian Gulf needed to be resolved. MacFarlane only hoped war could be avoided by giving the Russians some breathing room . . . time to see the error of their ways and retract their invasion forces. He knew the Pentagon thought the length of time he had given Bolotnikov to reconsider was foolhardy, though even they saw the tactical value of giving a militarily unprepared U.S. time to rearm. But his critics could be right. He had never faced a crisis like this before. Every move was a gamble.

In the meantime, as the fate of the world hung in the balance, all the president could do was watch his own personal fate played out upon the television screen as this day of days progressed.

# EIGHTY-NINE

Another back-alley rendezvous.

Another jumpy contact.

Blue Doc watched as the nervous young man hurried away into the falling snow.

He still couldn't figure the fellow's game, although he seemed on the level. A soft-spoken, intelligent-sounding kid uncomfortable with the cloak-and-dagger routine. The information he possessed, however, could categorize him as a first-class screwball.

That is . . . unless it was true.

Blue Doc scratched the perennial itch behind his left ear, then turned and walked away in the opposite direction.

Things were hot enough with the world situation. He didn't need this right now. If it were a bogus lead, it could wind up getting him killed. He especially didn't need that!

But he couldn't ignore it. Not something of this magnitude. He'd have to do some serious sidewalk pounding. Look under a few rocks. Play the Moscow spy game one last time . . . just in case the guy's info was on the level.

He only hoped he was back in the embassy when and if the call to pull out came. He didn't relish the idea of being stuck out in the streets of this city without the embassy to go home to. He knew the KGB too well.

---

MacFarlane marveled at Foster's aplomb. Recent events seemed not to have ruffled him in the least. He walked with that military cadence, poise and assurance in every statuesque inch, casting his vote as if it were the only one that mattered.

He was a cameraman's dream—waving and smiling, knowing just the proper angle to present to the lens.

He was a born winner!

And MacFarlane knew it could happen. Foster might win.

Exit polls throughout the East were trickling in, and the president was making a strong showing. But then everyone knew that would happen. In the South, however, Foster would be the overwhelming victor. There was no question about that. MacFarlane was confident he would carry his own home territory in the Northwest. But the Midwest and California were still a toss-up, along with Illinois, Texas, and Florida . . . they could go either way. Ohio of course was Foster's. Michigan and the industrial North would be MacFarlane's, following Wilson's surprise endorsement two days ago.

The thought of Harley Wilson reminded the president that he hadn't seen Dick Howard in several days. He was just glad Dick had finally dropped all that foolishness about putting Wilson on the cabinet.

Well . . . however the election turned out, the result rested in God's hands.

His future did not depend on the outcome of this plebiscite, no matter how troubling it was to watch Foster's smug countenance on the TV screen. He had felt God's leading more strongly than ever these past few days . . . almost as if he were being physically turned around and set upon a road toward . . . toward what he was still unsure.

Also, Vladimir Kudinsky had been on his mind a great deal in the last twenty-four hours. By rights they ought to be embarking on this new path together. Kudinsky's wisdom, his gentleness, the experience of his years would all have proven great assets to whatever lay ahead.

Yet he had to trust that God had removed his Russian friend for some even greater purpose.

---

Lvov Sanatorium lay thirty-two miles east of Moscow down a picturesque wooded road now bordered with banks of fresh, white snow.

Blue Doc drove past the hospital, noting the high red brick walls enclosing the grounds. He remained on the main road another two miles until he came to the nearest town, a burg of about twenty thousand. For the sake of his present business he would have preferred a large metropolis. But fortunately it wasn't so small that his arrival would instantly be noticed and rate a headline in the local edition of *Pravda.*

He pulled the car to a stop in front of a small cafe which had been specified by his Moscow contact. He was supposed to meet one Jozef Witos here, a Polish immigrant and a nurse at the sanatorium.

It was only seven in the evening, and already the place was nearly filled to shoulder-to-shoulder capacity, taking on the flavor of a small-town cabaret. As unobtrusively as possible he scanned the customers for the man "in the black Cossack hat," though as might be expected, there were several bobbing up and down in the crowd.

This was not going to be a fun evening, grimaced Blue Doc morosely.

He managed to locate a seat at a table already occupied by four others, grabbed the vacant stool, and sat down.

His man would have to come to him, he thought.

Good thing he was the only one wearing a black handkerchief in the breast pocket of his sport jacket. Come to think of it, he was probably the only one wearing a sport jacket!

About three minutes later one of the Cossacks wandered toward him.

"You are Andrivich's friend from Moscow?" the man asked in Russian. He was big, muscular, and young—thirty at the most.

"I am his cousin," Blue Doc replied in his own flawless dialect, using the code response they had agreed upon.

Jozef Witos grabbed a stool from an adjacent table and squeezed in next to the CIA agent. He signaled for a waitress. Blue Doc was hardly surprised at the immediate response he received. He hoped this gorilla turned out to be friendly.

When two glasses of dark beer had been sloshed down on the wooden table in front of them, Blue Doc ventured to speak.

"So . . . I understand we have many friends in common," he began, leaning close to Witos in order to be heard over the hubbub.

"It would seem so," replied the hulking man, nonchalantly sipping his beer. "But then I meet so many people at the hospital. Fine people, too."

"I had a friend who was hospitalized not long ago," ventured Blue Doc. "Perhaps you can tell me about him."

"It was my understanding you wanted to *see* him," said Witos cautiously, "perhaps arrange for some other accommodations for him—away from here . . . far away."

"That would be preferable," replied Blue Doc. "Yes, that was the original intent. But I understood that would be difficult."

"Difficult, yes . . . impossible, no. That is, it might be arranged for him to meet *you* . . . outside . . . perhaps in the small wood to the north of the facility. *If* you can have a vehicle there, it might be possible for us to arrange for our mutual friend to meet you there."

"A vehicle will be no problem. Has our friend recovered from his illness?"

"That will take some time, but he is able to travel."

"Will assistance be required in arranging for his furlough?" asked Blue Doc.

"Everything is being arranged to get him to you."

"By whom?"

"Our friend has many friends . . . even some who speak his own language."

Blue Doc eyed Witos intently, then took a long swallow of beer.

"But once our friend is with you, you are on your own," the Russian added.

"There are friends in many places," answered Blue Doc cryptically.

"You must be ready at a moment's notice. A week . . . a month . . . perhaps two. When the time is right, you will be contacted. But when the word comes, you must be ready. To be left in the woods too long can prove fatal.'"

"I understand," replied Blue Doc. "I will be there."

# NINETY

Three minutes after eight.

The polls were closed in the East. Rather and Jennings and the rest would be on the air any minute now. Then for three hours they would cleverly try to dance around the gathering flood of incoming returns, lest any West Coast votes be "swayed" by their reports.

Still, they would manage to fill up air time, finding ways to convey their predictions despite the open booths in that distant region known as Pacific Standard Time—until eleven o'clock Eastern, at which time all cats would escape from their regional bags.

At the White House, about a dozen people milled around the president's personal quarters.

Karen left Jeremy, who was talking to Duke Mathias and Peter Venzke in front of one of the four television sets, and walked over to her father. He was preparing to help himself to a cup of coffee from the buffet table set up along one wall.

"I'm so proud of you, Dad," she said, placing an arm affectionately over his shoulder. "It doesn't matter if you win or lose—I'm still proud of how you've allowed God to remain in control."

He smiled in reply and gave her a squeeze.

"Everyone can see the change," she went on, "the strength, the calm in the midst of all this. I really don't think you are worried at all about the election, are you?"

"It's a little late to worry now anyway," he said. "But thank you. I appreciate your words. By the way, have you seen Backman?"

"No," answered Karen. "Not yet."

Hardly had the words escaped her lips when Charlie Backman and his wife entered the room. The president immediately hurried toward them, shook Backman's hand warmly, and gave his wife a hug of greeting.

"Charlie!" said MacFarlane, "glad to see you. Ready to share our finale?"

"I appreciate your asking us, Mr. President." The vice-presidential candidate looked a bit bedazzled at his ready acceptance into this most elite of the hierarchies.

"You belong here, you know," said MacFarlane, leading him toward a comfortable chair in the corner, while Karen took Mrs. Backman over to Jeremy's group.

"I think all this will take some time getting used to," said Backman when they were seated. "The White House is a long way from Capitol Hill."

"Sometimes I think it's a long way from anywhere!" laughed MacFarlane. "Would you like a cup of coffee?"

Backman nodded. The president rose, and Backman started to follow.

"Sit still, Charlie," said MacFarlane, motioning with his hand. "I'll get it."

Moments later he returned with two cups.

"You know, that's exactly why I picked you for the VP spot," said the president as he handed Backman his coffee. "Your distance from the establishment, so to speak. You've been in the Senate all these years, but somehow you've remained above all the games Washington is famous for."

"How can you be sure that's not because I've not been asked to play?" said Backman, relaxing.

"No, no—that's not it. I'm no expert, but I know people. I've studied your record thoroughly, and I've watched you . . . as a person. You've had plenty of opportunity. But you've kept above the fray, Charlie, and retained a level of integrity and honor I'm proud of."

"I appreciate your confidence. I hope I can justify it."

"You will, I have no doubt. Integrity and honor—those are two of the most vital qualities a president must have. Along with maturity of judgment."

"Don't you mean vice-president?" said Backman.

"Yes—of course." MacFarlane paused thoughtfully. "But you know what they say . . . a heartbeat away from the Oval Office. And sometimes—" Again the president stopped. This was not the time for him to voice his own reservations about the office they were discussing.

"Let's pray that never happens, Mr. President," Backman went on earnestly. "Because one reason I decided to join you on the ticket was that I feel you've a great deal to offer this country. The last three years have been difficult ones. But I think your star is rising, as the saying goes, and I want to be part of your vision for the future."

"You will be, Charlie," replied the president with a strange glow in his eye. "Have no doubt—you will be."

Just then Jake Randolf approached. He greeted Backman cordially, but his mind was obviously on other matters.

"You have a call, Mr. President," he said. "From Bob Rhinwald," he added pointedly.

"What could he want tonight?" asked MacFarlane.

"Maybe to congratulate you."

"Or offer his condolences," added MacFarlane with a smile. "That would be just like the CIA—to know the outcome before I do!"

Despite the lighthearted exchange, the look in their eyes indicated that neither man expected this call to be over some trivial matter. With war threatening and the military on standby alert, the CIA director could only have portentous news.

MacFarlane excused himself and went to the nearby room where the call had been directed.

"Hello, Bob, this is the president," MacFarlane said, then listened for several moments while Rhinwald explained his reason for calling.

"Is our agent certain of the informant? . . . I see—yes, I know how that is, but in this case . . . I understand . . . but the risk must be taken despite Iran—"

Another long pause, during which the president's face wore a rigid expression halfway between excitement and fear.

"Yes, Bob . . . you have my full approval on the operation. But, Bob, I must emphasize how sensitive this is. If the wrong people in Moscow stumble on what your man's doing, it could be an excuse for them to retaliate. And you know what that means! So keep it on a need-to-know basis—a half-dozen persons at the most. And I want to personally clear each one. No foul-ups on this. I may want to bring a few of my own people in on it if something materializes—"

Another pause.

"Yes, I understand your concern, but I have some—some contacts that may be helpful—"

"Of course . . . cautions noted, Bob. But this is extremely important to me, and I have to do what I think best. Keep me informed—day or night. And, Bob . . . thanks."

When the president returned to the living room, his step was more buoyant than it had been fifteen minutes ago, and his eyes held an intense glow that no one, not even his daughter, could explain.

Suddenly the election results had grown anticlimactic for Jarvis MacFarlane.

# NINETY-ONE

The motorcade sped through the darkened Washington streets. The steady rain had stopped, but the streets were still slick with moisture. It was twenty minutes past midnight.

The cars had left 1600 Pennsylvania Avenue the moment California had been called. Texas had gone the other way, as had Ohio. But Florida, Illinois, and New Jersey had squeaked into their column about an hour earlier. Michigan still hadn't been called, but New York was the president's.

In five minutes the three limousines and three private cars pulled up at the back entrance of the Sheridan Arms Hotel, the Washington headquarters for the MacFarlane campaign. In all, twenty people poured out of the vehicles, with MacFarlane himself at the center of the congestion. The small throng tried to bump and jostle its way inside before the growing crowd outside, which had anticipated their arrival, grew too unwieldy. They squeezed through the narrow doorway two and three abreast, and then along the back corridors leading to the main ballroom.

As the entourage reached the end of the hallway, the door opened and Avery Lengyel appeared. He walked straight toward MacFarlane, his hand extended.

"I'm sorry you couldn't join us at the White House, Avery," said MacFarlane sincerely.

"It was important I be here," replied Lengyel. The campaign manager continued to grip MacFarlane's hand, and a large grin spread over his face. "Well . . . may I be the first to offer my official congratulations?"

"By all means!" beamed MacFarlane.

"Then, congratulations, *Mr. President,*" said Lengyel, "*and,* Mr. President-elect! Well done!"

"Thank you, Avery. But 'well-done' are the words I should offer you! We all have you to thank in many ways. Jordan . . . Sasso . . . Baker—all legends in your profession—but you outdid them all!"

A rousing applause went up in the hallway at the president's words.

"Well . . . they're all waiting for you inside, Mr. President," said Avery. "We shouldn't disappoint them!" He turned and led the way as two Secret Service men held open the double doors.

As they entered the ballroom, the din from the three or four hundred guests was almost deafening.

These were his people, thought MacFarlane. They had worked hard for him and had earned this moment of joyful abandon. Yet somehow it all appeared distant from his true self, like a scene from a hazy dream fading away just before consciousness returned. This which had once been his life was no longer his world.

How much longer could he live with one foot in the fading, hazy world of politics and the other in the bright new life where the sunshine was growing brighter all the time?

These pensive reflections passed through his brain in the twinkling of an eye, however. For almost immediately the pressing world of fog enveloped him and he was fully part of it once more.

Avery Lengyel had mounted the central podium, strode quickly toward the microphone, given it a tap, and received a loud squeal in response.

Then raising his arms jubilantly above his head, he shouted, "Ladies and gentlemen—our victor . . . the president of the United States!" Even had he hoped to say more he would not have been able to, for nothing could have penetrated the strident cheers that followed his brief introduction.

As the president began to move through the pressing crowd, those nearest his pathway did all within their power to touch their candidate. He grinned and shook hands and tossed out personal comments as he threaded his way forward, but in his eyes burned a faraway light which had no origins in these present proceedings.

Twelve minutes later, having delivered the speech Avery had

prepared for him, he closed his remarks with a reminder that a tense world situation still implored them to pray earnestly for peace. With his last word, the crowd went wild again with merrymaking that would last most of the night, and the champagne flowed freely.

The president beckoned for Charlie Backman to join him, and after a few moments sent the same signal to Karen and Mrs. Backman. They all raised their joined hands high in response to the cheers.

"Let's get home," said MacFarlane to Karen through his perfunctory smile. "I've had enough of the champagne atmosphere for one night."

Gradually they made their way off the platform to mingle and shake more hands, working toward the exit. They had managed about a third of the distance when Dick Howard sidled his way through the crowd.

"Where have you been keeping yourself, Dick?" said the president warmly.

"Man, oh man, but we did it, didn't we, Mac!" he half giggled, ignoring MacFarlane's question. He was red-faced and giddy, clearly having consumed more champagne than was good for his sensitive physique. "We smeared Foster from here to kingdom come!"

"The race was too close to go that far, Dick," said MacFarlane with a laugh. "They're only giving us 52% and 327 electoral votes so far. Hardly a landslide."

"Who cares, Mac? We won! And you won't squawk now about sharing your cabinet with Wilson."

"What do you mean?" MacFarlane's tone darkened. "I have no intention of doing such a thing."

"It's too late."

"Dick, don't tell me you've done something foolish!"

"Come on, Mac!" slurred Howard. "Don't be so naive! Where do you think that labor endorsement came from? You think you would have won tonight without the deal I made with Wilson?"

"You . . . you made a deal with Wilson?"

"You can thank me later, Mac! Right now—come on, loosen up! Enjoy the party. This is what we worked so hard for. It's time to celebrate! I'm going to get drunk enough for Jake and me together!"

# PART VI

# THE PEACEMAKER

*Peace I leave with you; my peace I give you. I do not give to you as the world gives. Do not let your hearts be troubled and do not be afraid. . . . Behold, I am coming soon!*

JOHN 14:27; REVELATION 22:7

# NINETY-TWO

It was not the first time Karen and Jeremy had been to Rock Creek Park. But it was easily the most memorable.

"Are you sure, Jeremy?" Karen asked, smiling through her tears. "You know, you had reservations about my father at first."

"That was before I knew you!"

"And before the Lord's work in our lives?"

"Yes . . . that too." Jeremy sighed. He had been slow to come around, he now acknowledged—a result of his analytical mind. But at last he saw everything clearly.

"I always feel an identification with that blind man Jesus healed in Mark 8. Remember?" he went on after a pause. "That's just how I felt, sort of gaining my spiritual sight in stages, seeing people at first, but thinking they were trees."

Karen laughed. "But your questions and doubts were honest," she said. "I always respected you for that. Better a walk with God built on solid thinking than a flimsy faith with nothing to support it. But you haven't answered my question."

"About being sure? You mean sure of my faith? Of course I'm sure. It may take me a while, but once I commit to something, I give it my all. For better or worse, the Lord has me now for the duration."

"I'm glad to hear it. But that's not what I meant."

"Oh—sure about your father you mean? Well, I think I've come to see—"

"Come on . . . you're teasing me! You know what I mean!"

"Let me finish," he admonished, his eyes filled with laughter—and something more. "What I was about to say is that I think I will be very pleased to have a man like your father as my father-in-law. Which is a roundabout way of saying . . . of course I'm sure, silly!"

"Positive?"

"I wouldn't have asked you to marry me if I wasn't sure I wanted you to spend the rest of your life as my wife! When I commit to something, I give it my all. It's for keeps!"

"Oh, Jeremy, I'm so happy!" Karen clutched his arm tightly and snuggled against his chest.

"So are you going to answer my question, or keep me in suspense?"

"Haven't you figured out my answer?"

"Well, judging from your mood, I would have to say I gather you might be interested. But it would still be nice to hear it from those beautiful lips of yours."

"Okay, then here's my answer," she said. "Yes . . . yes . . . yes! Of course I'll marry you!"

"That's all I wanted to know," he replied with a smug grin and drew her into his embrace.

For several minutes the lovers were lost in their own silent world, oblivious to the drippy essence of the quiet scene around them—dew-soaked trees, soggy ground, and rising streams preparing themselves for winter.

"What is your father going to do?" Jeremy asked at length, when they were once more walking along the path.

"I don't know. There's still been no response from the Soviets to his communique, as you know," she said. "Does it surprise you that all the criticism he's received from the rest of the world has been that he's being too soft? The U.N. has come out praising his restraint, but Israel is practically ready to go to war over the invasion if we don't."

"Understandable, I suppose. They feel threatened. From Iran, the Soviets would have a clear bead on Palestine and the Mediterranean, which is what a lot of people think Bolotnikov's ultimate goal is."

"I know Dad's wrestling with all that. But he's been awful quiet lately. I can tell he's really struggling about what role he personally is supposed to occupy in the unfolding of all these events. He's under terrible pressure from the Pentagon."

"Foster's not helping either," Jeremy complained. "He's still taking potshots at the administration. You'd think after his ploy with Bolotnikov—which, I think, could be construed as treasonous—*and* his defeat that he'd know enough to just shut up and go away."

"Well, he is still a senator."

"Yeah, a rebellious one who's not supporting his leader at a time of crisis!" said Jeremy. "What about Howard? He and your dad still on the outs?"

"I thought you knew—Dick resigned yesterday."

"No . . . I hadn't heard that. Any reasons given."

"Dad asked for his resignation. It almost killed him to do it. They were such close friends once. But he had to. I guess some things happened during the campaign that really severed their ability to work together. Dad didn't tell me any details."

"That's too bad. But Backman and your dad really seem to be hitting it off, don't they?"

"It's amazing! They've become best friends almost overnight. Dad is telling him *everything*—about the administration and everyone who works in it, about the White House, about all the negotiations last June."

"Everything?" asked Jeremy.

"I don't know about that. But if he hasn't, I wouldn't be surprised if he does someday. I hate to even think it, but it's almost like he's training Charlie to take over as president."

"I'm sure your father just wants him fully prepared to be an effective vice-president. Your dad had to step in immediately when Ryan died, and it probably wasn't that easy for him. I'm sure he just wants to make Backman's transition from the legislative to the executive as smooth as possible."

"I suppose you're right."

They walked on farther, enjoying the quiet of the park. When Karen spoke again, her voice rang with a touch of nostalgia.

"I don't think I ever did thank you, Jeremy," she said.

"For what?"

"For walking up to me that day at the university last May . . . and for asking if you could share my table."

"My pleasure—Miss MacFarlane," Jeremy said, bowing over her hand. "But I have to admit one thing," he went on laughingly.

"What?'

"I sure had no idea all I was getting myself into!"

# NINETY-THREE

From the darkness of the quiet sitting room on the top floor of the White House, Jarvis MacFarlane gazed out at the brightly lighted monument to the nation's first president.

He had woken suddenly an hour before, at 1:30, knowing he was being summoned. "Come, my son," the night seemed to say, "I am at last ready to reveal your destiny."

He had been sitting in this same spot since then, hardly moving.

There were no earthly visions tonight, but his eyes shone with the glow of revelation. Truly, the Presence was with him.

Tumbling through the brain of this world leader, this president of the United States, this late child of God, were the multitude of reflections that had been gathering momentum for the previous nine months. Out of a vague disorder they had slowly coalesced, taking gradual form. With every successive prayer from his lips, "Lord, show me Your wisdom . . . guide me into Your will for my life," had come an infinitesimal sharpening of the focus. But with every such prayer had also come a growing uneasiness—some undefined discomfort of soul which seemed to place him *as president* at odds with his true self *as a Christian*.

The victory celebration four weeks ago at the Sheridan had graphically elucidated the division in his spirit. When Dick Howard had broken his drunken news about Wilson, an explosion had gone off in MacFarlane's heart. Over him had flooded a sense of betrayal, of futility, of wasted effort, of friendship gone sour . . . of a presidency—on the very night of its external triumph—decayed and rotten. He could hardly wait to get out of there. He was no longer part of that world! It had grown dim and passing. And from that instant, his prayers began to sharpen into answers and renewed purpose and vision—though in directions he could never have predicted.

In the meantime, he was still president! What could be more ironic than the fact that he had just been reelected to another four years, while he himself felt more and more at odds with the very nature of politics!

It was not a pleasant dilemma, for Jarvis MacFarlane did not like playing games. He never had. And ever since that night he had felt like a double-sided man, offering to the public a mere facade of his true self. Day after day as he grappled over this intensifying dichotomy in his spirit, he had pleaded with God to clarify the truth for him, to reveal His wisdom to his own frail but hungry mind.

Tonight, the specific direction for which he had prayed had come. For the last hour, instead of questions and uncertainties, a single phrase had imprinted itself indelibly into his consciousness. Over and over the seven words came back to him—*My kingdom is not of this world.*

With that simple phrase, Jarvis MacFarlane knew God had spoken, and the fog that had clouded the direction of his future began to lift. Now he not only knew Who walked beside him, but also began to catch a glimpse of where they were bound together.

It was not what he had anticipated.

"O Lord, my God, I desire to be more fully Yours!" he prayed softly. "Make me Your child . . . Your servant. Transform my heart, Lord. In spite of my flaws and weaknesses and fears, make me into a son who reflects the nature of Your firstborn Son. Help me to more fully grasp that You are not doing so much *with* me or *through* me—but that You want to do Your work *in* me. You want to make me into a certain kind of person—into a man who reflects the character of Christ.

"O Lord! I've had so much of it wrong. Forgive my shortsightedness—thinking that You had a work to accomplish in the world through me. Your world is not man's world. Your world is the human heart—my heart! *That's* where Your great work is taking place, Lord! Your kingdom is not of this world. It's been in front of me all along. You told me as much when You first spoke to me. O Lord, now that I see that truth, give me strength and courage to walk in it. Make clear the path You have chosen for me to walk."

When Jarvis MacFarlane rose from his chair forty minutes later, he breathed in a deep sigh—one filled with contentment and peace. At last he knew what he had to do.

# NINETY-FOUR

Charlie . . . thanks for coming," said the president, standing and shaking hands warmly with the vice-president elect. "How's the transition going?"

"Lots to learn. But the people you assigned to help me are doing a great job."

"Good."

"You told me to clear my morning, so I'm at your service."

"What I have to talk to you about may take some time," said the president. "I wanted to make sure we weren't interrupted."

"Sounds urgent."

"Not urgent really, Charlie—but very important. I wanted to speak with you very personally about some rather dramatic and wholesale changes that have been occurring in my life, resulting in a hundred-and-eighty degree turnaround in my perspective on politics. I think it's important I share these realizations with you. But consider yourself warned. It won't be like anything you've heard on Capitol Hill."

"I'm intrigued!" said Backman.

"Well, let's pour ourselves a cup of coffee and then I'll plunge right in."

They walked over to the sideboard and the president poured them each a cup of coffee from the silver coffee service sitting there. Then rather than taking a seat behind his desk, MacFarlane led his guest over to two wingback chairs facing the formal fireplace.

Once they were situated, the president said, "I don't know exactly how to begin, Charlie. There is so much to tell. What it all boils down to, I suppose, is a simple statement Jesus made in the eighteenth chapter of John which I haven't been able to get out of my head, where He said, 'My kingdom is not of this world.' "

Backman merely nodded, acknowledging his familiarity with the passage.

"Ever since I began trying to take this job seriously in light of what I thought God wanted of me—since last spring—I somehow assumed He wanted me to do what I could to work for political and social change within the world, within the system, any way I could. I fought for reelection because I felt I needed to be president to bring about many of the changes I felt God desired in our country. I fought for peace with the summit in Moscow. And I prayed that somehow I would be used to accomplish God's purpose, thinking God wanted me to influence events and policies. With God's man in the White House, I thought, just imagine what might be accomplished!

"Yet for several months something has been eating away at me. Something about my efforts to change the world for the better was out of sync. I didn't know what it was, but something was troubling me."

He paused, took a sip from his cup, and continued.

"Several weeks ago things began to come into focus for me—about our country, our founders, our history, and our present plight!

"What I hadn't grasped is that politics doesn't fall within the realm of the spirit at all. There *is* a kingdom of man, a kingdom where politics is necessary. And everything in that kingdom isn't completely corrupt and bad. Politics and social programs accomplish a lot of worthwhile things. Where we go wrong, though, is thinking there's an overlap between the kingdoms. There isn't. God's kingdom is on an altogether different plane than man's.

"That isn't to say a man can't be a citizen of God's kingdom and still function in the world of man. We do . . . we must. But the point is, you can't expect to bring the principles of God to bear on man's kingdom and thereby change man's kingdom *into* the kingdom of God. Man's kingdom will always be just that—*man's*. You can do good in man's kingdom. You can help people. You can live out your call as a child of God. But that living out must be on an individual level—feeding the hungry, giving cups of cold water to the thirsty, Mother Teresa, that kind of personal ministry. How far it can go beyond that, into genuine societal change—well, that's what I'm questioning. I really don't know. I do know you will never turn man's realm into God's kingdom.

"It's a complex issue, Charlie," said the president with a sigh.

"And I'm not suggesting Christians pull out and divorce themselves from society. Jesus was involved with the people of the world and their cares from morning till night. But protesting this, banning that, legalizing this, passing a constitutional amendment about that . . . how much good is it all going to do—eternally? To think we're going to legislate the values of the kingdom of God into man's kingdom is a mirage. It'll never happen. You can't legislate morality into an essentially corrupt system, which the kingdom of man is at its core. Man cannot legislate the kingdom of God. The two kingdoms have different origins, pulsate with a different kind of life . . . and have different kings. Morality . . . righteousness—they are spiritual issues. Legislation can never impact righteousness. Morality is a matter of the heart. And politics doesn't change hearts.

"Certainly we are commanded to bring the kingdom of God to bear upon men's lives. But the goal is to draw men and women into the kingdom of God—by virtue of a change in their hearts. The goal isn't to change society. It's an individual work targeted at hearts, not at systems of politics or laws. We must do good in society, but not to society. You can't pass a law that says someone has to behave in a certain manner. That's why disciples like Billy Graham and Mother Teresa and C.S. Lewis never had a political agenda. They lived active lives in the world, but they understood that the true battleground of the kingdom of God is the heart of man. You can't legislate the things of God.

"That isn't to say that God's people shouldn't be active through all segments of society. Jesus said we must act as the salt of the earth—doing good, bringing the ways of His kingdom to bear on the people around us. Nor am I suggesting that the many dedicated Christians we have right now in the Congress and state legislatures throughout the country resign. I'm simply saying that as we try to bring salt to a needy world, we have to realize God's kingdom is not of this world.

"Can you imagine the impact on the world if we Christians lived—really lived!—the words of Jesus. If we treated every person we met like Jesus told us to, the world would be transformed overnight. I was just reading this morning—"

The president paused as he rose and walked over to his desk and picked up a small book.

"Here it is. I'll read it to you. Let's see—" Hurriedly he flipped through the pages.

"Listen to what this fellow says," he said when he had located the passage he wanted. " 'The cause of every man's discomfort is evil, moral evil—first of all evil in himself, his own sin, his own wrongness, his own unrightness; and then evil in those he loves: with this latter, the only way to get rid of it is for the man to get rid of his own sin. Foolish is the man, and there are many such men, who would rid himself or his fellows of discomfort by setting the world right, by waging war on the evils around him, while he neglects that integral part of the world where lies his business, his first business—namely, his own character and conduct. Even if it were possible—an absurd supposition—that the world should thus be righted from the outside, it would still be impossible for such a man, remaining what he was, to enjoy the perfection of the result, for he would yet be out of tune with the organ he had tuned. No evil can be cured in mankind except by its being cured in individual men.'

"And then listen to this last part, and how it applies to us, in our chosen field," said the president. "I can't say I *know* the guy is right, but it sure makes you think. Listen, he says Jesus 'did not care for government. No such kingdom would serve the ends of his Father in heaven . . . . Government was to him stale and unprofitable. . . . The Lord cares for no kingdom over anything this world calls a nation. The Lord would rather wash the feet of his weary brothers than be the one and only perfect monarch that ever ruled the world.'

"See what I mean, Charlie! That's amazing stuff for guys in our business. I hardly know what to make of it . . . But I didn't mean to start preaching. It's just that I've been asking myself very pointedly lately just what it is I am supposed to be involved in. What role does God want *me* to play? And I must confess I am beginning to wonder about the whole political arena—not in an absolute way, but insofar as it affects me.

"What does God want me to do now, in view of these discoveries I've been making? That is the critical question—and one I'm afraid will influence your future rather heavily, too, Charlie. That's why I have gone to such lengths explaining my position. I want you to understand where I'm coming from in all this."

The president exhaled a long sigh and fell silent. Finally Backman spoke.

"I think I understand your feelings, Mr. President," he said. "And to a degree I agree with you. However, I do think Christians can and should be involved at every level of society, trying to do the good they can—as long as they keep their own personal and spiritual priorities straight."

"Exactly my point," replied MacFarlane. "If God calls a Christian to involvement, he should answer that call. Just so long as he keeps in mind where the real battle must be waged, and that God's kingdom can't be imposed on man's society by legislation or executive fiat."

"But you agree good can be done?"

"Of course! Look at Wilberforce and slavery. Or our founding fathers. They fought for right and truth. But abolishing slavery didn't change men's hearts. That can only come as God speaks to the hearts of individuals. So where are we going to invest our efforts? In bolstering a society that's eventually going to crumble anyway, or in things more eternal? It's a question each must answer for himself personally."

"But God does lead some people into the social arena—into politics," said Backman. "I'm one of them, Mr. President. I love politics, and I believe I'm accomplishing something worthwhile."

"Which is exactly why I picked you, Charlie! I want you involved—and excited about what you're doing."

"Then what exactly is this conversation about? For a while I thought you were trying to talk me out of my love for politics."

MacFarlane laughed. "I'm sorry if I misled you," he said. "No, I don't want to talk you out of anything. I merely wanted to communicate the other side of the issue, because . . . well, to be honest with you, Charlie, I've been wrestling with my own role in all this."

"I see."

"It's entirely a personal thing, not a value judgment. Though it's a touchy issue, and I can see how it can be misinterpreted. God calls Christians into many different spheres of involvement. I'm merely trying to sort out where he is calling me—just me. I've got to tell you, I'm seriously questioning the direction of my future. And I wonder if it includes all this." He swung his arm through the air as if to indicate the whole White House. "I'm beginning to feel God may have something else—that my primary calling may not be the presidency at all."

"Yet a Christian in the White House *can* do good."

"Yes, and there has for months been my ambivalence," said the president. "Where do these new revelations fit in? Why did the Moscow treaty fail? True peace, the kind Jesus proclaimed, will never come through summits and treaties. His peace is on an altogether different level than I thought back in June when world *political* peace was my focus. There should be men and women fighting on the various fronts of the world for peace—keeping the forces of evil at bay. But now I am beginning to see that the peace He wants me to work toward is peace brought about because the kingdom of God has come—peace of the heart—eternal peace . . . peace *in* men because of their union with their Maker, not a superficial agreement not to kill each other. I believe God is calling me to the proclamation of His kingdom in a different arena."

"So what are you going to do, Mr. President?" asked Backman.

MacFarlane sighed thoughtfully. "Charlie," he replied with a slight laugh, "*that's* my sixty-four-thousand-dollar question! And though I think I've at last been shown the answer, I'm not quite ready to let you in on it yet. I just want to make sure I give the Lord ample time to speak to me if I'm misreading His signals about what I think I'm to do. In the meantime, I'm going to rely heavily upon you insofar as being an effective president is concerned. I have great confidence in you, and it's going to be a pleasure having a fellow-Christian to share the load with for a change."

# NINETY-FIVE

MacFarlane's next meeting did not take place in the White House.

What he wanted to discuss with Duke Mathias needed an entirely different setting—away from the incessant interruptions, and especially away from the aura of his position. He needed to slip into a different character for this conversation—that of a novice, a disciple. He and Karen and his future son-in-law were leaving day after tomorrow to spend the Christmas holidays in Washington state, but before he left, he had to get some things settled. He hoped talking with Duke would help.

The small presidential retinue had driven south, without a firm destination, hoping to keep the press at bay. Now here they were walking through the wooded park at Jamestown, under bare trees with two or three inches of snow crunching under foot. In a way it was fitting that times and decisions so momentous be given perspective at the very spot where the country had begun close to four hundred years earlier.

MacFarlane took the path slowly, cane in hand. When his advisor-friend suggested that the walking might be too tiring, the president replied that the exercise was good for his still-weak leg.

"I admit I feel a little foolish, Duke," said MacFarlane, getting down to cases. "Here I am president of the United States, yet it seems every day or two I have to run to one of my new spiritual counselors or friends with a trivial question. Three nights ago it was Peter. Today it's your turn!"

Duke laughed. "Think how Peter and I feel! You may feel foolish, but I'm out of my league. Jeremy and I were talking about that after our Bible study last week—how odd he feels when you and he are chatting away and it suddenly dawns on him all over again that you are the president."

Now it was MacFarlane's turn to laugh. "Where else am I going to turn! All my old friendships are no good for this sort of thing. And you, Duke—you and Peter both—you're not only friends, you're mature Christians who've been at it so much longer than I have."

"I don't mind," said Mathias sincerely. "Actually, you are helping me grow in my own faith in ways you're probably unaware of. But I remember when I was a young Christian—I practically camped out on my pastor's doorstep. There was so much I had to learn!"

"That's it! So much to learn!"

"It's a whole new way of life," Duke continued, "new values . . . priorities. It can be a little bewildering at first. So you need to talk about it, ask things, pray with people who've been at it long enough to have their feet more or less under them and are walking along the road of faith. Don't be embarrassed, Jarvis. I've never seen anyone grow in the faith as rapidly as you. You're truly God's man. You may be asking a lot of questions. And sure—there are things I've learned that you don't know yet. But your asking is indicative of your hunger, not your immaturity. You'll very soon find yourself in this mentor position with others. It's a natural progression as you grow and mature. Others will come into the faith as a result of you, and you'll help bring them along, even though you're still gaining guidance and help from others. It's a total support system—a family structure—where Christians at all stages of development nurture and develop along with everyone else. Even now you are aiding in the development of my own faith. And I've seen the look in Jeremy's eye when he listens to you. He's hungry to learn from you. He looks up to you as someone older and wiser in the faith."

MacFarlane chuckled. "Older and wiser! I've barely been groping along for six months!"

"The length of time is insignificant, for God's hand has been upon you. He has something mighty for you to do. I sense it. He's rapidly bringing you into great maturity."

"But why me, Duke? Why a heathen man who had hardly given God more than a passing consideration all his life?"

"I can't answer that. Only God knows, and His ways are beyond our knowing. But I do know that He sees our hearts," said Duke. "Why did God single out an insignificant shepherd boy named David to become the mightiest of Jewish kings and the ancestor of His own Son? Because somehow He knew David was His man. Why did God choose Abraham—one man in the midst of an entire city? Because something in the heart of Abraham told God that this was the man to father the entire nation of God's people. Why did God choose Moses out of all the men on the earth to reveal His presence face-to-face? Again, I don't know. God uses unexpected people for significant things. God chose each of these men long before they really knew Him. Just like you. He saw that they were destined for His purposes in their times. And if you can accept this, Jarvis, I think God's hand is on you in a unique way for our times."

"But what are our times, Duke? What's so special about this day and age? Maybe that's what I need to know in order to understand whatever it is God has in mind for me. I've had so much thrown at me this year. I think I'm really pretty sure of my personal course now—for the first time—what I'm to do. Yet there are so many aspects of the whole Christian perspective on life—the present, the future—it's just difficult to put it all together so that everything makes sense. In other words, most of my earlier confusion is fading, but I'm still eager to understand more. Does that make sense, Duke?"

"Of course. I understand perfectly."

"Take that tape we listened to, for instance," the president went on, "and everything it seems I've heard at the meetings of the Legation—they're always talking about the 'times.' Whenever Daniel speaks, it's 'preparation' for this . . . 'the hour is at hand' . . . the *time* is short. I've been taking all that as sort of a personal message to me as president—to work toward peace while there's still time, before war breaks out. 'The time is short' is a phrase I've associated with what in politics we call the 'window of opportunity'—a make-hay-while-the-sun-shines sort of thing. That's how my ears have heard that phrase all this year. Yet now I'm sensing maybe there's more to it—more meaning than my limited sight has been able to grasp."

MacFarlane paused and gazed up at the winter-bare branches above them. "I've been reading some things lately in the Bible," he went on, "things that make me wonder about these times in a far larger way than merely as they concern me. Something out of the ordinary is happening, and I'm eager to know what it all means."

"You want a lesson on Revelation, Jarvis?" grinned Mathias.

"Something like that."

"Haven't Daniel and Peter gone over all that with you? After all, the Legation majors in end times prophecy."

"Sketchily. But somehow it hasn't all come into focus for me. Maybe I just need a fresh approach. Daniel is kind of—" The President hesitated.

"Passionate?" suggested Duke.

MacFarlane smiled. "Actually, I was thinking of an even stronger term," he said. "Don't get me wrong. I love the group, and I've learned a great deal. But now I have to put it all together myself—gain a wider perspective." He paused, then added, "What do you think—is that wrong of me to say?"

"Certainly not," replied Duke. "That's the sensible, mature approach, and I think every one of those men would heartily encourage you in it. Most people are not so free from their own biases that they can perfectly and accurately discern truth. So truth comes to them tinged with their own personality, their own backgrounds, their own ways of responding. Thus the Legation has one kind of focus, which they've shared with you, but that's only one of the streams contributing to the whole river of truth. And whatever I tell you is the same—colored by my own perspective on things. You may find yourself letting go of some of Daniel's viewpoints eventually as you ask God to reveal a deeper and wider picture to you. You know, I go along with a great deal of it. Yet the Legation represents only a small part of God's body. There are obedient, godly men and women throughout this country, throughout the world, who would think Daniel was positively a crackpot. And they are active members of God's whole body too."

"Do you think he's a crackpot?" asked the president.

"Heavens no! I believe God is speaking to us today in a variety of ways, and I certainly think He's speaking prophetically through Daniel and people like him. I'm just saying that even though that's true, God's dealing with us as individuals is much more boundless and inclusive than any person or group or movement."

"You don't hear that point of view very often," mused MacFarlane.

"Most are so busy propping up and defending their own little corner of truth that they lose sight of everybody else. What might have begun as a genuine revelation of truth gradually turns into an all-absorbing system, which has to be protected and perpetuated. When a mind and heart are open to the influences of God's Spirit, then truth is continually coming in and revelation is constantly new and wisdom ever deepening. However, when a person or a movement makes the focus of its endeavors only the outgoing of truth—preaching, proclamation, witnessing, and various programs to spread their version of the 'gospel'—then gradually the inflowing lines become blocked. And without a continually fresh supply of incoming truth from God, stagnation results."

"It sounds like what you're saying is just the old adage—you have to find out the truth for yourself."

"In a way. But there's a danger in that phrase which is especially prevalent today—the modern theory of relativity I call it."

"Einstein?"

"Hardly! I borrowed it from a Christian writer and theologian by the name of Francis Schaeffer. Essentially it's this—modern man thinks that truth is relative. What's true for you may not be true for me. Do your own thing. And there's a huge falsehood beneath all those if-it's-right-for-you-do-it mentalities."

"Okay—I'm listening. Explain."

"It's just this. Truth isn't up for grabs. There *is* truth, and it's the opposite from what's false. Truth isn't relative."

"How does that apply to me . . . to Daniel . . . to Christians trying to grow and find truth in the midst of all kinds of various ideas and teachings and viewpoints?"

"Well, that's where the theory of relativity infiltrates the Christian church. You see, we must each establish a relationship with God in which we allow *Him* to reveal to us what the truth is in its completeness. It is not enough to take spoon-fed portions of truth from our teachers and pastors and spiritual mentors. Each one of us must listen to God speaking for ourselves. In that general sense, then, truth must be individually arrived at. But in no way does that give credence to the modern lie that truth is relative to each person individually—that truth for one person can be different from truth for another. Truth is truth. But each of us is individually responsible to discover it."

"That's a fine dividing line."

"Precisely why so many mistake it."

They walked for a few moments in silence.

"All right, Duke," said MacFarlane at length, "now tell me about Revelation."

"Okay, Jarvis, but hold on to your hat! What I'm about to tell you may seem incredible."

"After all that's happened lately, I would expect no less," said MacFarlane.

"When I first heard some of this stuff, I could hardly believe it."

"Why?"

"Because we live in far more significant times than most people think."

"So I've gathered!"

"I believe we are living in one of the two most significant eras in the whole history of man."

"Haven't people always said *their* time period was the most significant?"

"People have said it and been wrong. But today too many things are lining up, Jarvis. I believe our world—mankind—is about to reach a point of climax, a point of no return—the most significant turning point history has ever known."

"How can you be sure?"

"Because it's all been foretold." Duke paused, took a deep breath, then plunged ahead. "Tell me, Jarvis, have you ever heard of the *parousia*?"

"It sounds vaguely familiar."

"It's a Greek word which literally means *presence* or *arrival* or *coming,* and it's the term used to refer to the second coming of Christ." Duke eyed the president carefully. "Have you heard of the second coming? I mean, did you know that Jesus is going to return again to the earth?"

"Sure. I've heard that. Even before I was a Christian. Everyone's familiar with that idea, aren't they?"

"Perhaps," replied Duke. "But very few people think of it in practical terms—that is, both that it is *really* going to happen and that it could be imminent."

"You've got my attention, Duke. Don't keep me in suspense!"

"Well here's the point where you're going to have to seek God and ask Him to reveal the truth to you. I'm very reluctant to say *this* is going to happen or *that* is going to happen. Too many people take it upon themselves to speak categorically for God, and I don't want to do that. So I'm just going to lay out for you what some people are saying—"

"People like Daniel?"

"I'm sure he would definitely hold this view!" laughed Duke. "Anyway, I don't want to be guilty of saying that *I* know how it's going to be because I don't. I'm not sure God even wants us to try to figure out every detail. I think we're to be vigilant and alert and, beyond that, to trust Him, even beyond our own human understanding. Okay, with that disclaimer then, shall I proceed?"

"Yes! Get on with it, for heaven's sake!"

"Well, there are numerous schools of thought on Jesus' second coming," Duke began. "But I would say that most Christians' viewpoints could be classified into one of four groupings. One says that all the second coming talk is purely figurative because Jesus *is* alive on the earth already in the spiritual sense, and that's about all there is to it. Second is another whole range of Christians who don't think about it at all. They approach it as they do most aspects of their faith—impersonally—living from day to day without giving it a thought. Then third, there are those who believe in a literal second coming, but think it will be at some distant future time. And fourth, there are those who believe that Christ's coming is not only literal, but imminent."

They continued walking under the trees, occasionally pausing to brush the snow off a bench and sit for a rest, oblivious to the cold, as Duke imparted some of the most astounding things the president had ever heard. An hour later, MacFarlane still listened raptly to his advisor's animated discussion.

"It's the years," Mathias was saying, "it's all in the years! Six thousand of them since Adam and Eve. Whether the world was created right then, or whether God created the heavens, the earth, and the plant and animal kingdoms much earlier, is relatively insignificant. What's important is that six thousand years ago God breathed life into man. And following that, every two thousand years there has been a major cataclysmic occurrence which has forever and irreversibly altered eternal history. In other words, every two thousand years God has himself stepped *into* history and miraculously changed its entire course and direction. The point is, six thousand years ago God gave man life—His life. That would have been roughly 4,000 B.C. Two thousand years after that He called Abraham out of Ur and made His everlasting covenant with him. That covenant became the foundation for the entire Jewish nation and all of Old Testament history. Two thousand years after that, God sent His Son Jesus. Again, history was forever altered. And interestingly, throughout the entire span between Abraham and Jesus, the coming of the Messiah was foretold."

"Don't stop now, Duke," urged MacFarlane when his friend fell silent.

"Well—that's it. Surely you see what I'm driving at."

"Not exactly."

"Come on, Jarvis. Put it together. Two thousand years have passed since the birth of Christ."

"You're saying something is about to happen?"

"Remember, I'm simply giving you this particular line of biblical interpretation. Not all Christians believe this, but a good many believe that, yes, something huge is at hand. Something on the level of Jesus' birth!"

"And by that 'something' you mean—"

"It's all been foretold. What has been prophesied since the *last* time, since Jesus was here on earth? In fact, what did Jesus himself prophesy even before His death?"

"You mean that Greek word?"

"*Parousia.* Yes. Jesus foretold that He would come again, that He would return to earth."

"That's incredible!" said MacFarlane in amazement. "What

you're saying, then, is not only that Jesus is coming back to earth, but that He's coming back soon!"

"*I'm* not saying that, no. I earnestly want to make myself clear on this one point, Jarvis—that you must turn *solely* to God to reveal His truth to you. But this is a view that many, many Christians share today, with mounting enthusiasm and confirmation. Of course for every book written expounding this view of the imminent return of Jesus, there is another written arguing for a varying position. You will have to sort through that between you and the Lord. Jesus said that the Holy Spirit would guide us into all truth." Duke paused, then asked, "How much of Revelation have you read?"

"Most of it, but I couldn't quote you any details."

"Read the last chapter. In the next to last verse in the whole Bible, Jesus says, 'I am coming soon'—"

Even as the words left Duke's lips, the president recalled vividly the Lord's voice speaking those very words the previous February.

"And Matthew 24 conveys the same thing," Duke concluded.

"Haven't people been saying that for years?"

"Yes, but always overlooking one or more of the signs Jesus gave as indicators of His return, especially the vital significance of the year 2000. Most of what has passed for prophecy in the past has been more wishful thinking than accurate biblical and historical scholarship."

"So you're predicting the time for Christ's return has finally come?"

"I'm simply saying that a lot of factors are lining up which certain people—who hold to the fourth viewpoint I mentioned earlier—look to as significant. Factors in addition to the approach of the year 2000."

"For instance?"

"The Jews inhabiting their homeland and becoming a nation again. Any prophecies of the *parousia* prior to 1948 had to be false on that count alone. But after Israel became a nation for the first time in almost nineteen hundred years, the door was immediately open for many other signs to begin to unfold."

"What else?"

"Increased earthquake activity throughout the earth. Russian hostility to Israel. The moves toward a world economy. Men of peace rising up. All these things are predicted in both the book of Daniel and Revelation. I'm no expert in the study of the end times, Jarvis, but there are many who see great and solemn import to these developments. In God's timetable, of course, the year 2000 could be any time up to 2200 for all I know. We're not supposed to know for certain. And that no doubt explains the huge variety of interpretations. But there are certain points the Bible is clear on—that God labored for six days and on the seventh rested. It also says that with God a day is as a thousand years and a thousand years is as a day. Putting that together, there are those who read it to mean that God has been 'laboring' among man to bring about his redemption for six days, or six thousand years, from Adam to the present. They say that at this very moment we stand on the threshold of the seventh day, which will be a time of unprecedented peace and harmony on earth—the day of God's rest."

"Peace . . . throughout the earth?" repeated the president. He looked away, sighed deeply, and was silent a long while. Through his mind went the words he had heard so many months ago—*I am the Peacemaker.*

"This is all astounding," he said at length. "I suppose I have heard bits and pieces of it before. But it somehow didn't break in so clearly on me that—that we—*you and I,* might actually be alive to witness His return!"

"I know how you feel, Jarvis. I could hardly think about anything else for months after I first heard about all this. Listen to this Scripture." As he spoke, Duke pulled a small New Testament out of his pocket and flipped hurriedly through the pages. "Jesus has been telling His disciples about the signs that will foretell His coming, and this is how He ends the discussion," he said and began reading, " 'Now learn this lesson from the fig tree: As soon as its twigs get tender and its leaves come out, you know that summer is near. Even so, when you see all these things, you know that it is near, right at the door. I tell you the truth, this generation will certainly not pass away until all these things have happened. . . . Therefore keep watch, because you do not know on what day your Lord will come.' "

He stopped, closed the book, then looked at the president.

"There are those who say, Jarvis, that *we* are what is sometimes called 'the generation of the fig tree.' This generation now living upon the earth is the generation which is witnessing the fulfillment of all these signs that have for so long been prophesied. And Jesus clearly says that the generation of the fig tree will see the fulfillment of everything He has just been talking about—His return to earth. I tell you, Jarvis, these are exciting times. The stage is set. The time could be soon."

Shaking his head, Jarvis stopped walking, then clasped his hands together and held them up to his mouth in a silent gesture of intense thought. Alternately nodding and shaking his head, he struggled to assimilate the flood of new information pouring over him.

Suddenly he turned toward Duke. "Tell me," he said intensely, "is there anything else that has to come first—any sort of . . . of preparation which the prophecies say will . . . I don't know . . . pave the way for Jesus' coming?"

"There are two things. One is the rebuilding of the Jewish temple in Jerusalem on its original site. And now at last, just this year, that has begun. And the other has to do with Moses and Elijah, two of the Old Testament's most significant men in terms of the prophetic pattern."

"What do you mean?" the president asked.

"Well, they were both men whom God set apart by revealing himself to them. Moses was said to be the only man to look upon God's face and live. And it is said that the presence of the Lord passed by Elijah and then spoke to him in a gentle whisper. It was Moses and Elijah who appeared to Jesus, as recorded in Mark 9, and these two figures have always been associated with the 'two witnesses' who will come to prophesy prior to Jesus' return, as mentioned in Revelation 11."

"Will Moses and Elijah actually come back to the earth?" asked MacFarlane.

"Only God knows. There is that interpretation. But often God's means of fulfilling a prophecy are much different than people expect. Elijah was also expected to come prior to Jesus' birth two thousand years ago, to prepare the way and to call people's hearts to repentance. The Jews were expecting a literal Elijah to come in the flesh. Yet God sent John the Baptist instead, who became a symbol of Elijah. The prophecy was fulfilled, yet not as people expected. In the same way, perhaps the fulfillment of Revelation 11 will be unexpected as well. Perhaps it will come through men no one recognizes at first as bearing the message of preparation. But their message will be like John's, calling men and women throughout the world to ready themselves for the return of Jesus."

By now MacFarlane was scarcely listening. His thoughts were tumbling back in time as the words of the Voice in his vision played themselves over and over in his mind. Duke's disclosure had given them new perspective. He recalled everything he had heard during the past months—his talks with Peter, Daniel's prophetic words to him, the tape, the books he'd been given, scriptures he had read. Suddenly the words of the vision made more sense than they had at any time since he had first heard them. And with the deeper revelation of their meaning, all at once a huge fog began to lift from the consciousness of Jarvis MacFarlane and he at last saw the course that had been laid out for him.

"Duke, if you don't mind, I think I need a little time alone," the president said quietly.

"Certainly," replied Duke. "I'll just wait for you here."

Slowly the president turned and walked down the path, and as Duke watched him go, he somehow sensed that he had been privileged to share in a momentous moment. For though only one figure was visible to the human eye, Duke knew there were two present.

# NINETY-SIX

Before Jarvis MacFarlane had a chance to take any practical action on the resolve that had come to him following his talk with Duke, events once again swept him up in their dramatic pull.

Before he and Duke were halfway back to the city, a call came over the car phone.

"Yes, Bob—I understand," MacFarlane said after listening for a moment, and a smile gradually spread over his face. "Excellent—so his people are in place? . . . Good. When do you expect us to have to move . . . I see—I'm glad you got at least that much notice, but it doesn't give me much time."

He paused thoughtfully for a moment. "Okay, Bob, listen. I've had some people working on it from our end—they've got a network of their own that should—" The speaker at the other end interrupted him. "Okay, point well taken . . . yes, I know how you people work, but I have my reasons, Bob . . . That's right, I'm afraid that is how I want to proceed. They'll just have to coordinate with my people . . . Outsiders? . . . I suppose that's what you'd call them. Nevertheless, I want your people to cooperate . . . I know that—no guarantees . . . I'll accept responsibility . . . Okay. And thanks, Bob."

He hung up the phone, a deep light shining in his eyes.

---

That night when Jeremy Manning walked into the third floor sitting room of the White House, only the president was there. He had sent Karen to another part of the house.

"Thank you for coming over so quickly, Jeremy," said MacFarlane.

"It sounded serious."

"It is. I wanted to see you alone because this has nothing to do with Karen. In a way I suppose it doesn't have much to do with your job on my staff either," said the president. "I'm going to ask you to do something for me, Jeremy—as a Christian and as a friend. Don't ask me why you came into my mind for this assignment. I don't doubt there are a hundred more qualified persons in Washington. But for some reason I think you are the man the Lord wants. But once you've heard me out, I want you to feel perfectly free to say no. If you don't feel comfortable with it, your turning me down won't jeopardize your job or your future relationship with me in any way. Believe me, I want you to be confident in whatever decision you make."

"Go on, sir" said Jeremy.

MacFarlane drew in a deep breath, then began. "This has all come up suddenly," he said, "and there could be danger. For Karen's sake, I would rather send someone else. However, as I said, you were the one who came to my mind the moment I asked the Lord about it. I need someone I can trust implicitly, Jeremy, for this concerns a very dear friend of mine . . ."

---

Late the next afternoon, with a mixture of uncertainty and excitement, Jeremy settled back into his seat on the Lufthansa 747 bound for Frankfurt. He had hardly had time to pack, much less worry about a passport, necessary visas, or traveler's checks. Everything had been arranged, the president told him.

"As far as anyone knows this is nothing more than a last-minute Christmas holiday for you, Jeremy. You work for me, but no one must know that I sent you—that is, until you reach your destination. Also, there is another person on the plane with whom you are acquainted, although your seats are at opposite ends of the cabin. For his sake, and yours, you must not in any way let on that there is the slightest acquaintance between you—again, that is, until you are with his friends there. You will know when that time has come."

Here the president had paused and gazed even more seriously—if that was possible—into Jeremy's eyes.

"Once there, the man on the plane will be your contact, your lifeline—along with a CIA operative known as Blue Doc. Do whatever these two men tell you. Whatever comes, you may trust them. Above all, Jeremy, you must pray. That is your chief assignment as my liaison on this mission. For without His help, it cannot succeed.

# NINETY-SEVEN

Patrick Foster slammed down the phone and turned to Harv Bateman with fire in his eyes.

"We've got him! At last—at last we're going to bring that self-righteous so-and-so down to size!"

"A little late isn't it, Senator?" inquired Bateman cynically, draining off the last of his double Scotch. He still hadn't recovered from the sting of realizing he was not bound to the White House as the president's Chief of Staff.

"Too late?" sneered Foster. "He may have four more years to play a ridiculous figurehead, but I'm going to make sure every month of it is miserable for him! He'll get nothing through the Senate unless he plays by my rules. I've got the votes, and as Majority Leader, I'll run this town! Too late? Not when I see him coming to me to beg for support for one of his cockamamie fool notions! We'll see who's really got the power then! He's going to wish I'd won a hundred times in the next four years! But right now I've got something more important to deal with."

"What's it all about?" asked Bateman, still not enthusiastic but thawing somewhat to the idea of another scrap in the political mud.

But his boss hardly heard him, hardly even seemed aware of his presence in the room.

"I'm glad I kept those guys in place!" he muttered to himself, shuffling through some papers on his desk. "I knew they'd turn up something one of these days. But a sudden flight to Germany and then to Kiev?—I should have known he was up to something!"

Still mumbling, he tore madly through what looked to be a desk diary or address book. "I'm going to have to give that guy in the CIA a bonus—this is worth the five years I've been paying him off for little bits of nothing . . . this is the ball game—my way of evening the score, just for old time's sake, MacFarlane! I'll bring your little charade down around your ears!"

Finally in frustration he threw down the book, sending the papers on top of his desk flying in several directions. He grabbed his phone again, pushed the intercom button, and shouted at his secretary.

"I don't care what time it is there, or what you have to do to get through, get Bolotnikov on the line! . . . Moscow, you fool! . . . That's right. Where else do you think the Kremlin is?"

# NINETY-EIGHT

When Jeremy arrived in Kiev the next afternoon, he was exhausted. He had been on planes and in airports for twenty-four hours.

Dmitri had flown direct from Frankfurt also, but, as ordered, Jeremy had not acknowledged him. The moment they left the plane Jeremy saw Dmitri whisked off in one direction, and a few moments later he himself was greeted, by name, by two strangers who spoke perfect English and took him to a waiting car.

Within forty minutes he was between the sheets of a soft bed in the guest room of a second-floor apartment on the outskirts of the city. His only instructions had been, "Sleep now while you can, Manning. We'll be getting you up about one in the morning, and the drive's a long one."

---

While Jeremy still slept, the man known to him as Dmitri Mujznek, assistant to the Soviet ambassador to the United States, sat on an unpainted wooden chair in the small kitchen of a simple farmhouse outside the village of Mtsensk, north of Orel in the west-central plain of Soviet Russia. He had been cramped in a tiny Fiat for six hours and had only moments before arrived at his destination. It was 10:45 P.M. local time.

"It is good to see you, my old friend," said the farmer in the colloquial Russian dialect.

"It has been far too long," replied the guest with a smile.

"The years have been kind to you."

"And to you. The agrarian life still appeals to you, eh?"

"You forget," laughed the farmer, "in this country one has little choice. But yes, things have been better since *perestroika*. At last I feel as if some of the land and some of my work are really mine."

"I am happy for you."

"I never thought we would see one another again," said the farmer. "When the call came to alert the old network, my first thought was that it must be a trick to bring us out of hiding after all this time."

"It was I who arranged the call."

"I know that now. But why? There is so little persecution of our brothers and sisters now."

"The prisoner I have come to get out is political, not religious."

"Political! We are given to understand there are no more such prisoners in this era of tolerance and openness."

"Few perhaps—but the old ways die hard. And there remains one whom I must help liberate, whatever the cost," replied the visitor. "Has everyone along the way been notified?"

"They are ready."

"Good. Then I can get some sleep before morning."

"But is it not dangerous for you to be here?" asked the farmer. "Many of our old enemies are still in power. Some have risen to the very apex!"

"Yes, no doubt there is some danger. But he has known nothing of my whereabouts for sixteen years. Even in the embassy I have managed to conceal my steps and stay in the background. I'm sure he has forgotten me completely by now. And even if not, no one knows of my return. We will be out of here and across the Atlantic before our old KGB friend knows anything is amiss."

"Be careful, my friend. He swore vengeance the last time, and he is not a man who forgets."

"I do not even intend to set foot in Moscow."

"I am glad of that!"

# NINETY-NINE

Blue Doc arose at 5:10.

It would not be light for hours. The predicted storm was not due in for another thirty-six hours. He was glad of that at least. With everything else, especially all the loose jokers in the deck, he'd just as soon not have to worry about the weather. Though in this bleak land in the dead of winter, even with the sun shining they'd probably be lucky if the temperature got above one or two degrees Celsius.

He grabbed his heavy jacket, threw on his schapska, and headed out into the frigid early morning.

---

The woods north of Lvov Sanatorium were not thick, yet one could get lost in them if he tried. Blue Doc thought they should do nicely—that is if Jozef Witos managed to get here with his patient on schedule before the arrival of automobiles made this out of the way place look like a convention center. Crisscrossed as the wood was with narrow dirt car paths, escape should be easy as long as there was no trouble, though he'd feel a lot better about it if he could accompany the kid from the States at least as far as his first contact. What if something went wrong? Cut loose in the middle of the Soviet Union with no experience, a green civilian would never be able to get the plan back on track!

But the director had been insistent. "None of your people can make the connection with the second stage. It has to be a clean break—a two-phase operation. Their people still watch you and some of our boys pretty close. If they should happen to tail you, I want to make sure we minimize the risk of them following it through to the end." Blue Doc had learned to obey orders a long time ago, and he would do so now, even though the whole thing sounded ridiculous.

He climbed out of his car, shut the door, and leaned up against the fading blue paint. He glanced down at the luminous dial of his watch. Three minutes till six. His boys ought to be here in ten or fifteen minutes, and Witos was scheduled to appear with the patient at 6:25. How he was going to do it, Blue Doc didn't know. But he didn't need to.

It was at times like this that he sometimes wished he hadn't given up smoking. The waiting was always the worst.

---

Sitting in the back seat of the Mercedes—this one was green—Jeremy knew by this time that he was being escorted by two CIA agents. In the middle of the night they had awakened him from his exhausted slumber and driven him to a small airstrip, from which they had flown to Tula in a little six-seater. Once on the ground again, they had picked up the green Mercedes and had been driving ever since. Jeremy was certain they were headed northward toward Moscow.

He still knew nothing concerning the intrigue he had suddenly been thrown into, except that the two men would rather be making the journey without him. He had ascertained that much, but little else, from their conversation he had overheard as he pretended to sleep.

"They must've gone whacko!" the passenger in the front seat said to the driver. "They think a novice can do it better than us?"

"The whole deal's in civilian hands after we pass him off. After that, we're out of it. Then this guy and his people take over—whoever they are."

"But this guy doesn't know a thing! What good can he do anybody?"

"I'm just telling you what I was told. All we have to do is get him there safely and back up Doc."

"Kind of a crazy operation if you ask me."

"Not like the old days, that's for sure!"

---

At 6:14 headlights blared silently through the blackness and made their way slowly toward Blue Doc.

He stood his ground watching. Softly the tires crunched over the twig-strewn dirt path, then came to a stop. The lights went out, and all was black again.

Car doors opened and closed softly, and moments later three men stood beside Blue Doc. He knew the unfamiliar face had to be the civilian.

"Well, Manning," said Blue Doc, "I don't know who you are or how you carry so much clout, but I hope you know what you're doing."

"I don't know anything, except that I've been ordered to do

exactly what you tell me—that is, if you are the one they call Blue Doc."

"That's me. And they told you nothing?"

"Only that I'd be the go-between from you to the other network who are going to get him out of the country."

Blue Doc let out a sigh. "Okay—we don't have much time, so listen carefully, Manning. This is the craziest plan I've ever heard, but somebody high up seems to think it will work. Now, in a few minutes some guys are going to bring a man through a gate over there on the edge of the woods—you can't see it, but it's there. We're going to put that man in the back seat of the car you came in—" He stopped and turned to the agent who had driven the Mercedes. "Paul, get that thing turned around, will you, so it'll be all set for him to hightail it outta here."

As the agent moved to carry out his order, Blue Doc said to Jeremy, "You're going to be in the driver's seat, Manning, and once you've got him, you're gonna drive out just like you came in—straight ahead there until you reach the edge of the woods. At the paved road that runs perpendicular to this dirt one, you turn right and drive straight south for some five to eight miles until you see a man hitchhiking on the right side of the road. He's your contact, and I sure hope he's there."

Blue Doc paused and shook his head, then said, "When you leave here, that's the last time you'll see any of us. From then on you better hope that old Christian underground can still function, 'cause they're all you're gonna have."

The third agent, who had remained silent since they left the car, now spoke up. "I think they're coming, Doc. I can hear something through the trees there."

"Get in the car, Manning, just in case," said Blue Doc.

The man called Paul was just climbing out, and Jeremy took his place behind the wheel. The engine was still idling.

A moment or two more and soft voices and footsteps could be heard . . . then a wavering beam from a flashlight . . . and three figures came faintly into view, all dressed in white. Two of them appeared to be helping the third to walk.

"So, Witos, you are right on time," said Blue Doc.

"As promised."

"Any trouble?"

"We will know that in another hour."

"Well—good job! Get him in the car."

Suddenly out of the silent night sky the swooshing of giant helicopter blades bore in upon them with frightening speed and a searchlight began panning the area.

"Go, Manning, go!" shouted Blue Doc. "If that beam homes in on you, he's dead! We'll try to divert them. Go on—get outta here!"

Jeremy jammed the accelerator down the moment the passenger door slammed shut, spewing a cloud of dust behind him as the tires of the Mercedes spun and gradually found their traction. In another minute they were racing through the woods.

Glancing back quickly, Jeremy could see that the beam of the menacing helicopter had located the three agents and the two white-clad hospital personnel. He slowed slightly, hoping to lessen the chance that they would hear or see him speeding along the dirt road. He could barely see in the darkness without lights, but he kept straight on. When he came to the fork he braked and twisted the wheel hard to the right, squealing the tires slightly as they came into contact with the pavement. Then he accelerated again and was soon flying along the deserted road to the south. After about a mile he flipped on the headlights.

A voice spoke up behind him. "We are safe now, I think."

Jeremy gave a start. He had forgotten all about his passenger!

As Jeremy glanced into the back seat, the man said, "They will not follow. They think I am with your . . . what do you call him? . . . your Blue Doc? He is an agent all of our people know. They will expect him to see to me personally. An ingenious plan to use your top agent in Russia as a mere decoy."

Jeremy could not believe his eyes.

In the back seat sat Kudinsky!

# ONE HUNDRED

Mr.—Mr. Premier!" exclaimed Jeremy. "I—I thought you were . . . I had no idea it was—"

"My surprise is nearly as great as yours," replied the Russian. "But you are not an agent, I think," he went on, struggling with the English he had not used for some time. "I think you were in Moscow—I saw you with the president, did I not?"

"Yes, you did. But what do you mean by surprise?" asked Jeremy. "Isn't this your doing?"

"I knew nothing until thirty minutes ago. Two orderlies came to my cubicle and told me to come with them. Suddenly I am in the middle of the woods, being snatched away by one of the American president's bodyguards."

Jeremy laughed. "Hardly a bodyguard! I'm just a friend. Well, more than that—but believe me, this intrigue stuff is foreign to me too. I don't even know where we're going."

"Some team we will make," chuckled Kudinsky. "The blind man leading the dead! Then tell me, how do you come to be here?"

"The president said that he wanted me along because he could trust me."

"Did he give you no special instructions?"

"Only that I should pray."

"Ah," replied Kudinsky. "That perhaps explains everything." He paused thoughtfully, then chuckled again. "Just like my friend MacFarlane, sending in a novice with no instructions but to pray. Now I can see his hand in this! He knew it would come to this—you and me together. Me an outcast in my own country, and you—what is your name, son?"

"Manning . . . Jeremy Manning."

"Ah, yes, I remember now—Manning. You and me, Jeremy Manning. He knew we would wind up like this, alone and together, with no one else to turn to, no plan, no escape route. It is beautiful—your president is such a resourceful man!"

"I'm afraid I don't follow you, sir," said Jeremy. "As you said, we are alone and without a plan."

"Don't you see? He knew it would come to this—that you and I would be alone together with no one to turn to for deliverance except the God who protects and delivers His people. That is why he reminded you to pray. He knew we would be safer alone with God than with all the agents he could muster. And don't you see? It has worked already! I am certain the plan devised by your country's agents was foolproof. Yet the KGB learned of it, and no doubt even now they are interrogating your Blue Doc and his men. Had we depended on their plans, I would already be on my way back to the sanatorium—or worse. But your president knew best. He put my safety in the hands of God and His people."

"Those men back there don't know where we're headed either," added Jeremy.

"What instructions were you given?" asked Kudinsky.

"Only to drive south until we come to a man hitchhiking along the side of the road."

"I am certain he will be another of God's army," said Kudinsky. "We always used to wonder—back in the old days, you understand—how they kept funneling Christians out and across the border. I have the feeling I'm about to find out firsthand! Your president is an ingenious man. I cannot wait to set these tired old eyes on him again!"

"Aren't you being a bit optimistic, Mr. Premier?" laughed Jeremy.

"We will make it, young Manning. Do not forget—we are in God's hands now. Remember what the Book says—where two or three are gathered in His name, He is there in the midst of them."

"You may have to remind me often," said Jeremy. "I'm a brand-new Christian."

"As am I!" said Kudinsky. "But He is with us. It is also said that He uses the foolish to confound the wise, and perhaps we are the proof. But now I think we should perhaps pull off into these woods for a few minutes. They will have discovered I am not with your agents and will be scanning the surrounding area. Our headlights will be easily seen."

Instantly Jeremy applied the brakes and turned off the lights. He should have thought of it himself! They would spot them in a second on this deserted road! At the first opportunity he pulled off the pavement and drove several yards into the heavy cover of the nearby wood, then cut the engine.

Within a few minutes the sound of the helicopter slashed through the air and whizzed by them overhead. It circled over the area for several minutes, then finally flew on.

"I do not think we have been seen," sighed Kudinsky.

Jeremy exhaled and slumped down in the seat. "I'm glad you thought of the lights when you did."

"I can claim little credit. *He* put the danger of the lights into my brain. And now I think the time has come, young Manning, for us to heed your president's advice. We must ask God to guide our every step and our every thought."

Jeremy nodded, and both men bowed their heads.

For the next twenty minutes, the audible conversation in the car was carried on with the unseen third member in their midst.

# One Hundred One

Dmitri glanced down at his watch once more. He could not even see the time, but it was a habit he couldn't break. They should have been here long before now!

He heard the ominous sounds of a helicopter roaming swiftly through the skies and hurried off the road into the woods before it even came into sight. Slipping to the hard, frozen ground under some brush, he watched the spotlight rotating and scanning for any movement below. At least they were still searching, he thought, which meant they had not found their quarry.

"Blind their eyes, Lord, and bring Your people through to safety!" Dmitri prayed, as he had prayed so many times years ago.

In another minute the helicopter was gone, swinging in a wide arc back toward Lvov. When it had disappeared from sight, Dmitri rose and walked back to the road. He peered northward. They should have been here at least thirty minutes ago, he thought.

Suddenly in the distance he saw a flash of light, then darkness again. He waited. The flash came again, closer this time. Darkness once more, then again a moment of light. Yes—it was two lights! The headlights of a car!

Dmitri could hear the engine now, creeping along the deserted roadway. The driver was flashing on the lights only long enough to see the way for another minute of darkness. He only hoped it wasn't the KGB!

---

"There he is!" said Jeremy to the premier, who was still in the back seat. "Up there, beside the road."

He flashed the lights on one more time, then off, and gradually closed the distance, pulling to a stop beside the shadowy figure. In another instant the man was inside.

"Dmitri!" exclaimed Jeremy.

"Our Lord be praised, you made it safely!" said Dmitri. "But what kept you? I nearly froze out there praying for you. My contact dropped me off two hours ago."

"The helicopter—you must have seen it," answered Jeremy.

Dmitri nodded, rubbing his hands rapidly together.

"We didn't want to be seen, so after they had passed, we drove mostly in the dark."

"A wise plan. But the dawn is starting to break, so we will make better time now."

"Where are we going?" asked Jeremy.

"Not far for now—only another hour. We will rest by day at farms and other safe houses along our route and travel only by night. We will drive all the way to Warsaw, and we have many friends along the way. The border will be safer for us than the airports. But why don't you pull off, Jeremy. I'll drive. I have made this trek a thousand times. I can drive it with my eyes closed in the dead of night."

"This is not the first time you have used such a plan?" asked Jeremy as he slowed the car to a stop.

"First time!" laughed Dmitri. "More like the thousandth time! The specifics always varied at the point of initial departure, but everyone we took out of Moscow eventually went through this same series of farmhouses, back roads, and wooded dirt trails you will soon be familiar with. You will walk many miles, my friend, see much of our Russian countryside—even if at night, and ride in some of the most broken-down cars and wagons that you can imagine. Believe me, you will not forget these next six days of your life!"

Jeremy got out of the car and walked around to the passenger side, as Dmitri and he exchanged places.

"But surely such cloak-and-dagger routines haven't been required for years," Jeremy commented as the two men met and paused in front of the car.

"You are right," said Dmitri. "I have been in the States myself for sixteen years—though I had to get out because my cover had been penetrated and I would have jeopardized the entire network. That's why I returned myself for this mission. Not only is this the most important rescue we have ever attempted, but I needed to be here to make sure all the pieces of the thread held together after such a long period of inactivity."

"But your position at the embassy," said Jeremy. "If they knew who you were—?"

"Ah, there are ways, Jeremy," replied Dmitri. "Whether we were bringing Bibles across the border or smuggling Christians and dissidents out, our prayer always used to be, 'Blind their eyes Lord.' And He was able to do that for me also. It was important that I maintain my usefulness to the network, and I thought I could best do that in some official capacity. I never dreamed that with my new identity I would rise so high on the ambassador's staff. My position came in handy many times, but I had to keep my faith strictly hidden, and never once returned to Moscow. Too many people knew me there."

"Which explains the secretive meetings of the Legation whenever you were involved." Jeremy nodded in understanding.

"If anyone connected with the embassy, or the press—anyone!—had discovered that I had any connection with the Legation or an organized Christian group of any kind, it would only have been a matter of time before my former identity was uncovered. I could not put everything we had established at risk. But come—I have already been in this cold too long! And look, the morning is at hand. We must get to our destination!"

Soon they were speeding along once more, still with the lights extinguished. Jeremy hoped Dmitri did indeed know this road with his eyes closed!

"So, Mr. Manning," said the premier from the back seat. "Do you intend to introduce me to our deliverer?"

Jeremy turned around, but before he had a chance to say a word, Kudinsky spoke once more.

"But I think I already know him! We have not, of course, met face-to-face, but he was one of the chief adversaries of my government for so long—a thorn in the flesh, as it were—that I feel he is already my friend!"

"It is an honor to be on the same side with you at last," said Dmitri, glancing toward the back seat with a smile.

"The honor is entirely mine," replied Kudinsky, speaking in Russian. "To be counted one of you is a blessing and a joy, Brother—"

"Please, Mr. Premier," interrupted Dmitri. "I do not even want to hear the word until you are safe and free. And for his own safety, I do not want our young friend to even hear my name. And you too, for your own safety, must henceforth know me only as Dmitri Mujznek."

"As you wish," replied Kudinsky.

# ONE HUNDRED TWO

Ominous clouds of dark gray slowly approaching from the north portended the coming storm.

Staring out the window of his Kremlin office, General Secretary Leonid Bolotnikov seethed in silent fury. The phone call just ended had informed him that his old nemesis had been snatched from the sanatorium, right from under their noses. Five prisoners had been taken—three CIA agents and two hospital employees—and were being held, but all questioning had been to no avail. Meanwhile, the trail was growing colder by the minute!

It all came at such a bad time! Suddenly that fool MacFarlane had not only won the election, but was riding high in public opinion. He had backed off from any confrontation in Iran, playing the usual American role of wimp. Yet he had spoken with such authority and confidence, even in giving them two years to pull out their troops, that world opinion was quickly rushing to back him. If things continued in this vein, thought Bolotnikov, he would have to order the troops out of Iran just to keep peace with his many trading partners throughout the world.

It galled the Soviet leader to have to prostrate himself before such a weakling! And the way things presently stood, he wouldn't even be able to torture the truth out of those three agents they had nabbed! They'd scream for their release and he would have to grant it. Well, election or no election, at least that fool Foster was still proving of some use.

Also, something told him the old Christian escape network was involved. Back when he was head of the KGB he'd almost had them once. Bolotnikov remembered the day vividly when he'd squared off face-to-face against their leader. That was a face he'd never forget! He'd have had him too, if that moronic peasant hadn't jumped in the line of fire at the last instant. Suddenly his quarry was gone, and all the KGB director had to show for his months of surveillance, payoffs, investigations, and bribes was a dead Russian farmer in the middle of a cornfield.

Bolotnikov had never heard of him again. And with the thawing of East-West relations the escape network they'd never been able to penetrate dwindled into inactivity.

But this had the whiff of those people all over it! He was glad now that he'd kept a file active and persisted in his efforts to locate a crack in the chain that had remained unbroken for so many years. It was time he got involved actively again himself. This was a victory he wanted to savor *personally*!

He spun around, walked to his desk, and grabbed his phone.

---

Thirty-five minutes later, the general secretary's office door opened and a visitor was shown inside.

"Ah, Soroka," smiled Bolotnikov, "how does it go with you in your new assignment"

"Very well, Mr. President," Pavel replied. "I am most grateful for the promotion."

"Nothing you didn't deserve, Pavel," returned Bolotnikov. "You proved your loyalty to the new order in what I know was a most difficult way for you."

Inwardly a stab of pain pierced Pavel's heart at the memory, but he determinedly tried to keep from wincing at the thought of his dead friend.

"I summoned you this morning, Pavel, because I need a favor of you."

"Anything I can do, Mr. President."

"In my file—I merely ran across the information a short while ago when looking up some routine matter—I discover that you maintain connections with a good many people down in the Gomel-Bobrujsk region."

"Ah—yes—that is—"

"You were in charge of the Ministry of Agriculture for many years, Pavel, and you had strong ties to the area."

"Yes—yes—that is true," replied Pavel.

"There are a good many Christians there, I am given to understand?"

"I—that is—I have not made such persons—"

"Come, come, Pavel!" said Bolotnikov with a warm smile. "This is the new age of Soviet openness. You know you have nothing to fear for yourself or your friends. We encourage these groups now."

"Yes, Mr. President. It was simply that I did not wish you to misunderstand my—my position. I—I am still a devout party member."

"And I admire your devotion, Pavel. It is only that I, you see, am desirous of opening myself to understand our people. As president, you know, I must be sympathetic to the needs and aspirations of all segments of our diverse Motherland."

He paused, still smiling, then added almost as an afterthought, "There was said to be a farmer of wheat in the village of Svetlogorsk who engaged in the sideline of hiding Christians who were—well, you remember how it was, Pavel, back in those days when things were tense, back before the era of tolerance, how the KGB and certain Christian groups were constantly at odds?"

He paused, while Pavel nodded uncertainly.

"They were always trying to escape or bring illegal books *in*—and we—that is, the KGB—were duty bound to try to stop them. And of course we are all grateful that those days are behind us. But I am now involved in an attempt to widen my own horizons by understanding more of how these people think. Do you suppose—" He paused again, then glanced into Pavel's eyes with just the hint of a narrowing of his own gaze. "Do you suppose, Pavel, that you could obtain for me the name of that particular farmer?"

"I do not know that I could be helpful to—"

"I think you underestimate yourself, Pavel," said Bolotnikov, with a broad smile that could hardly varnish the forcefulness of his tone. "I am quite sure there are people there, persons who have grown to trust you over the years, who could give you the information we desire. I'm sure you have only to ask."

"It may be they still wish to remain anonymous," suggested Pavel lamely.

"But I wish the information," said Bolotnikov, his smile fading. "You have proven yourself faithful in the past. I have not disappointed you, have I, Pavel?"

"No, sir."

"I would not want to have to tell the Committee—that is, the next time your name came before them—that you were unwilling to do your part. They would not take kindly to such news. I fear I could not dissuade them from reconsidering your recent promotion. Does this make the urgency of my request more clearly understood, Pavel?"

"Yes, sir. I will do what I can."

"The matter is most urgent, Pavel. I need the information by this afternoon. If need be, I will arrange for you to fly down there in my own plane within the hour."

"I do not think that will be required, Mr. President. I will make some phone calls."

"Good, Pavel! I will be waiting!"

As Pavel exited the office of the Soviet Union's most powerful man, his head hung in shame. *What have I come to,* he thought, *that*

*I have become a mere pawn in this evil man's hand?*

Yet even as his tormented conscience asked the question, Pavel knew he would betray his friend Markus Tanicev, just as he had betrayed his friend Vladimir. He was caught in a web, and it was the only way he knew to survive.

# ONE HUNDRED THREE

Late in the afternoon of the third day, Dmitri wheeled the rusty Renault sedan around the final street corner of the small village of Svetlogorsk and headed again into the countryside. It was contrary to his pattern to drive during the day, but the snowfall of the recent storm, though neither bitter nor prolonged, had slowed their progress.

Three kilometers past the village he swung off onto a dirt road to the right. As he had explained to young Manning and the premier, they would leave the car next to the river, where someone would retrieve it and take it back to Gomel. Then they would walk along the bank of the Berezina for the two kilometers more it took to reach the Tanicev farm. In the morning they would be taken in a wagon behind Markus's tractor across several fields to another farm where they would spend the rest of the day in the loft of a barn. At night they would drive—in another borrowed car—north to Bobrujsk. From there they would travel southeast along the highway, leave the main road short of the border, drive north to Volkvovysk, and cross into Poland at Bobrowniki.

The distance was not great, he explained, but many of their connections were made field to field, footpath to footpath—and they would change automobiles another four times. But their flight out of Poland had already been arranged, and once in Poland there was nothing to fear. The KGB were hated there more than ever, and Poland was now more strongly linked to the West than the Kremlin would have dreamed possible ten years earlier.

---

Fifteen minutes after they had stashed the Renault, Dmitri led his two weary companions across the final desolate wheat field, where unploughed rubble from last season's crop poked through the two or three inches of snow that remained on the ground. It was slow going for the elderly premier, whose precarious health had been further weakened during his stay at Lvov.

They approached the farm from the field side, as was their standard procedure, and headed toward the small green door at the back of the barn. All was quiet.

It was too quiet, thought Dmitri. There was not even the sound of a chicken or goose or duck. And since when had Markus Tanicev been able to afford such a large automobile? But then, he had been away many years, and times had changed.

Besides, he was always nervous when they were out in plain view, especially in a barren field such as this. Twenty yards more and they would be in the safety of the barn until nightfall. Then he could relax and think out the final leg of their escape route. It would be good to see Markus again after sixteen years. . .

Suddenly the door in front of him flew open nearly in his face, crashing against the side of the barn with a loud clatter. The boot that had kicked it with such force stepped through from the barn into the paling light of the gray afternoon.

The three fugitives stopped in their tracks, and Kudinsky's face turned ashen.

"So, we meet again, Comrade Rostovchev! Somehow I knew it was you behind this brash scheme!"

"Bolotnikov!" muttered Dmitri through clenched teeth.

"And you," sneered Bolotnikov, looking at Kudinsky. "Our great leader—sunk to sneaking through fields and hiding in barns!"

"We can hurt you no longer, Leonid," said Kudinsky. "You have everything you wanted. What can you possibly want with us?"

"What indeed! You never really understood, did you? Never understood the real game," said Bolotnikov. "It's power, Vladimir—power! And now that I have it, don't you see, I can't let you go. They would make a hero of you in the West, and where would my power be then?"

"Then if it is me you are after, I will go with you willingly. Take me back to Lvov. But you can have no use for these two. They are innocent."

"Innocent! Vladimir, Vladimir!" laughed Bolotnikov. "You are the innocent. Don't you know who this man is—this man you would call innocent? This is our old antagonist, the head of the whole Christian network, Rostovchev. I had him once and he slipped through my fingers. But it shall not happen again! I always suspected him of being a CIA informant besides, and I have been waiting my day of retribution for years! You made me look like a stooge more than once, Rostovchev—and today you will pay!"

Kudinsky turned his head slightly in Jeremy's direction. "Do not forget your president's injunction, my son," he whispered in English.

Slowly, an inch at a time, Dmitri had been stepping backward until he was beside his two companions.

"Does he speak Jeremy's language?" Dmitri asked Kudinsky euphemistically in English.

"Not a word."

"Enough of this!" shouted Bolotnikov, pulling a pistol out of his belt. "Into the barn, all of you!"

As they began advancing slowly, Dmitri spoke to Jeremy and Kudinsky in a low tone, as though he might be reassuring him. "When we are at the door, I will attempt to disarm him. You two run around the outside of the barn. No doubt you will find Markus tied up in the house. I will try to keep this man occupied until you can get to him. Mr. Premier, you tell the farmer to drive you to Boris's. If Markus is hurt, his wife knows the way. I will try to meet you at Boris's. But if something—"

"We cannot leave you!" said Jeremy.

"Do as I say. I am not the reason for this mission. If I do not come, Boris will take you—"

"Silence!" cried Bolotnikov, waving his pistol in the air. "Now tell me—who is the young American, Rostovchev?"

"No one you need fear," answered Dmitri.

"I shall decide that! Who are you, American?" he demanded, advancing and yelling in Jeremy's face.

Not understanding the language, Jeremy remained silent.

They were almost at the door.

"It is time," whispered Dmitri. "In the name of Jesus," he added under his breath, then sprang forward. With a great thrust he crashed his shoulder into Bolotnikov's side, knocking him off balance just inside the barn door.

"Run!" yelled Dmitri. "Run . . . God go with you . . . run!"

Jeremy and Kudinsky obeyed as Dmitri slammed the door shut.

The enraged Bolotnikov lumbered to his feet and threw himself against the door from the inside, but he underestimated the strength of his adversary on the other side. His overweight body bounced off the door and he staggered backward like an angry bear.

Jeremy and Kudinsky were around the side of the barn now and making for the small farmhouse.

"I'll try the car," shouted Jeremy. "You go inside and see if Markus is there."

Out of breath and exhausted, Kudinsky obeyed.

Jeremy tore open the door of what had to be Bolotnikov's huge black Mercedes. The key was still in the ignition! He twisted the key and revved the engine into a fast idle!

He heard two shots. Had Dmitri been hit?

But Dmitri had stepped back from the door before Bolotnikov fired through it. Splinters of wood exploded off the thin wooden panels and the bolt shattered. For the second time in five minutes Bolotnikov's heavy booted foot crashed open the door of the barn, this time sending it flying off its hinges.

Pistol in hand, the angry ex-KGB strongman stepped through the opening, turning his head quickly to the left and right to see what had become of his prisoners.

He was just in time to hear the words, "God forgive me!" as Dmitri's fist smashed into the side of his face. Again Bolotnikov lost his balance and staggered backward into the wall, the pistol slipping from his grasp.

Dmitri seized the weapon, contemplated it for the briefest of moments, then—fearing necessity or passion might make its use inevitable—flung it from him in a mighty heave as he ran to join his friends.

Bolotnikov faltered to his feet, his mind groggy from the vicious blow. But the sight of blood on his hand when he rubbed it across his face brought him to his frenzied senses once more. He wobbled across the snowy field, and some preternatural instinct carried him straight to where his pistol lay. As his hand closed around its handle and his finger found the trigger, he turned and made for the corner of the barn with ever surer step.

He heard a car engine now, and tires skidding in the dirt and gravel!

---

Markus Tanicev and his wife were barely in the back seat when Jeremy jammed his foot to the floor. The powerful Mercedes sent rocks and dust flying in all directions.

Jeremy glanced around. There was Dmitri! He had gotten free!

Jeremy slammed on the brakes and the huge car jerked to a stop. He jumped out to open the door.

Dmitri ran toward them across the farmyard, then up the slight incline where the car waited. Suddenly in the distance Jeremy saw another figure round the corner of the barn in pursuit.

"Run, Dmitri . . . run!" he cried.

But even as the words were still warm in his mouth, the distant figure stopped, raised his arm, and took aim.

"No!" screamed Jeremy. But his cry was lost in the fiery explosion, and Dmitri fell as he ran—twenty yards from the car.

Jeremy started to run to him, when a voice from inside the car stopped him.

"Come, young Manning," said Kudinsky. His tone was sad but full of authority. "Come . . . or he will kill us all!"

Tears filling his eyes, Jeremy jumped back inside, yanked the car into gear, and slammed the gas pedal to the floor. Two more shots rang out. The second one shattered the rear window, spraying glass inside the car.

"Lord God, protect our brother!" prayed Kudinsky, while Tanicev and his wife clasped hands and began praying fervently for the fate of their dear friend.

As the black Mercedes sped away, none of its occupants saw Bolotnikov shaking his angry uplifted fist at them, nor heard his evil curses as he stood over the dead form of his longtime foe.

Even in victory, somehow he knew he had been defeated by one stronger than himself.

# ONE HUNDRED FOUR

Central Park seemed a quiet, peaceful wonderland, like a place immortalized in some fairy tale. No more perfect spot for the meeting could be imagined.

Besides, New York was a much more likely place to preserve anonymity, a useful factor when there might still be danger. The city's New Year's celebrations of a week ago were well past, and life was back to normal.

Snow fell gently on the tree-lined paths and drifted onto a few unfrequented patches of ground. Those resilient city dwellers who were out, clad in fur and woolen mufflers and boots, appeared not in the least intimidated by the cold. Even an occasional snowman added to the population of the landscape, standing as a silent sentinel of the barren beauty of winter.

An old man, slight of build, ambled harmoniously into the fairyland scene. His wool overcoat showed fray about the cuffs, but his brown fur Cossack cap lent him a regal bearing.

The man navigated casually over many paths, finally coming out into a clearing where several park benches were invitingly situated. He chose an unoccupied one, brushed away a bit of snow, then eased onto the bench. It hardly seemed the weather for such an activity, but the man then proceeded to pull a paperback copy of Louis L'Amour's *Comstock Lode* from his pocket. He leaned back, adjusted his wire-rimmed spectacles on his nose and ears, and began to read, seemingly unconscious of the activity in the park around him.

Neither did he take notice of the gradual influx of new arrivals into the clearing. Several lone men—dressed uncannily alike in heavy overcoats covering dark suits, leather gloves, and dark glasses—made their way into the area from opposite directions, milling around in awkward random fashion.

The occupier of the bench quietly turned a page in his book, engrossed in the western saga.

Soon another man sauntered onto the scene, followed closely by three more of the dark-suited men. Although his attendants appeared tense and vigilant, this latest park visitor walked in a relaxed manner, despite a decided limp. He casually approached the occupied park bench, tipped his hat, and smiled pleasantly.

"May I join you?" he asked.

"Of course," replied the first man in accented English. The conversation which followed, however, was in Russian.

"I have not dared believe it could be true until this very moment!" said the younger of the two men, grasping the other's hand and clutching it tightly.

"It is true, my friend," said the other with a warm smile. "But even I must, as you say, pinch myself occasionally to be assured I am out of that place. However did you manage it?"

"Some of our people are very resourceful. Although from what Jeremy tells me, our CIA had very little to do with it once you were out of the facility."

The older man laughed. "That young Manning is quite a compatriot! I must say I grew very attached to him in the short time we were together."

"And he you! He talks about nothing else. You have already become like a father to him."

"It is *he* to whom I owe my freedom more than anyone. More, I should say, than any other *earthly* person. Which reminds me, I must thank you for the instructions you gave Manning when you sent him to me. We owe our very lives to the Lord's intervention many times over, and often it was the thought of you which reminded us to pray and commit our way to Him once again."

"Jeremy tells me you saved his skin a time or two also."

"Nothing compared to his bravery."

"I heard you got out of the car and dressed down a police officer who had stopped you along the road. How does the story go?"

The old Russian laughed. "We could not have been more than four or five kilometers from the border. We were completely alone by then, making a run for an unprotected portion of the border we had been told about, when a policeman stopped us to ask for directions to a certain road—which, of course, we knew nothing about. Manning was driving and could not understand the man. I tried to speak up, but the officer insisted on trying to talk to the man behind the wheel. It was very awkward, and the fellow began to get worrisome and suspicious."

"What happened?"

"I got out and proceeded to chastise the man in the most abusive language I could think of, telling him we were working for Comrade Bolotnikov and that surely he'd heard of the escape from Lvov Sanatorium? He had heard something of it, now that he recalled, he said. And so I continued on, dropping enough official names and phrases that I suppose he believed my story. In a few more minutes we were on our way toward the border."

"And he never recognized you?"

"No, the poor fellow! When it does dawn on him, he's going to think he needs to go to Lvov himself! I am still considered dead there, you know."

"Here too. I think it best you remain that way for a time. That's why I arranged this little charade here in the park. For your safety, as well as for the sake of the peace negotiations we must continue with Bolotnikov, I do not want him to know I had any hand in it. For him to know you are here could endanger your life and worsen the situation in Iran."

"Yes, I am sure you are right. He has many loyalists who are still deeply planted in your country."

"We will be shown when the time is right to alter your public status. Until then, you will be my guest. I have arranged for you to be transferred to a small farm in Pennsylvania where you will have a cottage to yourself and can read, study, and write. All your needs will be provided for, and I will occasionally be able to visit you. You will be taken there tomorrow, and Jeremy will be there awaiting you. Word is already spreading around that a long-lost great uncle of his has been located and brought to live in this country. After today, my friend, your name will be Manniskyev."

"You are full of surprises!" said the older man with a smile. "And how grateful I am for everything you have done."

"Oh, it is *I* who am grateful! To our God for bringing you again to me. How I have felt the need for fellowship with you!"

"There will now be time, my friend. I have many things about which I must ask you."

"Just wait till you hear what I have to tell you!" replied the younger man. "I think I at last understand a little of what He wants us to do."

The elder man nodded, then began to chuckle softly. Finally he laughed outright. "Perhaps He has been telling us the same things—again!"

"I can honestly say I do not think anything He does will now surprise me!"

An hour and fifteen minutes later, the younger man rose.

"I must go now. But we will be together again very soon. All is being arranged, and you will be contacted at your hotel. It will not be long, my friend, before we are able to begin this new adventure in earnest!"

"God be with you!" said the older man, rising also.

The two men embraced warmly. Then the younger man turned to rejoin his three protectors. As they ambled off, the older man stood looking after them with a smile. Inside him was the strong sensation that their mutual destiny had at this moment begun anew.

# ONE HUNDRED FIVE

A buzz of speculation filtered through the White House press room.

With the inauguration only four days away, President MacFarlane had called for this nationally televised prime-time speech, with a press conference to follow. It was unprecedented.

Ever since the surprise announcement yesterday, rumors had been circulating rampantly around the city that the speech would be of momentous proportions, no small feat in an administration beset by more than its share of historical events. But what could the president possibly have to so urgently address the nation about, when his inauguration speech was only four days away? Only war seemed that urgent. And if there had been an outbreak in the tense Middle East situation, news of it would already have exploded across the networks.

None of the reporters on the White House beat could nail down any details. No one was talking. The scuttlebutt was that no one really knew anything—neither aides nor staff members.

The only things worthy of note—and given the approaching inauguration, it was probably not so unusual after all—were the daily meetings between President MacFarlane and his vice-president elect. These were given passing consideration in the media, but were not considered particularly noteworthy.

It wasn't as if the media was starved for news. There was plenty in the world to keep them busy, for the situation in Iran continued to keep the teletype humming.

The Russian invasion force had maintained its hold on Iran's key cities and ports, but had otherwise been unusually quiet. The Soviets did not seem anxious to try to extend their infiltration, and some sources speculated that the Soviet leaders had been thrown off-guard by President MacFarlane's surprisingly strong but lenient ultimatum the week of the invasion. It appeared they had anticipated either war with the United States or an unhindered aggression. But to suddenly find the onus of decision thrust back upon their own shoulders, with the whole world watching with a condemning eye, was unexpected.

The president's ultimatum to the Soviets was as simple as it was unusual in diplomatic history: "We don't want to go to war with you over a country that is neither our ally nor one with whom we have maintained tenuous diplomatic relations. Neither do we want to start a major war over a border incident, or because you have mistakenly ordered an invasion you will later see was ill-advised and will thus regret. Therefore, we will not go to war with you to drive you out of Iran, but will instead give you the opportunity to withdraw peacefully. We do, however, feel most strongly that you have breached both the freedom and integrity of another nation, something you have no right to do. The whole world condemns you, and we condemn you. We will not allow such injustices and such aggression to continue. Therefore, be warned—if you do not withdraw your troops from Iran and pull all military equipment and personnel north beyond the fortieth parallel, we will move upon the region with all the military might that the cause of freedom can muster, whether the whole free world supports us, or whether no one but our own freedom-loving people support our cause. No more will aggressors be allowed to swallow other nations, even those with whom we do not share an allegiance.

"You have two years from the day of your invasion to effect this complete withdrawal. During those two years, the United States will prepare itself for war. As commander in chief, I will order a mobilization of our forces immediately. It will be the earnest prayer of our people and people throughout the world that you seriously reevaluate your position, that you reconsider the terms of the Moscow peace initiative of last June, and that you withdraw your troops. We will defend the right of nations to govern themselves without fear of Soviet aggression.

"This is no bluff. Iran shall not be yours. Act now. Act promptly. Act wisely. Or the consequences will be yours to face."

Somehow, despite his belligerent threats and despite the laughter with which he initially greeted MacFarlane's stern communique, General Secretary Bolotnikov seemed to sense that this strange American president meant exactly what he said and was probably fool enough to back up his words. In spite of his stepped-up efforts to conclude "mutual assistance" treaties with Egypt, Libya, Ethiopia, Iraq, Yugoslavia, and several other nonaligned nations, the new Soviet leader was strangely noncommittal about specific future plans in the Persian Gulf region.

Most of the talk throughout the U.S. and Europe these days was talk of war, but the president still spoke fervently about the subject of the ill-fated Moscow treaty, even as he took steps to back up the substance of his ultimatum. After initial skepticism, by mid-December even the Pentagon recognized a new strength in their com mander in chief. Martin Tucker and Emmit Howson found themselves uncharacteristically supportive of the president's moves and decisions regarding the buildup, finding in him an admirable balance between strength and a desire for peace.

Israel had also been troublesome. Convinced the Soviets were planning an invasion either from the north or the east, the Israelis had begun their own military buildup, publicly saying they could not depend on anyone else to defend their freedom if a Russian invasion did occur.

The United European Community met in Rome, city of the Common Market's original founding in 1957, along with other Western nations, to discuss a joint response to the Iranian situation. The chief message to emerge from the hastily convened conference, in a spellbinding speech by the Italian delegate Flaavio, was that peace must be achieved and that new world leadership was called for that could effectively unite the nations of the globe. Flaavio himself emerged as one whom many hailed as the heir apparent to MacFarlane and Kudinsky, a man who might be able to effectively unify conflicting factions in the cause for peace. He vowed to meet jointly with the pope, the Soviet premier, the American president, and other religious and political leaders in order to arrive at a new and unprecedented framework for peace.

The news men and women of Washington D.C., therefore, had had plenty to occupy their commentaries and editorials. And against this backdrop of world events, they had been altogether unprepared for the president's surprise announcement that he would address the nation.

---

At exactly 7:45 P.M. Rick Bonner stepped into the noisy room.

"All right, ladies and gents," said the White House press secretary, "the show's on. Come this way. There should be plenty of seats for all."

The ensemble of reporters and journalists crushed out cigarettes, grabbed up purses, tape recorders, and other paraphernalia, and hurried after the press secretary.

The conference hall was already half full, cluttered with television cameras and crews, security agents, and many members of the White House staff and Congress. The room would hold five or six hundred people in a pinch, and over four hundred newsmen and lawmakers had been invited today.

In the front row Karen MacFarlane sat straight and tall, her face radiant and a look of pride in her eye. Her fiance, Jeremy Manning, beside her looked pensive and serene, as if he knew something he wasn't telling. The president's friend from Georgetown, Peter Venzke, sat beside Manning, and just beyond Venzke was Duke Mathias. Between Venzke and Mathias was a man with whom both seemed on very intimate terms, but whom no one else in the room had been able to identify. All of them wore the same look to be seen on the face of Manning and the President's daughter. It was a glow of anticipation for what lay ahead.

At exactly 8:00 P.M. Jarvis MacFarlane walked into the room and stepped before the cameras.

The moment the president took his place at the podium, a hush invaded every corner of the room. Before so much as a word was spoken, every person seemed to sense—from the set of his shoulders, from the steady gaze in his eyes, from the purposeful stride of his step—that before them stood a man of authority. Those who had been acquainted with him in the early days could give astounding witness to the amazing metamorphosis in this man during the past year. Somehow though, they said to themselves, it had only become apparent in recent weeks, even days. Now they wondered as they beheld the penetrating gaze of intensity and maturity emerging from his eyes . . . had they ever really known him at all?

A few even wondered how the nation, the Congress, the world could have been so deaf to the central message he had been trying to proclaim, especially now that the message seemed to be such a natural extension of his own character.

"Ladies and gentlemen," MacFarlane began, focusing on those present as if he were addressing each one personally, "and those of my fellow Americans and fellow citizens of this world who are viewing these proceedings on their television sets," —and here he gazed into the cameras stationed at the back of the room with the same effect—"the announcement I will make tonight is a decision that has been reached after weeks and months of deep and serious searching within the depths of my own soul, and with no little prayer as well. Believe me when I say it is not a lightly made decision, and I honestly confide in you that it is made with extremely conflicting emotions.

"As some of you know, but as many of you probably do not know, this past year I have had what many would term a 'religious experience'—"

The buzz of reaction which might have been expected among the crowd of listeners never came. The weight of MacFarlane's pres ence was too awe-inspiring and his words too sincere to give way to light murmurings. Truly a dropped pin could have been heard.

"I hesitate to attach such a label to it, knowing that labels are usually constricting and often lead to misunderstanding. Yet it is my hope that I have the opportunity in the coming months to make very clear to you much of what this experience means to me. For the moment, suffice it to say that my encounter with God has been a wonderfully personal one of great joy—and one which has caused my entire outlook on . . . well, on nearly everything, to change in many ways.

"As a result, my perspective on this job—the presidency—on the country, and on politics in general has changed as well. Everything about me either has been or is in the process of being made new. One of the areas of deepest impact has been my perspective on the future. That, too, will be an area about which I plan to address the people of the world in much greater detail in the times ahead.

"At this point, however, what I would say is simply this: these changes within me have seriously and irrevocably altered my life and my calling in life. I have attempted with everything I am to be a good president, to work toward justice, toward dignity for all men and women, and toward peace. However, no longer do I feel that this office is the primary podium from which I am to further proclaim the message I have been given. For it is primarily a spiritual message, rather than a social or political one, which I have been compelled to communicate. I am no longer my own man. God's mandate upon my life is one I take as of the utmost consequence, even more than the mandate of reelection from my fellow citizens.

"The words I have to say now are not uttered without some sadness, because I have been honored to serve in this most respected position. But with the sadness there is also great joy and anticipation for what lies ahead. For the future is exciting and filled with the promises of God. Therefore, it is with great assurance that this is indeed the proper step to take that I announce to you that effective January 21, Inauguration Day, I will resign the office of presidency of these beloved United States—"

With the word *resign,* a murmuring buzz broke out in a hushed wave throughout the room.

"Your new president," continued MacFarlane as soon as order had again settled over the audience, "the man of my choice and the man who shares in my mandate from you, the people of this nation, will be inaugurated in four days as President Backman. His will truly be a bipartisan administration, for he is well aware that he has been elected on a ticket representing the opposition party. I am optimistic and excited to see the results of this arrangement.

"The man whom we may now call President-elect Backman will be free to select his own staff. However, some of my own cabinet and advisors will remain. Dick Howard gave me his resignation two weeks ago, after he and I spent several hours together in discussions regarding the future. Oscar Friedman notified me this morning, when I told him what I intended to do, of his decision to resign, as did Eugene O'Shea. Mr. Backman has already asked Martin Tucker and Duke Mathias to stay on, and both have eagerly agreed. In addition, my good friend Jake Randolf will remain on the new president's advisory staff, and I know will be as invaluable in the new administration as he has been to me.

"As you know, several cabinet and other high-level appointees have been named since the election. Since Mr. Backman and I have jointly arrived at most of these decisions, this change at the top will not effect those nominations. There is one exception, however.

"Just an hour ago I spoke on the phone with Harley Wilson. As you know from reports that have leaked out, overtures had been made to him with regard to the transportation vacancy on the cabinet. Unfortunately, from the very beginning there had been a misunderstanding between Wilson and some of my people, and therefore—because of my resignation—I urged upon Mr. Wilson the recommendation that he withdraw his name from consideration for the post. He expressed his disappointment and sincere regret that things could not work out, but in the end consented that it would be wisest for him to withdraw.

"President-elect Backman and I have been working closely these past three weeks to insure a smooth transition in government. There is great unity of purpose in this administration, as well as between Mr. Backman and me, regarding the tense world situation as it now stands. I plan to work as closely with the new president as he desires. And I hope, furthermore, to be able to influence the situation in Iran for the good in my new nonpolitical role."

The president paused, took a deep breath, then continued.

"I would not take such a severe step if the strongest and most urgent of forces were not compelling me to do so. Seven months ago you listened as Soviet Premier Kudinsky and I spoke to the world of peace, and as we began to make unprecedented steps in that direction. Yet today, the world stands on the brink of war.

"For a long time I cherished the hope that this office could make a difference. But I have come to see that treaties and laws and politics and other superficialities of society are limited in what they can achieve in a permanent way—they cannot ever hope to bring lasting peace to our troubled world. Lasting peace will only come as individual hearts are changed.

"Peace, I have come to see, is an inner quality, not a legislated entity between nations. It happens as one man with a vision speaks face-to-face with another man—two men, two women, whose hearts yearn for truth together and are willing to sacrifice their own interests for the good of the other. That, my friends, is the process to which I now choose to dedicate my life.

"I have great hope for this nation, and my stepping down from this office is reflective of that hope. My earnest prayer is that I will be able to make a difference in the critical days ahead. Perhaps not on the world's battlefields—sadly, they may always exist—but in individual human hearts, the primary dwelling place of the God who is our Maker and the only source of true peace.

"God go with you one and all!"

# EPILOGUE

Outside, the noise of the assembling crowd gradually rose. The approaching roadways were snarled and the parking lot was already nearly filled to capacity. Inside, those who had come early and were already in their seats visited with one another in the pleasant August-evening shirtsleeve warmth.

Deep within the bowels of the stadium, in a small private room, two men waited.

"Your year of exile is about to end, my friend."

"And your seven months out of office."

"It has been a quiet time—wondering what will come next."

"We are about to find out!"

MacFarlane glanced down at his watch. "Forty minutes, and they will expect me . . . with my surprise guest! I truly pray this coming out of hiding does not endanger you."

"After all we have been through and seen, can you really be worried about my life, Jarvis?"

"The flesh is weak! How could I forget! But our friends are waiting to pray with us. I'll bring them in."

The former president rose, went to an adjoining room, and soon returned with Jeremy Manning, his new son-in-law of two months, along with Peter Venzke, Duke Mathias, and Daniel King and Richard Gregory from the Legation.

"Well, gentlemen, we have been waiting and praying for this moment for some time," said MacFarlane. "I only wish Dmitri could be here among us, though of course he is with us in spirit. We have prayed together many, many times over the past months, seeking God's guidance. But now, before we one last time commit our way to Him, I would like to ask if any of you, my dear friends who have helped me gain my footing in this new adventure of being God's son and servant—if any of you have a final word for me . . . for us. You all know me well enough by now to realize how prone I am to questions and self-doubts."

A couple in the group chuckled at his words.

"Your reservations are your salvation, Jarvis," said Peter. "They keep your ego out of the way—which is not something that can be said about very many Christian public figures. You hold on to your self-doubts, and you keep being willing to let God use you in spite of them, and you can be assured that God is walking beside you."

"Amen!" added Jeremy.

Next Daniel spoke up.

"When you first came to us, Jarvis, you were somewhat reluctant to accept a few of the things we spoke of. Though I respected you and could sense the openness of your heart, I wanted you to see everything *our* way. Perhaps I should say *my* way. But over the months our association together has changed me too. You have helped me see that what God has shown us is only one part of His message to His people. I now see that every Christian—every man and woman—must be faithful to the message God gives him in the circles where he finds himself. You and Vladimir have been chosen to carry the message of God's truth into far wider circles than any of us here will ever be able to, simply because of who you are. Your message, therefore, must be larger, deeper, more expansive than what I perhaps will ever see. I have been challenged in my own thinking as I have watched you these past six months seeking wisdom and counsel from so many parts of the Christian spectrum—from Protestants, Catholics, Pentecostals, from liberals and fundamentalists. I must admit, you have surprised me at every turn, Jarvis! Your openness to all Christians, coupled with your unflinching determination to listen only to God's voice in the end and to do everything He tells you—it has been a true witness to me about the kind of man whom God is able to use in His work. I have come to see clearly why He laid His hand on you. You two have been chosen as heralds of His message. Your voices will carry far."

Daniel stopped, and again there was silence.

"The Lord be praised," sighed Jarvis quietly.

"Yes!" whispered Kudinsky. "Amen!"

"Yet still I wonder if we know enough of the message to say anything clear about it," said MacFarlane.

"We are never required to see the whole," said Duke Mathias, "only to faithfully take the next step we do see."

"That is how He protects us," added Peter. "If we saw all, we would surely faint in fear. I believe following Him in the times ahead will involve danger for each one of us here—more than it has till now. The enemy will attempt to destroy the message the Lord has given you. He may attempt to destroy you. Or, what is often worse, he may seek to discredit you so that your words will be ignored. Therefore, we must never forget to pray for the protective hand of the Lord to be over and under us."

"He has shown you but the beginning," said Richard. "He told you He would give you the words to say. He will send you people.

He will continue to speak. I believe you can be confident and humble that He is speaking through you."

"That is one of the first lessons you taught me, Jarvis," added Jeremy, "when I was struggling to understand the most basic things of faith—that if we are faithful to give out what He has given, He will reveal what is to follow . . . in His time."

"Amen to all you say!" replied MacFarlane after a lengthy pause. "Vladimir and I thank you so much for everything. But now we have only a few minutes left. I think it is time we pray."

---

Forty minutes later, Jarvis MacFarlane, and Vladimir Kudinsky, flanked by an entourage of close companions, made their way down a corridor toward their appointment with the waiting throng.

"How I pray we are doing the right thing," said Jarvis.

"The open doors, the confirming counsel—they have all been unmistakable," replied Kudinsky. "Yet still you doubt?"

"I think I will always doubt," chuckled MacFarlane. "I do not doubt God's guiding hand, nor even the doors He opens. But I doubt *myself*. Therefore, I must always question. I must never allow myself the contentment of assuming I am in God's will."

"Perhaps your very uncertainties, your reluctance to depend upon yourself, is why God is able to use you."

"I do not know, Vladimir. Even now, as we are on the very threshold of our debut, so to speak, our first large public appearance together as spokesmen for God's kingdom, even now I am filled with doubts."

"Doubts that God is with us . . . in us?"

"No, not that. Doubts about this method, this large spectacle. It reminds me of a celebrity performance," said MacFarlane. "*Is* this God's way? Would Jesus—if He came to earth today—speak like this to thousands in a huge stadium? Would He go on TV to reach the masses? Would He even be a public figure? I don't know, Vladimir. I have the feeling He wouldn't do any of those things. Don't you think that He would simply walk the streets and roads and fields of the world, telling the people His truth?"

"It is a question I cannot answer, Jarvis. But you and I are public figures, even though we have left those offices we once filled. And is it not likely that God came to us as He did because He wanted us to proclaim His peace in some unique way? Surely He desires that we proclaim it as effectively as the means He gives us affords. Just think, Jarvis, of the people who will hear our voices throughout the world!"

"I know, my friend. I do not doubt God's hand in this meeting this evening. I truly am excited to be able to walk out there—not as a president, but as God's man—and tell them that you are alive and here with me as my brother. And to tell them that what we—you and I—could not achieve as world leaders, He can achieve in men's hearts. To tell that He is the Peacemaker of the world and that He is coming! Yes, Vladimir, it humbles me to think that God wants to use us—men who two years ago did not even know He really existed."

"Yet still you have doubts, is that it?" smiled Kudinsky.

"Let's say I want us to keep our inner ears tuned to *His* voice, not the voices clamoring for us to go here, go there, do this, do that. Something inside tells me big gatherings such as tonight are perhaps a doorway, but not the end. I think the time is not far off when you and I may be sent to walk the earth as He did—among the people, not in front of them—to proclaim His coming with our lives rather than our words."

"It may well be so," mused the Russian thoughtfully.

Two minutes later, in his first public appearance since leaving office, former President Jarvis MacFarlane strode to the podium before a crowd of 68,000, along with television cameras and radio mikes too numerous to count.

"Ladies and gentlemen, I am so glad you have come tonight! I have brought a special surprise guest to share the platform with me, and I will introduce him momentarily.

"But before I do that, I think I should begin by clarifying one thing for some of you, especially those of the news media. I realize this is my first public address since I left the presidency. However, my remarks this evening will not touch in any way upon political themes. The things you are about to be confronted with may be unlike anything many of you have ever heard before in your life. . . ."

*And I will give power to my two witnesses, and they will prophesy for 1,260 days.*

Revelation 11:3